THE UNIVERSITY OF VIRGINIA EDITION OF
THE WORKS OF STEPHEN CRANE

VOLUME VI

TALES OF WAR

Crane at Brede Place, 1899

STEPHEN CRANE

Title : TALES OF WAR

THE LITTLE REGIMENT
"AN EPISODE OF WAR"
WOUNDS IN THE RAIN
"SPITZBERGEN TALES"

EDITED BY
FREDSON BOWERS
LINDEN KENT PROFESSOR OF ENGLISH AT
THE UNIVERSITY OF VIRGINIA

WITH AN INTRODUCTION BY
JAMES B. COLVERT
PROFESSOR OF ENGLISH AT THE
UNIVERSITY OF GEORGIA

THE UNIVERSITY PRESS OF VIRGINIA
CHARLOTTESVILLE

CENTER FOR EDITIONS OF
AMERICAN AUTHORS
AN APPROVED TEXT
MODERN LANGUAGE
ASSOCIATION OF AMERICA

Editorial expenses for this volume have been supported by grants from the National Endowment for
the Humanities administered through the Center
for Editions of American Authors of the Modern
Language Association.

To
Clifton Waller Barrett

FOREWORD

THIS volume brings together all of Crane's published short stories concerned with war, except "Death and the Child," which was included in *Tales of Adventure*, Volume V of the University of Virginia edition of THE WORKS OF STEPHEN CRANE. The stories are arranged in chronological order of their collected publication: *The Little Regiment*, then the isolated "An Episode of War" that rounds off the Civil-War group, then the Spanish-American War stories collected in *Wounds in the Rain*, and finally the four Spitzbergen stories from *Last Words*.

The Introduction by Professor Colvert places these stories in the literary context of Crane's development as a writer. The Textual Introduction details the physical forms of the texts, their authority and transmission as well as their publishing history, and examines specific problems involved in the establishment of the texts in their present critical form. The general principles on which the editing has been based are stated in "The Text of the Virginia Edition" prefixed to Volume I of the WORKS, *Bowery Tales* (1969). This account should be supplemented by the extended discussion of specific problems offered in the Foreword to *Tales of Adventure* (WORKS, Volume V, 1970), since similar problems are found in the texts of these war stories. Particular mention should be made, perhaps, of the extension of the classic principles of authority and of copy-text required in this and the preceding volume by particularly complex circumstances of textual transmission.

The expenses of the preparation of the texts in this volume with their introductions and apparatus have been subsidized by a grant from the National Endowment for the Humanities administered through the Modern Language Association of America and its Center for Editions of American Authors, but with generous support, as well, from the University of Virginia.

The editor is grateful for assistance and various courtesies to Professor Robert Stallman of the University of Connecticut, Professor Joseph Katz and Professor Matthew J. Bruccoli of the University of South Carolina, Professor Bernice Slote of the University of Nebraska, and his colleagues Professors James B. Colvert of the University of Georgia and J. C. Levenson of the University of Virginia. Professor James Meriwether of the University of South Carolina, who examined this volume for the Center for Editions of American Authors seal, made several suggestions. Mr. Kenneth A. Lohf, Librarian for Rare Books and Manuscripts of the Columbia University Libraries, has been of unfailing and particular assistance. The editor is grateful to the librarians of Syracuse University, Yale University, and Dartmouth College for their courtesies in making available unpublished letters in their collections, and to the librarians of Harvard, the British Museum, and the London Library for the use of their collections. The constant assistance of the custodians of the Barrett Collection at the University of Virginia has been invaluable, and Miss Helena Koiner, Head of Interlibrary Loans, has placed the editor deeply in debt for her help over an extended period. The services as research assistants of Mrs. David Yalden-Thomson and Miss Gillian G. M. Kyles, and of Mr. Alan Day in London, have been essential and much appreciated, for in these days of relatively rapid editorial publication no single scholar can think of assuming the burden of the repeated checking for accuracy of notation enforced by the standards for CEAA editions.

The editor's personal debt to Mr. Clifton Waller Barrett and his magnificent collection at the University of Virginia remains constant and can be expressed only by the dedication of this edition to him.

For permission to use as copy-text the manuscript of "The Kicking Twelfth" and to illustrate it the editor is grateful to the Henry W. and Albert A. Berg Collection of the New York Public Library, Astor, Lenox and Tilden Foundations, and also to Alfred A. Knopf, Inc.; other illustrations are with the permission of the Columbia University Libraries and the University of Virginia Library, by whose permission, also, " 'And If He Wills, We Must Die' " is edited from the early typescript in the Barrett Collection.

F. B.

CONTENTS

x · Contents

INTRODUCTION

I

A T THE end of the year 1895 Crane found himself in a difficult literary situation. The brilliant success of *The Red Badge of Courage* that fall firmly established his reputation as a war novelist, and though the reviewers praised it enthusiastically for its graphic realism, it was, as Crane uncomfortably realized, hardly representative of the kind of realism described in the theories of his "literary fathers," William Dean Howells and Hamlin Garland. Crane pledged allegiance to their program shortly after he met Garland in Asbury Park, New Jersey, in 1892, when, as he later explained, he "developed all alone a little creed of art" and later "discovered" that it was "identical with the one of Howells and Garland." [1] Probably at Garland's suggestion he moved to New York City that fall to study the Bowery and the East Side tenements in preparation for his novels of "social realism," *Maggie: A Girl of the Streets* and *George's Mother.* Although what he wrote in these novels, and in his sketches and stories of city life, is hardly realism in Howells' sense of the term, it seemed—even to Crane's "literary fathers" —to honor an indispensable tenet of realistic theory: that "truth" in art is grounded in actual observation and experience. So far as Howells was concerned, the New York fiction proved that Crane was moving in the right direction, and he advised the author after reading *Maggie* that he "thoroughly respected" his "literary conscience." [2] But *The Red Badge of Courage* was another matter, as Crane himself believed. It was a pure invention of the fancy, apparently a mere celebration of those "clever and witty expedients" which he had contemptuously denounced in 1892

---

[1] Crane to Lily Brandon Munroe, New York, [March, 1894?], *Stephen Crane: Letters*, ed. R. W. Stallman and Lillian Gilkes (New York, 1960), p. 31.
[2] Howells to Crane, New York, April 8, 1893, *Letters*, p. 18.

when he declared himself on the side of "nature and truth" as an ally of the new realism.

Thus the novel was both a triumph and an embarrassment. In praising its realism the adulatory reviews merely advertised the author's apostasy, at least to Crane and, as he could correctly guess, to his mentor Howells. He was perhaps not much surprised when the critic wrote him early in 1896 to express his regret that Crane had chosen to abandon his career in favor of unconventional poetry (in *The Black Riders*, 1895) and fanciful war stories. "For me," Howells wrote, "I remain true to my first love, 'Maggie.' That is better than all the Black Riders and Red Badges." [3] Crane's reply to this suggests that he clearly understood the comment as a reproach for straying from the path of truth. "I am, mostly, afraid," he wrote Howells by way of explaining why he was not shouting "triumphant shouts" over the success of the novel. "Afraid that some small degree of talk will turn me ever so slightly from what I believe to be the pursuit of truth." [4] As the record suggests, Howells' point had already occurred to him. Some months earlier, when the growing fame of the novel had begun to focus the issue, he had felt obliged to reaffirm his literary aims, though in so doing he had admitted, in effect, that his original commitment to realism had been only "partially" fulfilled. "I decided," he said then in reference to his beginnings in 1892, "that the nearer a writer gets to life the greater he becomes as an artist, and most of my prose writings have been toward the goal partially described by that misunderstood and abused word, realism." [5] Shortly after he received Howells' note celebrating the superiority of *Maggie* over the war novel, he also reaffirmed—with a certain poignant uncertainty, as it appears in the context of his situation—his continuing regard for the opinions of the two men who had sponsored him at the beginning of his career. "The one thing that deeply pleases me in my literary life—brief and inglorious as it is—is the fact that men of sense believe me to be sincere. 'Maggie' . . . made me the friendship of Hamlin Garland and W. D. Howells, and the one thing that makes my life worth living . . . is the con-

[3] Same, Jan. 26, 1896, *Letters*, p. 102.
[4] Crane to Howells, Hartwood, N.Y., [1896], *Letters*, p. 106.
[5] Crane to an editor of *Leslie's Weekly*, [about November, 1895], *Letters*, p. 78.

sciousness that never for an instant have those friendships at all diminished." [6] And on the same day that he wrote to assure Howells of his loyalty to "sincere" literature, he advised his editor at Appleton's, who had apparently expressed doubts about publishing his recently completed novel, *The Third Violet*, "I dont think The Red Badge to be any great shakes but then the very theme of it gives it an intensity that a writer cant reach every day. The Third Violet is a quiet little story but then it is serious work and I should say let it go." [7]

The record of these months between October, 1895, and February, 1896, when he was living quietly at his brother Edmund's house in Hartwood, New York, and writing the transparent little novel about bohemian life in the art studios he frequented in his New York City years, shows an understandable reluctance to continue in the "false" direction pointed by *The Red Badge*. Its success seemed inevitably to demand a sequel, but he responded evasively and doubtfully to the proposals of various editors who wanted more war stories in order to exploit its fame. The McClure Syndicate requested a series of historical pieces on major Civil War battles, a request to which he responded with little enthusiasm. "Your project it seemed to me would require a great deal of study and a great deal of time. I would be required to give up many plans for this winter and this I am reluctant to do." [8] About this time he began to derogate *The Red Badge*, referring to it slightingly on various occasions as the "damned 'Red Badge,' " "that damned book," "the accursed 'Red Badge.' " He expressed the view, doubtless encouraged by Howells, that it was overrated. "I suppose I ought to be thankful to 'The Red Badge' but I am much fonder of my little book of poems, 'The Black Riders.' My aim was to comprehend in it the thoughts I have had about life in general, while 'The Red Badge' is a mere episode in life, an amplification." [9] It had not only, he seemed to think, pointed him in the wrong direction, but it had also exhausted his creative energy and undermined his attempt to return to realism in *The Third Violet*. "I have finished," he noted at

[6] Crane to John Northern Hilliard, [January, 1896?], *Letters*, p. 109.
[7] Crane to Ripley Hitchcock, Hartwood, N.Y., Jan. 27, [1896], *Letters*, p. 106–107.
[8] Crane to John Phillips, Hartwood, N.Y., Dec. 30, [1895], *Letters*, pp. 83–84.
[9] Crane to an editor of *Leslie's Weekly*, [about November, 1895], *Letters*, p. 79.

the end of December, "my new novel—'The Third Violet'—and
sent it to Appleton and Co., as per request, but I've an idea it
won't be accepted. It's pretty rotten work. I used myself up in the
accursed 'Red Badge.' " [10]

But dubious as he was about pursuing war as a subject for
fiction, he nevertheless agreed to provide McClure with more
stories, and in November he set to work on "The Little Regiment," the title story of the volume published late in 1896. "I am
writing a story—'The Little Regiment' for McClure," he complained. "It is awfully hard. I have invented the sum of my
invention with regard to war and this story keeps me in internal
despair." [11] He was still laboring over it in February when he
wrote his friend Nellie Crouse, "I am engaged in rowing with
people who wish me to write more war-stories. Hang all war-
stories. Nevertheless I submitted in one case and now I have a
daily battle with a tangle of facts and emotions." [12] He referred to
"Three Miraculous Soldiers" as a "little" story in a note to
McClure in January warning him that the agreement they had
made might not be altogether advantageous to him. "I am perfectly satisfied with my end of it," he advised, "but your end
somewhat worries me for I am often inexpressibly dull and
uncreative and these periods often last for days"; [13] and again, "I
feel for you when I think of some of the things of mine which
you will have to read or have read." [14] But by the end of February
he had written a total of five new war stories since the publication of *The Red Badge*: "Three Miraculous Soldiers," "An Indiana Campaign," "The Veteran," "An Episode of War," and "The
Little Regiment." [15] When he finished "The Little Regiment" at

[10] Crane to Curtis Brown, Hartwood, N.Y., Dec. 31, 1896 [for 1895], *Letters*,
p. 87.
[11] Crane to Willis Brooks Hawkins, Hartwood, N.Y., [about Nov. 12, 1895],
Letters, p. 72.
[12] Hartwood, N.Y., Feb. 5, [1896], *Letters*, p. 111.
[13] Hartwood, N.Y., Jan. 27, [1896], *Letters*, p. 108.
[14] Same, Jan. 28, [1896], *Letters*, p. 108.
[15] Two of the stories in *The Little Regiment* were written before *The Red
Badge of Courage* was published. "A Mystery of Heroism" was printed in the
Philadelphia Press, Aug. 1, 2, 1895; "A Grey Sleeve" appeared in the *Philadelphia Press*, Oct. 12, 14, 15, 1895. "An Episode of War," usually considered
uncertainly as a Spanish-American War story, was probably written during
this period. Although first published in December, 1899, in *The Gentlewoman*,
an English magazine, and then in *Last Words*, it is probably the story listed

the end of that month he described it loyally as "a novelette which represents my work at its best," but he also added emphatically, "and is positively my last thing dealing with battle." [16]

II

The history of the war fiction after *The Red Badge* begins, then, with the effect of the success of the novel on Crane's conception of himself as a writer. So far as *The Little Regiment* is concerned, the effect was severely demoralizing, for it merely compounded, as he thought, the literary error to which *The Red Badge* stood already as a conspicuous monument. The historian, who has the advantage of hindsight and perspective, sees the matter in a different light. In his view it appears clearly that the theory of realism, as Crane imperfectly understood it from Howells and Garland, was largely irrelevant to his vision and aims as a writer. There is no evidence that he fully grasped the implications of the documentary method the theory of realism advocated and in effect demanded of him, a method radically at odds with his own compositional practice. Nor did he understand fully, apparently, that Howells' equation of "truth" in art with the "authority" of first-hand knowledge of its subject matter was only indirectly and obliquely applicable to his practice. He was certain that his New York novels and stories correctly represented "social realism." The war stories after *The Little Regiment*, all based more or less on actual experience and observation, he would doubtless have felt also represented impeccable realism, though there is little evidence that he was much concerned after 1896 with the problem of reconciling literary theory and practice. As J. C. Levenson observes, considering the relation of Crane's art to real-life experience in the late Whilomville tales, references to "particular sources . . . contribute little to an understanding of Crane's fiction. Early and late, such items

---

in a record Crane made in 1897 as "Loss of an Arm" (see the Textual Introduction). According to the record, "Loss of an Arm" was published in the *Youth's Companion,* but none of Crane's works ever appeared in this magazine. Crane perhaps lost the manuscript and then found it later, after he went to England.

[16] Crane to the editor of *The Critic,* Hartwood, N.Y., Feb. 15, 1896, *Letters,* p. 117.

furnish evidence for a negative argument: despite his own simple ideas of art as literal representation, his work is not sufficiently accounted for in that way. Whatever else it may be, his realism is not simply a matter of direct rendering of an observed object." [17]

This holds true for his later war fiction as well; for, to put it simply, what he saw in real war is rendered not as history but as history transmuted by the resources of his imagination. These resources were the images, themes, motifs, and descriptive patterns he had already worked out by the time he came to see the real thing, the compositional devices of The Red Badge, of The Little Regiment, and more importantly of his very early Sullivan County sketches. This is to say in effect that he observed real war from a pre-established literary point of view, a view which largely determined what was seen and what the observed event signified. "Death and the Child," a story based on his first experience of real war at Velestino in 1897, is a rich example of the powerful control his purely literary resources could exercise over his observation—a remarkable variation on the themes and imagery of The Red Badge of Courage. He adapted these resources to a variety of styles ranging from the hyperbolic, elaborately rhetorical, reflexive style of the early fiction to the lean, open, sardonically understated style of such late stories as "The Upturned Face." This story attenuates his essentially mythic sense of war so severely that it seems all but absent except in the broad context of his characteristic feeling for the ambiguous crossing of horror and humor in a dreamlike suspension of the movement of time. But even at this extreme range of style and form, his composition draws obliquely on resources developed essentially in the experimental fiction of 1892, the radical origin of all of his fiction, even of the "realistic" studies of city low life in Maggie, George's Mother, and other New York stories and sketches. Thus the history of the work represented in this volume begins in this early fiction, especially in the Sullivan County sketches, written shortly before he denounced them in 1892 as merely "clever and witty expedients" and pledged his unsteady allegiance to Howells' and Garland's realism.

[17] Introduction to Tales of Whilomville, THE WORKS OF STEPHEN CRANE, VII (Charlottesville: University Press of Virginia, 1969), xiii.

III

The hero of the sketches is a literary version of the naïve, infinitely self-assured middle-class vacationers Crane studied as a newspaper reporter in Asbury Park, New Jersey, where he worked summers in the early nineties for his brother Townley's news agency. The vacationers were models for several satirical sketches in which he practiced the art of literary characterization. "The average summer guest," he wrote in one piece, "stands in his two shoes with American self-reliance, playing casually with his watch-chain, and looks at the world with a clear eye." He presumes a vast worldly knowledge, even as he foolishly submits to the "arrogant prices" and other practiced deceits of hotel proprietors. "However," Crane observes, "deliberately and baldly attempt to beat him out of fifteen cents and he will put his hands in his pockets, spread his legs apart and wrangle in a loud voice until sundown." [18] Another passage deals with the "summer youth," a "rose-tint and gilt-edge" swaggerer who appears on the beach with the "summer girl," described as "a bit of interesting tinsel flashing near the sombre-hued waves." [19] Again, Crane describes the millionaire owner of the beach, a pompous gentleman who loudly advertises his virtues and pieties and who considers it a matter of high import that his beach lies "adjacent to the Lord's ocean." [20]

The recurrent motif, as these examples show, is vain delusion in ironic contrast with a vast, remote, sombre nature. The Sullivan County sketches, written about this same time, develop the theme in an elaborate metaphor of man at war against nature. The hero is the unnamed "little man," a camper and hunter who wanders over the haunted countryside courageously challenging its apparently inimical spirit in ludicrous assaults on caves, bears, mountains, and forests. He is fond of melodramatic, self-assertive postures and resounding oratory celebrating his courage and other virtues, a demeanor which masks an almost hysterical fear and dread of what he takes to be the dark powers of

[18] *New York Tribune*, Aug. 14, 1892, p. 17.
[19] *Ibid.*
[20] *Ibid.*

the alien landscape. What makes it particularly sinister is its bewildering ambiguity, for it sometimes seems benign and sympathetic, a serene Edenic vision of the world in perfect harmony with the spirit of the "little man's" presumed virtues. It is this ambiguity which challenges him and moves him to master its secret meaning. His characteristic approach is to assault it violently, as if to overpower it and subdue it to his will.

The model for the landscape in which he pursues his adventures was the wild country of Sullivan County, New York, which Crane knew intimately as a hunter and fisherman; but in the fiction it is transmuted to a dreamlike symbolic evocation of the world of nature, an elusive and problematic event of the hero's distraught fancy. Crane's metaphors and images throw over it the weird light of heightened color and invest it with a savage and threatening animism:

All those things which come forth at night began to make noises. Unseen animals scrambled and flopped among the weeds and sticks. Weird features masqueraded awfully in robes of shadow.

It appears in contradictory moods with ironic contrasts between its vaguely sinister and idyllic aspects:

The sun gleamed merrily upon the waters, the gaunt, towering tree-trunks and the stumps lying like spatters of wood which had dropped from the clouds. Troops of blue and silver darning-needles danced over the surface. . . . Down in the water, millions of fern branches quavered and hid mysteries.[21]

Or again, it appears mute, stolid, indifferent, as in the ending of a story about the "little man's" assault on a supposedly malevolent hill: "The mountain under his feet was motionless." [22] There is also a recurring strain of religious imagery evoking a mournful, tender sentience in the landscape which is dramatically contrasted to the threat of demonic shadows and baleful setting suns:

In a field of snow some green pines huddled together and sang in quavers as the wind whirled among the gullies and ridges. . . . On the ridge-top a dismal choir of hemlocks crooned over one that had fallen. The dying sun created a dim purple and flame-colored

21 "The Octopush," *New York Tribune*, July 10, 1892, pt. 2, p. 17.
22 "The Mesmeric Mountain," in *Last Words* (London, 1902), p. 230.

tumult on the horizon's edge and then sank. . . . As the red rays retreated, armies of shadows stole forward.[23]

The problematical nature of the landscape is suggested further in images of obscuring mists, fogs, and cloaking darkness:

The sun slid down and threw a flare upon the silence, coloring it red. . . . Dusk came and fought a battle with the flare. . . . A ghost-like mist came and hung upon the waters. The pond became a grave-yard.[24]

Crane's irony appears most obviously in his mocking diminishment of the "little man," whose burlesque posturing as a hero of supreme virtue, knowledge, and courage is constantly belied in his various encounters with nature. His swagger, noble oratory, and outrageous self-esteem are merely hopeful shams, utterly vulnerable to the dreadful specters his fancy projects upon the countryside. But his moods are variable, and in serene, happy moments his fancy conjures an idyllic world in perfect accord with the supposed harmony of his soul. In these pieces, and later in the New York fiction, Crane experimented with a style of composition designed to emphasize these incongruous aspects of the hero's mind by fusing the apparent contradictions in his perception in single images, often with grotesque effect. A set description in "The Mesmeric Mountain," a Sullivan County fable that concentrates many of the motifs and images of Crane's fiction, early and late, illustrates the point.

A lazy lake lay asleep near the foot of the mountain. In its bed of water-grass some frogs leered at the sky and crooned. The sun sank in red silence, and the shadows of the pines grew formidable. The expectant hush of evening, as if some thing were going to sing a hymn, fell upon the peak and the little man.[25]

A passage in *George's Mother* shows how he adapted these images to the description of street scenes. In this example the religious motif becomes overt in the picture of a little chapel threatened by the lurid, mystical powers of the city:

In a dark street the little chapel sat humbly between two towering apartment-houses. A red street-lamp stood in front. It threw a marvel-

[23] "Killing His Bear," *New York Tribune*, July 31, 1892, pt. 2, p. 18.
[24] "The Octopush," p. 17.
[25] "The Mesmeric Mountain," in *Last Words*, p. 229.

lous reflection upon the wet pavements. It was like the death-stain of a spirit. Farther up, the brilliant lights of an avenue made a span of gold across the black street. A roar of wheels and a clangor of bells came from this point, interwoven into a sound emblematic of the life of the city. It seemed somehow to affront this solemn and austere little edifice. It suggested an approaching barbaric invasion. The little church, pierced, would die with a fine illimitable scorn for its slayers.[26]

The "little man's" war against nature becomes to his descendants, the heroes of *Maggie* and *George's Mother*, war against a man-made world, where the murky vistas of shadowy streets and looming buildings are demonic and potentially violent, like the objects of nature in the Sullivan County landscape. In the city fiction he developed another compositional device—suggested perhaps by the technique of impressionist artists in whose studios he lived when he was writing these novels and *The Red Badge*—a method of describing scenes from odd angles of vision, deliberately distorting the conventional realistic treatment of space and time and thus intensifying the sense of a threateningly incoherent order of reality which burdens so many of his fictional heroes. A passage from "An Experiment in Misery," a description of Bowery life written in 1894, illustrates this quasi-surrealistic effect of the method:

Through the mists of the cold and storming night, the cable cars went in silent procession, great affairs shining with red and brass, moving with formidable power, calm and irresistible, dangerful and gloomy, breaking silence only by the loud fierce cry of the gong. Two rivers of people swarmed along the sidewalks, spattered with black mud, which made each shoe leave a scar-like impression. Overhead, elevated trains with a shrill grinding of the wheels stopped at the station, which upon its leg-like pillars seemed to resemble some monstrous kind of crab squatting over the street. . . . Down an alley there were somber curtains of purple and black, on which street lamps dully glittered like embroidered flowers.[27]

This strange landscape of insubstantial objects appearing in constantly shifting guises—now demonic and threatening; again hopefully idyllic, benevolent, and mystically religious; and still

[26] *Bowery Tales*, THE WORKS OF STEPHEN CRANE, I, 156.7–16.
[27] "An Experiment in Misery," New York *Press*, April 22, 1894, pt. 3, p. 2.

again sternly indifferent and neutral—is the imaginary world technically perceived by the morally disoriented hero, though it also obliquely reflects Crane's own ironic sense of half-concealed, warring powers in the worlds of man and nature; and deeper than this, the Christian sense of the fallen world as the battle-ground of God and the Devil—the heritage of a minister's son. He deals with the subject directly in the religious poems of *The Black Riders*, less directly in the Sullivan County fables. In the New York fiction, where his metaphor of man and nature is shifted to a social context, the theme, though vaguely omnipresent, is shadowily transformed, as in the description of the wounded little chapel, already quoted, and in the following passage, which represents the hero's reflection on the mysterious city in *George's Mother*:

He had a vast curiosity concerning this city in whose complexities he was buried. It was an impenetrable mystery, this city. It was a blend of many enticing colours. He longed to comprehend it completely, that he might walk understandingly in its greatest marvels, its mightiest march of life, its sin. He dreamed of a comprehension whose pay was the admirable attitude of a man of knowledge.[28]

The immediate reference is to George's naïve yearning for worldly sophistication, but in the context of the myth of the "little man" it appears as an attenuation of a metaphor which springs from Crane's deep conviction that human vanity is poignantly vulnerable to the dark, ineffable powers of the world —a conviction which is the ultimate motive of his irony.

IV

The Red Badge of Courage is clearly an expansion of the fable of the "little man" at war against nature. The inimical spirit of the haunted glens of Sullivan County becomes in the novel the "swollen god" of war, the ghostly manifestation of a terrible, unseen enemy concealed in the obscuring mists and smoke of battle or tranformed grotesquely in the perspective of vast distances or odd angles of sight. The threatening landscape, as perceived in the hysterical fancy of Henry Fleming (an obvious

[28] WORKS, I, 135.35–136.2.

elaboration of the "little man") is the abode of the mysterious enemy, the "red and green monsters" that swarm in his imagination as he flees from his first battle.

> From far off in the darkness came the trampling of feet. The youth could occasionally see dark shadows that moved like monsters.

> Staring once at the red eyes [the campfires of the distant enemy] he conceived them to be growing larger, as the orbs of a row of dragons advancing.[29]

Henry is bewildered by the contradictory guises in which the landscape seems to appear and reappear:

> As he gazed around him the youth felt a flash of astonishment at the blue, pure sky and the sun gleamings on the trees and fields. It was surprising that Nature had gone tranquilly on with her golden process in the midst of so much devilment [63].

Having fled to a forest in the rear, he hopes to find consolation in what now appears to be a serene, idyllic prospect of nature:

> This landscape gave him assurance. A fair field holding life. It was the religion of peace. It would die if its timid eyes were compelled to see blood. He conceived Nature to be a woman with a deep aversion to tragedy [78].

In a little grotto he finds a temple of worship:

> At length he reached a place where the high, arching boughs made a chapel. He softly pushed the green doors aside and entered. Pine needles were a gentle brown carpet. There was a religious half light.

But in this hopeful green chapel he finds to his horror a decaying corpse, a thing of terror in the very temple of nature, a corruption in "the fair field holding life." Again he takes wild flight, pursued by frightful visions, imagining that "some strange voice would come from the dead throat and squawk after him in horrible menaces." From a distance, though, the whole affair seems a puzzling mystery. "The trees about the portal of the chapel moved soughingly in a soft wind. A sad silence was upon the little guarding edifice."

[29] *The Red Badge of Courage* (New York, 1895), pp. 21–22. Other quotations in this section are from the same edition.

His blind rush upon the enemy in his next battle, like the "little man's" assault on the "hostile" peak in the early fable, is figuratively a desperate assault on a traitorous and hostile nature; he celebrates this event, which earns him the name of hero, not as a triumph over enemy soldiers nor as a victory over his cowardice, but as a vengeful subjugation of "mountains."

He had fought like a pagan who defends his religion. Regarding it, he saw that it was fine, wild, and, in some ways, easy. He had been a tremendous figure, no doubt. By this struggle he had overcome obstacles which he had admitted to be mountains. They had fallen like paper peaks, and he was now what he called a hero [169].

Henry's state of mind at this point is equivalent to the vain delusion of his fictional ancestor, the "little man," who struts victorious on the brow of the motionless mountain. The logic of the metaphor requires a resolution in terms of the hero's relation to nature, but the concluding chapters of the novel evade this central dramatic issue. The story subtly shifts to another problem, Henry's commitment to his fellow soldiers, to the regiment as a community of man. But Henry, though a hero among men, wins no victory over nature. And the flurry of sentimental images of the landscape in the final paragraphs of the book, Henry's vision of "tranquil skies, fresh meadows, cool brooks—an existence of soft and eternal peace," is disturbingly reminiscent of the delusionary mood in which he took temporary solace in nature's little chapellike bower.

V

When *The Little Regiment* appeared in 1896, the reviewers almost unanimously declared it to be an expedient repetition of *The Red Badge*, a view largely echoed by historians up to our own time. The general opinion, then and now, is that it is also decidedly inferior to the novel, which it undoubtedly is. It was written grudgingly and apparently against what Crane took to be his artistic conscience. And it is repetitious, though chiefly in the sense that it draws heavily upon the system of rhetoric and symbology of *The Red Badge*. But the view that these stories are in all respects simply shorter versions of the war novel is mis-

leading. It is only partially true, as a representative critical comment phrases it, that they "clearly demonstrate the themes, the conflicts, the irony and imagery of *The Red Badge*, reduced to a series of fragile, synthetic miniatures." [30] In one respect they are radically different: they abandon the mythic theme which Crane found most congenial to his imagination. The poignantly alienated "little man" appears nowhere in these stories, and the haunted landscape of the sketches, which largely provides the settings, consequently appears as an elaborate and irrelevant backdrop in a different kind of story.

The aims and motives of the protagonists, who are generally more rational, critical, and reflective than the heroes modeled on the "little man," are defined in terms of a social rather than a mythic world. In this respect they seem to develop a tendency shown in the closing chapters of the war novel, where Crane solved the problem of a premature resolution of Henry's war against nature by subtly shifting the issue to the world of men. In *The Little Regiment* he modeled his characters roughly on that of Henry as he appears at the end of the novel, thus moving closer in his conception of the stories to the realism he was seeking in the fall and winter of 1895–96. *The Little Regiment*, in short, marks the point in the history of Crane's fiction where, in his suddenly heightened concern for theory, he begins to translate his semiallegorical "little man" into a credible social type, and the consequence of this was to alter radically the basic dramatic structure of his plots and to open the way to the development of a variant style. The title story centers on the problem two quarrelsome brothers have in communicating their mutual affection. "A Grey Sleeve" is about a brief, intense courtship conducted against a background of war. "An Indiana Campaign" describes the comical folkways of villagers in a false crisis created by a rumor. "The Veteran" tells how Henry Fleming as an old man sacrifices his life in an attempt to rescue his horses from a burning barn, the most interesting of all the stories from the point of view of the historian, as will be suggested later.

The story which most closely resembles *The Red Badge* in

30 Thomas A. Gullason, "The Significance of *Wounds in the Rain*," *Modern Fiction Studies*, V (Autumn, 1959), 235.

conception and incident is "A Mystery of Heroism," written probably in the early fall or late summer of 1895 before the war novel
brought Crane his disturbing fame; and since it represents more
subtly than any of the others the movement away from the fable
of the "little man," it is worth examination in some detail.[31] It
describes Fred Collins' heroic charge across a field under heavy
enemy fire to secure a bucket of water from a distant well, an
action reminiscent of Henry's wild charges in the novel. The
story opens with the familiar images ironically linking demonic
war and Edenic nature:

From beyond a curtain of green woods there came the sound of
some stupendous scuffle as if two animals of the size of islands were
fighting [49.3–5].

For the little meadow which intervened was now suffering a terrible
onslaught of shells. Its green and beautiful calm had vanished utterly.
Brown earth was being flung in monstrous handfuls. And there was a
massacre of the young blades of grass. . . . Some curious fortune
of the battle had made this gentle little meadow the object of the red
hate of the shells and each one as it exploded seemed like an imprecation in the face of a maiden [49.39–50.7].

The passage obviously draws upon the same source as do similar
descriptions in *The Red Badge*, but there is a difference both in
treatment and in dramatic significance. The image is not projected upon the landscape from the demoralized fancy of the
hero; it is merely a setting, constructed out of the materials of
Crane's myth but adapted to a nonmythic dramatic situation.
The hallucinatory sense—the violent colors, the mystical air of
dread, the hyperbolic evocation of the monstrous which symbol-
izes the distraught moral sense of Henry Fleming—is notably
subdued, though not altogether absent.

But this flattening of the metaphor is dramatically appropriate, for Collins is not like Henry as the "little man." Collins is
aware, though vaguely, of his self-serving pride, and this aware-
ness gives him the power of a certain critical detachment. He
can reflect as Henry cannot in the first part of the novel on the

[31] The story was probably written about the time he returned from Mexico in
May, 1895. He toured the West and Mexico as a correspondent for the Bacheller
Syndicate.

mystery of that pride which commits him to a senseless display of bravery. He knows, as Henry does not, that the definition of heroism as the absence of fear is incorrect, for although he has no fear he is compelled to admit that he has no heroic virtues:

> No, it could not be true. He was not a hero. Heroes had no shames in their lives and, as for him, he remembered borrowing fifteen dollars from a friend and promising to pay it back the next day, and then avoiding that friend for ten months [53.30–33].

The point is that Collins argues the matter in an ethical context, in the context of the world of men and social conduct. But it is not the world of man—not even of the enemy—that exercises the consciousness of Henry when he wrestles with the same problem on the eve of his first battle:

> A little panic-fear grew in his mind. As his imagination went forward to a fight, he saw hideous possibilities. He contemplated the lurking menaces of the future, and failed in an effort to see himself standing stoutly in the midst of them. He recalled his visions of broken-bladed glory, but in the shadow of the impending tumult he suspected them to be impossible pictures.[32]

Henry's adversary is the "red and green dragon," the "lurking menaces" that try the spirit in the difficult private relation of God and man. Collins' enemy is the Confederate artillery shelling the meadow he proposes to cross. The animistic manifestations of lurking menaces are in the consciousness of the narrator, not in his.

A passage in "An Indiana Campaign," a story about the crisis caused by a rumor that a "rebel" is hiding in the woods near old Major Tom Boldin's village of Migglesville, illustrates Crane's method of adapting the portentous imagery of the Sullivan County sketches and *The Red Badge* to a comedy of manners. A group of women and children, their eyes "large with excitement" at the "possible dangers [which] had for them a delicious element," follow the intrepid veteran out to the countryside to see him capture the enemy soldier, and Crane describes the scene much as Henry or the "little man" might have seen it, though its effect and meaning is radically altered:

[32] *The Red Badge*, pp. 13–14.

The familiar scene suddenly assumed a new aspect. The field of corn which met the road upon the left was no longer a mere field of corn. It was a darkly mystic place whose recesses could contain all manner of dangers. The long green leaves, waving in the breeze, rustled as from the passing of men. In the song of the insects there were now omens, threats.

There was a warning in the enamel blue of the sky, in the stretch of yellow road, in the very atmosphere. Above the tops of the corn loomed the distant foliage of Smith's woods, curtaining the silent action of a tragedy whose horrors they imagined [61.1–10].

The landscape appears in this sinister guise not only to the women and children but to the hero and his companion, Peter, as well; it is a vision common to the whole village crowd, and it thus represents not the hallucination of a profoundly disoriented consciousness wrestling with the definition of a deceitful nature, but simply the conventional mental response of these timid and unsophisticated rustics.

The relentless irony with which Crane reproaches the un-Christian vanity of the hero of *The Red Badge* appears in *The Little Regiment* in a lower key, gently and even affectionately directed against minor and venial foibles of character. The heroine of "Three Miraculous Soldiers" has certain heroic ambitions like her very distant fictional cousins, Henry and the "little man," but her homely common sense keeps her firmly attached to the real world of cause, effect, and probability, another instance of Crane's adjustment of his style toward a more open, realistic treatment of situation; thus the heroine's thoughts about the style of her conduct with respect to three friendly soldiers imprisoned in a barn are treated with a tender, ironic circumspection:

Heroines, she knew, conducted these matters with infinite precision and despatch. They severed the hero's bonds, cried a dramatic sentence, and stood between him and his enemies until he had run far enough away. She saw well, however, that even should she achieve all things up to the point where she might take glorious stand between the escaping and the pursuers, those grim troopers in blue would not pause. They would run around her, make a circuit. One by one she saw the gorgeous contrivances and expedients of fiction fall before the plain, homely difficulties of this situation [33.28–37].

The title story illustrates Crane's difficulty in adapting his rhetorical materials to a situation intended to reveal character. "The Little Regiment" is an anecdote about two brothers whose deep affection for one another is apparently belied by their constant bickering, and the function of the war setting, which is profusely elaborated, is merely to provide the crisis of danger which exposes unequivocally their true feelings. Though irrelevant to the dramatic issue, the war nevertheless appears as the familiar symbol of a radical violence in nature, fulsomely described in Crane's characteristic imagery and rhetoric of the haunted landscape—of lurking menace in obscure shadows, ambiguous vistas, the threatened little chapel:

> The town on the southern shore of the little river loomed spectrally, a faint etching upon the grey cloud-masses which were shifting with oily languor. A long row of guns upon the northern bank had been pitiless in their hatred, but a little battered belfry could be dimly seen still pointing with invincible resolution toward the heavens.
> The enclouded air vibrated with noises made by hidden colossal things [3.8–15].

> Ultimately the night deepened to the tone of black velvet. . . . There was little presented to the vision, but to a sense more subtle there was discernible in the atmosphere something like a pulse; a mystic beating which would have told a stranger of the presence of a giant thing–the slumbering mass of regiments and batteries [11.29–37].

The last phrase may indicate an unsuccessful attempt to solve a radical compositional problem by forcing symbolic evocations onto specific things, a tactic which negates both symbol and thing.

"The Little Regiment," it will be recalled, is the story that engaged Crane in a "daily battle with a tangle of facts and emotion," a difficulty which arose doubtless from his attempt to impose his reflexive style on an ineffectively conceived subject; but another story, "The Veteran," a very brief sequel to *The Red Badge* which tells how old Henry Fleming bravely sacrifices his life trying to save two colts from a burning barn, points clearly toward the new style Crane was apparently seeking. The rhetorical flourishes, the studied elaboration of chiaroscuro imagery, and the startling conceits of the fables of the "little man" are here largely abandoned. The lean, open, disciplined prose of "The Veteran" moves the story rapidly and precisely from the scene in which old Henry tells about running away from his first battle to the lucid and powerfully concentrated description of his final rush into the blazing barn, just before the roof falls in. Yet, faint as it is, there is behind the relatively circumstantial and enumerative style the ghost of Crane's metaphysical landscape. The story opens with a fleeting glimpse of "three hickory trees placed irregularly in a meadow that was resplendent in spring-time green," a faint echo of that spring long ago when young Henry once found the idyllic landscape suddenly filled with "red and green dragons." Farther away, standing now invincible, is the familiar little chapel, "the old, dismal belfry of the village church." Telling the story of his flight, old Henry now appreciates "some comedy in this recital." The enemy, he recalls, appeared as a "lot of flitting figures"; and he remembers thinking at the moment of panic that "the sky was falling down" and that "the world was coming to an end." Thus he names in a serene latterday vision the "red and green monsters."

The barn in which he meets his death is presented at first glance in "its usual appearance, solemn, rather mystic in the black night," but when he hurls aside the door, "a yellow flame leaped out at one corner and sped and wavered frantically up the old grey wall. It was glad, terrible, this single flame, like the wild banner of deadly and triumphant foes." The image of this satanic fire, "laden with tones of hate and death, a hymn of wonderful ferocity," crosses with the image of demonic war, and old Henry at last charges the enemy he was permitted to evade at the end of *The Red Badge*. The concluding paragraph of the story extends more appropriately to the metaphor of the "little man's" redemption, which is intrinsically tragic rather than comic, than does the ambiguous resolution of the war novel:

When the roof fell in, a great funnel of smoke swarmed toward the sky, as if the old man's mighty spirit, released from its body—a little bottle—had swelled like the genie of fable. The smoke was tinted rose-hue from the flames, and perhaps the unutterable midnights of the universe will have no power to daunt the color of this soul [86.29–34].

"The Veteran" is a skillful adaptation of Crane's symbolic materials to a new style, the style essentially of the fine story "The Open Boat," which bears, proudly perhaps, the subtitle "A Tale Intended to be after the Fact" but which also, like "The Veteran," is composed of elements obliquely drawn from his mythic imagination. When he wrote "The Veteran," the famous sea story was less than a year in the future, but he was now prepared for it—with a method, devised in the experimental stories of *The Little Regiment*, that seemed to atone for his apostasy from realism.

V

The one necessary requirement, though, was experience of the real thing. At the end of 1896 Crane had a method, earned in his painful struggle with *The Little Regiment*, but, according to theory, no subject matter on which to exercise it. He knew, or suspected, the opinion Howells might render years later in a comment on Crane's fiction: "He lost himself in a whirl of wild guesses at the fact from the ground of insufficient witness. . . . *The Red Badge of Courage*, and other things that followed it, were the throes of an art failing with material to which it could not render an absolute devotion from an absolute knowledge." [33] Crane himself would have had no reason to disagree. For whatever other motives he sought the experience of real war, this alone was sufficient.

Yet, as he came to realize after he had seen it in Greece and Cuba, war's final meaning was as elusive as the meaning of those imaginary wars he had described on the landscapes of Sullivan County and Chancellorsville. "But to get the real thing!" cries the narrator in Crane's reflective history of his experience in Cuba, "War Memories." "It seems impossible! It is because war is neither magnificent nor squalid; it is simply life, and an expression of life can always evade us. We can never tell life, one to another, although sometimes we think we can" (222.1–5). To "tell life," experienced or imagined, as he may not have fully realized when he departed for Greece in 1897, re-

---

[33] "Norris," *North American Review*, CLXXV (December, 1912), 770.

quires a coherent vision of the world and, in the case of the artist, a method for expressing it. The vision, as this brief history suggests, he had essentially from the very beginning, a sense of the world invested in a literary version of the serpent in the Edenic garden, and the method he had devised by the end of 1896 as an ingenious elaboration of the compositional patterns invented in the experimental fiction of 1892. By the time he came to see his first battle at Velestino in 1897 he had not only an attitude with which to frame its meaning, but also a practiced method for describing it.

What he saw at Velestino was, in a very important sense, what his literary sense of war compelled him to see. John Bass, correspondent for the New York *Journal*, asked him during the battle what impressed him most about it, and Crane replied by citing precisely the two radical elements of the imaginary wars described in his earlier fiction: "the attitude of the men" and the "mysterious force" which was their adversary. And he seemed also to allude to his characteristic symbolization of the mystical elements in his fictional landscapes:

> Between two great armies battling against each other the interesting thing is the mental attitude of the men. The Greeks I can see and understand, but the Turks seem unreal. They are shadows on the plain—vague figures in black, indications of a mysterious force.[34]

These are the basic elements of the one short story based on the experience, "Death and the Child," a curious elaboration in variant forms of the themes and symbols of *The Red Badge*. They figure largely in the composition of many of his war dispatches, as do other motifs drawn from the earlier fiction—or more precisely from the vision common to both the fiction and the dispatches. An incident reported in an article in the *Journal* on the battle of Velestino, for example, seems to cross exactly the image of war as the demon destroyer in the holy order of creation, as symbolized in *The Red Badge* in the famous scene in the chapel in the forest:

> The reserves coming up passed a wayside shrine. The men paused to cross themselves and pray. A shell struck the shrine and demol-

---

[34] Bass, "How Novelist Crane Acts on the Battlefield," New York *Journal*, May 23, 1897, p. 37.

ished it. The men in the rear of the column were obliged to pray to the spot where the shrine had been.[35]

The style, it may also be noted, is the spare, open, declarative style of "The Veteran" and "The Open Boat," the deceptively simple style Ernest Hemingway is often said to have invented.

It would be misleading, of course, to say that the experience of real war had no effect on Crane's art. For one thing, his experience in Greece and Cuba gave him a surer knowledge of the various instruments and accouterments of war and a certain confidence in naming and describing them. Thus the war stories after 1897 show a heightened sense of the reality of things like guns, caissons, trenches, and an understanding of the technical significance of terrain. He acquired also a practical knowledge of tactics and maneuvers and an interest in the politics of war which furnished subjects for dispatches from the front and even for one of the stories in *Wounds in the Rain*, "The Second Generation." The effect of all this on his style, in general, was to give it a certain technical authority notably absent in *The Red Badge* and *The Little Regiment*, where the things of war and the factual circumstances of military life are characteristically evoked, sometimes monotonously, in figurative rather than literal language. But the remarkable feature of the later war stories is the consistency with which they reflect the world of his imagination, the visionary landscapes which are the domains of ambiguously revealed spirits haunting his metaphysical sense of life.

The vision is severely attenuated usually, more severely often than in "The Veteran," where the firmly restrained specification of the pastoral setting and the demonic fire tends to give the style a feeling of realism. But it is nevertheless Crane's imagination which ultimately shapes the meaning of the observed event —and even seems to determine often the selection of events to be observed. The degree to which they are symbolically attenuated, as one might expect, varies widely. Thus a passage in "War Memories" describing a military hospital temporarily installed in a church, observed in El Caney in 1898, obviously elaborates a

35 "Stephen Crane at Velestino," New York *Journal*, May 11, 1897, p. 1.

Name	Where serialized - England	Where serialized - U.S.	Number words		
The Price of the Harness	Blackwood's	Cosmopolitan	6500		
The Lone Charge of William B. Perkins	Westminster Gazette	McClure's	1870		
The Clan of No-Name	Black and White	N.Y. Herald, etc	6150	21615	
God Rest Ye, Merry Gentlemen	Cornhill	Sat. Evening Post	7095	21615	
The Revenge of the Adolphus	Strand	Strand	6420		
This Majestic Lie	McClure	McClure	8600		
The Sergeant's Private Mad-house	Eng. Illustrated	Phila. Sat. E. Post	2870		
~~The Nothing of Insanity~~			5330 8180 9260	44835	
Virtue in War	Eng. Illustrated	Tillotson's Syn		53035	
Marines Signaling	—	McClure's	2700	55735	
The Second Generation	Cornhill	Phila. Sat. Ev. Post	8200		
The Cuban Campaign	Anglo-Saxon	Anglo-Saxon	20,000		

Autograph inventory for *Wounds in the Rain*

Stephen Crane on the *Three Friends* off Cuba, 1898

Crane and others on board ship for Puerto Rico, 1898

men who ~~sat~~ had sat smoking there.

This subtle essence, this soul of the life that had been, brushed like invisible wings the thoughts of the men in the swift columns that came up from the river.

Bivouac fires upon the side-walks, in the streets, in the yards, threw their ~~tall~~ wavering reflections which examined like slim red fingers the dingy shot-pierced walls and the piles of tumbled brick. A loud ~~hu~~ and endless humming of voices arose from the great blue crowds. From time to time a sharp spatter of firing from far picket lines entered this bass chorus. ~~and~~ The smell from the ~~burning~~ ~~fortress~~ smouldering ruins floated down the streets on the cold night breeze and mingled with the odors of frying bacon and the fragrance from countless little coffee-pails. The rifles, stacked in the shadows, infrequently ~~emitted~~ flashes of ~~steel~~ light. Wherever a colors lay horizontally from one stack to another was the bed of a fury-tempered eagle which was to lead men into the mystic smoke of many ~~morrows~~.

Dan came with an armful of wood derived from a garden fence. He shied around through the smoke and sparks until he arrived in a strategic position. Then he bestowed the wood dexterously upon the camp-fire. "Where's Billie — do you know? he said to the ring of men.

"Gone on picket."

"Get out! Has he? said Dan. "No business to go on picket. Why

Page 9 of an early draft of "The Little Regiment"

"And if He wills, we must die."

By Stephen Crane

A sergeant, a corporal and fourteen men of the Twelfth
Regiment of the line had been sent out to occupy a house on the
main highway. They would be at least a half of a mile in advance
of any other picket of their own people. Sergeant Morton was
deeply angry at being sent on this duty. He said that he was
over-worked. There were at least two sergeants, he claimed furiously, whose turn it should have been to go on this arduous
mission. He was treated unfairly: he was abused by his superiors;
why did any damn fool ever join the army: as for him he would get
out of it as soon as it was possible: he was sick of it: the life
of a dog. All this he said to the corporal who listened attentively, giving grunts of respectful assent. On the way to this post,
two privates took occasion to drop to the rear and pilfer in the
orchard of a deserted plantation. When the sergeant discovered
this absence, he grew black with a rage which was an accumulation
of all his irritations. "Run," you——" he howled, "bring them here!
I'll show them——" A private man swiftly to the rear. The others
of the squad began to shout personally at the two delinquents
whose figures they could see in the deep shade of the orchard,
curiously picking fruit from the ground and cramming it within
their shirts, next to their skins. The beseeching cries of their
comrades stirred the culprits more than did the bawling of the
sergeant. They ran to rejoin the squad, while holding their loaded
bosoms and with their mouths open with aggrieved explanations.

Jones faced the sergeant with a horrible cancer marked in
lumps on his left side. The disease of Patterson showed quite

aspect. About twenty windless men suddenly arrived and threw themselves upon the crest of the hill and breathed. And these twenty were joined by others and still others until almost ~~half~~ 1,100 men of the Twelfth lay upon the hill top while the ~~their~~ regiment's track was marked by body after body, in groups and singly. The first officer ~~backed~~ – perchance the first man – one never can be certain the first officer to gain the top of the hill was Timothy Lean and, such was the situation that he had the honor to receive his colonel with a bashful salute.

The regiment knew exactly what it had done. It did not have to wait to be told by the Spitzbergen newspapers. It had taken a formidable position with the loss of about 500 men and it knew it. It knew too that it was great glory for the Kicking Twelfth and as the men lay rolling on their bellies they expressed their joy in a wild cry. "Kim up the Kickers". For a moment there was nothing but joy and then suddenly company commanders were besieged by men who wished to go down the path of the charge and look ~~back~~ for their mates. The answers were without the quality of mercy. They were short, snapped quick words. "No; you can't."

The attack on the enemy's left was sounding in great rolling crashes. The shells in their flight through the air made a noise as of red hot iron plunged into water and stray bullets nipped near the ears of the Kickers.

The Kickers looked and saw. The battle was below them. The enemy was indicated by a long noisy line of gossamer smoke. Although there could be seen a toy battery with tiny men employed at the guns. All over the field the shrapnel was bursting making quick balls of white smoke. Far away two regiments of Spitzbergen infantry were charging and at the distance this charge looked like a casual stroll. It appeared that small black groups of men were walking meditatively toward the Rostina intrenchments.

A manuscript page of "The Kicking Twelfth" in Edith Richie's hand

(7.)

Now it came to pass that the Spitzbergen battery on the far right took occasion to mistake the identity of the Kicking Twelfth and the Captain of these guns, not having anything to occupy him in front, directed his six 3.2's upon the ridge where the tired Kickers lay side by side with the Rostina dead x A Shrapnel shell came swinging over the Kickers, seething and fuming x It burst directly over the trenches and the Shrapnel, of course, scattered forward, hurting nobody x But a man screamed out to his officer, "By God, Sir, That is one of our own batteries" The whole line quiv--ered with fright x Five more shells streaked overhead and one ~~[crossed out]~~ flung its hail into the middle of the 3rd Battalion's line and the Kicking Twelfth shuddered to the very ~~centre~~ of its heart — and arose like one man — and fled x

Col. Sponge, fighting, frothing at the mouth, dealing blows with his fists right & left found himself confronting a fury on horseback x Richie was as pale as death and his Eye sent out sparks x "What does this conduct mean"? he flashed out from between his fastened teeth x

Sponge could only gurgle, "The battery — the battery — the battery —

"The battery?" cried Richie in a voice which sounded like pistol shots x "Are you afraid of the guns you almost took yesterday? Go back there, you white-livered cowards! You swine! You dogs! Curs! — curs—

A manuscript page, in an unknown hand, of "The Shrapnel of Their Friends"

THE UPTURNED FACE.

By Stephen Crane

"What will we do now? "said the adjutant, troubled and
excited.

"Bury him," said Timothy Lean.

The two officers looked down close to their toes where lay
the body of their comrade. The face was chalk-blue; gleaming eyes
stared at the sky. Over the two upright figures was a windy sound
of bullets, and on the top of the hill, Lean's prostrate company
of Spitzbergen infantry was firing measured volleys.

"Don't you think it would be better——," began the adjutant,
"we might leave him until to-morrow."

"No," said Lean,"Wean't hold that post an hour longer. I've
got to fall back, and we've got to bury old Bill."

"Of course," said the adjutant at once. "Your men got in-
trenching tools?"

Lean shouted back to his little line, and two men came slowly,
one with a pick one with a shovel. They started in the direction
of the Rostina sharp-shooters. Bullets cracked near their ears.
"Dig here," said Lean gruffly. The men, thus caused to lower their
glances to the turf, became hurried and frightened merely because
they could not look to see whence the bullets came. The dull heat
of the pick striking the earth sounded amid the swift snap of
close bullets. Presently the other private began to shovel.

"I suppose," said the adjutant, slowly, "we'd better search
his clothes for—things."

Lean nodded; together in curious abstraction they looked at
the body. Then Lean stirred his shoulders suddenly, arousing himself.

First page of a typescript of "The Upturned Face"

pattern of imagery that can be traced to a Sullivan County sketch, "Four Men in a Cave":

The interior of the church was too cavelike in its gloom for the eyes of the operating surgeons, so they had had the altar-table carried to the doorway, where there was a bright light. Framed then in the black archway was the altar-table with the figure of a man upon it. He was naked save for a breech-clout, and so close, so clear was the ecclesiastic suggestion, that one's mind leaped to a fantasy that this thin pale figure had just been torn down from a cross. The flash of the impression was like light, and for this instant it illumined all the dark recesses of one's remotest idea of sacrilege, ghastly and wanton. I bring this to you merely as an effect—an effect of mental light and shade, if you like; something done in thought similar to that which the French Impressionists do in color; something meaningless and at the same time overwhelming, crushing, monstrous [254.19–33].

The passage suggest Crane's conception of art better perhaps than anything else he ever wrote about it, and "Four Men in a Cave" illustrates how consistently his late writing held to a principle grasped half-intuitively at the very beginning of his career. The sketch describes a nightmare adventure in a "haunted" cave where the "little man" and his companions are confronted by a mystical, priestlike creature threatening violence:

A great gray stone, cut squarely, like an altar, sat in the middle of the floor. Over it burned three candles in swaying tin cups hung from the ceiling. Before it, with what seemed to be a small volume clasped in his yellow fingers, stood a man. . . . He fixed glinting, fiery eyes upon the heap of men. . . .[36]

The priestlike man turns out to be a half-crazed recluse who forces the terrified men into a poker game at the point of a knife. The "small volume" is seen later as a deck of cards. The images common to both passages—the altar, the gloomy cave, the priestlike spectral man, the garish lights, and the vague aura of sacrilege—are radical elements of Crane's imagination.

[36] *New York Tribune*, July 3, 1892, pt. 2, p. 14.

More tenuous in its connection with his symbolic world is his description of his first-observed instrument of real war, a torpedo boat off the Cretan coast in 1897:

A scouting torpedo-boat as small as a gnat crawling on an enormous decorated wall came from the obscurity of the shore. Apparently it looked us over and was satisfied, for in a few moments it was returned to obscurity.[37]

Whether the image of the animistic boat, appearing in the perspective of a vast distance out of a mystic obscurity was an actual historical event rendered in casually figurative language or whether it was purely an event of the literary imagination is hard to determine, though one suspects the latter in view of the elaboration on the obscurity to which the boat returns: "It was lonely and desolate like a land of Despair. . . . Nothing lived there save the venomous torpedo-boat, which, after all, had been little more than a shadow on the water." [38]

Circumstantial as the later stories appear to be, casually considered, they are nevertheless in one degree or another energized by Crane's mythic imagination, though they may seem, out of the context of the earlier fiction, to be merely decorated narratives of random incidents of war. An example is the comical anecdote based on a real-life war adventure, "The Lone Charge of William B. Perkins." The story is a curious adaptation of the version of the fable of the "little man." The hero in real life was Ralph Paine, a war correspondent who foolishly wandered out of the trenches at Guantanamo to attack a Spanish sniper observed in a distant clump of mysterious trees; Paine retreated under heavy rifle fire to the safety of an abandoned sugar boiler and eventually returned unhurt to his own lines. In Crane's fictional version—and the story is fiction in the same sense "The Open Boat" is—the hero appears in the basic guise of the vainglorious "little man." Discovering the Spanish sniper, Perkins announces his "perception" in a "loud voice" and "declared hoarsely that if he only had a rifle he would go and possess himself of this particular enemy." Only when the hero finds himself in a sudden

---

[37] "An Impression of the 'Concert,' " *Westminster Gazette*, May 3, 1897, p. 81.
[38] *Ibid.*

storm of bullets does it occur to him that he is merely "an almshouse idiot plunging through hot crackling thickets on a June morning in Cuba." Then "the beauties of rural Minnesota illuminated his conscience with the gold of lazy corn, with the sleeping green of meadows, with the cathedral gloom of pine forests." He seeks refuge in the rusted sugar boiler, "a temple shining resplendent with safety." When the enemy rifle fire dies down, he strolls back to his trenches "with his hat not able to fit his head for the new bumps of wisdom that were on it." Later he is observed "wearing a countenance of poignant thoughtfulness."

The relation of the story to *The Red Badge* is clear enough. The vainglorious hero, the wild assault upon the concealed enemy, the mystical aspect of the adversary, the sudden panic, the yearning vision of a reassuring, idyllic nature, the retreat to the degraded temple, the reconstruction of pride to humility—all are major motifs in Crane's work, concentrated in *The Red Badge*. These figurations constantly recur in the Cuban stories and in the tales of the mythical Spitzbergen army in "The Kicking Twelfth," and though they are often more or less decorative in some of these stories, as if drawn expediently from cultivated literary resources, they also echo the portentous drama conceived in Crane's radical sense of man and his enigmatic world. Even though a story like "The Price of the Harness," based on the battle of San Juan Hill, celebrates the stoic devotion to duty of the professional soldier (an expansion, it might be noted, of the sense of character expressed in the conversion of the "loud soldier" in *The Red Badge* to a soldier of quiet, modest competency), it also obliquely defines war as the dark manifestation of a devil-corrupted world. Its realism accommodates the myth that haunted Crane's imagination from first to last. The shadows of the Cuban landscape, like those of Sullivan County and Chancellorsville, are "all grim and of ghostly shape." The setting Cuban sun throws its hostile glance upon the problematical landscape just as it does in the famous image at the end of Chapter IX in *The Red Badge*. The devoted regulars in "The Price of the Harness" perceive that their war is "not much like a battle with men" but "a battle with a bit of charming scenery, enigmatically potent for death."

It may be, as it has been said, that Crane's credo as an

observer of war was "only [to] say what I saw." [39] But what he said early in 1896, when he was trying painfully to reconcile his theoretical commitment to realism as he wrote the stories in *The Little Regiment*, is also true. "I understand that a man is born into the world with his own pair of eyes, and he is not at all responsible for his vision—he is merely responsible for his quality of personal honesty. To keep close to this personal honesty is my supreme ambition." [40] The war stories in this volume tell what he saw. But they tell also what he had been seeing for a long time—a long time before he saw real battlefields in Greece and Cuba.

J. B. C.

[39] In *The War Dispatches of Stephen Crane* (New York University Press, 1964), p. 107, R. W. Stallman and E. R. Hagemann remark: "Crane would agree with [war correspondent] George W. Steevens' credo as reporter: 'I only say what I saw.'"

[40] Crane to John Northern Hilliard, Hartwood, N.Y., Jan. 28, [1896], *Letters*, p. 108.

TEXTUAL INTRODUCTION

I

THE LITTLE REGIMENT

THE earliest certain reference to the book collection *The Little Regiment* comes in a letter from Crane in Hartwood to Ripley Hitchcock, his Appleton editor, on March 26, 1896: "As for Edward Arnold, his American manager is an old schoolmate and ten year's friend of mine and he conducted such a campaign against me as is seldom seen. Once I thought he was about to get 'The Little Regiment' when you stepped in and saved it" (*Letters*, p. 121).[1] Sometime, then, between mid-February when he was finishing the last story to be written—"The Little Regiment"—and late March, Appleton accepted the collection of Civil-War stories. On May 11, 1896, William Appleton from the firm's London office wrote to Heinemann: "We agree to let you have the publication in England etc. of Maggie and The Little Regiment and Other Stories on a royalty of 15 per cent of retail, you to pay an advance of £30 for each book. 'Maggie' we expect to publish in June, and I have no doubt that we shall be able to send you proofs very shortly. 'The Little Regiment' will be ready

---

[1] Earlier possible references appear to be to other books. For example, on January 12, 1896, Crane wrote to Nellie Crouse: "McClure is having one of his fits of desire to have me write for him and I am obliged to see him. Moreover, I have a new novel coming out in the spring and I am also obliged to confer with the Appleton's about that" (*Letters*, p. 100). Although in a footnote Stallman conjectures that this new novel is *The Little Regiment*, Crane must be referring to *The Third Violet*. He mailed the manuscript of *The Third Violet* to Ripley Hitchcock of Appleton either on December 27, 1895 (*Letters*, p. 83), or December 30 (*Letters*, p. 85) and would have every expectation at that time of early publication. It was the newspaper serialization later decided on that delayed its appearance between covers. On February 15, 1896, Crane wrote to the editor of *The Critic*: "This winter I wrote a novel 'The Third Violet,' which is to be published by Appletons. . . . I am now finishing a novelette for S. S. McClure called The Little Regiment" (*Letters*, p. 117). The novelette obviously is the revised short story, not the book collection, and thus the earlier letter must be dissociated from *The Little Regiment*.

in the autumn" (typed copy in Lilly Library, Indiana University). In the Lilly collection is the Heinemann answer on May 13 accepting the terms of this letter of May 11. The Lilly Library also has the contract for *The Little Regiment* between Crane and Appleton, dated May 26, 1896, in which the six stories comprising the volume are listed by title and the royalty is assigned as 15 per cent of retail. Furthermore, in the Lilly Library is an autograph letter from Crane written on Appleton stationery and dated July [16, 1896]: "Dear Mr. Appleton: I have written to Arnold that your arrangement with Heinemann concerning The Little Regiment and The Third Violet must stand—that it was a prior and just contract and that I intend to see that Heinemann's rights in the book shall be guarded. Very truly, Stephen Crane". No other mention of the book has been preserved save for a telegram from Jacksonville, Florida, to Appleton, dated February 24, 1897, asking for payment from the Heinemann edition to be wired Crane (*Letters*, p. 139), and a reference on February 4, 1899, about a plan to sequester royalties from his four Appleton books (*Letters*, p. 208).

Copyright was applied for on October 7, 1896, and deposit made in the Library of Congress on October 30. *Publishers' Weekly* announced it as 'just ready' on November 7, and it seems to have been published on or about that date and not on the announcement date in the *Weekly* of December 5. *The Bibliography of American Literature* notes receipt of copies by November 10; the Harvard copy AC85.C8507.896l is signed Chester Noyes Greenough and dated November 12, 1896. The price was one dollar.

The first edition, first printing, may be described as follows:

𝕿𝖍𝖊 𝕷𝖎𝖙𝖙𝖑𝖊 𝕽𝖊𝖌𝖎𝖒𝖊𝖓𝖙 | 𝕬𝖓𝖉 𝕺𝖙𝖍𝖊𝖗 𝕰𝖕𝖎𝖘𝖔𝖉𝖊𝖘 𝖔𝖋 𝖙𝖍𝖊 𝕬𝖒𝖊𝖗𝖎𝖈𝖆𝖓 | 𝕮𝖎𝖛𝖎𝖑 𝕸𝖆𝖗 | 𝕭𝖞 | 𝕾𝖙𝖊𝖕𝖍𝖊𝖓 𝕮𝖗𝖆𝖓𝖊 | 𝕬𝖚𝖙𝖍𝖔𝖗 𝖔𝖋 𝕿𝖍𝖊 𝕽𝖊𝖉 𝕭𝖆𝖉𝖌𝖊 𝖔𝖋 𝕮𝖔𝖚𝖗𝖆𝖌𝖊, 𝖆𝖓𝖉 𝕸𝖆𝖌𝖌𝖎𝖊 | [Appleton device] | 𝕹𝖊𝖜 𝖄𝖔𝖗𝖐 | 𝕯. 𝕬𝖕𝖕𝖑𝖊𝖙𝖔𝖓 𝖆𝖓𝖉 𝕮𝖔𝖒𝖕𝖆𝖓𝖞 | 1896

Collation: [1]⁸ 2–13⁸, pp. [i–vi] 1–196 [197–202]. Text paper is unwatermarked laid with vertical chainlines 31 mm. apart; leaf measures 7¼ × 4⅞″, top edge stained yellow, all other edges untrimmed. The first leaf of the flyleaf fold is pasted down on the cover under the front endpaper leaf, its conjugate appearing after the free endpaper, and vice versa in the back. Both endpapers and flyleaves, front and back, are the laid text paper, unwatermarked, ordinarily with vertical chainlines but with horizontal chains known.

Contents: p. i: half-title, 'THE LITTLE REGIMENT | AND OTHER EPISODES OF THE AMERICAN | CIVIL WAR'; p. ii: advt. for 14th edition of *The Red Badge of Courage* and the 4th edition of *Maggie*; p. iii: title; p. iv: 'COPYRIGHT, 1896, | BY D. APPLETON AND COMPANY. | Copyright, 1895, 1896, by Stephen Crane.'; p. v: contents; p. vi: blank. p. 1: text begins with 'THE LITTLE REGIMENT.'; on p. 196: 'THE END.'; p. 197: publisher's advts. beginning 'GILBERT PARKER'S BEST BOOKS.'; on p. 202: last advt. for 'THE LILAC SUNBONNET.' (The plate for the Gilbert Parker advt. is the same as that in the earlier Appleton *Maggie*.)

The Little Regiment, p. 1   An Indiana Campaign, p. 128
Three Miraculous Soldiers, p. 45   A Gray Sleeve, p. 151
A Mystery of Heroism, p. 106   The Veteran, p. 185

Binding: Tan buckram. *Front cover*: '[orn.] | T²HE LITTLE | REGI-MENT | BY | STEPHEN CRANE | [orn.]'. *Spine*: '[orn.] | THE | LITTLE | REGIMENT | [orn.] | CRANE | [orn.] | APPLETONS'. *Back cover*: blank. T² on front cover in red within panel of gold lozenges; ornaments and all initial letters on cover and spine except 'B' of 'BY' in red, other lettering in black.

Copies: University of Virginia Barrett copy PS1449.C85.L5 1896b (551404) preserves dust jacket, buff paper, lettered and ornamented like the binding except the panel for T² has black instead of gold lozenges. Back cover and flaps are blank. This same dust jacket, less perfectly preserved, also in UVa McGregor copy A1896. C7L5 (281464). Columbia (B812.C85.S7 1896a), with dust jacket. Yale (dated December 25, 1896).

Variants: Harvard (AC85.C8507.896l) with endpapers and flyleaves of unwatermarked laid text paper but horizontal chainlines; University of Virginia (Taylor [508330]) with front endpaper and flyleaf of unwatermarked wove paper and back leaves of unwatermarked vertical-chainline text paper.

A later printing, or series of printings, distinguishes itself by changed advertisements. Page 197 is headed by an advt. for The Beginners of a Nation series by Edward Eggleston, the first item *The Seats of the Mighty*; and page 202 ends with the announcement of a series called The Story of the West. At least two distinct printings with these altered advertisements may be differentiated in one by the use for the text of the unwatermarked laid paper of the first printing(s) but in the other of a similar laid paper with vertical chainlines but watermarked with the Appleton device. The priority of the two printings with different paper has not been established. The endpapers and flyleaves may vary between laid and wove paper.

Copies: Columbia (B812.C85.S7 1896a), text laid paper no watermark, endpapers and flyleaves laid, no watermark. Harvard (AC 85.C8507.896la), text laid paper no watermark, endpapers laid with watermark, flyleaves laid without watermark. University of Virginia, Barrett (551402), watermarked laid paper in text, wove endpapers and flyleaves. British Museum (012704.f.13), text laid paper no watermark, endpapers laid no watermark, flyleaves wove, date-stamped May 19, 1897.

Advance copies: In the Barrett Collection at the University of Virginia is preserved an advance copy (551403) of the American sheets as issued in the first printing, the text with unwatermarked laid paper, vertical chainlines, and the advertisements for Gilbert Parker and *The Lilac Sunbonnet* respectively. The sheets are bound without endpapers in plain paper wrappers perhaps once white but now aged to buff. In England the Bodleian Library (Fic.2712.e.13-28) preserves the same form of advance copy but with a cancellans title-page reading 'THE LITTLE REGIMENT | And Other Episodes of the American | Civil War | BY | STEPHEN CRANE | AUTHOR OF "THE RED BADGE OF COURAGE," | AND "MAGGIE" | LONDON | WILLIAM HEINEMANN | 1896', the verso blank. This title was printed in England, as shown by the laid paper with vertical chainlines and the watermark 'Abbey Mills | Greenfield'. The half-title pp. i–ii has been removed, presumably because of the Appleton advertisements on its verso, and the three final leaves of Appleton advertisements, pp. 197–202, have also been canceled. This deposit copy is stamped November 13, 1896. A similar copy, but with the wrappers removed upon rebinding, is preserved in the British Museum (012601.i.30/17), date-stamped October 30, 1896. This represents, quite clearly, Heinemann's copyright deposit while his own edition was printing.

The first English edition by Heinemann was announced in the *Publishers' Circular* of February 13, 1897. The Williams and Starrett *Bibliography* is in error in stating that this edition was date-stamped in the British Museum on October 30, 1896, since that deposit copy was the advance Appleton sheets with a cancellans Heinemann title-page, and at present date the British Museum does not own a copy of the 1897 Heinemann edition.

The edition, which sold for 3/– cloth and 2/6 wrappers, may be described as follows:

The Little Regiment | And Other Episodes of the | American Civil War | By | Stephen Crane | Author of | "The Red Badge of Courage," "Maggie" | Etc. | London | William Heinemann | 1897

Collation: [a]⁴ A–I⁸ K⁴, pp. [i–vi] vii [viii], [1–2] 3–150 [151–152], misnumbering p. vii as '5'. Text paper is unwatermarked laid with vertical chainlines 25 mm. apart; leaf measures 7½ × 4¾", top edge untrimmed and other edges rough trimmed. Sixteen pages of publisher's catalogue bound in.

Contents: p. i: advt. for *The Red Badge of Courage*; p. ii: advt. for *Maggie*; p iii: half-title, 'The Little Regiment'; p. iv: advts. for the Pioneer Series; p. v: title; p. vi: '*All rights reserved*'; p. vii: contents; p. viii: blank; p. 1: half-title 'The Little Regiment'; p. 2: blank; p. 3: text; on p. 150: '*Printed by* BALLANTYNE, HANSON & Co. | *Edinburgh and London*'; pp. 151–152: blank.

Binding: The 2/6 wrappered copy was published with the front wrapper lettered and decorated '[green] THE PIONEER SERIES. | [short rule] | [black] The Little Regiment | [panel illustrating four Japanese figures, in black, green, tan, yellow] | [green] London: WILLIAM HEINEMANN.' In the 3/– cloth copies wove endpapers are present and the front wrapper is bound in as a flyleaf, the back wrapper being removed. The cloth is dark green. Front cover: '[within a decorative panel] *The* | *Little* | *Regiment* | *Stephen Crane*'. Spine: *The* | *Little* | *Regiment* | [orn.] | *Stephen Crane* | HEINEMANN'. Back cover: '[within a decorative panel] *The Pioneer Series*'. All lettering in white.

Copies: University of Virginia, Barrett (551405) in cloth. Columbia University (SC Collection) in wrappers; in Crane's hand on front leaf: 'Crane | Brede Place |||'. Then in Cora's hand, 'This book belongs to | Mʳˢ Stephen Crane | Brede Place | Sussex | 1897 ||| '. London Library, rebound and wants pp. i–ii, 151–152, and publisher's catalogue. Date-stamped February 20, 1897.

Variant: In the Barrett Collection, University of Virginia, is a copy (551406) bound in orange cloth, front and back covers blank, spine lettered in black 'THE | LITTLE REGIMENT | STEPHEN CRANE | [Heinemann's device within frame] | HEINEMANN'. The endpapers are wove. The wrappered front cover is not present, but the publisher's catalogue is appended.

Published perhaps on July 9, 1898, although not announced in the *Publishers' Circular* until July 16, at a price of 6/–, is Heinemann's *Pictures of War*, collecting *The Red Badge of Courage* and *The Little Regiment*. The edition may be described as follows:

Pictures of War | By | Stephen Crane | Author of | "The Open Boat," "The Third Violet," etc. | London | William Heinemann | 1898

Collation: [a]⁴ b⁸ A–I⁸ K–U⁸ X⁸ Y⁴, pp. [i–viii] ix–xxiv, [1] 2–344. Text paper is unwatermarked wove; leaf measures 7⁷⁄₁₆ × 5″, bottom edge trimmed but other edges untrimmed; endpapers unwatermarked wove. 32 pp. publisher's catalogue bound in.

Contents: pp. i–ii: advts. for Stephen Crane's Works; p. iii: half-title, 'Pictures of War'; p. iv: advt. 14 Heinemann novels for 1898; p. v: title; p. vi: '*NEW EDITION* | *The Red Badge of Courage, 1st Impression, 1895* | *2nd, 3rd, 4th, 5th, and 6th Impressions, 1896* | *The Little Regiment, and other Stories, 1st* | *Impression, 1897* | *This Edition enjoys Copyright in all countries* | *signatory to the Berne Treaty, and is* | *not to be imported into the United States* | *of America.*'; p. vii: contents; p. viii: blank; pp. ix–xxiv: 'An Appreciation' signed 'GEORGE WYNDHAM'; p. 1: The Red Badge of Courage; p. 196: blank; p. 197: The Little Regiment; on p. 344: 'Printed by BALLANTYNE, HANSON & Co. | Edinburgh & London'.

Binding: Tan linen. Front cover: '[black] Pictures of War | [orange] *By Stephen Crane* | [orange sword orn.]'. *Spine*: '[black] Pictures | [black] of War | [orange] *By Stephen* | [orange] *Crane* | [Heinemann device in orange and black] | [black] *Heinemann*'. Back cover: sword orn. in orange.

Copies: University of Virginia–Barrett (551450); Columbia University.

In the regular edition, as above, the Contents list does not notice the Wyndham Appreciation, which seems to have been in the nature of an afterthought.

A Colonial Edition was also published, from the same plates but with the Contents corrected to include notice of the Wyndham Appreciation.

PICTURES OF WAR | THE RED BADGE OF COURAGE | THE LITTLE REGIMENT, Etc. | BY | STEPHEN CRANE | WITH AN APPRECIATION BY | GEORGE WYNDHAM, M.P. | LONDON | WILLIAM HEINEMANN | 1898

Contents: pp. i–ii: blank; p. iii: advts. for Colonial Library; p. iv: advt. for Crane's Works; p. v: title; p. vi: '*All rights reserved*'; p. vii: contents; p. viii: blank. Rest as in trade edition. No publisher's catalogue.

Binding: Buff paper wrappers: Front wrapper: '𝕳𝔢𝔦𝔫𝔢𝔪𝔞𝔫𝔫'𝔰 𝕮𝔬𝔩𝔬-𝔫𝔦𝔞𝔩 𝕷𝔦𝔟𝔯𝔞𝔯𝔶 | [short rule] | Pictures of War | BY | STEPHEN CRANE | *Author of "THE OPEN BOAT," ETC.* | LONDON | WILLIAM HEINEMANN | *Published for sale in the British Colonies and India only* | *** *This volume may also be had in Cloth Binding, price Three Shillings* | *and Sixpence*'.
On the inside of the front wrapper are advertisements for the Colonial Library, and these are continued on the inside and outside of the back wrapper. Wove paper, all edges trimmed.

Copies: Columbia (front wrapper signed 'Mrs Stephen Crane | 6, Milborne Grove, The Boltons | S.W.' Copy is from Crane's private library.)

Variant: Also from Crane's private library and signed from Brede Place by Cora Crane in the Columbia University Libraries Special Collections is a copy of the trade edition text sheets (contents without the Appreciation) bound in Colonial wrappers but with a conjugate variant title-page: 'PICTURES OF WAR | BY | STEPHEN CRANE | AUTHOR OF "THE OPEN BOAT," ETC. | LONDON | WILLIAM HEINEMANN | 1898'.

Pictures of War (1898) was printed from the plates—repaged and resigned—of the Heinemann *The Little Regiment* edition of 1897. No textual change was made in the plates between these 'editions.'

In the preparation of the present text the five University of Virginia examples of the 1896 Appleton edition were collated on the Hinman Machine, using the advance copy (Barrett 551403) as the control. No change whatever was made in the plates between the advance copy and the other examples of the printing(s) with the Gilbert Parker advertisement on page 197, or in the later printing(s) with The Beginners of a Nation series advertised on page 197.

The two University of Virginia—Barrett copies of the 1897 Heinemann edition were collated against each other on the Hinman Machine and showed no textual variation. In addition, Barrett 551405 of the 1897 edition was collated on the Hinman Machine against the Barrett 551450 copy of *Pictures of War* (1898) and against the 1916 reprint of *Pictures* from the Yale University Library collection but with no textual change in the plates revealed. On the evidence, the text of the American and English first editions of *The Little Regiment* may be taken as established in invariant form.

THE LITTLE REGIMENT

"The Little Regiment" appeared first in *McClure's Magazine*, VII (June, 1896), 12–22, advertised as by the author of *The Red Badge of Courage*.[2] Simultaneously it was published in England in *Chapman's Magazine*, IV (June, 1896), 214–232, copyrighted by Stephen Crane, also noted as the author of *The Red Badge*. In August, 1896, *Current Literature*, XX, 145–146, digested it under the section "The Sketch Book: Character in Outline," with the heading 'In the Heat of Battle.' The excerpts comprise 3.1–4.26, 16.11–17.10, and 17.20–18.2 in the present edition. *McClure's Magazine* was credited as the source but collation discloses that, instead, the *Chapman's* text was reprinted. In the 1896 Appleton collection *The Little Regiment* the story occupied pages 1–44, and in the Heinemann *Little Regiment* (1897) it took up pages 1–32. Finally, Heinemann reprinted it in his collection *Pictures of War* (1898), pages 197–226. In an autograph list preserved at Columbia University, perhaps to be dated

---

2 Two illustrations and a decorative initial were drawn by I. W. Tower. The illustrations have the legends: 'IN ONE MYSTIC CHANGING OF THE FOG . . . A SMALL GROUP OF THE GRAY SKIRMISHERS . . . WERE SUDDENLY DISCLOSED TO DAN AND THOSE ABOUT HIM' and 'THE LINE, GALLOPING, SCRAMBLING, PLUNGING LIKE A HERD OF WOUNDED HORSES, WENT OVER A FIELD THAT WAS SOWN WITH CORPSES.'

near August, 1896, the story is listed below "Three Miraculous Soldiers" with ditto marks beneath its notation 'English rights.' Among Crane's manuscript fragments in the Columbia University Libraries is a holograph leaf that seems to be the opening paragraph of what may represent the very earliest attempt at what was to become "The Little Regiment." At least, the name Dempster, the drizzle, the standing in the mud, and the swearing from a rich vocabulary are parts of "The Little Regiment" (3.26–29; 4.27–29; 6.9–13). This reads:

Dempster began the war with no small and valueless collection of epithets which were his by right of creation and construction and reconstruction. Moreover, he was a man quick to adapt the better part of another's thought and as he was a pleasant fellow, both pious and impious according to the crisis, he had made much talk with other soldiers and soon acquired all that was skilful and profound in the language of the entire corps. Standing ankle-deep in mud and with a cold insistent drizzle flinging it's fine drops at his neck, he used his [stored *deleted*] vocabulary in a description of his emotion.

However, regardless of the assignment of this fragment, a piece of the actual story in an advanced draft state is preserved in a single leaf, also in the Columbia University Libraries Special Collections. This is paged 9 and is written in black ink on the recto of a leaf of cheap wove unwatermarked ruled paper, 253 × 201 mm., the rules 10 mm. apart. On the verso in Crane's hand is the penciled word count 240. The text, which is associated with 9.9–25 and 18.14–18, reads as follows:

men who had ᵃ sat smoking there.
This subtle essence, this soul of the life that had been, brushed like invisible wings the thoughts of the men in the swift columns that came up from the river.
Bivouac fires upon the side-walks, in the streets, in the yards, threw high ᵇ their wavering ᶜ reflections which examined like slim red fingers the dingy shot-pierced walls and the piles of tumbled brick. A loud and ᵈ endless humming of voices arose from the great blue crowds. From time to time a sharp spatter of firing from far picket lines entered this bass chorus. The ᵉ smell from the smouldering ᶠ ruins floated down the streets on the cold night breeze and mingled with the odor ᵍ of frying bacon and the fragrance from countless little coffee-pails. The rifles, stacked in the shadows, infrequently emitted ʰ

flashes of steely [1] light. Wherever a colors lay horizontally from one stack to another was the bed of a fury-tempered eagle which was to lead men into the mystic smoke of many morrows.

Dan came with an armful of wood derived from a garden fence. He shied around through the smoke and sparks until he arrived in a strategic position. Then he bestowed the wood dexterously upon the camp-fire. "Where's Billie—do you know?" he said to the ring of men.

"Gone on picket."

"Get out! Has he?" said Dan. "No business to go on picket. Why

[a] had] *preceded by deleted* 'sat'
[b] high] *interlined with a caret*
[c] wavering] *preceded by deleted* 'tall'
[d] and] *preceded by deleted* 'hu'
[e] The] *preceded by deleted* 'and'
[f] smouldering] *preceded by deleted* 'burning factories'
[g] odor] *final* 's' *deleted*
[h] emitted] *interlined above deleted* 'caught'
[i] steely] *interlined above deleted* 'silver'

It is just possible that the manuscript fragment is from an early version of the story mentioned in a letter to Willis Brooks Hawkins: "I am writing a story—"The Little Regiment" for McClure. It is awfully hard. I have invented the sum of my invention in regard to war and this story keeps me in internal despair. However I am coming on with it very comfortably after all" (*Letters*, p. 72). This letter has been conjecturally dated November 12, 1895, but seems to be somewhat later, perhaps after the December 30 letter to John Phillips of McClure, although this latter sounds more as if a series of articles had been proposed for Civil-War battles, not stories (*Letters*, pp. 83–84). However, on January 9, 1896, Crane is writing to Phillips about Fredericksburg and his intense interest in this battle (*Letters*, p. 98), and in a letter to Nellie Crouse conjecturally dated January 26 (*Letters*, p. 102) he has returned from Virginia. On January 27 (p. 107) he writes to McClure that "I am getting the Fredericksburg row into shape," but it is also shown here that he had already written and had had accepted "Three Miraculous Soldiers." Perhaps it is "The Little Regiment" that is referred to in terms that show it was nearing completion in a letter on February 5 to Nellie Crouse: "I am engaged in rowing with people who wish me to write more war-stories. Hang all war-stories! Nevertheless I submitted in one case and now I have a daily battle with a tangle of facts and emotions. I am however doing the thing in a way that is not without a mild satisfaction to me" (p. 111). It would seem likely that the war story "The Little Regiment" started in November–December, 1895, was revised consequent upon his visit to Fredericksburg; and indeed the rearrangement of the material in the story's printed form from that in the early manuscript fragment suggests a thorough recasting in January and February, 1896, for it was still unfinished on February 15 (*Letters*, p. 117).

The *McClure's Magazine* text (McC) was presumably printed from a typescript made from Crane's final manuscript. *Chapman's Magazine* (Ch) varies substantively on a number of occasions from *McClure's*, but the general closeness of the accidentals suggests that the two texts are related in some manner. One possible hypothesis is that McClure, acting as Crane's agent, sent the carbon abroad for sale through its English office, although the possibility must be considered that, instead, an early stage of the *McClure's* proof formed the English printer's copy. This question is best considered after the ground has been cleared by an examination of the relation of the Appleton 1896 version (A1) to *McClure's*.

Since *McClure's* appeared in June, 1896, and *The Little Regiment* copyright was applied for on October 7, 1896, with deposit in the Library of Congress on October 30, one would normally expect that a clipping from the magazine would have been available as printer's copy. But some confused and confusing evidence suggests that "The Little Regiment" was in book proof by the time the magazine appeared, or shortly thereafter. In a letter from Hartwood to the Appleton editor Ripley Hitchcock that Stallman dates June 6 or June 13, 1896 (but is perhaps in July), Crane writes: "Through the fault of the U.S.P.O. Dept.—no less —proofs did not reach me until today. I return them herewith." Then after a remark that he has asked someone at Arnold's (which published *George's Mother* and was angling for the English rights of *The Little Regiment* and *The Third Violet*) to come to Hartwood, he apparently signed the letter. But the signature (and just possibly some text) has been cut out, and hence the final and important statement may not be complete, or it may be all there since it is in the nature of a postscript. At any rate, when the paper is once more intact, the letter concludes, "The copy was not complete. Used June McClure's" (*Letters*, p. 125). The difficulty of the date remains, for it seems clear that there is an intimate connection between this and the July letter in the Lilly Library, quoted above, which ought to link a visit of Arnold's representative to Hartwood (prior to July 16) with the attempt of Arnold's to secure the English rights for *The Little Regiment* and *The Third Violet*. However, under any circumstances the reference to the June *McClure's* would seem to establish the proof he was returning as that for the book form of "The Little Regiment," which had appeared in the June issue of the magazine. Yet the exact meaning of 'the copy' is obscure, and even more obscure is the question how and where it was incomplete. That is, if Crane meant that the original printer's copy he had submitted was incomplete and he had pieced it out with the June *McClure's*, the evidence of the A1 text would be against him (unless it were some minor lacunae) and the conjectural date of the letter would be much too early. Moreover, it would seem pointless to add a postscript on the subject at this late date. On the other hand, Crane may have been remarking that the copy of the story sent him with the proof was incomplete and that he had had to read proof for part of it against the text in the June *McClure's*. This could be but may somewhat strain the actual words of the postscript. The third possibility is that he was answering some query of Hitchcock's about the nature of the printer's copy for this story, in which case he could have been remarking that his own copy (manuscript) was incomplete and he had therefore provided copy from the magazine. (One may note that the next story, "Three Miraculous Soldiers," had been sent to Appleton in typescript.) No certain judgment can be made between these various speculations, although the third may seem the most probable. Whether Crane sent his manuscript to McClure, who had the typing done, or himself provided McClure with a typescript and carbon, he would have had no copy left except his manuscript; but he would almost certainly have had a spare set of the magazine proofs to send to Appleton, and in the letter carelessly used the phrase 'June McClure's' when he meant the proof of the story that had (or was to) come out in the June number of the magazine.

Some evidence exists of a connection between *Chapman's* and the Appleton text that would support a hypothesis that, in considerable part at least, an early or intermediate set of the McC magazine proofs did indeed serve as Appleton printer's copy. Although both Ch and A1 have a number of readings unique with each, they join against *McClure's* in three interesting substantive variants: McC reads *matched* against their *match* (11.7), *skin* against their *face* (20.34), and *sat* against their *saw* (21.11). Both *match* and *saw* are misprints, or common errors derived from some source, and might have been mended independently in McC even though the odds might seem distinctly against independent correction of *match*, which makes sufficient sense. But the reading *skin* in McC for *face* is more difficult to assign to fortune, and we may take it with some confidence that these three readings stood in the printer's copy both for *Chapman's* and for *The Little Regiment,* and that the McC variants represent a later stage of the text, whether from authorial or editorial correction. If this is so, in these sections of "The Little Regiment" Crane could not have provided Appleton with an actual clipping of the June *McClure's,* but he could have furnished for the text in which these readings appear either a magazine proof before the corrections were made or else a typescript (or carbon) that had the errors in it. Only general probability can be appealed to, but it may seem that the odds would favor Crane's having in his possession an extra copy of the proof, on the analogy of the preserved *McClure's* proofsheets of "The Veteran" among his possessions that Cora sold after his death,[3] instead of an incomplete carbon copy.[4] If so, the McC forms of these three readings must represent final proof corrections.

Other evidence also suggests that A1 was printed from proofs of McC. At 14.14–16 McC and A1 read, *leaving a history of*

---

[3] These sheets are preserved in the Special Collections of the Columbia University Libraries. They are early proofs, before editorial correction, and one of them bears a request for its return to the magazine. See the Textual Introduction to "The Veteran."

[4] That is, if Crane had a typescript and carbon made up to sell to McClure, it would seem that he would have handed both of them over since McClure would be acting as his agent for foreign sale, unless it was privately understood that McClure would send proof to England. On the other hand, if McClure made up the typescript (as may seem more probable), Crane would have been returned, normally, only his manuscript.

*many movements in the wet yellow turf, cursing the atmos-
phere, blazing away every time they could identify the enemy.*
Ch agrees except that it has *damning the atmosphere*. Again, at
21.7–8 *He made a gesture then of irritation and rage. Curse
it! Don't I know it?*" but Ch reads *Damn it!* It seems almost
inevitable that *damn* in Ch derived from Crane's manuscript and
that the common substitute *curse* represents *McClure's* censorship. (American family magazines of this era were very cautious
indeed, as the history of Crane's text illustrates.) Although it is
possible that both Appleton and *McClure's* hit upon the same
substitute for *damn*, it is simpler to take it that A1 copied McC in
these readings. If so, A1 would need to have been set from an
early proof, not a clipping of the magazine, for the second *damn*
occurs in A1 only four lines before the error *saw* that A1 shares
with Ch against the McC correction *sat*.[5]

The evidence of the accidentals is relatively neutral between
McC and A1. No bibliographical transfer of manifest printer's
error from McC to A1 occurs to demonstrate beyond question
that A1 was set from McC proof, but the accidentals are close
enough to make the hypothesis tenable. The unique substantive
variants of A1 strongly suggest the same editorial smoothing of
faulty reference (3.1) and incoherence (7.25), and the desire to
avoid craggy syntax (6.32), verbal repetition (9.8), and split
infinitives (18.2) that had characterized Ripley Hitchcock's editing work on the revised Appleton *Maggie* published in the spring
of 1896, and probably in *The Red Badge of Courage* and *The
Third Violet* as well. These editorial changes were no doubt
marked in the margins of the copy sent to the Appleton printer,
or made in the last stages of proof. They are generally pervasive
and even though Crane read proof for this story no single A1
unique variant can be attributed to him with any certainty.

The unique variants of Ch are partly in a different category. A

[5] A further inference can then be drawn. If it was the McC compositor who
twice substituted *curse* for *damn*, then only one stage of proof was furnished
Crane and the three readings *matched*, *skin*, and *sat* probably represent his
own corrections. Under these circumstances Ch would need to have been set
from a typescript or carbon in order for the *damn* to be preserved. On the other
hand, if the evidence were to suggest that Ch also derived from a McC proof,
we should need to posit two stages: the first proof in a form much like the
typescript text and then a revise in which Crane, presumably, made the three
substantive changes which he did not transfer to the extra copy he retained.

few seem simple misprints like *white-hatted* for *wide-hatted* (9.9), a few either simple sophistications or inadvertences like *flushed* for *rushed* (6.1), *after* for *at* (8.3), *the men* for *men* (12.30) or *arose* for *aroused* (13.4). A few are so completely neutral that their exact status cannot be determined, like *the regiment* for *his regiment* (7.12) or *an enemy* for *the enemy* (14.16). But several are almost certainly authorial. The most definite of these is the Ch reading *blue clouds* at 9.14, which is *blue crowds* in McC and A1. For instance, in "Three Miraculous Soldiers" Crane wrote, *Soldiers hovered in blue clouds about the bright splendor of the fires in the orchard* (35.18–20), and in "The Clan of No-Name" *A cloud of blue figures far up this dignified shaded avenue fired at once* (128.23–24). With these parallels, it is inevitable that Ch at 9.13–14 cannot be corrupt when it reads, *In the darkness a loud and endless humming arose from the great blue clouds bivouacked in the streets*, despite the fact that when this passage is deliberately echoed later at 18.12–13 all three texts read *The droning of voices again arose from the great blue crowds*, and (significantly) *crowds* is here the reading of the manuscript fragment as well.

Other evidence accumulates that Ch in some manner preserves original Crane readings. Most unusual is the appearance in Ch of the rare *slidering* (properly 'sliddering') at 8.1 for McC,A1 *sliding*. Even though the present editor has not yet found another example of *sliddering* in Crane, it is a reading difficult to attribute to the Ch compositor. The Marlovian use of *applaud* as a noun in Ch at 10.11 (for McC,A1 *applause*) is also interesting, except here it may be a fossil of some alteration and thus a verb after all. Not altogether explicable in terms of compositorial sophistication is the odd difference between McC,A1 *A soldier had chanced upon a hoop-skirt, and arrayed in it he was performing a dance* (10.9–11) and Ch *a pair of hoop-skirts, and, arrayed in them . . .* With these to go on, one can query whether the English version of 3.16–20 was, after all, not original instead of the work of the Ch editor or compositor. McC,A1 read: *Guns on distant heights thundered from time to time with sudden, nervous roar, as if unable to endure in silence a knowledge of hostile troops massing, other guns going to position. These sounds, near and remote, defined . . .* On the other hand, Ch prints, *troops massing and of other guns getting into position. These various sounds defined* . . . As another example of rearrangement that would seem unlikely to have been caused by an editor's or compositor's concern one may cite 9.1–3 where McC,A1 read, *its quaint individuality, poised in the air above the ruins, defying the guns, the sweeping volleys; holding in contempt those avaricious blazes*, whereas Ch has *defied the guns and the sweeping volleys, and held in contempt* . . .

If, then, certain of the *Chapman's* unique variants are taken to represent the text in a somewhat different stage from that in McC, the problem arises of the order of change and the nature of the transmissional process. The difficulty of forming a hypothesis that would take the Ch variants to be revisions is too acute to entertain, and the general direction of alteration does seem to place McC at a later stage. The question thus narrows to the means by which earlier textual readings could be found in Ch than in McC and the identity of the agent who made these changes. Two possibilities exist. In some respects the simpler conjecture would be that Ch was set up from a carbon of the typescript used as copy for McC, but after it had been mailed to England Crane retrieved the original and made some revisions before it was sent to the printer. His comments about the story in letters seem to indicate that he had more than ordinary difficulty in writing it, and evidence exists that he revised it at least once before publication and in a major way from the form represented by the preserved manuscript leaf. Moreover, a parallel might be present with "An Indiana Campaign," in which the hypothesis for textual transmission requires Crane to have recovered and worked over the typescript that was about to be set for newspaper syndication but to have neglected the (presumed) carbon that had been sent to the *Pocket Magazine*. "Three Miraculous Soldiers" also seems to have been worked over, although at a later stage in its transmission, since this story represents the only one in which A1 was apparently set from a typescript and not from proofs or clippings of the magazine texts. Internally, some slight evidence in "The Little Regiment" might be taken as pointing to Ch setting from a typescript. The lighter system of punctuation is closer to Crane's than the heavier *McClure's* pointing; the Ch use of the parenthetical dash for internal McC commas occasionally seems typical, but could easily be compositorial. It is interesting to see *side-walk* hyphenated in Ch as in the manuscript leaf, though not in McC, and to notice that Ch prints Crane's characteristic spelling *dern* for McC *durn*. These may be straws in the wind, but they remain straws.

More pertinent, perhaps, are some difficulties that would appear if Ch were set up from an early proof of McC since in that case the Ch unique variants taken to be authorial and not Ch corruptions would need all to have been changed in a proof that was earlier than the proof that almost certainly was sent to Appleton as printer's copy. We should need to suppose either that—like the change from *damn* to *curse*—all the McC variants represent the editor's alterations and only the three unique McC variants are Crane's made in the one set of proofs he ever saw, or else that the *McClure's* editor did his own work on the proofs after Crane had marked and returned them and then supplied Crane with revises, a copy of which was later sent to Appleton. In this connection the evidence of "The Veteran" is not altogether applicable, chiefly because of the question whether Crane ever returned to McClure its proofs that he was supposed to correct. It seems fairly clear that "The Veteran" proofs supplied Crane were the originals and that little or no editing had been done on the printer's copy before typesetting. Instead, the McClure editor subsequently went over the punctuation system and marked the proof, supplying heavier pointing; in addition to the correction of some errors he also altered a neutral word and added another, apparently on his own authority. Since it may be that Crane had not returned the originals, it is likely that no revises were sent to him—at least the early proofs are what he preserved. But the special circumstances prevent any hypothesis that McClure would not ordinarily supply revises. We simply do not know.

The difficulties of the theory that *Chapman's* was set from the original proofsheets of the *McClure's* text (as A1 was set from the penultimate set) involve the amount of resetting that was ordered and the requirement that Crane at least in some part would be responsible for these revisions and received a set of revises in which, presumably, he made three further alterations —although these last could perhaps be editorial. However, the resetting was, in the last analysis, not exorbitant for the times, and it may well be that for a story that had given him so much difficulty Crane did indeed request revises, even though he was usually a careless and generally uninterested proofreader. In favor of the hypothesis are the parallels from the other stories in *The Little Regiment* collection. "The Veteran," from McClure's, was sold in England in the form of early proofsheets; and McClure also sent proofs abroad of "Three Miraculous Soldiers," although in this case the analogy is less exact since these were the same proofs that were supplied the subscribing American newspapers. The Bacheller syndicate also sent to England such master proofs for newspapers, not a typescript or its carbon. Whether there is one further piece of evidence is difficult to assess. The alteration already noticed in the passage at 3.16–20 consisted of substituting in McC the more elegant *going to position* for *getting into position* (a quite possible editorial change) but also the addition of *sounds, near and remote,* for *various sounds* (almost certainly authorial). It is just possible that the omission of *and of* before *other* (and perhaps of *various*) was consequential; that is, the compositor to avoid resetting more than a line or two in order to insert *near and remote* chopped out some words and thereby saved himself a rearrangement of type to the end of the paragraph. On the other hand, tempting as this conjecture would be if applied to a more modern author harried by the severe expenses of proof correction, it has little or no application to conditions in the late nineteenth century. The inference is, then, that the total revision is literary in this passage and of no evidential value in respect to the copy.

The general impression an editor receives is that *Chapman's* might well have been set from a typescript. The evidence is small but perhaps of cumulative importance. Ch does indeed preserve some authorial readings, other than the profanity, that are not necessarily revisions in McC, such as *young* for *younger* (15.25; see the Textual Note). Not all of these can properly be laid at the door of the McC proofreader or of Crane; and it is perhaps significant that Ch retains the typical Crane spelling *derned* for McC *durned,* a difference one might suppose more likely to be compositorial in McC than the marked alteration of a proofreader. To such matters must be added the various occasions in which Ch (although perhaps by chance or its own styling) preserves a lighter system of punctuation characteristic of Crane than is found in McC.

Against this hypothesis may be placed a certain amount of external evidence favoring the general custom of sending early proofs abroad for English sale. It is also possible, given the evidence of "The Veteran" proofs in which word-division as well as punctuation was altered, that certain familiar accidentals in Ch could represent their forms in the early McC proof in the state sent to England although editorially altered, together with some substantives (as in "The Veteran"), before revises. Yet on examination this evidence for a custom of sending proofs abroad as copy may not apply to the present case. In all other occurrences English publication was not timed to coincide with that in American newspapers, or, in the case of "The Veteran," with the publication of the story in *McClure's Magazine*, and thus the delay in making the English sale from a copy of early proofs was of no consequence. But with "The Little Regiment" the simultaneous publication in England and America seems to have been planned for copyright protection, possibly; and since *McClure's* could not schedule the story until it was known what month would be agreeable to whatever English magazine was to buy it, there was every reason for haste and for sending a carbon across the Atlantic for early sale instead of waiting for the copy to be set into proof. This hypothesis, moreover, simplifies the difficulties present in the American revision of proof, since it does not require Crane to have read proof twice, a most unlikely procedure. On the whole, then, the weight of the internal textual evidence plus external probability seems to favor the theory that *Chapman's* was set from a carbon of the typescript used for the *McClure's Magazine* printer's copy.

The matter is, actually, of considerable importance for the editorial treatment of the text. If Ch were set from a typescript, its accidentals and certain of its substantives are of equal theoretical authority with those of McC, and an editor can emend his McC copy-text by conflation with Ch. On the other hand, if Ch had been set from the McC proof, in the broadest sense it would have had no authority since it would be a derived text except for whatever accidentals and substantives one might conjecture were altered by the McC proofreader in his copy of this same proof. However, the textual theory of transmission adopted for the present edition is based on the belief that Ch was set from a carbon of the McC typescript and hence that both magazine texts radiate from the same basic source.

McClure's Magazine, then, is chosen as copy-text since its American styling, in general, places it in the closest relation of all preserved documents to the lost original typescript. But since *Chapman's* is also of authority, certain of its accidentals are admitted when they represent what are known to be Crane's normal characteristics. The case of the substantives is more difficult. In a few readings it seems reasonably clear that Ch preserves pure readings that were corrupted by the McC compositor. However, these occur in a substantive texture which has certainly undergone English styling and sophistication that cannot be accepted as authoritative. The problem is also complicated by the difficulty of estimating the nature and amount of the proof alterations in McC. We know of three, two of which correct errors in the typescript and its carbon reproduced in Ch and in the proof behind A1, and one that appears to be a stylistic alteration of an authoritative original repeated in the typescript from manuscript. It is not beyond reason to suggest that these represent Crane's own changes in the proof. What is not clear, however, is whether they represent the only alterations that he made. If they do, then the proof that served as printer's copy for A1 was the original, and the magazine proofreader made no substantive changes after Crane returned the galleys. In this case the McC variants in all substantive readings where Ch is assumed to retain the original typescript authority would sort themselves into (a) McC compositorial lapses and sophistications or (b) designed changes whether by Crane or by the McC editor.

The problem is then posed in plain terms. In order to explain such variation as does not seem to be compositorial, the typescript used to set McC (but not the carbon sent to Ch) must have been altered either by Crane or the editor, or by both, before typesetting, since these changes could not have been made in proof. If the evidence of the preserved galleys of "The Veteran" is applicable to "The Little Regiment," the McC proofreader made his changes in the proof in the same state sent to the author; and perhaps for "The Veteran" with more attention to the substantives because Crane, apparently, either had not marked or had not returned the proof. On the analogy of Crane's dissatisfaction with the original typescript of "The Monster" and his desire to make revisions in it, and on the analogy of the changes that he seems to have made in "An Indiana Campaign" in one form of the typescript after submission but before typesetting, it is not unreasonable to take it that he could have made the noncompositorial revisions in "The Little Regiment" typescript and that no need exists to suppose that an editor went over the copy first to make his own unauthoritative changes. If this is so, variants in McC from Ch that do not seem to be compositorial in their origin must be accepted as authoritative. The only substantive variants in Ch, then, that can be used to emend the copy-text are those conjectured to retain the typescript readings that were corrupted during the typesetting of McC. Such a working hypothesis considerably narrows the area of editorial discretion and leads to a relatively conservative treatment of the copy-text.

On the other hand, if the three identified proof changes in McC are conjectured to have been made in a stage of the proof later than that gone over by Crane and the original proofreader, no such simplified working hypothesis would be possible since the various stylistic changes from Ch found in McC might then prove to be editorial and unauthoritative. However, the working hypothesis for the present text discounts this possibility and adheres to the simpler reconstruction of the textual transmission.

The task of identifying hypothetical Crane proof-alterations in the book form (A1) and separating them from the Appleton editorial changes is basically impossible. Because of the likelihood that Crane's hurried reading of the book proof was cursory, and because none of the A1 variants can be clearly assigned to him, the group has been conjectured to be without authority. The Heinemann collection E1 is only a faithful resetting of A1 without independent authority, and the E2 *Pictures of War* merely reprints the E1 plates.

The editorial position can be summarized briefly. *McClure's Magazine* is accepted as the copy-text. A few accidentals emendations are made from *Chapman's* when an assumption can be made that the Ch text in these respects is closer to the typescript and its carbon than is the McC typesetting. Substantive emendation from A1 is barred except as correction. A number of substantive variants in Ch are assessed as English compositorial or editorial styling, with the remaining taken to represent the forms of the original typescript carbon. However, authentic as these are in their origin, when the McC variant is conjectured to be the result of Crane's subsequent revision of the typescript, the assumed revision within the copy-text has been retained. Hence substantive variants from *Chapman's* used to emend the copy-text are conjectured to be pure readings from the typescript that were altered by the compositor in the course of setting the McC text. The three readings of McC that can be identified as proof corrections by the agreement of Ch and A1 against McC are, of course, accepted.

THREE MIRACULOUS SOLDIERS

"Three Miraculous Soldiers" is mentioned in Crane's correspondence only once, but with information that gives a terminal date for its composition. On January 27, 1896, Crane wrote to McClure from Hartwood, "I dont know how much you were going to pay me for the little 'Three Miraculous Soldiers' but if you can send me twenty-five more dollars to last until my February ship comes in, it would assist the Cranes of Sullivan County very greatly. I think the agreement with you is a good thing. I am perfectly satisfied with my end of it but your end somewhat worries me for I am often inexpressibly dull and uncreative and these periods often last for days" (*Letters*, pp. 107–108).

The story was syndicated in a shortened version by S. S. McClure, Ltd., in a number of newspapers, generally appearing on Sunday, March 15, 1896.[6] The identified newspapers are the

[6] Two illustrations accompanied the proofsheets mailed to newspapers, with the legends ' "I Knowed You'd Holler" ' and ' "He Can't Be Dead." ' In the *Boston Globe* because the original legend for the first illustration came in text that had been cut, the newspaper changed the legend to read 'WHAT SHE FOUND IN THE BARN'. No special mat was provided for the heading, but the Chicago *Inter Ocean*, the San Francisco *Examiner*, and the *Philadelphia Inquirer* made up their own illustrated titles. The *Kansas City Star* advertised 'Now First Published' and by the author of *The Red Badge of Courage*.

Saint Paul Pioneer Press (N¹), March 15, 1896, p. 24; Chicago *Inter Ocean* (N²), March 15, pp. 33–34; *Kansas City Star* (N³), March 15, p. 16; San Francisco *Examiner* (N⁴), March 15, p. 25; *Omaha Daily Bee* (N⁵), March 14, p. 12 (morning edition) and reprinted in the same setting in *Omaha Weekly Bee*, March 18, p. 1; *Boston Globe* (N⁶), March 15, p. 34; *Philadelphia Inquirer* (N⁷), March 15, p. 26; and *Pittsburgh Leader* (N⁸), March 15, p. 22. The story was cut further independently in N⁶ and N⁷. In England the story appeared in the normal syndicated form in the *English Illustrated Magazine*, XV (May, 1896), 104–115 (EIM).⁷ Finally, with a complete text it was collected in the 1896 Appleton *Little Regiment* volume (A1), pages 45–105; in the 1897 Heinemann *Little Regiment* (E1), pages 33–77; and in the 1898 Heinemann *Pictures of War* (E2), pages 227–271. In an autograph list of stories preserved in the Columbia University Libraries Special Collections, and to be dated perhaps about August, 1896, it is recorded with the notation beside it, 'English rights'. Below is "The Little Regiment" with ditto marks under the rights notation, then "The Veteran," and then various syndicated sketches.

The syndicated newspaper versions were individually set up from a common proof sent out by McClure. The question arises whether this proof contained the original version so that the more complete form in the 1896 book collection was a revised and expanded text, or whether the newspaper omissions represent cuts. The evidence favors the hypothesis that a long story was cut by McClure for publication in Sunday newspapers. The only suggestion that A1 could be an expanded text comes at 23.8 where *A voice* in all versions oddly repeats *A voice* at 23.3 beginning a paragraph found only in A1. One would have expected 23.8 to read *The voice* if it had been written at the same time as 23.3. But the evidence of 42.23–29 is conclusive for cutting. Part V begins with Mary waiting some distance from the barn for the three soldiers to reach it and begin a fight. In A1 she then has an impulse to beg them to come away, and she runs toward the building. This vital fact that she *sped toward the*

⁷ The McClure copyright notice was printed. In addition to a decorative title Arthur Jule Goodman drew a full-page illustration with the legend 'SITTING THERE COMFORTABLY, THE THREE SURVEYED HER WITH AMUSEMENT.'

barn is omitted by the N cut, in which the text reads, with manifest discontinuity: *The girl waiting in the darkness expected to hear the sudden crash and uproar of a fight as soon as the three creeping men should reach the barn. When she arrived, however, she gazed about her bewildered.*

The nature of the copy from which the master proof was set up is not demonstrable, but the evidence would favor a rather careless typescript that probably had not been reviewed by the author—although this last is far from certain, even given Crane's occasional indifference to detail in such matters. The number of substantive variants, including manifest errors, between the N text and A1 is extraordinarily large, perhaps too large to be laid exclusively to the McClure compositor(s). The hypothesis would fit the evidence that Crane delivered his manuscript to McClure, who had a typescript made from it to send to the printer. The manuscript would then have been returned to Crane.[8]

The *English Illustrated Magazine* text was set from a copy of the McClure proof. It agrees completely with all the N cuts and with every substantive difference between the two lines of the text except for the correction of two errors. Moreover, until it begins independent paragraphing toward the end when it had space to fill, it agrees with the N paragraphing system in all cases of variation from A1. The two substantives in which EIM agrees with the A1 correct reading against N are *Expressions* (44.19) for *Expression,* and *grimy* (46.23) for *grimly.* The first was sufficiently obvious to attract the independent correction of the San Francisco *Examiner* even though the other newspapers followed the error faithfully. As for the second, some evidence exists to suggest that this was a manuscript error that was separately corrected—but without authority—by EIM and by A1 (see Textual Note). The case would not even be worth discussion were it not for a perhaps slight preponderance of agreement in accidentals between EIM and A1 as against the majority N system but particularly for a handful of EIM-A1 concurrences

---

[8] The comparative correctness of the A1 text prevents any working hypothesis that it was set from a carbon of the typescript that was used as McClure copy before cutting. The evidence seems to point without difficulty to the A1 setting from the manuscript itself or (possibly) from a new typescript prepared from it. However, if Crane had himself had a typescript prepared for McClure, his carbon might have been preserved to send to Appleton. Further discussion of this point occurs below.

in cases that could be significant as evidence for a special relationship between the two documents. The most unexpected agreement, and therefore the strongest piece of evidence, comes at 44.30 when in the disjointed speech of the three troopers, separated by dashes, an uncharacteristic exclamation point appears after *devil of a row* and before the dash in EIM and A1 but not in any example of N. It is also interesting that at 27.13 and regularly thereafter EIM joins A1 in *No, m'm* as against the invariable N *No'm'm*. Significant capitalization and punctuation could be argued for at 28.31–32 where the three soldiers delicately suggest to Mary in EIM and A1, *If you could bring us a little snacklike—just a snack—we'd——* whereas in N all texts read *snacklike. Just a snack. We'd——*. Capitalization and the dash agree in EIM and A1 at 31.16–17 *"Ma," the girl exclaimed, "and now they want to use the barn—and our men in the feed box!* whereas N reads *exclaimed. "And . . . barn, and our men . . . box.*; and again EIM and A1 join at 44.21 in *Now —now* although N reads *Now! Now* (N[1] *Now, now*). Capitals but not dashes vary at 43.33 between EIM and A1 *and at ——? and at* versus N *And at ——? And at . . .* Finally, although EIM agrees in its use of exclamation marks with A1 against N periods or commas about as often as it joins N, the exact sequence of selected points in both seems unusual at 29.9–11. Here EIM and A1 read *"Wait a minute," whispered a grey soldier excitedly. "Maybe they're going along by. No, by thunder, they hain't! They're halting. Scoot, boys!"* whereas N in all but one version has periods.

However, this evidence turns out to be suspect. The last illustration of the unusual agreement in what was and what was not exclamatory is, oddly enough, repeated against all the other newspaper texts by the *Boston Globe* (N[6]). Four of the remaining agreements concern the use of capitals versus N lower case, a concentration of evidence that suggests common styling more than common copy; and indeed some evidence does exist in favor of assigning the N capitals in this text, elsewhere, as more authoritative and the lower case in A1 as editorial or compositorial (see Textual Note to 43.26). If this evidence, then, is less than demonstrative, the fact that these concurrences represent the only individual cases that might have any textual validity— except for the two corrections of substantive error—makes the hypothesis too weak to consider: the unusual agreements are far fewer than ought to be found if in some manner there had been a closer link between A1 and EIM than between N and EIM.[9] The final piece of evidence, although it is negative in its procedure, is almost a *reductio ad absurdum*. That is, EIM varies uniquely in fifteen substantive readings from the agreement of N and A1.[10] These are evidently EIM compositorial departures from copy, and the proportion is by no means excessive. On the contrary, if both N and EIM radiate from a common typescript, then in comparison with EIM the master proof that can be reconstructed from the composite N texts varies from both EIM and A1 only in the two errors at 44.19 and 46.23 that are correct in EIM and A1. This being so, these would necessarily represent the only substantive departures of the master proof from its typescript copy. Such fidelity to copy is difficult to credit. Therefore, since the positive evidence is so small in quantity and in its quality is explicable in other terms, the negative evidence must be taken as sufficient to dispose of any hypothesis other than that EIM was set from the McClure proof in exactly the same manner as were the various newspapers.

Although a number of manifest errors exist in the N line of the text [11] and a handful of identifiable compositorial mistakes or sophistications in A1,[12] a considerable number cannot be brought under a simple hypothesis of compositorial error—even with the addition of authorial revision—to permit N and A1 to derive from common copy (cuts aside) like a typescript and its carbon. The neutral variants of a kind not likely to have received au-

[9] The most plausible hypothesis for such a link would be that McClure sent the original cut typescript to England instead of a copy of the proof. This would have been such an odd procedure as to be explained only as an attempt to give EIM the option of printing the full or the shortened version. That EIM—if so—chose the shorter version cut for cut may seem difficult to credit in these circumstances, especially when toward the end the EIM compositor was obviously spacing out his copy to the best of his ability by paragraphing at every opportunity but he still preserved all the cuts. As it was, he still had a fair amount of white space at the foot of his final page.

[10] In two of these EIM agrees fortuitously with one newspaper version and once with two; but these are clear-cut cases of independent styling.

[11] Typical, for example, are N *stream* for A1 *streak* (23.11), *head* for *heels* (24.15), *pig* for *peg* (26.27), *flight* for *plight* (36.14), and *across* for *arose* (46.10).

[12] As, for example, A1 *whence* for N *from whence* (23.32–33), *close* for *closer* (29.29), *circle* for *circles* (35.38), *from which* for *from whence* (38.33–34), *were* for *was* (44.9), or *in* for *at* (45.39).

thorial attention bulk too large not to require some relatively different line of transmission to account for them. On the evidence of the number of memorial errors or misreadings in N, like *stream* for *streak* (23.11), *and dreaming* for *of dreaming* (33.20), *even* for *ever* (39.3), or *their* for *this* (40.31), it is reasonable to assume that similar variants that make more sense may also be assigned as errors, like *when* for *where* (22.17), *occasionally* for *occasional* (22.20), *continuing* for *contriving* (23.22), *intercepted* for *intersected* (29.5), *showed* for *shone* (29.32), *song* for *sound* (36.17), and so on. The general texture of error being thus established, various quite neutral variants come under suspicion, like *in* for *into* (23.14), *a* for *the* (25.24), *On* for *In* (25.29), *the* for *a* (31.24), *the* for *his* (40.11), *the* for *this* (40.16), and the like, although some of these may, instead, be unidentifiable A1 departures from copy. Nevertheless, when controls exist for the A1 compositors, as in "The Little Regiment" or "A Mystery of Heroism" or "The Veteran," the incidence of substantive error in A1 is shown to be admirably low. Under these circumstances, the majority of errors in the N line can be attributed to a very careless typist compounded by a less than scrupulous typesetting.

No evidence can be advanced to suggest whether the Appleton text was set from Crane's original manuscript or from a fresh and relatively accurate typescript made from it.[13] What is clear, however, is that A1 goes back to the manuscript independently —whether or not through an intermediary document—and in substantive readings is much the superior text as a result either of a more immediate descent or of transmission through more careful agents, or of both. That it has been styled in its accidentals by the Appleton compositors is to be expected, and evidence to this effect is present that coincides well enough with what can be learned from simpler control texts where comparison may be made with A1's exact printer's copy. That some attention to substantives and to syntax was probably given to it by the Appleton editor(s) so that N can sometimes be taken as preserving

[13] For a straw in the wind, however, see the Textual Note for 35.37. An even lighter straw is the A1 use of *bent* for Crane *bended,* the value of which cannot be assessed in this particular connection because *bent* could be compositorial or editorial.

the manuscript readings is clear not only from control texts but also from evidence in "Three Miraculous Soldiers" itself. This editorial ministration—again on the evidence of the controls—is not likely to be pervading; but it is probable that at least as many of the editorial alterations have gone unidentified in the present text as have been isolated and corrected.[14]

Two separate problems involving possible revision arise. The first, and more speculative, is the question whether in the typescript copy or in the proofs for McClure Crane made any revisions of his manuscript readings that were not recorded and transferred back to the manuscript itself.[15] These could be verbal substitutions, such as *rolling* for *rioting* (46.1), *hollow* for *mellow* (44.9); they could be the omission of *fine* (31.31) or of *some* (46.34); or they could be the addition of *still upon it* (27.30) and of *brown* (27.30). They could perhaps extend to the two somewhat larger additions at 40.27–28 and 41.21, for which see the respective Textual Notes. Much of this is a question of plus or of minus and very difficult indeed to adjudicate for the simple reason that, in reverse, they could be revisions in the A1 copy.[16] For instance, that Crane sometimes revised his

[14] Substantive emendation of the generally superior A1 text can properly be undertaken only on the basis of some tangible evidence. When this is wanting, who can say whether it should be A1 *half a mile* or N *a half mile* (22.17), *see now* or *now see* (39.2), *wail* or *wailed* (31.15)? Is the clash of arms *mellow* or *hollow* (44.9), do people at a tragedy love the *rioting* or the *rolling* of a tempest (46.1), did the prisoner *slip* or *slide* from the feed box (43.23)?

[15] A lack of care can be documented in various Crane texts. For instance, in the Heinemann collection *The Open Boat* he regularly annotated copy sent to the printer in the form of clippings from magazines, but he did not request these revisions in the American *Open Boat*, nor did he insert in the Heinemann collection the changes he made in the proof of the American edition. Although he was sent proof for "The Veteran" by *McClure's Magazine*, he seems to have made no substantive revision in it. Since it seems somewhat more probable that he gave his manuscript of "Three Miraculous Soldiers" to McClure, who returned it to him after a typescript was made, perhaps alterations in the McClure proof would be easier to credit if a hypothesis were to be advanced for this authorial intervention; but the case is far from certain, nor is it certain that he made any changes in either copy.

[16] With a very few exceptions—principally where Appleton editing is in question—the exchange of words is almost impossible to decide in favor of the N reading. (But see the Textual Note to 25.24 for evidence that authenticates the A1 reading as Crane's.) On the other hand, some of the N 'additions' or A1 'deletions' are probably not N revisions. That Mary knelt *weeping* (46.27) seems to be taken care of sufficiently by her *lamenting eyes* (46.28). At 27.30 the specification of one soldier's slouch hat as *brown* is not an improvement if the intention was to have one soldier wearing a Union cap, one a gray Con-

work between magazine and book publication is best exemplified in "The Pace of Youth" (see *Tales of Adventure*, WORKS, V), but this is a special case of bringing an early story up to date. We know that he revised "The Five White Mice" in the process of making a fair copy from the Hartwood manuscript. We know that he wanted to make changes in "The Monster" before publication. That in the brief interval between sale of "Three Miraculous Soldiers" to McClure and preparation of copy for *The Little Regiment* collection he might review the manuscript and change a few words or add a word or so is not difficult to credit, and there is a good chance that he did so, although only to a limited extent. If *better* to remove repetition of *all right* at 46.36 is not an editor's switch, we may have such a revision. *Sound* for *song* at 36.17 may be another attempt to avoid the overuse of a word; at 38.39–39.1 *blackness* certainly goes better with *velvet* than *darkness* (see 11.29). At 42.17—if it is not an N omission—the addition of *Oh, no, m'm* is probably intended to represent the words of a second or third soldier in a communal speech. *Rolling* at 46.1 may be too allusive in reference to stage-thunder (Crane usually specifies the theatrical drums) and *rioting* more effective. A few of these A1 variants do arouse suspicion as to their source. It is more likely, perhaps, that *some* at 46.34 was omitted in N than added in A1 (except perhaps by error of contamination). *Shrill* is a common word with Crane for a woman's voice or scream. But its addition at 36.11 seems superfluous. At 43.23 *slipped* is not obviously an improvement on *slid*. However, the mother's *O John, John! why did you, why did you?* at 24.35 is almost certainly not an addition in A1 but an editorial subtraction in N since it would be meaningless without the information provided at 27.37–38 that he is her husband—but this identification occurs in a passage cut from the N copy.[17]

federate slouch hat (see "The Little Regiment" 14.26, 30), and the other to be hatless. At 47.6–7 the elided phrase *worst kind of rebel* fits better with the shorthand of the young officer's first omission of an article before *Girl* than does N *of a rebel*. To specify *three* at 39.36 before *miraculous soldiers* at that late point may seem otiose. No single case for revision can be approved without reservation, although it must be admitted that a few of the cases offer some difficulty in reverse. The best arguments could be made for the readings in N at 40.27–28 and 41.21 as N revisions and not A1 deletions; but see the Textual Notes for the possibility that these two passages were present in the manuscript.

[17] The real anomaly is the unique appearance here of *O* instead of the *Oh* spelling that is invariable not only in Crane's manuscripts (except in *The*

In the present editor's opinion Crane could have made no more than a handful of changes in the typescript for A1 or in his manuscript after it had been used as copy for the McClure master proof (through the intermediary typescript) and it may well be that some of these variants that seem to be authentic in A1 and not necessarily N errors come from the Appleton editor, who might have been inclined toward greater freedom in the alteration of a typescript than of a magazine clipping. In a relatively few cases the N substantives must be chosen to repair the A1 compositorial errors or certain recognizable Appleton sophistications. But on the whole, whenever relevant evidence can be brought to bear on the nature of the variants, the A1 text appears to be the superior.

For convenience A1 is chosen as the copy-text, partly because it is the most complete form of the story but chiefly because it is at least equidistant from the manuscript with the reconstructed proof of N [18] if both were set from different typescripts, and there is at least a possibility that it may be one step closer if the manuscript were the printer's copy. In some respects the accidentals of the reconstructed proof seem closer to Crane's customary characteristics than do those of A1; but the bulk of these consist of the more obvious and formal features of the A1 styling such as its English spellings, particularly of words ending in -*our*, its use of commas instead of colons to introduce dialogue, and its heavier pointing of compound sentences and exclamatory speech. These are readily identifiable and can be emended when N preserves more faithfully the Crane accidentals texture. Abominably careless the typist of the copy for the McClure typesetting must have been, but the corruption of the substantives seems to have gone hand in hand with a general almost

---

O'Ruddy, where a few *O* spellings slip in under English influence) but also here in N and A1. If it were not for the reason given why the sentence is presumably an N editorial cut, it would be tempting to speculate that an Appleton editor who was an O-speller exercised his literary fancy here. But that would be idle daydreaming.

[18] One must emphasize that any individual newspaper text, and also the EIM text, is one step farther from the manuscript than A1 since a second typesetting (the proof) has intervened. On the other hand, sufficient copies of settings from the master proof have been discovered to reconstruct with some confidence most details of this proof. Hence the comparison is actually to be made between this reconstructed proof and A1, which removes the second compositors.

naïve faithfulness to the accidentals of the typescript made from manuscript in just those characteristics that A1 was most inclined to restyle. Moreover, there are certain advantages to recording a cross section of the variable accidentals of both lines of the text, a process that is best done by recording the necessary emendation of the A1 version.[19] Since E1 and E2 are completely derived texts, it has been unnecessary to call upon them for emendations.

The text of the present edition, therefore, through an eclectic treatment of the A1 copy-text by reference to the independent N line attempts a partial reconstruction of the manuscript so far as the preserved documents permit. This procedure is possible because the two typesettings radiate in different lines of descent from the lost manuscript. Common readings may thus be taken as those of the manuscript (faithfully passed through the intermediary typescript[s]). Differences may be adjudicated on the basis of Crane's known characteristics.

A MYSTERY OF HEROISM

"A Mystery of Heroism," copyrighted by Irving Bacheller, was syndicated in various newspapers, generally in two parts, on August 1, 2, 1895.[20] It is listed in no known Crane inventory or

---

[19] The list of Emendations shows a common pattern of $N^{1,3-5,7-8}$ agreeing in considerable part with each other in what may be taken as faithfulness to the light Crane punctuation that filtered through the McClure typescript and into the master proof. Of course it is possible that these compositors were normally light punctuators, but it is also possible that they were more inclined to follow copy without restyling than such a compositor as set N^2, who is usually much heavier in his pointing than the other workmen. Indeed, some evidence is available about the lack of impulse to restyle: as an example, at 29.15 $N^{1-2,4,7-8}$ agree in the unique use of *haint* without the apostrophe found in other appearances, surely a faithful reproduction of an error in the master proof (or more likely of a Crane form that had somehow survived in the transmission). Again, $N^{1-3,5,7-8}$ conservatively follow the copy error *express* at 24.26. At 26.8 $N^{1,3,5}$ repeat what must have been the proof error *Of*, so obvious that the rest automatically corrected it to *Oh*. At 27.15 $N^{3-5,7-8}$ print the error *Keh-pluck*; at 33.7 $N^{1,3,5-8}$ repeat the error *three* for *the three*; and at 44.19 $N^{1-3,7}$ follow the wrong singular *Expression*. These make something of a pattern that can then be extrapolated to a similar treatment of accidentals.

[20] Bacheller provided the newspapers with two illustrations for each part. In Part I the legends are 'In a Great Convulsive Death-Leap' (*variant*: Death Leap) and 'Precisely Like a Stake'; in Part II, 'The Regiment Had Just Turned Its Many Faces Toward Him' and 'Collins Ran like a Farmer Chased by a Bull'. (In the *Philadelphia Press* the first legend reads 'Death-Trap' in error.) These illustrations did not appear in the *San Francisco Chronicle* of August 14,

notes for a collection. The subtitle "A Detail of an American Battle" is confined to the newspaper texts. Newspaper appearances identified and collated for the present edition are the *Philadelphia Press* (N¹), August 1, 1895, p. 11, and August 2, p. 9; *Minneapolis Tribune* (N²), August 1, 2, p. 4; *Omaha Daily Bee* (N³), August 1, 2, p. 7; *Kansas City Star* (N⁴), August 1, p. 8, and August 2, p. 10; *San Francisco Chronicle* (N⁵), August 14, 15, p. 11; and the Chicago *Times-Herald* (N⁶), in one part, on Sunday, October 27, p. 33.

In cut form the story also appeared in an advertising pamphlet for Dr. Greene's patent medicine *Nervura*, presumably published from his offices in New York and in Boston. The text agrees with none of the unique variants in any known newspaper version and appears to have been set from the Bacheller master proof and therefore authorized. This rare pamphlet, which has been preserved in the Barrett Collection of the University of Virginia Library (PS1449.C85M7 1896 [574822]), consists of a gathering in 16's on wove paper, paged [1] 2–32. It is stapled in buff paper wrappers, the front reading, in the form of an artist's drawing: '[within a rule frame] NOVELS | AND | STORIES | [illustration of a woman against a winter landscape containing a rectangle rule frame within which is 'FREE NUMBER'] | COMPLETE STORIES. | FORTUNE'S WHEEL, by THE DUCHESS. | A MODERN PYGMALION, by GRANT ALLEN. | PEACE HATH ITS VICTORIES, by EUGENE FIELD. | A MYSTERY OF HEROISM, by STEPHEN CRANE | THE SECRET OF THE ABANDONED SHIP, by | W. CLARK RUSSELL.' Since the versos of the leaves advertise *Nervura*, "A Mystery of Heroism" is printed on pages 17, 19, 21, 23 with the head-title, 'A MYSTERY OF HEROISM. | [short rule] | BY STEPHEN CRANE. | [short rule] | COPYRIGHTED. | [short rule]'.

The story was printed as pages 106–127 in the Appleton *Little Regiment* collection (1896), as pages 79–95 in the Heinemann *Little Regiment*, and as pages 273–290 in the Heinemann *Pictures of War* (1898).

---

15. The Chicago *Sunday Times-Herald*, for October 27, used three of the cuts, but instead of the plain type-heading of the other newspapers it provided its own illustrative heading showing Collins with his pail against a background of bursting shells. In this heading the author's name is mysteriously given as 'Stephen A Crane'.

Whether the copy provided Bacheller was a manuscript or a typescript cannot be determined. The Appleton text (A1) was set from the same master proof sent to the newspapers and very likely not from a clipping since it follows no unique reading in an identified newspaper version. The substantive variants in A1 appear to be editorial 'improvements' or compositorial errors without authority. The Heinemann *Little Regiment* (E1) was set from a copy of A1, and the 1898 *Pictures* (E2) reprints E1.

The textual situation is relatively simple. The preserved documents permit no more than a reconstruction of the Bacheller proof from the six newspaper texts, joined by A1, all of which radiate independently from this lost proof and thus are technically of equal authority. The English editions are derived and without authority. For convenience the *Philadelphia Press* printing has been selected as copy-text, since it is representative. It is reprinted here, emended as necessary by reference to the other authorities when it appears to wander whether in accidentals or in substantives from the majority view, which should ordinarily represent the readings of the Bacheller proof.

An Indiana Campaign

"An Indiana Campaign" was syndicated by Bacheller, Johnson and Bacheller in a series of newspapers, appearing in two parts on May 23 and May 25, 1896, and credited to the author of *The Red Badge of Courage*.[21] The identified and collated newspaper versions are the *Kansas City Star* (N¹), May 23, 25, 1896, p. 7;[22] *Buffalo Commercial* (N²), May 23, p. 4, and May 25, p. 5; *Nebraska State Journal* (N³), May 23, p. 5, and May 25, p. 4; *Minneapolis Tribune* (N⁴), May 23, p. 6, and May 25, p. 4; *San Francisco Chronicle* (N⁵), in one part, June 14, p. 12; and *St. Louis Post-Dispatch* (N⁶), in one part, June 23, p. 9. Bacheller

---

[21] Two illustrations were provided for each part. In Part I the legends read 'He Gave a Shrill Whoop' and ' "All I Know Is, That I'm A-Goin' After 'Im" '; in Part II, 'Once He Turned His Head and Asked: "What?" ' and 'He Was Bounding at a Great Speed'. The *St. Louis Post-Dispatch* did not use these illustrations. The *San Francisco Chronicle* made up its own illustrative heading showing the major climbing over the fence with his gun, and a single five-column drawing with the legend, ' "Come On, Jeroozel. You're a Man" '.

[22] The title in this newspaper has a preliminary heading, 'A STORY OF THE CIVIL WAR.'

printed the story in his *Pocket Magazine*, II (September, 1896), 92–114, and presumably sold it for Crane in England, where it appeared in the *English Illustrated Magazine*, XVI (December, 1896), 320–326.[23] In the Appleton *Little Regiment* (1896) the story occupied pages 128–150, in the Heinemann *Little Regiment* (1897), pages 97–114, and in the Heinemann *Pictures of War* (1898), pages 291–308.

All the newspaper versions radiate from a common original, the lost Bacheller master proof that was set up from Crane's typescript or manuscript, as do also the *English Illustrated Magazine* (EIM) and the Appleton *Little Regiment* (A1).[24] The Heinemann *Little Regiment* (E1) is a reprint of A1, and *Pictures of War* (E2) is from the E1 plates. The newspapers, EIM, and A1 are substantive texts and theoretically each is of equal authority with the others. The English book line is derived and lacks all authority.

The *Pocket Magazine* (PM) version is an anomaly since it does not use the Bacheller proof for copy as one would ordinarily have expected. The transmissional problem raised is whether it radiates from the same archetype as does the lost Bacheller proof, in which case PM would be of equal authority with the text of this proof reconstructed from the amalgamated evidence of $N, EIM, and A1. On the other hand, if either the reconstructed proof or else PM derives from a still earlier archetype—as one from the manuscript and the other from a typescript—then the earlier derivation would have a peculiar and superior authority.[25] General probability would suggest radiation from a common source. That is, the only reason why Bacheller would not use the syndicate proof as printer's copy for his *Pocket Magazine* would seem to be that he wanted to get the story into type for PM without delay (despite its later appearance) and felt that he had an equally satisfactory printer's copy. Thus if Crane sold him the typescript and a carbon, he would seem to have used one for PM

---

[23] For this publication Arthur Jule Goodman drew two illustrations with the legends ' " 'GOT.' GOT A REBEL OVER IN THE WOODS," ROARED THE MAJOR' and ' "I THOUGHT I HEERED SOMEBODY HOLLER" '.

[24] A1 does not follow the unique variants of any identified newspaper version and thus was more likely set up from an extra copy of the Bacheller proof in Crane's possession than from a clipping.

[25] Of course, if both lines derive from typescripts independently made up from the manuscript, then each would be of equal authority; see note 29 below.

and the other for his syndicated proof. If, instead, Crane sold him the manuscript, he would have had a typescript and its carbon made from it for printer's copy. To send a manuscript to one printer and a typescript to the other creates a logical problem unless one wishes to engage in such idle guesses as that no carbon was made and thus the manuscript had to be used.

However, the evidence of the two texts must be evaluated in the construction of a working hypothesis. Certain oddities exist for either theory. If both texts had a common origin in a typescript and its carbon, the percentage of substantive variation due to the compositors is very high. That is, if we consider clear-cut unique substantive error alone, PM has at least seven and $N at least nine such mistakes.[26] In addition to these, and of greater importance as evidence, must be recorded at least twenty-three other substantive variant readings of a more neutral cast, some of which may be authorial changes and some compositorial or editorial alterations. Certain of these substantive differences could be explained by a theory of revision at some stage. The question might arise whether still others can be attributed merely to compositorial waywardness on both sides. For instance, ten variants occur in which N prints a dialect form like *th'* or *an'* or *'im* and PM prints the normal *the, and,* and *him*; as well as six such variants in which PM prints the dialect but N the normal form. An intermediate stage of transmission to introduce some other corrupting agent than the two compositors would be useful in such a situation.

A few pieces of evidence (albeit negative and therefore difficult to evaluate) suggest a common origin, however. Several minor agreements of a peculiar nature occur that might not have survived a typist as well as a compositor. For instance, although *yeh* is the invariable form of speech of all characters, both N and PM agree in *you* at 62.18: *If yeh hear anythin', you come*

---

[26] The relatively identifiable PM errors are *sort of* for N *sort of an* (57.7), *which* for *who* (57.29), *peg* for *pegs* (58.35), *Peterson* for *Petersen* (60.18 *et seq.*), *top* for *tops* (61.8), *or* for *nor* (62.19), and the omission of *of* (62.25). The N errors are *Migglesville* for PM *the Migglesville* (57.6), *field* for *fields* (57.22), *boys* for *the boys* (59.9), *moment* for *movement* (59.36), the omission of *as* (61.5), *importance* for *the importance* (61.24), *the dignity* for *dignity* (61.24), *lift* for *shift* (63.29), *glittering* for *gliding* (64.27), and *other* for *the other* (65.26).

a-runnin', *will yeh?* [27] Correspondingly, *hain't* is the invariable usage except for two *ain't* forms in PM one of which (63.18) surely not by chance coincides with the only appearance of *ain't* in N. A very unusual concurrence to escape the normalizing process, and one that must go back to common copy at some point, appears in the two different lines of text at 66.4–5. The major, returning from his mission, bounds along shouting: *"It's all right! It's all right,"* . . . *"It's all right."* This is the PM form. The exact agreement of $N in the first exclamation point and the final period is significant, as well as the fact that four newspaper versions agree with PM in the comma after the second *right* despite the pull that was felt by N[5-6], and also by EIM and A1, toward repeating here the initial exclamation. Hence the Bacheller proof must have agreed with PM throughout this sequence except for reading *it's* instead of PM *It's*. For this triple anomaly to have survived a typist when it failed with four compositors may be thought unusual. Moreover, in view of Crane's invariable use of the preterite *bended*, if one or other of the two lines of text had been set from manuscript, either the Bacheller or the PM compositor might perhaps have retained this form instead of the invariable sophistication *bent* at 63.21,27.

Perhaps the keystone to the argument for a common copy and not the independent radiation of one line in some manner from the manuscript appears at 63.1–4. The paragraph starts, *The two then began a wary journey through the corn.* Then in both PM and $N,EIM it continues: *One by one the long aisles between the rows appeared as they glanced along each of them. It seemed as if some gruesome thing had just previously vacated it.* The editor of the A1 collection presumably saw the error and altered the sentences to read, as they must: *One by one the long aisles between the rows appeared. As they glanced along each of them it seemed as if some gruesome thing had just previously vacated it.* Although one might speculate that Crane could have misconstrued his meaning and inscribed the PM-N version in writing out a fair-copy manuscript, the more likely explanation puts the blame on a typist working from manuscript. If so, PM

[27] Here no question of special emphasis can rationalize the agreement in *you*. The only other joint use of *you* in this story is at 58.26, but here in PM the emphasis italic (impossible to set in newspaper cases) shows why both texts retain the form. PM reads *you* for N *yeh*, however, at 63.22.

and N would have been set from the typescript and its carbon in which the error had been made.

This working hypothesis fits the general probability of the textual transmission from the point of view of publication. It also fits two slender pieces of evidence suggesting that an anomaly in the two texts derives from a change made in common copy, or, instead, imperfectly made in a carbon and its typescript. At 65.21–23 Peter Witheby reproves the two little boys for not bringing the powder horn and bullet container and asserts, in PM, *I told yeh to bring it.* In $N^{2-4,6}$ and EIM the phrase is printed in error as *t' bring 'im*; only in $N^{1,5}$ and A1 is it properly *t' bring 'em.* Whatever the origin of the A1 *'em* (probably editorial), it is clear that the Bacheller proof read *'im* and that the *'em* of $N^{1,5}$ represents independent corrections. The association of the error *'im* with the unique PM *it* as against *'em* suggests the possibility that the original copy read *it* as in PM and that a reviser in altering the *t* to *m* forgot to change the vowel. Unfortunately, this line of argument is reversible.[28]

No great difficulty obtains in assessing a number of the N variants as on the whole more likely to be revisions than their readings in PM. Although various could have originated with an alert editor, such as the useful substitution of *the gun* for *it* at 65.19 or the omission of *slowly* at 63.22 to avoid a jingle with *Finally* beginning the sentence, a few would seem to show, instead, the presence of the author. Among these one would place the reservation of the impact of *supreme* (found at 61.33 and in a favorite Crane phrase at 65.12) by changing *supremely* at 57.26 to *extremely*; the choice of *hold* for *grip* at 58.30, of *clambered* for *climbed* (62.15); possibly the addition of *silken* (65.34) and of *little* (58.3), and even the preference for *said* to replace *replied* (63.16) and *asked* (63.23); and possibly the

[28] A simpler alternative exists, of course, and may be true. That is, both forms of the typescript copy could have read *'im* in error, and the PM *it* may be only an attempt at correction like the change to *'em* of $N^{1,5}$. Demonstration is impossible whether the $N^{1,5}$ change is not so natural as to cast doubt on this hypothesis of PM sophistication. One must also consider that revision of some sort between PM and N is not dependent upon such a possible slip but is amply attested to in a number of substantive variants that seem to go beyond what would ordinarily be found without authorial intervention. The point under inquiry is in what document and at what stage these alterations were made, and the admittedly tenuous evidence of *it* and *'im* is intended to bear only on that problem.

omission of *still* before *mopping* at 66.13. On the other hand, a number are so neutral as almost certainly to be the unauthoritative products of textual transmission, such as *this* or *the* (64.5), *upon* or *on* (64.9), and *swiftest* or *the swiftest* (64.33–34). The particular difficulty is to find a suitable principle for the choice among these indifferent variants, for the percentage of ascertainable substantive error is about the same in both lines of the text and is higher than one usually encounters in prints deriving from a single document. In general, however, the fact that the copy behind N seems to have been given a final revision by Crane either in proof or before it was put into type [29] leads an editor to play the odds and to place a greater value on the N variant in cases where no reason exists to suppose that PM is the more authoritative. As it is, a surprisingly large number of PM variant readings are selected, a testimony to what appears to have been undeniable carelessness in the compositor of the lost Bacheller proof, although the PM compositor was by no means blameless himself.

[29] Superficially something of the same textual situation seems to hold in "An Indiana Campaign" as in "Three Miraculous Soldiers," and it may seem disturbing that different conclusions are drawn from what might appear to be the same kind of evidence. The differences between the two cases are more substantial than their agreement, however. Primary is the fact that the second line of the text for the "Soldiers" originated with the copy for Appleton after magazine publication was complete, whereas in the "Campaign" the two lines originate in the prepublication stage. Second, the verbal differences between the two lines of each story are similar only insofar as careless transcribers have corrupted the text in similar ways. The sort of tangible evidence that has implied revision in the "Campaign" is absent in the "Soldiers" except as an indication of nonrevision, as most notably in the question of the authority behind the correct variant *grimy* at 46.23. Moreover, the possibility of minor revision, although at a different stage, is not barred by the textual transmission posited for the "Soldiers." Nevertheless, the working hypothesis for the textual transmission of the "Campaign" is not strongly based. If the collations were viewed in a vacuum, they could readily lead to the theory that the large number of indifferent variants requires an extra typist as well as a compositor and a revising author to intervene in the transmission. That is, the evidence would be most susceptible of explanation if the PM and the N lines were each set from an independent typescript made up from the manuscript. The links between them that have been discussed above would then have originated in the manuscript itself, faithfully reproduced in each typescript. It is only the difficulty of accounting for two such independent typescripts in the prepublication period and in connection with the Bacheller syndicate that prevents the adoption of this hypothesis. Fortunately, the question of PM as copy-text is not altered since in either case it is at least equidistant with the reconstructed Bacheller proof from the manuscript. The partial uncertainty about the transmission, however, does encourage more than ordinary eclecticism in the acceptance of substantives from either line.

Since the working hypothesis adopted for the transmission of the text places PM and the N-line on an equal basis of authority for the accidentals, the choice of PM as copy-text is justified only by its generally closer conformity to the usual texture of Crane's punctuation (and thus to the characteristics of the archetypal typescript that are being partially reconstructed) than seems to be true for the more heavily edited and thus conventional N accidentals. The PM copy-text is emended in its accidentals, however, when a good chance holds that its own editing or compositorial corruption has obscured features of Crane's normal habits that happen to be preserved more faithfully in N. For the substantives an attempt is made to substitute correct readings in N for what appear to be compositorial departures from copy in PM. In addition, when both texts appear to vary neutrally or to represent two stages of authority—original and casually revised readings—what are taken to represent Crane's final revisory intentions are taken from N to emend the PM copy-text. The result is intended to approximate as closely as the preserved documents permit the revised typescript (or the typescript plus proof revisions) from which was set the Bacheller proof that served as copy for the newspapers, for the *English Illustrated Magazine*, and for the Appleton *Little Regiment*.

A GREY SLEEVE

"A Grey Sleeve" was syndicated in October, 1895, in a number of newspapers and generally in three parts, copyrighted by Irving Bacheller. The identified and collated examples are the *Kansas City Star* (N[1]), October 10–12, 1895, p. 7; *Minneapolis Tribune* (N[2]), October 10–12, pp. 6, 6, 8; *Philadelphia Press* (N[3]), October 12, 14, 15, p. 11; *Omaha Weekly Bee* (N[4]), three parts in one, October 30, 1895, p. 1; *San Francisco Chronicle* (N[5]), three parts in one, January 19, 1896, p. 13; and the Chicago *Times-Herald* (N[6]), three parts in one, March 22, 1896, p. 38. The Bacheller syndication included mats for a decorative heading 'A Grey Sleeve | By Stephen Crane' [30] and two crude illustrations for

---

[30] 'Grey' is Crane's invariable manuscript spelling. Despite the form of the heading, most of the American versions normalize to *gray* in their text.

each part.[31] These newspaper versions, whatever their dates, radiate from the lost master proof that Bacheller had set up from Crane's typescript or manuscript. Except for a random hit or two, no variant reading in one version is repeated in another, and thus all are theoretically of equal authority.

Bacheller followed by printing the story in his *Pocket Magazine* (PM), II (May, 1896), 69–103. Thereafter it appeared in *Frank Leslie's Weekly* (FLW), LXXXII (May 28, 1896), 367–369, with an illustration,[32] the same text then being reprinted in *Demorest's Family Magazine* (DFM), XXXII (September, 1896), 627–632, with the same illustration but without the decorative initial found in FLW. In England the story appeared in the *English Illustrated Magazine* (EIM), XIV (January, 1896), 437–447, with illustrations by Arthur Jule Goodman.[33] Except for DFM, which descends from *Leslie's Weekly*, these magazine texts all were set from copies of the basic Bacheller proof and thus they join the newspaper versions as independent authorities.

In the 1896 Appleton *Little Regiment* (A1) the story occupies pages 151–184. The printer's copy was a clipping of the *Pocket Magazine*. The evidence includes a general agreement between

---

[31] Part I legends are 'Sharpshooter' and 'Like a Flight of Harnessed Demons'; Part II has 'Directly in Front of the Captain Was a Young Girl' and ' "Don't Cry Like That" '; Part III are ' "Oh, Harry, He Was Good to Me" ' and ' "Get Out of My House, You Thieves!" '. For Crane's comment on these, see note 33 below. The *Philadelphia Press* used a selection but added an illustration of its own to Part I with the legend, 'The Mad Rush of Battle'. The *San Francisco Chronicle* made up its own illustrated heading and had one large illustration with the legend, 'He Leaned Toward the Shaking Girl and Said, Gently'. The *Chicago Times-Herald* also had made its own illustrated heading and two illustrations with the legends, 'The Troopers Threw Themselves on the Grove' and ' "What Are You Holding Behind You?" '

[32] By Benjamin West Clinedinst. The legend is, ' "What Are You Holding Behind You?" He Said, Suddenly'.

[33] The legends are, ' "Go In Hard Now!" He Roared in a Voice of Hoarse Fury', 'She Wavered To and Fro Upon Her Feet, and Held Her Hands Behind Her', ' "Will You Tell Me What You Were Going to Do With This Pistol?" ', and ' "Am I Never Going to See You Again?" ' '. On January 6, 1896, Crane wrote to Nellie Crouse: "I am sending you by this mail a newspaper clipping of 'A Grey Sleeve.' It is not in any sense a good story and the intolerable pictures make it worse. In England it comes out in a magazine and if I had a copy I would send you one, in order to make you think it was a better story but unfortunately I have not yet seen the English periodical." And on January 12 he wrote again: "It is good of you to like 'A Grey Sleeve.' Of course, they are a pair of idiots. But yet there is something charming in their childish faith in each other. That is all I intended to say" (*Letters*, pp. 97, 99).

their accidentals,[34] but more particularly the fact that A1 alone repeats the two independent PM variants, which must be unauthoritative, *rail* for *railing* (77.14) and *Oh*, for *hi!* (78.26), and it also follows PM in the unauthoritative variant *heed* for *need* (79.11), although here it is also in agreement with N[5], DFM, and EIM. A1 diverges from PM in nine substantive readings and three forms of words. If these are not viewed in isolation but as part of the total evidence for the A1 variants in the entire volume, they may be identified as errors or as shrewd editorial guesses but not authorial revisions.[35] The 1897 Heinemann *Little Regiment* (E1) version, pages 115–140, was set from A1, and the 1898 Heinemann *Pictures of War*, pages 309–334, reprints E1. Since both are derived texts the only point of interest is the single verbal difference of E1 from its copy, the error *you* for *we* at 80.11, in which it fortuitously joins the same mistake in another derived text, DFM.

Of the eleven noticed texts, the six newspaper versions, plus PM, FLW, and even EIM (corrupt as it is), are all authoritative for the reconstruction of the accidentals as well as the substantives of the Bacheller master proof, which is as far back as a critical text can reach. The version that seems to reproduce with best general faithfulness the texture of this master proof is the *Kansas City Star* (N[1]). This has been selected as the copy-text, therefore, but emendation from the other eight collated authorities has been made as needed in order to bring N[1] into as exact conformity as possible with the reconstructed Bacheller proof.

THE VETERAN

"The Veteran" appeared first in *McClure's Magazine* (McC), VII (August, 1896), 222–224. In the Columbia University Libraries Special Collections are preserved two sets of proofsheets (McC[p]) in identical slip galleys numbered 462 and 463, both

---

[34] Including such unique agreements as a dash after *thing* at 70.9, the reading *You won't hurt him, will you?* (77.20–21), *distinctly*, "*we* (78.4), and a comma instead of a dash after *no* (80.13).
[35] The nine unique substantive readings in A1 are at 68.5, 68.15, 68.22, 69.9, 72.20, 72.35, 77.24, 78.28, and 79.15. The forms are *burned* for *burnt* (69.20), *girded* for *girted* (70.11), and *bent* for *bended* (80.23), for which last also see N[6], FLW+.

uncorrected. One set has written at its head, 'Please return as soon as possible.' The first paragraph of the magazine has been reset, with one small variation,[36] in order to admit a seven-line ornamental initial replacing the two-line heading capital of the proof. Farther down, eight lines of type (*turned . . . calamity.* 84.28–33) have been reset without change in wording to nine lines in order to improve the spacing.

In England the story was printed in the Christmas number of the *St. James's Budget* (December, 1896), pages 81–82 (SJB).[37] An illustrative heading showing Fleming in flight at Chancellorsville and a two-column illustration with the legend 'The old man hurled aside the great doors, and a yellow flame leaped out' were drawn by Everard Hopkins. No copyright notice was appended. On December 22, 1896, the *Chicago Tribune* (N^1) ran the piece on page 10 under the heading "Short Story of the Day." Again no copyright notice appeared but credit was given to the *St. James's Budget.* The story concluded the 1896 Appleton collection *The Little Regiment*, pages 185–196, the Heinemann *Little Regiment* (1897), pages 141–150, and the 1898 *Pictures of War*, pages 335–344. In an autograph list of stories in the Columbia University Libraries Special Collections, probably to be dated about August, 1896, "The Veteran" appears, under "Three Miraculous Soldiers" and "The Little Regiment" with the single word 'Magazine' beside it, whereas the other two have the notation 'English rights'.

Whether the copy for *McClure's* was the manuscript or a typescript cannot be determined. The *McClure's Magazine* text exhibits the following twenty-five variants from the galley proofs, the reading to the left of the bracket being that of the proofsheets:

82.3 Further] Farther   82.13 grocer. His] grocer–his   82.14 weight.] ~ —   82.16 manner₍] ~ ,   82.29 frightened₍] ~ , 83.2 sir.] ~ ,   83.3 particular₍] ~ ,   83.17 now,] ~ ; 83.29,84.1,2 Sickleses] Sickles's   84.4 to] into   84.5–6

---

[36] This is the change from *Further* to *Farther* at 82.3, unless, instead, the editor marked this alteration in connection with the other correction of the proof.

[37] This publication and the *Chicago Tribune* reprint have not previously been recorded.

county seat] ~ - ~   84.11 sleep$_\wedge$] ~ ,   84.24 door$_\wedge$] ~ ,
84.34–35 brampling, and] trampling, and   85.8 it, but] ~ ; ~
85.18 blanket$_\wedge$] ~ ,   85.20 himself$_\wedge$] ~ ,   85.23 pail-
ful$_\wedge$] ~ ,   85.24 barn$_\wedge$] ~ ,   85.29 themselves;] ~ :
85.32 Here$_\wedge$ . . . well$_\wedge$] ~ , . . . ~ ,   85.38 unconscious$_\wedge$] ~ ,
86.12 sky$_\wedge$] ~ ,

These proofsheets came from Cora's hoard of Crane's possessions. Hence the presence there of two copies of the galleys, and
particularly of the one labeled to be returned, makes it difficult
to know whether Crane had sent back a third set. It is of prime
importance, of course, to identify the agent who made the
changes that are printed in the magazine. Those in the accidentals are certainly not Crane's, for they increase the weight of his
characteristic light punctuation and, in one case of the substitution of a colon for a semicolon, they insert a punctuation mark
he seldom used except as a preface to dialogue. Even the change
of *Further* to *Farther* (if made in proof and not in the resetting
of the paragraph) is away from his usual form. Outside of the
correction of the literal error *brampling*, then, there remains
only one reading—the change of *lapsed to* to *lapsed into*—that
could possibly have been made by Crane; but in the absence of
better evidence it is probably wise to attribute this to the
McClure's editor as well.

   The copy-text therefore becomes the *McClure's* proofsheets,
which stand closer to the accidentals of the manuscript than any
other known version and would appear to be virtually unstyled.
This copy-text is emended by the two necessary *McClure's*
corrections. The *St. James's Budget* derives from the *McClure's*
proofsheets in their preserved uncorrected form, and the *Chicago Tribune* from the *Budget*. The copy for the Appleton *Little
Regiment* was a clipping of *McClure's Magazine*. The single A1
substantive variant at 83.17 is—on the evidence of the rest of the
volume—more likely to be editorial than authorial.[38] The Heinemann *Little Regiment* text was set from the Appleton, and the
Pictures of War reprinted from its plates. Hence all editions are
derived and only the *McClure's* proof is substantive.

---

[38] At 83.17 McC *pretty flustered* becomes A1 *pretty well flustered*, but this
added *well* merely brings the phrase into conformity with *pretty well scared*
earlier at 82.18.

II

AN EPISODE OF WAR

In the Columbia University Libraries Special Collections is preserved an autograph inventory of stories, to be dated in the summer of 1897,[39] that contains the first mention of "An Episode of War." In this listing it is placed as number five, under the title 'The Loss of an Arm', is given a count of 1,500 words, and its place of publication is noted as 'Youth's Companion'. On October 31, 1895, the corresponding editor of the *Companion* had written Crane indicating a strong interest in publishing his tales (*Letters*, pp. 67–68), and in an advertisement for the seventy-first anniversary of publication printed in the New York *Press*, November 28, 1896, page 5, Crane had been listed among the ten 'Leading Writers' for the magazine. Nevertheless, although search of the *Youth's Companion* fails to disclose publication of this or of any other Crane story, Crane's inventory mention does not seem to represent either a lapse of memory or wishful thinking. Something of a hypothesis can, in fact, be constructed. When in his inventory lists Crane does not get a title right, it may result, as in "War Memories," from his indecision about its final form, but ordinarily it means that he did not have the manuscript in his possession, as probably with "A Tale of Mere Chance," and was recalling its contents as a form of title. It is odd that except for the 1897 inventory mention, under "The Loss of an Arm," this story does not appear by title in Crane's various lists when he was thinking of different collections. However, it does ultimately show up in one of the lists preserved in the Columbia University Libraries, to be dated in early January, 1900, but without title. This is the list that notes the nine Midnight Sketches for a total of 20,000 words and then proceeds with nine other tales, mostly noted as unpublished, beginning with "A Dark Brown Dog" and ending with "The Pursuit of the Tiles" (A Tale of Mere Chance) and including "Moonlight on the Snow" and "Twelve O'Clock" as well as the Wyoming Tales.

---

[39] See Professor J. C. Levenson's Introduction in *Tales of Adventure*, p. liv, n42.

Below "Twelve O'Clock" and in sixth place in this list Crane left
a blank for a title but noted the place of publication in parentheses as 'Gentlewoman' and the word count as 1,500. Since the
word count is the same as for "An Episode of War" and since
this is the only story that Crane published in *The Gentlewoman*,
the identification may be taken as definite.[40]

So far as is known, thus, "An Episode of War" was first
published in the English magazine *The Gentlewoman*,[41] the
Christmas issue, December, 1899, pages 24–25, where it is noted
as copyrighted in the United States and Canada by Messrs.
Perry, Mason and Co. Its other printed appearance was in the
posthumous collection *Last Words* (Digby, Long & Co., 1902),
pages 294–300. The copyright notice in *The Gentlewoman*
seems to provide the evidence for a reconstruction of the earlier
events, for the firm of Perry, Mason and Co. published the
Youth's Companion. It would seem, then, that "An Episode of
War," perhaps under the title "The Loss of an Arm," had indeed
been sold to the *Companion*, maybe in late 1896 when the
advertisement for Crane appeared, but for some reason was then
thought to be unsuitable for that periodical and its publication
hung fire until the owners retrieved some of their outlay by
selling the rights in England. If so, it may well be that Crane had
mislaid his manuscript and had no copy of the story; moreover,
the *Companion's* failure to publish it kept him from contemplating it for a collection until, apparently, he heard of the proposed
Gentlewoman publication and once more listed it as a possibility.

At any rate, whether or not composition was actually in late
1896 as seems to be indicated, the 1897 inventory mention of
what must certainly be the story we know as "An Episode of
War" demonstrates what has not always been clear to critics:

[40] Fol. 10 of the holograph manuscript of *The O'Ruddy*, owned by Mrs.
Donald Klopfer, is inscribed on the other side of a piece of foolscap paper that
had originally contained a list of magazines under columns headed English
and U.S. *The Gentlewoman* is the last of the six English magazines listed,
which include the *Strand, Anglo-Saxon Review, English Illustrated Magazine,
Pall Mall Magazine,* and *Harper's* (sic). In the U.S. side is listed only the
Saturday Evening Post.

[41] J. M. Flagg was the artist for an illustrated title that also carries the legend,
'His hoarse breathing was plainly audible'; a large illustration reads, 'Tenderly
placed it in the scabbard'. The soldiers are drawn in Spanish-American War
uniform. A clipping of the story from this magazine is in a Crane scrapbook in
the Columbia University Libraries Special Collections.

the story is a Civil-War and not a Spanish-American War piece, and it was written, presumably, too late for the McClure agreement and then for inclusion in *The Little Regiment* collection.

In the Barrett Collection of the University of Virginia Library is preserved the blue-ribbon copy of a typescript on the rectos of five leaves of unruled white wove foolscap, 328 × 199 mm., watermarked 'INDIAN | & | COLONIAL'. The typing was done on the Crane typewriter but the document is not one of Cora's typescripts. The typist has put the title into capitals and under it placed a decorative line composed of colons intersected by hyphens and then, underlined, 'by Stephen Crane.' The paging is without parentheses, and the title is repeated in the upper left corner of each leaf, within parentheses. At the end a row of five decorative marks has been made by typing left and right parentheses in the same spaces and intersecting them by hyphens. Since the typewriter had no margin release, the occasional letter or two of the start of a word in the right margin is x'd out or deleted with a slant but is sometimes simply left. The typist is prepared to break a word with or without correct syllabification, and when a word is thus hyphenated at the end of a line it almost always follows that the remaining letters beginning the next line in the left margin are preceded by a hyphen also. This, it may be remarked, is a characteristic of the manuscript of "The Kicking Twelfth" inscribed by Edith Richie, who was a guest at Brede from early July of 1899 into the new year, and also of Crane's own manuscripts.

Some corrections are made in the typescript *currente calamo*. For example, at 90.18 *power* has a final *s* deleted by a typed slant; at 91.13 the *of* following the word *slant* was first typed as *on* but then altered; at 91.16 the final *s* in *onwards* is deleted by a slant; at 91.19 an *a* before *man's* is deleted by a slant, and another *a* is so deleted at 91.25 before *bush-fires*. Two cases appear of apparent anticipations: at 91.5 *orderlies* was x'd over before proceeding with *a bugler, two or three orderlies*, and at 93.8 *so* is typed over *as*.

On the verso of the fifth leaf in Cora's hand is written in black ink the vertical 'For book | 1600 words'. The notation 1,600 words, also in Cora's hand, appears as well in the upper left corner of the first leaf. No blue-crayon numbering occurs as in some of the other Barrett typescripts for stories in *Last Words* from the same source, nor are word counts written on the versos of the leaves.

In the same black ink with which she noted the word count, Cora has supplied missing letters in the right margin at 91.33 with the addition of *rs* and a period to complete *others*. At 92.11 the break in the right margin is *for-|ground*, but Cora placed an *e* over the first hyphen. Within the text at 90.9 *men* is inscribed over an illegible typed word of three letters and at 91.26 the missing *er* after *b* in *reverberated* has been added with a caret. Four missing marginal letters are overlooked: at 89.7 *crevices* is typed as *crevice*, at 89.21 *had* as *ha*, at 90.39 *over* as *ove*, and at 91.25 *with* as *wit* without ink correction. Of more textual concern, perhaps, are three places where, in pencil and hence presumably at a later time, Cora altered readings. The first of these is the deletion of *in* and the interlineation of *with* before *wonder* (91.35) and the second the interlineation with a caret of *that* (92.20). Also in pencil Cora made three periods into exclamation marks in the doctor's speech (92.37).[42]

The Barrett typescript (TMsᵃ) is a part of a purchase that was made from the publisher Coates, of Philadelphia, with whom Paul Reynolds on behalf of Cora Crane was negotiating for an American edition of *Last Words*. Coates demanded that examples of the proposed material be sent to him, and at one point had accepted the book for publication but then withdrew, apparently, for no edition has ever been discovered. Since these negotiations were being carried on during the preparation of *Last Words* for English publication, it is clear that Cora had to supply duplicate copy. The *Last Words* text (E1) is so close to the typescript, particularly in the singularities of punctuation, as to suggest that it was set from the lost carbon copy (TMsᵇ) of the Barrett typescript, which the evidence shows must have been

---

[42] Some interest inheres in the fact that Cora changed the periods to exclamations not as a part of the ink correction but of the pencil revision at a later time. Properly speaking, however, these markings should not be classed as revisions, for the lower-case letters twice following the original periods indicate that exclamations were always intended. The Crane typewriter had a curved apostrophe that could not be used to form an exclamation point by backspacing and typing above a period. Hence in the preserved typescripts of material from this typewriter all exclamation points are added by altering periods by hand.

altered by Cora in a manner identical with the alterations she wrote in the preserved TMsᵃ. Particularly, the three pencil changes appear in *Last Words*; but though these are also present in the G text, *Last Words* does not repeat the unique variants of G but does reflect two minor though significant errors in TMs. For instance, at 90.17 the word *existence* ends a line in TMsᵃ without punctuation, although two spaces remained before the right margin. *The Gentlewoman* punctuates with a comma, which seems to be correct; but an anomalous dash is found in E1, which is incorrect because it never supplies (what was not present in TMs) another dash properly to close the parenthetical material thus opened up. This faulty E1 emendation would seem to indicate that its copy, like TMsᵃ, lacked marginal punctuation here and thus that Cora had passed over the error in TMsᵇ as well. Similarly, at 93.1, although one space was available before the right margin, the typist omitted the necessary period after *wrathfully*. *The Gentlewoman* corrects this mistake easily, since the first word in the next line of TMs is *His* with a capital. But the E1 compositor seems to have been thrown off his stride and, mistaking the syntax, he set a comma after *wrathfully* and continued the sentence with lowercase *his*.

That *Last Words* was derived immediately from TMsᵇ, the carbon of the Barrett typescript, seems demonstrable. The relationship between TMs and *The Gentlewoman* is not quite so obvious. That there is an intimate connection, however, is clear from the appearance in both of common errors. For example, together with E1 the text of G repeats the erroneous comma after *Well* at 90.14 which quite distorts the syntax. Moreover, where E1 corrects the error, G and TMs agree in the repetition of *white* in TMs *little white puffs of white smoke* (89.18–19). Finally, G and E1 repeat the TMs error *has* at 89.15. Both G and TMs are very close indeed in their accidentals. On the other hand, G prints four unique substantive variants: *moment* but TMs *instant* (89.24), *them* but TMs *him* (90.28), as well as *at once* (89.27) and *miraculously* (90.2), both of which are not present in TMs.

The similarities between the two texts are so marked as strongly to suggest that one must have been the printer's copy for the other. Under ordinary circumstances one would automatically assume that TMs must have been the copy; but these circumstances are not ordinary. Perhaps no great difficulty exists in a speculation that the printer's copy TMs[b] was recovered from *The Gentlewoman* and preserved so that ultimately it was sent to the printer for *Last Words*.[43] On the other hand, the example of three Spitzbergen stories—"The Kicking Twelfth," "The Upturned Face," and "The Shrapnel of Their Friends"— which have typescripts or carbon copies in the Barrett Collection from the same source, as well as other material also in typescript that appeared in *Last Words*, practically demonstrates that all of these typescripts were made by or for Cora after Crane's death when she was actively engaged in the preparation of the volume. No preserved typescript from the Coates source can be dated positively before June, 1900.

At first sight the typescript for "An Episode of War" appears as if it might be an exception. That is, although the copy was definitely made on the Crane typewriter, it was not typed by Cora or by at least one and possibly two other typists whose work is suggested in the Barrett typescripts. In fact, the decorations and other characteristics are unusual. It has already been remarked that the double hyphenation of words divided between lines is found in the Edith Richie manuscript of "The Kicking Twelfth" and the spelling of the typescript in such matters as *grey* and *serjeant* is the same in both. These are also Crane spellings, incidentally, and the typescript also has his spelling *trajedy*. Yet the typescript cannot be Edith Richie's, in part because of the date that must be assigned to it owing to its connection with other typescripts prepared for *Last Words* (see below) and in part because the physical characteristics of this typist appear to correspond (except for the decorations) with those of the typist for part of Chapter XXIV of *The O'Ruddy* preserved in a ribbon copy and three carbons in the Columbia University Libraries, a typescript that must have been prepared no earlier than April, 1900, long after Edith Richie had left Brede. This typist also

---

[43] Of course, a second carbon may have existed; but in all research so far engaged in about Crane's printer's copy no suggestion occurs that more than a single carbon was made along with a typescript. The three carbon copies that Cora typed for *The O'Ruddy* seem to represent a special case connected with the need for extra copies to offer for prospective serialization and to several publishers at once.

seems to have been responsible for the late unfinished Spitzbergen story "The Fire Tribe and the Pale Face" also preserved at Columbia. She may have been Helen Crane.

Small matters of punctuation such as TMs's typical hyphenation of *school-house* and *good-morning*, which G prints as one and as two words, or its typical omission of the comma before the *and* of a series of three after *saluted* at 91.2, where G prints a comma, suggest that TMs could derive from a Crane manuscript. The common errors of TMs and of G would need to have originated in TMs, but the four unique substantive variants in G, which appear to be authentic enough, would need to be set down either as proof corrections in G or as alterations of TMs[b] not made in the preserved TMs[a].

Nevertheless, insuperable difficulties arise for any such hypothesis. One does not need to appeal to probability that more of the egregious TMs errors ought to have been corrected by the G compositor or caught in proof, or to the slight oddity that the typescript would have been retained when no immediate use was planned for it. Instead, two physical facts make it highly improbable that this typescript differs in its manufacture from the general date of the other *Last Words* typescripts and carbons that were made up for the specific purpose of serving as printer's copy for the volume in England and in the United States. First, Cora's markings—whether the supplying of missing letters at the ends of lines or of altered words—are made in the same ink as in the other typescripts, and even her pencil changes reflect the same second round of review and alteration in pencil observed in some of the other typescripts. These relate TMs to the rest in a manner difficult to negate. Secondly, the wove paper watermarked 'INDIAN & COLONIAL' is found in other of these Barrett typescripts, specifically in "At Clancy's Wake," "Why Did the Young Clerk Swear," "A Tale of Mere Chance," and in part in "London Impressions." Six Columbia University typescripts, one for *Last Words* but the others not published or else copies of early newspaper material, are also on this paper. Interestingly, one of these—"An Auction Sale of Real Estate in Texas U.S.A." —has 6 Milborne Grove as the return address, a lodging Cora engaged in the late summer of 1900 after her husband's death. Another—"An American Tramp's Excursion"—has the same mixture of this wove watermarked paper with a laid paper watermarked Britannia with a bust in right profile as is found in the Barrett "London Impressions," this Britannia paper also being found in the Barrett typescripts of "The Kicking Twelfth" and "Silver Pageant." Neither paper appears in the Whilomville manuscript series.

All the physical evidence, therefore, supports the hypothesis that the Barrett typescript of "An Episode of War" was made up at the same time as the other typescripts that can be traced back to Coates, and for the same purpose. If so, its carbon cannot have been the copy for the *Gentlewoman* text. The relationship between this typescript and *Gentlewoman* is no doubt established by the example of "The Kicking Twelfth," "The Upturned Face," and "The Shrapnel of Their Friends," all of which are typescripts that were copied from the printed texts in order to provide printer's copy for *Last Words*. Why Cora did not utilize clippings we do not know, but the fact is incontrovertible that "The Kicking Twelfth" typescript derived from the magazine text, and the evidence of the others is as suggestive as the unusual common errors of G and of TMs are now seen to be in "An Episode of War."

Under these circumstances the typescript of "An Episode" has no textual authority whatever. Its alterations, particularly the second round in pencil, merely help to bring it into conformity with the printed text, and the four unique substantive variants between the two can be nothing but errors of the typist. The copy-text for the present edition, therefore, is the text in *The Gentlewoman*, which represents the only preserved authority. The Barrett typescript derives from it, and the *Last Words* text was printed from the carbon of this typescript.

III

WOUNDS IN THE RAIN

On August 4, 1899, Crane wrote to Pinker: "The U.S. book-rts of the war-stories were promised to Stokes last year when I was in America. He is to advance $1000" (*Letters*, p. 223). The agreement, then, appears to date from the hectic days between Crane's arrival from Cuba at Hampton Roads on July 13, 1898, and the end of the month when he went to Pensacola to take part in the Puerto Rican campaign. No story was on paper at this point, but in September and October he began to mail war anecdotes from Havana to Paul Reynolds, his American agent, and on November 1, 1898, in a note accompanying the manuscript of "Marines Signaling Under Fire at Guantanamo," he asked Reynolds to "convey to Stokes the pleasing information that I have completed about 15000 words of Cuban stories and that he shall have the book for spring, and govern your placing of these articles accordingly" (typed copy, Syracuse University Library). The 15,000 words mentioned on November 1 covered "The Lone Charge of William B. Perkins" (1,870 words, sent September 14), "The Price of the Harness" (6,500 words, sent September 27), "The Clan of No-Name" (6,150 words, sent in October), and "Marines Signaling" (2,700 words, sent November 1), for an actual total of 17,220 words.

Spring publication proved as illusory as most of Crane's optimistic plans for literary production. " 'God Rest Ye, Merry Gentlemen' " followed in February, 1899, on his return to England, but thereafter a hiatus developed. In a list in the Columbia University Libraries on cheap unruled wove paper 265 × 212(?) mm. (the right margin is torn and the widest part of the leaf measures 195 mm.), Crane first sets down the titles of various Whilomville stories and then under the heading of 'War Stories, etc' he notes "The Price of the Harness," "The Blue Hotel," "The Clan of No-Name," " 'God Rest Ye, Merry Gentlemen,' " and then four miscellaneous items before concluding with a later addition, "The Lone Charge of William B. Perkins." This list in its original form may be dated as of March, 1899 (*Tales of Whilomville*, WORKS, VII, liii). A slightly later Columbia list on the same paper is headed 'New Collection' and starts with "The Blue Hotel" but then includes only the four war stories in order.

"The Revenge of the *Adolphus*" came next, in April-May of 1899. Then on August 4 he wrote Pinker in the same letter in which he stated that the American rights belonged to Stokes that he would get to work on the battle articles (later to become *Great Battles of the World*) "as soon as I finish the war-stories" (*Letters*, p. 223). Not much later, in a letter that must be redated to

August, he advised Pinker: "My short stories are developing in three series. I. The Whilomville stories. (always to Harpers.) | II. The war tales. | III. Tales of western life similar to 'Twelve O'Clock.' It might be well to remember this. For instance if you could provisionally establish the war tales with one magazine and the western tales with another as the Whilomville yarns are fixed with Harper's, it would be very nice" (*Letters*, p. 214). Crane is here reviving what had been the original plan for his war stories. Probably as a consequence of a loan pledged against his work that had got him from England to Cuba, *Blackwood's* earlier had had the English rights and had published "The Price of the Harness". But after the magazine had rejected "The Lone Charge," "The Clan of No-Name," and "Marines Signaling," the agreement seemingly lapsed, at least from Crane's point of view, and thus he began to urge Pinker to find a *Blackwood's* kind of publisher for his series.

Later, on August 31 Cora requested Pinker: "Mr. Crane says please let him know what you have done with the stories. He is hastening to get the war book ready for the publisher and has 67000 words done now. When this is done he will have certain sums due from Stokes & Co. in America but in the meantime he is going to run very short" (*Letters*, p. 226). This statement is useful in dating the completion of "War Memories" as prior to August 31, and "This Majestic Lie" as after, for without the mysterious 5,330 words assigned a story (which is probably "The Making of the 307th") in Crane's autograph final list of his Cuban stories (for which see below), the word counts given there total 67,200. It also indicates that "Virtue in War" and "The Second Generation" had already been written by this date and, of course, "The Serjeant's Private Mad-house," which was published on September 30 in the *Saturday Evening Post* and may date back to April or May. Cora's inquiry about what Pinker has 'done with the stories' may refer to his failure always to notify Crane of sales (see Crane's letter of November 4, 1899, protesting he had not been informed of the sale of "The Second Generation," *Letters*, pp. 239–240). That is, Crane at this date seems to believe that various of the stories have been placed in magazines but that Pinker has not kept him advised. This may be thought more likely than a reference to the collection of copy for the book, particularly since—at this time—Pinker was not dealing with Stokes about *Wounds in the Rain* although he was probably in touch with Methuen.

Crane's letter to Pinker of September 22, 1899, "I am anxious to get the 80000 words ready for Stokes" (*Letters*, p. 231), suggests that Stokes had set this figure as a general minimum of acceptability and that Crane was concerned to meet it in order to secure his advance. He continues, "and your letter received in Paris filled me with an idea that I had missed a few thousand words—in short that I had written a story and then absolutely forgotten it as I often do." This reference to a confusion in his mind between "The Second Generation" and "Virtue in War" and to the nearness of his reaching the mark of 80,000 words suggests that "This Majestic Lie" was in the last stages of preparation, for on October 4 Robert McClure, in London, received a copy from Pinker (McClure to Pinker, TLS Dartmouth). In fact, although Crane believed, according to his autograph list, that he had ended by providing copy totaling 83,935 words, Stokes later discovered that the computation was arrived at by the duplication of "Virtue in War" under the title of "The Making of the 307th," thus reducing the volume to 75,735 words; and on June 15, 1900, he complained to Pinker, "This serious falling off in the number of words will make the book a small one" (TLS, Dartmouth).

Within a day or two of September 22, 1899, if not on the very day, "This Majestic Lie" must have been completed, since Crane cabled Stokes that the book was finished and he wanted his advance. Then ensued a misunderstanding that is revealed in the following letter of Robert Barr to Crane on October 2:

As I see myself as a boy in those incomparable boys stories you are writing for Harper's Mag. (no one has ever touched the innards of the actual boy until those stories were written) so I also see myself in every line of the letter you wrote to Stokes. The Lord gave me a rockier temper than you've got, as you very well know. . . .

I have read both your letter and Stokes' over three or four times to get the hang of the thing, and this is my understanding of it.

1. Crane and Stokes. (Mutually agreeing.) £100 paid on receipt of copy.
2. Crane. (Cabling.) "Book finished. Will you cable money."

3. Stokes. (Cabling.) "Yes on receipt of complete MS."
4. S Crane. (Cabling.) "I withdraw the book."
5. Stokes (Writing.) "We stand by the London Convention of 1884."
6. BLOODY WAR.

Now it is quite plain that a misapprehension arose after No. 2. If the word "now" or "Today" had been added to your cablegramme there would have been no chance of a misunderstanding, but as the cable reads the mistake was liable to occur. The situation after No. 3. is that Stokes thinks he has acceded to your request, and I can imagine his amazement when you cable withdrawing the book.

I wouldn't break with Stokes on this, if I were you. He is a thoroughly honorable man, and the more I know of other publishers, the more I appreciate him. God Almighty, I should be glad if other publishers would keep to the letter of their agreement. . . . You were asking Stokes to do what they would not do for any other living man. They did it once for Frederic, but they refused to do it a second time, and they would have lost their money if they had. . . .

You are all right when you stick to your pen, and are apt to be all wrong when you meddle with business. . . .

You have got things on exactly the right basis now, in leaving Pinker to deal with editors and publishers. Write, write, write, anything but business letters [*Letters,* pp. 233–234].

The flare-up over the payment of the advance was apparently resolved by Stokes's capitulation as indicated in his letter to Pinker on October 9, which also shows that Crane had taken Barr's advice to leave his affairs to Pinker:

We have just received instructions from Stephen Crane, Esqr. that our correspondence regarding his affairs with us shall in the future be conducted with you.

We are very much gratified that this is to be the case.

We have just made to him an advance payment for a volume of short stories of the Spanish-American War.

We have contracted with him for a long novel of the American Revolution, to follow the short stories above mentioned and for first offer of following work.

We are to make him advance payments on this novel on receipt of each instalment.

We mention these details for your guidance, and shall appreciate it very much if you will secure the additional copy and the title for the volume of short stories, and send them to us as soon as possible, together with word as to the date of publication of this book.

Undoubtedly you can secure information as to other details connected with the long novel from Mr. Crane, and we shall be pleased to send them to you whenever you wish it.

We regret that our correspondence with Mr. Crane seems to have been mutually unsatisfactory, and we are glad, for this reason, to deal with you in the matter in the future [TLS, New York Public Library—Berg Collection].

Evidently Pinker responded on October 17, for in an undated letter that should have been written in the last week of October Stokes provides Pinker with information that had been requested:

Answering your letter of the 17th ult. we would say that we have advanced Mr. Crane £100. on account of royalties on the volume of short stories of the Spanish-American War, and shall be glad to have the further copy mentioned by you as you receive the proofs.

We are glad to learn that the book is to come out next spring, and shall be indebted for more definite information as to the time whenever you find it possible to give it to us.

We shall be glad to hear from Messrs. Methuen as to their taking plates from us.

We have not yet received any word from them on this subject . . . [TLS, New York Public Library—Berg Collection].

The October 9 letter from Stokes indicates that some copy had already been received. This was presumably clippings of "The Price of the Harness" (*Blackwood's*, December, 1898), "Marines Signaling Under Fire" (*McClure's Magazine*, February, 1899), "The Lone Charge of William B. Perkins" (*McClure's Magazine*, July, 1899), "'God Rest Ye, Merry Gentlemen'" (proofsheets from *Cornhill*, May, 1899), all stories that were noted in a letter of May 23, 1900, to Pinker, as in Stokes's possession in letterpress (TLS, Dartmouth).

It must have been in late October or early November, 1899, that Crane wrote out a list for Stokes of the contents of the volume. Apparently he sent this list directly to Stokes, for on December 29 Stokes mailed to Pinker, at Pinker's request, the list of the stories "as made up at present" (TLS, Dartmouth). The autograph list preserved in the Special Collections of the Columbia University Libraries (reproduced in this volume) was undoubtedly the precursor of the list for Stokes, although it was not written all at one time and was altered in some details at a later date. The original list was written in blue ink (the vertical lines between categories are in pencil) and noted the titles of the stories from "The Price of the Harness" through "The Serjeant's Private Mad-house" and then, after a space, "The Making of the 307th." The magazines named both for England and America are given in this ink only through "The Revenge of the *Adolphus*"; those for "This Majestic Lie" and "The Serjeant's Private Mad-house" were added subsequently in a black ink. The word-count column is in blue ink down through 2,870 for "The Serjeant's Private Mad-house," including the change of the count for "The Clan of No-Name" from 6,000 to 6,150 words. This blue ink extends further to the count of 5,330 for whatever story this is supposed to be attached to, and to the cumulative total 44,835 to the right of this figure. The remaining four story titles from "Virtue in War" to "The Cuban Campaign" (i.e., "War Memories") are written in a black ink, which is also used to delete "The Making of the 307th." The three magazines listed in England and the three in America are also in black, except that 'Phila Sat Ev Post' and the count 8,200 added later are in blue ink for "The Second Generation." In the word-count column the black ink inscribes the 8,100 count that ultimately seems to apply to "Virtue in War" and the figure 8,200 that was originally placed after "Virtue in War" is also in black but deleted in blue. The same 8,200 squeezed in above it and below the 8,100 is written in blue and deleted in blue. The cumulative totals 53,035 and 55,735 are in black.

We know that by October Crane was aware that the *Strand Magazine* had accepted "The Revenge of the *Adolphus*," but he did not hear about the acceptance of "The Second Generation" by *Cornhill* until November 4 (*Letters*, pp. 239–240), so that the black ink, at any rate, must come after that date, with the final blue-ink alterations probably toward the end of the month. The arrangement of the list differs from that which Stokes sent to Pinker on May 22 and May 23, 1900, which is arranged in the published order. But in the autograph, "This Majestic Lie" and "The Second Generation" are out of position. Some of the information is erroneous. For instance, Crane may have thought at first that the *Strand* controlled international rights to "The Re-

venge of the *Adolphus*," but he did not alter the American serialization column to take account of its publication in *Collier's* on
October 28, 1899. "This Majestic Lie" assigned to *McClure's* is
understandable since it appears that *McClure's* bought it in early
October but relinquished rights to it at some indeterminate time
before publication of *Wounds in the Rain*. It is also interesting
that "War Memories" is called "The Cuban Campaign," especially
since in the Stokes lists of May, 1900, it is denominated only
"Story for Lady Churchill," a note that must reproduce what
Crane had written originally. Very likely the title was not decided
on before the final proof stage, which would have been in November for the December issue of the *Anglo-Saxon Review*.

The word-count column has its difficulties. It is clear that the
cumulative total of 21,615 after " 'God Rest Ye' " was written
after the count for "The Clan of No-Name" had been altered
from 6,000 to 6,150. The next cumulative total 44,835 appears
to the right of the anomalous 5,330 figure and includes it. The
addition should have been 44,770, however, and this slight error
persists in the remaining figures. The cumulation then includes
8,200 words for "Virtue in War" and stops at 55,735 and the
count for "Marines Signaling." Thereafter it was evident that
with the lengthy "War Memories" and "The Second Generation"
still to go, Crane had over 80,000 words. The deletion of the
5,530 count was made, of course, after the last total had been
added.

The history now switches to the Stokes lists of May 22 and
May 23, 1900, sent to Pinker, which give the titles in the final
order found in the volume, except that both lists have a story
entitled "The Making of the 307th" ahead of "Virtue in War."
The May 22 letter (actually a later letter than the postdated May
23 communication) merely names the stories; the earlier, which
accompanies a discussion of the available printer's copy, gives
the English magazines of publication "with the exception of 'The
Making of the 307th,' 'This Majestic Lie' and 'The Second Generation,' regarding which we have no information" (TLS, Dartmouth). In this list a line of typed dashes appears in the column
for the magazine names of "The Making of the 307th" and "The
Second Generation." The column opposite "Marines Signaling"
has the typed notation '(unsold)' but deleted by hand with a line

of dashes; opposite "This Majestic Lie" is a typed-in name that has been heavily deleted and is now illegible. Then on June 15 Stokes wrote to Pinker, among other matters concerning the volume: "Another difficulty is that the printer has discovered that two stories in Mr. Crane's own list, given by him as 'The Making of the 307th,' and 'Virtue in War,' respectively, are one and the same story, although in the column for the number of words opposite the titles in this MS. list he has given the number of 8100 words for the former and 8200 words for the latter" (TLS, Dartmouth).

Certain of the events can be conjecturally reconstructed. Although the list of stories that Stokes sent Pinker in December, 1899, has not been preserved, it may not have been the list in the form sent in May, 1900, as 'Mr. Crane's own list,' because "Virtue in War" is noted in the May list as in the *English Illustrated Magazine*, which did not publish the story until June, 1900. Hence in November, 1899, Crane must have furnished Stokes with a partial list of titles that could have approximated those titles in the Columbia autograph list written in blue ink. In this December 29 letter to Pinker Stokes remarked that the list he is enclosing is "as made up at present" and he continued, "He promised us that he would make some addition to these, and we should be glad to have them." Perhaps Crane listed, the first time, only those stories for which he could provide copy and waited for the rest, as in the black ink, until he knew their place of publication.

It seems clear from Crane's letters to Pinker in September, 1899, worrying whether "Virtue in War" and "The Second Generation" were not the same story, that part of the confusion lay in the fact that the original title for "Virtue in War" had been "The Making of the 307th" and the magazine title was to be "West Pointer and Volunteer; Or, Virtue in War." At any rate, it is evident that by the time Crane wrote the black-ink entries in his autograph list, the question of "Virtue in War" as distinct from "The Second Generation" had been settled, so that he added the title when he knew that the *English Illustrated Magazine* had taken it but before he had been informed about *Leslie's*. And about that time he provided Stokes with a final copy of the autograph list, rearranged in order, and comprising what he thought was to be the complete group of stories. That Stokes was not altogether happy with the size of the volume, even though it at first seemed to meet his minimum word requirements, is evident from a postscript to the May 22 letter: "We have here a memorandum that was given us originally by Mr. Crane, and which contains a list of these stories; but we have always looked upon this as merely a preliminary and imperfect memorandum, subject to change. If we are to follow the order as given in that memorandum and you will cable us to that effect, this will expedite matters greatly." He was more unhappy, of course, when he discovered on June 15 that owing to the duplication of "The Making of the 307th" and "Virtue in War" his volume was 8,200 words less than he had thought in May, and was under the 80,000 words agreed upon. But by that time Crane was dead.

The problem must now be faced of the mysterious 5,330 word count in Crane's autograph list, the deletion of "The Making of the 307th," and the deletion of the two notations of 8,200 words. An undated letter, no. 272 (*Letters*, p. 211), from Crane to Pinker from Brede reads as follows: "I send you a rattling good war story—I think 5330 words. Please send me a checque for £40 so that I will get it on Sunday morning. If you have to dispose of the U.S. rights of any of the stories you had better consult me. I know my U.S. market. Yours faithfully *S.C.* PS: I should think this would go to the Strand. How am I going? Strong?" Professor Stallman dates this conjecturally as February 16, 1899, and footnotes the information that "The Revenge of the *Adolphus*" was published by the *Strand Magazine* in September, 1899. However, the reference to Pinker disposing of American rights places this letter, instead, after late July, 1899, when the break with Reynolds seems to have occurred and Pinker took over the handling of Crane's stories in the United States. Thus the letter is probably to be dated in August, at which time it takes its place beside letter no. 278, which has been redated by Professor J. C. Levenson in August partly on the basis of a similar allusion, "Today I will dictate for you some information as to my U.S. market," and partly on the identification of the Whilomville story that was enclosed (see Introduction to *Tales of Whilomville*, pp. lii ff.). Moreover, the word count of "The Revenge of the *Adolphus*" is 6,420 by his reckoning, and Crane did not make such miscalculations as this against himself when estimating the length of his stories.

This war story of 5,330 words in no. 272 checks exactly with the word count in blue ink in the autograph list for *Wounds in the Rain*, which was included in the cumulative total after "Virtue in War" and "Marines Signaling" had been added below in black ink at a later time. No other war story that Crane wrote has a word count nearer than a thousand words to this figure of 5,330. It would seem almost certain that the blue-ink 5,330 is intended to apply to the blue-ink title "The Making of the 307th" even though it is not quite on a line with the title. We know from Stokes's letter of June 15, 1900, that he had been furnished a typescript of "The Making of the 307th" but when the duplication was discovered he preferred to use the letterpress copy of "Virtue in War" from *Frank Leslie's Popular Monthly* of November, 1899, that had been sent him. But he also states that "The Making of the 307th" had been noted in Crane's list of stories as 8,100 words as against 8,200 for "Virtue in War." It is an odd fact that in the autograph list 5,330 is deleted in the later black ink and 8,100 placed on a line in this same ink opposite the title. But it is odder that the hand that wrote the 8,100 is probably to be identified as Cora's.

If the story of 5,330 words that accompanied letter no. 272 to Pinker was "The Making of the 307th," as suggested by the autograph list and by the lack of any other war story that would qualify, then one may conjecture that Crane subsequently took the manuscript back, expanded it, and retitled it "Virtue in War," or—at first—"West Pointer and Volunteer." It is possible that the revision and expansion to the present form represented by "Virtue in War" involved the addition of the conflict between Lige and Gates and that the published title "West Pointer and Volunteer" reflected the changed emphasis from the macrocosm of the regiment to the microcosm of the two individuals. It may be suggested that the confusion in Crane's mind in mid-September whether "Virtue in War" and "The Second Generation" were one and the same story may have arisen because "The Making" may have had the same subtitle as was found in "West Pointer" and Pinker referred to it by its subtitle whereas Crane continued to think in terms of "The Making of the 307th" title.

If this is so, the order of events may have been something like this. In late October or early November the autograph list in blue ink was made up, including "The Making of the 307th" with its word count of 5,330. The space between this title and "The Serjeant's Private Mad-house" would seem to indicate that Crane was uncertain about the order and was reserving a place for other stories between the two. Later in November, or in early December, he added the next two stories in black ink, "Virtue in War" and "Marines Signaling" with their cumulative total that included the 5,330 figure. Somewhat later he completed the list in black ink but left the American place of publication and the word count vacant for "The Second Generation." Probably about this time the revised word count for "The Making of the 307th" was added in the black ink. Probably in December of 1899, or January, 1900, the final changes were made in the list in blue ink. Following the news of publication of "The Second Generation" in the *Saturday Evening Post* for December 2, 1899, this fact and the word count were filled in. Perhaps at the same time, or close to it, the discovery was made that "The Making of the 307th" and "Virtue in War" were identical. The sequence is not clear, since it is possible that this revelation came earlier and that the title "The Making of the 307th" was deleted in black ink at some point after the cumulative total of 55,735 was written, that is, after the last two items had been added and perhaps concurrent with them. The word count 5,330 one may conjecture had been deleted earlier in favor of the 8,100 count for the revised version. But now, in blue ink, the 8,200 word count for "Virtue in War" seems to have been deleted in favor of the 8,100 count above it, although at some point 8,200 was restored in the blue ink, squeezing it into the available space but then deleting it in the same ink. One might conjecture that what triggered this discovery was the receipt of a copy of *Frank Leslie's Monthly*, published in the United States in November, containing "West Pointer and Volunteer." It is something of a mystery how this clipping got to Stokes, for otherwise the only letterpress copy provided him came from English magazines when a choice existed. Yet, obviously, the information was not passed on to Stokes that "Virtue in War" had replaced the typescript provided him of "The Making of the 307th," and so the error persisted until his printer discovered the coincidence in June, 1900.

As early as October 9, 1899, Stokes had been concerned to
know the title of the collection. It would seem that final copy was
in Stokes's hands probably in December, 1899, either in clipping,
proof, or in typescript form for those stories that were to be
published in December. It is interesting to observe that Cora
(who at this point was thinking that Methuen would set the book
independently instead of using American plates) told Pinker on
January 9, 1900, "can *you* see Methuen and say that now they
have or can get at any time the ms. for war stories" (*Letters*, p.
262), this being, of course, part of a request for an advance on
some sort of literary security. Methuen did, indeed, advance
£100 on account of royalties, but it is likely that this advance
was not made until the contract was signed on June 24, 1900
(TLS, Plant to Pinker, May 21, 1901, and March 2, 1905, Dartmouth). Although Stokes kept hoping that more stories would be
written for the volume and perhaps delayed typesetting in this
hope, in December, 1899, he began taking some preliminary
action. On December 1 he wrote to Pinker, "Can you give us the
title for the volume of 'War Stories' by Stephen Crane, and the
date of publication?" (TLS, Dartmouth) and on December 5 he
addressed Crane directly asking for "a brief description of your
new volume of 'War Stories' that we have the honor of publishing" ('volume of "War Stories" ' is written in hand above deleted
typed 'novel') and asking for general information of publicity
value. On December 29, enclosing a list of the stories to Pinker,
Stokes still is asking for the title and the date of publication
(TLS, Dartmouth). In response to some lost Stokes letter, no
doubt, Pinker wrote Cora on January 9, 1900, asking "Have you
a copy of the story written for Lady Randolph Churchill for me
to send to Stokes? It is, as you know, included in the book, and I
have no copy here" (*Letters*, p. 261), to which Cora replied
briefly on January 10, "Stokes and Co. have a copy of the article
in Lady Churchill's magazine. I sent it to them" (*Letters*, p.
263).

In January and February a dispute began about the exact
form of the title. The main difficulty, apparently, was not in
relation to the title *Wounds in the Rain* but to the subtitle.
Stokes's London representative, Dominick, had expressed himself on this point, and on February 1, 1900, Pinker passed on to

Crane his opinion: "He thinks so long a title as the one you have chosen would seriously affect the sale of the volume, and he tells me that in view of the glut of books on the Cuban war which has appeared in America he thinks it unwise to proclaim in your title that your book deals with the same subject" (*Letters*, p. 264, n. 25). On February 5 Crane exploded:

> I spent two months trying to find an effective title to the book of War Stories. I decided upon *"Wounds in the Rain."* This seemed to me *very effective.*
>
> Dominick's views are of no account to me whatever and I am surprised that Methuen found occasion to agree with him on any point.
>
> The sub-title—the books on the Cuban War have for more than a year terrified the Stokes firm and they have not the slightest idea that they are now in possession of the only fairly decent book on the Cuban War which has yet been written—the sub-title, I say, can be dispenced with for America and become this: 'A collection of War Stories.' As for Methuen, he can adopt the same sub-title if he likes.
>
> But as for the premier title, "Wounds in the Rain," I shall not change that unless I am *compelled* to do so [*Letters*, p. 264].

In a letter conjecturally dated April 23, 1900, Cora enclosed to Pinker the dedication to Frewen which she requested be placed in both the American and English editions (*Letters*, p. 276), and on May 4 Stokes acknowledged to Pinker receipt of the dedication (TLS, Dartmouth). The subtitle, however, was still a source of friction. In an undated letter, but probably after August 3, 1900, Cora wrote from 47 Gower Street to Pinker, "I also enclose a *copy* of his note on the title. It would be very stupid not to use it and I must ask you to say that, I hope this note will be used" (ALS, Dartmouth). The note she referred to may be that preserved as an insert in a copy of the Methuen edition recently turned up in Jacksonville, Florida, which in Crane's hand reads as follows:

Wounds in the Rain.
A collection of stories relating to the Spanish-American war of 1898
By Stephen Crane.

Note: The intermediate descriptive phrase should certainly appear on the cover of the book as well as on the title page. Otherwise, *rain* rhymes atrociously with *Crane* and ruins the entire effect of the singular and sinister brutality of the title. The intermediate sentence should also be made to appear in any advertisement. S. C. [G. W. Hallam, *Studies in Bibliography*, XX (1967), 266]

To Cora's letter Pinker, in an undated response, wrote, "I have urged Messrs Methuen to follow your wishes regarding the subtitle" (TLS, Dartmouth). As it turned out, the Stokes edition carried the brief subtitle "War Tales," but Methuen followed Crane's note except that neither publisher paid any attention to the request to have the subtitle on the cover.

As of the end of May, Stokes was still preparing to send copy to the printer. In a letter postdated May 23, 1900, he addressed Pinker hoping to be sent more printed copy from English periodicals since—Crane doubtless having read proof on these—Stokes could then omit to send book proof to England and save much time and trouble. He enclosed a list of the stories in their final order with the English magazines in which they had appeared. Opposite "The Making of the 307th" is only a line of typed dashes; typed '(unsold)' has been deleted by hand opposite "Marines Signaling," a short typed word after "This Majestic Lie" has been heavily deleted, and a line of typed dashes appears after "The Second Generation." He then lists the letterpress copies in his possession: "The Price of the Harness," "The Lone Charge," " 'God Rest Ye,' " "Virtue in War," and "Marines Signaling." "The Lone Charge" and "Virtue in War" were listed as from American magazines and not from the English otherwise noted. Obviously, copy for "Marines" had arrived after the outdated entry 'unsold' of the list of which this is a copy. He hopes that he will not need to send proofs of these, at least (TLS, Dartmouth). In a prior dictated letter, of May 22, about another matter Stokes adds a postscript. Methuen wants publication on August 14, a date that means Pinker will need to cable to confirm the order of the stories. It will also expedite matters if he will cable to confirm that proofs need not be sent to England (TLS, Dartmouth).

By June 15 preparation for typesetting had been completed since the printer had discovered that the typescript copy for "The Revenge of the *Adolphus*" was incomplete, and Stokes writes to Pinker for a copy from the *Strand* in case one cannot be located in New York. The printer had also discovered the duplication between the typescript of "The Making of the 307th" at 8,100 words and the letterpress copy of "Virtue in War" at 8,200, and Stokes proposes to utilize the latter (no doubt on the grounds it had been proofread).

This serious falling off in the number of words will make the book a small one. Is there not something else by Mr. Crane in the same field that can be added to the volume, to run it out so as to make it a larger book? If so, please send the copy for this immediately. We have purchased a copy of 'The Anglo-Saxon Review', and have sent this to the printer to use in setting up "War Memories". We have typescript copy only for the following, however:—'The Clan of No Name'; 'The Revenge of the Adolphus'; 'The Sergeant's Private Mad House'; and 'This Majestic Lie'. We have tried our best to find these in the various magazines, but without success. If you have been able to carry out our suggestion as to sending us letter-press copy for them, it will help matters greatly [TLS, Dartmouth].

On June 26 Stokes writes Pinker that a copy of the *Strand* has been found for "The Revenge" "so that the work of making our plates of 'Wounds in the Rain' is now progressing as rapidly as possible" (TLS, Dartmouth). Pinker responded later with the *Strand* clipping but not with clippings to replace the typescripts that had been assembled to send to Stokes before the December publication of several stories, and on July 5 Stokes acknowledges the clipping and continues (taking cognizance of the break between Cora and Pinker):

We are sorry to learn from Messrs. Methuen & Co. that we have turned to you improperly in the matter of 'Wounds in the Rain'. You will remember that Mr. Crane instructed us to correspond with you in the matter, and, owing to the imperfect state of the copy and the difficulty in regard to the title of the work, we were compelled to trouble you as we did. Surely, we were entitled to receive complete copy in a responsible state of perfection from some one, and as the author's instructions were to turn to you, we naturally did so" [TLS, Dartmouth].

The Stokes correspondence then ceases with a coda to Pinker on July 26 when after complaining that Pinker has not sent him copy for a story by another author, Stokes continues, "We fear that when the time comes for us to have our edition in readiness, there will be the same uncomfortable circumstances existing as

in the case of 'Wounds in the Rain', due to no fault of ours"
(TLS, Dartmouth). But perhaps the last letter to quote had
better be Stokes to Pinker, earlier, on May 4, 1900, in which he
acknowledges receipt of Pinker's letter of April 24 with the
dedication for *Wounds in the Rain*. He continues: "We are quite
anxious to have some news as to Mr. Crane's condition, as we
have heard nothing concerning it for some weeks. In the absence
of continued bad news, our hope is that he is recovering. Not-
withstanding the friction that we have had with him, we trust
you will please tell him of the inquiry that we have made and
express our great sympathy with him in his illness,— this entirely apart from any business matters" (TLS, Dartmouth). At
the foot of this letter Pinker has written, to be typed in reply, "I
am much obliged to you for your kind letter of the 4th inst. I am
glad to tell you that Mr Crane is very much better, and my last
news is that they hope to get him away this week. I will not fail
to tell him of your sympathetic inquiries."

Only a few odds and ends of references have any further
bearing on the publication of *Wounds in the Rain*. On August
10, 1900, Methuen wrote to Pinker asking for a list of Crane's
works to face the title and stating that they had the copy for the
dedication. To this Pinker wrote in pencil at the foot, probably as
a note for a response, "Is there not a sub-title?" (ALS, New York
Public Library). In early August Cora was trying to persuade
Pinker to send her proofs of *Wounds* (no doubt already printed
at that time), and as late as October 20 she was requesting the
same of her new agent Perris. Stokes applied for copyright on
the volume September 1, 1900, with deposit made on September 4. It was advertised in the *Publishers' Weekly* for October 13,
the price $1.50.

The Stokes edition may be described as follows:

[within a black rule-frame] [red] WOUNDS IN | THE RAIN [black
rule] | [black] *War Stories* | [rule] | BY | [red] STEPHEN CRANE |
[black] *Author of* | "The Red Badge of Courage," "Active Service," |
"War is Kind," etc. || [leaf orn.] || 𝕹𝖊𝖜 𝖄𝖔𝖗𝖐 | [red] Frederick A.
Stokes Company | [black] *Publishers*

Collation: [1² 2–23⁸] (signed π⁴ [1]⁸ 2–21⁸ 22⁶, misnumbering 17 as
18), pp. [i–viii], [1] 2–347 [348]. Text paper unwatermarked laid
with vertical chainlines 22 mm. apart; leaf measures 7⁵⁄₁₆ × 4¹⁵⁄₁₆",
all edges trimmed, top edge gilt; wove endpapers.

Contents: p. i: half-title, '[red thick-thin rule] | [black] WOUNDS *in the* RAIN | [red thin-thick rule]'; p. ii: blank; p. iii: title; p. iv: 'Copyright, 1899, by | S. S. McClure Company. | Copyright, 1899, by | The Curtis Publishing Company. | Copyright, 1899, by | Frank Leslie Publishing House (Incorporated). | Copyright, 1900, by | Frederick A. Stokes Company. | [short rule] | *All Rights Reserved.*'; p. v: 'TO | 𝔐𝔬𝔯𝔢𝔱𝔬𝔫 𝔉𝔯𝔢𝔴𝔢𝔫 | THIS SMALL TOKEN OF THINGS | WELL REMEMBERED BY | HIS FRIEND | STEPHEN CRANE. | Brede Place, Sussex, *April*, 1900.'; p. vi: blank; p. vii: contents; p. viii: blank; p. 1: text with head-title 'WOUNDS IN THE RAIN | [short rule]'; on p. 347: 'THE END.'; p. 348: blank.

The Price of the Harness	The Sergeant's Private
The Lone Charge of	Madhouse
William B. Perkins	Virtue in War
The Clan of No-Name	Marines Signalling under Fire
God Rest Ye, Merry	at Guantanamo
Gentlemen	This Majestic Lie
The Revenge of the	War Memories
Adolphus	

The Second Generation

Binding: Dark green cloth, all lettering in gold. *Front cover*: '[within a chain border] WOUNDS *in* | THE RAIN | *By* Stephen Crane | [leaf orn.]' *Spine*: 'Wounds | *in the* | Rain | Crane | [leaf orn.] | Stokes'. *Back cover*: blank.

Dust jacket: Off-white paper lettered in red. *Front*: '[within a chain border] WOUNDS *in* | THE RAIN | WAR STORIES | *By* Stephen Crane | *Author of* "THE RED BADGE OF | COURAGE," "ACTIVE SERVICE," etc. | Brilliant and thrilling work in the best vein of one who | has been called by Robert Barr "the greatest modern writer | on war." | While the author's experience and observations have been | drawn on, the result is exciting and interesting, and by no | means in the nature of a dry record of events. | The book has added interest because it is the latest work | of the late Stephen Crane, with the exception of "The O'Ruddy," a long novel to be published next year. | *The Publishers.*' *Spine*: like cover. *Back*: within a thick-thin rule-frame advertisements for *Active Service* at $1.25 and *War is Kind* at $2.50 in the limited "Bradley" edition. Advertisements on front and back flaps.

Copies: University of Virginia–Barrett PS1449.C85W6 1900 (551478), with dust jacket; Barrett (451623); Taylor 1900.C73W6 (508750).

Note: A fourth edition was advertised in the *New York Evening Post* on November 13, 1900, and in the *New York Tribune*, December

15, 1900. Professor Joseph Katz and Professor Matthew Bruccoli own copies of *Wounds in the Rain* identical in every respect with the first printing except that 'Third Editon' appears at the foot of p. iv, the copyright page. Barrett copy 576814 is of the fourth printing, with 'Fourth Edition' replacing 'Third Editon' on p. iv.

The English edition, priced at six shillings, was deposited for copyright in the British Museum on September 1, 1900, and announced in the *Publishers' Circular* of September 22, 1900. It was printed from the plates of the Stokes edition.

WOUNDS IN THE RAIN | A COLLECTION OF STORIES RELATING TO | THE SPANISH-AMERICAN WAR OF 1898 | BY | STEPHEN CRANE | METHUEN & CO. | 36 ESSEX STREET W. C. | LONDON | 1900

Collation: π⁴ 1–21⁸ 22⁶, pp. [i–viii], [1] 2–347 [348], plus bound-in publisher's catalogue dated August, 1900 (October has also been observed), of 48 pp. Text paper is laid unwatermarked with vertical chainlines 25 mm. apart; leaf measures 7½ × 5", top edge trimmed; wove endpapers.

Contents: p. i: half-title, 'WOUNDS IN THE RAIN'; p. ii: 'BY THE SAME AUTHOR' (10 titles, including *Great Battles of the World* but not *The O'Ruddy*); p. iii: title; p. iv: blank; p. v: dedication; p. vi: blank; p. vii: contents; p. viii: blank; p. 1: text; on p. 347: '[rule] | *Printed from American Plates* | Edinburgh: T. & A. CONSTABLE, Printers to Her Majesty.'; p. 348: blank.

Binding: Red cloth, all lettering in gold. *Front cover*: '[within a rule-frame] WOUNDS | IN THE | RAIN | BY | STEPHEN CRANE.' *Spine*: '[within a rule-frame] WOUNDS | IN THE | RAIN | STEPHEN CRANE | [within a rule-frame] METHUEN.' Back cover: blank.

Copies: University of Virginia–Barrett PS1449.C85W6 1900a (551479). British Museum, deposit copy, 012641.c.40.

NOTE: Correspondence is preserved in the Dartmouth College Library about a cheap edition. On March 2, 1905, Plant (the solicitor for the estate) wrote Pinker: "The Agreement with Messrs. Methuen & Co. of the 24th June 1899 provides for the issue of a cheap edition of 'Wounds in the Rain' at a royalty of 12½ per cent on the published price and I am quite willing to assent to this." On March 4, 1905, Methuen wrote Pinker that they could not pay more than 1d. royalty on the proposed one-shilling edition or 1½d. on the proposed one-shilling and sixpence edition and added: "this is far better than selling copies at remainder price. . . . Otherwise . . . we shall have to omit the volume from the series." On April 26, 1905, in a letter to Pinker Plant accepted the Methuen terms.

In the preparation of the present edition the control University of Virginia–Barrett copy 551478 was collated on the Hinman Collating Machine against the Taylor copy (508750) and the Barrett copy of the fourth printing (576814) without evidence appearing of any changes in the American plates. However, when the control copy (551478) was collated against the Barrett copy (551479) of the Methuen printing from duplicate plates, a number of plate changes were observed. In the following list the first page-line reference is to the present edition and the second, within parentheses, to the Stokes-Methuen page-line. The reading to the left of the bracket is that of the Stokes plates and that to the right is that of the Methuen plates. Since these changes were not made by the time of the Stokes fourth printing, the assumption must follow that Methuen was responsible for the alterations, which should then be classified as corrections without authority.

133.24   (69.2–3)   Pobrecetto] Pobrecito
144.27   (88.1)   and] an
147.33   (93.27)   late] late.
149.4   (96.8)   Daqueri] Daiquiri
156.11   (109.7)   said] said:
156.31   (110.5)   leaward] leeward
163.30–31   (123.12)   conflict,] conflict.
166.24   (128.18)   gun.] gun:
167.31   (131.1)   steamed] streamed
177.29   (148.21)   When] While
177.29   (148.21)   guard] watched
190.5   (170.27)   regulars] regular
202.27   (193.1)   was] were
204.7   (195.23)   plentitude] plenitude
204.27   (196.22)   elapse.] elapse."
210.27   (208.8)   too.] too."
210.31   (208.12–13)   Valladolid] Valladolid,
233.22   (250.26)   camp. Leaving] camp, leaving
234.35   (253.13)   leaward] leeward
234.38, 235.4   (253.18, 23)   Fort] Port

Each state of the plates for the American and the English first-editions seems to be established, therefore.

THE PRICE OF THE HARNESS

The manuscript of "The Price of the Harness" was sent to Paul Reynolds from Havana on September 27, 1898, with the usual enthusiastic plug and the note, 'English copy goes to Blackwood's' (*Letters*, pp. 187–188). From Havana on November 3, 1898, Crane wrote to Reynolds:

> Just received letter concerning "The Price of the Harness." If Blackwood can't take it for Dec. ask them to give it to Pinker. Somebody must have it. With Pinker it is worth £36. We can't lose it.
>
> Damn Walker. The name of the story is "The Price of the Harness" because it *is* the price of the harness, the price the men paid for wearing the military harness, Uncle Sam's military harness; and they paid blood, hunger and fever. Let him if he likes conjure some inflammatory secondary title. He is a fool [*Letters*, p. 193].

This second letter explains the unauthoritative title editorially adopted in the *Cosmopolitan*, "The Woof of Thin Red Threads," when the story was published in December, 1898 (XXVI, 164–172).[44] As "The Price of the Harness" it appeared simultaneously in *Blackwood's Edinburgh Magazine*, CLXIV (December, 1898), 829–840. This is also the title Crane gave it in three manuscript lists preserved in the Columbia University Libraries Special Collections. In the first, after a group of Whilomville materials headed 'The Harper's book' comes the heading 'War Stories, etc', of which "The Price of the Harness" is the first. To the left is the notation 'Published' and to the right the memorandum that it is 6,000 words and appeared in *Cosmopolitan* and *Blackwood's*. Both lists may be dated, probably, in March of 1898 (see *Tales of Whilomville*, p. liii). The third list comprises the eleven stories complete for *Wounds in the Rain*, although not quite in their final order. Here "The Price of the Harness" comes first, the two magazine appearances are given, but the word count now is 6,500 words.

[44] The *Cosmopolitan* title was drawn from Crane's sentence at 109.34–36, *It [the noise of battle] reminds one always of a loom, a great grand steel loom, clinking, clanking, plunking, plinking, to weave a woof of thin red threads, the cloth of death.*

On receipt of the manuscript Reynolds presumably had a typescript and its carbon made, one of which was sold to the *Cosmopolitan* and the other mailed to *Blackwood's*, which did manage to publish it on time. Crane, in Havana, would not have seen proof. The two texts, then, derive quite clearly from this typed copy, the *Blackwood's* variants being no more than the usual 'improvements' that English editors allowed themselves, particularly with American scripts. However, *Blackwood's* preserves most usefully one sentence, *He laid his face to his rifle as if it were his mistress* (110.18–19), which seems to have been cut (with a consequential change in the next sentence) in the *Cosmopolitan* in deference to the prudery expected of a 'family magazine.'

Each version, then, is of equal textual authority. The *Cosmopolitan* has been selected as copy-text, however, mainly because its American typesetting may be presumed to agree more closely with the characteristics of the basic typescript, which is as far back as an editor can reach. Yet in some respects of accidentals *Blackwood's* reproduces more faithfully certain punctuation characteristics that accord with Crane's habits but seem to have been overlaid by *Cosmopolitan* styling. The copy-text, thus, has been emended conservatively on the authority of *Blackwood's* from time to time in an attempt by eclectic selection to approximate, so far as the preserved documents permit, the details of the basic typescript commissioned by Reynolds. The 1900 Stokes collection *Wounds in the Rain* (A1) printed the story on pages 1–32. The Stokes letter to Pinker of May 23, 1900, indicates that a clipping from *Blackwood's* was in their possession, and collation demonstrates that this clipping was used as printer's copy without authoritative alteration. The book edition, therefore, is purely derived and has no textual standing.

THE LONE CHARGE OF WILLIAM B. PERKINS

"The Lone Charge of William B. Perkins" seems to have been the first of the Cuban stories that Crane wrote after establishing himself in Havana. From Havana on September 14, 1898, he wrote Reynolds: "I send you The Lone Charge of William B. Perkins. McClure ought to give you £20 for U.S. rights. The

English rts belong to Blackwoods Magazine. Please make copy and send to them. Hold money for U.S. rts subject to my cabled order" (Syracuse, typed transcript). From London the Authors' Syndicate wrote Reynolds on November 9, 1898: "We acknowledge receipt of Lone Charge and note it is to appear in January McClure's. We will endeavor to synchronise an English appearance and get £30" (Syracuse, typed transcript). The result of this negotiation was the publication in the *Westminster Gazette*, XIII, no. 1819 (January 2, 1899), 1–2, with the prefixed note, '*Copyright U.S.A.*', reprinted in the same typesetting (with only minor resetting and no variation) in the *Westminster Budget*, January 6, 1899, p. 20. From Ravensbrook on January 19, 1899, Crane wrote indignantly to Reynolds: " 'The Lone Charge of William B. Perkins' was published over here by the 'Westminster Gazette' Where did they get it and who reaped the money"; on March 16, appeased, he wrote to Reynolds from Brede, "I note that you have instructed the Authors Syndicate to pay me money due for 'The Lone Charge of Wm. B. Perkins' " (Syracuse, typed transcripts). Magazine publication was completed when it appeared in *McClure's Magazine*, XIII (July, 1899), 279–282.[45] In the first of the two lists of March, 1899, the story comes at the end of the group headed 'War Stories, etc,' separated from the other Spanish-American War tales. It is noted as 'Published', the *Gazette* and *McClure's* are named, and the word count is 2,000. In the second list, 'New Collection,' the entry is copied but it is placed fourth and last of the *Wounds* tales noted. In the third and final list of early 1900 it appears as the second story but with the word count now 1,810.

One copy of Reynolds' typescript or carbon would have gone to *Blackwood's* and then, presumably on rejection, to the Authors' Syndicate; the other went to *McClure's*. Although the accidentals show the effect of styling in both periodicals, nothing in the evidence would prevent the assumption that each was set from such common copy. The substantive variants, as well, except for the usual editorial alterations on both sides, although principally

[45] Four illustrations were drawn by W. J. Glackens. In the first illustration the date '98' follows the name. The legends are: ' "*Come on*," *he shouted*'; '*Perkins flung himself through that hole*'; '*An apparitional figure*'; and '*Then he told them*'. The title advertises Crane as 'Author of "The Red Badge of Courage," "The Open Boat," etc.'

in the *Gazette*, do not require any hypothesis that one or other version was printed from a fresh typescript independently made up from the manuscript. At the most, a noneditorial variant or two might be put down to Crane's review of one of the copies, but even this suggestion is not needed except for a single reading. This definitely must have been changed by such review, by proof alteration, or by special instruction. In the *Gazette* the penultimate sentence reads, *The party then laid down in the brush and laughed until every face was blazing red*, but in *McClure's* it comes out as, *The patrol then marveled at the truthfulness of war correspondents until they were almost blind* (118.14–15).

Both are manifestly Crane's, and thus the problem resolves itself to finding the reason for the change and deciding the priority. Since *McClure's* was published six months later than the *Gazette* one might take it that Crane had changed his mind after January about the merits of the sentence and substituted a new one in the copy sent to *McClure's*. And indeed at first sight such a hypothesis might seem to be confirmed by the apparent reason for the substitution. In "Lynx-Hunting" after Jimmie told Fleming that he had thought the shot cow was a lynx, *Old Fleming and his Swede at once lay down in the grass and laughed themselves helpless*. As Professor Levenson has determined (*Tales of Whilomville*, p. xlvi), "Lynx-Hunting" was written after January 19, 1899, although before January 31, and thus follows the publication in the *Westminster Gazette* of "The Lone Charge." One may take it, then, that finding himself in some difficulty to conclude "Lynx-Hunting," Crane borrowed the violent laughter and the rolling in the grass from "The Lone Charge" but thereupon altered the conclusion of the first story— easily enough done—in order not to have two stories end with the identical action. The only difficulty in applying this conjecture to "The Lone Charge" is the fact that the dated illustration places copy with *McClure's* in late 1898. However, on the evidence of the preserved McClure proofsheets of "The Veteran," *McClure's Magazine* was accustomed to sending proof to Crane. Since the July publication date allows plenty of time for Crane to have received and returned proof, we must suppose that he supplied the new sentence not in the printer's copy but in proof sometime in the early months of 1899, or by mailed instructions.

"The Veteran" proofsheets offer ample evidence to identify the heavy styling Crane's accidentals received from the *McClure's* editors. Although the *Westminster Gazette* text of "The Lone Charge" is substantively less reliable than the *McClure's*, its accidentals texture appears on the whole to reflect Crane's usual characteristics more faithfully than does *McClure's*. Since the two versions are of equal authority in respect to their accidentals owing to their equal distance from a common copy, the *Westminster Gazette* has been selected as copy-text inasmuch as it is generally less in need of accidentals emendation than *McClure's*. Into this texture have been placed the *McClure's* variant substantives that appear to reproduce what we may suppose to have been the manuscript readings without benefit of English editorial tinkering. Moreover, since it seems certain that Crane revised the *McClure's* proof in respect to the penultimate sentence, in case he took the opportunity to make minor changes at the same time they would be included by a general reliance upon the *McClure's* substantives.[46] As for the altered sentence, the *McClure's* version must presumably be accepted as representing Crane's final intentions. On the other hand, the original sentence seems to have been changed for reasons extraneous to its own literary merit and hence one may feel some reluctance at the necessity to reject on nonliterary grounds the original version.

The *Gazette* and *McClure's* are the only textual documents of any authority. The collected *Wounds in the Rain* derives from McC and has no independent authority either in accidentals or in substantives. Collation confirms the Stokes report to Pinker dated May 23, 1900, that his firm had the *McClure's* clipping for the story. The present text, therefore, attempts by an eclectic choice of materials from the two original authorities to reconstruct as nearly as may be the original typescript that, with its carbon, served as their printers' copy, plus the substitution of the one identifiable authorial proof change in *McClure's*.

The Clan of No-Name

With the undated letter from Havana in late October, 1898, in which Crane inquired of Reynolds whether he had received "The

---

[46] The most difficult case involves WG *splutter* vs. McC *sputter* (115.38), for which see the Textual Note.

Price of the Harness," he enclosed the manuscript of "The Clan of No-Name."⁴⁷ His comment is typical: "I am now sending you a *peach*. I love it devotedly. Sell it to anybody if the price is grand enough. Otherwise remember that *Blackwood's* have a call on me. . . . I *love* this story" (*Letters*, p. 188). The story is not, in fact, titled in the letter, but that it was "The Clan of No-Name" is certain. The dispatch of all of the Spanish-American War stories written in Havana is accounted for save for the "Clan" in letters that definitely refer to their titles up to " 'God Rest Ye, Merry Gentlemen,' " which was the first of the *Wounds in the Rain* stories to be written in England. Corroboration is given by a typescript copy of a subsequent undated letter—but one assignable to October—now in the Syracuse University Library collection of Crane, which encloses a third article for the *New York Journal* and remarks, "You have not yet receipted for that superb masterpiece The Clan of No-Name." Reynolds apparently found no ready sale for the story since it did not appear until March 19, 1899, and then in syndicated newspaper form. From Ravensbrook on January 19, 1899, Crane wrote to Reynolds a plea for money, including the statement, "I depend on you for something like £75.—counting 'The Clan of No Name' and Harpers miserly £25.—" (Syracuse, typed transcript). Apparently this does not refer to a sale, but on February 13, 1899, he writes, "I note what you say in regard to getting 60— for the 'Clan of No-Name' " in connection with some dissatisfaction with the price (Syracuse), which indicates that Reynolds had disposed of the story; and on March 2, 1899, in a postscript he compliments Reynolds, "I think you did mighty well with 'The Clan of No Name' " (Syracuse).

The story was syndicated, copyrighted in 1899 by Crane, in the *New York Herald* (N¹) on Sunday, March 19, 1899, sec. 8, p. 2. It has also been located in the Chicago *Times-Herald* (N²), March 19, 1899, sec. 5, pp. 1–2 and, in cut form, in the San Francisco *Examiner* (N³), the Sunday Magazine section, March

---

⁴⁷ In his correspondence Crane refers to the story without distinction as *Clan of No Name* or *Clan of No-Name*. The newspaper decorative headings and the heading in *Black and White* read *No Name*, although the hyphenated form is found in the collection *Wounds in the Rain*. It is probably decisive that in the three autograph lists of stories in which the title appears Crane gives it as *No-Name*.

19, 1899, p. 29.[48] The evidence suggests that a master proof of the *Herald* typesetting was sent out to the other newspapers. Whether the *Herald* itself bought the story for syndication on a cash and royalty basis is not entirely clear. In response to a letter from Crane dated March 30, 1899, hoping that he has collected 'by this time' the money for the "Clan" (Syracuse), Reynolds responds on April 11 that he has not 'got in all the money from the papers' but will send it to Pinker later (Columbia University Libraries). Then on April 17 Reynolds writes that all the money has been received 'except for a paper in San Francisco' (Columbia).

Whether or not Reynolds tried for a 'grand price' is unknown, but it is certain that, whether immediately or after a delay, he sent on the story to *Blackwood's*, for on March 17, 1899, Crane wrote to Pinker from Brede, "Please tell me when Mr. Meldrum was kind enough to loosen his talons on the 'Clan of No Name.' " [49] How long *Blackwood's* had been considering the story is not to be determined; but at any rate on March 20 Pinker was able to telegraph news of the sale to *Black and White* and in a letter he added that the price was fifteen guineas. *Blackwood's*, he said, had returned it on March 9 (*Letters*, p. 219). *Black and White* (BW) held the story until the Christmas number, 1899,

---

[48] The *Herald* had a decorative heading drawn and gave it a three-column illustration with the legend, 'HE THRUST A CARTRIDGE INTO THE REMINGTON AND CREPT UP BESIDE THE TWO UNHURT MEN'. The Chicago *Times-Herald* had a different and very elaborate heading and gave it six illustrations with the legends, 'MARGHARITA WALKED ALONE IN THE MOONLIT GARDEN', 'HE SCREAMED AN ALARM AND FELL INTO THE BLOCKHOUSE', ' "POR DIOS, HOMBRES! POR DIOS! FUEGO!" ', 'HE THRUST A CARTRIDGE INTO THE REMINGTON AND CREPT UP BESIDE THE TWO UNHURT MEN. EVEN AS HE DID SO THREE OR FOUR BULLETS CUT SO CLOSE TO HIM THAT ALL HIS FLESH TINGLED', ' "MARGHARITA," HE MURMURED. "I WANT YOU TO MARRY ME" ', and 'THAT NIGHT SHE TOOK A STAINED PHOTOGRAPH FROM HER DRESSING TABLE AND HOLDING IT OVER THE CANDLE BURNED IT TO NOTHING'. The *Examiner* has an illustrative heading showing Smith kissing Margharita and an illustration with the legend, 'The Lieutenant closed his eyes. He did not want to see the flash of the machete'.

[49] He continues: "I think my relations with the Blackwoods is about the most expensive friendship I have yet devised. Please let me know if the 'Clan of No Name' is not sold by the 20th. Let me know by wire. In that case I shall come to London and wrestle with some newspaper friends. I should think Black and White or the London Illustrated News are extremely likely people. I have myself sold them stories of much the same character without any trouble. . . . If you can get £30 cash for both those stories now [" 'God Rest Ye' " and 'Clan'] I would rather have it than £50 next month, although they brought in America a trifle like £106" (*Letters*, p. 218).

when it appeared in pages 13–16 without copyright notice.[50] In the two early lists of his war stories, Crane included the "Clan" below "The Price of the Harness" with the notation 6,500 words and publication in 'Herald etc' and in *Black and White*. In the final list for *Wounds* it is third, with the same publications but with a word count of 6,150. In the 1900 Stokes *Wounds in the Rain* (A1) the story occupied pages 42–73.

Since Crane had sent the manuscript from Havana, Reynolds would have had a typescript made for American sale, and since he had been requested to send a copy to *Blackwood's*, the normal assumption would be that he mailed either the ribbon copy or a carbon and that this, eventually, became the printer's copy for *Black and White*. Whether the textual evidence supports this simple conjecture is in question. Moreover, since neither a clipping from the *Herald* (or any other known newspaper) nor from *Black and White* served as copy for the Stokes book collection, the transmission to A1 is also in question together with A1's authority. That is, collational evidence and the statement by Stokes on June 15, 1900, that he possessed typescript copy for this story establishes the kind of copy he had, since there is no indication that Pinker ever responded to his pleas for printed copy instead of the typescripts. The origin of this typescript and its place in the transmissional history of the text is of prime importance.

At first sight two lines of text—one English and one American —seem to develop. In substantives alone *Black and White* (BW) and *Wounds* (A1) agree against the *Herald* (N^1) in thirty-five readings, whereas BW and N^1 agree against A1 only ten times, all of these being A1 errors. Moreover, the accidentals of BW and A1 are sometimes closer to each other than to N^1.[51] On the other hand, it is odd indeed that N^1 and A1 concur against BW in thirty-one readings. The latter anomaly may be partly resolved by the observation that a considerable number of the BW unique

---

[50] It was advertised as illustrated by W. Dewar, who drew a heading for it portraying the three principals and also a full-page illustration with the legend 'IT WAS AS IF SOME GIANT HAD STRUCK HIM ON THE CHEST WITH A BEAM'.

[51] For example, BW and A1 agree some forty-eight or more times in word-division versus N^1, whereas N^1,A1 agree against BW and N^1,BW against A1 only half a dozen times apiece, or less. However, see below for the lack of significance in this evidence after analysis.

variants are obviously editorial; for example, four rectify Crane's split infinitives and others are concerned to smooth his craggy syntax and idiom. Various are simple errors, like *surprised* for *surprise* (124.15), *moved* for *mowed* (129.26), or *single* for *singular* (132.10). We end with no more than a handful that are so neutral as in some part to defy critical classification and a very few (to be considered later) that must be examined as proof alterations. In short, the variants in which N^1 and A1 concur against BW are largely clear cut BW departures from copy, and thus the unusual agreement of N^1 and A1 has no significant bearing on the problem of multiple lines of transmission—that is, multiple copy—each with its own distinctively grouped readings. Except for the ten unique errors in A1 and for some special BW unique readings, the statement still remains true that when A1 disagrees with N^1 it is joined by BW.

Whether this pairing signifies an American and an English line of the text, emanating from two different basic typescripts as in "Death and the Child," is almost impossible to demonstrate. Since N^1 stands alone,[52] no way exists to show by its agreement with another American text that radiates, with it, from some common original whether certain of its readings derive from different copy or are, instead, N^1 errors or corrections.[53] In this situation the problem of the N^1 unique readings can be attacked only like those of BW, on a critical basis. That N^1 has had editorial attention is manifest. It can be no accident that, the Spanish-American War then over, N^1 reduces some of Crane's anti-Spanish detail, such as the description of the foulness of the Spanish tongue (125.9–10) or of the corrupt Spanish colonel (133.5–6). If the BW,A1 description of how Margharita *rumpled him [Smith] at once to squalid slavery* (135.5–6) is Crane's —and it is surely no one else's—then $N^{1'}$s *reduced him to abject*

---

[52] N^1 does not radiate with the other newspapers from the common copy of a lost proof; instead, the N^1 text is itself in a sense this proof, and the other newspapers have no more authority than if they had been set from an actual clipping of N^1.

[53] That is, when at 121.36 N^1 gets the Cuban name wrong as *Manriel*; or has the mistake of *several* for *severed* (127.6) or of *a lone* for *along* a (128.24); or the substitution of *one* for *task* (123.2); or omissions like that of *disconsolately* (128.33); the N^{2-3} repetitions are meaningless. But concurrence in any of these readings by another text that derived from the copy used by N^1 itself would prove the two-tradition hypothesis.

slavery shows the bland editorial hand, which is perhaps to be seen also in the translation *kept at bay* (123.4) for BW,A1 *bayed* which is also found in *The O'Ruddy*. The long cut from 127.36 to 128.21 seems editorial or mechanical. Since it is observed by N[2-3] as well, it is not a last-moment shortening of the story to fit the *Herald* space, but instead an early shortening. It is definitely not an addition in BW,A1: the opening sentence of Part VII (128.22) depends upon the missing material. In addition, the N[1] variants represent a number of mistakes in the typesetting such as *impossible* for *possible* (129.18), *familiar* for *unfamiliar* (which may be editorial, however, since it is repeated [131.7,15]), and *lines of* for *lies and* (136.3), plus a liberal sprinkling of such typos as *dum* for *dun* (126.30), or *emotioned* for *emotional* (129.22). The ten omissions of single words or phrases seem wholly unauthoritative. In short, when the obvious errors of typesetting and editorial interference are weeded out, there remain no more than seven or eight readings so neutral that they might have come from different copy than that behind BW,A1, and these, of course, are suspect.

The analysis of the accidentals reveals something of the same standoff in evidence bearing on two lines of transmission. That is, although in punctuation variants alone BW and A1 join against N[1] some 84 or more times, it is also true that N[1] and BW together disagree with A1 in punctuation some 83 or so times; hence no real quantitative tradition of BW and A1 on the one side can be set against N[1] that cannot be laid to N[1] styling, or common BW and A1 styling.[54] The evidence both for substantives and for accidentals joins with the external evidence that Reynolds probably sent a copy of this story to *Blackwood's* and the mate (whether the carbon or ribbon) to the *New York Herald* to

---

[54] For instance, although it is true—as remarked above—that BW,A1 agree about forty-eight times in word-division versus N[1], whereas N[1],A1 agree only four times against BW, and N[1],BW only five times against A1, a qualitative analysis reduces the significance of this quantitative imbalance. Except for five cases of division such as *blockhouse* or *block house* and *forever* or *for ever*, the variants all represent hyphenated compounds in BW,A1 versus nonhyphenation in N[1]. Indeed, N[1] never hyphenates a compound against an unhyphenated form in either BW or A1, and its general refusal to hyphenate seems as rigid a compositorial styling as to present no evidence about the nature of the N[1] copy. In contrast, the selectivity in hyphenation (to some extent) shared by BW and A1 may give us some glimpse as to the forms in the copy despite a general tendency on both parts, perhaps, to hyphenate more freely than the copy may have warranted.

discourage any hypothesis that a separate textual tradition, based on different copy, distinguishes BW and A1 from N[1].

If BW and N[1] may be taken as radiating from the same typescript, then the copy for A1 must be determined. The possibilities would seem to lie between A1 set from a fresh typescript made from the manuscript or set from the typescript behind the *Herald* or *Black and White*.

Any speculation that A1 could have come from some early form of BW proof founders not only on the Stokes statement of June 15, 1900, that his firm had the typescript but also on the noneditorial variant readings revealed by collation. Such a hypothesis would be an easy way of accounting for the substantive agreements between BW and A1 versus N[1],[55] but it would require some indifferent and also some inferior variants to have been produced later by BW editorial action along with the restyling that can be understood. It would also require A1 to have corrected automatically such errors as *single* at 132.10, not wholly obvious perhaps. Although it would explain the common error *struck* at 119.28 in BW and A1, no other common error of a similar kind seems to exist.

That A1 was set from a fresh typescript presupposes that when Crane was assembling copy for *Wounds in the Rain* the "Clan" had not yet appeared in *Black and White* and so no clipping was available to him.[56] The correspondence does indeed suggest that preparation of the volume and negotiations with Stokes were actively pursued in October and November, 1899, and thus that Crane might have had to make up fresh copy for the volume. If so, the question poses itself of the source for such a copy. If Crane had had any form of typescript, no need would exist for a copy, and thus the manuscript itself as the source of

[55] As well as for some of the accidentals agreements. For example, it is tempting to wonder if the high proportion of semicolon sentences in A1 could not be accounted for by derivation in some manner from BW. Of the approximately thirteen sentence-structure variants between BW and joint N[1],A1, at least nine are produced by semicolon structures in BW. Of the approximately eight sentence variants in which N[1] differs from BW,A1, six are due to semicolons in the latter. However, only one case appears in which A1 uses a semicolon construction versus BW and N[1].

[56] For example, on March 25, 1899, he wrote in a postscript to Reynolds: "Living over here in England I find considerable trouble in getting copies of my stories as they appear in the States. I would not want to worry you with such a small matter but if you find it coming your way at times, I would appreciate any mailed copy of the American publication" (Syracuse, typed transcript).

the new copy would seem to be the only answer. Yet this hypothesis would require Reynolds to have sent the manuscript to Crane in England in early 1899 at some time after his return—perhaps an odd procedure when small evidence exists that Crane had any idea of collecting his published manuscripts for their own sake and when a typescript form was in the hands of his English agent.[57] Nevertheless, a hypothesis for a new typescript has a certain superficial attractiveness since the rather extraordinary number of punctuation variants that separate A1 from the agreement of BW with N^1 (and thus perhaps with the basic copy) would be more readily accounted for. The 83 or more accidentals variants in which A1 varies from BW,N^1 as compared with the 84 or more in which N^1 differs from BW,A1 (or the 55 or so in which BW goes contrary to N^1,A1) are more than would ordinarily be expected from simple compositorial styling, perhaps. Qualitatively, however, positive evidence in favor of the A1 text as independent from joint N^1,BW is wanting,[58] and negative evidence suggests that what we know of the external history correctly reflects the transmission. Once the spate of N^1 newspaper paragraphings in Part 1 is over with, only one difference in paragraphing at 135.8 exists (and it does not mark off dialogue) to separate BW,A1 from N^1 until the spacing-out paragraph indention of BW at 135.25. Typists may follow the paragraphing of copy this faithfully, but they may not. Moreover, the careful distinction of hyphenated compounds that joins BW and A1, with only a very few disagreements, would be odd if a typist

[57] This also presupposes that on receipt of Crane's manuscript from Havana Reynolds then mailed directly to *Blackwood's* one of the copies of the typescript he had made up, as Crane had suggested for the "Clan" and had requested for the preceding "Lone Charge of William B. Perkins" and "The Price of the Harness" (September 14, 1898, from Havana accompanying the "Charge" MS: "The English rts belong to Blackwoods magazine. Please make copy and send to them"). In return for a loan to get him to Cuba, Crane seems to have made an agreement that *Blackwood's* would have the refusal of his war stories, an agreement lasting at least through "Marines Signaling Under Fire" that followed the "Clan." That Pinker intervened to recover the "Clan" from Meldrum (*Blackwood's*) does not signify that he had handled it from the beginning and would have received the story. See Crane to Reynolds from Havana on November 3 about "The Price of the Harness": "If Blackwood can't take it for Dec. ask them to give it to Pinker."

[58] The failure of A1 to capitalize any military title versus the BW,N^1 agreement in giving capitals to the general and the colonel, though not to the lieutenant, is not really evidence in the light of observed compositorial styling in this matter in other texts. Moreover, BW does not follow N^1 in capitalizing the captain.

had intervened between them; and so perhaps would the frequent concurrence of A1 with N^1 in semicolon and other details of sentence structure as compared with BW, and also A1's concurrence with BW against N^1 in the matter of the semicolon sentences. In substantives, a different typist might be expected to substitute words for BW,N^1 copy agreements, but all we have are the ten misprints and minor restylings in A1 that could well be compositorial alone. To sum up, if BW were set from a carbon of the typescript that was copy for N^1 (or vice versa), then insufficient differences exist between BW and A1 to demonstrate a different kind of printer's copy for each so long as the hypothesis holds that the substantive variants in BW are in considerable part editorial as well as compositorial. In turn, N^1 in combination with BW differs from A1 about as much as it differs from BW in combination with A1 in the matter of accidentals and also in substantives once adjustment is made for the editorial treatment of BW. Two textual traditions, in whatever combination of authorities, cannot be demonstrated.

If, then, all three authorities radiate from the typescript and its carbon, we could suppose that, in need of copy for A1, Crane recovered the typescript from BW when proof was sent him, or afterward.[59] The textual transmission thus conjectured places each of the preserved documents as technically equal in authority with the others in respect to the accidentals. In fact, of course, they are of different degrees of reliability. BW is far the heaviest punctuator, since it increases the weight of punctuation versus N^1,A1 some 40-odd times as against only about 7 decreases. Ordinarily, therefore, BW runs counter to Crane's characteristics and is of little independent authority.[60] In contrast, N^1 lightens

[59] If so, the editorial alterations in BW were made in proof and not marked in the typescript. For a somewhat similar case, see "The Second Generation." But, of course, Reynolds may have sent Crane two carbons. It would be natural enough.

[60] BW's most distinctive lightening of punctuation is the four times it removes commas setting off parenthetical phrases, which represent over half its changes in the direction of less weight. Once it substitutes a comma for an exclamation, and once an exclamation for a period. It makes four commas into semicolons and five commas into dashes while reducing two dashes to commas. In adding commas its favorite practice is to set off the parts of a compound predicate (9 times), and next the clauses of a compound sentence (7 times). It sets off six parenthetical phrases, three appositional phrases, three inverted phrases, four dependent clauses, and one inverted dependent clause. It never adds commas in a series of three.

the punctuation of joint BW,A1 some 36 times and increases the weight only 17. Qualitatively the circumstances are interesting because they serve as a useful guide to editorial emendation. For instance, N^1 never removes any commas in a series of two or more adjectives before a noun, whereas it adds such commas three times. It once removes a comma before *and* in a series of three but never adds any.[61] For the rest it is fairly uniform in lightening punctuation, four times removing commas setting off appositional phrases, four times in compound predicates, five times in parenthetical phrases, six times in compound sentences before *and* or *or*, five times after inverted phrases, five times before the dependent clause of a complex sentence, and six times after the inverted dependent clause of a complex sentence. In contrast, about half of the increased punctuation in N^1 concentrates on adding commas before dependent clauses, which it does eight times, chiefly to relatives. Then there is a marked drop in incidence of change when three commas are added in adjectival series and two apiece in setting off appositional, parenthetical, and inverted phrases. No punctuation is added to mark compound predicates or after inverted dependent clauses. N^1 also uses commas instead of semicolons four times and never independently makes a comma into a semicolon. Three times it substitutes an exclamation for a period or comma and once for a dash. It never removes a BW,A1 exclamation point, but it does use a question mark for one exclamation, and once for a period. It substitutes parenthetical dashes for commas twice.

All the N^1 decreases in the weight and amount of punctuation are in line with Crane's characteristics and may provisionally be accepted as reproducing the typescript with some faithfulness. Except for the distinctive treatment of setting off relative clauses and adding commas to adjective series—both of which run counter to Crane's practices—the other increases in the punctuation must be assigned either to N^1 styling or to reproduction of the copy. The freer use of exclamation points is probably N^1 styling. Definitely N^1 styling is the distinctive use of a dash after a colon to introduce dialogue. The strong disinclination to hy-

---

[61] Crane's manuscripts seldom punctuate between two adjectives, or even three, before a noun; and he regularly fails to punctuate between the second and third element of a series of three before the *and* or *or*.

phenate compounds is not characteristic of Crane and almost certainly does not represent the copy. The characteristics of N^1 are, in general, uniformly distributed and suggest that only one compositor set the type.

Quantitatively, A1 shows weightier punctuation habits since it adds about 37 commas while removing about 24. These statistics are deceptive, however, because A1 seems to have been set by at least two, and perhaps three, compositors of differing character-istics. The first compositor set Parts I–V. He alone accounts for over half of the added commas. In his stint only once does he remove a comma found in N^1 and BW, but he adds 20, eight of these setting off appositional phrases, six prepositional phrases, three inverted phrases, and three compound predicates. He does not depart from N^1,BW in other respects. In contrast, the com-positor who set Parts VI–VII was a remarkable lightener of punc-tuation. No less than eleven of the eighteen commas he removes had set off the clauses of a compound sentence. Otherwise, he takes away the commas from two compound predicates and one apiece from parenthetical phrases, dependent clauses, inverted dependent clauses, a series of three before *and*, and an adjective series. This compositor does add commas to set off three in-verted phrases (he had removed none), two dependent clauses, one appositive phrase, one parenthetical phrase, and one in-verted dependent clause. The third compositor is more balanced in all respects. He adds more commas (9) than he removes (5), but these additions are confined to setting off appositive phrases (3), dependent clauses (3), inverted phrases (2), and inverted dependent clauses (1). He removes commas from three inverted dependent clauses, two compound sentences, one parenthetical phrase, one dependent clause, and one adjective series. The whole of A1 is relatively conventional otherwise: it substitutes a comma for a semicolon once, and the reverse once; it substitutes two semicolons for dashes, two exclamation points for commas, one comma for an exclamation, and one dash for a comma.

Since a typescript was the common printer's copy, one cannot assert confidently that any single authority must be following the copy when it agrees with Crane's known characteristics against the other two. Nonetheless, although the concurrence of two of the independently radiating documents is significant evidence, it is far from presenting a prima facie case that this agreement must reproduce the exact details of the copy: too many of these shifting agreements go contrary to Crane's habits to be invariably right. The independent accidentals of BW can be almost wholly ignored as evidence. What is less clear is the authority of the concurrence of BW and A1 in heavy punctuation against the minority N^1 light punctuation. Here an editor may be partly guided by the compositorial analysis of A1. In Parts I–V the strong characteristic of the first A1 compositor to add commas to set off appositional and parenthetical phrases (8 and 6) joins with a similar tendency in the BW compositor (3 and 6) to suggest that in cases where these commas are not present in N^1 then N^1 is more than likely to preserve the copy detail even against the combined evidence of BW and A1. Similarly commas dividing compound predicates (A1–3, BW–2) and inverted phrases (A1–3, BW–1) in this section are only slightly less suspicious. Reservations may be expressed about any BW,A1 comma separating a compound sentence when N^1 is wanting the comma. In these cases an editor may well feel justified in upholding the integrity of N^1 against the known styling tendencies of BW,A1 even though these may be in the majority. On the contrary, the distinctive tendency of N^1 to punctuate dependent clauses, particularly relatives, joins with a similar tendency in BW (although not, in this section, in A1) to give some authority to A1's lightness here when it fails to punctuate.

In the work of the second A1 compositor in Parts VI–VII the editorial position changes slightly. The present editor would like to believe that the extraordinary difference in no commas between the clauses of compound sentences in A1 and the commas in joined N^1,BW reflects the more faithful reproduction of copy in A1. But the steep fall in A1 is itself suspicious as more likely to result from compositorial styling than lack of styling; and to take it that A1 is authoritative here would be to denigrate the general superior authority of N^1 more severely than the facts permit, especially since throughout the whole text N^1 never adds a comma in this situation when no comma is present in BW,A1. Hence the minority view of A1 here would seem to carry little or no authority, and commas cannot be removed on the example of

A1 alone, no matter how much Crane's manuscript habits would be approximated. In this section N^1 is the best authority. Some slight tendency on the part of A1 and BW to add commas to set off inverted phrases suggests that N^1 can offer a good minority case for authority when it does not punctuate. Some attention can be paid to any minority document that does not set off dependent clauses (especially relatives) owing to N^1's slight tendency to style with commas joined to an equal tendency both in A1 and BW. Finally, in Parts VIII–IX with the return of A1 to a somewhat heavier cast of punctuation that links it to BW more closely, N^1 minority failure to punctuate appositional and inverted phrases, and dependent clauses, has good odds in favor of duplicating the typescript practice.

The usual moderate position of N^1 in respect to what may be reconstructed as the accidentals of the lost typescript makes it the most satisfactory and convenient copy-text, with A1 filling in as copy-text for the N^1 cut of the material ending Part VI. However, according to the analysis presented above the authority of the agreement of any two documents in emending N^1 accidentals must vary according to the different compositorial stints in A1 combined with the noticed styling tendencies in N^1 and BW to encourage selective emendation, as necessary, on the example of only one document—or, often, of a refusal to emend.

The situation in respect to the substantive emendation of the N^1 copy-text differs radically. Here it is demonstrable that neither N^1 nor A1 has been altered by Crane in any reading not represented in the typescript and thus that their unique variants must in every case represent compositorial departure, even where reason exists to suspect a typescript mistake like *struck* at 119.28, or possibly independent styling that fortuitously agrees, as may have happened in the idiom involving *half* (see the Textual Note to 122.18). Thus agreement in any substantive reading by N^1 and BW against A1 or by BW and A1 against N^1 is ordinarily decisive.

A peculiar difficulty arises in connection with a few of BW's unique readings, however. The general texture of compositorial error and of editorial sophistication is so pervasive as to cast doubt on the authority of any BW unique verbal, and it would be possible to include these under the general principle governing

N¹ and A1 above were it not for the single variant: the alteration of N¹,A1 *Polite people always babbled at each other like two brooks* (134.28) to BW *like two coffee-mills*. This is not only a change difficult to credit to compositor or editor but also one that substitutes something like a Crane idiom (see the Textual Note) for a normally conventional comparison. Since it is impossible to believe that *coffee-mills* stood in the typescript and that N¹ and A1 independently hit upon altering it to *brooks*, the authority of at least one unique BW reading could be conjectured; and the argument could be advanced to explain it that it represents an authorial alteration in the BW proof. If one, perhaps more. Fortunately the majority of the BW variants are so obviously non-authorial that one may narrow the other reasonable possibilities to only four. Of these the strongest case can be made for the BW substitution at 127.5 of *leaving a bit of his trousers in passing on the lively serpentine ends of the severed wires* for the N¹,A1 *tearing his trousers in passing . . .* It is difficult to see why an editor would wish to change the original, whereas one can understand, perhaps, the extra precision that Crane might have inserted. This variant, then, might be accepted on the same basis as *coffee-mills*. Considerably less certain, but still within the margin of possibility, is the addition at 134.6 of BW *or down to hell* after *heaven* in the N¹,A1 sentence, *with the dull fear in his breast that her mother would enter and indifferently announce that she had gone up to heaven or off to New York with one of his dream-rivals . . .* At first sight it would seem difficult to have the mother announce Margharita's descent to hell, after death, as indifferently as her ascent to heaven; but this is one of Smith's fantasies and hence not subject to the ordinary tests of rational behavior—as shown by the use of *indifferently* to announce the girl's death. As remarked in the Textual Note to this reading, the addition fits with Smith's later-revealed assumption of Margharita's treachery. The chief uneasiness about adopting it is that it chimes so patly with the second half of a traditional phrase and thus may have proved irresistible to the BW editor, even though it is worth notice that he does not interfere in any such manner elsewhere.

The remaining two possibilities are omissions and thus more difficult to evaluate. The first comes at 127.15–16 in the description of the lieutenant's running toward the blockhouse and deletes the words *from the enemy and others* [A1 *the others*] *were only three hundred yards away*. The Textual Note discusses in detail the reasons why the excision, though tempting, is probably not authoritative and so has not been adopted. The second, which removes *in the wisdoms* [$N *wisdom*] *of bushwhacking* after *experience* at 130.2, is least certain of all and on the whole appears to be quite unauthoritative (see its Textual Note, also).

These five comprise the only BW variants that have any claim to consideration. Yet it is clear that the *-mills* part of *coffee-mills* was a British editorial change, for Crane used the American term *coffee grinder*. Moreover, the only parallels that have been observed are not really pertinent ones (see the Textual Note). The BW text is exceedingly corrupt in other respects, and the only other story that BW printed in Crane's lifetime—"Death and the Child"—was not authorially altered in proof. On the whole, the case for Crane's having made these three changes in BW proof is not strong enough to influence editorial procedure.

The text of "A Clan of No-Name," then, by an eclectic choice of accidentals variants emending as advisable the *New York Herald* copy-text attempts a near reconstruction of the underlying typescript that Paul Reynolds commissioned from the Crane manuscript. Into this established texture of accidentals are admitted those variant substantives that, in turn, represent the readings of the lost manuscript on the evidence of any two of the authorities. In practice this means with only one or two exceptions the joint readings of N^1 and A1.

"GOD REST YE, MERRY GENTLEMEN"

The first mention of " 'God Rest Ye, Merry Gentlemen' " comes in a letter on February 1 from Crane at Ravensbrook to Pinker in which he encloses a Whilomville story, "The Angel-Child," and adds: "You will be glad to know that I am now writing a story with which you can have good game: 'God Rest Ye, Merry Gentlemen.' We are sure you will like it" (*Letters*, p. 206). On February 4 he reports to Pinker that the story "is coming on finely" (*Letters*, p. 208). On February 13 he addresses Reynolds: "I enclose you the story 'God Rest Ye Merry Gentlemen' which is

7000-words in length. I note what you say about getting 60- for 'The Clan of No Name' and I think that if you have difficulty with the story I am now sending you, you had better use it on the newspapers. They should like it better by all odds. This new story (a copy) has already been handed to Pinker for the sale of the English rights" (Syracuse, typescript copy). On March 2 in a lengthy letter to Pinker enclosing a Whilomville story, "The Lover and the Tell-Tale," and noting progress on *Active Service*, he inquires, "What has become of 'God Rest Ye Merry Gentlemen'?" (Syracuse, typescript copy). Reynolds cabled on March 5 that the story was sold for $300, and as a consequence Cora wrote Pinker to withdraw the story from the English market until the question of international copyright was clarified (*Letters*, p. 216). Pinker responded on March 9 with a complaint (*Letters*, p. 217). By March 16 Crane was in a position to write Reynolds that Pinker had been instructed that the *Saturday Evening Post* wished to use the story in April if possible and to try to see that some English magazine printed it in the same month (Syracuse, typescript copy). Actually, it was March 17 before Crane wired Pinker and followed with a letter that he could hold the story until May but no longer. Pinker still had "The Clan of No-Name" on his hands, and in the letter Crane urges him to sell both stories for £30 cash immediately, which he would prefer to £50 the following month (*Letters*, p. 218). Mention of the story then ceases except for a late inquiry to Pinker by Cora, after Crane's death, undated but from her Gower Street lodgings and therefore in late July or in August of 1900, asking whether four of the *Wounds* stories including " 'God Rest Ye' " had been sold by him in the United States. On May 23, 1900, however, Stokes lists it as in his possession in a letterpress copy from the *Cornhill*.

Publication of the story was achieved simultaneously in the *Saturday Evening Post*, CLXXI (May 6, 1899), 705–707,[62] and in the *Cornhill Magazine*, n.s., VI (May, 1899), 577–592, where it was stated to be 'Copyright, 1899, by Stephen Crane, in the

[62] Three illustrations were provided by C. D. Williams with the legends, ' "NO, 'TIS NOT SO DEEP AS A WELL, NOR SO WIDE AS A CHURCH DOOR; BUT 'TIS ENOUGH, D'YOU SEE?" ', '*It was like being burned out of a boarding-house and having to carry one's trunk eight miles to the nearest neighbor*', and '*Little Nell took the dispatch. It was: "Tell Nell can't understand his inaction"* '.

United States of America.' In the two March lists preceding collection of *Wounds in the Rain* it is one of the four stories mentioned, the word count being given as 7,095 and publication in the *Saturday Evening Post*. In the earlier list the paper is torn in the right margin so that nothing more can be seen, but in the second list a blank space has been left after the *Post* and a suffixed *and*. The third and last list gives both magazines and retains the same word count of 7,095. In the Stokes *Wounds in the Rain* of 1900 (A1) it occupies pages 74–106.

The February 13, 1899, letter to Reynolds specifies that a *copy* has been handed to Pinker. This word does not signify that Reynolds is being sent the manuscript itself but instead that Pinker had been given the carbon of the ribbon copy which was Reynolds'. Although the accidentals of the *Saturday Evening Post* (SP) and of *Cornhill* (C) vary considerably owing to their separate styling, they are not so distant as to preclude common copy. The frequent manufacture of small sections in SP—without regard for the narrative—marked off by a space and central dot are characteristic of the magazine and have no relation to copy. Also characteristic and without reference to copy is the frequent breaking down of long into short paragraphs. The punctuation in SP is often heavier than is customary with Crane, but this is also found in other SP printings of his stories. The *Post* editor cut the story expertly, but it is evident that these major omissions are cuts and not additions in *Cornhill*. It is also certain that the SP censorship of the profanity is editorial. Less certain are the omissions of short sentences like *It was warm, very warm* (140.21), of short phrases like *on the steps* (141.6), or single words like *fiercely* (142.21). Although some of the six such sentences may be cuts (especially two that contain profanity), and some of the eight phrases, especially toward the end when the cuts increase, the omission of ten single words is difficult to account for. Some of these could be authorial additions in the *Cornhill* proof; yet the occasional omission of such words in "The Serjeant's Private Mad-house" and "The Second Generation" in their SP texts leads to the conviction that they are not necessarily C proof additions and are probably SP editorial or compositorial doings, or both, of a piece with the other SP variants. The use of dots in SP between sentences may be authorial since a similar habit is seen in the A1 text of "The Revenge of the *Adolphus*" (169.26,27,30,31) and in other substantive texts.

The *Cornhill* text has itself undergone some sophistication to substitute English idiom, the most obvious being the use of *tin* for *can* (137.18; 144.30,34); but more subtle stylistic alterations seem to have been made as well, as in the substitution of *one* for the repetitive *canteens* at 142.37 or of *was* for *were* at 145.8. That it was proofread by Crane may be assumed on the basis of a letter to Pinker later in the year on November 4, 1899, remarking that he has received proof for "The Second Generation" from *Cornhill* (*Letters*, p. 239). The changes could not have been many, and their identification is not always easy owing to the question whether a variant between both magazines that seems satisfactory is a proof revision in *Cornhill* or an unauthoritative change in the *Post*. But whether Tailor was shot in the *right* (SP) or the *left* (C) lung, as at 152.13,33, and whether at 146.33 the order was *Tailor and Point* (SP) or *Point and Tailor* (C) would seem to rest upon authorial second thoughts. And just possibly a few of the omitted single words are C additions and not SP subtractions.

The *Cornhill Magazine* was the copy for A1, but the evidence suggests that, unusually, the copy was not a clipping from the magazine itself. (On May 23, 1900, Stokes reported only that he had 'letter-press' copy for this and several other stories.) The most obvious piece of evidence is the long cut in C 147.30–148.34 of the description of the captain and the young lieutenant who gave the correspondents breakfast—a description containing material of little interest to English readers, with the consequential cut of the sentence at 149.1–2, *They never saw the captain again.* This text is found both in SP and in A1. In the stories in *Wounds in the Rain* to this point there has been no suggestion that Crane made changes in the copy sent to Stokes (except in the unusual case of "The Revenge of the *Adolphus*"), and no reason exists here to suppose that he restored the cut in a C clipping by a typescript addition. Moreover, other evidence bears on the matter. In only two substantive readings does C depart from SP in a case where A1 retains the SP reading. If these were simple errors in C, the agreement of A1 with SP would be understandable as ordinary A1 correction, but they are not. The clearest as applied to the question of A1 copy is the verb for the action of the two English correspondents who befriended Nell on the veranda after the theft of his mackintosh. In SP and A1 the correspondents *lying awake to smoke a last pipe, reared and looked at him lazily* (143.36–38). In C this reads *half rose and looked . . .* At 142.23–25 in SP and A1 Nell *found only* [A1: *only found*] *about fifty men who had been the first American soldier to set foot on Cuba,* whereas in C the reading is *first American soldiers . . .* This last shows, quite clearly, a misunderstanding of the irony and a literal-minded determination to match plural with plural. Apparently *reared* was thought to be objectionable applied to human beings and *half rose* more genteel. These readings plus the cut would seem to belong to a late stage of the proof, just before printing, and very likely one never seen by Crane. If so, the copy that Crane sent to Stokes for A1 must have been an extra set of an earlier proof he had retained —whether a revise or an annotated copy containing his corrections cannot be determined.

Despite the undoubtedly heavy styling that the *Saturday Evening Post* version has received, it is the most satisfactory and convenient copy-text for the accidentals, although it has been emended when the *Cornhill* text appears to preserve characteristics of Crane's accidentals that may be taken to refer back to the typescript copy for both. However, the *Cornhill* version has superior authority for the substantives owing to its status as a proofread text, and thus those substantive *Cornhill* variants conjectured to be correct readings of *Post* errors or else authorial proof revisions have been incorporated in the SP copy-text. The eclectic text contrived for this edition, therefore, attempts to reconstruct as far as possible the original typescript and to substitute for this typescript's verbal readings what seem to be Crane's final intentions as expressed in the changes he made in the *Cornhill* proof.

THE REVENGE OF THE *Adolphus*

The United States Naval Attaché in London, Commander J. C. Colwell, who had been Crane's weekend guest at Brede a few days before, returned with comments on May 27, 1899, a copy of

"The Revenge of the *Adolphus*" he had been requested to look over for technical details (*Letters*, pp. 221–222). In July– August, 1900, the story was among the four from *Wounds in the Rain* that Cora listed for Pinker in an inquiry whether he had sold them in the United States and to what magazines. The autograph list of stories for *Wounds in the Rain* places it fourth, giving the word count as 6,420 and the *Strand* as the place of publication in both England and America. Since Colwell's advice came after the typescript copy (or carbon) for Reynolds had been mailed off, the date of the story is probably April or early May, but could have been March. An illuminating reference comes on June 15, 1900, in a letter from Stokes to Pinker: "In setting up 'Wounds in the Rain' we have struck another obstacle. The story that Mr. Crane gave us entitled 'The Revenge of the Adolphus' is incomplete. We are trying to find the number of the Strand Magazine in which this was printed, but a search at the International News Company's has, as yet, proved futile. Will you not, in any case, please send us copy of this story as soon as possible?" (TLS, Dartmouth). On June 26 Stokes was able to report, "We have been able to find in the Astor Library here a copy of the number of the Strand Magazine containing 'The Revenge of the Adolphus' which was the story that was incomplete in the 'copy' sent us by Mr. Crane so that work of making our plates of 'Wounds in the Rain' is now progressing as rapidly as possible" (TLS, Dartmouth). On July 5 Stokes acknowledges, "It was very kind on your part to send us a copy of 'The Revenge of the Adolphus' from one of the numbers of 'The Strand Magazine' " (TLS, Dartmouth).

These are the only preserved early references to the story. The conjecture that it may be the story referred to in Letter 272 (*Letters*, p. 211) is a red herring, since the story mentioned there is only 5,330 words, and the letter should be dated in August, 1899.

The first publication was in the United States in *Collier's Weekly*, XXIV (October 28, 1899), 13–14, 19, 24–25,[63] and then,

[63] H. Reuterdahl drew an illustrative heading of Pent at the aft gun of the *Chicken* with the legend, ' "IF WE DON'T SILENCE THAT FIELD-GUN SHE'LL SINK US, BOYS" '. Copyright by Crane, 1899, was noted.

in England, in the *Strand Magazine*, XVIII (December, 1899), 724–733.[64] The Stokes *Wounds in the Rain* (1900) printed it on pages 107–137.

The copy for *Collier's Weekly* (CW) and the *Strand Magazine* (S) presents no problem. The accidentals are so extremely close between these two texts, with differences only in a stray comma here and there (allowing for *Collier's* more frequent paragraphing required by its narrow measure in a three-column page), that a typescript and its carbon furnish the only possible answer. The substantives are quite another matter, however. Commander Colwell's letter of May 27, 1899, is worth quoting in detail since it accounts for most of the alterations that Crane made in the *Strand* text from the common typescript and carbon as preserved in the *Collier's* text.

Dear Mr. Crane: I return the copy of the story of the "Adolphus" which I have read with much amusement and pleasure. You have hit off the local color of that sort of thing admirably and the unconscious humour of the actors on the little stage is quite true to life. . . .

I would suggest that (p. 1) the correspondents sit in the deck house or on a bench in the shade of the galley as the latter is a very crowded and uncomfortable place in a small craft in hot weather and in 99 vessels out of 100 has no more room than is necessary for the cook and his pots.

The "Chancellorville" answers to the DETROIT, MARBLEHEAD, MONT- GOMERY class, and they are Commanders' commands.

"Flagship" is only used to describe a ship flying an Admiral's flag or a Commodore's board-pennant. In all other cases when two or more vessels are in company it is "Senior Officer's ship," or "S.O." or "S.O.P." "Senior Officer's pennant."

Chicken's captain (p. 9). Captain is a generic term afloat and means anything from the person commanding a canal boat to one commanding a battleship. Commander means a specific rank to which certain duties appertain.

P. 9. The boatswain would not remain in the cabin after the official

[64] The Starrett and Williams *Bibliography* gives the month as September, 1899, an error followed by subsequent writers on Crane. C. J. Staniland drew an illustrative heading and seven illustrations with the legends, ' "THAT THERE IS A UNITED STATES CRUISER" ', 'THE "CHANCELLORVILLE" ', 'THE SHOT KICKED UP A HIGH JET OF WATER INTO THE AIR', 'A MARINE ORDERLY APPEARED', 'THEY PROMPTLY ELIMINATED THEMSELVES', 'THE "CHICKEN" ROUNDED THE "HOLY MOSES" AND STARTED IN-SHORE', and ' "GIVE IT 'EM HOT!" '

business was finished, but after looking unhappy for a bit would slide out the door and hunt the more congenial company of his confrères, the warrant-officers mess. The executive officer would undoubtedly add himself to the gathering in the cabin and the four then there would probably be about the same age and with naval academy affinities.

P. 10. The crew of the natty gig of the yacht would probably pull a "steady stroke," but the "three men" in the heavy life boat of the tug would only wobble along.

P. 11. A cruiser of the "Chancellorville" class would have a couple of buglers on board and always go to "quarters" by bugle accompanied by the drum beat. The boatswain's whistle and call of the boatswain's mates is used in small craft with no bugles or drummers. I would suggest the opening of that chapter something like the following which is what would really happen: "Beat to quarters!" from Surrey.

A quick patter of feet, a clanging of scuttle plates, rattle of ammunition hoists, and the energetic chug of breech-plugs followed as the guns are loaded and swung into extreme train ahead. Then everybody looked a little bored. Scarcely a word was spoken after the first order beyond the sharp repetition "shell-common" at each ammunition scuttle by the impatient carriers and the quiet "4000 yards" of the gun-division officers. The ship and her crew were ready &c &c. . . .

The "Adolphus" is a good story and will 'go.' Let me know when and where it is to appear. Very truly yours, *J. C. Colwell* [*Letters*, pp. 221–222].

Crane correctly altered Surrey's rank as Colwell had suggested.[65] He altered the incorrect references to the *Chancellorville* as a flagship (except for the oversight at 162.2), adopted *Senior Officer* or *S.O.* or *S.O.P.*, straightened out the term *captain*, removed the boatswain from Surrey's cabin after the official conference, expanded the call to quarters with drums and bugles instead of piping, and took account of other details suggested by Colwell. Crane must have retrieved the typescript in early June and corrected his naval terminology before the *Strand* put the story into type. Whether the few other changes found in the *Strand* text were made at this time or in proof is not to be

[65] That is, he altered the title in the copy for the *Strand*, and also made other corrections, but not in the basic manuscript, and not in *Collier's Weekly*. That A1 at 171.9 assigns the title *Commander* is explained by the fact that the *Strand* was copy for A1 at this point.

determined.[66] Although there should have been time if he had wished, he seems to have made no effort to alter the *Collier's* copy before publication as a result of Colwell's letter. On the other hand, as discussed below, he seems to have made other changes in the typescript sent to America that were not transferred to his manuscript and were not copied in the retained typescript probably because it had already left his hands for Pinker's office.

The 1900 *Wounds in the Rain* text (A1) was not printed from a clipping or a proof of CW or of S, but instead (except for the ending) from a fresh typescript made from the manuscript. Except for a few of the changes in naval terminology the A1 substantives agree with CW or else vary independently from the common CW,S reading. Grammatical infelicities like *sung* for *sang* (166.37) apparently come from the manuscript and not from an extra carbon of the basic typescript separately corrected by CW and S.[67] Crane does not seem to have kept (or been able to find) the Colwell letter, nor had he made notes in his manuscript of the alterations performed in the copy for the *Strand*. As a consequence he remembered simple details like the avoidance of *flagship*, and the use of *captain* not *commander* for the senior officer on each vessel, and he had some recollection of his change of *engineer*; but for the rest he either retained the manuscript version as found in CW [68] or else he altered the manuscript in the direction of Colwell's suggestions as he recalled them but, of course, with different wording from what he had earlier written in the copy for S.[69]

[66] Among these may be mentioned such variants as S *swift* for *gruff* (164.24) and the correction of what seems to have been the manuscript error *complete* (166.3) to S *complex*. He continued the revision of naval terminology by substituting other words for *engineer* in describing engine-room personnel on board the *Chicken*. This was not mentioned in Colwell's letter but—if one wants to guess—might have been suggested by Conrad. The *Chicken* had too small a crew to afford the luxury of more than one 'engineer,' if that.

[67] Also in favor of a different reference back to the manuscript origin and not to a common basic typescript is the typical Crane *was* at 167.3 instead of the CW,S *were*, which seems to reflect their typescript.

[68] This process passed over the S addition of the executive officer (162.33–34), the nice touch Colwell had suggested about the boatswain's uneasiness after official business was over and his departure from the cabin (163.14–16), or the details of the beating to quarters on a cruiser of the *Chancellorville* class (163.35–164.2).

[69] As in *senior officer* and *S.O.* for S *senior officer's ship* (162.24), or *stoker* for S *man* (168.30), or the confusing change of *vessels* to *gunboats* (163.5).

The need for a new copy for A1 associates this story with others, like "The Clan of No-Name," "The Serjeant's Private Mad-house," and "The Second Generation," which all had December publication in England and are all set in A1 from something other than the clippings of the magazine texts that served for earlier published stories. That is, as suggested in the earlier Textual Introduction treating the assembly of copy for Stokes, Crane seems to have got together copy for much of *Wounds in the Rain* before these December publications were available to him and thus was forced to adopt various expedients according to the circumstances. The pattern is too clear for other explanation.

The textual situation for "The Revenge of the *Adolphus*" is somewhat complex. The fidelity of both *Collier's* and the *Strand* to the accidentals of their typescript is attested by the comparatively few variants between them. This typescript in some respects did not reflect all of Crane's accidentals habits, particularly in its regular setting off with commas of two adjectives before a noun and its punctuation of a series of three with a comma before the *and*. It is weightier than the manuscript would have been in punctuating the two clauses of a compound sentence; nevertheless, it is sufficiently close to the presumed details of the manuscript in a number of other respects so that neither magazine can be called heavily styled. The A1 text seems to have been set by two compositors. The first set Parts I–III (just possibly Part IV) and in his lightness and other characteristics is almost certainly the same compositor who set Parts VI–VII of "The Clan of No-Name." Part V, and just possibly Part IV, seems to be the work of the first compositor of "The Clan" since parenthetical phrases become regularly punctuated. Parts VI–VII may well be the work of the third compositor, although the original workman would not be an impossibility; at any rate, the punctuation is lighter than in Part V. Since the working hypothesis has it that A1 reverts independently to the manuscript for its text through a typescript intermediary, A1 radiates from the ultimate manuscript authority (except for its final pages) in a different line from the typescript and its carbon that links CW and S. Of the two lines, A1 is definitely closer in its accidentals to Crane's known system and therefore becomes the copy-text. However, when the lightness of CW,S in such matters as inverted phrases, which even the first compositor of A1 preferred to punctuate, suggests that their line is closer to the lost manuscript, emendation has been made, especially in Part V where the heavier-styling A1 compositor has a short stint. However, A1 loses any independent authority at the point where the Stokes compositor had to complete the story from the *Strand* copy. The exact place cannot be determined with precision, but the general area is clear enough. The substitution at 170.3 in S of *men* for typescript (CW,A1) *engineers* is the last identifiable independent reading of A1 from S. The first positively identifiable common reading comes at 170.27 when, contrary to its previous practice, A1 follows S in hyphenating *gun-boats*. Somewhere in between, the typescript stopped and setting from S copy began. Fortunately, no variants appear between the two texts in this indeterminate interval, and so an editorial problem involving their relationship does not arise. However, as a result of this shift in copy that destroys the evidence of CW,A1 concurrence, CW becomes the only authority for the longer statement of how the correspondents secured the news story, a passage that seems to have been the result of a cut in S in order to fit the ending of the story snugly on the last line of the last page without a three- or four-line run-over, a cut that just possibly may have had the cooperation of the author when requested by the *Strand* because of the added S specification that the correspondents on the cruiser were *two*. A1 also ceases to be an independent witness in a crux in the possible area of the shift from typescript to letterpress copy. At 170.16 the retention by S of the past perfect tense in *had sent* to parallel preceding *had been unable*, as against the CW preterite can no longer be confirmed by A1 if A1 copy at this point had shifted to S. Although the case is a little doubtful, this evidence encourages the emendation of S by reversion to CW, which is less sophisticated and may well represent the true reading. If this is so, then the switch in copy must have taken place somewhere between 170.3 and 170.16.

The neutral substantive variants like *board* or *board of* (159.35) seem to be no more nor less authoritative in any single line than in the other. However, when CW and S agree substantively against A1, A1 must be (a) the accurate reading of the manuscript which had been corrupted in the typescript behind the magazine texts; (b) an A1 typescript or compositorial error; or (c) a Crane alteration in the new typescript for A1 of the original manuscript reading represented by CW,S agreement. Actually, a further category (d) should be mentioned as a possibility; that is, unique A1 readings might theoretically represent manuscript readings that had been altered in both the original typescript and carbon when Crane read over copy before sending it off for sale.

In a small way (a) is probably reflected in the A1 reading *days* at 155.5 for the more sophisticated *days'* of CW,S; perhaps the A1 *git* for *get* and *kin* for *can* (157.28) represent typescript faults in CW,S rather than Crane revisions in A1; but A1 *sung* for *sang* (166.37) is almost certainly in this category. The A1 preservation of the profanity does not quite fall here since it seems to have been present in the first typescript but to have been censored separately by the two magazines. The misunderstanding of the sense at 158.35 which leads to A1 *Sure, take the glass* instead of *Sure. Take the glass* is a good example of (b), or such A1 errors as the sophistication *sent* for *set* (165.5); and perhaps *'m* for *'em* (166.28) and *back of the shoals* (160.29) for *at the back of the shoals*. Some difficulty arises in separating (c) from hypothetical (d). Practically no evidence is preserved to indicate how much revision Crane was likely to make in a typescript and its carbon immediately after the manuscript had been prepared for sale. Edith Richie testified that he made few if any such changes (see the Textual Introduction to "The Kicking Twelfth"), and what evidence there is is largely negative. In some respects it would be simpler to take it that except for the attempt at reproducing Colwell's advice about naval terminology Crane made no alterations in the manuscript or, on review, in the new typescript. But the evidence of his change of manuscript *like charging horsemen* to *like charging bantams* in A1 (165.13) indicates a real review of the language. Under these circumstances no clear-cut evidence for (d) appears; and thus the neutral variants in A1 like *shake* for *hook* (157.12,15,20) may join others not so neutral like the revision of the signal orders (165.11–12), the relocation of the galley (155.22), and stylistic changes like *nondescripts* for *ships* (164.30) as category (c), further alterations made on the occasion of the typing of the new manuscript for Stokes.

The copy-text, thus, has been emended substantively in classes (a) and (c); that is, when the typescript behind CW,S seems to have been in error, or when A1 has revised the original as represented by this typescript.

When A1 and CW agree against S, the case is relatively simple: either (a) the compositor of S has made an error, or (b) S had revised the reading of the original manuscript whether by annotation of its typescript or in proof, or both. There is only one ascertainable example of (a), the venial change in S of *toward* to the English form *towards* (160.21), to which can be added the softer *blazes* (157.25) where CW slipped up and allowed *hell* to be printed as in A1. The major revision that Crane gave this story comes in category (b) in which the *Strand* typescript was very considerably altered in respect to naval terminology and once or twice in other matters. These revisions are accepted, of course, and substituted for the original readings of the copy-text.

When A1 and S agree against CW (except at the very end) the normal inference would be (a) that CW is in error since the common reading of S and of A1 derives from the manuscript by two different intermediaries. The failure of CW to italicize emphasized words as at 155.12 or 155.16–17 is the most obvious example, to which may be added small variants like CW's omission of *fort* (166.31). Special circumstances—all connected with the revision of naval detail—can (b) produce S,A1 agreement against an originally accurate CW representation of the manuscript, such as the change from CW *commander* to S *captain* (162.22,29,39). A serious problem results, however, when a unique reading in CW does not fall under (a) or (b) above as a CW error or a good manuscript reading revised by S and A1. Just one or two seem in this category, if one assumes as one must that the passage about the correspondents at 170.31–34 and its odd consequential change involving *Two* at 170.31 is an S editorial cut to fit the space at the end and not, instead, a last-minute addition to the CW typescript before it was mailed to America. The most difficult to explain is the homely, comic touch that one of the correspondents had carried a pair of *opry glasses* to war (155.26), granting that the phrase was not intended to be deprecatory for binoculars. It might be understood as a cut in S alone, but how it got omitted in A1 as well is mysterious unless it is taken as a CW addition. And then there is the puzzling case of the one use of emphasis italics in CW in *won't* at 156.36, which occurs in a place where they are not present in S,A1. This is not very much to go on. Such as it is, however, the evidence suggests that a change or two was indeed made in the typescript for CW that was not transferred to the other or to the manuscript. This being so, it may be that *sprang up* (159.11) and *to the sky* (157.34), particularly the latter, deserve more serious attention as CW variants; and *Titanic* (158.14) might not, in the end, be merely a compositorial or editorial capitalization.[70] On the other hand, since the typescript may have read 3.2 (as in the Spitzbergen stories), the CW *three-decimal-twos* for *three-point-twos* is almost surely editorial (162.13–14); and given its adverb *elaborately,* then *strolled* (156.25) is more likely correct than CW *strode.*

There remain the cases in which all three authorities differ. These occur when S has altered the naval technicalities and, later, Crane had to change the manuscript readings for the copy for A1 but forgot what his S revisions had been and set down something else. This situation poses something of a problem. Chronologically and literally the A1 variant would represent Crane's final intention; but 'final intention' in a textual sense implies knowledge of previous readings and hence a conscious rejection of them in favor of a different form. When Crane grew dissatisfied with his account of the signals sent by the *Chancellorville* at 165.11–12 and revised it in A1, he knew what he was doing since CW and S agree and hence represent the manuscript reading. The case is altered as at 162.24, however. Here the manuscript, as represented by CW, read *flagship . . . flagship.* On Colwell's advice that this was an improper word, in the typescript for the *Strand* Crane altered it to *senior officer's ship . . . senior officer's ship.* But when he came to prepare copy for A1 all he remembered was that *flagship* in the manuscript was wrong, and since reference to his S change was impossible he came up with *senior officer . . . S.O.* In cases where Crane

---

[70] See the same minority capitalization of *Titanic* in "Death and the Child," *Tales of Adventure,* p. 125.6.

forgot in any way to alter his copy as he had done for S, obviously one must rely on the authority of the S change. This authority may also hold as a working principle for A1 changes when S had also modified its copy. That is, the terms that immediately came to Crane's mind when he had Colwell's letter before him and was revising his S copy may seem to be better worth preserving in an established text than the promptings of an inconsistent and less exact memory some months later. Ordinarily the same sense results, but on a few occasions phrasing of some stylistic significance is involved. For example, at 163.5 he originally wrote that there was a danger the Spanish fort would divide its fire between *the flagship and the vessels*. In the S changes of *flagship* he altered this to read *the S.O.P.'s ship and the vessels;* for A1 he substituted *cruiser* for *flagship* but then continued and altered *vessels* to *gunboats*. It is unlikely that he would have made this change of *vessels* if he had not been in process of correcting *flagship* throughout. Moreover, the revision *gunboats* was careless because the American craft had never been called this before and it was a word reserved for the Spanish boats. Here an editor may have little difficulty in justifying the retention of CW,S *vessels*. That the present edition chooses S's *the S.O.P.'s ship* instead of A1 *the cruiser* is only because some principle must be adopted, and it has seemed best to give higher authority in these changes to the consistent S text instead of the inconsistent A1. This principle also moves the editor to accept S *tumultuously* at 165.13, which altered CW *like charging horsemen* despite Crane's objection to the MS,CW phrase when he came to prepare A1 and his later version *like charging bantams*. Whether he would still have made the A1 change if he had known that he had once written *tumultuously* is unknowable. On only one occasion when somewhat more precision is gained by A1 *stoker* at 168.30 for S *man* and CW *engineer* is the A1 reading adopted.

The present text, then, is a highly eclectic one. The foundation is the A1 copy-text accidentals, with infrequent and controlled emendation from what would have been the first typescript reading in CW,S. But each of the three documents has substantive authority stemming from Crane alterations made at different times. The CW variants are accepted that are taken to be those that Crane added to the typescript copy before it was mailed to the United States but after copy for English sale had been delivered to Pinker. The S variants are accepted almost uniformly except when they represent conjectured typescript departures from the manuscript, S compositorial error, or the censorship of profanity. The A1 final variants are accepted when they do not appear to be mistakes by the compositor (or possibly by the typist) and when they do not conflict with substantive alterations already decided on by S. The result approximates no document that could have existed; but the procedures are calculated to give a composite text as close as can be contrived to the ideal of Crane's verbal intentions combined with the accidentals of his manuscript that filtered through two independent intermediaries.

THE SERJEANT'S PRIVATE MAD-HOUSE

Almost no record is preserved of "The Serjeant's Private Mad-house." In a letter to Pinker conjecturally dated October 24, 1899, enclosing a Whilomville story, Crane in a postscript adds, "By the Phila. Sat Evening Post printing 'The Sergeant's Private Mad-House' on Sept 30, the English copyright of it is lost of course" (*Letters*, p. 236). It is among the *Wounds* stories of which Cora inquired in July–August, 1900, as to whether Pinker had sold any in the United States and in what magazines. In the list that preceded *Wounds in the Rain* it is placed after "This Majestic Lie," is given as 2,810 words, and as published in 'Eng Illustrated' and 'Phila. Sat. E. Post'. The first appearance in print was in the *Saturday Evening Post,* CLXXII (September 30, 1899), 214–215; then in the *English Illustrated Magazine,* XXII (December, 1899), 243–249;[71] and then in the 1900 Stokes *Wounds in the Rain,* pages 138–151.

---

[71] The title form *Mad-house* is drawn from the autograph list for *Wounds in the Rain.* In the letter to Pinker it is *Mad-House.* The hyphenated form is used in the title and text of the *English Illustrated Magazine;* the title's capitals are ambiguous but in the text it is *mad-house.* Both the *Saturday Evening Post* and *Wounds in the Rain* normalize throughout to *madhouse.* The spelling *serjeant* is found in the autograph list and is probably customary with Crane. (See the evidence of the typescript of " 'And If He Wills, We Must Die.' ") In the *Post* the story was noted as '*Copyright, 1899, in Great Britain*'. George Gibbs drew a picture of Dryden, with rifle at the ready, to go with the title, and Howard

The accidentals characteristics of the *Saturday Evening Post* (SP) and of the *English Illustrated Magazine* (EIM) are sufficiently close to make tenable the hypothesis that they were printed from a typescript and its carbon. As with "The Clan of No-Name," "The Revenge of the *Adolphus*," and "The Second Generation," the December publication of the English magazine text precluded the use of a clipping as the copy for *Wounds in the Rain* (A1), and the collational evidence suggests that a fresh typescript was made up for the collection, a theory that may be confirmed by the Stokes statement of June 15, 1900, that he had a typescript.[72] Two textual traditions, then, are present, the one represented by joint SP,EIM and the other by A1.

The question then arises whether the fifteen unique substantive variants in SP, the thirteen in EIM, and the twenty-five in A1 were produced by editorial and compositorial action or whether at least some of them represent authorial revision. For such a brief story the proportion in each is surprisingly high. The *Post* probably represents the simplest case. As in "The Revenge of the *Adolphus*," authorial proofreading can be discarded as a hypothesis here, but the possibility exists that, as in "The Revenge," Crane might have altered the typescript before mailing it to

Chandler Christy an illustration with the legend, 'AT LAST THE SERGEANT WAS IN A POSITION FROM WHICH HE WAS ABLE TO REACH OUT AND TOUCH DRYDEN ON THE ARM'. The *English Illustrated Magazine* has no copyright notice. Its illustrations, by F. S. Wilson, have the legends, '*Dryden paid no heed*', '*The sergeant grabbed his private asylum by the scruff of the neck*', '*They fought more like Red Indians*', and '*The lieutenant arose among them. . . . "Now where is that idiot, sergeant?"*'

[72] As found once in "The Revenge of the *Adolphus*," the A1 compositor sets *O* for *oh* (178.9), the only two places this spelling occurs in *Wounds in the Rain*. But whether this anomaly represents a reproduction of his copy (in which case it would be an English typescript) or a compositorial preference cannot be determined. In certain respects of styling and readings A1 is closer to EIM than it is to SP, and some odd joint readings develop that might suggest a more intimate connection than simple radiation from the manuscript through two different typescripts. But enough neutral variants occur not imputed entirely to compositorial interference to indicate that radiation is the proper conjecture and that one text could not have derived from the other as by a typescript, or carbon, no matter how altered. For instance, the following selected readings offer sufficient evidence: SP and A1 *gurgh-ugh* but EIM *gurgh—ugh* (178.10), or SP, and A1 "*You seem to be fond of singing, Dryden?*" but EIM *Dryden.*" (179.6–7), or SP "*Halt! Who's there? Halt, or I'll fire!*", EIM "*Halt!—who's there? Halt—or I'll fire!*" and A1 "*Halt—who's there—halt or I'll fire!*" (175.32), or such readings as SP,EIM *his stern hail* but A1 *the stern hail* (173.7–8) or SP,EIM *as yet* but A1 *yet* (173.10), which seem to represent a textual tradition for A1 different from that of SP and EIM.

America. Yet although the date of composition is not known, it is at least possible that by the time "The Serjeant's Private Madhouse" was ready for sale Crane had broken with Reynolds and would have dealt with the *Post* through Pinker. Such speculations are not necessary, however, for with one possible exception the SP unique variants versus EIM,A1 are almost certainly editorial.[73] Any special authorial marking of the typescript used by the *Post* as printer's copy, separate from marking of the copy for EIM, cannot be demonstrated. The case for EIM in respect to its unique variants from SP and A1 is simple also in the same manner. No one of these readings suggests more than the faint possibility of a proof alteration,[74] not a copy revision, and most are plainly editorial.[75] The evidence would suggest that both typescript and carbon were sent out in identical condition.

[73] It is interesting to see the SP editor normalizing *cactus plant* to *cactus bush* at 172.24, censoring even such profanity as was represented by two dashes at 179.23, and even substituting *idiot* for *devil* at 178.17 after reducing *hell* to *deuce* at 177.33. Perhaps compositorial are such variants as the error in the placement of the comma at 173.25 that quite changes the sense, the addition of normalizing *the* before *outposts* (174.25), the rearrangement of *promptly would* to *would promptly* (177.8), and so on. The reversal of the order of the carol "While shepherds" (177.29–32) and the song "The minstrel boy" (178.1–4) is odd but seems to be unauthoritative since the beginning of the third song "Please, oh, please, do not let me fall" (178.9–10) follows naturally on the Minstrel Boy excerpt but not on the carol except by the most metaphysical of associations. One can only guess as to the reason for the exchange. Very likely the religious subject of the carol made the editor jittery about possible blasphemy so that he thought the reader had better be introduced to the mad singing by the Minstrel Boy, with its clearer application to the immediate situation, before the shock effect of the carol. The single reading that might go back to the author is SP *the swift searchlight flashed through the foliage* for EIM,A1 *the swift search-light flashes tore through the foliage* (174.23–24). However, one can only speculate here that the editor or compositor felt the verb *tore* was inappropriate for a searchlight gleam and altered the description conventionally.

[74] However, not a single EIM unique variant is so clearly authorial as to lead to its adoption in the present text as a Crane revision in proof. The present editor does not believe that Crane—if he read proof, as probably he did—interfered with anything but typos, with one possible exception. That is, the SP version of 173.15–16 is indubitably clumsy, *Finally he arrived at a point where he could see him seated in the shadow*; but whether it was Crane or the compositor who substituted *the man* in EIM for *him* is not to be determined. The EIM phrase is characteristic enough of Crane, but a compositor could have drawn it from a few lines before, *he knew that the man would be hidden in a way practiced by sentry marines* (173.10–11).

[75] EIM *particularly* for SP,A1 *particular* (172.11) seems to be a clear-cut misunderstanding, and this would affect one's view of the authority of *simply a* for *a simple* a few lines earlier (172.8) and also of *hardly* for *hard* (178.18). The transfer of the men's prayer for daybreak to the lieutenant by omitting his own

The situation in respect to the more numerous variants in A1 is more complex. That A1 through its typescript goes back to the manuscript independently of the SP,EIM line seems demonstrable. Under these circumstances the categories into which the A1 unique variants might fall are (a) the original readings of the manuscript that have been corrupted in the first typescript from which SP and EIM derive; [76] (b) A1 compositorial errors, in which case the typescript forms reproduced in SP,EIM would be taken as correct; [77] (c) Crane alterations in both typescript and carbon on review before he mailed the two copies for SP and EIM—whether separately or both to Pinker; (d) revisions in A1 in the manuscript copy or in the new typescript made to send Stokes for *Wounds in the Rain*; and (e) a combination of (c) and (d).

Although some readings like A1 *glistening* for *glisten in* (172.21), or the single words in A1 not present in SP,EIM like *slowly* (172.22), *then* (174.10), and *somewhat* (177.35), are uncertain enough to fall indifferently into classes (a) or (c) or (d), various are clear-cut revisions like A1 *faintest* for SP,EIM *slightest* (172.20), *hyena* for *coyote* (175.12), *admonition* for *caution* (176.10), and *hard* for *swift* (176.25). Here it is a question somewhat like that of plus or of minus. That is, is *hyena* preferable to *coyote* and *admonition* to *caution*, or the reverse. A Ouija-board would be useful in such decisions. It is probably accurate to remark, however, that if one were to evaluate the variants *en bloc*, one would prefer to avoid the position that all A1 unique variants not to be assigned as errors represent the original readings of the manuscript and that the SP,EIM

---

prayer about the ammunition (177.21–22) seems due to eyeskip. No virtue inheres to EIM *the affairs* for *affairs* (172.28), *dwarfed* for *dwarf* (172.31), or *talking* for *talk* (176.18). Syntactical rearrangements like *could not even be* for *could be not even* (175.8) are scarcely authorial, and the substitution of *Cuban* as an adjective for *Cubans* as a noun at 177.3,4 with its consequential change of *insurgent* to *insurgents* seems to represent only editorial or compositorial tinkering with a slight clumsiness in copy.

[76] Representative of such indifferent variants are A1 *rock* for *rocks* (172.6), *the stern* for *his stern* (173.7–8), and perhaps *yet* for *as yet* (173.10) or *knew* for *knew that* (176.19), although these last two may be reversible. For the probable authority of *rocks* see the parallel at 140.16–17, however.

[77] These may range from such an obvious misprint as A1 *pen* for *ken* (176.21), through a fairly obvious error in context as *required* for *require* (176.16), to relatively indifferent readings like *small* for *a small* (174.13), *soldiers* for *soldier* (176.37), and *increased* for *increase* (177.24).

readings are revisions made in their typescript and its carbon. "The Revenge of the *Adolphus*" shows that in at least one case when Crane was forced to make up fresh copy for A1 he took the occasion to revise, although he had not done so when for "The Clan of No-Name" he used an additional carbon or retrieved the actual typescript printer's copy from the English magazine. But "The Revenge" presents a special case since the impetus to revise was provided by the need to alter some naval details, and it is unknowable whether Crane otherwise would have troubled himself to make the nontechnical revisions that are also found. Other stories present conflicting evidence.[78] Yet at 173.15, however easy it is to assign to an authorial proof correction or a compositorial alteration the change to *the man* of the awkward SP (and presumably manuscript) *him,* the A1 repetition of the name *Dryden* as a variant seems more authorial and may represent the one case in which this story repeats the occasional circumstances of "The Revenge of the *Adolphus*" whereby Crane, having forgotten what changes he had made in the typescript copy for the *Strand,* independently changed the copy for A1 to something else.

The balance of the evidence, thus, suggests that in "The Serjeant's Private Mad-house" the new typescript made up from the manuscript for A1 printer's copy had been in some part reviewed and revised before dispatch to Stokes. The question then arises whether, as was true for "The Revenge," some of the A1 variants instead reproduce the original manuscript readings, although here they would have been revised in the magazine publications by alteration of the typescript and carbon at the same time. This is not impossible; and indeed the change or two that Crane seems to have made in the copy of "The Revenge of the *Adolphus*" for America might be taken to support it were it not that there is no evidence in "The Revenge" that he had earlier reviewed and altered *both* copies after typing—indeed, the reverse. (The alterations in S as a result of Colwell's letter are too special a case to bear on "The Serjeant's Private Mad-house.")

One variant in particular suggests the possibility, nevertheless. In SP,EIM 176.24–27 reads: *The forty marines lay in an*

---

[78] "The Second Generation" for instance has something of the same situation (see below, p. clxvi).

irregular oval. From all sides the Mauser bullets sang low and swift. The occupation of the Americans was to prevent a rush, and to this end they potted carefully at the flash of a Mauser. . . . It could be argued that *the occupation of the Americans* was a copy revision in SP,EIM of the manuscript reading *their occupation*, as found in A1, in order to avoid the ambiguity of referring *their* back to the *forty marines* after the intervening sentence with the subject the *Mauser bullets* which, momentarily, seems to be the referent of *their*. Something of the same sort of ambiguity had already called itself to Crane's attention at least once and perhaps twice at 173.15. If this is so, other A1 variants might be brought in question. Whether *earned* at 174.19 and *somewhat* at 177.35 (if they are A1 additions and not mistaken omissions in the first typescript) are otiose is not wholly clear. It is difficult to decide whether the literally accurate *told* of SP,EIM at 174.29 with its reference back to 174.8–9 is not preferable to A1 *tell* and its awkward repetition; and if so, whether A1 *tell* is a compositorial mistake by contamination from the second *tell*, a fancied improvement revising *told*, or the original manuscript reading revised in the SP,EIM typescript to *told*. This list might be expanded, but the plain fact is that with the possible exception of 176.26 and the ambiguity of its pronominal reference, the case for A1 reproducing unrevised manuscript readings is too tenuous to affect editorial policy—and even 176.26 is sufficiently uncertain to discourage the adoption of *The occupation of the Americans* from SP,EIM.[79] Under these conditions when the absence of a control as in "The Revenge of the *Adolphus*" leads only to uncertain speculation, it seems best to accept the working hypothesis that the A1 unique variants are either printing corruptions or Crane's final intentions, and to attempt to choose among them on this black-and-white basis alone.

The accidentals of *Wounds in the Rain* for the major part of the story seem to have been set by the compositor whose characteristics are remarkably like Crane's own, or who was an unusually faithful follower of copy. This superior fidelity to the assumed accidentals of the manuscript copy, even if an interme-

---

[79] However, the reading *told* is adopted at 174.29 from SP,EIM but on the theory that A1 is in error.

diary typescript intervened, leads to the choice of A1 as the copy-text. However, as usual, since both SP and EIM are authoritative in their own right as stemming from the original typescript made from the manuscript, controlled emendation has been made from their accidentals in cases where the compositorial habits of A1 appear to diverge from the assumed A1 copy, or when this second typescript copy seems less faithful to the manuscript than the first typescript. The revised substantives of A1 are taken to be generally authoritative, but emendation from SP,EIM is admitted in the case of assumed error either in the A1 compositor or in his copy. However, such emendation is permitted only from joint SP,EIM agreement: the unique readings of SP and of EIM are taken to be unauthoritative departures from copy with a slight question holding about *the man* in EIM at 173.15 as a possible proof correction. If so, it is the only identifiable such correction in EIM but has not been adopted because of a superior A1 variant for the same unsatisfactory SP original. The text of this story, therefore, attempts to reconstruct so far as the preserved documents permit the copy behind A1.

VIRTUE IN WAR

On September 30, 1899, Crane wrote to Pinker from Brede: "I cannot express how worried I am over 'Virtue in War' and 'The Second Generation.' I can only remember writing one story and I would almost bet the two titles cover one story. We may be making a hideous blunder. Please find out"; and again on the same day or, very likely the next, at the end of another letter he adds, "I am still nervous about Virtue in War and The Second Generation" (*Letters*, pp. 232–233). These remarks apparently have nothing to do with any news that the stories had been sold, although the horrible possibility of two English magazines printing the same story is certainly in Crane's thoughts. Instead, they go back to a lost letter from Pinker earlier in the month that had occasioned a telegram about the stories on September 21. In a letter from Brede on September 22, Crane writes: "I know that you are amused by my telegram of yesterday. The fact is that I am anxious to get the 80000 words ready for Stokes and your letter recieved in Paris filled me with an idea that I had missed a few thousand words—in short that I had written a story and then absolutely forgotten it as I often do" (*Letters*, p. 231).

It may be that the different versions of the title that were extant confused Crane as they were later to confuse Cora. For instance, probably in early August, 1900, she wrote to Pinker from 47 Gower Street inquiring about the details of his sale of Crane's stories, most of these in *Wounds*, which had not been included in a statement sent her, and continued, "And have the following been published here?" The first to be mentioned is "Virtue in War" but this has been deleted (ALS, Dartmouth). The reason seems to come to light in a letter, probably in early December, 1900, to Pinker: "Will you please let me know if you sold the story 'The making of the 307th,' serially in America. Was it sold to the Saturday Evening Post?" (ALS, Dartmouth). Pinker must have set her right, for on December 19 she addressed her new agent Perris from 6 Milborne Grove, "I find that the story 'The making of the 307th' has been published under another name in 'Wounds in the Rain,' so it must be left out of the book of short stories [i.e., *Last Words*]" (ALS, Yale).

The autograph list that Crane made up for *Wounds in the Rain*, now preserved in the Columbia University Libraries (and reproduced in this volume), seems to suggest that "The Making of the 307th" had originally been a much shorter story that was later expanded and retitled. This story is probably to be identified as the war story of 5,330 words that Crane sent to Pinker in August, 1899 (*Letters*, no. 272, p. 211, redated). It is also mentioned in Stokes's lists as "The Making of the 307th" and as 8,100 words, a change that appears to be reflected in the autograph list that preceded the memorandum sent to Stokes. It would seem, however, that the title had been changed to "West Pointer and Volunteer; Or, Virtue in War" for magazine sale. One may suspect, then, that Pinker had referred to the story under its subtitle in the lost letter that triggered Crane's worried responses in September, 1899, whether "Virtue in War" and "The Second Generation" were the same (a confusion perhaps abetted by the fact that they had the identical word count of 8,200), whereas Crane was still thinking of the story under its original title. (The conjectural reconstruction of the revision of the story and the alterations in the autograph list is sketched above on pages xciv–xcviii in the account of the assembling of the collection *Wounds in the Rain.*) How it was that the story is noted as "Virtue in War" in the autograph list for *Wounds in the Rain* and in the memorandum of the titles of the stories and their order that was sent to Stokes, although it was published in the magazines in the United States and England as "West Pointer and Volunteer," a title never mentioned in letters or lists, is not to be explained. Equally difficult to explain is why Stokes was not informed when—according to the autograph list—the error was discovered that "The Making of the 307th" was the same story as "Virtue in War," and even how a clipping of the American publication in *Leslie's* was sent as printer's copy to Stokes but a typescript of "The Making of the 307th." It is also something of a matter of conjecture why 'Tillotson's Syn' is given in the autograph list under the column for American publication.[80] At any rate, as "West Pointer and Volunteer; Or, Virtue in War" the story had its first publication in *Frank Leslie's Popular Monthly*, XLIX (November, 1899), 88–101, and this is the title that heads the posthumous appearance in the *Illustrated London News*, CXVI (June 16, 1900), 809–811.[81] As "Virtue in War" it appeared in the Stokes *Wounds in the Rain* (1900), pages 152–177; but Stokes must have ignored the *Leslie's* title of his copy in favor of "Virtue in War" in

---

[80] The English firm of Tillotson's, or the Northern Newspaper Syndicate, had a New York office and it may be that Pinker disposed of the story to the Syndicate, which negotiated the sale to *Frank Leslie's Popular Monthly*. Unfortunately, *Leslie's* has no copyright notice.

[81] Warren B. Davis drew for *Leslie's* five illustrations with the legends, ' "GO BACK TO YOUR QUARTERS!" ', 'THE SKIPPER MEANT THAT HE WAS RUNNING HIS SHIP AS HE DEEMED BEST', 'AFTER THEY HAD VIOLENTLY ADJURED HIM TO LIE DOWN AND HE HAD GIVEN WEAK BACKS A COLD STIFF TOUCH, THE 307TH CHARGED IN RUSHES', 'THE DYING MAJOR DREW HIS REVOLVER, COCKED IT AND AIMED UNSTEADILY AT LIGE'S HEAD', and ' "SAY, GENTS, ANY OF YE GOT A BOTTLE?" ' In the *London Illustrated News* H. C. Seppings Wright drew an illustrative title showing the advance of the column and two illustrations with the legends, ' "Well, Maje," said the newcomer genially, "how goes it?" ' and ' "Oh, I'm so-o-o tired!" ' No copyright notice appears in either publication. Since Crane died on June 5, the *News* must have made a last-minute series of changes. Under a vignette giving a photograph of Crane as part of the title drawing the type legend reads, 'THE LATE STEPHEN CRANE', and under his name as author the following has been inserted: *'Mr. Stephen Crane's death was understandably hastened by the hardships he endured in the Spanish-American War. It is particularly interesting that Mr. H. C. Seppings Wright, the illustrator of this story, acted as our Special Artist during the campaign in Cuba, where he met Mr. Crane.'*

Crane's memorandum so that the title in the book cannot be said to have any special authority. Crane's list is what authenticates it.

The Cincinnati *Enquirer*, June 10, 1900, p. 9 (N^1), picked up the story and reprinted it from *Leslie's* with two illustrations after the magazine. The headline advertised it as 'CRANE'S LAST WAR STORY. | Based on His Cuban Campaign With | the Sixth Infantry. | Keen Observation the Basis | of Clever Fiction From | Pen of the Dead | Writer.' The story itself was prefaced by the following: "Mr. Stephen Crane, the news of whose death at the early age of 30 has just been cabled from Baden, was one of the most promising of America's younger writers. The story which follows is in his best style, and it will be of particular interest since one of the regular regiments in the brigade which the writer describes was the Sixth Infantry, which was stationed for a number of years at Ft. Thomas. The story appeared in the Frank Leslie's Magazine of November, 1899, under the title of 'West Pointer and Regular, or Virtue in War.'" The text reprints that in *Leslie's* with only the usual errors found in newspaper publication.

The variants in this story are few and minor. *Leslie's Monthly* (FL) and the *Illustrated London News* (ILN) seem to have been set from a typescript and its carbon. *Wounds in the Rain* (A1) was printed from a clipping of FL, the collational evidence and Stokes's letter about copy agreeing. No evidence suggests that Crane revised any one of the three publications whether in proof or by special annotation of their copy. Although ILN is technically of equal authority, the copy-text has been chosen as *Leslie's Monthly* because of its American styling, but this has been emended in the accidentals from ILN as seems advisable. As a derived and unrevised text, A1 has no authority. The attempt is, then, to reconstruct as nearly as may be from the preserved documents the typescript behind FL and ILN.

MARINES SIGNALING UNDER FIRE AT GUANTANAMO

The sole early reference to "Marines Signaling Under Fire" comes in a letter from Havana to Reynolds on November 1, 1898, in which Crane encloses a newspaper article (Syracuse, typed copy). In it he remarks, "The English rts on the marines go to Blackwoods," thus establishing his dispatch of the manuscript to Reynolds in late October. This letter, then, would seem to identify as "Marines Signaling" the piece sent Reynolds on October 20: "I enclose a 'personal anecdote' thing for McClure. Hit him hard. Hit him beastly hard. I have got to have at least fifteen hundred dollars this month, sooner the better. For Christ's sake get me some money quick here by cable" (*Letters*, p. 189).[82] In the list of stories for *Wounds in the Rain* the title is given simply as 'Marines Signaling', the column for serialization in England is left blank but McClure's is noted for America, and the word count is given as 2,700. The piece came out in *McClure's Magazine*, XII (February, 1899), 332–336.[83] So far as is known it was not separately printed in England; hence its history concludes with the publication in *Wounds in the Rain* (1900), pages 178–189.

The *McClure's* version has the only direct connection with the lost manuscript through the typescript that Reynolds would have had made and therefore becomes the copy-text. The *Wounds* version is a close reprint of *McClure's*, from a clipping or a

[82] This view differs from that of R. W. Stallman, who conjecturally identifies "This Majestic Lie" with 'the personal anecdote sort of thing' sent to Reynolds on October 20 (*Stephen Crane: A Biography* [New York, Braziller, 1968], p. 425). What seems decisive is not alone the fact that "Marines" is told in the first person, whereas "This Majestic Lie" is straight third-person narrative, but also Crane's letter of November 1. Before the paragraph informing Reynolds that the English rights of "Marines" belong to *Blackwood's* appears this: "Convey to Stokes the pleasing information that I have completed about 15000 words of Cuban stories and that he shall have the book for spring, and govern your placing of these articles accordingly." The stories that Crane is known to have written in Havana are "The Lone Charge of William B. Perkins" (September 14, 1898), "The Price of the Harness" (September 27), "The Clan of No-Name" (early October), and "Marines Signaling Under Fire" (before November 1). According to the count given in the list Crane made up for *Wounds in the Rain*, these four stories total 16,860 words. Since "This Majestic Lie" is given in the list as 8,600 words, it could not possibly be included in this November 1 cumulative total of about 15,000 words. See the Textual Introduction to "This Majestic Lie," also, for the indication that it dates from the autumn of 1899, not of 1898.

[83] The *McClure's* printing advertises it as by the 'Author of "The Red Badge of Courage," "The Open Boat," etc.' W. J. Glackens drew an illustrative heading of a wigwagger on the ridge that was placed above the title. Four illustrations appear with the legends, '*The enemy shoot at you from an adjacent thicket*', '*When the man stood up to signal, the colonel stood beside him*', '*The situation demanded that he face the sea and turn his back to the Spanish bullets*', and '*Early morning coffee!*'.

proof, and is of no independent authority since it was without authorial alteration of any sort.

THIS MAJESTIC LIE

Some unknown difficulty seems to have attended the sale of "This Majestic Lie." On October 4, 1899, Robert McClure in London wrote to Pinker: "I beg to acknowledge your letter of October 3rd which correctly sets forth the understanding come to between us regarding . . . Mr Stephen Crane's 'THE MAJES-TIC LIE,' the latter of which, according to our computation in this office, extends to 9,000 words. With regards to date of publication, it is understood that you are to be at liberty to arrange a convenient date for issue in this country, giving us notice in advance of at least . . . three months in respect of Mr Crane's story" (TLS, Dartmouth). On October 6 McClure wrote to Pinker again: "Replying to your letter of the 5th int., I beg to acknowledge receipt of the original MS of Mr Crane's story "The Majestic Lie," which I return herewith. I find that the story runs to 8,300 words and that the total price, therefore, should be £78:15:0. I am unable to send you a cheque at once, as you suggest, particularly in view of the fact that the story may not be published for sometime" (TLS, Dartmouth). The other references are posthumous. In July–August, 1900, Cora wrote to Pinker about a statement he had provided her in which she asks, "And have the following been published here?" and includes "The Majestic Lie." Then on September 12, 1900, she wrote to the agent Perris, "I enclose you some statements which will show you the prices recieved by Mʳ. Crane for his short stories. Please return them to me after you have looked them over carefully. "The Majestic Lie" was paid for above the rate I named (£10– a thousand words.) Mr. Crane would not write for less than that, and you can use that as an average" (ALS, New York Public Library).

Some difficulty must have resulted from McClure's demurring about present payment, and it may be either that the New York office ultimately took advantage of the loophole to decline the story or else Crane may have instructed Pinker to attempt to sell it elsewhere for cash, not promises. It is odd that as late as the autograph contents list for *Wounds in the Rain* Crane still noted McClure as the publisher in both countries (the word count in this list is 8,600 words), yet when it was published posthumously in the *Herald* it was not syndicated by McClure and was copyrighted by Paul Reynolds. No known publication appeared in England. In the United States, the *New York Herald* printed it (with the title as in Crane's list of "This Majestic Lie") in its sixth section on Sunday, June 24, 1900, p. 10, with the conclusion on July 1, p. 3.[84] The story was syndicated, though not widely. Two other appearances not previously recorded have been found: N^2 in the *Chicago Tribune*, June 24, 1900, pp. 41–42, and July 1, p. 43; and N^3 in the *St. Louis Daily Globe-Democrat*, June 24, pp. 4–5, complete in one installment.[85] Both used the same copy, which must have been a master proof set up by the *New York Herald* which, with only a handful of final changes, printed its text from the same setting of type. This master proof was used for copyright deposit in the Library of Congress, where it is still preserved.[86] N^2 and N^3 faithfully repeat most of the readings of the early master proof that were corrected in the final *Herald* text;[87] but it is possible that a still earlier form of the proof was

[84] In June 24 a special banner headline advertised its decorative title as 'STEPHEN CRANE'S LAST STORY', and drawings from two photographs are provided, one from the picture of Crane as a cadet at the Hudson River Institute in 1888 (Stallman, no. 1) and the other—so far as can be told—a free rendering of a picture of 1896 (Stallman, no. 8), with the legend that it represented Crane's last portrait. Each installment carried a four-column illustration with the legends, ' "WHAT HAVE YE GOT?" HE ASKED BEFORE COMMITTING HIMSELF' and 'AGAIN THE TWO MEN SURVEYED EACH OTHER DURING A PERIOD OF SILENCE'.

[85] Very likely additional search will reveal other newspaper versions. Forty copies were ordered of the proofs. The *Chicago Tribune* printed a large illustrated heading with three joined illustrations beneath the title for the first installment on June 24, with the legends, ' "WHOEVER HEARD OF IT?" ', ' "AND A LITTLE THING FOR THE WAITER?" ', and ' "WHO AM I, ANYHOW?" '; in the second installment, on July 1, a different illustrative heading was used and two separate illustrations with the legends, ' "HOW'S LITTLE ALFRED?" ' and '. . . SMOKING A CIGAR IN THE PRESENCE OF A WAITER.' The *St. Louis Globe-Democrat* used a single large illustration with the legend, 'HE HELD UP A SOLEMN HAND.'

[86] The two statutory copies are stamped 8258 and 8259; each has the handwritten notation 'A 14939 June 16–1900' and the stamped register of copyright as June 18. The proof heading is dated Monday June 11, and forty proofs are noted to be sent as soon as possible to E. Marshall.

[87] The substantive changes between proof (N^{1a}) and the published *Herald* text (N^{1b}) are listed in the Historical Collation. The complete notation of changes is as follows, the proof reading being to the left of the bracket: 202.12 one-hundredth] one one-hundredth 202.26 pyjama] pajama 206.28

sent them. Only a single piece of evidence suggests the existence
of such a form, but it is hard to explain on other terms. At 204.7
as a common error N^{2-3} print *plentitude* whereas correct *plenitude* is found both in the Library of Congress proofs and in the
Herald. Significantly, the *Wounds in the Rain* Stokes text also
reads *plentitude*, no doubt repeating the spelling in the typescript which thus, seemingly from a lost earlier proof, seems to
have been passed on to N^{2-3}. (This Stokes reading was corrected
among the plate changes made in the Methuen *Wounds.*)

Since the *Chicago Tribune* and the *St. Louis Globe-Democrat*
texts derive from an early proof of the *New York Herald*
publication [88] and have no independent authority, the choice of
copy-text lies between the 1900 *Wounds* text ($A1$) and the *Herald*
(N^1), more specifically the N^1 copyrighted proofsheets. These two
authorities seem to derive from a typescript and its carbon since
the substantive differences are few and of the kind to be expected in the course of normal textual transmission, and the
accidentals are sufficiently close. (Stokes had the story in typescript in his possession on June 15, 1900.) In general the $A1$
styling is slightly more characteristic of Crane's manuscript habits in the accidentals than is N^1, perhaps in part because the

---

life.] life   208.14   blame] blamed   208.24   end??] end?   212.5   remember"——] remember"—   213.1,22; 214.32   Aquacate] Aguacate   215.5
flyer] flier   215.25   minutes, are] minutes. Are   216.1   blocaded] block-
aded   219.39   was] were   220.11   was] were   220.31   puz-|zling]
puz|zling

[88] Certain readings indicate that N^{2-3} were set up from common-copy proofsheets that were in at least as early a state as the Library of Congress deposit
galleys, and not from the corrected form used to print the *Herald* text. For instance, at 202.12 N^{2-3} agree with N^{1a} (the Congress proof) in *one-hundredth* as
against N^{1b} (the *Herald*) *one one-hundredth*. In this case $A1$ confirms the N^{1a}
reading as the correct one and the N^{1b} as sophistication. The same situation
holds at 208.14 with N^{1a},$A1$ *blame* but N^{1b} *blamed*, and at 219.39 with N^{1a},$A1$
was but N^{1b} *were* (at 220.11 $A1$ joins N^{1b} in the sophistication *were* for N^{1a}
was). At 213.1,22 and 214.32 N^2 (for the first reading) and N^{2-3} (for the second and third) follow the N^{1a} error *Aquacate* corrected in N^{1b} to *Aguacate*. A
very odd reading occurs at 204.7 when N^{2-3} join in the error *plentitude* (indicating that this was the reading of their copy), although it is *plenitude*, correctly, in both N^{1a} and N^{1b}. Moreover, that *plentitude* was probably the reading
of Crane's copy is suggested by the appearance of this erroneous form in $A1$
(see the Textual Note to 204.7). The evidence would suggest that this single
change was made in the Congress proof galleys before deposit but after earlier
pulls had been mailed to the newspapers containing the *plentitude* reading.
That this was the only difference between the Congress galleys and the newspaper copy is indicated by the fact that nowhere else do N^{2-3} agree with $A1$
against N^1.

light-punctuating compositor of A1 had most to do with it. Nevertheless, some emendations in the accidentals are adopted from N¹, particularly to adjust this compositor's penchant for setting off inverted phrases with commas, although it has been impossible to decide fairly between his generally heavier hyphenation of compounds and N¹'s usual failure to hyphenate. Only one or two substantive variants from N¹ need be considered since Crane intervened with neither text after the typescript stage and the A1 readings ordinarily prove to be superior except where, as at 210.8 with *abjuring*, A1 too faithfully repeats a common Crane error that must have been copied in the typescript from the manuscript. The present edition, therefore, by a controlled conflation of the two authorities attempts to reconstruct as closely as possible the typescript from which A1 and N¹ independently derive.

War Memories

On August 4, 1899, Crane wrote to Pinker from Brede about various financial matters and casually interjected, "Lady Churchill has asked me to write for her Review. I have consented of course. It is not a commercial transaction" (*Letters*, p. 223). Despite this disclaimer, payment for the article "War Memories" became a later necessity, as shown by a letter from Cora to Pinker, conjecturally dated October 21, 1899, in which she sums up various monies due Crane and adds: "Then there is *at least* £50 due from John Lane for the Lady Churchill article. . . . Please let me know what you can do for us. Can't you manage to send Mr. Crane £50 on receipt of this & go and make John Lane pay you?" (*Letters*, pp. 235–236). "War Memories" was published in the *Anglo-Saxon Review*, X (December, 1899), 10–38. It was not reprinted in the United States so far as is known. Although listed in the autograph inventory for *Wounds in the Rain* in last place, when finally collected in the book, pages 229–308, it is next to last, as in the later list Crane provided Stokes, followed by the concluding story, "The Second Generation." Probably the title "War Memories" was not arrived at until the final proof. In the list preserved at Columbia University it is called 'The Cuban Campaign', but in the Stokes list it is simply, 'The Story for Lady Churchill'.

The nature of the copy for the *Wounds* volume (A1) is more than an academic question since the crucial choice of copy-text is involved. That is, if A1 were printed from a clipping or a proof of the *Review* (AS), it would have no independent authority in the accidentals, and very likely none in the substantives, and could not be used as a source of emendation save as a convenience to repair error. On the other hand, if one were set from a typescript and the other from its carbon,[89] both would be of equal authority and an eclectic text could be contrived that would attempt, from features of both, to reconstruct the salient details of this lost typescript.

Important in any inquiry into this matter is the fact that in no other story published in England in December was Crane able to provide a clipping, thus suggesting that he had assembled copy for Stokes before this date. Moreover, the *Anglo-Saxon Review* cuts (or A1 additions) prevent any hypothesis that nothing but a clipping was the copy for A1 unless one wishes to hypothesize that Crane took the trouble to restore cuts by a typescript addition at the crucial points. This care would be extraordinary but not impossible. It could be envisaged for the three major cuts, each involving several A1 pages, but it is most difficult to credit in the small variants involving only a few sentences describing his reactions to the army doctor on shipboard found at 260.18–22 and 260.23–26. Taking these two objections together, one may discard with no reluctance any hypothesis involving the use of an initially provided clipping.

The same objections would not necessarily apply to a proof, however, if the variants could be shown to represent cuts made in the proof itself and not in the copy before AS was set. This case of plus or minus is almost impossible to decide authoritatively on the available evidence relating to these gaps. The major cuts at 223.16–225.25 (the anecdote of the *Machias*), 255.23–257.24 (the anecdote of Bos'n but prefaced by a brief anecdote of General Shafter), and 261.24–263.28 (the last part

---

[89] The two versions seem to be too close to support any hypothesis that one was from the manuscript and the other from a typescript.

of the shipboard description and the entire account of the arrival home) might well have been editorial since none involves the fighting in the campaign. It would be idle to suggest that other episodes were equally eligible.[90] To speculate what an editor might or might not do is scarcely profitable. More to the point, perhaps, is to suggest that the curious alterations of a few sentences about the army doctor could not have been made for reasons of conserving space since the article ends very shortly with a number of lines to spare.[91] The theory that the AS cuts were made in proof, thus, is not an attractive one: the common-sense reconstruction would be that the *Review* editor marked the cuts in the typescript, perhaps with Crane's assistance but perhaps not, so that this material was never set by the printer.

Although the external evidence does not, in fact, settle the question of the textual transmission, it does assist in reconstructing the copy that Stokes's printer eventually received. On January 9, 1900, Pinker wrote Cora: "Have you a copy of the story written for Lady Randolph Churchill for me to send to Stokes? It is, as you know, included in the book, and I have no copy here"; to this Cora responded on January 10: "Stokes and Co. have a copy of the article in Lady Churchill's magazine. I sent it to them" (*Letters*, pp. 261, 263). Unfortunately, Cora did not specify when she had sent copy to Stokes, nor what kind of copy. The probability is that she had earlier included "War Memories" in the second batch of stories that had been mailed to Stokes, and that the copy was neither a proof nor a clipping but

[90] However, if the last one were a cut, and made after the setting into proof, it is as possible for the editor as for Crane to have written the AS transition passage that intervenes between 261.23 and 263.28: *Ultimately we arrived. We landed at Old Point Comfort—saintly name!* But space considerations would not have dictated the exact dimensions of this late cut, for the *Review* ends on page 38 with 32 lines of type, whereas its page holds 46 lines, and the editor could have preserved the 261.24–27 continuation of shipboard life (except that it begins a paragraph and so may have seemed a convenient place to start a cut). More important, still within space limitations, *Thus they lived until the ship reached Hampton Roads* (261.27–28) that immediately follows would seem to offer as good a transition to the last paragraph *The episode was closed . . .* (263.29–30) as the one that was apparently specially devised as a bridge, particularly if *we* were to be substituted for *they.*

[91] Indeed, it could theoretically be that the small variants about the army doctor are revisions in A1 even though the others are editorial cuts, or they might even be authorial proof alteration in AS (including the final AS transition bit) if A1 were set from different copy. The substantive variants between the two texts are discussed below.

instead the carbon of the typescript that had been sold to the *Anglo-Saxon Review*. The evidence as to the latter point appears to be decisive. In the May 23 letter of Stokes to Pinker, "War Memories" is not in the group of five stories that are noted as in his possession in letterpress form. On June 15 it is not listed among the four Stokes has in typescript for which he is endeavoring to secure printed copy, but this omission is explained in the preceding sentence, "We have purchased a copy of 'The Anglo-Saxon Review', and have sent this to the printer to use in setting up 'War Memories'." It is significant that in the May 23 Stokes list of stories and their places of publication, 'The Anglo-Saxon' is noted, but the title is not provided and instead there is the entry '(Story for Lady Churchill)'. This must mean that the title was unknown at that date to Stokes (in Crane's own list it was not titled either) since the copy in his possession did not have one: in this case Stokes could not have had a clipping and very likely not a proof. However, the notice in the June 15 letter that he has purchased the *Anglo-Saxon Review* and sent it to his printer is revelatory. If Stokes had had the story in any letterpress form he would not have needed to purchase the *Review*. That he had previously had some form of copy is suggested by his list of May 23. The evidence is clear that this copy could only have been the untitled typescript carbon that Cora had mailed him probably in November, 1899, or a little later. Otherwise he could not have learned about the cuts in the *Review* text.

We know that Stokes's printer, thus, had both the typescript and the printed version in his possession when he came to set copy. It is evident that in some manner, perhaps when working out word counts, either Stokes or the printer discovered the fact that the typescript contained passages not in the *Review* and so was able to include them in the book version. However, this fact does not tell us whether the printer, as a consequence, set from the typescript copy exclusively or else whether he set from the *Review* printed text and referred to the typescript only for the extra material. (Although it is theoretically possible that two simultaneously setting compositors were given sections of each, no positive evidence supports such a hypothesis.) Under these circumstances, the possible evidence contained in the magazine and the book texts must be explored.

That in favor of AS printed copy throughout except for the additions is hard to assess. The two texts in their accidentals are extremely close, allowing for normal compositorial punctuation preferences. The paragraphing is identical save for 260.27, where A1 creates a paragraph and none exists in AS.[92] The constant A1 agreement in punctuation with AS except where known compositorial habits interfere is so exact as to lead to the query whether both texts could coincide so closely in this manner if they derived from a typescript and its carbon and whether, indeed, A1 must not in some way stem from AS to produce this result. A1's acceptance of the AS British spelling *waggon* at 252.6,9 is unusual, as may also be the spelling *spirt* (226.4,8). It may be significant that at 227.16 both texts agree in the unusual capitalization of the second *It* in the sentence *It—what shall I say?—It interested him, this coincidence.* Although several times A1 and AS agree in the phrase *sort of*, both print *sort of a* at 237.34, a Crane idiom often sophisticated by compositors. After diverging with *afterward* from the English form *afterwards* at 230.3, A1 agrees with AS *afterwards* at 231.10 and in *towards* at 238.22. In other stories A1 ordinarily uses the American, not the English forms. Whether *blacked-hull* at 237.15 is a derived error in A1 from AS is not altogether clear. Possibly significant is the fact that AS reads *San Juan Hill* and A1 *San Juan hill* at 250.3–4 and 251.17–18, but A1 agrees in *Hill* at 257.25. Yet evidence such as this is uncertain. For instance, at 249.1 both AS and A1 print *hill* and thus the reading of the typescript—whether *hill* or *Hill*—is in doubt even granting that it would be consistent, as is the question of which text is departing from copy and which following it. (In "The Second Generation" two independently set texts read *Hill*.) As another example, A1 and AS disagree occasionally in their hyphenation or nonhyphenation of compounds, but A1 is not always consistent. At 255.9 A1 reads *operating table* and AS *operating-table*; thus when at 255.20 A1 joins in the hyphenated form it is tempting to conjecture that AS copy has influenced the compositor when he repeated the words. But A1 is inconsistent without regard for AS

[92] Whether this has anything to do with the variants of plus or minus in the preceding paragraph is obscure, but it is difficult not to take it that there was some connection.

copy. In two passages where AS is wanting and A1 is the only authority, A1 at 256.22 reads *riding breeches* but *riding-breeches* at 257.22; and *yellow-flag* at 261.30 but *yellow flag* at 261.34.

The prime difficulty in putting any weight on specific unusual agreements between the two texts like *waggon* or *blacked-hull* is that they could just about as easily go back to common copy as to AS transmitting a detail to A1. One may turn, then, to what would be a series of unusual differences if AS had provided the printer's copy for A1. This evidence is also difficult to assess since it is negative; that is, agreement is not present that one would expect to be present if AS were the copy. Although controls are wanting to demonstrate that the divergences resulted from AS's departure from common copy instead of from A1's departure from AS, several examples could appear to have possible significance. At 249.12–13 A1 repeats the series clause *who was pegging along at the heels of still another man* but AS prints it only once. Given the extreme repetition within this sentence, it could be simpler to conjecture AS omission of a unit present in common copy than A1 addition. Perhaps a stronger case occurs at 239.33–34, which in AS reads, *They baulk at trifles when a blockhead cries 'Go on.'* but in A1 is *. . . when a blockhead cries go on.* That A1 would omit the quotes in dialogue found in its AS copy is difficult to credit, whereas it is less troublesome to envisage the AS compositor making a quote out of the A1 form in his typescript.[93] Another anomaly occurs at 252.9–11. Here A1 reads, rather abruptly: *"You can make room for her," said the private of the Second Cavalry. A young, young man with a straight mouth.* This is typical enough of Crane's style; but one would not expect it from the A1 compositor faced with the normal AS *. . . Second Cavalry, a young, young man with a straight mouth.* Another anomaly in A1 if AS had been the copy comes at 253.6–7 in the anecdote of the refugee family, where in AS the sentence reads, *In the meantime the pimple face approached me,* but in A1 appears the curious error *the pimple-faced.* One might speculate that some disruption had occurred here in the typescript, such as the deletion of a noun after *-faced*

---

[93] The question of a misunderstanding of the AS single quotes cannot enter here, for AS puts all dialogue in single quotes although A1, more conventionally, chooses double quotes. Thus the A1 compositor would have known that this was intended to be quoted speech if he had the AS copy before him.

without the correction of the adjective in A1 as was seen necessary in AS. But daydreaming like this is not evidence: all that can be said is that it is a not impossible error in A1 if AS were the copy.

Additional minor disagreements can be mentioned. AS and A1 usually agree in emphasis italics except at 242.10 and 253.3 where A1 has roman. It may be, then, that nothing is involved but compositorial styling when A1 does not follow the AS italics for *attaché* (245.14) and *fête* (254.4), which Crane would not himself have italicized. Although both texts usually agree, also, in the dashes that mark Crane's nervous conversational style in this piece, there are differences which may or may not result from independent compositorial action in AS, just as such differences occur in other stories in A1. Two instances may be cited, however, where the A1 dashes could represent unusual compositorial initiative in A1 if AS, which wants the dashes, had been the copy. It is perhaps somewhat easier to understand the AS compositor passing them over in his copy than the A1 compositor adding them each in a typical Crane situation: *But—we put to sea in a dug-out* (238.39) and *A noiseless campaign—on his part* (240.10). At 242.8–10 AS reads *my plate was there, you know, and—Fate provides some men greased opportunities for making dizzy jackasses of themselves*, whereas A1 correctly prints *my plate was there, you know, and—— Fate provides . . .* It seems likely that the capitalized *Fate* was taken by the AS compositor as a personification and the dash as an interval. But the context indicates that *Fate* is capitalized because it begins a sentence and that the A1 long dash with following space that provides this syntax is the correct reading.[94] If so, AS would not be the copy for A1 unless the A1 compositor was perspicuous indeed.[95]

[94] For a similar suspension and new sentence one may compare 231.38–39 in both texts: *But unfortunately—— In the meantime I had given up . . .*

[95] Finally, one may suggest that when controls are present it is usually the text without exclamation points that is more faithful to copy. That is, compositors more commonly add such marks at appropriate places than reduce them to periods or commas. From the various instances in which A1 prints periods and AS exclamations although one would expect A1 to follow the exclamations if AS had been its copy, one may select especially *He didn't need them—bless your heart!* (240.19) and *Isolate yourself, sir! Isolate yourself!* (261.1).

Such internal evidence as has been detailed can scarcely be taken as demonstrating one or other case, however. Except for a few common errors that might possibly be explained as readily by their presence in the basic typescript as by A1 copying AS, the vast majority of the variants are mistakes in one or other text, like A1 *violent* for AS *violet* (227.21); or they are indifferent like AS *protection* versus A1 *protections* (233.33) or AS *a right* for A1 *the right* (241.23) or AS *pale* versus A1 *as pale* (247.4). The brief cuts AS made in the diatribe against the army doctor (260.18–22,23–26) do not appear to be evidence about the nature of the A1 copy since they are probably to be linked with the major AS cut that follows beginning with the next paragraph and hence cannot qualify as A1 revisory additions. Only two substantive readings might be significant: these are AS *bulk* but A1 *honest pounds* (222.17) and AS *great* but A1 *attractive* (229.34).[96] In A1 *attractive* produces an unsuccessful and not wholly characteristic wordplay and appears in conjunction with a grammatical correction not likely to be authorial (see the Textual Note to 229.34), whereas *great*, though an undistinguished word, is reasonably characteristic. Perhaps this variant can be ignored as evidence. On the other hand, the phrase *honest pounds* applied to a bunch of bananas is puzzling if AS *bulk* had been the copy.

It is tempting, especially for this latter reading, to suggest that if AS and A1 each was set from the typescript and its carbon, *honest pounds* and perhaps *attractive* could represent the original Crane readings and *bulk* and *great* the AS proof corrections. But the matter is highly speculative and the evidence insufficient to form the basis for a theory of textual transmission against the probability that AS would, in general, be used as the printer's copy for A1. (What contamination from the typescript might be possible even with A1 providing the usual copy can only be guessed at, and just possibly could explain *honest pounds*.) It is clear from Stokes's letters that the main reason he tried to insist on letterpress copy was not for greater ease in typesetting. On the contrary, the single reason he advances is that he prefers not to send proofs of the book to England, with

[96] This is to regard AS *lithe* but A1 *light* (241.24) as a mistake in A1, not a revision.

consequent delay. Hence if he can set from magazine copy that Crane had proofread and approved, he will read proof in the United States for simple error and produce the volume with less difficulty. Thus it is reasonable to expect that the printer would be instructed to utilize the authorially proofread and presumptively correct revised A1 copy instead of the typescript assumed to be less perfect in its characteristics except when he was forced to refer to it. This assumption is supported by small pieces of internal evidence such as the common errors and some agreement in variation, but particularly the British styling of some forms of words in A1 that seem to derive from the AS copy since they do not appear thus elsewhere in the book.

As a consequence, the present editor's working hypothesis is that, for the general run of the typesetting, A1 was set from the AS copy that Stokes had purchased in New York for the purpose. Given this conjectured textual transmission, AS is the only authoritative text except when the cuts are being restored in A1 from the typescript that Cora had provided. Under these circumstances readings from A1 can be used to emend the AS copy-text only when correction is involved, not revision, except for the added material. Outside of these additions, therefore, all an editor can do is to reprint AS as correctly as possible and with desirable uniformity of texture. In this last connection, English spellings present in both texts have been put into Crane's American forms for the sake of consistency.

THE SECOND GENERATION

"The Second Generation" seems to have been linked in Pinker's mind, if not in Crane's, with "Virtue in War," and it is possible that both were written close to each other in point of time. It is these two stories that are referred to in a letter from Pinker to Crane in Paris about mid-September, 1899, causing Crane to telegraph Pinker on September 21 from Brede and to write him on September 30 and October 1 begging him to straighten out the situation in case "Virtue in War" and "The Second Generation" were the same story under two different titles. The last reference is on November 4 in which he remarks: "Please write me at some length about various stories and in particular always gladden my heart when you have news of sale. For instance the information that you had sold 'The Second Generation' to the Cornhill magazine was conveyed to me when I received the proofs. It is only a matter of a few pounds but anyhow it was pleasant to know it and I might have had the pleasure earlier" (*Letters*, pp. 231, 232, 233, 239–240). The story appeared in the *Cornhill Magazine*, n.s., VII (December, 1899), 734–753, and in the *Saturday Evening Post*, CLXXII (December 2, 1899), 449–452.[97] In the list made up for *Wounds in the Rain* "The Second Generation" is next to the last in order, noted as published in *Cornhill* and the *Post*, and the word count is given as 8,200. Finally, the story is one of the four in *Wounds* of which Cora wrote Pinker in July-August, 1900, asking if he had sold them in the United States and to what magazines. In *Wounds in the Rain* (1900) it is the final story, on pages 309–347.

The textual history of "The Second Generation" is of some complexity, like the rest of the stories that were published in December, 1899, after copy had been assembled for *Wounds in the Rain* and thus clippings from the English magazines could not be utilized. The copy for *Cornhill* (C) and the *Saturday Evening Post* (SP) seems to have been the usual typescript and its carbon. Allowing for the rather heavy editing in the *Post* and for the *Cornhill* styling, which was also heavy, the accidentals are close enough to have derived from this single source. The substantives occasionally diverge sharply. A number of these verbal variants can be traced to *Post* editing, with a particular emphasis upon censorship. Most obviously, the profanity that is freely reproduced in the *Cornhill* pages is either omitted or turned into innocuous phrases like *blamed, blanked, the deuce*, or *by Jove*. Even such mild soldiers' abuse as *low-down* and *pie-faced* (271.27–28) is excised. Less obviously, certain details that might reflect on a United States Senator's dignity are omitted or altered. For instance, that the Senator *drank a neat*

---

[97] In the *Cornhill* it was stated to be 'Copyright 1899 by Stephen Crane in the United States of America' and in the *Post* 'Copyright, 1899, by The Curtis Publishing Company. Copyrighted in Great Britain'. C. D. Williams drew an illustration of the troops on San Juan below the *Post* title and also three illustrations with the legends, ' "Has any one seen my saddle-bags? Why, if I lose 'em I'm ruined" ', ' "General! General! Cadogan is off there in the bushes eating potted ham and crackers" ', and ' "Senator, they say they don't give a cuss whether your son's dead or not" '.

whisky before lighting a cigar (265.1) is deleted. Any suggestion that bribery existed in Washington is altered. This motive seems to govern the otherwise curious changes of *penny* to *bun* and of *amount* to *thing* (266.13–15). Even the senatorial speech is made correct: such slurrings as *fightin'*, *goin'*, *nothin'* are expanded, and the Senator's address to a friend *Henery* becomes *Henry*. A more subtle because at first seemingly motiveless series of excisions occurs in SP as of *I'll do my best with it* (267.3–4), or *somewhere* (268.6), or *unlocked his teeth* (271.23), or *He's all right* (272.26), or *his face* (278.14). However, because of evidence detailed below connecting *Wounds in the Rain* (A1) with the *Post*, these can be demonstrated to have been present in the SP copy although later excised in proof. The purpose seems to have been to save space here and there a line at a time. It is significant that each of the examples given occurs at the end of an SP paragraph and the omission prevents a run-over on an extra line. The pattern of these cuts in the last sentence of a paragraph is too obvious not to have a mechanical explanation, since no critical one is possible.[98]

In the *Post* such compositorial changes and editorial alterations in the proof can be distinguished since something of a control exists in the A1 text. The book publication associates itself very clearly in its accidentals with the *Post* as against *Cornhill*, and also in a number of substantive variants. So close is this concurrence, indeed, that a theory that A1 was set from a proof of SP would be quite viable were it not for two sets of significant evidence to the contrary. The first is subject to two interpretations and so cannot be considered apart from the second. A1 does not follow a number of unique SP omissions, particularly those that occur at the ends of paragraphs and that were made in order to save a half dozen or so lines. It would be possible to suggest, however, that this cutting was done in a later state of the proof and that it was the original state of the galleys —before this editorial intervention—that furnished printer's copy for A1. (Obviously, cutting of the story to fit the available space would take place after proof was ready and space could be

___

[98] The *Post* ends the story with twenty-three lines of extra space in the column, which is filled by a short poem. One may guess that the story originally left insufficient space for any kind of filler, and hence the editor in proof made such alterations as would enable the three-stanza poem to fit the space.

calculated exactly.) This hypothesis would then permit the numerous readings in which SP,A1 disagree with C when C does not seem to be manifestly in error to be assessed as changes by the SP editor in the pre-typesetting, or copy, stage so that the earliest proof would contain them. Of these the most conspicuous are the variants between SP,A1 on the one hand and C on the other in respect to the profanity. It is true one might conjecture that at 272.22 Crane added *Hell!* in the *Cornhill* proof, not that the *Post* editor deleted it from the typescript before setting. But to believe that Crane, for instance, originally wrote SP,A1 *blamed* for C *damn* (267.32), *a rip* for *three whoops in Hades* (268.25–26), *dash* for *damn* (269.23), *cuss* for *gawd dam* (275.1,6), *deuce* for *devil* (276.21), *Jove* for *gawd* (277.24,31), *blamed* for *damned* (278.38), or *the deuce* for *hell* (281.24) and then altered these in proof to the full-blown C readings would be to believe nonsense. Indeed, one can see the SP editor at work after typesetting, weeding out from the proof profanity that had escaped his blue-pencil in the typescript copy, when at 264.20 C reads *damned*, A1 *d—d*, but SP omits the word, or at 272.33 when for C *damned* and A1 *d—d*, SP reduces to *blanked*. It seems evident that in these last two cases A1 is following copy that antedates the final SP proof. This copy could still have been the original proofs, however, not the revises.

On the other hand, evidence accumulates that is not readily explicable by the hypothesis that A1 was set from early proofs of SP. A few substantive readings find A1 agreeing with C against SP when it would have been strange indeed for the A1 compositor to have objected to the SP reading and to have invented fortuitously the exact reading of *Cornhill*. In this group one can single out C,A1 *while* but SP *though* (265.4); C,A1 *somewhere* omitted by SP (268.6); possibly *shocked* in C,A1 omitted by SP (271.22) unless this is a case of the SP cutting in proof; C,A1 *had* but SP *would* (278.26); and C,A1 *should* but SP *would* (279.27). To these may perhaps be added the twofold profanity represented in SP by the double long dashes versus the single dash in C,A1 (274.27), and possibly the difficulty in the original reading that seems to be represented by the complete disagreement at 268.21 of C *fetlessly*, the A1 error *bootlessly*, but the correct SP *footlessly*. One or two of these might be explained as part of the continuing proof alteration of the SP editor as exemplified in the two initially overlooked cases of profanity, but it may seem difficult to assign all of them to his ministrations. Even more difficult to attribute to this editor is a series of minor dialect changes in quoted speech such as C,A1 *eatin'* but SP *eating* (269.15); C,A1 *b'cause* but SP *because* (272.31; 273.12); C *a'*, A1 *o'*, but SP *of* (272.32; 273.10); C,A1 *'im* but SP *him* (273.9,12), and in reverse direction C,A1 *them* but SP *'em* (267.22). Since most of these occur in the speech of common soldiers intermixed with similar contractions, it would be odd for an editor to interfere so arbitrarily in highly colloquial dialogue. This would seem to be a very different case from the attention given to the Senatorial speech in marking up the typescript.

The conclusion one may draw is that for some unknown reason Crane did not have a fresh typescript made from his manuscript for A1 as he had done with "The Revenge of the *Adolphus*," nor apparently was an English proof available as with the *Cornhill* proof that was copy for A1 " 'God Rest Ye, Merry Gentlemen.' " Instead, either at Pinker's or at Crane's request the *Post* must have turned over to Stokes the typescript copy it had used for its typesetting, and thus in its full editorially marked form. This being so, the editorial problem is in part simplified. When SP disagrees with joint C,A1 readings, the unique SP variants, whether compositorial or editorial, can have no authority. Correspondingly, unique A1 variation from joint SP,C agreement is exposed as A1 compositorial error.

This serves to narrow the field of inquiry to only those readings in which C on the one hand differs from joint SP,A1 on the other. Since SP and A1 go back independently to a common copy, under ordinary circumstances their agreement would automatically force unique C divergence into the category either of C errors or of authorial proof alteration.[99] But the case is not so

---

[99] The possibility might exist of independent review of the *Cornhill* copy before printing. But this possibility occurs only when Crane was himself sending off two copies, one to his English agent and the other to Reynolds in New York, and thus had the opportunity to review one at greater leisure if it were not immediately dispatched in the same mail. At the time of "The Second Generation" he had broken with Reynolds, and Pinker was handling the United States sales. Thus Crane would send to Pinker either the manuscript for typed copies to be made or, more economically at this particular time, the typescript and carbon that Cora or some houseguest like Edith Richie would have made

simple, for an editor must contend with the heavy hand of the *Post* editor who had marked the copy for the printer. In many respects this editor attended to purely formal matters like the paragraphing, and just possibly some specific matters of punctuation. As remarked above, he deleted or defused the profanity of Crane's soldiers and upheld the dignity of the United States Senate. These are all demonstrable editorial alterations since A1 and SP agree in them and C's readings would seem to have been drawn from the original typescript. The SP,A1 concurrences can be firmly distinguished, of course, from the compositorial or the further editorial work on the text in proof where SP is not followed by A1.

But the more the SP editor is taken to have interfered with purely stylistic considerations, the more the critic approaches the gray area where the possibility of *Cornhill* editorial or compositorial styling and also of Crane's proof alteration begins to offer a reasonable alternative and where (in most cases) the joint SP,A1 concurrence may represent the purer reading of the typescript from which the English text departs. Some few unique C variants are clearly British styling, such as the substitution of *kindly* for *kind* (267.6), of *underclothing* for *underwear* (270.1), of *eh, Gory?* for *Hey, Gory!* (270.19), or of *roller-topped* for *roll-top* (274.9). Some are simple errors of the C compositor, like *strutted* for *sputtered* (278.11) or *abode* for *adobe* (283.24), and no doubt *does* for *dare* (266.11), *fronted* for *confronted* (271.7), and *more* for *rather* (272.15). In theory a few could be Crane's proof revisions, but no single one of these can be identified. The best candidate at first sight would be his praise of American manhood as outmatching the best in Europe (265.33–34); yet odd as it may seem for an American editor to excise such innocent chauvinism, the context suggests the strong possibility that this change may be credited to the SP editor and that the C version stood in the typescript.[100] For the

---

up for him. For example, in a letter to Pinker which Professor Levenson has redated in August, 1899 (see *Tales of Adventure*, p. cxix, n 113), Crane begins, "I am sending you 2 copies of a short story". More important, however, we know from his remark to Pinker that he received *Cornhill* proof for this story.

[100] The case is obscure at best. The C version reads, *They were fine men. Individual to individual, American manhood overmatches the best in Europe; but manhood is only an essential part of a lieutenant, a captain or a major.*

most part the direction of change tends toward 'improvement' in the SP,A1 text, as in the substitution of *this arrangement* for *it* detailed in note 100 above. Another possible example is the substitution of *cheek* in SP,A1 for *face* at 283.10. In C the last sentence of the paragraph reads, *The Senator's face was flushed with enthusiasm, and he looked eagerly and confidently at his son.* Then the next paragraph begins, *But Casper had pulled a long face.* It is difficult to conceive of an English editor or of Crane removing *cheek* in proof and substituting *face*, but easy for the SP editor to object to the weak repetition and to make a suitable alteration.[101] Further editing may very likely be found in the SP,A1 version *officer called to officer, classmate to classmate, and in these greetings rang a note of everything, from West Point to Alaska* which is smoother than the graceless C text, *classmate to classmate, in which rang a note . . .* (270.12–13).

Here the reference to *manhood* in the first clause is completed by its application, repeating the word, in the second. But the SP,A1 text, where the first reference to *manhood* is omitted and only the application—altered to apply to *fine men*—appears, is more amorphous: *They were fine men, though manhood is only an essential part . . .* Possibly this was the typescript version, improved in proof when its intention was seen to be unsatisfactorily conveyed; possibly the dislocation in SP,A1 reveals a cut. It may be that this variant cannot be considered without reference to others in the paragraph. Above, at 265.28–30, C's *A German field-marshal would have beamed with joy if he could have seen them—to send to school* might not read in a wholly satisfying way, if C were a revised passage, in comparison to the more natural SP,A1 *could have had them—to send to school*. If the *manhood* passage is a cut in SP, then, it is probable that the editor 'improved' the C reading. Following the *manhood* cut, the paragraph concludes, in C, *But at any rate, it had all the logic of going to sea in a bathing-machine* (265.35–36). Here the referent for the pronoun *it* goes well back to the first sentence in the paragraph (265.25–27) describing the *large number of well-bred handsome young men* [who] *were receiving appointments as lieutenants, as captains, and occasionally as majors*. The reference requires an effort to locate when *it* is the only clue. Hence one would scarcely expect Crane or the *Cornhill* editor to substitute the *it* for typescript *this arrangement*, and instead the SP phrase appears to reflect the revision given by the editor to this paragraph for reasons of his own. (Just possibly he felt Crane's satire reflected on the dignity of the American legislative and administrative process and on the ability of the American volunteers in the war, and he partly legitimized it as an *arrangement* just as he had cleaned up the picture of Senator Cadogan.

[101] The alternative is to take it that this is a C error whereby *face* anticipating *a long face* got fixed in the compositor's mind and his memorial failure contaminated the reading. If this is an SP change, on the other hand, as seems more probable, it may just possibly help to explain the very odd omission in SP,A1 of *his face* in the C text, *The senator lifted his eyes and his face darkened* (283.32). One can only speculate that this too was to be part of the change of *face* to *cheek* (perhaps *cheek* being transferred here) but was only partly completed and then overlooked.

In fact, so generally more acceptable by ordinary standards are many of these SP,A1 variants that a critic might be tempted to view them as SP authorial corrections if the time element did not almost forbid such a conjecture as well as the lack of any evidence throughout the *Wounds in the Rain* volume that Crane saw proof for the American magazine publications. He complained to Reynolds, indeed, that he was not even sent clippings.

The editorial problem, then, is straightforward only up to a point. Because of its independent derivation from a copy of the typescript, A1 in accidentals is of equal authority with the other two texts, and inferior to C only when the SP editor seems to have altered the typescript copy, as in the paragraphing and seemingly in a few small details of punctuation. The *Cornhill* text, though set from what seems to have been a less heavily edited copy of the basic typescript, has nevertheless been subjected by the compositor to English styling. On the whole, especially when appropriate accidentals emendations from *Cornhill* are admitted, A1 forms the most satisfactory copy-text and has been selected as the textual basis for the accidentals. In these accidentals, therefore, when SP and A1 agree against C, they should reflect the forms of the typescript in all cases where (a) the SP editor has not intervened, or (b) both compositors have not fortuitously restyled the typescript in the same manner. Some suspicion may be aroused that the SP editor added commas to Crane's unpunctuated adjective series, but in most other respects his ministrations in the accidentals remain invisible. Other combinations are more trustworthy, such as agreement of C with SP against A1, or of C and A1 against SP. Most of these have been honored, even when they entail making the punctuation heavier, unless reason exists to suspect similar though independent compositorial styling.

Less straightforward is the question of capitalization. The two American texts capitalize all military titles in a manner that is alien to Crane's earlier practice, whereas *Cornhill* agrees with him. The capitalization in SP and A1 is carried further, however, into *Commissary, Senator, Administration, Machine, Guv'nor, State,* and *National.* Here more uncertainty exists whether these may not represent the typescript forms reduced in C instead of raised by the SP editor, as seems probable with the military

titles.[102] Perhaps these capitalizations are not indivisible. The
evidence, such as it is, is conflicting. At 276.9 A1 departs from
SP and its own practice to print *department* without the invariable capital. This may represent only compositorial styling, however, and not a reflection of copy. More pertinent is what seems
to be a slip in C at 274.22 in which it assigns a capital to *State*
against its otherwise invariable practice, suggesting that the
compositor had been reducing a typescript capital for this word.
The whole matter is so obscure and the difficulties of distinguishing between the edited and unedited capitalized categories are so
great that the present editor has chosen to follow the *Cornhill*
uncapitalized words in almost every case save for the convention
of direct address, since on the whole—without regard for the
hypothetical features of the lost typescript or its SP editing—
these represent most fairly Crane's usual practice, even though
he may possibly have modified it for this story. Two exceptions
have been made. In the one, on the evidence of C's slip, *State* has
been capitalized. In the other the capitalization of *Senator* in
SP,A1 has been preserved in the belief that, like the capitalization of *General* and of *Colonel* in "The Clan of No-Name," Crane
here had in mind something like the equivalent of a name.
Throughout, the American *Caspar* has been preferred to C's
Casper.

For substantives, as remarked above, the case is quite straightforward that all A1 unique variants must be errors and all
unique SP variants are either compositorial departures from
copy or editorial alteration in the proof. Neither class can be
accepted. The unique C substantive variants from SP,A1 must in
each case—in a far from straightforward process—be judged on
their individual merits as well as on their possible place in a
pattern of alteration. On purely critical and philological grounds,
therefore, the present edition either retains the A1 copy-text

[102] It is worth notice that in " 'God Rest Ye, Merry Gentlemen,' " printed
earlier in the *Post* and in *Cornhill*, military titles are capitalized in SP but not
in C. This agrees with the practice in "The Second Generation." But in " 'God
Rest Ye,' " which seems to have been set in A1 from a proof of C, the titles are
not capitalized. This suggests only that the typescript had capitals for these
titles in "The Second Generation," but it does not reveal whether they were an
original part of the typescript or were editorial markings. In the manuscript of
The O'Ruddy, which is mixed in many characteristics, titles are sometimes
capitalized and sometimes not.

substantives which concur with SP, on the theory that C has strayed from copy, or else evaluates them as SP editorial alteration, in which case the purer readings of the typescript must be restored by emendation from *Cornhill*. The eclectic method attempts, then, to reconstruct from the preserved documents the presumed features of the original basic typescript, which is as far back as one can journey toward the lost Crane manuscript.

One last word may be said about the choice of copy-text. The case for A1 as being set from the retrieved *Post* typescript has fewer difficulties than the hypothesis that, instead, an early stage of the SP proof was used as copy for the book. The latter hypothesis would require the SP editor to have worked over the story extensively in the typescript, and then to have made a number of further changes in the proof which, being set only in revises, were not present in the proof copy passed on to Stokes. Although somewhat more complicated, the latter hypothesis is by no means impossible. If it were to be true, the purist would opt for SP as the copy-text, but with the presumed changes made in the typescript emended by reference to *Cornhill*, and the presumed changes made in the later proof emended by reference to A1, which would be taken as preserving the earlier proof readings. The problem is a nice one and susceptible of varying argument. Given the uncertain situation, however, it may be thought that A1, still, is the superior copy-text. If the hypothesis is correct that, like SP, it was set from the typescript, then it is an acceptable copy-text. On the other hand, even if a doubt remains that A1 might have been set from an early SP proof, a case could still be made for it as copy-text on the grounds that, on the whole, it could preserve more faithfully the characteristics of the typescript copy than the editorially modified SP final setting. This would be a most unusual case, but it would have something to be said in its favor. But the question is in such legitimate doubt that no clear objection seems to hold against the selection of A1 as the most satisfactory compromise copy-text.

IV

SPITZBERGEN TALES

THE KICKING TWELFTH

On January 9, 1900, Pinker wrote to Cora protesting a letter he had received from Crane that he took as a threatened breach of contract and enclosing a statement of unsold stories, among which he placed "three 'Spitzbergen' tales; making together 7,800 words (the British rights of the first has been sold, as you will see from the account)" (*Letters*, p. 260). The first Spitzbergen tale in point of composition, then, as well as in its order of narrative, was "The Kicking Twelfth," here distinguished from the other two of the reference as having been sold in England. As early as January 13, 1899, Conrad had referred to "The Upturned Face" as the story of the "Dead Man" (*Letters*, p. 205) but in terms that made it clear the story was at that time only an idea and very likely with another background; thus this early reference to a Spitzbergen tale is of no service in dating "The Kicking Twelfth." Indeed, the earliest date for any subsequent reference to a Spitzbergen story is November 4, 1899, about eleven months later, when Crane sent to Pinker an unnamed story but one that must be "The Upturned Face," followed by a letter from Cora to Pinker, conjecturally dated November 7, in which she reports Crane's advice to offer it and " 'And If He Wills, We Must Die' " to the *New Magazine* (*Letters*, pp. 238–239, 241). By early November, apparently, the series was complete. According to a letter of January 9, 1900, from Crane to Pinker, the search for a sale of the series in the United States was still continuing, for Crane had been in touch with the London representative of the *New Magazine* and he suggests again to Pinker that "It might be another good place for the Spitzbergen Stories" (*Letters*, p. 261). The first publication of "The Kicking Twelfth" was in the *Pall Mall Magazine*, XX (February, 1900), 173–179. It appeared in the United States, later, in *Ainslee's Magazine*, VI (August, 1900), 46–51,[103] and finally

---

[103] In the *Pall Mall Magazine* (not the *Gazette*, as recorded in the Williams and Starrett *Bibliography*) the story is noted as 'Copyright 1900 by Stephen

in the collection *Last Words* (Digby, Long & Co., 1902), pages 35–52, where the Spitzbergen Tales have a special section. In the New York Public Library is preserved the untitled manuscript, dictated to Edith Richie and inscribed in her hand (including all corrections) on the rectos of six numbered leaves of cheap unwatermarked wove quarto paper 265 × 208 mm., the rules at intervals of 9 mm. On the first leaf, in which the hand is extremely small, the word count for each line is given in the left margin. This manuscript is accompanied by the following letter from Edith Richie Jones to her brother-in-law Mark Barr, dated April 26, 1942, and written on a leaf of stationery headed 10 Tucker Street, Marblehead, Mass.:

> Burning up old letters & papers these days. Among 1000000 others I came across the enclosed. Can you read it? I just have. When you are through with it, tear it up. As far as I can remember, S. Crane dictated it to me as he sprawled on the couch with the dogs in the big hall. Why I wrote it in that tiny script I know not.[104] I must have typed it later. Sometimes in a train or out-doors or in a room he'd say: "Anyone got a pencil & paper? I've just thought of something." Then Cora or I wd write it down & afterwards type it. He rarely altered any of it but seemed to have it all straight in his mind when he began. I have an old magazine somewhere with this story in it. Note the General Richie (after me) & Colonel Sponge (after the dog).
>
> Much love, old Brudder—
Lovingly
E.

Preserved in the Barrett Collection of the University of Virginia Library is a carbon of a typescript, now laminated, of eleven leaves, numbered within spaced parentheses at top center, of foolscap laid paper 325 × 202 mm., with horizontal chainlines and the watermark in gothic lettering 'Britannia | [Britannia's head] | Pure Linen'. This is typed on the Crane typewriter and is now a faded black. The title is in full capitals and followed by a

---

Crane.' No copyright notice is present in *Ainslee's*, where Crane is advertised as 'Author of "The Red Badge of Courage," "The Open Boat," etc., etc.' *Ainslee's* provided a full-page illustration drawn by Charles Grunwald with the legend 'It was running down hill this time. The mob of panting men poured over the stones'.

[104] Actually, only the first leaf is written in a tiny script. Leaves 2–4, 6 follow the ruled paper. Leaf 5, though filling each ruled interval with about two lines, is much larger than the first leaf.

period. The typist was no professional since in the right margin letters and punctuation are often omitted when the measure has been filled. The spelling is English in its use of *-our* endings. An identifying characteristic is the typing of dashes with a single hyphen character, not two or more. The generally correct spelling with only a few lapses and the careful breaking of words at the ends of lines by syllables joins with the distinctive treatment of the dash to indicate that Cora was not the actual typist. However, in black ink in the upper left corner of the first leaf Cora wrote '4200 words' and in Cora's hand under the title (which she underlines) is written 'By | Stephen Crane.'; also in her hand in the upper right corner is '(Spitzbergen Tales)'. In the left margin is a small 'gg' opposite the fifth line from the foot. To the right of the title, in blue crayon, is a large 5. Cora has reviewed the typescript, supplying missing letters and punctuation at the ends of lines in the black ink she used throughout, strengthening weakly typed letters, supplying missing words, strengthening typed deletions, separating run-together words and joining letters with a skip between them, supplying the vertical stroke of exclamation marks over typed periods, and in general preparing the copy for the press. One or two of these alterations are made with a dark pencil, probably as an afterthought. Cora also put the word count for each page within a circle on the verso together with the cumulative count up to 4,191.

As will be indicated below, this typescript is not Edith Richie's nor does it transcribe her manuscript.

Collational evidence suggests that the *Pall Mall Magazine* (PMM) and *Ainslee's Magazine* (AM) versions were set from a typescript and its carbon, presumably the one that had been made up from the Richie manuscript. This typescript seems to have been reviewed by Crane but not seriously revised. In all, twelve substantive variants were made in the typescript as evidenced by the agreement of AM and PMM against MS. Of these, *sped* for MS *hurried* (287.12) is perhaps the clearest authorial change. Several necessary corrections were made. The word *along* omitted in MS at 288.34 is obviously required, and so is a choice at 295.24 between MS *terrible* before *fire* or before *cyclone* (an example of an incomplete MS revision). Probably inadmissible is *advance* for MS *advanced* (296.15); but *clank* for *clink* (290.18), and at 288.8 the addition of *there* before *would sound*, are more typical of Crane than not. At 288.24 the omission of *of* and the substitution of a comma after *name* may well represent an authentic change in the typescript. The rest would seem to be typist's sophistications with small chance of authorial initiative: *or* for *nor* (288.2), *into* for *in* (289.14), *information* for *informations* (291.4), *a great* for *great* (294.11), and *dropped* for *drooped* (295.17).

In substantives PMM differs from AM and MS some twenty-three times. Most of these variants should almost certainly be discarded as the editorial or compositorial styling given by many English magazines, especially to American scripts. It is significant that Crane's typical split infinitive is adjusted at 287.5, and an attempt to adjust another at 288.10 seems to underlie the loss of the word *seriously*. The changes in Crane's indicatives to subjunctives at 293.32, 295.21, and 296.33 and the use of the British collective plural at 294.24 are also obviously none of Crane's doing. However, we must assume that Crane saw proof, and it would seem that the author alone would be responsible for the alteration of *the men came to attention* to *the men wearily adjusted themselves* (296.20–21) that emphasizes a few lines later Colonel Sponge's standing at attention. This being so, other less readily identifiable variants that had passed scrutiny in the original typescript need survey, among which the necessary alteration of *guns* to *horses* (291.17) must have a high place. Although one or two of the rest are useful and could perhaps represent Crane tinkering with his style, the odds seem to favor editorial revision in various details of a text that seemed carelessly written.[105]

[105] For instance, it may be that at 289.7–8 the excision of *in the camp* completes an initially unfinished revision of its position, on the order of the deletion in the typescript of *terrible* at 295.24. The removal of the repeated *But* at 291.5 is necessary, whether authorial or editorial. On the other hand, at 287.21–22 the apparently linked omission in PMM of *in fact* and the change from *transformed* to *transferred*, or the shift at 290.28–29 from *what it would look like* to *how it would look*, might tempt one to assign Crane as the agent were it not for the pervasive influence of the editor elsewhere in somewhat the same smoothing out of careless style, such as *the moment came* for *it came the moment* (288.29); and if this seems authorial, then one could evidence the nonauthorial objection to the MS and AM *back of* that led to the substitution of *behind* at 291.7 and of the British *at the back of* at 292.3. At 287.22 why

Collation of the Barrett typescript reveals the extraordinary fact that it is a copy of the *Pall Mall Magazine* printed text and therefore to be dated after February, 1900, in fact considerably later and at a time when Cora was assembling copy for *Last Words*. The evidence is too definite for any doubt, and the evidence in this typescript may be supported by the typescripts of "The Upturned Face" and "The Shrapnel of Their Friends," all by the same typist and all with the same evidence of derivation from their English magazine publication. The immediately suspicious fact is that PMM has no substantive that is unique in the sense that it is not shared on the one hand by AM or on the other by the Barrett typescript-carbon (TMs^b).[106] If TMs^a, or its carbon TMs^b, had been PMM copy, this fidelity of PMM to its source would be amazing, but TMs^{a-b} could not have been its copy because all of the various omitted words in TMs^b (in which PMM agrees with MS,AM) could scarcely have been supplied by hand in TMs^a, and the direction of the sophistication at 292.3 mentioned in note 106 is not easily reversible. Similarly, TMs agrees with PMM in what appear to be purely typographical variants from the MS,AM norm. What may be a misprint *repositaries* (287.12) is present in both,[107] as is the variant spelling *podgy* for *pudgy* (296.25) and the convention *d——* for *damn* (296.31). Hyphen for hyphen TMs matches the PMM treatment of compounds, and it is equally exact in its correlation of semicolons, of variant paragraphing, and even of the only two times that PMM introduces the unusual colon (*tide:* 293.26; *blood:* 293.36). In fact, fewer than a dozen punctuation variants exist between the two documents. Especially noteworthy is the unusual agreement of three variants in the space of a few words where at 288.30 for AM *cry, "Kim up the Kickers"—there* PMM and TMs read *cry,—"Kim up, the Kickers!"—there*.[108] The sub-

---

transformed should be altered to the less desirable *transferred* except as a misreading is not to be determined; but one can guess that *in fact* was sacrificed because of the chime with preceding *in Rostina* and because the editor thought the phrase superfluous since he missed Crane's purposed irony.

[106] Literally, the PMM variant for MS,AM *back of* is *at the back* (292.3), whereas TMs has *at the backs*; but this is a TMs sophistication of a PMM sophistication and the intention remains the same between the two.

[107] Only possibly a misprint in PMM since it could have been an error in the typescript that was its copy but one that was automatically corrected by AM.

[108] Actually, TMs^a has a period, not an exclamation; but since a period here would be anomalous, it is evident that Cora merely overlooked inserting the

stantive readings, however, settle the direction of derivation, for TMs agrees with every PMM departure from AM—including those assigned to the PMM editor or compositor—even though it is extremely careless in its omissions of words to form unique variants of its own, and in some alterations that are unique.

This typescript came to the Barrett Collection ultimately from Coates in Philadelphia, the proposed American publisher of *Last Words*, and like other typescripts in the Collection was evidently dispatched to Reynolds by Cora for his negotiations first with Stokes and then with Coates. Its ribbon copy (TMs^a) was the printer's copy for the London *Last Words* (E1), the only book edition as it turned out. The readings—including the unique omissions of the typist (also a feature of "The Upturned Face") —demonstrate this fact, but it is useful also to notice the E1 error of a hyphen to form a false compound *wheel-struggled* (291.21) which resulted from the compositor's misunderstanding of a TMs hyphen used as a dash. In view of the trouble that Pinker seems to have had from time to time to secure copies of out-of-date magazines (as in his efforts to secure a copy of "War Memories" to send to Stokes for *Wounds in the Rain*) it would seem that Cora found it more convenient, or cheaper, to have the friendly typist transcribe what was probably her one example of the magazine text of these stories to provide the *Last Words* publishers, both English and American whom she was trying to interest, with their copies. This seems to be a more probable explanation than that she was endeavoring to conceal from them the prior magazine publication of the stories, although this possibility cannot be entirely discarded.

This ordering of the textual transmission of "The Kicking Twelfth" clears the ground of what would otherwise be much confusing substantive variation in the preserved documents. It seems clear that only one manuscript ever existed—the Edith Richie inscription from dictation now deposited in the Berg Collection at NYPL. This has the only basic authority and is the mandatory selection as copy-text.[109] Both the *Ainslee's* and the

---

ink vertical stroke with which elsewhere she completed the exclamations from periods.

[109] It is true that the texture of accidentals, especially in a few spellings, is Edith Richie's, not Crane's. Nevertheless, the highly characteristic light punctuation which is identical with that of his autograph manuscripts suggests that he dictated to her the punctuation as well as the words, and no doubt the capitali-

Pall Mall Magazine versions derive from a lost typescript and its carbon that must have been made from this manuscript. Their concurring substantive variants from MS probably represent Crane's correction of this typescript, although the possibility exists that certain of them could repeat the typist's departure from copy. These seven variants have been incorporated, as authoritative, in the substantive readings of the copy-text as well as a few necessary accidentals corrections of the manuscript. It is assumed that Crane read proof for PMM and that one or two of its distinctive substantive variants are his authoritative alterations that should be adopted but that the vast majority of the PMM differences stem from unauthoritative editorial and compositorial styling. No AM substantive variant from MS can be authoritative, including its odd variant *Spitzenberg*. At this point all authority ceases. Since TMs is only a transcript of PMM made after Crane's death, its variants attest to nothing but the extreme carelessness of the typist in copying substantives (not all repaired by Cora's review) as against the extraordinary care in reproducing the accidentals. The *Last Words* variants from TMs must be taken merely as compositorial errors or else, perhaps in a few cases, as the reproduction of readings that Cora had marked by hand in TMs[a] but not in the Barrett TMs[b].

The present edition is able to reproduce the maximum of accidentals authority from its MS copy-text and to incorporate in its substantives the relatively few alterations from the lost typescript (AM-PMM agreement) and the proof changes Crane is conjectured to have made in PMM so that his final intentions have been recovered as nearly as critical and bibliographical procedure can identify them.

The Upturned Face

The idea for "The Upturned Face" had been in Crane's head as early as January 13, 1899, when Conrad referred to the "Dead Man" as something Crane would need to put aside while "you unload your new experience" (*Letters*, p. 205). Almost eleven

---

zation as well. However, for better or for worse, the accidentals of this manuscript are more authoritative than those of the two magazine prints deriving from the lost typescript made from this manuscript.

months later the story was sent to Pinker, on November 4, 1899, with Crane's usual plug but also the interesting information that he was trying to see if it could not be dramatized as a sketch for Sir Johnston Forbes-Robertson.[110] In a letter conjecturally dated November 7, Cora passed on to Pinker Crane's advice "to offer the New Magazine in New York both the 'Burial' and 'And if He Wills We Must Die' ", and on December 7 she inquired, "You got my word about selling 'The Upturned Face?' " (*Letters*, pp. 241, 248). Although in the United States sale to *Ainslee's* must have been quick (it was the first to be published and presumably the first to be accepted of the three tales that *Ainslee* printed), the English rights took longer. On August 8, 1900, *Black and White* returned the story to Pinker, although accepting "The Shrapnel of Their Friends" (TLS, University of Virginia–Barrett). It was immediately offered to the *Illustrated London News*, whose editor on August 13 queried Pinker: "In the event of our accepting Stephen Crane's story, 'The Up-turned Face', I suppose you would let us have it on the same terms as the last [" 'And If He Wills We Must Die' "], namely three guineas per thousand." At the foot of the letter Pinker wrote: "Yes, the terms for Stephen Crane's story 'The Up-turned Face' shall be the same as for the last. By the way, may I have a cheque for that?" (TLS, Dartmouth). On August 18 the editor returned the story to Pinker with the comment: "I am sorry that the Stephen Crane story

---

[110] The story is not named in the letter but no possibility other than "The Upturned Face" seems to exist. Nothing came of the proposal to Forbes-Robertson. The pertinent part of the letter is as follows: "I am enclosing a double extra special good thing. At the same time I am sending a copy to Forbes Robertson in an attempt to make him see that in a thirty minute sketch on the stage he could so curdle the blood of the British public that it would be the sensation of the year, of the time. As soon as I get word from Robertson I will communicate the word to you but I suppose there is no intermediate reason against sending the story out to magazines since we can always prevent calamity by refusing their terms. These remarks of course apply merely to some difficulty over the copyright in America which would have to be protected in case of a possible rendering by Forbes Robertson appearing before the story was published in America. ¶ I will not disguise from you that I am wonderfully keen on this small bit of 1500 words. It is so good—for me—that I would almost sacrifice it to the best magazine in England rather than see it appear in the best paying magazine. I suppose many men stir you with tumultuous sentiments concerning work which they have just completed but—anyhow take a copy of this story home with you and read it and let me know your opinion. This is something that you do not always do. I can go all over the place and write fiction about almost anything and if you give me a racing tip from time to time it is extremely handy."

"The Up-turned Face" is scarcely likely to support the late author's reputation. I, therefore, return it with many thanks" (TLS, Dartmouth). In an undated letter from Milborne Grove, but probably about mid-September, Cora wrote Pinker, "Please let me know at what price you sold The Upturned Face to the Crystal Palace Magazine" (ALS, Dartmouth). The story is presumably among those referred to in a letter of November 28, 1900, from the solicitor Alfred Plant to Pinker: "Have you any short stories in hand still unpublished? I hear from Mrs Crane that you have sold the Spitzbergen Stories and 'Manacled'. I shall be glad to know what prices you obtained for them." At the bottom Pinker wrote: "I have no unpublished short stories in my possession. You will I think find the amounts received for the stories in the statement rendered" (TLS, Dartmouth).

It would seem that "The Upturned Face" was the last of the four Spitzbergen tales to be written. "The Kicking Twelfth" was almost certainly the story referred to by Pinker as the first (*Letters*, p. 260). In a letter of January 9, 1900, he asks for another copy of "the second Spitzbergen story, 'The Shrapnel of Their Friends'" (*Letters*, p. 261). If the conjectural date of November 7, 1899, is correct for Cora's letter to Pinker asking him to submit the "Burial" and " 'And If He Wills We Must Die' " to the *New Magazine*, then the November 4 letter to Pinker enclosing "The Upturned Face" must imply that " 'And If He Wills' " had been in his hands before that date. The first publication was in *Ainslee's Magazine*, VI (March, 1900), 108–110, followed in England by appearance in the first number of the *Crystal Palace Magazine*, October, 1900, pp. 2–3,[111] and finally in *Last Words* (1902), pages 52–59.

Preserved in the Barrett Collection in the University of Virginia Library is a ribbon typescript in blue ink of "The Upturned Face" on the rectos of six leaves of cheap unwatermarked ruled wove quarto paper 265 × 208 mm., the rules 9 mm. apart. This

---

[111] The volume number of *Ainslee's* is VI, not V as recorded in the Williams and Starrett *Bibliography*. For *Ainslee's* Campbell J. Phillips drew a large illustration with the legend ' "Go to the rear," he said to the wounded man', and he was probably responsible for the unsigned illustrative heading of an officer with helmet removed and bowed head. No copyright notice is given here or in the *Crystal Palace Magazine*. In the latter as part of a decorative title heading it is stated to be a 'New Story by *Stephen Crane*'.

is the same paper used in the Barrett typescript of "A Poker Game" (see *Tales of Adventure*), the Richie manuscript of "The Kicking Twelfth," and the fragment of "The Shrapnel of Their Friends." The leaves are numbered within spaced parentheses centered at the head, the title is in full capitals followed by a period. The typing was done on the Crane typewriter and by the same typist who had copied "The Kicking Twelfth." The same generally correct but not impeccable spelling appears (although there was trouble twice about *aggrieved*), with *-our* endings. Words are broken by syllables at the ends of lines but when the measure was full final letters and punctuation are omitted in the right margin. The same use of the single hyphen for a dash occurs as in "The Kicking Twelfth," but in this typescript a few are typed as two hyphens, and the long dash at the end of suspended speech may be one, two, or three hyphens. This typescript does not resemble the examples that Cora herself seems to have produced. However, Cora in a black ink has underlined the title and beneath it written 'By Stephen Crane.', double underlined. She has also added necessary letters and punctuation in the right margin, separated run-together words by vertical lines, made exclamations from periods, interlined for clarity some words that had been corrected in spelling in the course of typing, and supplied two words omitted by the typist, a third being added later in a dark pencil. This pencil inscribed 'nn' at the foot of the first leaf under the left margin on the final line. A large blue-crayon 10 is written in the upper right corner. Cora wrote on the versos the usual circled word count for each page and the cumulative totals up to 1,450. Vertically, in pencil, on the last verso she added the note: 'The Upturned Face | For book | 1450 words—'.

The two magazine versions are sufficiently close to have been set from the lost typescript and its carbon that would have been made from the manuscript. The several omissions in *Ainslee's* may be accounted for by editorial cuts designed to fit the brief story into three two-columned pages and to make room as well for the large illustration without running a few lines over on a fourth page. As in "The Kicking Twelfth" the Barrett typescript proves to be a copy of the English magazine text made, with its carbon, to serve as printer's copy for the proposed English and

American editions of *Last Words*.[112] The textual situation, with this fact established, becomes simplified. Because of its American typesetting the *Ainslee's* (AM) version has been selected as the copy-text, but it is emended in certain features of the accidentals from the equally authoritative *Crystal Palace Magazine* (CP) when this seems to preserve more faithfully than the sometimes heavy *Ainslee's* styling what may be assumed to be the characteristics of the lost typescript. The cuts in AM are restored on the authority of CP as well. The Barrett typescript (TMs), being a copy of CP, has no authority at all, nor does the *Last Words* text (E1), which was set from the carbon of the Barrett typescript and faithfully reproduces its errors while slightly increasing the textual corruption on its own hook. By combining the most authoritative features of the two magazine versions the present text attempts to reconstruct as nearly as possible from the preserved documents the readings, both in accidentals and in substantives, of the lost typescript that had been the printer's copy.

The Shrapnel of Their Friends

The earliest preserved reference to "The Shrapnel of Their Friends" comes on January 9, 1900, when Pinker in a letter to

---

[112] The evidence of exact concurrence in TMs with what appear to be typographical features of CP is of the same order as that in "The Kicking Twelfth." Significant examples are the comma after the dash following *and* at 299.14 but particularly the agreement at 299.25 in no comma after the dash but in a comma at 299.26. Particularly significant is the agreement in the incorrect *field—Go* (300.7–8) instead of the correct form which would be *field— Go*. Both agree in not setting off *too* at 299.19 with commas, but both do set off *too* at 300.13. (Actually, TMs types the first comma but the second has been supplied by Cora in ink, although it is possible that she is only strengthening a weakly typed comma.) The variants are not reversible. For example, the unique TMs substantive readings at 297.16 and 298.3 are not reproduced in CP, which instead agrees with AM. At 299.11 the CP comma after *death* is wanting in TMs because there was no room in the right margin and Cora missed it in her repair of the typist's omissions. The TMs anomalous period after *you* at 300.8 indicates that Cora forgot to add the vertical stroke of the exclamation that is found in CP, and no doubt this is the reason for the CP exclamation but TMs period after *in* at 298.22. It is interesting to observe that in E1 the comma after *death* is present, whether by compositorial initiative or by Cora's marking of the TMs[b] is uncertain. However, on the evidence of E1 she did not mark either of the two exclamations found in CP at 300.27 or 298.22 which also remain as periods in the Barrett TMs[a].

Cora states that he has three unsold Spitzbergen stories, with the British rights sold for a fourth (the first), and adds, "Can you let me have another copy of the second Spitzbergen story, 'The Shrapnel of Their Friends'?" (*Letters*, pp. 260–261). On August 8, 1900, the editor of *Black and White* accepted the piece in a letter to Pinker: "I beg to acknowledge receipt of your letter dated August 7th, and to accept the story by Mr. Stephen Crane called 'The Shrapnel of His Friends' at the price you mention, namely, three guineas per thousand words for the British and Colonial serial rights. This will appear in our issue of September 29th. I beg to return 'The Upturned Face'" (TLS, University of Virginia–Barrett). In an undated letter from 47 Gower Street, probably in July-August, 1900, Cora inquired of Pinker if the story, among others she was tracing, had been sold in England (ALS, Dartmouth), and later, perhaps in September, 1900, in an undated letter from Milborne Grove whether "Shrapnel" among other stories had been sold serially in England (ALS, Dartmouth).

The first publication was in *Ainslee's Magazine*, V (May, 1900), 303–305, followed by the appearance, previously unrecorded, in *Black and White*, XVII (September, 1900), 490–491,[113] and then in the collection *Last Words* (1902), pages 59–69, where it is the third of the four Spitzbergen Tales.

Preserved in the Columbia University Libraries Special Collections are three leaves, numbered 7, 8, and 9, concluding the story, the text starting with 305.12 of the present edition. This is written in pencil on the rectos of cheap wove unwatermarked ruled paper 265 × 208 mm., the rules 9 mm. apart, which is the same as that used by Edith Richie to write out the manuscript of "The Kicking Twelfth." The story was dictated by Crane, evidently;[114] the scribe could, but need not, have been an

[113] *Ainslee's* records that the story was 'Copyright by Street & Smith. Copyright in Great Britain'; Charles Grunwald provided a full-page illustration with the legend 'But a man screamed. . . . "By God, sir, that is one of our own batteries."' *Black and White* is without copyright notice. W. H. Holloway drew the illustration with the legend 'THE TWELFTH BIVOUACKED ON THE RIDGE'.

[114] One small and uncertain piece of evidence might go contrary to the hypothesis of dictation. The first time *shrapnel* is written (as *Shrapnel*), the *h* is mended over some other letter that just possibly is a *c*. This brings to mind the spelling *schrapnel* in the two Cora letters to Pinker, now preserved at Dartmouth, that inquire about this story. However, it is undemonstrable whether in this spelling Cora, whose spelling was atrocious, was reproducing a Crane misspell-

clxxxiv · Textual Introduction

American: the -or spelling is used for *honor* (306.22) but the *s* for *z* in *apologised* (306.18,20). This unidentified hand also wrote the manuscript of the dramatization of the third chapter of Crane's unfinished Spitzbergen story "The Fire Tribe and the Pale Face" preserved in the Columbia University Libraries Special Collections. The text is so very close to the final form of "The Shrapnel of Their Friends" that it is likely this is the only manuscript that ever existed and that a typescript for publication was made directly from it.[115] Revisions—not all of them *currente calamo* but perhaps made on reading over the manuscript to Crane—appear in pencil in the same hand.

In the Barrett Collection of the University of Virginia Library is preserved a faded black typescript-carbon of seven numbered leaves, now laminated. The paper is laid foolscap, 325 × 202 mm. with horizontal chainlines and the watermark in gothic lettering, 'Britannia | [Britannia's head] | Pure Linen'. This paper is identical with the Barrett typescript of "The Kicking Twelfth." Using the Crane typewriter, the same typist made this carbon as was responsible for "The Kicking Twelfth" and "The Upturned Face." As with the other typescripts, Cora went over the text in black ink and later in pencil to prepare it for the printer by

---

ing (inadvertently followed for a moment by the scribe of the present manuscript) or was inventing one of her own, as is more likely. In favor of dictation is not only the example of "The Kicking Twelfth" and of other manuscripts but also the internal evidence of the "Shrapnel" manuscript, such as it is. Most of the changes by the scribe seem to have been made on review. But two were definitely current and indicate dictation, since otherwise one would need to suppose that the scribe was himself altering a manuscript he was copying, and in a major way. The clearest-cut case comes at 305.32, where a period was initially inscribed after *Richie* but then the following *in* of the continuation was written over it. At 305.21 after *and one* the scribe first wrote down *fo* (query: the start of *following*) but then deleted the two letters and wrote *burst*, only to delete that and continue with *flung*.

[115] For example, AM repeats (without the intrusive comma) the unusual dash after *frankly* in MS *But the men of the battery told the Kickers to go to the devil—frankly,—freely, placidly, told the Kickers to go to the devil* (306.34), whereas BW makes the adverbs into a series of three with only the one dash after *devil*. It is difficult to conceive of Crane really intending the *frankly*, in its position, modifying only the first *told* and then the two adverbs *freely*, *placidly* modifying only the second. It may be that as he first thought of the phrases he intended each to be followed by a dash but changed his intention after the first. At any rate, the typescript, on the evidence of AM, must have followed the manuscript anomaly, but the BW editor or compositor properly turned the adverbs into a conventional series of three, which appears to reflect the original intention.

strengthening uncertain letters, adding missing letters and punctuation omitted in the right margin, separating run-together words and joining skips, strengthening typed-out deletions, making exclamations of periods, and adding missing words. She underlined the title and wrote beneath it 'By | Stephen Crane.', with a double underline. A torn-off corner at the upper left preserves of the word count, in pencil, only the figures 575. In the upper right corner Cora wrote in the black ink '(Spitzbergen Tale.)'. In the left margin of the first leaf, opposite the last line, is a miniscule *g* in black ink repeated below in pencil. To the right of the title is a large blue-crayon figure 9. The versos of the leaves are blank, without the customary word count.

The *Ainslee's Magazine* (AM) text and the *Black and White* (BW) appear to have been set from a lost typescript and its carbon, which is not the Barrett document. On the evidence of the preserved three leaves of manuscript from which this typescript was conjecturally made without intermediary, the typescript fell into a few errors that were not detected, such as the plural *eyes* for *eye* (305.27), and the singular *wrong* for *wrongs* (306.20). However, it was very slightly revised on review as in the substitution of *decoration* for *Order* (306.26), and at least one of its errors—*nearer* for *near* (306.23)—was corrected. The status of the omission of MS *shell* at 305.16 is uncertain. The AM text made a serious eyeskip at 305.16–18, sophisticated a reading or two like *wag-wig* (303.25), and fell into a few misreadings or memorial errors like *steps* for *steeps* (304.35) and *streamed* for *streaked* (305.21). Unless a few other variants are AM errors—a proposition that for at least two does not seem likely—before his death Crane must have made an alteration or two in the typescript copy that was later to be used by *Black and White*, notably the substitution of *a good* for *an* (301.8) and *at that time* (301.11–12).[116] The omission of *otherwise* (301.19) in BW and of *too* (302.3) are taken to be BW errors, as is *died* for *dived* (302.32). BW almost certainly sophisticated *sat* to *sat on* (303.14), but the status of its substitution of *the* for *its* (304.10) is less certain in the absence of the manuscript.

As in the Barrett typescript of "The Kicking Twelfth" and "The

---

[116] Conjecturally these could have been altered when Pinker requested the second copy of the story on January 9, 1900 (*Letters*, p. 261).

Upturned Face," the typescript-carbon (TMs[b]) of "The Shrapnel of Their Friends" represents a transcript of the English magazine version: the faithful reproduction of variant details that seem to have originated in the typescript that was the printer's copy [117] or are typographical in origin is the same and needs no further rehearsal. It is, once more, significant that BW has no substantive variant from joint TMs,AM as would be almost inevitable if TMs had had an independent origin, although TMs makes the usual errors in its transcript of BW. The printer's copy for *Last Words* (E1) was quite definitely the ribbon copy (TMs[a]) of the Barrett carbon. Certain of the changes that Cora made in TMs[b], principally in the later pencil, could not have been present in TMs[a]. For instance, she interlined in TMs[b] *that* for *and* (301.7), but E1 prints the original *and*; she added a *d* to TMs[b] *jingle*, but E1 prints *jingle* (303.4). Various errors were missed, like *carefully* for *cheerfully* (304.2); others were manufactured: at 301.25 the typist had come to the end of the line with *rejoic* and Cora, not checking MS, guessed wrongly by adding *ing* instead of *ed* and E1 follows her error. At 304.10 in TMs[b] she corrected Crane's false grammar *laid* by interlining *lay*, but this was a too late interposition since all texts, including E1, read *laid*.[118] In the course of its typesetting E1 produced a few minor further corruptions of the text.

Because of its American typesetting, *Ainslee's* has been chosen as the copy-text throughout. However, when *Black and White* seems to preserve more faithfully than AM the presumed accidentals of the underlying typescript, emendations have been made from this equal authority. When MS is available it is used to emend the AM texture on the assumption that Crane was generally inclined to dictate punctuation and paragraphing as well as words. (The concurrence of AM,BW in some commas not found in MS indicates that the typescript was more heavily styled than the manuscript, but of course without any demonstra-

[117] For instance, if the typescript followed the manuscript, it would have capitalized military titles. Both AM and BW reduce these to lower case except at 302.6,7, where BW, followed by TMs, prints *General*, contrasting with *general* —also followed by TMs—at 303.11.
[118] The single difficulty comes at 301.17, where the typist had originally written *feelings* but then deleted the final *s* with a typed slant, yet E1 prints the plural. One can only speculate that the E1 compositor (who could readily see the *s* under the slant) preferred the rejected plural.

ble authority.) The capitalization system of MS is not acceptable, however, because in capitalizing such words as *Shrapnel* and consistently capitalizing military titles it seems to go contrary to the general practice of these Spitzbergen stories as indicated in the various magazine prints and in the Richie manuscript—and perhaps even in the typescript made from this "Shrapnel" manuscript except for the possible slip at 302.6,7 (unless, on the evidence of *Infantry* at 301.4 we must take it that BW like AM restyled the capitals present throughout the typescript).

In the substantives the occasionally more correct readings of BW are substituted for AM errors, and the two BW readings conjecturally representing later revision in the copy are accepted. The general intent of the present text is to reconstruct as closely as possible the lost copy of the typescript used by the AM and BW printers, but when MS is available this reconstructed typescript in certain respects of accidentals and of substantives yields to what is taken to be the superior authority on the whole of the manuscript. The text, then, is an eclectic one, constructed from a choice of variants between two equal authorities; but in its latter part beginning with 305.12 utilizing the readings of three authorities with considerable reliance on the manuscript.

"AND IF HE WILLS, WE MUST DIE"

The first that is heard of " 'And If He Wills, We Must Die' " is in a letter conjecturally dated November 7, 1899, in which Cora passes on to Pinker Crane's advice "to offer to the New Magazine in New York both the 'Burial' and 'And if He Wills We Must Die' " (*Letters*, p. 241). As of January 9, 1900, Pinker had not sold the story (*Letters*, p. 260). In an undated letter, probably written in September, 1900, Cora from 6 Milborne Grove asks if " 'And If He Wills' " as well as "The Shrapnel of Their Friends" have been sold serially in England and to whom (ALS, Dartmouth). On August 25, 1900, Nops Electrotyping Agency wrote to Pinker requesting him to set a fee for a Norwegian translation. Pinker originally wrote at the foot, "I would suggest five guineas", but then altered it to read "Mrs Crane suggests five guineas" (TLS, University of Virginia–Barrett). Finally, when

Reynolds and Cora were assembling material for the proposed American edition of *Last Words*, the title appears in a list of stories of which he had copies, as he wrote her on October 23, 1900 (TLS, Columbia). The first publication was in the *Illustrated London News*, CXVII (July 28, 1900), 121–122, reappearing without change also in the issue for August 11, 1900, pages 185–186. This was followed by American publication in *Frank Leslie's Popular Monthly*, L (October, 1900), 533–538,[119] and then by collection in *Last Words* (1902), pages 69–78, as the last of the Spitzbergen section.

In the Barrett Collection of the University of Virginia Library is a typescript of eight leaves made with the Crane typewriter on cheap wove unwatermarked ruled quarto paper 265 × 208 mm., the rules 9 mm. apart. This is the same paper as the Barrett typescript of "The Upturned Face." The title is typed in caps and lower case, ' "And if He Wills, we must die." ', and has a line of dashes a double space below. The foliation is in unspaced parentheses centered at the top. Some final letters are missing in the right margin, and letters may be x'd out there that had started a word not conveniently to be broken at the margin. The highly uncertain spelling suggests that Cora was the typist. In black ink Cora signed the story 'By Stephen Crane' on the line of dashes and she placed the word count 2,178 at the upper left. In the left margin at the foot of the first leaf appears a miniscule *o*. A black-crayon figure 2 is in the upper right corner. Cora reviewed the typing and in black ink and then in dark pencil she supplied missing letters and punctuation in the right margin, made periods into exclamations, separated run-together words, strengthened weakly typed letters, and altered a few words. The final line of text that runs over on folio 8 is supplied with page number in handwriting. No word count appears on the versos, but on the verso of the last leaf is written 'for book in U.S.'

119 For the *News* Ernest Sherie drew an illustrative title showing Johnston's dead body hanging from the window and two large illustrations with the legends, 'In returning he came to a sentry, Jones, munching an apple. He sternly commanded him to throw it away' and 'Then he entered and stood across the body of Knowles, and fired vigorously into a group of charming plum-trees'. No copyright notice is present here or in *Leslie's*. F. P. Klitz drew for *Leslie's* two illustrations with the legends, ' "A NICE PAIR!" SAID THE SERGEANT' and 'A YOUNG SUBALTERN OF THE ENEMY'S INFANTRY . . . BURST INTO THIS REEKING INTERIOR'. An illustrative tailpiece shows the dead Hussar lying beside the road,

Cora must have attempted to make an accurate copy even though she fell short of the mark. One paraphrase, a fault to which she seems to have been prone, she caught and altered in the typing: at 307.8 after *arduous* she typed *duty* but then deleted it before carrying on with *mission*. Several others she noticed during her review, which—even though imperfectly—must have involved some manner of collation. At 307.9 in ink she added *ed* with a caret to *damn*, deleted *it was* before *possible* at 307.10, and at 312.19 deleted *fell* and interlined *dropped* with a caret. Her review also picked up other errors. In pencil she substituted *face* for *force* at 308.31, and *whose* for *who's* at 307.7. She began the typing with the spelling *sergent* but at 308.6 went over to *sergeant* and then at 308.22 (with only one lapse at 309.37) to *serjeant*, which seems to have been Crane's spelling. The misspelling in the opening words of the story had also included a failure to space *Asergent*. In ink she interlined *A serjeant*, but the other *sergent* misspellings she was content to mend by the simple interlineation of an *a* with a caret.

The *Illustrated London News* (ILN) and *Leslie's Monthly* (FL) texts were set from a different typescript and its carbon. The major source of substantive variation is the cutting, with some bridgework, engaged in by the *Leslie's* editor to make enough room for the illustrative tailpiece. The lost typescript and its carbon had one certain error, *spilling* for *spitting* (309.35). Whether other variants from the Barrett typescript (TMs) such as ILN,FL *as* for TMs *as if* (310.9) or *that* for *who* (311.14) are TMs errors or mistakes in the typescript that was printer's copy for ILN and FL is not demonstrable.

Unlike the three other Barrett typescripts of the Spitzbergen stories sent to Reynolds for *Last Words*, this one is not a copy of the English magazine publication; moreover, it is also by a different typist. Since "The Upturned Face" had been typed out from the *Crystal Palace Magazine* as late as October, 1900—if not from a proof—the fact that " 'And If He Wills' " was not published until late July might not have been an overriding consideration. Some factor connected with the typist perhaps dictated the difference, and it is perhaps not wholly by chance that this story, with its different typescript, is the only one of the Spitzbergen group for which Reynolds had a copy on October 23,

1900. At any rate, Cora seems to have used the original manuscript in making up this typescript for *Last Words*: in various respects the punctuation system is closer to Crane's, and it is possible that some of the readings were merely faithful renditions of copy, such as the spelling *serjeant* that she finally adopted instead of her own initial preference, or the appearance of Crane's typical error *who's* for *whose*.

If this is so, the Barrett typescript has equal authority with the two magazine texts in respect to substantives, and theoretically superior authority in respect to the accidentals since it is only one step removed from the manuscript instead of two. Hence the variants between the two lines of the text deserve careful scrutiny. The censorship imposed by the magazines on the profanity is obvious enough. The one or two neutral variants provide insufficient evidence for anything but opinion.[120] The chief differences between the magazine texts and TMs lie in the number of words that are omitted in TMs (or added in the lost typescript, or both). That Cora was prone to omissions is clear from 308.14–15 in which TMs is wanting the parenthetical clause *here the serjeant wrathfully imitated the voice of his captain*— although its presence in the manuscript is attested to by the vestigial double quotes after *say* and the succeeding dash. The two-sentence omission in TMs at 308.26–27 could be an eyeskip since the sentence just before it had also ended with *barracks*. These examples of carelessness in full transcription, then, do not promote confidence in her accuracy when single words are in question, like the omission of *casually* (307.13), *much* (308.32), *little* (309.24), *charming* (311.7), or *stealthy* (312.3). However, the evidence is insufficiently clear for anyone to try to distinguish TMs errors from alterations made in the lost typescript before it and its carbon were sent off for sale.

Because of its conjectural closeness to the manuscript, the Barrett typescript becomes the copy-text. This choice is not the most convenient one since it entails a larger than usual list of emendations because of TMs imperfections. It is also true that the virtues of TMs could be adequately preserved by emendation

---

[120] That is, on the evidence of 307.10 and her own deletion of the intrusive *it was*, perhaps *as if* for *as* at 310.9 is an equally unconscious expansion that she did not notice on review, and likewise perhaps *a dangerous* for *dangerous* at 307.30.

from them of another copy-text, like *Leslie's*, at a considerable saving in the number of recorded alterations. But if FL were chosen as copy-text, the unique qualities of the TMs would be lost in their details since most would not be of the kind that are recorded in the Historical Collation. Since it is evident that on some occasions Cora typed Crane's manuscripts from early 1899 on, and hence that his text in the preserved printed documents may sometimes have been transmitted through her, it may be well in some place to record completely the characteristics of one of her typescripts in comparison with the printed versions. The present is as good a place as any. The errors of TMs have been corrected by adoption of certain joint readings of FL and ILN, which must represent the lost typescript, with due regard for the possibility of error originating in this document and perpetuated in the magazines. (Since the *Last Words* version [E1] was set from the carbon of Cora's typescript it has no authority whatever.) The text in the present edition by these eclectic means attempts a partial reconstruction of the lost manuscript, but it also is calculated to include any substantive alterations that might have been made in the lost typescript that derived from this manuscript before it and its carbon were released for sale to English and American magazines.

F. B.

The Little Regiment

THE LITTLE REGIMENT

I

THE fog made the clothes of the column of men in the roadway seem of a luminous quality. It imparted to the heavy infantry overcoats a new color, a kind of blue which was so pale that a regiment might have been merely a long, low shadow in the mist. However, a muttering, one part grumble, three parts joke, hovered in the air above the thick ranks, and blended in an undertoned roar, which was the voice of the column.

The town on the southern shore of the little river loomed spectrally, a faint etching upon the grey cloud-masses which were shifting with oily languor. A long row of guns upon the northern bank had been pitiless in their hatred, but a little battered belfry could be dimly seen still pointing with invincible resolution toward the heavens.

The enclouded air vibrated with noises made by hidden colossal things. The infantry tramplings, the heavy rumbling of the artillery, made the earth speak of gigantic preparation. Guns on distant heights thundered from time to time with sudden nervous roar, as if unable to endure in silence a knowledge of hostile troops massing, other guns going to position. These sounds, near and remote, defined an immense battle-ground, described the tremendous width of the stage of the prospective drama. The voice of the guns, slightly casual, unexcited in their challenges and warnings, could not destroy the unutterable eloquence of the word in the air, a meaning of impending struggle which made the breath halt at the lips.

The column in the roadway was ankle-deep in mud. The men swore piously at the rain which drizzled upon them, compelling them to stand always very erect in fear of the drops that would sweep in under their coat-collars. The fog was as cold as wet clothes. The men stuffed their hands deep in their pockets and huddled their muskets in their arms. The machinery of orders had rooted these soldiers deeply into the mud precisely as almighty nature roots mullein stalks.

They listened and speculated when a tumult of fighting came from the dim town across the river. When the noise lulled for a time, they resumed their descriptions of the mud and graphically exaggerated the number of hours they had been kept waiting. The general commanding their division rode along the ranks, and they cheered admiringly, affectionately, crying out to him gleeful prophecies of the coming battle. Each man scanned him with a peculiarly keen personal interest, and afterward spoke of him with unquestioning devotion and confidence, narrating anecdotes which were mainly untrue.

When the jokers lifted the shrill voices which invariably belonged to them, flinging witticisms at their comrades, a loud laugh would sweep from rank to rank, and soldiers who had not heard would lean forward and demand repetition. When were borne past them some wounded men with grey and blood-smeared faces, and eyes that rolled in that helpless beseeching for assistance from the sky which comes with supreme pain, the soldiers in the mud watched intently, and from time to time asked of the bearers an account of the affair. Frequently they bragged of their corps, their division, their brigade, their regiment. Anon, they referred to the mud and the cold drizzle. Upon this threshold of a wild scene of death they, in short, defied the proportion of events with that splendor of heedlessness which belongs only to veterans.

"Like a lot of wooden soldiers," swore Billie Dempster, moving his feet in the thick mass, and casting a vindictive glance indefinitely; "standing in the mud for a hundred years."

"Oh, shut up!" murmured his brother Dan. The manner of his words implied that this fraternal voice near him was an indescribable bore.

"Why should I shut up?" demanded Billie.

"Because you're a fool," cried Dan, taking no time to debate it; "the biggest fool in the regiment."

There was but one man between them, and he was habituated. These insults from brother to brother had swept across his chest, flown past his face, many times during two long campaigns.

Upon this occasion he simply grinned first at one, then at the other.

The way of these brothers was not an unknown topic in regimental gossip. They had enlisted simultaneously, with each sneering loudly at the other for doing it. They left their little town and went forward with the flag, exchanging protestations of undying suspicion. In the camp life they so openly despised each other that when entertaining quarrels were lacking, their companions often contrived situations calculated to bring forth display of this fraternal dislike.

Both were large-limbed, strong young men, and often fought with friends in camp unless one was near to interfere with the other. This latter happened rather frequently, because Dan, preposterously willing for any manner of combat, had a very great horror of seeing Billie in a fight; and Billie, almost odiously ready himself, simply refused to see Dan stripped to his shirt and with his fists aloft. This sat queerly upon them, and made them the objects of plots.

When Dan would jump through a ring of eager soldiers and drag forth his raving brother by the arm, a thing often predicted would almost come to pass. When Billie performed the same office for Dan, the prediction would again miss fulfilment by an inch. But indeed they never fought together, although they were perpetually upon the verge.

They expressed longing for such conflict. As a matter of truth, they had at one time made full arrangement for it, but even with the encouragement and interest of half of the regiment they somehow failed to achieve collision.

If Dan became a victim of police duty, no jeering was so destructive to the feelings as Billie's comment. If Billie got a call to appear at the headquarters, none would so genially prophesy his complete undoing as Dan. Small misfortunes to one were, in truth, invariably greeted with hilarity by the other, who seemed to see in them great reënforcement of his opinion.

As soldiers, they expressed each for each a scorn intense and blasting. After a certain battle, Billie was promoted to corporal. When Dan was told of it, he seemed smitten dumb with astonishment and patriotic indignation. He stared in silence, while the dark blood rushed to Billie's forehead, and he shifted his weight from foot to foot. Dan at last found his tongue, and said: "Well, I'm derned!" If he had heard that an army mule had been appointed to the post of corps commander, his tone could not have had more derision in it. Afterward, he adopted a fervid insubordination, an almost religious reluctance to obey the new corporal's orders, which came near to developing the desired strife.

It is here finally to be recorded also that Dan, most ferociously profane in speech, very rarely swore in the presence of his brother; and that Billie, whose oaths came from his lips with the grace of falling pebbles, was seldom known to express himself in this manner when near his brother Dan.

At last the afternoon contained a suggestion of evening. Metallic cries rang suddenly from end to end of the column. They inspired at once a quick, business-like adjustment. The long thing stirred in the mud. The men had hushed and were looking across the river. A moment later the shadowy mass of pale-blue figures was moving steadily toward the stream. There could be heard from the town a clash of swift fighting and cheering. The noise of the shooting coming through the heavy air had its sharpness taken from it, and sounded in thuds.

There was a halt upon the bank above the pontoons. When the column went winding down the incline, and streamed out upon the bridge, the fog had faded to a great degree, and in the clearer dusk the guns on a distant ridge were enabled to perceive the crossing. The long whirling outcries of the shells came into the air above the men. An occasional solid shot struck the surface of the river and dashed into view a sudden vertical jet. The distance was subtly illuminated by the lightning from the deep-booming guns. One by one the batteries on the northern shore aroused, the innumerable guns bellowed in angry oration at the distant ridge. The rolling thunder crashed and reverberated as a wild surf sounds on a still night, and to this music the column marched across the pontoons.

The waters of the grim river curled away in a smile from the ends of the great boats, and slid swiftly beneath the planking. The dark, riddled walls of the town upreared before the troops, and from a region hidden by these hammered and tumbled houses came incessantly the yells and firings of a prolonged and close skirmish.

When Dan had called his brother a fool, his voice had been so decisive, so brightly assured, that many men had laughed, considering it to be great humor under the circumstances. The incident happened to rankle deep in Billie. It was not any strange thing that his brother had called him a fool. In fact, he often called him a fool with exactly the same amount of cheerful and prompt conviction, and before large audiences, too. Billie wondered in his own mind why he took such profound offence in this case; but, at any rate, as he slid down the bank and on to the bridge with his regiment, he was searching his knowledge for something that would pierce Dan's blithesome spirit. But he could contrive nothing at this time, and his impotency made the glance which he was once able to give his brother still more malignant.

The guns far and near were roaring a fearful and grand introduction for this column which was marching upon the stage of death. Billie felt it, but only in a numb way. His heart was cased in that curious dissonant metal which covers a man's emotions at such times. The terrible voices from the hills told him that in this wide conflict his life was an insignificant fact, and that his death would be an insignificant fact. They portended the whirlwind to which he would be as necessary as a waved butterfly's wing. The solemnity, the sadness of it came near enough to make him wonder why he was neither solemn nor sad. When his mind vaguely adjusted events according to their importance to him, it appeared that the uppermost thing was the fact that upon the eve of battle, and before many comrades, his brother had called him a fool.

Dan was in a particularly happy mood. "Hurray! Look at 'em shoot," he said, when the long witches' croon of the shells came into the air. It enraged Billie when he felt the little thorn in him, and saw at the same time that his brother had completely forgotten.

The column went from the bridge into more mud. At this southern end there was a chaos of hoarse directions and commands. Darkness was coming upon the earth, and regiments were being hurried up the slippery bank. As Billie floundered in the black mud, amid the swearing, sliddering crowd, he suddenly resolved that, in the absence of other means of hurting Dan, he would avoid looking at him, refrain from speaking to him, pay absolutely no heed to his existence; and this done skilfully would, he imagined, soon reduce his brother to a poignant sensitiveness.

At the top of the bank the column again halted and rearranged itself, as a man after a climb rearranges his clothing. Presently the great steel-backed brigade, an infinitely graceful thing in the rhythm and ease of its veteran movement, swung up a little narrow, slanting street.

Evening had come so swiftly that the fighting on the remote borders of the town was indicated by thin flashes of flame. Some building was on fire, and its reflection upon the clouds was an oval of delicate pink.

II

All demeanor of rural serenity had been wrenched violently from the little town by the guns and by the waves of men which had surged through it. The hand of war laid upon this village had in an instant changed it to a thing of remnants. It resembled the place of a monstrous shaking of the earth itself. The windows, now mere unsightly holes, made the tumbled and blackened dwellings seem skeletons. Doors lay splintered to fragments. Chimneys had flung their bricks everywhere. The artillery fire had not neglected the rows of gentle shade-trees which had lined the streets. Branches and heavy trunks cluttered the mud in driftwood tangles, while a few shattered forms had contrived to remain dejectedly, mournfully upright. They expressed an innocence, a helplessness, which perforce created a pity for their happening into this cauldron of battle. Furthermore, there was under foot a vast collection of odd things reminiscent of the charge, the fight, the retreat. There were boxes and barrels filled with earth, behind which riflemen had lain snugly, and in these little trenches were the dead in blue with the dead in grey, the poses eloquent of the struggles for possession of the town until the history of the whole conflict was written plainly in the streets.

And yet the spirit of this little city, its quaint individuality, poised in the air above the ruins, defying the guns, the sweeping volleys; holding in contempt those avaricious blazes which had attacked many dwellings. The hard earthen side-walks proclaimed the games that had been played there during long lazy days, in the careful shadows of the trees. "General Merchandise," in faint letters upon a long board, had to be read with a slanted glance, for the board dangled by one end; but the porch of the old store was a palpable legend of wide-hatted men, smoking.

This subtle essence, this soul of the life that had been, brushed like invisible wings the thoughts of the men in the swift columns that came up from the river.

In the darkness a loud and endless humming arose from the great blue clouds bivouacked in the streets. From time to time a sharp spatter of firing from far picket lines entered this bass chorus. The smell from the smouldering ruins floated on the cold night breeze.

Dan, seated ruefully upon the doorstep of a shot-pierced house, was proclaiming the campaign badly managed. Orders had been issued forbidding camp-fires.

Suddenly he ceased his oration, and scanning the group of his comrades, said: "Where's Billie? Do you know?"

"Gone on picket."

"Get out! Has he?" said Dan. "No business to go on picket. Why don't some of them other corporals take their turn?"

A bearded private was smoking his pipe of confiscated tobacco, seated comfortably upon a horse-hair trunk which he had dragged from the house. He observed: "Was his turn."

"No such thing," cried Dan. He and the man on the horse-hair trunk held discussion, in which Dan stoutly maintained that if his brother had been sent on picket it was an injustice. He ceased his argument when another soldier, upon whose arms could faintly be seen the two stripes of a corporal, entered the circle. "Humph," said Dan, "where you been?"

The corporal made no answer. Presently Dan said: "Billie, where you been?"

His brother did not seem to hear these inquiries. He glanced at the house which towered above them, and remarked casually to the man on the horse-hair trunk: "Funny, ain't it? After the pelting this town got, you'd think there wouldn't be one brick left on another."

"Oh," said Dan, glowering at his brother's back. "Getting mighty smart, ain't you?"

The absence of camp-fires allowed the evening to make apparent its quality of faint silver light in which the blue clothes of the throng became black, and the faces became white expanses, void of expression. There was considerable excitement a short distance from the group around the doorstep. A soldier had chanced upon a hoop-skirt, and arrayed in it he was performing a dance amid the applause of his companions. Billie and a greater part of the men immediately poured over there to witness the exhibition.

"What's the matter with Billie?" demanded Dan of the man upon the horse-hair trunk.

"How do I know?" rejoined the other in mild resentment. He arose and walked away. When he returned he said briefly, in a weather-wise tone, that it would rain during the night.

Dan took a seat upon one end of the horse-hair trunk. He was facing the crowd around the dancer, which in its hilarity swung this way and that way. At times he imagined that he could recognize his brother's face.

He and the man on the other end of the trunk thoughtfully talked of the army's position. To their minds, infantry and artillery were in a most precarious jumble in the streets of the town; but they did not grow nervous over it, for they were used to having the army appear in a precarious jumble to their minds. They had learned to accept such puzzling situations as a consequence of their position in the ranks, and were now usually in possession of a simple but perfectly immovable faith that somebody understood the jumble. Even if they had been convinced that the army was a headless monster, they would merely have nodded with the veteran's singular cynicism. It was none of their business as soldiers. Their duty was to grab sleep and food when occasion permitted, and cheerfully fight wherever their feet were planted, until more orders came. This was a task sufficiently absorbing.

They spoke of other corps, and this talk being confidential, their voices dropped to tones of awe. "The Ninth"—"The First"—

"The Fifth"—"The Sixth"—"The Third"—the simple numerals rang with eloquence, each having a meaning which was to float through many years as no intangible arithmetical mist, but as pregnant with individuality as the names of cities.

Of their own corps they spoke with a deep veneration, an idolatry, a supreme confidence which apparently would not blanch to see it matched against everything.

It was as if their respect for other corps was due partly to a wonder that organizations not blessed with their own famous numeral could take such an interest in war. They could prove that their division was the best in the corps, and that their brigade was the best in the division. And their regiment—it was plain that no fortune of life was equal to the chance which caused a man to be born, so to speak, into this command, the proud keystone of the defending arch.

At times Dan covered with insults the character of a vague unnamed general to whose petulance and busy-body spirit he ascribed the order which made hot coffee impossible.

Dan said that victory was certain in the coming battle. The other man seemed rather dubious. He remarked upon the fortified line of hills which had impressed him even from the other side of the river. "Shucks," said Dan. "Why, we——" He pictured a splendid overflowing of these hills by the sea of men in blue. During the period of this conversation Dan's glance searched the merry throng about the dancer. Above the babble of voices in the street a far-away thunder could sometimes be heard—evidently from the very edge of the horizon—the boom-boom of restless guns.

III

Ultimately the night deepened to the tone of black velvet. The outlines of the fireless camp were like the faint drawings upon ancient tapestry. The glint of a rifle, the shine of a button might have been of threads of silver and gold sewn upon the fabric of the night. There was little presented to the vision, but to a sense more subtle there was discernible in the atmosphere something like a pulse; a mystic beating which would have told a stranger of the presence of a giant thing—the slumbering mass of regiments and batteries.

With fires forbidden, the floor of a dry old kitchen was thought to be a good exchange for the cold earth of December, even if a shell had exploded in it and knocked it so out of shape that when a man lay curled in his blanket his last waking thought was likely to be of the wall that bellied out above him as if strongly anxious to topple upon the score of soldiers.

Billie looked at the bricks ever about to descend in a shower upon his face, listened to the industrious pickets plying their rifles on the border of the town, imagined some measure of the din of the coming battle, thought of Dan and Dan's chagrin, and, rolling over in his blanket, went to sleep with satisfaction.

At an unknown hour he was aroused by the creaking of boards. Lifting himself upon his elbow, he saw a sergeant prowling among the sleeping forms. The sergeant carried a candle in an old brass candlestick. He would have resembled some old farmer on an unusual midnight tour if it were not for the significance of his gleaming buttons and striped sleeves.

Billie blinked stupidly at the light until his mind returned from the journeys of slumber. The sergeant stooped among the unconscious soldiers, holding the candle close, and peering into each face.

"Hello, Haines," said Billie. "Relief?"

"Hello, Billie," said the sergeant. "Special duty."

"Dan got to go?"

"Jameson, Hunter, McCormack, D. Dempster. Yes. Where is he?"

"Over there by the winder," said Billie, gesturing. "What is it for, Haines?"

"You don't think I know, do you?" demanded the sergeant. He began to pipe sharply but cheerily at men upon the floor. "Come, Mac, get up here. Here's a special for you. Wake up, Jameson. Come along, Dannie, me boy."

Each man at once took this call to duty as a personal affront. They pulled themselves out of their blankets, rubbed their eyes, and swore at whoever was responsible. "Them's orders," cried the sergeant. "Come! Get out of here." An undetailed head with dishevelled hair thrust out from a blanket, and a sleepy voice said: "Shut up, Haines, and go home."

When the detail clanked out of the kitchen, all but one of the remaining men seemed to be again asleep. Billie, leaning on his elbow, was gazing into darkness. When the footsteps died to silence, he curled himself into his blanket.

At the first cool lavender lights of daybreak he aroused again and scanned his recumbent companions. Seeing a wakeful one he asked: "Is Dan back yet?"

The man said: "Hain't seen 'im."

Billie put both hands behind his head and scowled into the air. "Can't see the use of these cussed details in the night-time," he muttered in his most unreasonable tones. "Darn nuisances. Why can't they——" He grumbled at length and graphically.

When Dan entered with the squad, however, Billie was convincingly asleep.

IV

The regiment trotted in double time along the street, and the colonel seemed to quarrel over the right of way with many artillery officers. Batteries were waiting in the mud, and the men of them, exasperated by the bustle of this ambitious infantry, shook their fists from saddle and caisson, exchanging all manner of taunts and jests. The slanted guns continued to look reflectively at the ground.

On the outskirts of the crumbled town a fringe of blue figures were firing into the fog. The regiment swung out into skirmish lines, and the fringe of blue figures departed, turning their backs and going joyfully around the flank.

The bullets began a low moan off toward a ridge which loomed faintly in the heavy mist. When the swift crescendo had reached its climax, the missiles zipped just overhead, as if piercing an invisible curtain. A battery on the hill was crashing with such tumult that it was as if the guns had quarrelled and had fallen pell-mell and snarling upon each other. The shells howled on their journey toward the town. From short-range distance there came a spatter of musketry, sweeping along an invisible line and making faint sheets of orange light.

Some in the new skirmish lines were beginning to fire at various shadows discerned in the vapor, forms of men suddenly revealed by some humor of the laggard masses of clouds. The crackle of musketry began to dominate the purring of the hostile bullets. Dan, in the front rank, held his rifle poised, and looked into the fog keenly, coldly, with the air of a sportsman. His nerves were so steady that it was as if they had been drawn from his body, leaving him merely a muscular machine; but his numb heart was somehow beating to the pealing march of the fight.

The waving skirmish line went backward and forward, ran this way and that way. Men got lost in the fog, and men were found again. Once they got too close to the formidable ridge, and the thing burst out as if repulsing a general attack. Once another blue regiment was apprehended on the very edge of firing into them. Once a friendly battery began an elaborate and scientific process of extermination. Always as busy as brokers, the men slid here and there over the plain, fighting their foes, escaping from their friends, leaving a history of many movements in the wet yellow turf, damning the atmosphere, blazing away every time they could identify the enemy.

In one mystic changing of the fog, as if the fingers of spirits were drawing aside these draperies, a small group of the grey skirmishers, silent, statuesque, were suddenly disclosed to Dan and those about him. So vivid and near were they that there was something uncanny in the revelation.

There might have been a second of mutual staring. Then each rifle in each group was at the shoulder. As Dan's glance flashed along the barrel of his weapon, the figure of a man suddenly loomed as if the musket had been a telescope. The short black beard, the slouch hat, the pose of the man as he sighted to shoot, made a quick picture in Dan's mind. The same moment, it would seem, he pulled his own trigger, and the man, smitten, lurched forward, while his exploding rifle made a slanting crimson streak in the air, and the slouch hat fell before the body. The billows of the fog, governed by singular impulses, rolled between.

"You got that feller sure enough," said a comrade to Dan. Dan looked at him absent-mindedly.

V

When the next morning calmly displayed another fog, the men of the regiment exchanged eloquent comments; but they did not abuse it at length, because the streets of the town now contained enough galloping aides to make three troops of cavalry, and they knew that they had come to the verge of the great fight.

Dan conversed with the man who had once possessed a horse-hair trunk; but they did not mention the line of hills which had furnished them in more careless moments with an agreeable topic. They avoided it now as condemned men do the subject of death, and yet the thought of it stayed in their eyes as they looked at each other and talked gravely of other things.

The expectant regiment heaved a long sigh of relief when the sharp call, "Fall in!" repeated indefinitely, arose in the streets. It was inevitable that a bloody battle was to be fought, and they wanted to get it off their minds. They were, however, doomed again to spend a long period planted firmly in the mud. They craned their necks and wondered where some of the other regiments were going.

At last the mists rolled carelessly away. Nature made at this time all provisions to enable foes to see each other, and immediately the roar of guns resounded from every hill. The endless crackling of the skirmishers swelled to rolling crashes of musketry. Shells screamed with panther-like noises at the houses. Dan looked at the man of the horse-hair trunk, and the man said: "Well, here she comes!"

The tenor voices of young officers and the deep and hoarse voices of the older ones rang in the streets. These cries pricked like spurs. The masses of men vibrated from the suddenness with which they were plunged into the situation of troops about to fight. That the orders were long-expected did not concern the emotion.

Simultaneous movement was imparted to all these thick bodies of men and horses that lay in the town. Regiment after regiment swung rapidly into the streets that faced the sinister ridge.

This exodus was theatrical. The little sober-hued village had been like the cloak which disguises the king of drama. It was now put aside, and an army, splendid thing of steel and blue, stood forth in the sun-light.

Even the soldiers in the heavy columns drew deep breaths at

the sight, more majestic than they had dreamed. The heights of the enemy's position were crowded with men who resembled people come to witness some mighty pageant. But as the column moved steadily to their positions, the guns, matter-of-fact warriors, doubled their number, and shells burst with red thrilling tumult on the crowded plain. One came into the ranks of the regiment, and after the smoke and the wrath of it had faded, leaving motionless figures, every one stormed according to the limits of his vocabulary, for veterans detest being killed when they are not busy.

The regiment sometimes looked sideways at its brigade companions composed of men who had never been in battle; but no frozen blood could withstand the heat of the splendor of this army before the eyes on the plain, these lines so long that the flanks were little streaks, this mass of men of one intention. The recruits carried themselves heedlessly. At the rear was an idle battery, and three artillerymen in a foolish row on a caisson nudged each other and grinned at the recruits. "You'll catch it pretty soon," they called out. They were impersonally gleeful, as if they themselves were not also likely to catch it pretty soon. But with this picture of an army in their hearts, the new men perhaps felt the devotion which the drops may feel for the wave; they were of its power and glory; they smiled jauntily at the foolish row of gunners, and told them to go to blazes.

The column trotted across some little bridges and spread quickly into lines of battle. Before them was a bit of plain, and back of the plain was the ridge. There was no time left for considerations. The men were staring at the plain, mightily wondering how it would feel to be out there, when a brigade in advance yelled and charged. The hill was all grey smoke and fire-points.

That fierce elation in the terrors of war, catching a man's heart and making it burn with such ardor that he becomes capable of dying, flashed in the faces of the men like colored lights, and made them resemble leashed animals, eager, ferocious, daunting at nothing. The line was really in its first leap before the wild, hoarse crying of the orders.

The greed for close quarters which is the emotion of a bayonet charge came then into the minds of the men and developed until it was a madness. The field, with its faded grass of a Southern winter, seemed miles in width to this fury.

High, slow-moving masses of smoke, with an odor of burning cotton, engulfed the line until the men might have been swimmers. Before them the ridge, the shore of this grey sea, was outlined, crossed, and re-crossed by sheets of flame. The howl of the battle arose to the noise of innumerable wind-demons.

The line, galloping, scrambling, plunging like a herd of wounded horses, went over a field that was sown with corpses, the records of other charges.

Directly in front of the black-faced, whooping Dan, carousing in this onward sweep like a new kind of fiend, a wounded man appeared, raising his shattered body, and staring at this rush of men down upon him. It seemed to occur to him that he was to be trampled; he made a desperate, piteous effort to escape; then finally huddled in a waiting heap. Dan and the soldier near him widened the interval between them without looking down, without appearing to heed the wounded man. This little clump of blue seemed to reel past them as bowlders reel past a train.

Bursting through a smoke-wave, the scampering, unformed bunches came upon the wreck of the brigade that had preceded them, a floundering mass stopped afar from the hill by the swirling volleys.

It was as if a necromancer had suddenly shown them a picture of the fate which awaited them; but the line with a muscular spasm hurled itself over this wreckage and onward, until men were stumbling amid the relics of other assaults, the point where the fire from the ridge consumed.

The men, panting, perspiring, with crazed faces, tried to push against it; but it was as if they had come to a wall. The wave halted, shuddered in an agony from the quick struggle of its two desires, then toppled and broke into a fragmentary thing which has no name.

Veterans could now at last be distinguished from recruits. The new regiments were instantly gone, lost, scattered, as if they never had been. But the sweeping failure of the charge, the battle, could not make the veterans forget their business. With a last throe, the band of maniacs drew itself up and blazed a volley at the hill, insignificant to those iron intrenchments, but nevertheless expressing that singular final despair which enables men to coolly defy the walls of a city of death.

After this episode the men renamed their command. They called it the Little Regiment.

VI

"I seen Dan shoot a feller yesterday. Yes, sir. I'm sure it was him that done it. And maybe he thinks about that feller now, and wonders if *he* tumbled down just about the same way. Them things come up in a man's mind."

Bivouac fires upon the side-walks, in the streets, in the yards, threw high their wavering reflections, which examined, like slim, red fingers, the dingy, scarred walls and the piles of tumbled brick. The droning of voices again arose from great blue crowds.

The odor of frying bacon, the fragrance from countless little coffee-pails floated among the ruins. The rifles, stacked in the shadows, emitted flashes of steely light. Wherever a flag lay horizontally from one stack to another was the bed of an eagle which had led men into the mystic smoke.

The men about a particular fire were engaged in holding in check their jovial spirits. They moved whispering around the blaze, although they looked at it with a certain fine contentment, like laborers after a day's hard work.

There was one who sat apart. They did not address him save in tones suddenly changed. They did not regard him directly, but always in little sidelong glances.

At last a soldier from a distant fire came into this circle of light. He studied for a time the man who sat apart. Then he hesitatingly stepped closer and said: "Got any news, Dan?"

"No," said Dan.

The new-comer shifted his feet. He looked at the fire, at the sky, at the other men, at Dan. His face expressed a curious despair; his tongue was plainly in rebellion. Finally, however, he contrived to say: "Well, there's some chance yet, Dan. Lots of the wounded are still lying out there, you know. There's some chance yet."

"Yes," said Dan.

The soldier shifted his feet again, and looked miserably into the air. After another struggle he said: "Well, there's some chance yet, Dan." He moved hastily away.

One of the men of the squad, perhaps encouraged by this example, now approached the still figure. "No news yet, hey?" he said, after coughing behind his hand.

"No," said Dan.

"Well," said the man, "I've been thinking of how he was fretting about you the night you went on special duty. You recollect? Well, sir, I was surprised. He couldn't say enough about it. I swan, I don't believe he slep' a wink after you left, but just lay awake cussing special duty and worrying. I was surprised. But there he lay cussing. He——"

Dan made a curious sound, as if a stone had wedged in his throat. He said: "Shut up, will you?"

Afterward the men would not allow this moody contemplation of the fire to be interrupted.

"Oh, let him alone, can't you?"

"Come away from there, Casey!"

"Say, can't you leave him be?"

They moved with reverence about the immovable figure, with its countenance of mask-like invulnerability.

VII

After the red round eye of the sun had stared long at the little plain and its burden, darkness, a sable mercy, came heavily upon it, and the wan hands of the dead were no longer seen in strange frozen gestures.

The heights in front of the plain shone with tiny camp-fires, and from the town in the rear, small shimmerings ascended from the blazes of the bivouac. The plain was a black expanse upon which, from time to time, dots of light, lanterns, floated slowly here and there. These fields were long steeped in grim mystery.

Suddenly, upon one dark spot, there was a resurrection. A strange thing had been groaning there, prostrate. Then it suddenly dragged itself to a sitting posture, and became a man.

The man stared stupidly for a moment at the lights on the hill, then turned and contemplated the faint coloring over the town. For some moments he remained thus, staring with dull eyes, his face unemotional, wooden.

Finally he looked around him at the corpses dimly to be seen. No change flashed into his face upon viewing these men. They seemed to suggest merely that his information concerning himself was not too complete. He ran his fingers over his arms and chest, bearing always the air of an idiot upon a bench at an almshouse door.

Finding no wound in his arms nor in his chest, he raised his hand to his head, and the fingers came away with some dark liquid upon them. Holding these fingers close to his eyes, he scanned them in the same stupid fashion, while his body gently swayed.

The soldier rolled his eyes again toward the town. When he arose, his clothing peeled from the frozen ground like wet paper. Hearing the sound of it, he seemed to see reason for deliberation. He paused and looked at the ground, then at his trousers, then at the ground.

Finally he went slowly off toward the faint reflection, holding his hands palm outward before him, and walking in the manner of a blind man.

VIII

The immovable Dan again sat unaddressed in the midst of comrades, who did not joke aloud. The dampness of the usual morning fog seemed to make the little camp-fires furious.

Suddenly a cry arose in the streets, a shout of amazement and delight. The men making breakfast at the fire looked up quickly. They broke forth in clamorous exclamation: "Well! Of all things! Dan! Dan! Look who's coming! Oh, Dan!"

Dan the silent raised his eyes and saw a man, with a bandage of the size of a helmet about his head, receiving a furious demonstration from the company. He was shaking hands and explaining and haranguing to a high degree.

Dan started. His skin of bronze flushed to his temples. He seemed about to leap from the ground, but then suddenly he sank back, and resumed his impassive gazing.

The men were in a flurry. They looked from one to the other. "Dan! Look! See who's coming!" some cried again. "Dan! Look!"

He scowled at last, and moved his shoulders sullenly. "Well, don't I know it?"

But they could not be convinced that his eyes were in service. "Dan! Why can't you look? See who's coming!"

He made a gesture then of irritation and rage. "Damn it! Don't I know it?"

The man with a bandage of the size of a helmet moved forward, always shaking hands and explaining. At times his glance wandered to Dan, who sat with his eyes riveted.

After a series of shiftings, it occurred naturally that the man with the bandage was very near to the man who saw the flames. He paused, and there was a little silence. Finally he said: "Hello, Dan."

"Hello, Billie."

THREE MIRACULOUS SOLDIERS

I

THE girl was in the front room on the second floor, peering through the blinds. It was the "best room." There was a very new rag carpet on the floor. The edges of it had been dyed with alternate stripes of red and green. Upon the wooden mantel there were two little puffy figures in clay—a shepherd and a shepherdess probably. A triangle of pink and white wool hung carefully over the edge of this shelf. Upon the bureau there was nothing at all save a spread newspaper, with edges folded to make it into a mat. The quilts and sheets had been removed from the bed and were stacked upon a chair. The pillows and the great feather mattress were muffled and tumbled until they resembled great dumplings. The picture of a man terribly leaden in complexion hung in an oval frame on one white wall and steadily confronted the bureau.

From between the slats of the blinds she had a view of the road as it wended across the meadow to the woods and again where it reappeared crossing the hill, a half mile away. It lay yellow and warm in the summer sunshine. From the long grasses of the meadow came the rhythmic click of the insects. Occasional frogs in the hidden brook made a peculiar chug-chug sound as if somebody throttled them. The leaves of the wood swung in gentle winds. Through the dark-green branches of the pines that grew in the front yard could be seen the mountains, far to the southeast and inexpressibly blue.

Mary's eyes were fastened upon the little streak of road that appeared on the distant hill. Her face was flushed with excitement and the hand which stretched in a strained pose on the sill trembled because of the nervous shaking of the wrist. The pines whisked their green needles with a soft hissing sound against the house.

At last the girl turned from the window and went to the head of the stairs. "Well, I just know they're coming, anyhow," she cried argumentatively to the depths.

A voice from below called to her angrily: "They ain't. We've never seen one yet. They never come into this neighborhood. You just come down here and 'tend to your work insteader watching for soldiers."

"Well, ma, I just know they're coming."

A voice retorted with the shrillness and mechanical violence of occasional housewives. The girl swished her skirts defiantly and returned to the window.

Upon the yellow streak of road that lay across the hillside there now was a handful of black dots—horsemen. A cloud of dust floated away. The girl flew to the head of the stairs and whirled down into the kitchen.

"They're coming! They're coming!"

It was as if she had cried "Fire!" Her mother had been peeling potatoes while seated comfortably at the table. She sprang to her feet. "No—it can't be—how you know it's them—where?" The stubby knife fell from her hand and two or three curls of potato skin dropped from her apron to the floor.

The girl turned and dashed up stairs. Her mother followed, gasping for breath and yet contriving to fill the air with questions, reproach and remonstrance. The girl was already at the window eagerly pointing. "There! There! See 'em! See 'em!"

Rushing to the window, the mother scanned for an instant the road on the hill. She crouched back with a groan. "It's them, sure as the world. It's them!" She waved her hands in despairing gestures.

The black dots vanished into the wood. The girl at the window was quivering and her eyes were shining like water when the sun flashes. "Hush! They're in the woods. They'll be here directly." She bended down and intently watched the green archway from whence the road emerged. "Hush! I hear 'em coming," she swiftly whispered to her mother, for the elder woman had dropped dolefully upon the mattress and was sobbing. And indeed the girl could hear the quick, dull trample of horses. She stepped aside with sudden apprehension, but she bended her head forward in order to still scan the road.

"Here they are!"

There was something very theatrical in the sudden appearance of these men to the eyes of the girl. It was as if a scene had been shifted. The forest suddenly disclosed them—a dozen brown-faced troopers in blue, galloping.

"Oh, look," breathed the girl. Her mouth was puckered into an expression of strange fascination as if she had expected to see the troopers change into demons and gloat at her. She was at last looking upon those curious beings who rode down from the North—those men of legend and colossal tale—they who were possessed of such marvellous hallucinations.

The little troop rode in silence. At its head was a youthful fellow with some dim yellow stripes upon his arm. In his right hand he held his carbine, slanting upward with the stock resting upon his knee. He was absorbed in a scrutiny of the country before him. At the heels of the sergeant the rest of the squad rode in thin column with creak of leather and tinkle of steel and tin. The girl scanned the faces of the horsemen, seeming astonished vaguely to find them of the type she knew.

The lad at the head of the troop comprehended the house and its environments in two glances. He did not check the long, swinging stride of his horse. The troopers glanced for a moment like casual tourists, and then returned to their study of the region in front. The heavy thudding of the hoofs became a small noise. The dust, hanging in sheets, slowly sank.

The sobs of the woman on the bed took form in words which, while strong in their note of calamity, yet expressed a querulous mental reaching for some near thing to blame. "And it'll be lucky fer us if we ain't both butchered in our sleep—plundering and running off horses—old Santo's gone—you see if he ain't—plundering——"

"But, ma," said the girl, perplexed and terrified in the same moment, "they've gone."

"Oh, but they'll come back," cried the mother without pausing her wail. "They'll come back—trust them for that—running off horses. Oh John, John! why did you, why did you?" She suddenly lifted herself and sat rigid, staring at her daughter. "Mary," she said in tragic whisper, "the kitchen door isn't locked." Already she was bended forward to listen, her mouth agape, her eyes fixed upon her daughter.

"Mother——" faltered the girl.

Her mother again whispered: "The kitchen door isn't locked." Motionless and mute they stared into each other's eyes.

At last the girl quavered: "We better—we better go and lock it." The mother nodded. Hanging arm in arm they stole across the floor toward the head of the stairs. A board of the floor creaked. They halted and exchanged a look of dumb agony.

At last they reached the head of the stairs. From the kitchen came the bass humming of the kettle and frequent sputterings and cracklings from the fire. These sounds were sinister. The mother and the girl stood incapable of movement. "There's somebody down there," whispered the elder woman.

Finally, the girl made a gesture of resolution. She twisted her arm from her mother's hands and went two steps downward. She addressed the kitchen: "Who's there?" Her tone was intended to be dauntless. It rang so dramatically in the silence that a sudden new panic seized them as if the suspected presence in the kitchen had cried out to them. But the girl ventured again: "Is there anybody there?" No reply was made save by the kettle and the fire.

With a stealthy tread the girl continued her journey. As she neared the last step the fire crackled explosively and the girl screamed. But the mystic presence had not swept around the corner to grab her, so she dropped to a seat on the step and laughed. "It was—was only the—the fire," she said, stammering hysterically.

Then she arose with sudden fortitude and cried: "Why, there isn't anybody there. I know there isn't." She marched down into the kitchen. In her face was dread, as if she half expected to confront something, but the room was empty. She cried joyously: "There's nobody here. Come on down, ma." She ran to the kitchen door and locked it.

The mother came down to the kitchen. "Oh, dear, what a fright I've had. It's given me the sick headache. I know it has."

"Oh, ma," said the girl.

"I know it has—I know it. Oh, if your father was only here! He'd settle those Yankees mighty quick—he'd settle 'em! Two poor helpless women——"

"Why, ma, what makes you act so? The Yankees haven't——"

"Oh, they'll be back—they'll be back. Two poor helpless women! Your father and your uncle Asa and Bill off galavanting around and fighting when they ought to be protecting their home! That's the kind of men they are. Didn't I say to your father just before he left——"

"Ma," said the girl, coming suddenly from the window, "the barn door is open. I wonder if they took old Santo?"

"Oh, of course they have—of course—— Mary, I don't see what we are going to do. I don't see what we are going to do."

The girl said: "Ma, I'm going to see if they took old Santo."

"Mary," cried the mother, "don't you dare!"

"But think of poor old Sant, ma."

"Never you mind old Santo. We're lucky to be safe ourselves, I tell you. Never mind old Santo. Don't you dare to go out there, Mary—Mary!"

The girl had unlocked the door and stepped out upon the porch. The mother cried in despair, "Mary!"

"Why, there isn't anybody out here," the girl called in response. She stood for a moment with a curious smile upon her face as of gleeful satisfaction at her daring.

The breeze was waving the boughs of the apple trees. A rooster with an air importantly courteous was conducting three hens upon a foraging tour. On the hillside at the rear of the grey old barn the red leaves of a creeper flamed amid the summer foliage. High in the sky clouds rolled toward the north. The girl swung impulsively from the little stoop and ran toward the barn.

The great door was open and the carved peg which usually performed the office of a catch lay on the ground. The girl could not see into the barn because of the heavy shadows. She paused in a listening attitude and heard a horse munching placidly. She gave a cry of delight and sprang across the threshold. Then she suddenly shrank back and gasped. She had confronted three men in grey seated upon the floor with their legs stretched out and their backs against Santo's manger. Their dust-covered countenances were expanded in grins.

II

As Mary sprang backward and screamed, one of the calm men in grey, still grinning, announced: "I knowed you'd holler." Sitting there comfortably the three surveyed her with amusement.

Mary caught her breath, throwing her hand up to her throat. "Oh," she said. "You—you frightened me."

"We're sorry, lady, but couldn't help it no way," cheerfully responded another. "I knowed you'd holler when I seen you coming yere, but I raikoned we couldn't help it no way. We hain't a-troubling this yere barn, I don't guess. We been doing some mighty tall sleeping yere. We done woke when them Yanks loped past."

"Where did you come from? Did—did you escape from the— the Yankees?" The girl still stammered and trembled. The three soldiers laughed. "No'm'm. No'm'm. They never cotch us. We was in a muss down the road yere about two mile. And Bill yere they gin it to him in the arm. Keh-plunk. And they pasted me thah, too. Curious. And Sim yere, he didn't get nothing, but they chased us all quite a little piece, and we done lose track of our boys."

"Was it—was it those who passed here just now? Did they chase you?"

The men in grey laughed again. "What—them? No, indeedee. There was a mighty big swarm of Yanks and a mighty big swarm of our boys, too. What—that little passel? No'm'm."

She became calm enough to scan them more attentively. They were much begrimed and very dusty. Their grey clothes were tattered. Splashed mud had dried upon them in reddish spots. It appeared, too, that the men had not shaved in many days. In the hats there was a singular diversity. One soldier wore the little blue cap of the Northern infantry, with corps emblem and regimental number; one wore a great slouch hat with a wide hole in the crown, and the other wore no hat at all. The left sleeve of one man and the right sleeve of another had been slit and the arms were neatly bandaged with a clean cloth. "These hain't no more than two little cuts," explained one. "We stopped up yere to Mis' Leavitts—she said her name was—and she bind them for us. Bill yere, he had the thirst come on him. And the fever too. We——"

"Did you ever see my father in the army?" asked Mary. "John Hinckson—his name is."

The three soldiers grinned again, but they replied kindly:

"No'm'm. No'm'm, we hain't never. What is he—in the cavalry?"

"No," said the girl. "He and my uncle Asa and my cousin—his name is Bill Parker—they are all with Longstreet—they call him."

"Oh," said the soldiers. "Longstreet? Oh, they're a good smart ways from yere. 'Way off up nawtheast. There hain't nothing but cavalry down yere. They're in the infantry, probably."

"We haven't heard anything from them for days and days," said Mary.

"Oh, they're all right in the infantry," said one man, to be consoling. "The infantry don't do much fighting. They go beller-ing out in a big swarm and only a few of 'em get hurt. But if they was in the cavalry—the cavalry——"

Mary interrupted him without intention. "Are you hungry?" she asked.

The soldiers looked at each other, struck by some sudden and singular shame. They hung their heads. "No'm'm," replied one at last.

Santo, in his stall, was tranquilly chewing and chewing. Some-times he looked benevolently over at them. He was an old horse and there was something about his eyes and his forelock which created the impression that he wore spectacles. Mary went and patted his nose. "Well, if you are hungry, I can get you some-thing," she told the men. "Or you might come to the house."

"We wouldn't dast go to the house," said one. "That passel of Yanks was only a scouting crowd, most like. Just an advance. More coming, likely."

"Well, I can bring you something," cried the girl eagerly. "Won't you let me bring you something?"

"Well," said a soldier with embarrassment, "we hain't had much. If you could bring us a little snack-like. Just a snack. We'd ——"

Without waiting for him to cease, the girl turned toward the door. But before she had reached it she stopped abruptly. "Lis-ten," she whispered. Her form was bended forward, her head turned and lowered, her hand extended toward the men in a command for silence.

They could faintly hear the thudding of many hoofs, the clank of arms and frequent calling voices.

"By cracky, it's the Yanks." The soldiers scrambled to their feet and came toward the door. "I knowed that first crowd was only an advance."

The girl and the three men peered from the shadows of the barn. The view of the road was intersected by tree trunks and a little henhouse. However, they could see many horsemen streaming down the road. The horsemen were in blue. "Oh, hide—hide —hide," cried the girl with a sob in her voice.

"Wait a minute," whispered a grey soldier excitedly. "Maybe they're going along by. No, by thunder, they hain't. They're halting. Scoot, boys."

They made a noiseless dash into the dark end of the barn. The girl standing by the door heard them break forth an instant later in clamorous whispers. "Where'll we hide? Where'll we hide? There hain't a place to hide." The girl turned and glanced wildly about the barn. It seemed true. The stock of hay had grown low under Santo's endless munching and from occasional levyings by passing troopers in grey. The poles of the mow were barely covered, save in one corner where there was a little bunch.

The girl espied the great feed box. She ran to it and lifted the lid. "Here! Here!" she called. "Get in here."

They had been tearing noiselessly around the rear part of the barn. At her low call they came and plunged at the box. They did not all get in at the same moment without a good deal of a tangle. The wounded men gasped and muttered, but they at last were flopped down on the layer of feed which covered the bottom. Swiftly and softly the girl lowered the lid and then turned like a flash toward the door.

No one appeared there, so she went closer to survey the situation. The troopers had dismounted and stood in silence by their horses. A grey-bearded man, whose red cheeks and nose shone vividly above the whiskers, was strolling about with two or three others. They wore double-breasted coats and faded yellow sashes were wound under their black leather sword belts. The grey-bearded soldier was apparently giving orders, pointing here and there.

Mary tip-toed to the feed box. "They've all got off their horses," she said to it. A finger projected from a knothole near the top and said to her very plainly: "Come closer." She obeyed, and then a muffled voice could be heard: "Scoot for the house, lady, and if we don't see you again, why, much obliged for what you done."

"Good-bye," she said to the feed box.

She made two attempts to walk dauntlessly from the barn, but each time she faltered and failed just before she reached the point where she could have been seen by the blue-coated troopers. At last, however, she made a sort of a rush forward and went out into the bright sunshine.

The group of men in double-breasted coats wheeled in her direction at the instant. The grey-bearded officer forgot to lower his arm which had been stretched forth in giving an order.

She felt that her feet were touching the ground in a most unnatural manner. Her bearing, she believed, was suddenly grown awkward and ungainly. Upon her face she thought that this sentence was plainly written: "There are three men hidden in the feed box."

The grey-bearded soldier came toward her. She stopped; she seemed about to run away. But the soldier doffed his little blue cap and looked amiable. "You live here, I presume?" he said.

"Yes," she answered.

"Well, we are obliged to camp here for the night, and as we've got two wounded men with us I don't suppose you'd mind if we put them in the barn."

"In—in the barn?"

He became aware that she was agitated. He smiled assuringly. "You needn't be frightened. We won't hurt anything around here. You'll all be safe enough."

The girl balanced on one foot and swung the other to and fro in the grass. She was looking down at it. "But—but I don't think ma would like it if—if you took the barn."

The old officer laughed. "Wouldn't she?" said he. "That's so. Maybe she wouldn't." He reflected for a time and then decided cheerfully: "Well, we will have to ask her anyhow. Where is she? In the house?"

"Yes," replied the girl, "she's in the house. She—she'll be scared to death when she sees you."

"Well, you go and ask her then," said the soldier, always wearing a benign smile. "You go and ask her and then come and tell me."

When the girl pushed open the door and entered the kitchen, she found it empty. "Ma," she called softly. There was no answer. The kettle still was humming its low song. The knife and the curl of potato skin lay on the floor.

She went to her mother's room and entered timidly. The new lonely aspect of the house shook her nerves. Upon the bed there was a confusion of coverings. "Ma," called the girl, quaking in fear that her mother was not there to reply. But there was a sudden turmoil of the quilts and her mother's head was thrust forth. "Mary," she cried, in what seemed to be a supreme astonishment, "I thought—I thought——"

"Oh, ma," blurted the girl, "there's over a thousand Yankees in the yard, and I've hidden three of our men in the feed box." The elder woman, however, upon the appearance of her daughter had begun to thresh hysterically about on the bed and wailed.

"Ma," the girl exclaimed. "And now they want to use the barn, and our men in the feed box. What shall I do, ma? What shall I do?"

Her mother did not seem to hear, so absorbed was she in her grievous flounderings and tears. "Ma," appealed the girl. "Ma!"

For a moment Mary stood silently debating, her lips apart, her eyes fixed. Then she went to the kitchen window and peeked. The old officer and the others were staring up the road. She went to another window in order to get a proper view of the road, and saw that they were gazing at a small body of horsemen approaching at a trot and raising much dust. Presently she recognized them as the squad that had passed the house earlier, for the young man with the dim yellow chevrons still rode at their head. An unarmed horseman in grey was receiving their close attention. As they came very near to the house she darted to the first window again. The grey-bearded officer was smiling a fine broad smile of satisfaction. "So you got him?" he called out. The young sergeant sprang from his horse and his brown hand moved in a salute. The girl could not hear his reply. She saw the unarmed horseman in grey stroking a very black mustache and looking about him coolly and with an interested air. He appeared so indifferent that she did not understand he was a prisoner until she heard the grey-beard call out: "Well, put him in the barn. He'll be safe there, I guess." A party of troopers moved with the prisoner toward the barn.

The girl made a sudden gesture of horror, remembering the three men in the feed box.

III

The busy troopers in blue scurried about the long lines of stamping horses. Men crooked their backs and perspired in order to rub with cloths or bunches of grass these slim equine legs, upon whose splendid machinery they depended so greatly. The lips of the horses were still wet and frothy from the steel bars which had wrenched at their mouths all day. Over their backs and about their noses sped the talk of the men.

"Moind where yer plug is steppin', Finerty! Keep 'im aff me!"

"An ould elephant! He shtrides like a schoolhouse."

"Bill's little mar'—she was plum beat when she come in with Crawford's crowd."

"Crawford's the hardest-ridin' cavalryman in the army. An' he don't use up a horse, neither—much. They stay fresh when the others are most a-droppin'."

"Finerty, will yeh moind that cow a yours?"

Amid a bustle of gossip and banter, the horses retained their air of solemn rumination, twisting their lower jaws from side to side and sometimes rubbing noses dreamfully.

Over in front of the barn three troopers sat talking comfortably. Their carbines were leaned against the wall. At their side and outlined in the black of the open door stood a sentry, his weapon resting in the hollow of his arm. Four horses saddled and accoutred were conferring with their heads close together. The four bridle reins were flung over a post.

Upon the calm green of the land, typical in every way of peace, the hues of war brought thither by the troops shone strangely. Mary, gazing curiously, did not feel that she was contemplating a familiar scene. It was no longer the home acres. The new blue, steel, and faded yellow thoroughly dominated the old green and brown. She could hear the voices of the men, and it seemed from their tone that they had camped there for years. Everything with them was usual. They had taken possession of the landscape in such a way that even the old marks appeared strange and formidable to the girl.

Mary had intended to go and tell the commander in blue that her mother did not wish his men to use the barn at all, but she paused when she heard him speak to the sergeant. She thought she perceived then that it mattered little to him what her mother wished, and that an objection by her or by anybody would be futile. She saw the soldiers conduct the prisoner in grey into the barn, and for a long time she watched the three chatting guards and the pondering sentry. Upon her mind in desolate weight was the recollection of the three men in the feed box.

It seemed to her that in a case of this description it was her duty to be a heroine. In all the stories she had read when at boarding school in Pennsylvania, the girl characters, confronted with such difficulties, invariably did hair breadth things. True, they were usually bent upon rescuing and recovering their lovers, and neither the calm man in grey nor any of the three in the feed box was lover of hers, but then a real heroine would not pause over this minor question. Plainly a heroine would take measures to rescue the four men. If she did not at least make the attempt, she would be false to those carefully constructed ideals which were the accumulation of years of dreaming.

But the situation puzzled her. There was the barn with only one door, and with four armed troopers in front of this door, one of them with his back to the rest of the world, engaged no doubt in a steadfast contemplation of the calm man and, incidentally, of the feed box. She knew, too, that even if she should open the kitchen door, three heads and perhaps four would turn casually in her direction. Their ears were real ears.

Heroines, she knew, conducted these matters with infinite precision and despatch. They severed the hero's bonds, cried a dramatic sentence, and stood between him and his enemies until he had run far enough away. She saw well, however, that even should she achieve all things up to the point where she might take glorious stand between the escaping and the pursuers, those grim troopers in blue would not pause. They would run around her, make a circuit. One by one she saw the gorgeous contrivances and expedients of fiction fall before the plain, homely difficulties of this situation. They were of no service. Sadly, ruefully, she thought of the calm man and of the contents of the feed box.

The sum of her invention was that she could sally forth to the commander of the blue cavalry, and confessing to him that there were three of her friends and his enemies secreted in the feed box, pray him to let them depart unmolested. But she was beginning to believe the old grey-beard to be a bear. It was hardly probable that he would give this plan his support. It was more probable that he and some of his men would at once descend upon the feed box and confiscate her three friends. The difficulty with her idea was that she could not learn its value without trying it, and then in case of failure it would be too late for remedies and other plans. She reflected that war made men very unreasonable.

All that she could do was to stand at the window and mournfully regard the barn. She admitted this to herself with a sense of deep humiliation. She was not then made of that fine stuff, that mental satin, which enabled some other beings to be of such mighty service to the distressed. She was defeated by a barn with one door, by four men with eight eyes and eight ears—trivialities that would not impede the real heroine.

The vivid white light of broad day began slowly to fade. Tones of grey came upon the fields and the shadows were of lead. In this more sombre atmosphere the fires built by the troops down in the far end of the orchard grew more brilliant, becoming spots of crimson color in the dark grove.

The girl heard a fretting voice from her mother's room. "Mary!" She hastily obeyed the call. She perceived that she had quite forgotten her mother's existence in this time of excitement.

The elder woman still lay upon the bed. Her face was flushed and perspiration stood amid new wrinkles upon her forehead. Weaving wild glances from side to side, she began to whimper. "Oh, I'm just sick—I'm just sick! Have those men gone yet? Have they gone?"

The girl smoothed a pillow carefully for her mother's head. "No, ma. They're here yet. But they haven't hurt anything—it doesn't seem. Will I get you something to eat?"

Her mother gestured her away with the impatience of the ill. "No—no—just don't bother me. My head is splitting, and you know very well that nothing can be done for me when I get one of these spells. It's trouble—that's what makes them. When are those men going? Look here, don't you go 'way. You stick close to the house now."

"I'll stay right here," said the girl. She sat in the gloom and listened to her mother's incessant moaning. When she attempted to move, her mother cried out at her. When she desired to ask if she might try to alleviate the pain, she was interrupted shortly. Somehow her sitting in passive silence within hearing of this illness seemed to contribute to her mother's relief. She assumed a posture of submission. Sometimes her mother projected questions concerning the local condition, and although she labored to be graphic and at the same time soothing, unalarming, her form of reply was always displeasing to the sick woman, and brought forth ejaculations of angry impatience.

Eventually the woman slept in the manner of one worn from terrible labor. The girl went slowly and softly to the kitchen. When she looked from the window, she saw the four soldiers still at the barn door. In the west, the sky was yellow. Some tree trunks intersecting it appeared black as streaks of ink. Soldiers hovered in blue clouds about the bright splendor of the fires in the orchard. There were glimmers of steel.

The girl sat in the new gloom of the kitchen and watched. The soldiers lit a lantern and hung it in the barn. Its rays made the form of the sentry seem gigantic. Horses whinnied from the orchard. There was a low hum of human voices. Sometimes small detachments of troopers rode past the front of the house. The girl heard the abrupt calls of sentries. She fetched some food and ate it from her hand, standing by the window. She was so afraid that something would occur that she barely left her post for an instant.

A picture of the interior of the barn hung vividly in her mind. She recalled the knotholes in the boards at the rear, but she admitted that the prisoners could not escape through them. She remembered some inadequacies of the roof, but these also counted for nothing. When confronting the problem, she felt her ambitions, her ideals tumbling headlong like cottages of straw.

Once she felt that she had made her mind up to reconnoitre at any rate. It was night; the lantern at the barn and the camp-fires made everything without their circles into masses of heavy mystic blackness. She took two steps toward the door. But there she paused. Innumerable possibilities of danger had assailed her mind. She returned to the window and stood wavering. At last she went swiftly to the door, opened it and slid noiselessly into the darkness.

For a moment she regarded the shadows. Down in the orchard the camp-fires of the troops appeared precisely like a great painting, all in reds upon a black cloth. The voices of the troopers still hummed. The girl started slowly off in the opposite direction. Her eyes were fixed in a stare; she studied the darkness in front for a moment before she ventured upon a forward step. Unconsciously, her throat was arranged for a sudden shrill scream. High in the tree branches she could hear the voice of the wind, a melody of the night, low and sad, the plaint of an endless incommunicable sorrow. Her own distress, the plight of the men in grey—these near matters as well as all she had known or imagined of grief—everything was expressed in this soft mourning of the wind in the trees. At first she felt like weeping. This sound told her of human impotency and doom. Then later the trees and the wind breathed strength to her, sang of sacrifice, of dauntless effort, of hard carven faces that did not blanch when Duty came at midnight or at noon.

She turned often to scan the shadowy figures that moved from time to time in the light at the barn door. Once she trod upon a stick and it flopped, crackling in the intolerable manner of all sticks. At this noise, however, the guards at the barn made no sign. Finally she was where she could see the knotholes in the rear of the structure gleaming like pieces of metal from the effect of the light within. Scarcely breathing in her excitement she glided close and applied an eye to a knothole. She had barely achieved one glance at the interior before she sprang back shuddering.

For the unconscious and cheerful sentry at the door was swearing away in flaming sentences, heaping one gorgeous oath upon another, making a conflagration of his description of his troop horse.

"Why," he was declaring to the calm prisoner in grey, "you ain't got a horse in your hull —— —— army that can run forty rod with that there little mar'."

As in the outer darkness Mary cautiously returned to the

knothole, the three guards in front suddenly called in low tones: "Sssh." "Quit, Pete, here comes the lieutenant." The sentry had apparently been about to resume his declamation, but at these warnings he suddenly posed in a soldierly manner.

A tall and lean officer with a smooth face entered the barn. The sentry saluted primly. The officer flashed a comprehensive glance about him. "Everything all right?"

"All right, sir."

This officer had eyes like the points of stilettoes. The lines from his nose to the corners of his mouth were deep and gave him a slightly disagreeable aspect, but somewhere in his face there was a quality of singular thoughtfulness as of the absorbed student dealing in generalities which was utterly in opposition to the rapacious keenness of the eyes which saw everything.

Suddenly he lifted a long finger and pointed. "What's that?"

"That? That's a feed box, I suppose."

"What's in it?"

"I don't know. I——"

"You ought to know," said the officer sharply. He walked over to the feed box and flung up the lid. With a sweeping gesture he reached down and scooped a handful of feed. "You ought to know what's in everything when you have prisoners in your care," he added scowling.

During the time of this incident, the girl had nearly swooned. Her hands searched weakly over the boards for something to which to cling. With the pallor of the dying she had watched the downward sweep of the officer's arm, which after all had only brought forth a handful of feed. The result was a stupefaction of her mind. She was astonished out of her senses at this spectacle of three large men metamorphosed into a handful of feed.

IV

It is perhaps a singular thing that this absence of the three men from the feed box at the time of the sharp lieutenant's investigation should terrify the girl more than it should joy her. That for which she had prayed had come to pass. Apparently the escape of these men in the face of every improbability had been granted her, but her dominating emotion was fright. The feed box was a mystic and terrible machine, like some dark magician's trap. She felt it almost possible that she should see the three weird men floating spectrally away through the air. She glanced with swift apprehension behind her and, when the dazzle from the lantern's light had left her eyes, saw only the dim hillside stretched in solemn silence.

The interior of the barn possessed for her another fascination because it was now uncanny. It contained that extraordinary feed box. When she peeped again at the knothole, the calm grey prisoner was seated upon the feed box, thumping it with his dangling careless heels, as if it were in no wise his conception of a remarkable feed box. The sentry also stood facing it. His carbine he held in the hollow of his arm. His legs were spread apart and he mused. From without came the low mumble of the three other troopers. The sharp lieutenant had vanished.

The trembling yellow light of the lantern caused the figures of the men to cast monstrous wavering shadows. There were spaces of gloom which shrouded ordinary things in impressive garb. The roof presented an inscrutable blackness save where small rifts in the shingles glowed phosphorescently. Frequently old Santo put down a thunderous hoof. The heels of the prisoner made a sound like the booming of a wild kind of drum. When the men moved their heads, their eyes shone with ghoulish whiteness and their complexions were always waxen and unreal. And there was that profoundly strange feed box, imperturbable with its burden of fantastic mystery.

Suddenly from down near her feet the girl heard a crunching sound, a sort of a nibbling, as if some silent and very discreet terrier was at work upon the turf. She faltered back; here was no doubt another grotesque detail of this most unnatural episode. She did not run, because physically she was in the power of these events. Her feet chained her to the ground in submission to this march of terror after terror. As she stared at the spot from whence this sound seemed to come, there floated through her mind a vague, sweet vision, a vision of her safe little room in which at this hour she usually was sleeping.

The scratching continued faintly and with frequent pauses, as if the terrier was then listening. When the girl first removed her eyes from the knothole the scene appeared of one velvet blackness; then gradually objects loomed with a dim lustre. She could see now where the tops of the trees joined the sky and the form of the barn was before her dyed in heavy purple. She was ever about to shriek, but no sound came from her constricted throat. She gazed at the ground with the expression of countenance of one who watches the sinister-moving grass where a serpent approaches.

Dimly she saw a piece of sod wrenched free and drawn under the great foundation beam of the barn Once she imagined that she saw human hands, not outlined at all, but sufficient in color, form or movement to make subtle suggestion.

Then suddenly a thought that illuminated the entire situation flashed in her mind like a light. The three men, late of the feed box, were beneath the floor of the barn and were now scraping their way under this beam. She did not consider for a moment how they could come there. They were marvelous creatures. The supernatural was to be expected of them. She no longer trembled, for she was possessed upon this instant of the most unchangeable species of conviction. The evidence before her amounted to no evidence at all, but nevertheless her opinion grew in an instant from an irresponsible acorn to a rooted and immovable tree. It was as if she was on a jury.

She stooped down hastily and scanned the ground. There she indeed saw a pair of hands hauling at the dirt where the sod had been displaced. Softly, in a whisper like a breath, she said: "Hey!"

The dim hands were drawn hastily under the barn. The girl reflected for a moment. Then she stooped and whispered: "Hey! It's me!"

After a time there was a resumption of the digging. The ghostly hands began once more their cautious mining. She waited. In hollow reverberations from the interior of the barn came the frequent sounds of old Santo's lazy movements. The sentry conversed with the prisoner.

At last the girl saw a head thrust slowly from under the beam. She perceived the face of one of the miraculous soldiers from the feed box. A pair of eyes glinted and wavered; then finally settled upon her, a pale statue of a girl. The eyes became lit with a kind of humorous greeting. An arm gestured at her.

Stooping, she breathed: "All right." The man drew himself silently back under the beam. A moment later the pair of hands resumed their cautious task. Ultimately the head and arms of the man were thrust strangely from the earth. He was lying on his back. The girl thought of the dirt in his hair. Wriggling slowly and pushing at the beam above him he forced his way out of the curious little passage. He twisted his body and raised himself upon his hands. He grinned at the girl and drew his feet carefully from under the beam. When he at last stood erect beside her, he at once began mechanically to brush the dirt from his clothes with his hands. In the barn the sentry and his prisoner were evidently engaged in an argument.

The girl and the first miraculous soldier signaled warily. It seemed that they feared that their arms would make noises in passing through the air. Their lips moved, conveying dim meanings. In this sign language the girl described the situation in the barn. With guarded motions, she told him of the importance of absolute stillness. He nodded and then in the same manner he told her of his two companions under the barn floor. He informed her again of their wounded state and wagged his head to express his despair. He contorted his face to tell how sore were their arms and jabbed the air mournfully to express their remote geographical position.

This signaling was interrupted by the sound of a body being dragged or dragging itself with slow swishing sound under the barn. The sound was too loud for safety. They rushed to the hole and began to semaphore wildly at it, but the swishing continued with serene indifference until a shaggy head appeared with rolling eyes and quick grin.

With frantic downward motions of their arms they suppressed this grin and with it the swishing noise. In dramatic pantomime they informed this head of the terrible consequences of so much noise. The head nodded, and painfully but with extreme care the second man pushed and pulled himself from the hole.

In a faint whisper the first man said: "Where's Sim?"

The second man made low reply. "He's right here." He motioned reassuringly toward the hole.

When the third head appeared, a soft smile of glee came upon each face and the mute group exchanged expressive glances. When they all stood together free from this tragic barn, they breathed a long sigh that was contemporaneous with another smile and another exchange of glances.

One of the men tip-toed to a knothole and peered into the barn. The sentry was at that moment speaking. "Yes, we know 'em all. There isn't a house in this region that we don't know who is in it most of the time. We collar 'em once in awhile—like we did you. Now, that house out yonder, we——"

The man suddenly left the knothole and returned to the others. Upon his face, dimly discerned, there was an indication that he had made an astonishing discovery. The others questioned him with their eyes, but he simply waved an arm to express his inability to speak at that spot. He led them back toward the hill, prowling carefully. At a safe distance from the barn he halted and as they grouped eagerly about him, he exploded in an intense undertone. "Why, that—that's Cap'n Sawyer they got in yonder."

"Cap'n Sawyer!" incredulously whispered the other men.

But the girl had something to ask. "How did you get out of that feed box?" A man turned to her at once. "Oh! The feed box?" He smiled. "Well, when you put us in there, we was just in a minute when we allowed it wasn't a mighty safe place, and we allowed we'd get out. And we did. We skedaddled 'round and 'round until it 'peared like we was going to get cotched, and then we flung ourselves down in the cow stalls where it's low-like—just dirt floor—and then we just naturally went a-whooping under the barn floor when the Yanks come. And we didn't know Cap'n Sawyer by his voice nohow. We heard 'im discoursing, and we allowed it was a mighty pert man, but we didn't know that it was him. No'm'm."

These three men so recently from a situation of peril seemed suddenly to have dropped all thought of it. They stood with sad faces looking at the barn. They seemed to be making no plans at all to reach a place of more complete safety. They were halted and stupefied by some unknown calamity.

"How do you raikon they cotch him, Sim?" one whispered mournfully.

"I don't know," replied another in the same tone.

Another with a low snarl expressed in two words his opinion of the methods of Fate: "Oh, hell!"

The three men started then as if simultaneously stung and gazed at the young girl who stood silently near them. The man who had sworn began to make agitated apology: "Pardon, miss! 'Pon my soul I clean forgot you was by. 'Deed, and I wouldn't swear like that if I had knowed. 'Deed, I wouldn't."

The girl did not seem to hear him. She was staring at the barn. Suddenly she turned and whispered: "Who is he?"

"He's Cap'n Sawyer, m'm," they told her sorrowfully. "He's our own cap'n. He's been in command of us yere since a long time. He's got folks about yere. Raikon they cotch him while he was a-visiting."

She was still for a time and then, awed, she said: "Will they—will they hang him?"

"No'm'm. Oh, no'm'm. Don't raikon no such thing. No'm'm."

The group became absorbed in a contemplation of the barn. For a time no one moved nor spoke. At last the girl was aroused by slight sounds, and turning she perceived that the three men who had so recently escaped from the barn were now advancing toward it.

V

The girl waiting in the darkness expected to hear the sudden crash and uproar of a fight as soon as the three creeping men should reach the barn. She reflected in an agony upon the swift disaster that would befall any enterprise so desperate. She had an impulse to beg them to come away. The grass rustled in silken movements as she sped toward the barn.

When she arrived, however, she gazed about her bewildered. The men were gone. She searched with her eyes, trying to detect some moving thing, but she could see nothing.

Left alone again, she began to be afraid of the night. The great stretches of darkness could hide crawling dangers. From sheer desire to see a human, she was obliged to peep again at the knothole. The sentry had apparently wearied of talking. Instead he was reflecting. The prisoner still sat on the feed box, moodily staring at the floor. The girl felt in one way that she was looking

at a ghastly group in wax. She started when the old horse put
down an echoing hoof. She wished the men would speak; their
silence reinforced the strange aspect. They might have been two
dead men.

The girl felt impelled to look at the corner of the interior
where were the cow stalls. There was no light there save the
appearance of peculiar grey haze which marked the track of the
dimming rays of the lantern. All else was sombre shadow. At last
she saw something move there. It might have been as small as a
rat or it might have been a part of something as large as a man.
At any rate it proclaimed that something in that spot was alive.
At one time she saw it plainly and at other times it vanished,
because her fixture of gaze caused her occasionally to greatly
tangle and blur those peculiar shadows and faint lights. At last,
however, she perceived a human head. It was monstrously di-
sheveled and wild. It moved slowly forward until its glance could
fall upon the prisoner and then upon the sentry. The wandering
rays caused the eyes to glitter like silver. The girl's heart
pounded so that she put her hand over it.

The sentry and the prisoner remained immovably waxen and
over in the gloom the head thrust from the floor watched them
with its silver eyes.

Finally the prisoner slipped from the feed box and raising his
arms, yawned at great length. "Oh, well," he remarked, "you boys
will get a good licking if you fool around here much longer.
That's some satisfaction anyhow. Even if you did bag me. You'll
get a good walloping." He reflected for a moment and decided:
"I'm sort of willing to be captured if you fellows only get a
damned good licking for being so smart."

The sentry looked up and smiled a superior smile. "Licking,
hey? Nixey." He winked exasperatingly at the prisoner. "You
fellows are not fast enough, my boy. Why didn't you lick us
at —— ? And at —— ? And at —— ?" He named some of the great
battles.

To this the captive officer blurted in angry astonishment.
"Why, we did."

The sentry winked again in profound irony. "Yes—I know you
did. Of course. You whipped us, didn't you? Fine kind of whip-
ping that was. Why, we——"

He suddenly ceased, smitten mute by a sound that broke the stillness of the night. It was the sharp crack of a distant shot that made wild echoes among the hills. It was instantly followed by the hoarse cry of a human voice, a far-away yell of warning, singing of surprise, peril, fear of death. A moment later there was a distant fierce spattering of shots. The sentry and the prisoner stood facing each other, their lips apart, listening.

The orchard at that instant awoke to sudden tumult. There was the thud and scramble and scamper of feet, the mellow, swift clash of arms, men's voices in question, oath, command, hurried and unhurried, resolute and frantic. A horse sped along the road at a raging gallop. A loud voice shouted: "What is it, Ferguson?" Another voice yelled something incoherent. There was a sharp, discordant chorus of command. An uproarious volley suddenly rang from the orchard. The prisoner in grey moved from his intent listening attitude. Instantly the eyes of the sentry blazed, and he said with a new and terrible sternness: "Stand where you are."

The prisoner trembled in his excitement. Expressions of delight and triumph bubbled to his lips. "A surprise, by Gawd! Now! Now, you'll see!"

The sentry stolidly swung his carbine to his shoulder. He sighted carefully along the barrel until it pointed at the prisoner's head, about at his nose. "Well, I've got you, anyhow. Remember that. Don't move."

The prisoner could not keep his arms from nervously gesturing. "I won't; but——"

"And shut your mouth."

The three comrades of the sentry flung themselves into view. "Pete—devil of a row—can you——"

"I've got him," said the sentry calmly and without moving. It was as if the barrel of the carbine rested on piers of stone. The three comrades turned and plunged into the darkness.

In the orchard it seemed as if two gigantic animals were engaged in a mad floundering encounter, snarling, howling in a whirling chaos of noise and motion. In the barn the prisoner and his guard faced each other in silence.

As for the girl at the knothole, the sky had fallen at the beginning of this clamor. She would not have been astonished to see the stars swinging from their abodes, and the vegetation, the barn, all blow away. It was the end of everything, the grand universal murder. When two of the three miraculous soldiers who formed the original feed-box corps emerged in detail from the hole under the beam and slid away into the darkness, she did no more than glance at them.

Suddenly she recollected the head with silver eyes. She started forward and again applied her eyes to the knothole. Even with the din resounding from the orchard, from up the road and down the road, from the heavens and from the deep earth, the central fascination was this mystic head. There to her was the dark god of the tragedy.

The prisoner in grey at this moment burst into a laugh that was no more than a hysterical gurgle. "Well, you can't hold that gun out forever. Pretty soon you'll have to lower it."

The sentry's voice sounded slightly muffled, for his cheek was pressed against the weapon. "I won't be tired for some time yet."

The girl saw the head slowly rise, the eyes fixed upon the sentry's face. A tall black figure slunk across the cow stalls and vanished back of old Santo's quarters. She knew what was to come to pass. She knew this grim thing was upon a terrible mission and that it would reappear again at the head of the little passage between Santo's stall and the wall, almost at the sentry's elbow, and yet when she saw a faint indication as of a form crouching there a scream from an utterly new alarm almost escaped her.

The sentry's arms after all were not of granite. He moved restively. At last he spoke in his even, unchanging tone. "Well, I guess you'll have to climb into that feed box. Step back and lift the lid."

"Why, you don't mean——"

"Step back."

The girl felt a cry of warning arising to her lips as she gazed at this sentry. She noted every detail of his facial expression. She saw, moreover, his mass of brown hair bunching disgracefully about his ears, his clear eyes lit now with a hard cold light, his forehead puckered in a mighty scowl, the ring upon the third finger of the left hand. "Oh, they won't kill him. Surely they won't kill him." The noise of the fight at the orchard was the loud music, the thunder and lightning, the rioting of the tempest which people love during the critical scene of a tragedy.

When the prisoner moved back in reluctant obedience, he faced for an instant the entrance of the little passage and what he saw there must have been written swiftly, graphically in his eyes. And the sentry read it and knew then that he was upon the threshold of his death. In a fraction of time, certain information went from the grim thing in the passage to the prisoner and from the prisoner to the sentry. But at that instant the black formidable figure arose, towered and made its leap. A new shadow flashed across the floor when the blow was struck.

As for the girl at the knothole, when she returned to sense she found herself standing with clinched hands and screaming with her might.

As if her reason had again departed from her, she ran around the barn, in at the door and flung herself sobbing beside the body of the soldier in blue.

The uproar of the fight became at last coherent, inasmuch as one party was giving shouts of supreme exultation. The firing no longer sounded in crashes; it was now expressed in spiteful crackles, the last words of the combat, spoken with feminine vindictiveness.

Presently there was a thud of flying feet. A grimy, panting, red-faced mob of troopers in blue plunged into the barn, became instantly frozen to attitudes of amazement and rage, and then roared in one great chorus: "He's gone!"

The girl who knelt beside the body upon the floor turned toward them her lamenting eyes and cried: "He's not dead, is he? He can't be dead?"

They thronged forward. The sharp lieutenant who had been so particular about the feed box knelt by the side of the girl and laid his head against the chest of the prostrate soldier. "Why, no," he said, rising and looking at the man. "He's all right. Some of you boys throw some water on him."

"Are you sure?" demanded the girl, feverishly.

"Of course. He'll be better after awhile."

"Oh," said she softly, and then looked down at the sentry. She started to arise and the lieutenant reached down and hoisted rather awkwardly at her arm.

"Don't you worry about him. He's all right."

She turned her face with its curving lips and shining eyes once more toward the unconscious soldier upon the floor. The troopers made a lane to the door, the lieutenant bowed, the girl vanished.

"Queer," said a young officer. "Girl very clearly worst kind of rebel and yet she falls to weeping and wailing like mad over one of her enemies. Be around in the morning with all sorts of doctoring—you see if she ain't. Queer."

The sharp lieutenant shrugged his shoulders. After reflection he shrugged his shoulders again. He said: "War changes many things, but it doesn't change everything, thank God."

A MYSTERY OF HEROISM:
A DETAIL OF AN AMERICAN BATTLE

THE dark uniforms of the men were so coated with dust from the incessant wrestling of the two armies that the regiment almost seemed a part of the clay bank which shielded them from the shells. On the top of the hill a battery was arguing in tremendous roars with some other guns and to the eye of the infantry, the artillerymen, the guns, the caissons, the horses, were distinctly outlined upon the blue sky. When a piece was fired a red streak as round as a log flashed low in the heavens, like a monstrous bolt of lightning. The men of the battery wore white duck trousers, which somehow emphasized their legs, and when they ran and crowded in little groups at the bidding of the shouting officers, it was more impressive than usual to the infantry.

Fred Collins of A Company was saying: "Thunder, I wisht I had a drink. Ain't there any water round here?" Then somebody yelled: "There goes th' bugler!"

As the eyes of half of the regiment swept in one machine-like movement there was an instant's picture of a horse in a great convulsive leap of a death wound and a rider leaning back with a crooked arm and spread fingers before his face. On the ground was the crimson terror of an exploding shell, with fibres of flame that seemed like lances. A glittering bugle swung clear of the rider's back as fell headlong the horse and the man. In the air was an odor as from a conflagration.

Sometimes they of the infantry looked down at a fair little meadow which spread at their feet. Its long, green grass was rippling gently in a breeze. Beyond it was the grey form of a house half torn to pieces by shells and by the busy axes of soldiers who had pursued firewood. The line of an old fence was now dimly marked by long weeds and by an occasional post. A shell had blown the well-house to fragments. Little lines of grey smoke ribboning upward from some embers indicated the place where had stood the barn.

From beyond a curtain of green woods there came the sound of some stupendous scuffle as if two animals of the size of islands were fighting. At a distance there were occasional appearances of swift-moving men, horses, batteries, flags, and, with the crashing of infantry volleys were heard, often, wild and frenzied cheers. In the midst of it all, Smith and Ferguson, two privates of A Company, were engaged in a heated discussion, which involved the greatest questions of the national existence.

The battery on the hill presently engaged in a frightful duel. The white legs of the gunners scampered this way and that way and the officers redoubled their shouts. The guns, with their demeanors of stolidity and courage, were typical of something infinitely self-possessed in this clamor of death that swirled around the hill.

One of a "swing" team was suddenly smitten quivering to the ground and his maddened brethren dragged his torn body in their struggle to escape from this turmoil and danger. A young soldier astride one of the leaders swore and fumed in his saddle and furiously jerked at the bridle. An officer screamed out an order so violently that his voice broke and ended the sentence in a falsetto shriek.

The leading company of the infantry regiment was somewhat exposed and the colonel ordered it moved more fully under the shelter of the hill. There was the clank of steel against steel.

A lieutenant of the battery rode down and passed them, holding his right arm carefully in his left hand. And it was as if this arm was not at all a part of him, but belonged to another man. His sober and reflective charger went slowly. The officer's face was grimy and perspiring and his uniform was tousled as if he had been in direct grapple with an enemy. He smiled grimly when the men stared at him. He turned his horse toward the meadow.

Collins of A Company said: "I wisht I had a drink. I bet there's water in that there ol' well yonder!"

"Yes; but how you goin' to git it?"

For the little meadow which intervened was now suffering a

terrible onslaught of shells. Its green and beautiful calm had vanished utterly. Brown earth was being flung in monstrous handfuls. And there was a massacre of the young blades of grass. They were being torn, burned, obliterated. Some curious fortune of the battle had made this gentle little meadow the object of the red hate of the shells and each one as it exploded seemed like an imprecation in the face of a maiden.

The wounded officer who was riding across this expanse said to himself: "Why, they couldn't shoot any harder if the whole army was massed here!"

A shell struck the grey ruins of the house and as, after the roar, the shattered wall fell in fragments, there was a noise which resembled the flapping of shutters during a wild gale of winter. Indeed the infantry paused in the shelter of the bank, appeared as men standing upon a shore contemplating a madness of the sea. The angel of calamity had under its glance the battery upon the hill. Fewer white-legged men labored about the guns. A shell had smitten one of the pieces and after the flare, the smoke, the dust, the wrath of this blow was gone, it was possible to see white legs stretched horizontally upon the ground. And at that interval to the rear, where it is the business of battery horses to stand with their noses to the fight awaiting the command to drag their guns out of the destruction or into it or wheresoever these incomprehensible humans demanded with whip and spur—in this line of passive and dumb spectators, whose fluttering hearts yet would not let them forget the iron laws of man's control of them—in this rank of brute-soldiers there had been relentless and hideous carnage. From the ruck of bleeding and prostrate horses, the men of the infantry could see one animal raising its stricken body with its fore-legs and turning its nose with mystic and profound eloquence toward the sky.

Some comrades joked Collins about his thirst. "Well, if yeh want a drink so bad, why don't yeh go git it?"

"Well, I will in a minnet if yeh don't shut up."

A lieutenant of artillery floundered his horse straight down the hill with as great concern as if it were level ground. As he galloped past the colonel of the infantry, he threw up his hand in swift salute. "We've got to get out of that," he roared angrily. He was a black-bearded officer, and his eyes, which resembled beads, sparkled like those of an insane man. His jumping horse sped along the column of infantry.

The fat major standing carelessly with his sword held horizontally behind him and with his legs far apart, looked after the receding horseman and laughed. "He wants to get back with orders pretty quick or there'll be no batt'ry left," he observed.

The wise young captain of the second company hazarded to the lieutenant colonel that the enemy's infantry would probably soon attack the hill, and the lieutenant colonel snubbed him.

A private in one of the rear companies looked out over the meadow and then turned to a companion and said: "Look there, Jim." It was the wounded officer from the battery, who some time before had started to ride across the meadow, supporting his right arm carefully with his left hand. This man had encountered a shell apparently at a time when no one perceived him and he could now be seen lying face downward with a stirruped foot stretched across the body of his dead horse. A leg of the charger extended slantingly upward precisely as stiff as a stake. Around this motionless pair the shells still howled.

There was a quarrel in A Company. Collins was shaking his fist in the faces of some laughing comrades. "Dern yeh! I ain't afraid t' go. If yeh say much, I will go!"

"Of course, yeh will! Yeh'll run through that there medder, won't yeh?"

Collins said, in a terrible voice: "You see, now!" At this ominous threat his comrades broke into renewed jeers.

Collins gave them a dark scowl and went to find his captain. The latter was conversing with the colonel of the regiment.

"Captain," said Collins, saluting and standing at attention. In those days all trousers bagged at the knees. "Captain, I want t' git permission to go git some water from that there well over yonder!"

The colonel and the captain swung about simultaneously and stared across the meadow. The captain laughed. "You must be pretty thirsty, Collins?"

"Yes, sir; I am."

"Well—ah," said the captain. After a moment he asked: "Can't you wait?"

"No, sir."

The colonel was watching Collins's face. "Look here, my lad," he said, in a pious sort of a voice. "Look here, my lad." Collins was not a lad. "Don't you think that's taking pretty big risks for a little drink of water?"

"I dunno," said Collins, uncomfortably. Some of the resentment toward his companions, which perhaps had forced him into this affair, was beginning to fade. "I dunno wether 'tis."

The colonel and the captain contemplated him for a time.

"Well," said the captain finally.

"Well," said the colonel, "if you want to go, why go."

Collins saluted. "Much obliged t' yeh."

As he moved away the colonel called after him. "Take some of the other boys' canteens with you an' hurry back now."

"Yes, sir. I will."

The colonel and the captain looked at each other then, for it had suddenly occurred that they could not for the life of them tell whether Collins wanted to go or whether he did not.

They turned to regard Collins and as they perceived him surrounded by gesticulating comrades the colonel said: "Well, by thunder! I guess he's going."

Collins appeared as a man dreaming. In the midst of the questions, the advice, the warnings, all the excited talk of his company mates, he maintained a curious silence.

They were very busy in preparing him for his ordeal. When they inspected him carefully it was somewhat like the examination that grooms give a horse before a race; and they were amazed, staggered by the whole affair. Their astonishment found vent in strange repetitions.

"Are yeh sure a-goin'?" they demanded again and again.

"Certainly I am," cried Collins, at last furiously.

He strode sullenly away from them. He was swinging five or six canteens by their cords. It seemed that his cap would not remain firmly on his head, and often he reached and pulled it down over his brow.

There was a general movement in the compact column. The long animal-like thing moved slightly. Its four hundred eyes were turned upon the figure of Collins.

"Well, sir, if that ain't th' derndest thing. I never thought Fred Collins had the blood in him for that kind of business."

"What's he goin' to do, anyhow?"

"He's goin' to that well there after water."

"We ain't dyin' of thirst, are we? That's foolishness."

"Well, somebody put him up to it an' he's doin' it."

"Say, he must be a desperate cuss."

When Collins faced the meadow and walked away from the regiment he was vaguely conscious that a chasm, the deep valley of all prides, was suddenly between him and his comrades. It was provisional, but the provision was that he return as a victor. He had blindly been led by quaint emotions and laid himself under an obligation to walk squarely up to the face of death.

But he was not sure that he wished to make a retraction even if he could do so without shame. As a matter of truth he was sure of very little. He was mainly surprised.

It seemed to him supernaturally strange that he had allowed his mind to maneuver his body into such a situation. He understood that it might be called dramatically great.

However, he had no full appreciation of anything excepting that he was actually conscious of being dazed. He could feel his dulled mind groping after the form and color of this incident.

Too, he wondered why he did not feel some keen agony of fear cutting his sense like a knife. He wondered at this because human expression had said loudly for centuries that men should feel afraid of certain things and that all men who did not feel this fear were phenomena, heroes.

He was then a hero. He suffered that disappointment which we would all have if we discovered that we were ourselves capable of those deeds which we most admire in history and legend. This, then, was a hero. After all, heroes were not much.

No, it could not be true. He was not a hero. Heroes had no shames in their lives and, as for him, he remembered borrowing fifteen dollars from a friend and promising to pay it back the next day, and then avoiding that friend for ten months. When at home his mother had aroused him for the early labor of his life on the farm, it had often been his fashion to be irritable, childish, diabolical, and his mother had died since he had come to the war.

He saw that in this matter of the well, the canteens, the shells, he was an intruder in the land of fine deeds.

He was now about thirty paces from his comrades. The regiment had just turned its many faces toward him.

From the forest of terrific noises there suddenly emerged a little uneven line of men. They fired fiercely and rapidly at distant foliage on which appeared little puffs of white smoke. The spatter of skirmish firing was added to the thunder of the guns on the hill. The little line of men ran forward. A color-sergeant fell flat with his flag as if he had slipped on ice. There was hoarse cheering from this distant field.

Collins suddenly felt that two demon fingers were pressed into his ears. He could see nothing but flying arrows, flaming red. He lurched from the shock of this explosion, but he made a mad rush for the house, which he viewed as a man submerged to the neck in a boiling surf might view the shore. In the air, little pieces of shell howled and the earthquake explosions drove him insane with the menace of their roar. As he ran the canteens knocked together with a rhythmical tinkling.

As he neared the house each detail of the scene became vivid to him. He was aware of some bricks of the vanished chimney lying on the sod. There was a door which hung by one hinge.

Rifle bullets called forth by the insistent skirmishers came from the far-off bank of foliage. They mingled with the shells and the pieces of shells until the air was torn in all directions by hootings, yells, howls. The sky was full of fiends who directed all their wild rage at his head.

When he came to the well he flung himself face downward and peered into its darkness. There were furtive silver glintings some feet from the surface. He grabbed one of the canteens and, unfastening its cap, swung it down by the cord. The water flowed slowly in with an indolent gurgle.

And now as he lay with his face turned away he was suddenly smitten with the terror. It came upon his heart like the grasp of claws. All the power faded from his muscles. For an instant he was no more than a dead man.

The canteen filled with a maddening slowness in the manner of all bottles. Presently he recovered his strength and addressed a screaming oath to it. He leaned over until it seemed as if he intended to try to push water into it with his hands. His eyes as he gazed down into the well shone like two pieces of metal and in their expression was a great appeal and a great curse. The stupid water derided him.

There was the blaring thunder of a shell. Crimson light shone through the swift-boiling smoke and made a pink reflection on part of the wall of the well. Collins jerked out his arm and canteen with the same motion that a man would use in withdrawing his head from a furnace.

He scrambled erect and glared and hesitated. On the ground near him lay the old well bucket, with a length of rusty chain. He lowered it swiftly into the well. The bucket struck the water and then turning lazily over, sank. When, with hand reaching tremblingly over hand, he hauled it out, it knocked often against the walls of the well and spilled some of its contents.

In running with a filled bucket, a man can adopt but one kind of gait. So through this terrible field over which screamed practical angels of death Collins ran in the manner of a farmer chased out of a dairy by a bull.

His face went staring white with anticipation—anticipation of a blow that would whirl him around and down. He would fall as he had seen other men fall, the life knocked out of them so suddenly that their knees were no more quick to touch the ground than their heads. He saw the long blue line of the regiment, but his comrades were standing looking at him from the edge of an impossible star. He was aware of some deep wheel ruts and hoof prints in the sod beneath his feet.

The artillery officer who had fallen in this meadow had been making groans in the teeth of the tempest of sound. These futile cries, wrenched from him by his agony, were heard only by shells, bullets. When wild-eyed Collins came running, this officer raised himself. His face contorted and blanched from pain, he was about to utter some great beseeching cry. But suddenly his face straightened and he called: "Say, young man, give me a drink of water, will you?"

Collins had no room amid his emotions for surprise. He was mad from the threats of destruction.

"I can't," he screamed, and in this reply was a full description of his quaking apprehension. His cap was gone and his hair was riotous. His clothes made it appear that he had been dragged over the ground by the heels. He ran on.

The officer's head sank down and one elbow crooked. His foot in its brass-bound stirrup still stretched over the body of his horse and the other leg was under the steed.

But Collins turned. He came dashing back. His face had now turned grey and in his eyes was all terror. "Here it is! Here it is!"

The officer was as a man gone in drink. His arm bended like a twig. His head drooped as if his neck was of willow. He was sinking to the ground, to lie face downward.

Collins grabbed him by the shoulder. "Here it is. Here's your drink. Turn over! Turn over, man, for God's sake!"

With Collins hauling at his shoulder, the officer twisted his body and fell with his face turned toward that region where lived the unspeakable noises of the swirling missiles. There was the faintest shadow of a smile on his lips as he looked at Collins. He gave a sigh, a little primitive breath like that from a child.

Collins tried to hold the bucket steadily, but his shaking hands caused the water to splash all over the face of the dying man. Then he jerked it away and ran on.

The regiment gave him a welcoming roar. The grimed faces were wrinkled in laughter.

His captain waved the bucket away. "Give it to the men!"

The two genial, sky-larking young lieutenants were the first to gain possession of it. They played over it in their fashion.

When one tried to drink the other teasingly knocked his elbow. "Don't, Billie! You'll make me spill it," said the one. The other laughed.

Suddenly there was an oath, the thud of wood on the ground, and a swift murmur of astonishment from the ranks. The two lieutenants glared at each other. The bucket lay on the ground empty.

AN INDIANA CAMPAIGN

I

WHEN the able-bodied citizens of the village formed a company and marched away to the war, Major Tom Boldin assumed in a manner the burden of the village cares. Everybody ran to him when they felt obliged to discuss their affairs. The sorrows of the town were dragged before him. His little bench at the sunny side of the Migglesville tavern became a sort of an open court where people came to speak resentfully of their grievances. He accepted his position and struggled manfully under the load. It behooved him as a man who had seen the sky red over the quaint low cities of Mexico and the compact Northern bayonets gleaming on the narrow roads.

One warm summer day the major sat asleep on his little bench. There was a lull in the tempest of discussion which usually enveloped him. His cane, by use of which he could make the most tremendous and impressive gestures, reposed beside him. His hat lay upon the bench and his old bald head had swung far forward until his nose actually touched the first button of his waistcoat.

The sparrows wrangled desperately in the road, defying perspiration. Once a team went jangling and creaking past, raising a yellow blur of dust before the soft tones of the fields and sky. In the long grass of the meadow across the road the insects chirped and clacked eternally.

Suddenly a frowzy-headed boy appeared in the roadway, his bare feet pattering rapidly. He was extremely excited. He gave a shrill whoop as he discovered the sleeping major and rushed toward him. He created a terrific panic among some chickens who had been scratching intently near the major's feet. They clamored in an insanity of fear and rushed hither and thither seeking a way of escape, whereas in reality all ways lay plainly open to them.

This tumult caused the major to rouse with a sudden little jump of amazement and apprehension. He rubbed his eyes and gazed about him. Meanwhile some clever chicken had discovered a passage to safety and led the flock into the garden where they squawked in sustained alarm.

Panting from his run and choked with terror, the little boy stood before the major, struggling with a tale that was ever upon the tip of his tongue.

"Major—now—Major——"

The old man, aroused from a delicious slumber, glared impatiently at the little boy. "Come, come! What's th' matter with yeh?" he demanded. "What's th' matter? Don't stand there shaking. Speak up."

"Lots is th' matter," the little boy shouted valiantly with a courage born of the importance of his tale. "My ma's chickens 'uz all stole an'—now—he's over in th' woods."

"Who is? Who is over in th' woods? Go ahead."

"Now—th' rebel is!"

"What?" roared the major.

"Th' rebel," cried the little boy with the last of his breath.

The major pounced from his bench in tempestuous excitement. He seized the little boy by the collar and gave him a great jerk. "Where? Are yeh sure? Who saw 'im? How long ago? Where is he now? Did *you* see 'im?"

The little boy, frightened at the major's fury, began to sob. After a moment he managed to stammer: "He—now—he's in the woods. I saw 'im. He looks uglier'n anythin'."

The major released his hold upon the boy and pausing for a time, indulged in a glorious dream. Then he said: "By thunder, we'll ketch th' cuss. You wait here," he told the boy, "an' don't say a word t' anybody. Do yeh hear?"

The boy, still weeping, nodded and the major hurriedly entered the inn. He took down from its pegs an awkward, smoothbore rifle and carefully examined the enormous percussion cap that was fitted over the nipple. Mistrusting the cap he removed it and replaced it with a new one. He scrutinized the gun keenly as if he could judge in this manner of the condition of the load. All his movements were deliberate and deadly.

When he arrived upon the porch of the tavern he beheld the yard filled with people. Peter Witheby, sooty-faced and grinning, was in the van. He looked at the major. "Well?" he said.

"Well?" returned the major bridling.

"Well, what 'che got?" said old Peter.

" 'Got'? Got a rebel over in th' woods," roared the major. At this sentence the women and the boys who had gathered eagerly about him, gave vent to startled cries. The women had come from adjacent houses but the little boys represented the entire village. They had miraculously heard the first whisper of rumor and they had performed wonders in getting to the spot. They clustered around the important figure of the major and gazed in silent awe. The women, however, burst forth. At the word "rebel," which represented to them all terrible things, they deluged the major with questions which were obviously unanswerable.

He shook them off with violent impatience. Meanwhile, Peter Witheby was trying to force exasperating interrogations through the tumult to the major's ears. "What? No! Yes! How d' I know?" the maddened veteran snarled as he struggled with his friends. "No! Yes! What? How in thunder d' I know?" Upon the steps of the tavern, the landlady sat weeping forlornly.

At last the major burst through the crowd and went to the roadway. There, as they all streamed after him, he turned and faced them. "Now, look a' here, I don't know any more about this than you do," he told them forcibly. "All I know is there's a rebel over in Smith's woods an' all I know is that I'm a-goin' after 'im."

"But, hol' on a minnet," said old Peter. "How do yeh know he's a rebel?"

"I know he is," cried the major. "Don't yeh think I know what a rebel is?"

Then, with a gesture of disdain at the babbling crowd, he marched determinedly away, his rifle held in the hollow of his arm. At this heroic movement a new clamor arose, half admiration, half dismay. Old Peter hobbled after the major, continually repeating "Hol' on a minnet."

The little boy who had given the alarm was the center of a throng of lads who gazed with envy and awe, discovering in him a new quality. He held forth to them eloquently. The women stared after the figure of the major and old Peter his pursuer. Jerozel Bronson, a half-witted lad who comprehended nothing save an occasional genial word, leaned against the fence and grinned like a skull. The major and the pursuer passed out of view around the turn in the road where the great maples lazily shook at the dust that lay on their leaves.

For a moment the little group of women listened intently as if they expected to hear a sudden shot and cries from the distance. They looked at each other, their lips a little ways apart. The trees sighed softly in the heat of the summer sun. The insects in the meadow continued their monotonous humming, and, somewhere, a hen had been stricken with fear and was cackling loudly.

Finally Mrs. Goodwin said: "Well, I'm goin' up to th' turn a' th' road, anyhow." Mrs. Willets and Mrs. Joe Petersen, her particular friends, cried out at this temerity, but she said: "Well, I'm goin' anyhow."

She called Bronson. "Come on, Jeroozel. You're a man an' if he should chase us, why, you mus' pitch inteh 'im. Hey?"

Bronson always obeyed everybody. He grinned an assent and went with her down the road.

A little boy attempted to follow them, but a shrill scream from his mother made him halt.

The remaining women stood motionless, their eyes fixed upon Mrs. Goodwin and Jerozel. Then at last one gave a laugh of triumph at her conquest of caution and fear and cried: "Well, I'm goin' too."

Another instantly said: "So am I." There began a general movement. Some of the little boys had already ventured a hundred feet away from the main body, and at this unanimous advance they spread out ahead in little groups. Some recounted terrible stories of rebel ferocity. Their eyes were large with excitement. The whole thing with its possible dangers had for them a delicious element. Johnnie Petersen, who could whip any boy present, explained what he would do in case the enemy should happen to pounce out at him.

The familiar scene suddenly assumed a new aspect. The field of corn which met the road upon the left was no longer a mere field of corn. It was a darkly mystic place whose recesses could contain all manner of dangers. The long green leaves, waving in the breeze, rustled as from the passing of men. In the song of the insects there were now omens, threats.

There was a warning in the enamel blue of the sky, in the stretch of yellow road, in the very atmosphere. Above the tops of the corn loomed the distant foliage of Smith's woods, curtaining the silent action of a tragedy whose horrors they imagined.

The women and the little boys came to a halt, overwhelmed by the impressiveness of the landscape. They waited silently.

Mrs. Goodwin suddenly said: "I'm goin' back." The others, who all wished to return, cried at once disdainfully: "Well, go back, if yeh want to."

A cricket at the roadside exploded suddenly in his shrill song and a woman who had been standing near shrieked in startled terror. An electric movement went through the group of women. They jumped and gave vent to sudden screams. With the fear still upon their agitated faces, they turned to berate the one who had shrieked. "My, what a goose you are, Sallie. Why, it took my breath away. Goodness sakes, don't holler like that again."

II

"Hol' on a minnet," Peter Witheby was crying to the major, as the latter, full of the importance and dignity of his position as protector of Migglesville, paced forward swiftly. The veteran already felt upon his brow a wreath formed of the flowers of gratitude and as he strode, he was absorbed in planning a calm and self-contained manner of wearing it. "Hol' on a minnet," piped old Peter in the rear.

At last the major, aroused from his dream of triumph, turned about wrathfully. "Well, what?"

"Now, look a' here," said Peter. "What 'che goin' t' do?"

The major with a gesture of supreme exasperation wheeled again and went on. When he arrived at the cornfield he halted and waited for Peter. He had suddenly felt that indefinable menace in the landscape.

"Well?" demanded Peter, panting.

The major's eyes wavered a trifle. "Well," he repeated. "Well, I'm goin' in there an' bring out that there rebel."

They both paused and studied the gently swaying masses of corn, and behind them, the looming woods sinister with possible secrets.

"Well?" said old Peter.

The major moved uneasily and put his hand to his brow. Peter waited in obvious expectation.

The major crossed through the grass at the roadside and climbed the fence. He put both legs over the top-most rail and then sat perched there, facing the woods. Once he turned his head and asked: "What?"

"I hain't said anythin'," answered Peter.

The major clambered down from the fence and went slowly into the corn, his gun held in readiness. Peter stood in the road.

Presently, the major returned and said in a cautious whisper: "If yeh hear anythin', you come a-runnin', will yeh?"

"Well, I hain't got no gun nor nuthin'," said Peter, in the same low tone. "What good 'ud I do?"

"Well, yeh might come along with me an' watch," said the major. "Four eyes is better 'n two."

"If I had a gun——" began Peter.

"Oh, yeh don't need no gun," interrupted the major, waving his hand. "All I'm afraid of is that I won't find 'im. My eyes ain't so good as they was."

"Well——"

"Come along," whispered the major. "Yeh hain't afraid, are yeh?"

"No, but——"

"Well, come along then. What's th' matter with yeh?"

Peter climbed the fence. He paused on the top rail and took a prolonged stare at the inscrutable woods. When he joined the major in the cornfield he said with a touch of anger: "Well, you got th' gun. Remember that. If he comes fer me, I hain't got a blame thing."

"Shucks," answered the major. "He hain't a-goin' t' come for yeh."

The two then began a wary journey through the corn. One by one the long aisles between the rows appeared. As they glanced along each of them it seemed as if some gruesome thing had just previously vacated it. Old Peter halted once and whispered: "Say, look a' here, supposin'—supposin'——"

"Supposin' what?" demanded the major.

"Supposin'——" said Peter. "Well, remember you got th' gun an' I hain't got anythin'."

"Thunder!" said the major.

When they got to where the stalks were very short because of the shade cast by the trees of the wood, they halted again. The leaves were gently swishing in the breeze. Before them stretched the mystic green wall of the forest, and there seemed to be in it eyes which followed each of their movements.

Peter at last said: "I don't believe there's anybody in there."

"Yes, there is, too," said the major. "I'll bet anythin' he's in there."

"How d' yeh know?" asked Peter. "I'll bet he hain't within a mile o' here."

The major suddenly ejaculated: "Lissen!"

They bent forward scarce breathing, their mouths agape, their eyes glinting. Finally the major turned his head. "Did yeh hear that?" he said hoarsely.

"No," said Peter, in a low voice. "What was it?"

The major listened for a moment. Then he turned again. "I thought I heered somebody holler," he explained cautiously.

They both bent forward and listened once more. Peter in the intentness of his attitude lost his balance and was obliged to shift his foot hastily and with some noise. "Sssh," hissed the major.

After a minute Peter spoke quite loudly. "Oh, shucks, I don't believe yeh heered anythin'."

The major made a frantic downward gesture with his hand. "Shet up, will yeh!" he said, in an angry undertone.

Peter became silent for a moment, but presently he said again: "Oh, yeh didn't hear anythin'."

The major turned to glare at his companion in despair and wrath.

"What's th' matter with yeh? Can't yeh shet up?"

"Oh, this here hain't no use. If you're goin' in after 'im, why don't yeh go in after 'im?"

"Well, gimme time, can't yeh?" said the major, in a growl. And as if to add more to this reproach he climbed the fence that compassed the woods, looking resentfully back at his companion.

"Well?" said Peter, when the major paused.

The major stepped down upon the thick carpet of brown leaves that stretched under the trees. He turned then to whisper: "You wait here, will yeh?" His face was red with determination.

"Well, hol' on a minnet," said Peter. "You—I—we'd better——"

"No," said the major. "You wait here."

He went stealthily into the thickets. Peter watched him until he grew to be a vague slow-moving shadow. From time to time he could hear the leaves crackle and twigs snap under the major's awkward tread. Peter, intent, breathless, waited for the peal of sudden tragedy. Finally the woods grew silent in a solemn and impressive hush that caused Peter to feel the thumping of his heart. He began to look about him to make sure that nothing should spring upon him from the sombre shadows. He scrutinized this cool gloom before him, and at times he thought he could perceive the moving of swift silent shapes. He concluded that he had better go back and try to muster some assistance to the major.

As Peter came through the corn, the women in the road caught sight of the gliding figure and screamed. Many of them began to run. The little boys, with all their valor, scurried away in clouds. Mrs. Joe Petersen, however, cast a glance over her shoulder as she, with her skirts gathered up, was running as best she could. She instantly stopped and, in tones of deepest scorn, called out to the others: "Why, it's on'y Pete Witheby." They came faltering back then, those who had been naturally the swiftest in the race avoiding the eyes of those whose limbs had enabled them to flee only a short distance.

Peter came rapidly, appreciating the glances of vivid interest in the eyes of the women. To their lightning-like questions which hit all sides of the episode, he opposed a new tranquility gained from his sudden ascent in importance. He made no answer to their clamor. When he had reached the top of the fence, he called out commandingly: "Here you, Johnnie, you an' George, run an' git my gun. It's hangin' on th' pegs over th' bench in th' shop."

At this terrible sentence, a shuddering cry broke from the women. The boys named sped down the road, accompanied by a retinue of envious companions.

Peter swung his legs over the rail and faced the woods again. He twisted his head once to say: "Keep still, can't yeh? Quit scufflin' aroun'." They could see by his manner that this was a supreme moment. The group became motionless and still. Later, Peter turned to say "Sssh" to a restless boy, and the air with which he said it smote them all with awe.

The little boys who had gone after the gun came pattering along hurriedly, the weapon borne in the midst of them. Each was anxious to share in the honor. The one who had been delegated to bring it was bullying and directing his comrades.

Peter said "Sssh." He took the gun and poised it in readiness to sweep the cornfield. He scowled at the boys and whispered angrily: "Why didn't yeh bring th' powder-horn an' th' thing with th' bullets in? I told yeh t' bring 'em. I'll send somebody else next time."

"Yeh didn't tell us," cried the two boys shrilly.

"Sssh! Quit yeh noise," said Peter with a violent gesture.

However, this reproof enabled the other boys to recover that peace of mind which they had lost when seeing their friends loaded with honors.

The women had cautiously approached the fence and, from time to time, whispered feverish questions, but Peter repulsed them savagely, with an air of being infinitely bothered by their interference in his intent watch. They were forced to listen again in silence to the weird and prophetic chanting of the insects and the mystic silken rustling of the corn.

At last the thud of hurrying feet in the soft soil of the field came to their ears. A dark form sped toward them. A wave of a mighty fear swept over the group and the screams of the women came hoarsely from their choked throats. Peter swung madly from his perch and turned to use the fence as a rampart.

But it was the major. His face was inflamed and his eyes were glaring. He clutched his rifle by the middle and swung it wildly. He was bounding at a great speed for his fat, short body.

"It's all right! It's all right," he began to yell, some distance away. "It's all right. It's on'y ol' Milt' Jacoby!"

When he arrived at the top of the fence, he paused and mopped his brow.

"What?" they thundered in an agony of sudden unreasoning disappointment.

Mrs. Joe Petersen, who was a distant connection of Milton Jacoby, thought to forestall any damage to her social position by saying at once disdainfully: "Drunk, I s'pose!"

"Yep," said the major, still on the fence and mopping his brow. "Drunk as a fool. Thunder, I was surprised. I—I—thought it was a rebel sure."

The thoughts of all these women wavered for a time. They were at a loss for precise expression of their emotion. At last, however, they hurled this one superior sentence at the major:

"Well, yeh might have known."

A GREY SLEEVE

I

IT LOOKS as if it might rain this afternoon," remarked the
lieutenant of artillery.

"So it does," the infantry captain assented. He glanced
casually at the sky. When his eyes had lowered to the green-
shadowed landscape before him, he said fretfully: "I wish those
fellows out yonder would quit pelting at us. They've been at it
since noon."

At the edge of a grove of maples, across wide fields, there
occasionally appeared little puffs of smoke of a dull hue in this
gloom of sky which expressed an impending rain. The long wave
of blue and steel in the field moved uneasily at the eternal
barking of the far-away sharpshooters, and the men, leaning
upon their rifles, stared at the grove of maples. Once a private
turned to borrow some tobacco from a comrade in the rear rank,
but, with his hand still stretched out, he continued to twist his
head and glance at the distant trees. He was afraid the enemy
would shoot him at a time when he was not looking.

Suddenly the artillery officer said: "See what's coming!"

Along the rear of the brigade of infantry a column of cavalry
was sweeping at a hard gallop. A lieutenant riding some yards to
the right of the column bawled furiously at the four troopers just
at the rear of the colors. They had lost distance and made a little
gap, but at the shouts of the lieutenant they urged their horses
forward. The bugler, careering along behind the captain of the
troop, fought and tugged like a wrestler to keep his frantic
animal from bolting far ahead of the column.

On the springy turf the innumerable hoofs thundered in a
swift storm of sound. In the brown faces of the troopers their
eyes were set like bits of flashing steel.

The long line of the infantry regiments standing at ease underwent a sudden movement at the rush of the passing squad-

ron. The foot soldiers turned their heads to gaze at the torrent of horses and men.

The yellow folds of the flag fluttered back in silken shuddering waves, as if it were a reluctant thing. Occasionally a giant spring of a charger would rear the firm and steady figure of a soldier suddenly head and shoulders above his comrades. Over the noise of the scudding hoofs could be heard the creaking of leather trappings, the jingle and clank of steel and the tense low-toned commands or appeals of the men to their horses. And the horses were mad with the headlong sweep of this movement. Powerful underjaws bended back and straightened so that the bits were clamped as rigidly as vises upon the teeth, and glistening necks arched in desperate resistance to the hands at the bridles. Swinging their heads in rage at the granite laws of their lives which bended even their angers and their ardors to chosen directions and chosen paces, their flight was as a flight of harnessed demons.

The captain's bay kept its pace at the head of the squadron with the lithe bounds of a thoroughbred, and this horse was proud as a chief at the roaring trample of his fellows behind him. The captain's glance was calmly upon the grove of maples from whence the sharpshooters of the enemy had been picking at the blue line. He seemed to be reflecting. He stolidly rose and fell with the plunges of his horse in all the indifference of a deacon's figure seated plumply in church. And it occurred to many of the watching infantry to wonder why this officer could remain imperturbable and reflective when his squadron was thundering and swarming behind him like the rushing of a flood.

The column swung in a saber-curve toward a break in a fence and dashed into a roadway. Once a little plank bridge was encountered, and the sound of the hoofs upon it was like the long roll of many drums. An old captain in the infantry turned to his first lieutenant and made a remark which was a compound of bitter disparagement of cavalry in general and soldierly admiration of this particular troop.

Suddenly the bugle sounded and the column halted with a jolting upheaval amid sharp, brief cries. A moment later the men had tumbled from their horses and carbines in hand were running in a swarm toward the grove of maples. In the road, one of every four of the troopers was standing with braced legs and pulling and hauling at the bridles of four frenzied horses.

The captain was running awkwardly in his boots. He held his saber low so that the point often threatened to catch in the turf. His yellow hair ruffled out from under his faded cap. "Go in hard now," he roared in a voice of hoarse fury. His face was violently red.

The troopers threw themselves upon the grove like wolves upon a great animal. Along the whole front of the wood there was the dry crackling of musketry, with bitter, swift flashes and smoke that writhed like stung phantoms. The troopers yelled shrilly and spanged bullets low into the foliage.

For a moment, when near the woods, the line almost halted. The men struggled and fought for a time like swimmers encountering a powerful current. Then with a supreme effort they went on again. They dashed madly at the grove, whose foliage from the high light of the field was as inscrutable as a wall.

Then suddenly each detail of the calm trees became apparent and with a few more frantic leaps the men were in the cool gloom of the woods. There was a heavy odor as from burnt paper. Wisps of grey smoke wound upward. The men halted and, grimy, perspiring and puffing, they searched the recesses of the woods with eager, fierce glances. Figures could be seen flitting afar off. A dozen carbines rattled at them in an angry volley.

During this pause the captain strode along the line, his face lit with a broad smile of contentment. "When he sends this crowd to do anything, I guess he'll find we do it pretty sharp," he said to the grinning lieutenant.

"Say, they didn't stand that rush a minute, did they?" said the subaltern. Both officers were profoundly dusty in their uniforms, and their faces were soiled like those of two urchins.

Out in the grass behind them were three tumbled and silent forms.

Presently the line moved forward again. The men went from tree to tree like hunters stalking game. Some at the left of the line fired occasionally and those at the right gazed curiously in that direction. The men still breathed heavily from their scramble across the field.

Of a sudden a trooper halted and said: "Hello! there's a

house!" Everyone paused. The men turned to look at their leader. The captain stretched his neck and swung his head from side to side. "By George, it is a house!" he said.

Through the wealth of leaves there vaguely loomed the form of a large, white house. These troopers, brown-faced from many days of campaigning, each feature of them telling of their placid confidence and courage, were stopped abruptly by the appearance of this house. There was some subtle suggestion—some tale of an unknown thing which watched them from they knew not what part of it.

A rail fence girted a wide lawn of tangled grass. Seven pines stood along a driveway which led from two distant posts of a vanished gate. The blue-clothed troopers moved forward until they stood at the fence peering over it.

The captain put one hand on the top rail and seemed to be about to climb the fence when suddenly he hesitated and said in a low voice: "Watson, what do you think of it?"

The lieutenant stared at the house. "Derned if I know!" he replied.

The captain pondered. It happened that the whole company had turned a gaze of profound awe and doubt upon this edifice which confronted them. The men were very silent.

At last the captain swore and said: "We are certainly a pack of fools. Derned old deserted house halting a company of Union cavalry and making us gape like babies."

"Yes, but there's something—something——" insisted the subaltern in a half stammer.

"Well, if there's 'something—something' in there, I'll get it out," said the captain. "Send Sharpe clean around to the other side with about twelve men, so we will sure bag your 'something—something,' and I'll take a few of the boys and find out what's in the damned old thing."

He chose the nearest eight men for his "storming party," as the lieutenant called it. After he had waited some minutes for the others to get into position, he said "come ahead" to his eight men and climbed the fence.

The brighter light of the tangled lawn made him suddenly feel tremendously apparent and he wondered if there could be some mystic thing in the house which was regarding this approach.

His men trudged silently at his back. They stared at the windows and lost themselves in deep speculations as to the probability of there being, perhaps, eyes behind the blinds—malignant eyes, piercing eyes.

Suddenly a corporal in the party gave vent to a startled exclamation, and half threw his carbine into position. The captain turned quickly and the corporal said: "I saw an arm move the blinds. An arm with a grey sleeve!"

"Don't be a fool, Jones, now," said the captain sharply.

"I swear t'——" began the corporal, but the captain silenced him.

When they arrived at the front of the house the troopers paused, while the captain went softly up the front steps. He stood before the large front door and studied it. Some crickets chirped in the long grass and the nearest pine could be heard in its endless sighs. One of the privates moved uneasily and his foot crunched the gravel. Suddenly the captain swore angrily and kicked the door with a loud crash. It flew open.

II

The bright lights of the day flashed into the old house when the captain angrily kicked open the door. He was aware of a wide hallway carpeted with matting and extending deep into the dwelling. There was also an old walnut hat rack and a little marble-topped table with a vase and two books upon it. Further back was a great venerable fireplace containing dreary ashes.

But directly in front of the captain was a young girl. The flying open of the door had obviously been an utter astonishment to her and she remained transfixed there in the middle of the floor, staring at the captain with wide eyes.

She was like a child caught at the time of a raid upon the cake. She wavered to and fro upon her feet and held her hands behind her. There were two little points of terror in her eyes as she gazed up at the young captain in dusty blue, with his reddish, bronze complexion, his yellow hair, his bright saber held threateningly.

These two remained motionless and silent, simply staring at each other for some moments.

The captain felt his rage fade out of him and leave his mind limp. He had been violently angry, because this house had made him feel hesitant, wary. He did not like to be wary. He liked to feel confident, sure. So he had kicked the door open and had been prepared to march in like a soldier of wrath.

But now he began, for one thing, to wonder if his uniform was so dusty and old in appearance. Moreover, he had a feeling that his face was covered with a compound of dust, grime and perspiration. He took a step forward and said: "I didn't mean to frighten you." But his voice was coarse from his battle-howling. It seemed to him to have hempen fibers in it.

The girl's breath came in little, quick gasps, and she looked at him as she would have looked at a serpent.

"I didn't mean to frighten you," he said again.

The girl, still with her hands behind her, began to back away.

"Is there anyone else in the house?" he went on, while slowly following her. "I don't wish to disturb you, but we had a fight with some rebel skirmishers in the woods, and I thought maybe some of them might have come in here. In fact, I was pretty sure of it. Are there any of them here?"

The girl looked at him and said: "No!" He wondered why extreme agitation made the eyes of some women so limpid and bright.

"Who is here besides yourself?"

By this time his pursuit had driven her to the end of the hall, and she remained there with her back to the wall and her hands still behind her. When she answered this question she did not look at him, but down at the floor. She cleared her voice and then said: "There is no one here."

"No one?"

She lifted her eyes to him in that appeal that the human being must make even to falling trees, crashing bowlders, the sea in a storm, and said: "No, no, there is no one here." He could plainly see her tremble.

Of a sudden he bethought him that she had always kept her hands behind her. As he recalled her air when first discovered, he remembered she appeared precisely as a child detected at one of the crimes of childhood. Moreover, she had always backed away from him. He thought now that she was concealing something which was an evidence of the presence of the enemy in the house.

"What are you holding behind you?" he said suddenly.

She gave a little quick moan as if some grim hand had throttled her.

"What are you holding behind you?"

"Oh, nothing—please. I am not holding anything behind me; indeed I'm not."

"Very well. Hold your hands out in front of you, then."

"Oh, indeed, I'm not holding anything behind me. Indeed, I'm not."

"Well," he began. Then he paused, and remained for a moment dubious. Finally, he laughed. "Well, I shall have my men search the house, anyhow. I'm sorry to trouble you, but I feel sure that there is some one here whom we want." He turned to the corporal, who, with the other men, was gaping quietly in at the door, and said: "Jones, go through the house."

As for himself, he remained planted in front of the girl, for she evidently did not dare to move and allow him to see what she held so carefully behind her back. So she was his prisoner.

The men rummaged around on the ground floor of the house. Sometimes the captain called to them, "Try that closet," "Is there any cellar?" But they found no one, and at last they went trooping toward the stairs which led to the second floor.

But at this movement on the part of the men the girl uttered a cry, a cry of such fright and appeal that the men paused. "Oh, don't go up there! Please don't go up there!—ple-ease! There is no one there! Indeed—indeed there is not! Oh, ple-ease!"

"Go on, Jones," said the captain, calmly.

The obedient corporal made a preliminary step, and the girl bounded toward the stairs with another cry.

As she passed him, the captain caught sight of that which she had concealed behind her back, and which she had forgotten in this supreme moment. It was a pistol.

She ran to the first step, and standing there, faced the men, one hand extended with perpendicular palm, and the other holding the pistol at her side. "Oh, please, don't go up there. Nobody is there—indeed, there is not. P-l-e-a-s-e." Then suddenly she sank swiftly down upon the step, and, huddling forlornly, began to weep in the agony and with the convulsive tremors of an infant. The pistol fell from her fingers and rattled down to the floor.

The astonished troopers looked at their astonished captain. There was a short silence.

Finally, the captain stooped and picked up the pistol. It was a heavy weapon of the army pattern. He ascertained that it was empty.

He leaned toward the shaking girl, and said gently: "Will you tell me what you were going to do with this pistol?"

He had to repeat the question a number of times, but at last a muffled voice said, "Nothing."

"Nothing!" He insisted quietly upon a further answer. At the tender tones of the captain's voice, the phlegmatic corporal turned and winked gravely at the man next to him.

"Won't you tell me?"

The girl shook her head.

"Please tell me?"

The silent privates were moving their feet uneasily and wondering how long they were to wait.

The captain said, "Please won't you tell me?"

Then this girl's voice began in stricken tones half-coherent, and amid violent sobbing: "It was grandpa's. He—he—he said he was going to shoot anybody who came in here—he didn't care if there were thousands of 'em. And—and I know he would, and I was afraid they'd kill him. And so—and—so I stole away his pistol—and I was going to hide it when you—you—you kicked open the door."

The men straightened up and looked at each other. The girl began to weep again.

The captain mopped his brow. He peered down at the girl. He mopped his brow again. Suddenly he said: "Ah, don't cry like that."

He moved restlessly and looked down at his boots. He mopped his brow again.

Then he gripped the corporal by the arm and dragged him some yards back from the others. "Jones," he said, in an intensely earnest voice, "will you tell me what in the devil I am going to do?"

The corporal's countenance became illuminated with satisfaction at being thus requested to advise his superior officer. He adopted an air of great thought and finally said: "Well, of course, the feller with the grey sleeve must be upstairs, and we must get past the girl and up there somehow. Suppose I take her by the arm and lead her——"

"What!" interrupted the captain from between his clinched teeth. As he turned away from the corporal, he said fiercely over his shoulder: "You touch that girl and I'll split your skull!"

III

The corporal looked after his captain with an expression of mingled amazement, grief and philosophy. He seemed to be saying to himself that there unfortunately were times, after all, when one could not rely upon the most reliable of men. When he returned to the group he found the captain bending over the girl and saying: "Why is it that you don't want us to search upstairs?"

The girl's head was buried in her crossed arms. Locks of her hair had escaped from their fastenings and these fell upon her shoulder.

"Won't you tell me?"

The corporal here winked again at the man next to him.

"Because—" the girl moaned. "Because—there isn't anybody up there."

The captain at last said timidly: "Well, I'm afraid—I'm afraid we'll have to——"

The girl sprang to her feet again and implored him with her hands. She looked deep into his eyes with her glance which was at this time like that of the fawn when it says to the hunter: "Have mercy upon me."

These two stood regarding each other. The captain's foot was on the bottom step, but he seemed to be shrinking. He wore an air of being deeply wretched and ashamed. There was a silence.

Suddenly the corporal said in a quick, low tone: "Look out, captain!"

All turned their eyes swiftly toward the head of the stairs. There had appeared there a youth in a grey uniform. He stood looking coolly down at them. No word was said by the troopers. The girl gave vent to a little wail of desolation. "Oh, Harry!"

He began slowly to descend the stairs. His right arm was in a white sling and there were some fresh blood stains upon the cloth. His face was rigid and deathly pale, but his eyes flashed like lights. The girl was again moaning in an utterly dreary fashion as the youth came slowly down toward the silent men in blue.

Six steps from the bottom of the flight he halted and said: "I reckon it's me you're looking for."

The troopers had crowded forward a trifle and, posed in lithe, nervous attitudes, were watching him like cats. The captain remained unmoved. At the youth's question he merely nodded his head and said: "Yes."

The young man in grey looked down at the girl and then, in the same even tone which now, however, seemed to vibrate with suppressed fury, he said: "And is that any reason why you should insult my sister?"

At this sentence the girl intervened, desperately, between the young man in grey and the officer in blue. "Oh, don't, Harry, don't! He was good to me! He was good to me, Harry—indeed, he was."

The youth came on in his quiet, erect fashion until the girl could have touched either of the men with her hand, for the captain still remained with his foot upon the first step. She continually repeated: "Oh, Harry! Oh, Harry!"

The youth in grey maneuvered to glare into the captain's face first over one shoulder of the girl and then over the other. In a voice that rang like metal, he said: "You are armed and un-wounded, while I have no weapons and am wounded, but——"

The captain had stepped back and sheathed his saber. The eyes of these two men were gleaming fire, but otherwise the captain's countenance was imperturbable. He said: "You are mistaken. You have no reason to——"

"You lie!"

All save the captain and the youth in grey started in an electric movement. These two words crackled in the air like shattered glass. There was a breathless silence.

The captain cleared his throat. His look at the youth contained a quality of singular and terrible ferocity, but he said in his stolid tone: "I don't suppose you mean what you say now."

Upon his arm he had felt the pressure of some unconscious little fingers. The girl was leaning against the wall as if she no longer knew how to keep her balance, but those fingers—he held his arm very still. She murmured: "Oh, Harry, don't! He was good to me! Indeed he was!"

The corporal had come forward until he in a measure confronted the youth in grey, for he saw those fingers upon the captain's arm and he knew that sometimes very strong men were not able to move hand nor foot under such conditions.

The youth had suddenly seemed to become weak. He breathed heavily and hung to the railing. He was glaring at the captain, and apparently summoning all his will power to combat his weakness. The corporal addressed him with profound straightforwardness: "Don't you be a derned fool!" The youth turned toward him so fiercely that the corporal threw up a knee and an elbow like a boy who expects to be cuffed.

The girl pleaded with the captain. "You won't hurt him? Will you? He don't know what he's saying. He's wounded, you know. Please don't mind him!"

"I won't touch him," said the captain with rather extraordinary earnestness. "Don't you worry about it at all. I won't touch him!"

Then he looked at her and the girl suddenly withdrew her fingers from his arm.

The corporal contemplated the top of the stairs and remarked without surprise: "There's another of 'em coming!"

An old man was clambering down the stairs with much speed. He waved a cane wildly. "Get out of my house, you thieves! Get out! I won't have you cross my threshold! Get out!" He mumbled and wagged his head in an old man's fury. It was plainly his intention to assault them.

And so it occurred that a young girl became engaged in protecting a stalwart captain, fully armed, and with eight grim troopers at his back, from the attack of an old man with a walking stick.

A blush passed over the temples and brow of the captain and he looked particularly savage and weary. Despite the girl's efforts he suddenly faced the old man.

"Look here," he said distinctly. "We came in because we had been fighting in the woods yonder and we concluded that some of the enemy were in this house, especially when we saw a grey sleeve at the window. But this young man is wounded and I have nothing to say to him. I will even take it for granted that there are no others like him upstairs. We will go away, leaving your damned old house just as we found it. And we are no more thieves and rascals than you are."

The old man simply roared: "I haven't got a cow nor a pig nor a chicken on the place. Your soldiers have stolen everything they could carry away. They have torn down half my fences for firewood. This afternoon some of your accursed bullets even broke my window panes!"

The girl had been faltering: "Grandpa! Oh, grandpa!"

The captain looked at the girl. She returned his glance from the shadow of the old man's shoulder. After studying her face a moment, he said: "Well, we will go now." He strode toward the door and his men clanked docilely after him.

At this time there was the sound of harsh cries and rushing footsteps from without. The door flew open and a whirlwind composed of blue-coated troopers came in with a swoop. It was headed by the lieutenant. "Oh, here you are," he cried, catching his breath. "We thought—— hi! look at the girl!"

The captain said intensely: "Shut up, you fool!"

The men settled to a halt with a clash and bang. There could be heard the dulled sound of many hoofs outside of the house.

"Did you order up the horses?" inquired the captain.

"Yes, we thought——"

"Well, then, let's get out of here," interrupted the captain, morosely.

The men began to filter out into the open air. The youth in grey had been hanging dismally to the railing of the stairway. He now was climbing slowly up to the second floor. The old man was addressing himself directly to the serene corporal.

"Not a chicken on the place," he cried.

"Well, I didn't take your chickens, did I?"

"No, maybe you didn't, but——"

The captain crossed the hall and stood before the girl in rather a culprit's fashion. "You are not angry at me, are you?" he asked timidly.

"No," she said. She hesitated a moment and then suddenly held out her hand. "You were good to me—and I'm—much obliged."

The captain took her hand and then he blushed, for he found himself unable to formulate a sentence that applied in any way to the situation.

She did not seem to need that hand for a time.

He loosened his grasp presently, for he was ashamed to hold it so long without saying anything clever. At last with an air of charging an intrenched brigade, he contrived to say: "I would rather do anything than frighten you or trouble you."

His brow was warmly perspiring. He had a sense of being hideous in his dusty uniform and with his grimy face.

She said: "Oh, I'm so glad it was you instead of somebody who might have—might have hurt brother Harry and grandpa!"

He told her: "I wouldn't have hurt 'em for anything!"

There was a little silence.

"Well, good-bye," he said at last.

"Good-bye!"

He walked toward the door past the old man who was scolding at the vanishing figure of the corporal. The captain looked back. She had remained there watching him.

At the bugle's order, the troopers standing beside their horses swung briskly into the saddle. The lieutenant said to the first sergeant:

"Williams, did they ever meet before?"

"Hanged if I know."

"Well, say——"

The captain saw a curtain move at one of the windows. He cantered from his position at the head of the column and steered his horse between two flower beds.

"Well, good-bye!"

The squadron trampled slowly past.

"Good-bye."

They shook hands.

He evidently had something enormously important to say to her, but it seems that he could not manage it. He struggled heroically. The bay charger with his great mystically solemn eyes looked around the corner of his shoulder at the girl.

The captain studied a pine tree. The girl inspected the grass beneath the window. The captain said hoarsely: "I don't suppose —I don't suppose—I'll ever see you again!"

She looked at him affrightedly and shrank back from the window. He seemed to have woefully expected a reception of this kind for his question. He gave her instantly a glance of appeal.

She said: "Why, no, I don't suppose we will."

"Never?"

"Why, no—'tain't possible. You—you are a—Yankee!"

"Oh, I know it, but——" Eventually he continued: "Well, some day, you know, when there's no more fighting, we might——" He observed that she had again withdrawn suddenly into the shadow so he said: "Well, good-bye!"

When he held her fingers she bowed her head and he saw a pink blush steal over the curves of her cheek and neck.

"Am I never going to see you again?"

She made no reply.

"Never!" he repeated.

After a long time he bended over to hear a faint reply: "Sometimes—when there are no troops in the neighborhood—grandpa don't mind if I—walk over as far as that old oak tree yonder—in the afternoons."

It appeared that the captain's grip was very strong, for she uttered an exclamation and looked at her fingers as if she expected to find them mere fragments. He rode away.

The bay horse leaped a flower bed. They were almost to the drive when the girl uttered a panic-stricken cry.

The captain wheeled his horse violently and upon this return journey went straight through a flower bed.

The girl had clasped her hands. She beseeched him wildly with her eyes. "Oh, please, don't believe it. I never walk to the old oak tree. Indeed, I don't. I never—never—never walk there."

The bridle drooped on the bay charger's neck. The captain's figure seemed limp. With an expression of profound dejection and gloom he stared off at where the leaden sky met the dark green line of the woods. The long-impending rain began to fall with a mournful patter, drop and drop. There was a silence.

At last a low voice said: "Well—I might—sometimes I might—perhaps—but only once in a great while—I might walk to the old tree—in the afternoons."

THE VETERAN

OUT of the low window could be seen three hickory trees placed irregularly in a meadow that was resplendent in spring-time green. Further away, the old dismal belfry of the village church loomed over the pines. A horse meditating in the shade of one of the hickories lazily swished his tail. The warm sunshine made an oblong of vivid yellow on the floor of the grocery.

"Could you see the whites of their eyes?" said the man who was seated on a soap-box.

"Nothing of the kind," replied old Henry warmly. "Just a lot of flitting figures, and I let go at where they 'peared to be the thickest. Bang!"

"Mr. Fleming," said the grocer. His deferential voice expressed somehow the old man's exact social weight. "Mr. Fleming, you never was frightened much in them battles, was you?"

The veteran looked down and grinned. Observing his manner the entire group tittered. "Well, I guess I was," he answered finally. "Pretty well scared, sometimes. Why, in my first battle I thought the sky was falling down. I thought the world was coming to an end. You bet I was scared."

Every one laughed. Perhaps it seemed strange and rather wonderful to them that a man should admit the thing, and in the tone of their laughter there was probably more admiration than if old Fleming had declared that he had always been a lion. Moreover, they knew that he had ranked as an orderly sergeant, and so their opinion of his heroism was fixed. None, to be sure, knew how an orderly sergeant ranked, but then it was understood to be somewhere just shy of a major-general's stars. So when old Henry admitted that he had been frightened there was a laugh.

"The trouble was," said the old man, "I thought they were all shooting at me. Yes, sir. I thought every man in the other army was aiming at me in particular and only me. And it seemed so darned unreasonable, you know. I wanted to explain to 'em what an almighty good fellow I was, because I thought then they might quit all trying to hit me. But I couldn't explain, and they kept on being unreasonable—blim!—blam!—bang! So I run!"

Two little triangles of wrinkles appeared at the corners of his eyes. Evidently he appreciated some comedy in this recital. Down near his feet, however, little Jim, his grandson, was visibly horror-stricken. His hands were clasped nervously, and his eyes were wide with astonishment at this terrible scandal, his most magnificent grandfather telling such a thing.

"That was at Chancellorsville. Of course, afterward I got kind of used to it. A man does. Lots of men, though, seem to feel all right from the start. I did, as soon as I 'got on to it,' as they say now, but at first I was pretty flustered. Now, there was young Jim Conklin, old Si Conklin's son—that used to keep the tannery —you none of you recollect him—well, he went into it from the start just as if he was born to it. But with me it was different. I had to get used to it."

When little Jim walked with his grandfather he was in the habit of skipping along on the stone pavement in front of the three stores and the hotel of the town and betting that he could avoid the cracks. But upon this day he walked soberly, with his hand gripping two of his grandfather's fingers. Sometimes he kicked abstractedly at dandelions that curved over the walk. Any one could see that he was much troubled.

"There's Sickles's colt over in the medder, Jimmie," said the old man. "Don't you wish you owned one like him?"

"Um," said the boy, with a strange lack of interest. He continued his reflections. Then finally he ventured: "Grandpa—now —was that true what you was telling those men?"

"What?" asked the grandfather. "What was I telling them?"

"Oh, about your running."

"Why, yes, that was true enough, Jimmie. It was my first fight, and there was an awful lot of noise, you know."

Jimmie seemed dazed that this idol, of its own will, should so totter. His stout boyish idealism was injured.

Presently the grandfather said: "Sickles's colt is going for a drink. Don't you wish you owned Sickles's colt, Jimmie?"

The boy merely answered: "He ain't as nice as our'n." He lapsed then to another moody silence.

.   .   .   .   .   .

One of the hired men, a Swede, desired to drive to the county seat for purposes of his own. The old man loaned a horse and an unwashed buggy. It appeared later that one of the purposes of the Swede was to get drunk.

After quelling some boisterous frolic of the farm-hands and boys in the garret, the old man had that night gone peacefully to sleep when he was aroused by clamoring at the kitchen door. He grabbed his trousers, and they waved out behind as he dashed forward. He could hear the voice of the Swede, screaming and blubbering. He pushed the wooden button, and, as the door flew open, the Swede, a maniac, stumbled inward, chattering, weeping, still screaming. "De barn fire! Fire! Fire! De barn fire! Fire! Fire! Fire!"

There was a swift and indescribable change in the old man. His face ceased instantly to be a face; it became a mask, a grey thing, with horror written about the mouth and eyes. He hoarsely shouted at the foot of the little rickety stairs, and immediately, it seemed, there came down an avalanche of men. No one knew that during this time the old lady had been standing in her night-clothes at the bed room door yelling: "What's th' matter? What's th' matter? What's th' matter?"

When they dashed toward the barn it presented to their eyes its usual appearance, solemn, rather mystic in the black night. The Swede's lantern was overturned at a point some yards in front of the barn doors. It contained a wild little conflagration of its own, and even in their excitement some of those who ran felt a gentle secondary vibration of the thrifty part of their minds at sight of this overturned lantern. Under ordinary circumstances it would have been a calamity.

But the cattle in the barn were trampling, trampling, trampling, and above this noise could be heard a humming like the song of innumerable bees. The old man hurled aside the great doors, and a yellow flame leaped out at one corner and sped and wavered frantically up the old grey wall. It was glad, terrible, this single flame, like the wild banner of deadly and triumphant foes.

The motley crowd from the garret had come with all the pails of the farm. They flung themselves upon the well. It was a leisurely old machine, long dwelling in indolence. It was in the habit of giving out water with a sort of reluctance. The men stormed at it, cursed it, but it continued to allow the buckets to be filled only after the wheezy windlass had howled many protests at the mad-handed men.

With his opened knife in his hand old Fleming himself had gone headlong into the barn, where the stifling smoke swirled with the air-currents, and where could be heard in its fulness the terrible chorus of the flames, laden with tones of hate and death, a hymn of wonderful ferocity.

He flung a blanket over an old mare's head, cut the halter close to the manger, led the mare to the door, and fairly kicked her out to safety. He returned with the same blanket and rescued one of the work-horses. He took five horses out, and then came out himself with his clothes bravely on fire. He had no whiskers, and very little hair on his head. They soused five pailfuls of water on him. His eldest son made a clean miss with the sixth pailful because the old man had turned and was running down the decline and around to the basement of the barn where were the stanchions of the cows. Some one noticed at the time that he ran very lamely, as if one of the frenzied horses had smashed his hip.

The cows, with their heads held in the heavy stanchions, had thrown themselves, strangled themselves, tangled themselves; done everything which the ingenuity of their exuberant fear could suggest to them.

Here as at the well the same thing happened to every man save one. Their hands went mad. They became incapable of everything save the power to rush into dangerous situations.

The old man released the cow nearest the door, and she, blind drunk with terror, crashed into the Swede. The Swede had been running to and fro babbling. He carried an empty milk-pail, to which he clung with an unconscious fierce enthusiasm. He shrieked like one lost as he went under the cow's hoofs, and the milk-pail, rolling across the floor, made a flash of silver in the gloom.

Old Fleming took a fork, beat off the cow, and dragged the paralyzed Swede to the open air. When they had rescued all the cows save one, which had so fastened herself that she could not be moved an inch, they returned to the front of the barn and stood sadly, breathing like men who had reached the final point of human effort.

Many people had come running. Someone had even gone to the church, and now, from the distance, rang the tocsin note of the old bell. There was a long flare of crimson on the sky which made remote people speculate as to the whereabouts of the fire.

The long flames sang their drumming chorus in voices of the heaviest bass. The wind whirled clouds of smoke and cinders into the faces of the spectators. The form of the old barn was outlined in black amid these masses of orange-hued flames.

And then came this Swede again, crying as one who is the weapon of the sinister fates. "De colts! De colts! You have forgot de colts!"

Old Fleming staggered. It was true; they had forgotten the two colts in the box-stalls at the back of the barn. "Boys," he said, "I must try to get 'em out." They clamored about him then, afraid for him, afraid of what they should see. Then they talked wildly each to each. "Why, it's sure death!" "He would never get out!" "Why, it's suicide for a man to go in there!" Old Fleming stared absent-mindedly at the open doors. "The poor little things," he said. He rushed into the barn.

When the roof fell in, a great funnel of smoke swarmed toward the sky, as if the old man's mighty spirit, released from its body—a little bottle—had swelled like the genie of fable. The smoke was tinted rose-hue from the flames, and perhaps the unutterable midnights of the universe will have no power to daunt the color of this soul.

AN EPISODE OF WAR

AN EPISODE OF WAR

THE lieutenant's rubber blanket lay on the ground, and upon it he had poured the company's supply of coffee. Corporals and other representatives of the grimy and hot-throated men who lined the breastwork had come for each squad's portion.

The lieutenant was frowning and serious at this task of division. His lips pursed as he drew with his sword various crevices in the heap until brown squares of coffee, astoundingly equal in size, appeared on the blanket. He was on the verge of a great triumph in mathematics and the corporals were thronging forward, each to reap a little square, when suddenly the lieutenant cried out and looked quickly at a man near him as if he suspected it was a case of personal assault. The others cried out also when they saw blood upon the lieutenant's sleeve.

He had winced like a man stung, swayed dangerously, and then straightened. The sound of his hoarse breathing was plainly audible. He looked sadly, mystically, over the breastwork at the green face of a wood where now were many little puffs of white smoke. During this moment, the men about him gazed statue-like and silent, astonished and awed by this catastrophe which had happened when catastrophes were not expected—when they had leisure to observe it.

As the lieutenant stared at the wood, they too swung their heads so that for another moment all hands, still silent, contemplated the distant forest as if their minds were fixed upon the mystery of a bullet's journey.

The officer had, of course, been compelled to take his sword at once into his left hand. He did not hold it by the hilt. He gripped it at the middle of the blade, awkwardly. Turning his eyes from the hostile wood, he looked at the sword as he held it there, and seemed puzzled as to what to do with it, where to put it. In short this weapon had of a sudden become a strange thing to him. He looked at it in a kind of stupefaction, as if he had been miraculously endowed with a trident, a sceptre, or a spade.

Finally, he tried to sheath it. To sheath a sword held by the left hand, at the middle of the blade, in a scabbard hung at the left hip, is a feat worthy of a sawdust ring. This wounded officer engaged in a desperate struggle with the sword and the wobbling scabbard, and during the time of it, he breathed like a wrestler.

But at this instant the men, the spectators, awoke from their stone-like poses and crowded forward sympathetically. The orderly-sergeant took the sword and tenderly placed it in the scabbard. At the time, he leaned nervously backward, and did not allow even his finger to brush the body of the lieutenant. A wound gives strange dignity to him who bears it. Well men shy from this new and terrible majesty. It is as if the wounded man's hand is upon the curtain which hangs before the revelations of all existence, the meaning of ants, potentates, wars, cities, sunshine, snow, a feather dropped from a bird's wing, and the power of it sheds radiance upon a bloody form, and makes the other men understand sometimes that they are little. His comrades look at him with large eyes thoughtfully. Moreover, they fear vaguely that the weight of a finger upon him might send him headlong, precipitate the tragedy, hurl him at once into the dim grey unknown. And so the orderly-sergeant while sheathing the sword leaned nervously backward.

There were others who proffered assistance. One timidly presented his shoulder and asked the lieutenant if he cared to lean upon it, but the latter waved them away mournfully. He wore the look of one who knows he is the victim of a terrible disease and understands his helplessness. He again stared over the breastwork at the forest, and then turning went slowly rearward. He held his right wrist tenderly in his left hand, as if the wounded arm was made of very brittle glass.

And the men in silence stared at the wood, then at the departing lieutenant—then at the wood, then at the lieutenant.

As the wounded officer passed from the line of battle, he was enabled to see many things which as a participant in the fight were unknown to him. He saw a general on a black horse gazing over the lines of blue infantry at the green woods which veiled his problems. An aide galloped furiously, dragged his horse suddenly to a halt, saluted, and presented a paper. It was, for a wonder, precisely like an historical painting.

To the rear of the general and his staff, a group, composed of a bugler, two or three orderlies, and the bearer of the corps standard, all upon maniacal horses, were working like slaves to hold their ground, preserve their respectful interval, while the shells bloomed in the air about them, and caused their chargers to make furious quivering leaps.

A battery, a tumultuous and shining mass, was swirling toward the right. The wild thud of hoofs, the cries of the riders shouting blame and praise, menace and encouragement, and, last, the roar of the wheels, the slant of the glistening guns, brought the lieutenant to an intent pause. The battery swept in curves that stirred the heart; it made halts as dramatic as the crash of a wave on the rocks, and when it fled onward, this aggregation of wheels, levers, motors, had a beautiful unity, as if it were a missile. The sound of it was a war-chorus that reached into the depths of man's emotion.

The lieutenant, still holding his arm as if it were of glass, stood watching this battery until all detail of it was lost, save the figures of the riders, which rose and fell and waved lashes over the black mass.

Later he turned his eyes toward the battle where the shooting sometimes crackled like bush-fires, sometimes sputtered with exasperating irregularity, and sometimes reverberated like the thunder. He saw the smoke rolling upward and saw crowds of men who ran and cheered, or stood and blazed away at the inscrutable distance.

He came upon some stragglers and they told him how to find the field hospital. They described its exact location. In fact these men, no longer having part in the battle, knew more of it than others. They told the performance of every corps, every division, the opinion of every general. The lieutenant, carrying his wounded arm rearward, looked upon them with wonder.

At the roadside a brigade was making coffee and buzzing with talk like a girls' boarding-school. Several officers came out to him and inquired concerning things of which he knew nothing. One, seeing his arm, began to scold. "Why, man, that's no way to do.

You want to fix that thing." He appropriated the lieutenant and the lieutenant's wound. He cut the sleeve and laid bare the arm, every nerve of which softly fluttered under his touch. He bound his handkerchief over the wound, scolding away in the meantime. His tone allowed one to think that he was in the habit of being wounded every day. The lieutenant hung his head, feeling, in this presence, that he did not know how to be correctly wounded.

The low white tents of the hospital were grouped around an old school-house. There was here a singular commotion. In the foreground two ambulances interlocked wheels in the deep mud. The drivers were tossing the blame of it back and forth, gesticulating and berating, while from the ambulances, both crammed with wounded, there came an occasional groan. An interminable crowd of bandaged men were coming and going. Great numbers sat under the trees nursing heads or arms or legs. There was a dispute of some kind raging on the steps of the school-house. Sitting with his back against a tree a man with a face as grey as a new army blanket was serenely smoking a corn-cob pipe. The lieutenant wished to rush forward and inform him that he was dying.

A busy surgeon was passing near the lieutenant. "Good morning," he said with a friendly smile. Then he caught sight of the lieutenant's arm and his face at once changed. "Well, let's have a look at it." He seemed possessed suddenly of a great contempt for the lieutenant. This wound evidently placed the latter on a very low social plane. The doctor cried out impatiently. What mutton-head had tied it up that way anyhow. The lieutenant answered: "Oh, a man."

When the wound was disclosed the doctor fingered it disdainfully. "Humph," he said. "You come along with me and I'll 'tend to you." His voice contained the same scorn as if he were saying: "You will have to go to jail."

The lieutenant had been very meek but now his face flushed, and he looked into the doctor's eyes. "I guess I won't have it amputated," he said.

"Nonsense, man! nonsense! nonsense!" cried the doctor. "Come along, now. I won't amputate it. Come along. Don't be a baby."

"Let go of me," said the lieutenant, holding back wrathfully. His glance fixed upon the door of the old school-house, as sinister to him as the portals of death.

And this is the story of how the lieutenant lost his arm. When he reached home his sisters, his mother, his wife, sobbed for a long time at the sight of the flat sleeve. "Oh, well," he said, standing shamefaced amid these tears, "I don't suppose it matters so much as all that."

Wounds in the Rain

THE PRICE OF THE HARNESS

I

TWENTY-FIVE men were making a road out of a path up the hillside. The light batteries in the rear were impatient to advance, but first must be done all that digging and smoothing which gains no incrusted medals from war. The men worked like gardeners, and a road was growing from the old pack-animal trail. Trees arched from a field of guinea-grass which resembled young wild corn. The day was still and dry. The men working were dressed in the consistent blue of United States regulars. They looked indifferent, almost stolid, despite the heat and the labor. There was little talking. From time to time a government pack-train, led by a sleek-sided tender bell-mare, came from one way or the other way, and the men stood aside as the strong, hard, black-and-tan animals crowded eagerly after their curious little feminine leader.

A volunteer staff officer appeared, and, sitting on his horse in the middle of the work, asked the sergeant in command some questions which were apparently not relevant to any military business. Men straggling along on various duties almost invariably spun some kind of a joke as they passed.

A corporal and four men were guarding boxes of spare ammunition at the top of the hill, and one of the number often went to the foot of the hill swinging canteens.

The day wore down to the Cuban dusk in which the shadows are all grim and of ghastly shape. The men began to lift their eyes from the shovels and picks, and glance in the direction of their camp. The sun threw his last lance through the foliage. The steep mountain range on the right turned blue and as without detail as a curtain. The tiny ruby of light ahead meant that the ammunition guard were cooking their supper. From somewhere in the world came a single rifle-shot. Figures appeared, dim in the shadow of the trees. A murmur, a sigh of quiet relief, arose from the working party. Later, they swung up the hill in an unformed formation, being always like soldiers, and unable even to carry a spade save like United States regular soldiers. As they passed through some fields, the bland white light of the end of the day feebly touched each hard bronze profile.

"Wonder if we'll git anythin' to eat," said Watkins, in a low voice.

"Should think so," said Nolan, in the same tone. They betrayed no impatience; they seemed to feel a kind of awe of the situation.

The sergeant turned. One could see the cool grey eye flashing under the brim of the campaign hat. "What in hell you fellers kickin' about?" he asked. They made no reply, understanding that they were being suppressed.

As they moved on, a murmur arose from the tall grass on each hand. It was the noise from the bivouac of ten thousand men, although one saw practically nothing from the low-cut roadway. The sergeant led his party up a wet clay bank and into a trampled field. Here were scattered tiny white shelter-tents, and in the darkness they were luminous like the rearing stones in a graveyard. A few fires burned blood-red, and the shadowy figures of men moved with no more expression of detail than there is in the swaying of foliage on a windy night.

The working party felt their way to where their tents were pitched. A man suddenly cursed; he had mislaid something and he knew he was not going to find it that night. Watkins spoke again with the monotony of a clock. "Wonder if we'll git anythin' to eat."

Martin, with eyes turned pensively to the stars, began a treatise. "Them Spaniards——"

"Oh, quit it," cried Nolan. "What th' piper do you know about th' Spaniards, you fat-headed Dutchman? Better think of your belly, you blunderin' swine, an' what you're goin' to put in it, grass or dirt."

A laugh, a sort of a deep growl, arose from the prostrate men. In the mean time the sergeant had reappeared and was standing over them. "No rations to-night," he said gruffly, and turning on his heel walked away.

This announcement was received in silence. But Watkins had flung himself face downward, and putting his lips close to a tuft of grass, he formulated oaths. Martin arose and going to his shelter, crawled in sulkily. After a long interval Nolan said aloud, "Hell!" Grierson, enlisted for the war, raised a querulous voice. "Well, I wonder when we *will* git fed?"

From the ground about him came a low chuckle full of ironical comment upon Grierson's lack of certain qualities which the other men felt themselves to possess.

II

In the cold light of dawn the men were on their knees, packing, strapping and buckling. The comic toy hamlet of shelter-tents had been wiped out as if by a cyclone. Through the trees could be seen the crimson of a light battery's blankets, and the wheels creaked like the sound of a musketry fight. Nolan, well gripped by his shelter-tent, his blanket and his cartridge belt, and bearing his rifle, advanced upon a small group of men who were hastily finishing a can of coffee.

"Say, give us a drink, will yeh?" he asked wistfully. He was as sad-eyed as an orphan beggar.

Every man in the group turned to look him straight in the face. He had asked for the principal ruby out of each one's crown. There was grim silence. Then one said, "What fer?" Nolan cast his glance to the ground and went away abashed.

But he espied Watkins and Martin surrounding Grierson, who had gained three pieces of hard-tack by mere force of his audacious inexperience. Grierson was fending his comrades off tearfully. "Now, don't be damn pigs," he cried. "Hold on a minute." Here Nolan asserted a claim. Grierson groaned. Kneeling piously, he divided the hard-tack with minute care into four portions. The men, who had had their heads together like players watching a wheel of fortune, arose suddenly, each chewing. Nolan interpolated a drink of water and sighed contentedly.

The whole forest seemed to be moving. From the field on the other side of the road a column of men in blue was slowly pouring; the battery had creaked on ahead; from the rear came a hum of advancing regiments. Then from a mile away rang the noise of a shot, then another shot; in a moment the rifles there were drumming, drumming, drumming. The artillery boomed out suddenly. A day of battle was begun.

The men made no exclamations. They rolled their eyes in the direction of the sound, and then swept with a calm glance the forests and the hills which surrounded them, implacably mysterious forests and hills which lent to every rifle-shot the ominous quality which belongs to secret assassination. The whole scene would have spoken to the private soldiers of ambushes, sudden flank attacks, terrible disasters if it were not for those cool gentlemen with shoulder-straps and swords who, the private soldiers knew, were of another world and omnipotent for the business.

The battalion moved out into the mud and began a leisurely march in the damp shade of the trees. The advance of two batteries had churned the black soil into a formidable paste. The brown leggings of the men, stained with the mud of other days, took on a deeper color. Perspiration broke gently out on the reddish faces. With his heavy roll of blanket and the half of a shelter-tent crossing his right shoulder and under his left arm, each man presented the appearance of being clasped from behind, wrestler fashion, by a pair of thick white arms. There was something distinctive in the way they carried their rifles. There was the grace of an old hunter somewhere in it, the grace of a man whose rifle has become absolutely a part of himself. Furthermore, almost every blue shirt-sleeve was rolled to the elbow, disclosing fore-arms of almost incredible brawn. The rifles seemed light, almost fragile, in the hands that were at the end of these arms, never fat but always with rolling muscles and veins that seemed on the point of bursting. And another thing was the silence and the marvelous impassivity of the faces as the column made its slow way toward where the whole forest spluttered and fluttered with battle.

Opportunely, the battalion was halted astraddle of a stream, and before it again moved most of the men had filled their canteens. The firing increased. Ahead and to the left a battery was booming at methodical intervals, while the infantry racket was that continual drumming which, after all, often sounds like rain on a roof. Directly ahead one could hear the deep voices of field-pieces.

Some wounded Cubans were carried by in litters improvised from hammocks swung on poles. One had a ghastly cut in the throat, probably from a fragment of shell, and his head was turned as if Providence particularly wished to display this wide and lapping gash to the long column that was winding toward the front. And another Cuban, shot through the groin, kept up a continual wail as he swung from the tread of his bearers. "Ay—ee! Ay—ee! Madre mia! Madre mia!" He sang this bitter ballad into the ears of at least three thousand men as they slowly made way for his bearers on the narrow wood-path. These wounded insurgents were, then, to a large part of the advancing army, the visible messengers of bloodshed, death, and the men regarded them with thoughtful awe. This doleful sobbing cry, "Madre mia," was a tangible consequent misery of all that firing on in front into which the men knew they were soon to be plunged. Some of them wished to inquire of the bearers the details of what had happened, but they could not speak Spanish, and so it was as if fate had intentionally sealed the lips of all in order that even meager information might not leak out concerning this mystery—battle. On the other hand, many unversed private soldiers looked upon the unfortunate as men who had seen thousands maimed and bleeding, and absolutely could not conjure up any further interest in such scenes.

A young staff officer passed on horseback. The vocal Cuban was always wailing, but the officer wheeled past the bearers without heeding anything. And yet he never before had seen such a sight. His case was different from that of the private soldiers. He heeded nothing because he was busy, immensely busy and hurried with a multitude of reasons and desires for doing his duty perfectly. His whole life had been a mere period of preliminary reflection for this situation, and he had no clear idea of anything save his obligation as an officer. A man of this kind might be stupid; it is conceivable that in remote cases certain bumps on his head might be composed entirely of wood; but those traditions of fidelity and courage which have been handed to him from generation to generation, and which he has tenaciously preserved despite the persecution of legislators and the indifference of his country, make it incredible that in battle he should ever fail to give his best blood and his best thought for his general, for his men and for himself. And so this young officer in the shapeless hat and the torn and dirty shirt failed to heed the wails of the wounded man, even as the pilgrim fails to heed the world as he raises his illumined face toward his purpose—rightly or wrongly his purpose—his sky of the ideal of duty; and the wonderful part of it is that he is guided by an ideal which he has himself created, and has alone protected from attack. The young man was merely an officer in the United States regular army.

The column swung across a shallow ford and took a road which passed the right flank of one of the American batteries. On a hill it was booming and belching great clouds of white smoke. The infantry looked up with interest. Arrayed below the hill and behind the battery were the horses and limbers, the riders checking their pawing mounts, and behind each rider a red blanket flamed against the fervent green of the bushes. As the infantry moved along the road, some of the battery horses turned at the noise of the trampling feet and surveyed the men with eyes deep as wells, serene, mournful, generous eyes, lit heart-breakingly with something that was akin to a philosophy, a religion of self-sacrifice—oh, gallant, gallant horses!

"I know a feller in that battery," said Nolan musingly. "A driver."

"Damn sight rather be a gunner," said Martin.

"Why would ye?" said Nolan opposingly.

"Well, I'd take my chances as a gunner b'fore I'd sit 'way up in th' air on a raw-boned plug an' git shot at."

"Aw——" began Nolan.

"They've had some losses t'-day all right," interrupted Grierson.

"Horses?" asked Watkins.

"Horses an' men too," said Grierson.

"How d'yeh know?"

"A feller told me there by the ford."

They kept only a part of their minds bearing on this discussion because they could already hear high in the air the wire-string note of the enemy's bullets.

III

The road taken by this battalion as it followed other battalions is something less than a mile long in its journey across a heavily wooded plain. It is greatly changed now; in fact it was metamorphosed in two days; but at that time it was a mere track through dense shrubbery from which rose great dignified arching trees. It was, in fact, a path through a jungle.

The battalion had no sooner left the battery in rear than bullets began to drive overhead. They made several different sounds, but as they were mainly high shots it was usual for them to make the faint note of a vibrant string touched elusively, half dreamily.

The military balloon, a fat, wavering yellow thing, was leading the advance like some new conception of war-god. Its bloated mass shone above the trees, and served incidentally to indicate to the men at the rear that comrades were in advance. The track itself exhibited for all its visible length a closely knit procession of soldiers in blue with breasts crossed by white shelter-tents. The first ominous order of battle came down the line. "Use the cut-off. Don't use the magazine until you're ordered." Non-commissioned officers repeated the command gruffly. A sound of clicking locks rattled along the column. All men knew that the time had come.

The front had burst out with a roar like a brush fire. The balloon was dying, dying a gigantic and public death before the eyes of two armies. It quivered, sank, faded into the trees amid the flurry of a battle that was suddenly and tremendously like a storm.

The American battery thundered behind the men with a shock that seemed likely to tear the backs of their heads off. The Spanish shrapnel fled on a line to their left, swirling and swishing in supernatural velocity. The noise of the rifle bullets broke in their faces like the noise of so many lamp chimneys or sped overhead in swift cruel spitting. And at the front the battle-sound, as if it were simply music, was beginning to swell and swell until the volleys rolled like a surf.

The officers shouted hoarsely. "Come on, men! Hurry up, boys! Come on, now! Hurry up!" The soldiers, running heavily in their accouterments, dashed forward. A baggage guard was swiftly detailed; the men tore their rolls from their shoulders as if the things were afire. The battalion, stripped for action, again dashed forward.

"Come on, men! Come on!" To them the battle was as yet merely a road through the woods crowded with troops who lowered their heads anxiously as the bullets fled high. But a moment later the column wheeled abruptly to the left and entered a field of tall green grass. The line scattered to a skirmish formation. In front was a series of knolls treed sparsely like orchards, and although no enemy was visible, these knolls were all popping and spitting with rifle-fire. In some places there were to be seen long grey lines of dirt intrenchments. The American shells were kicking up reddish clouds of dust from the brow of one of the knolls where stood a pagoda-like house. It was not much like a battle with men; it was a battle with a bit of charming scenery, enigmatically potent for death.

Nolan knew that Martin had suddenly fallen. "What——" he began.

"They've hit me," said Martin.

"Jesus!" said Nolan.

Martin lay on the ground, clutching his left fore-arm just below the elbow with all the strength of his right hand. His lips were pursed ruefully. He did not seem to know what to do. He continued to stare at his arm.

Then suddenly the bullets drove at them low and hard. The men flung themselves face down in the grass. Nolan lost all thought of his friend. Oddly enough, he felt somewhat like a man hiding under a bed, and he was just as sure that he could not raise his head high without being shot as a man hiding under a bed is sure that he cannot raise his head without bumping it.

A lieutenant was seated in the grass just behind him. He was in the careless and yet rigid pose of a man balancing a loaded plate on his knee at a picnic. He was talking in soothing paternal tones.

"Now don't get rattled. We're all right here. Just as safe as being in church. . . . They're all going high. Don't mind them.

. . . Don't mind them. . . . They're all going high. We've got them rattled and they can't shoot straight. Don't mind them."

The sun burned down steadily from a pale sky upon the crackling woods and knolls and fields. From the roar of musketry it might have been that the celestial heat was frying this part of the world.

Nolan snuggled close to the grass. He watched a grey line of intrenchments, above which floated the veriest gossamer of smoke. A flag lolled on a staff behind it. The men in the trench volleyed whenever an American shell exploded near them. It was some kind of infantile defiance. Frequently a bullet came from the woods directly behind Nolan and his comrades. They thought at the time that these bullets were from the rifle of some incompetent soldier of their own side.

There was no cheering. The men would have looked about them wondering where the army was if it were not that the crash of the fighting for the distance of a mile denoted plainly enough where that army was.

Officially, the battalion had not yet fired a shot; there had been merely some irresponsible popping by men on the extreme left flank. But it was known that the lieutenant-colonel who had been in command was dead, shot through the heart, and that the captains were thinned down to two. At the rear went on a long tragedy in which men, bent and hasty, hurried to shelter with other men, helpless, dazed and bloody. Nolan knew of it all from the hoarse and affrighted voices which he heard as he lay flattened in the grass. There came to him a sense of exultation. Here, then, was one of those dread and lurid situations which in a nation's history stand out in crimson letters, becoming tales of blood to stir generation after generation. And he was in it and unharmed. If he lived through the battle, he would be a hero of the desperate fight at —— and here he wondered for a second what fate would be pleased to bestow as a name for this battle.

But it is quite sure that hardly another man in the battalion was engaged in any thoughts concerning the historic. On the contrary, they deemed it ill that they were being badly cut up on a most unimportant occasion. It would have benefited the conduct of whoever were weak if they had known that they were engaged in a battle that would be famous forever.

IV

Martin had picked himself up from where the bullet had knocked him and addressed the lieutenant. "I'm hit, sir," he said.

The lieutenant was very busy. "All right, all right," he said, heeding the man just enough to learn where he was wounded. "Go over that way. You ought to see a dressing-station under those trees."

Martin found himself dizzy and sick. The sensation in his arm was distinctly galvanic. The feeling was so strange that he could wonder at times if a wound was really what ailed him. Once, in this dazed way, he examined his arm; he saw the hole. Yes, he was shot; that was it. And more than in any other way it affected him with a profound sadness.

As directed by the lieutenant, he went to the clump of trees, but he found no dressing-station there. He found only a dead soldier lying with his face buried in his arms and with his shoulders humped high as if he was convulsively sobbing. Martin decided to make his way to the road, deeming that he thus would better his chances of getting to a surgeon. But he suddenly found his way blocked by a fence of barbed wire. Such was his mental condition that he brought up at a rigid halt before this fence and stared stupidly at it. It did not seem to him possible that this obstacle could be defeated by any means. The fence was there and it stopped his progress. He could not go in that direction.

But as he turned he espied that procession of wounded men, strange pilgrims, which had already worn a path in the tall grass. They were passing through a gap in the fence. Martin joined them. The bullets were flying over them in sheets, but many of them bore themselves as men who had now exacted from fate a singular immunity. Generally there were no outcries, no kicking, no talk at all. They too, like Martin, seemed buried in a vague but profound melancholy.

But there was one who cried out loudly. A man shot in the head was being carried arduously by four comrades, and he continually yelled one word that was terrible in its primitive strength. "Bread! Bread! Bread!" Following him and his bearers were a limping crowd of men less cruelly wounded, who kept their eyes always fixed on him, as if they gained from his extreme agony some balm for their own sufferings.

"Bread! Give me bread!"

Martin plucked a man by the sleeve. The man had been shot in the foot and was making his way with the help of a curved, incompetent stick. It is an axiom of war that wounded men can never find straight sticks.

"What's the matter with that feller?" asked Martin.

"Nutty," said the man.

"Why is he?"

"Shot in th' head," answered the other impatiently.

The wail of the sufferer arose in the field amid the swift rasp of bullets and the boom and shatter of shrapnel. "Bread! Bread! Oh, God, can't you give me bread? Bread!" The bearers of him were suffering exquisite agony, and often exchanged glances which exhibited their despair of ever getting free of this tragedy. It seemed endless.

"Bread! Bread! Bread!"

But despite the fact that there was always in the way of this crowd a wistful melancholy, one must know that there were plenty of men who laughed, laughed at their wounds whimsically, quaintly inventing odd humors concerning bicycles and cabs, extracting from this shedding of their blood a wonderful amount of material for cheerful badinage, and with their faces twisted from pain as they stepped, they often joked like music-hall stars. And perhaps this was the most tearful part of all.

They trudged along a road until they reached a ford. Here under the eave of the bank lay a dismal company. In the mud and in the damp shade of some bushes were a half-hundred pale-faced men prostrate. Two or three surgeons were working there. Also there was a chaplain, grim-mouthed, resolute, his surtout discarded. Overhead always was that incessant maddening wail of bullets.

Martin was standing gazing drowsily at the scene when a surgeon grabbed him. "Here, what's the matter with you?" Martin was daunted. He wondered what he had done that the surgeon should be so angry with him.

"In the arm," he muttered, half shamefacedly.

After the surgeon had hastily and irritably bandaged the injured member he glared at Martin and said, "You can walk all right, can't you?"

"Yes, sir," said Martin.

"Well, now, you just make tracks down that road."

"Yes, sir." Martin went meekly off. The doctor had seemed exasperated almost to the point of madness.

The road was at this time swept with the fire of a body of Spanish sharpshooters who had come cunningly around the flanks of the American army, and were now hidden in the dense foliage that lined both sides of the road. They were shooting at everything. The road was as crowded as a street in a city, and at an absurdly short range they emptied their rifles at the passing people. They were aided always by the over-sweep from the regular Spanish line of battle.

Martin was sleepy from his wound. He saw tragedy follow tragedy, but they created in him no feeling of horror.

A man with a red cross on his arm was leaning against a great tree. Suddenly he tumbled to the ground and writhed for a moment in the way of a child oppressed with colic. A comrade immediately began to bustle importantly. "Here," he called to Martin, "help me carry this man, will you?"

Martin looked at him with dull scorn. "I'll be damned if I do," he said. "Can't carry myself, let alone somebody else."

This answer, which rings now so inhuman, pitiless, did not affect the other man. "Well, all right," he said. "Here comes some other fellers." The wounded man had now turned blue-grey; his eyes were closed; his body shook in a gentle, persistent chill.

Occasionally Martin came upon dead horses, their limbs sticking out and up like stakes. One beast, mortally shot, was besieged by three or four men who were trying to push it into the bushes where it could live its brief time of anguish without thrashing to death any of the wounded men in the gloomy procession.

The mule train, with extra ammunition, charged toward the front, still led by the tinkling bell-mare.

An ambulance was stuck momentarily in the mud, and above the crack of battle one could hear the familiar objurgations of the driver as he whirled his lash.

Two privates were having a hard time with a wounded captain whom they were supporting to the rear. He was half cursing, half wailing out the information that he not only would not go another step toward the rear, but was certainly going to return at once to the front. They begged, pleaded at great length as they continually headed him off. They were not unlike two nurses with an exceptionally bad and headstrong little duke.

The wounded soldiers paused to look impassively upon this struggle. They were always like men who could not be aroused by anything further.

The visible hospital was mainly straggling thickets intersected with narrow paths, the ground being covered with men. Martin saw a busy person with a book and a pencil, but he did not approach him to become officially a member of the hospital. All he desired was rest and immunity from nagging. He took seat painfully under a bush and leaned his back upon the trunk. There he remained thinking, his face wooden.

V

"My Gawd," said Nolan, squirming on his belly in the grass, "I can't stand this much longer."

Then suddenly every rifle in the firing line seemed to go off of its own accord. It was the result of an order, but few men had heard the order; in the main they had fired because they heard others fire, and their sense was so quick that the volley did not sound too ragged. These marksmen had been lying for nearly an hour in stony silence, their sights adjusted, their fingers fondling their rifles, their eyes staring at the intrenchments of the enemy. The battalion had suffered heavy losses, and these losses had been hard to bear, for a soldier always reasons that men lost during a period of inaction are men badly lost.

The line now sounded like a great machine set to running frantically in the open air, the bright sunshine of a green field. To the prut of the magazine rifles was added the under-chorus of the clicking mechanism, steady and swift as if the hand of one operator was controlling it all. It reminds one always of a loom, a great grand steel loom, clinking, clanking, plunking, plinking, to weave a woof of thin red threads, the cloth of death. By the men's shoulders under their eager hands dropped continually the yellow empty shells, spinning into the crushed grass blades to remain there and mark for the belated eye the line of a battalion's fight.

All impatience, all rebellious feeling, had passed out of the men as soon as they had been allowed to use their weapons against the enemy. They now were absorbed in this business of hitting something, and all the long training at the rifle ranges, all the pride of the marksman which had been so long alive in them, made them forget for the time everything but shooting. They were as deliberate and exact as so many watchmakers.

A new sense of safety was rightfully upon them. They knew that those mysterious men in the high far trenches in front were having the bullets sping in their faces with relentless and remarkable precision; they knew, in fact, that they were now doing the thing which they had been trained endlessly to do, and they knew they were doing it well. Nolan, for instance, was overjoyed. "Plug 'em," he said. "Plug 'em." He laid his face to his rifle as if it were his mistress. He was aiming under the shadow of a certain portico of a fortified house; there he could faintly see a long black line which he knew to be a loophole cut for riflemen, and he knew that every shot of his was going there under the portico, mayhap though the loophole to the brain of another man like himself. He loaded the awkward magazine of his rifle again and again. He was so intent that he did not know of new orders until he saw the men about him scrambling to their feet and running forward, crouching low as they ran.

He heard a shout. "Come on, boys! We can't be last! We're going up! We're going up!" He sprang to his feet and, stooping, ran with the others. Something fine, soft, gentle, touched his heart as he ran. He had loved the regiment, the army, because the regiment, the army, was his life. He had no other outlook; and now these men, his comrades, were performing his dream-scenes for him. They were doing as he had ordained in his visions. It is curious that in this charge he considered himself as rather unworthy. Although he himself was in the assault with the rest of them, it seemed to him that his comrades were dazzlingly courageous. His part, to his mind, was merely that of a man who was going along with the crowd.

He saw Grierson biting madly with his pincers at a barbed-wire fence. They were half-way up the beautiful sylvan slope; there was no enemy to be seen, and yet the landscape rained bullets. Somebody punched him violently in the stomach. He thought dully to lie down and rest, but instead he fell with a crash.

The sparse line of men in blue shirts and dirty slouch hats swept on up the hill. He decided to shut his eyes for a moment because he felt very dreamy and peaceful. It seemed only a minute before he heard a voice say, "There he is." Grierson and Watkins had come to look for him. He searched their faces at once and keenly, for he had a thought that the line might be driven down the hill and leave him in Spanish hands. But he saw that everything was secure and he prepared no questions.

"Nolan," said Grierson clumsily, "do you know me?"

The man on the ground smiled softly. "Of course I know you, you chowder-faced monkey. Why wouldn't I know you?"

Watkins knelt beside him. "Where did they plug you, boy?"

Nolan was somewhat dubious. "It ain't much, I don't think, but it's somewheres there." He laid a finger on the pit of his stomach. They lifted his shirt and then privately they exchanged a glance of horror.

"Does it hurt, Jimmie?" said Grierson, hoarsely.

"No," said Nolan, "it don't hurt any, but I feel sort of dead-to-the-world and numb all over. I don't think it's very bad."

"Oh, it's all right," said Watkins.

"What I need is a drink," said Nolan, grinning at them. "I'm chilly—lyin' on this damp ground."

"It ain't very damp, Jimmie," said Grierson.

"Well, it is damp," said Nolan, with sudden irritability. "I can feel it. I'm wet, I tell you—wet through—just from lyin' here."

They answered hastily. "Yes, that's so, Jimmie. It *is* damp. That's so."

"Just put your hand under my back and see how wet the ground is," he said.

"No," they answered. "That's all right, Jimmie. We know it's wet."

"Well, put your hand under and see," he cried, stubbornly.

"Oh, never mind, Jimmie."

"No," he said in a temper. "See for yourself." Grierson seemed to be afraid of Nolan's agitation, and so he slipped a hand under the prostrate man, and presently withdrew it covered with blood. "Yes," he said, hiding his hand carefully from Nolan's eyes, "you were right, Jimmie."

"Of course I was," said Nolan, contentedly closing his eyes. "This hillside holds water like a swamp." After a moment he said: "Guess I ought to know. I'm flat here on it, and you fellers are standing up."

He did not know he was dying. He thought he was holding an argument on the condition of the turf.

VI

"Cover his face," said Grierson in a low and husky voice, afterward.

"What'll I cover it with?" said Watkins.

They looked at themselves. They stood in their shirts, trousers, leggings, shoes; they had nothing.

"Oh," said Grierson, "here's his hat." He brought it and laid it on the face of the dead man. They stood for a time. It was apparent that they thought it essential and decent to say or do something. Finally Watkins said in a broken voice, "Aw, it's a damn shame." They moved slowly off toward the firing line.

.   .   .   .   .   .

In the blue gloom of evening, in one of the fever tents, the two rows of still figures became hideous, charnel. The languid movement of a hand was surrounded with spectral mystery, and the occasional painful twisting of a body under a blanket was terrifying, as if dead men were moving in their graves under the sod. A heavy odor of sickness and medicine hung in the air.

"What regiment are you in?" said a feeble voice.

"Twenty-ninth Infantry," answered another voice.

"Twenty-ninth! Why, the man on the other side of me is in the Twenty-ninth."

"He is? . . . Hey there, partner, are you in the Twenty-ninth?"

A third voice merely answered wearily: "Martin of C Company."

"What? Jack, is that you?"

"It's part of me. . . . Who are you?"

"Grierson, you fat-head. I thought you were wounded."

There was the noise of a man gulping a great drink of water, and at its conclusion Martin said, "I am."

"Well, what you doin' in the fever place, then?"

Martin replied with drowsy impatience. "Got the fever too."

"Gee!" said Grierson.

Thereafter there was silence in the fever tent save for the noise made by a man over in a corner, a kind of man always found in an American crowd, a heroic, implacable comedian and patriot, of a humor that has bitterness and ferocity and love in it, and he was wringing from the situation a grim meaning by singing the Star-Spangled Banner with all the ardor which could be procured from his fever-stricken body.

"Billie," called Martin in a low voice, "where's Jimmie Nolan?"

"He's dead," said Grierson.

A triangle of raw gold light shone on a side of the tent. Somewhere in the valley an engine's bell was ringing, and it sounded of peace and home as if it hung on a cow's neck.

"An' where's Ike Watkins?"

"Well, he ain't dead, but he got shot through the lungs. They say he ain't got much show."

Through the clouded odors of sickness and medicine rang the dauntless voice of the man in the corner:

". . . Long may it wave. . . ."

THE LONE CHARGE
OF WILLIAM B. PERKINS

HE COULD not distinguish between a 5-inch quick-firing gun and a nickel-plated ice-pick, and so, naturally, he had been elected to fill the position of war correspondent. The responsible party was the editor of the *Minnesota Herald*. Perkins had no information of war and no particular rapidity of mind for acquiring it, but he had that rank and fibrous quality of courage which springs from the thick soil of Western America.

It was morning in Guantanamo Bay. If the marines encamped on the hill had had time to turn their gaze seaward they might have seen a small newspaper despatch-boat wending its way toward the entrance of the harbor over the blue sun-lit waters of the Caribbean. In the stern of this tug Perkins was seated upon some coal-bags, while the breeze gently ruffled his greasy pyjamas. He was staring at a brown line of entrenchments surmounted by a flag, which was Camp McCalla. In the harbor were anchored two or three grim grey cruisers and a transport. As the tug steamed up the radiant channel Perkins could see men moving on shore near the charred ruins of a village. Perkins was deeply moved; here already was more war than he had ever known in Minnesota. Presently he, clothed in the essential garments of a war correspondent, was rowed to the sandy beach. Marines in yellow linen were handling an ammunition supply. They paid no attention to the visitor, being morose from the inconveniences of two days and nights of fighting. Perkins toiled up the zig-zag path to the top of the hill and looked with eager eyes at the trenches, the field pieces, the funny little Colts, the flag, the grim marines lying wearily on their arms. And still more he looked through the clear air over a thousand yards of mysterious woods from which had emanated at inopportune times repeated flocks of Mauser bullets.

Perkins was delighted. He was filled with admiration for these jaded and smoky men who lay so quietly in the trenches waiting for a resumption of guerilla enterprise. But he wished they would heed him. He wanted to talk about it. Save for sharp inquiring glances no one acknowledged his existence.

Finally he approached two young lieutenants, and in his innocent Western way he asked them if they would like a drink. The effect on the two young lieutenants was immediate and astonishing. With one voice they answered: "Yes, we would." Perkins almost wept with joy at this amiable response, and he exclaimed that he would immediately board the tug and bring off a bottle of Scotch. This attracted the officers, and in a burst of confidence one explained that there had not been a drop in camp. Perkins lunged down the hill and fled to his boat, where in his exuberance he engaged in a preliminary altercation with some whisky. Consequently he toiled again up the hill in the blasting sun with his enthusiasm in no ways abated. The parched officers were very gracious, and such was the state of mind of Perkins that he did not note properly how serious and solemn was his engagement with the whisky. And because of this fact, and because of his antecedents, there happened the lone charge of William B. Perkins.

Now as Perkins went down the hill something happened. A private in those high trenches found that a cartridge was clogged in his rifle. It then becomes necessary with most kinds of rifles to explode the cartridge. The private took the rifle to his captain and explained the case. But it would not do in that camp to fire a rifle for mechanical purposes and without warning, because the eloquent sound would bring six hundred tired marines to tension and high expectancy. So the captain turned, and in a loud voice announced to the camp that he found it necessary to shoot into the air. The communication rang sharply from voice to voice. Then the captain raised the weapon and fired. Whereupon—and whereupon—a large line of guerillas lying in the bushes decided swiftly that their presence and position were discovered, and swiftly they volleyed.

In a moment the woods and the hills were alive with the crack and sputter of rifles. Men on the warships in the harbor heard the old familiar *flut-flut-fluttery-fluttery-flut-flut-flut* from the entrenchments. Incidentally the launch of the *Marblehead,* commanded by one of our headlong American ensigns, streaked for the strategic woods like a galloping marine dragoon, peppering away with its blunderbus in the bow.

Perkins had arrived at the foot of the hill where began the arrangement of one hundred and fifty marines that protected the short line of communication between the main body and the beach. These men had all swarmed into line behind fortifications improvised from the boxes of provisions. And to them were gathering naked men who had been bathing, naked men who arrayed themselves speedily in cartridge belts and rifles. The woods and the hills went *flut-flut-flut-fluttery-fluttery-flut-flllllutt-ery-flut.* Under the boughs of a beautiful tree lay five wounded men thinking vividly.

And now it befell Perkins to discover a Spaniard in the bush. The distance was some five hundred yards. In a loud voice he announced his perception. He also declared hoarsely that if he only had a rifle he would go and possess himself of this particular enemy. Immediately an amiable lad, shot in the arm, said: "Well, take mine." Perkins thus acquired a rifle and a clip of five cartridges.

"Come on!" he shouted. This part of the battalion was lying very tight, not yet being engaged, but not knowing when the business would swirl around to them.

To Perkins they replied with a roar. "Come back here, you —— fool. Do you want to get shot by your own crowd? Come back! ——!! ——!!" As a detail, it might be mentioned that the fire from a part of the hill swept the journey upon which Perkins had started.

Now behold the solitary Perkins adrift in the storm of fighting, even as a champagne jacket of straw is lost in a great surf. He found it out quickly. Four seconds elapsed before he discovered that he was an almshouse idiot plunging through hot crackling thickets on a June morning in Cuba. *Sss-s-s-swing-sing-ing-Pop* went the lightning-swift metal grasshoppers over him and beside him. The beauties of rural Minnesota illuminated his conscience with the gold of lazy corn, with the sleeping green of meadows, with the cathedral gloom of pine forests. *Sshsh-swing-Pop.* Perkins decided that if he cared to extract himself from a tangle of imbecility he must shoot. The entire situation was that he must shoot. It was necessary that he should shoot. Nothing would save him but shooting. It is a law that men thus decide when the waters of battle close over their minds. So with a prayer that the Americans would not hit him in the back nor the left side, and that the Spaniards would not hit him in the front, he knelt like a suppliant alone in the desert of chaparral and emptied his magazine at his Spaniard before he discovered that his Spaniard was a bit of dried palm-branch.

Then Perkins flurried like a fish. His reason for being was a Spaniard in the bush. When the Spaniard turned into a dried palm-branch, he could no longer furnish himself with one adequate reason. Then did he dream frantically of some anthracite hiding place, some profound dungeon of peace where blind mules live placidly chewing the far-gathered hay.

"*Sss-swing-wing-Pop. Prut-prut-prrrut.*" Then a field-gun spoke. "Boom-*Ra-swow-ow-ow-ow*-Pum." Then a Colt automatic began to bark. "*Crack-crk-crk-crk-crk-crk*" endlessly. Raked, enfiladed, flanked, surrounded, and overwhelmed, what hope was there for William B. Perkins of the *Minnesota Herald*?

But war is a spirit. War provides for those that it loves. It provides sometimes death and sometimes a singular and incredible safety. There were few ways in which it was possible to preserve Perkins. One way was by means of a steam-boiler.

Perkins espied near him an old rusty steam-boiler lying in the bushes. War only knows how it was there, but there it was, a temple shining resplendent with safety. With a moan of haste Perkins flung himself through that hole which expressed the absence of the steam-pipe.

Then ensconced in his boiler, Perkins comfortably listened to the ring of a fight which seemed to be in the air above him. Sometimes bullets struck their strong swift blow against the boiler's sides, but none entered to interfere with Perkins's rest.

Time passed. The fight, short anyhow, dwindled to *prut* . . . *prut* . . . *prut-prut* . . . *prut.* And when the silence came, Perkins might have been seen cautiously protruding from the boiler. Presently he strolled back toward the marine lines with his hat not able to fit his head for the new bumps of wisdom that were on it.

The marines, with an annoyed air, were settling down again when an apparitional figure came from the bushes. There was great excitement. "It's that crazy man," they shouted, and as he drew near they gathered tumultuously about him and demanded to know How He Had Accomplished It.

Perkins made a gesture, the gesture of a man escaping from an unintentional mud-bath, the gesture of a man coming out of battle, and then he told them.

The incredulity was immediate and general. "Like hell you did! What? In an old boiler? An old boiler? Out in that brush? Well, we guess not." They did not believe him until two days later, when a patrol happened to find the rusty boiler, relic of some curious transaction in the ruin of the Cuban sugar industry. The patrol then marveled at the truthfulness of war correspondents until they were almost blind.

Soon after his adventure Perkins boarded the tug, wearing a countenance of poignant thoughtfulness.

THE CLAN OF NO-NAME

Unwind my riddle.
Cruel as hawks the hours fly,
Wounded men seldom come home to die,
The hard waves see an arm flung high,
Scorn hits strong because of a lie,
Yet there exists a mystic tie.
Unwind my riddle.

I

SHE was out in the garden. Her mother came to her rapidly. "Margharita! Margharita, Mr. Smith is here! Come!" Her mother was fat and commercially excited. Mr. Smith was a matter of some importance to all Tampa people, and since he was really in love with Margharita he was distinctly of more importance to this particular household.

Palm trees tossed their sprays over the fence toward the rutted sand of the street. A little foolish fish-pond in the centre of the garden emitted a sound of red-fins flipping, flipping. "No, mamma," said the girl, "let Mr. Smith wait. I like the garden in the moonlight."

Her mother threw herself into that state of virtuous astonishment which is the weapon of her kind. "Margharita!"

The girl evidently considered herself to be a privileged belle, for she answered quite carelessly: "Oh, let him wait."

The mother threw abroad her arms with a semblance of great high-minded suffering and withdrew. Margharita walked alone in the moonlit garden. Also an electric light threw its shivering gleam over part of her parade.

There was peace for a time. Then suddenly through the faint brown palings was stuck an envelope, white and square. Margharita approached this envelope with an indifferent stride. She hummed a silly air, she bore herself casually, but there was something that made her grasp it hard, a peculiar muscular exhibition, not discernible to indifferent eyes. She did not clutch it, but she took it—simply took it in a way that meant everything, and to measure it by vision it was a picture of the most complete disregard.

She stood straight for a moment. Then she drew from her bosom a photograph and thrust it through the palings. She walked rapidly into the house.

II

A man in garb of blue and white—something relating to what we call bed-ticking—was seated in a curious little cupola on the top of a Spanish blockhouse. The blockhouse sided a white military road that curved away from the man's sight into a blur of trees. On all sides of him were fields of tall grass studded with palms and lined with fences of barbed wire. The sun beat aslant through the trees and the man sped his eyes deep into the dark tropical shadows that seemed velvet with coolness. These tranquil vistas resembled painted scenery in a theatre, and, moreover, a hot, heavy silence lay upon the land.

The soldier in the watching place leaned an unclean Mauser rifle in a corner and, reaching down, took a glowing coal on a bit of palm bark handed up to him by a comrade. The men below were mainly asleep. The sergeant in command drowsed near the open door, the arm above his head showing his long keen-angled chevrons attached carelessly with safety-pins. The sentry lit his cigarette and puffed languorously.

Suddenly he heard from the air around him the querulous, deadly-swift spit of rifle bullets and an instant later the poppety-pop of a small volley sounded in his face close, as if it were fired only ten feet away. Involuntarily he threw back his head quickly as if he were protecting his nose from a falling tile. He screamed an alarm and fell into the blockhouse. In the gloom of it men with their breaths coming sharply between their teeth were tumbling wildly for positions at the loop-holes. The door had been slammed, but the sergeant lay just within, propped up as when he drowsed, but now with blood flowing steadily over the hand that he pressed flatly to his chest. His face was in stark yellow agony. He chokingly repeated: "Fuego! Por Dios, hombres!"

The men's ill-conditioned weapons were jammed through the loop-holes and they began to fire from all four sides of the blockhouse from the simple data apparently that the enemy were in the vicinity. The fumes of burnt powder grew stronger and stronger in the little square fortress. The rattling of the magazine locks was incessant, and the interior might have been that of a gloomy manufactory if it were not for the sergeant down under the feet of the men, coughing out: "Por Dios, hombres! Por Dios! Fuego!"

III

A string of five Cubans in linen that had turned earthy brown in color slid through the woods at a pace that was neither a walk nor a run. It was a kind of a rack. In fact the whole manner of the men as they thus moved bore a rather comic resemblance to the American pacing horse. But they had come many miles since sun-up over mountainous and half-marked paths, and were plainly still fresh. The men were all practicos—guides. They made no sound in their swift travel, but moved their half-shod feet with the skill of cats. The woods lay around them in a deep silence such as one might find at the bottom of a lake.

Suddenly the leading practico raised his hand. The others pulled up short and dropped the butts of their weapons calmly and noiselessly to the ground. The leader whistled a low note, and immediately another practico appeared from the bushes. He moved close to the leader without a word, and then they spoke in whispers.

"There are twenty men and a sergeant in the blockhouse."

"And the road?"

"One company of cavalry passed to the east this morning at seven o'clock. They were escorting four carts. An hour later one horseman rode swiftly to the westward. About noon ten infantry soldiers with a corporal were taken from the big fort and put in the first blockhouse to the east of the fort. There were already twelve men there. We saw a Spanish column moving off toward Mariel."

"No more?"

"No more."

"Good. But the cavalry?"

"It is all right. They were going a long march."

"The expedition is half a league behind. Go and tell the General."

The scout disappeared. The five other men lifted their guns and resumed their rapid and noiseless progress. A moment later no sound broke the stillness save the thump of a mango as it dropped lazily from its tree to the grass. So strange had been the apparition of these men, their dress had been so allied in color to the soil, their passing had so little disturbed the solemn rumination of the forest, and their going had been so like a spectral dissolution, that a witness could have wondered if he dreamed.

IV

A small expedition had landed with arms from the United States and had now come out of the hills and to the edge of a wood. Before them was a long-grassed rolling prairie marked with palms. A half-mile away was the military road and they could see the top of a blockhouse. The insurgent scouts were moving somewhere off in the grass. The General sat comfortably under a tree, while his staff of three young officers stood about him chatting. Their linen clothing was notable from being distinctly whiter than those of the men who, one hundred and fifty in number, lay on the ground in a long brown fringe, ragged—indeed, bare in many places—but singularly reposeful, unworried, veteran-like.

The General, however, was thoughtful. He pulled continually at his little thin mustache. As far as the heavily patrolled and guarded military road was concerned, the insurgents had been in the habit of dashing across it in small bodies whenever they pleased, but to safely scoot over it with a valuable convoy of arms was decidedly a more important thing. So the General awaited the return of his practicos with anxiety. The still pampas betrayed no sign of their existence.

The General gave some orders and an officer counted off twenty men to go with him and delay any attempt of the troop of cavalry to return from the eastward. It was not an easy task, but it was a familiar task—checking the advance of a greatly superior force by a very hard fire from concealment. A few rifles had often bayed a strong column for sufficient length of time for all strategic purposes. The twenty men pulled themselves together tranquilly. They looked quite indifferent. Indeed, they had the supremely casual manner of old soldiers, hardened to battle as a condition of existence.

Thirty men were then told off whose function it was to worry and rag at the blockhouse and check any advance from the westward. A hundred men carrying precious burdens—besides their own equipment—were to pass in as much of a rush as possible between these two wings, cross the road and skip for the hills, their retreat being covered by a combination of the two firing parties. It was a trick that needed both luck and neat arrangement. Spanish columns were for ever prowling through this province in all directions and at all times. Insurgent bands —the lightest of light infantry—were kept on the jump even when they were not incommoded by fifty boxes, each one large enough for the coffin of a little man and heavier than if the little man were in it, and fifty small but formidable boxes of ammunition.

The carriers stood to their boxes and the firing parties leaned on their rifles. The General arose and strolled to and fro, his hands behind him. Two of his staff were jesting at the third, a young man with a face less bronzed and with very new accoutrements. On the strap of his cartouche were a gold star and a silver star placed in a horizontal line, denoting that he was a second lieutenant. He seemed very happy; he laughed at all their jests although his eye roved continually over the sunny grass-lands where was going to happen his first fight. One of his stars was bright, like his hopes; the other was pale, like death.

Two practicos came racking out of the grass. They spoke rapidly to the General; he turned and nodded to his officers. The two firing parties filed out and diverged toward their positions. The General watched them through his glasses. It was strange to note how soon they were dim to the unaided eye. The little patches of brown in the green grass did not look like men at all.

Practicos continually ambled up to the General. Finally he

turned and made a sign to the bearers. The first twenty men in
line picked up their boxes, and this movement rapidly spread to
the tail of the line. The weighted procession moved painfully out
upon the sunny prairie. The General, marching at the head of it,
glanced continually back as if he were compelled to drag behind
him some ponderous iron chain. Besides the obvious mental
worry, his face bore an expression of intense physical strain, and
he even bent his shoulders, unconsciously tugging at the chain
to hurry it through this enemy-crowded valley.

V

The fight was opened by eight men who, snuggling in the
grass within three hundred yards of the blockhouse, suddenly
blazed away at the bed-ticking figure in the cupola and at the
open door where they could see vague outlines. Then they
laughed and yelled insulting language, for they knew that as far
as the Spaniards were concerned the surprise was as much as
having a diamond bracelet turn to soap. It was this volley that
smote the sergeant and caused the man in the cupola to scream
and tumble from his perch.

The eight men, as well as all other insurgents within fair
range, had chosen good positions for lying close, and for a time
they let the blockhouse rage, although the soldiers therein could
occasionally hear above the clamor of their weapons shrill and
almost wolfish calls coming from men whose lips were laid
against the ground. But it is not in the nature of them of Spanish
blood and armed with rifles to long endure the sight of anything
so tangible as an enemy's blockhouse without shooting at it—
other conditions being partly favorable. Presently the steaming
soldiers in the little fort could hear the sping and shiver of
bullets striking the wood that guarded their bodies.

A perfectly white smoke floated up over each firing Cuban, the
penalty of the Remington rifle, but about the blockhouse there
was only the lightest gossamer of blue. The blockhouse stood
always for some big, clumsy and rather incompetent animal,
while the insurgents, scattered on two sides of it, were little
enterprising creatures of another species, too wise to come too
near, but joyously ragging at its easiest flanks and dirling the

lead into its sides in a way to make it fume and spit and rave like the tomcat when the glad, free-band foxhound pups catch him in the lane.

The men, outlying in the grass, chuckled deliriously at the fury of the Spanish fire. They howled opprobrium to encourage the Spaniards to fire more ill-used, incapable bullets. Whenever an insurgent was about to fire he ordinarily prefixed the affair with a speech. "Do you want something to eat? Yes? All right." Bang! "Eat that." The more common expressions of the incredibly foul Spanish tongue were trifles light as air in this badinage which was shrieked out from the grass during the spin of bullets and the dull rattle of the shooting.

But at some time there came a series of sounds from the east that began in a few disconnected pruts and ended as if an amateur was trying to play the long roll upon a muffled drum. Those of the insurgents in the blockhouse attacking party who had neighbors in the grass turned and looked at them seriously. They knew what the new sound meant. It meant that the twenty men who had gone to the eastward were now engaged. A column of some kind was approaching from that direction and they knew by the clatter that it was a solemn occasion.

In the first place, they were now on the wrong side of the road. They were obliged to cross it to rejoin the main body, provided, of course, that the main body succeeded itself in crossing it. To accomplish this the party at the blockhouse would have to move to the eastward until out of sight or good range of the maddened little fort. But judging from the heaviness of the firing the party of twenty who protected the east were almost sure to be driven immediately back. Hence travel in that direction would become exceedingly hazardous. Hence a man looked seriously at his neighbor. It might easily be that in a moment they were to become an isolated force and wofully on the wrong side of the road.

Any retreat to the westward was absurd, since primarily they would have to widely circle the blockhouse, and more than that they could hear even now in that direction Spanish bugle calling to Spanish bugle, far and near, until one would think that every man in Cuba was a trumpeter and had come forth to parade his talent.

VI

The insurgent General stood in the middle of the road gnawing his lips. Occasionally he stamped a foot and beat his hands passionately together. The carriers were streaming past him, patient, sweating fellows, bowed under their burdens, but they could not move fast enough for him when others of his men were engaged both to the east and to the west, and he, too, knew from the sound that those to the east were in a sore way. Moreover, he could hear that accursed bugling, bugling, bugling in the west.

He turned suddenly to the new lieutenant who stood behind him, pale and quiet. "Did you ever think a hundred men were so many?" he cried, incensed to the point of beating them. Then he said longingly: "Oh, for a half an hour! Or even twenty minutes!"

A practico racked violently up from the east. It is characteristic of these men that, although they take a certain roadster gait and hold it for ever, they cannot really run, sprint, race. "Captain Rodriguez is attacked by two hundred men, señor, and the cavalry is behind them. He wishes to know——"

The General was furious. He pointed. "Go! Tell Rodriguez to hold his place for twenty minutes, even if he leaves every man dead."

The practico shambled hastily off.

The last of the carriers were swarming across the road. The rifle-drumming in the east was swelling out and out, evidently coming slowly nearer. The General bit his nails. He wheeled suddenly upon the young lieutenant. "Go to Bas at the blockhouse. Tell him to hold the devil himself for ten minutes and then bring his men out of that place."

The long line of bearers was crawling like a dun worm toward the safety of the foot-hills. High bullets sang a faint song over the aide as he saluted. The bugles had in the west ceased, and that was more ominous than bugling. It meant that the Spanish troops were about to march, or perhaps that they had marched.

The young lieutenant ran along the road until he came to the bend which marked the range of sight from the blockhouse. He

drew his machete, his stunning new machete, and hacked feverishly at the barbed wire fence which lined the north side of the
road at that point. The first wire was obdurate, because it was
too high for his stroke, but two more cut like candy, and he
stepped over the remaining one, tearing his trousers in passing
on the lively serpentine ends of the severed wires. Once out in
the field and bullets seemed to know him and call for him
and speak their wish to kill him. But he ran on because it was his
duty, and because he would be shamed before men if he did not
do his duty, and because he was desolate out there all alone in
the fields with death.

A man running in this manner from the rear was in immensely greater danger than those who lay snug and closer. But
he did not know it. He thought because he was five hundred—
four hundred and fifty—four hundred yards away from the enemy and others were only three hundred yards away that they
were in far more peril. He ran to join them because of his opinion.
He did not care to do it, but he thought that was what men of his
kind would do in such a case. There was a standard and he must
follow it, obey it, because it was a monarch, the Prince of
Conduct.

A bewildered and alarmed face raised itself from the grass
and a voice cried to him: "Drop, Manolo! Drop! Drop!" He recognized Bas and flung himself to the earth beside him.

"Why," he said, panting, "what's the matter?"

"Matter?" said Bas. "You are one of the most desperate and
careless officers I know. When I saw you coming I wouldn't have
given a peseta for your life."

"Oh, no," said the young aide. Then he repeated his orders
rapidly. But he was hugely delighted. He knew Bas well. Bas was
a pupil of Maceo. Bas invariably led his men. He never was a
mere spectator of their battle; he was known for it throughout
the western end of the island. The new officer had early achieved
a part of his ambition—to be called a brave man by established
brave men.

"Well, if we get away from here quickly it will be better for
us," said Bas bitterly. "I've lost six men killed and more wounded.
Rodriguez can't hold his position there, and in a little time more
than a thousand men will come from the other direction."

He hissed a low call, and later the young aide saw some of the men sneaking off with the wounded, lugging them on their backs as porters carry sacks. The fire from the blockhouse had become a-weary, and as the insurgent fire also slackened, Bas and the young lieutenant lay in the weeds listening to the approach of the eastern fight which was sliding toward them like a door to shut them off.

Bas groaned. "I leave my dead. Look there." He swung his hand in a gesture and the lieutenant looking saw a corpse. He was not stricken as he expected. There was very little blood; it was a mere thing.

"Time to travel," said Bas suddenly. His imperative hissing brought his men near him. There were a few hurried questions and answers; then, characteristically, the men turned in the grass, lifted their rifles, and fired a last volley into the blockhouse, accompanying it with their shrill cries. Scrambling low to the ground, they were off in a winding line for safety. Breathing hard, the lieutenant stumbled his way forward. Behind him he could hear the men calling each to each: "Segue! Segue! Segue! Go on! Get out! Git!" Everybody understood that the peril of crossing the road was compounding from minute to minute.

VII

When they reached the gap through which the expedition had passed, they fled out upon the road like scared wild-fowl tracking along a sea-beach. A cloud of blue figures far up this dignified shaded avenue fired at once. The men already had begun to laugh as they shied one by one across the road. "Segue! Segue!" The hard part for the nerves had been the lack of information of the amount of danger. Now that they could see it, they accounted it all the more lightly for their previous anxiety.

Over in the other field Bas and the young lieutenant found Rodriguez, his machete in one hand, his revolver in the other, smoky, dirty, sweating. He shrugged his shoulders when he saw them and pointed disconsolately to the brown thread of carriers moving toward the foot-hills. His own men were crouched in line just in front of him, blazing like a prairie fire.

Now began the fight of a scant rear-guard to hold back the

pressing Spaniards until the carriers could reach the top of the ridge, a mile away. This ridge, by the way, was more steep than any roof; it conformed more to the sides of a French war-ship. Trees grew vertically from it, however, and a man burdened only with his rifle usually pulled himself wheezingly up in a sort of ladder-climbing process, grabbing the slim trunks above him. How the loaded carriers were to conquer it in a hurry, no one knew. Rodriguez shrugged his shoulders as one who would say with philosophy, smiles, tears, courage: "Isn't this a mess!"

At an order the men scattered back for four hundred yards with the rapidity and mystery of a handful of pebbles flung in the night. They left one behind, who cried out, but it was now a game in which some were sure to be left behind to cry out.

The Spaniards deployed on the road, and for twenty minutes remained there, pouring into the field such a fire from their magazines as was hardly heard at Gettysburg. As a matter of truth the insurgents were at this time doing very little shooting, being chary of ammunition. But it is possible for the soldier to confuse himself with his own noise, and undoubtedly the Spanish troops thought throughout their din that they were being fiercely engaged. Moreover, a firing-line—particularly at night or when opposed to a hidden foe—is nothing less than an emotional chord, a chord of a harp that sings because a puff of air arrives or when a bit of down touches it. This is always true of new troops or stupid troops, and these troops were rather stupid troops. But the way in which they mowed the verdure in the distance was a sight for a farmer.

Presently the insurgents slunk back to another position, where they fired enough shots to stir again the Spaniards into an opinion that they were in a heavy fight. But such a misconception could only endure for a number of minutes. Presently it was plain that the Spaniards were about to advance, and, moreover, word was brought to Rodriguez that a small band of guerillas were already making an attempt to worm around the right flank. Rodriguez cursed despairingly; he sent both Bas and the young lieutenant to that end of the line to hold the men to their work as long as possible.

In reality the men barely needed the presence of their officers. The kind of fighting left practically everything to the discretion of the individual, and they arrived at concert of action mainly because of the equality of experience in the wisdoms of bushwhacking.

The yells of the guerillas could plainly be heard, and the insurgents answered in kind. The young lieutenant found desperate work on the right flank. The men were raving mad with it, babbling, tearful, almost frothing at the mouth. Two terrible bloody creatures passed him, creeping on all fours, and one in a whimper was calling upon God, his mother, and a saint. The guerillas, as effectually concealed as the insurgents, were driving their bullets low through the smoke at sight of a flame, a movement of the grass or sight of a patch of dirty brown coat. They were no column-o'-four soldiers; they were as slinky and snaky and quick as so many Indians. They were, moreover, native Cubans, and because of their treachery to the one-star flag they never by any chance received quarter if they fell into the hands of the insurgents. Nor, if the case was reversed, did they ever give quarter. It was life and life, death and death; there was no middle ground, no compromise. If a man's crowd was rapidly retreating and he was tumbled over by a slight hit, he should curse the sacred graves that the wound was not through the precise centre of his heart. The machete is a fine broad blade, but it is not so nice as a drilled hole in the chest; no man wants his death-bed to be a shambles. The men fighting on the insurgent right knew that if they fell they were lost.

On the extreme right the young lieutenant found five men in a little saucer-like hollow. Two were dead, one was wounded and staring blankly at the sky, and two were emptying hot rifles furiously. Some of the guerillas had snaked into positions only a hundred yards away.

The young man rolled in among the men in the saucer. He could hear the barking of the guerillas and the screams of the two insurgents. The rifles were popping and spitting in his face, it seemed, while the whole land was alive with a noise of rolling and drumming. Men could have gone drunken in all this flashing and flying and snarling and din, but at this time he was very deliberate. He knew that he was thrusting himself into a trap whose door, once closed, opened only when the black hand knocked, and every part of him seemed to be in panic-stricken revolt. But something controlled him; something moved him inexorably in one direction; he perfectly understood, but he was only sad, sad with a serene dignity, with the countenance of a mournful young prince. He was of a kind—that seemed to be it—and the men of his kind, on peak or plain, from the dark northern ice-fields to the hot wet jungles, through all wine and want, through all lies and unfamiliar truth, dark or light, the men of his kind were governed by their gods, and each man knew the law and yet could not give tongue to it; but it was the law, and if the spirits of the men of his kind were all sitting in critical judgment upon him even then in the sky, he could not have bettered his conduct; he needs must obey the law, and always with the law there is only one way. But from peak and plain, from dark northern ice-fields and hot wet jungles, through wine and want, through all lies and unfamiliar truth, dark or light, he heard breathed to him the approval and the benediction of his brethren.

He stooped and gently took a dead man's rifle and some cartridges. The battle was hurrying, hurrying, hurrying, but he was in no haste. His glance caught the staring eye of the wounded soldier, and he smiled at him quietly. The man—simple doomed peasant—was not of his kind, but the law on fidelity was clear.

He thrust a cartridge into the Remington and crept up beside the two unhurt men. Even as he did so, three or four bullets cut so close to him that all his flesh tingled. He fired carefully into the smoke. The guerillas were certainly not now more than fifty yards away.

He raised him coolly for his second shot, and almost instantly it was as if some giant had struck him in the chest with a beam. It whirled him in a great spasm back into the saucer. As he put his two hands to his breast, he could hear the guerillas screeching exultantly, every throat vomiting forth all the infamy of a language prolific in the phrasing of infamy.

One of the other men came rolling slowly down the slope, while his rifle followed him, and striking another rifle, clanged out. Almost immediately the survivor howled and fled wildly. A whole volley missed him, and then one or more shots caught him as a bird is caught on the wing.

The young lieutenant's body seemed galvanized from head to foot. He concluded that he was not hurt very badly, but when he tried to move he found that he could not lift his hands from his breast. He had turned to lead. He had had a plan of taking a photograph from his pocket and looking at it.

There was a stir in the grass at the edge of the saucer, and a man appeared there looking where lay the four insurgents. His negro face was not an eminently ferocious one in its lines, but now it was lit with an illimitable blood-greed. He and the young lieutenant exchanged a singular glance; then he came stepping eagerly down. The young lieutenant closed his eyes, for he did not want to see the flash of the machete.

VIII

The Spanish Colonel was in a rage, and yet immensely proud —immensely proud, and yet in a rage of disappointment. There had been a fight, and the insurgents had retreated leaving their dead, but still a valuable expedition had broken through his lines and escaped to the mountains. As a matter of truth, he was not sure whether to be wholly delighted or wholly angry, for well he knew that the importance lay not so much in the truthful account of the action as it did in the heroic prose of the official report, and in the fight itself lay material for a purple splendid poem. The insurgents had run away—no one could deny it; it was plain even to whatever privates had fired with their eyes shut. This was worth a loud blow and splutter. However, when all was said and done, he could not help but reflect that if he had captured this expedition, he would have been a brigadier-general, if not more.

He was a short, heavy man with a beard, who walked in a manner common to all elderly Spanish officers and to many young ones. That is to say, he walked as if his spine was a stick and a little longer than his body; as if he suffered from some disease of the backbone which allowed him but scant use of his legs. He toddled along the road, gesticulating disdainfully and muttering, "Ca! Ca! Ca!"

He berated some soldiers for an immaterial thing, and as he approached the men stepped precipitately back as if he were a fire-engine. They were most of them young fellows, who displayed when under orders the manner of so many faithful dogs. At present they were black, tongue-hanging, thirsty boys, bathed in the nervous weariness of the after-battle time.

Whatever he may truly have been in character, the Colonel closely resembled a gluttonous and libidinous old pig, filled from head to foot with the pollution of a sinful life. "Ca!" he snarled as he toddled. "Ca! Ca!" The soldiers saluted as they backed to the side of the road. The air was full of the odor of burnt rags. Over on the prairie guerillas and regulars were rummaging the grass. A few unimportant shots sounded from near the base of the hills.

A guerilla, glad with plunder, came to a Spanish captain. He held in his hand a photograph. "Mira, señor. I took this from the body of an officer whom I killed machete to machete."

The captain shot from the corner of his eye a cynical glance at the guerilla, a glance which commented upon the last part of the statement. "M-m-m," he said. He took the photograph and gazed with a slow faint smile, the smile of a man who knows bloodshed and homes and love, at the face of a girl. He turned the photograph presently, and on the back of it was written: "One lesson in English I will give you—this: I love you, Margharita." The photograph had been taken in Tampa.

The officer was silent for a half-minute, while his face still wore the slow faint smile. "Pobrecito," he murmured finally with a philosophic sigh which was brother to a shrug. Without deigning a word to the guerilla he thrust the photograph in his pocket and walked away.

High over the green earth, in the dizzy blue heights, some great birds were slowly circling with down-turned beaks.

IX

Margharita was in the garden. The blue electric rays shone through the plumes of the palm and shivered in feathery images on the walk. In the little foolish fish-pond some stalwart fish was apparently bullying the others, for often there sounded a frantic splashing.

Her mother came to her rapidly. "Margharita, Mr. Smith is here! Come!"

"Oh, is he?" cried the girl. She followed her mother to the

house. She swept into the little parlor with a grand air, the egotism of a savage. Smith had heard the whirl of her skirts in the hall, and his heart, as usual, thumped hard enough to make him gasp. Every time he called he would sit waiting, with the dull fear in his breast that her mother would enter and indifferently announce that she had gone up to heaven or off to New York with one of his dream-rivals, and he would never see her again in this wide world. And he would conjure up tricks to then escape from the house without any one observing his face break up into furrows. It was part of his love to believe in the absolute treachery of his adored one. So whenever he heard the whirl of her skirts in the hall he felt that he had again leased happiness from a dark fate.

She was rosily beaming and all in white. "Why, Mr. Smith!" she exclaimed, as if he was the last man in the world she expected to see.

"Good evenin'," he said, shaking hands nervously. He was always awkward and unlike himself at the beginning of one of these calls. It took him some time to get into form.

She posed her figure in operatic style on a chair before him and immediately galloped off a mile of questions, information of herself, gossip and general outcries, which left him no obligation but to look beamingly intelligent and from time to time say: "Yes?" His personal joy, however, was to stare at her beauty.

When she stopped and wandered as if uncertain which way to talk, there was a minute of silence which each of them had been educated to feel was very incorrect—very incorrect indeed. Polite people always babbled at each other like two brooks.

He knew that the responsibility was upon him, and although his mind was mainly upon the form of the proposal of marriage which he intended to make later, it was necessary that he should maintain his reputation as a well-bred man by saying something at once. It flashed upon him to ask: "Won't you please play?" But the time for the piano ruse was not yet; it was too early. So he said the first thing that came into his head: "Too bad about young Manolo Prat being killed over there in Cuba, wasn't it?"

"Wasn't it a pity?" she answered.

"They say his mother is heartbroken," he continued. "They're afraid she's goin' to die."

"And wasn't it queer that we didn't hear about it for almost two months?"

"Well, it's no use tryin' to git quick news from there."

Presently they advanced to matters more personal, and she used upon him a series of star-like glances which rumpled him at once to squalid slavery. He gloated upon her, afraid, afraid, yet more avaricious than a thousand misers. She fully comprehended; she laughed and taunted him with her eyes. She impressed upon him that she was like a will-o'-the-wisp, beautiful beyond compare, but impossible, almost impossible, but at least very difficult; then again, suddenly, impossible—impossible—impossible. He was glum; he would never dare propose to this radiance; it was like asking to be Pope.

A moment later there chimed into the room something that he knew to be a more tender note. The girl became dreamy as she looked at him; her voice lowered to a delicious intimacy of tone. He leaned forward; he was about to outpour his bully-ragged soul in fine words, when—presto—she was the most casual person he had ever laid eyes upon, and was asking him about the route of the proposed trolley line.

But nothing short of a fire could stop him now. He grabbed her hand. "Margharita," he murmured gutturally, "I want you to marry me!"

She glared at him in the most perfect lie of astonishment. "What do you say?"

He arose, and she thereupon arose also and fled back a step. He could only stammer out her name. And thus they stood, defying the principles of the dramatic art.

"I love you," he said at last.

"How—how do I know you really, truly love me?" she said, raising her eyes timorously to his face, and this timorous glance, this one timorous glance, made him the superior person in an instant. He went forward as confident as a grenadier, and, taking both her hands, kissed her.

That night she took a stained photograph from her dressing-table, and, holding it over the candle, burned it to nothing, her red lips meanwhile parted with the intentness of her occupation. On the back of the photograph was written: "One lesson in English I will give you—this: I love you."

For the word is clear only to the kind who on peak or plain, from dark northern ice-fields to the hot wet jungles, through all wine and want, through lies and unfamiliar truth, dark or light, are governed by the unknown gods, and though each man knows the law no man may give tongue to it.

"GOD REST YE, MERRY GENTLEMEN"

LITTLE NELL, sometimes called the Blessed Damosel, was a war correspondent for the *New York Eclipse,* and at sea on the dispatch-boats he wore pyjamas, and on shore he wore what fate allowed him, which clothing was in the main unsuitable to the climate. He had been cruising in the Carribean on a small tug, awash always, habitable never, wildly looking for Cervera's fleet, although what he was going to do with four armored cruisers and two destroyers in the event of his really finding them had not been explained by the managing editor. The cabled instructions read: "Take tug. Go find Cervera's fleet." If his unfortunate nine-knot craft should happen to find these great twenty-knot ships, with their two spiteful and faster attendants, Little Nell had wondered how he was going to lose them again. He had marveled both publicly and in secret on the uncompromising asininity of managing editors at odd moments, but he had wasted little time. The *Jefferson G. Johnson* was already coaled, so he passed the word to his skipper, bought some canned meats, cigars and beer, and soon the *Johnson* sailed on her mission, tooting her whistle in graceful farewell to some friends of hers in the bay.

So the *Johnson* crawled giddily to one wave height after another, and fell, aslant, into one valley after another for a longer period than was good for the hearts of the men, because the *Johnson* was merely a habor tug, with no architectural intention of parading the high seas, and the crew had never seen the decks all white water like a mere sunken reef. As for the cook, he blasphemed hopelessly hour in and hour out, meanwhile pursuing the equipment of his trade frantically from side to side of the galley. Little Nell dealt with a great deal of grumbling, but he knew it was not the real, evil grumbling. It was merely the unhappy words of men who wished expression of comradeship for their wet, forlorn, half-starved lives, to which, they explained, they were not accustomed, and for which, they explained, they were not properly paid. Little Nell condoled and condoled without difficulty. He laid words of gentle sympathy before them, and smothered his own misery behind the face of a reporter of the *New York Eclipse*. They tossed themselves in their cockleshell even as far as Martinique; they knew many races and many flags, but they did not find Cervera's fleet. If they had found that elusive squadron this timid story would never have been written; there would probably have been a lyric. The *Johnson* limped one morning into the Mole St. Nicholas, and there Little Nell received this dispatch: "Can't understand your inaction. What are you doing with the boat? Report immediately. Fleet transports already left Tampa. Expected destination near Santiago. Proceed there immediately. Place yourself under orders. ROGERS, *Eclipse*."

One day, steaming along the high luminous blue coast of Santiago province, they fetched into view the fleets, a knot of masts and funnels, looking incredibly inshore, as if they were glued to the mountains. Then mast left mast, and funnel left funnel, slowly, slowly, and the shore remained still, but the fleets seemed to move out toward the eager *Johnson*. At the speed of nine knots an hour the scene separated into its parts. On an easily rolling sea, under a crystal sky, black-hulled transports—erstwhile packets—lay waiting, while grey cruisers and gunboats lay near shore, shelling the beach and some woods. From their grey sides came thin red flashes, belches of white smoke, and then over the waters sounded boom—boom—boom-boom. The crew of the *Jefferson G. Johnson* forgave Little Nell all the suffering of a previous fortnight.

To the westward, about the mouth of Santiago harbor, sat a row of castellated grey battle-ships, their eyes turned another way, waiting.

The *Johnson* swung past a transport whose decks and rigging were a-swarm with black figures as if a tribe of bees had alighted upon a log. She swung past a cruiser indignant at being left out of the game, her deck thick with white-clothed tars watching the play of their luckier brethren. The cold blue lifting seas tilted the big ships easily, slowly, and heaved the little ones in the usual sinful way, as if very little babes had surreptitiously mounted sixteen-hand trotting hunters. The *Johnson* leered and tumbled her way through the community of ships. The bombardment ceased, and some of the troopships edged in near the land. Soon boats black with men and towed by launches were almost lost to view in the scintillant mystery of light which appeared where the sea met the land. A disembarkation had begun. The *Johnson* sped on at her nine knots, and Little Nell chafed exceedingly, gloating upon the shore through his glasses, anon glancing irritably over the side to note the efforts of the excited tug. Then at last they were in a sort of a cove, with troopships, newspaper boats and cruisers on all sides of them, and over the water came a great hum of human voices, punctuated frequently by the clang of engine-room gongs as the steamers manœuvred to avoid jostling.

In reality it was the great moment—the moment for which men, ships, islands and continents had been waiting for months —but somehow it did not look it. It was very calm; a certain strip of high green rocky shore was being rapidly populated from boat after boat; that was all. Like many preconceived moments, it refused to be supreme.

But nothing lessened Little Nell's frenzy. He knew that the army was landing—he could see it; and little did he care if the great moment did not look its part—it was his virtue as a corre-spondent to recognize the great moment in any disguise. The *Johnson* lowered a boat for him and he dropped into it swiftly, forgetting everything. However, the mate, a bearded philan-thropist, flung after him a mackintosh and a bottle of whisky. Little Nell's face was turned toward those other boats filled with men, all eyes upon the placid, gentle, noiseless shore. Little Nell saw many soldiers seated stiffly beside upright rifle barrels, their blue breasts crossed with white shelter-tent and blanket-rolls. Launches screeched; jack-tars pushed or pulled with their boat-hooks; a beach was alive with working soldiers, some of them stark naked. Little Nell's boat touched the shore amid a babble of tongues, dominated at that time by a single stern voice which was repeating: "Fall in, B Company!"

He took his mackintosh and his bottle of whisky and invaded Cuba. It was a trifle bewildering. Companies of those same men in blue and brown were being rapidly formed and marched off across a little open space—near a pool—near some palm trees—near a house—into the hills. At one side a mulatto in dirty linen and an old straw hat was hospitably using a machete to cut open some green cocoanuts for a group of idle invaders. At the other side—up a bank—a blockhouse was burning furiously, while near it some railway sheds were smouldering, with a little Rogers engine standing amid the ruins, grey, almost white with ashes until it resembled a ghost. Little Nell dodged the encrimsoned blockhouse and proceeded to where he saw a little village street lined with flimsy wooden cottages. Some ragged Cuban cavalrymen were tranquilly tending their horses in a shed which had not yet grown cold of the Spanish occupation. Three American soldiers were trying to explain to a Cuban that they wished to buy drinks. A native rode by, clubbing his pony, as always. The sky was blue; the sea talked with a gravelly accent at the feet of some rocks; upon its bosom the ships sat quiet as gulls. There was no mention, directly, of invasion, invasion for war, save in the roar of the flames at the blockhouse; but none even heeded this conflagration, excepting to note that it threw out a great heat. It was warm, very warm. It was really hard for Little Nell to keep from thinking of his own affairs, his debts, other misfortunes, loves, prospects of happiness. Nobody was in a flurry; the Cubans were not tearfully grateful; the American troops were visibly glad of being released from those ill transports, and the men often asked with interest: "Where's the Spaniards?"

And yet it must have been a great moment! . . . It was a *great* moment! . . . It seemed made to prove that the emphatic time of history is not the emphatic time of the common man, who throughout the changing of nations feels an itch on his shin, a pain in his head, hunger, thirst, a lack of sleep, the influence of his memory of past firesides, glasses of beer, girls, theatres, ideals, religions, parents, faces, hurts, joys.

Little Nell was hailed from a comfortable veranda, and, looking up, saw Walkley of the *Eclipse,* stretched in a yellow-and-green hammock, smoking his pipe with an air of having always lived in that house, in that village. "Oh, dear Little Nell, how glad I am to see your angel face again. There—don't try to hide it! I can see it. Did you bring a corkscrew, too? You're superseded as master of the slaves. Did you know it? And by Rogers, too! Rogers is a Sadducee, a cadaver and a pelican, appointed to the post of chief correspondent, no doubt, because of his rare gift of incapacity. Never mind."

"Where is he now?" asked Little Nell, taking seat on the steps.

"He is down interfering with the landing of the troops," answered Walkley, swinging a leg. "I hope you have the *Johnson* well stocked with food as well as with cigars, cigarettes and tobaccos, ales, wines and liquors. We shall need them. There is already famine in the house of Walkley. I have discovered that the system of transportation for our gallant soldiery does not strike in me the admiration which I have often felt when viewing the management of an ordinary bun-shop. A-hunger, stifling, jammed together amid odors and everybody irritable—ye gods, how irritable! And so I—— Look! Look!"

The *Jefferson G. Johnson*, well known to them at an incredible distance, could be seen striding the broad sea, the smoke belching from her funnel, headed for Jamaica. "The Army Lands in Cuba!" shrieked Walkley. "Shafter's Army Lands near Santiago! Special type! Half the front page! Oh, the Sadducee! The cadaver! The pelican!"

Little Nell was dumb with astonishment and fear. Walkley, however, was at least not dumb. "That's the pelican! That's Mr. Rogers making his first impression upon the situation. He has engraved himself upon us. We are tattooed with him. There will be a fight to-morrow sure, and we will cover it even as you found Cervera's fleet. No food, no horses, no money. I am transport-lame; you are sea-weak. We will never see our salaries again. Whereby Rogers is a fool."

"Anybody else here?" asked Little Nell wearily.

"Only young Point." Point was an artist on the *Eclipse*. "But he has nothing. Pity there wasn't an almshouse here in this God-forsaken country. Here comes Point now." A sad-faced little man came along carrying much luggage. "Hello, Point, lithographer *and* genius; have you food—food? Well, then, you had better return yourself to Tampa by wire. You are no good here. Only one more little mouth to feed."

Point seated himself near Little Nell. "I haven't had anything to eat since daybreak," he said gloomily, "and I don't care much, for I am simply dog-tired!"

"Don't tell *me* you are dog-tired, my talented friend," cried Walkley from his hammock. "Think of me. And now, what's to be done?"

They stared for a time disconsolately at where, over the rim of the sea, trailed black smoke from the *Johnson*. From the landing-place below and to the right came the howls of a man who was superintending the disembarkation of some mules. The burning blockhouse still rendered its hollow roar. Suddenly the man-crowded landing set up its cheer, and the steamers all whistled long and raucously. Tiny black figures were raising an American flag over a blockhouse on the top of a great hill.

"That's mighty fine Sunday stuff," said Little Nell. "Well, I'll go and get the order in which the regiments landed, and who was first ashore, and all that. Then I'll go and try to find General Lawton's headquarters. His division has got the advance, I think."

"And, lo! I will write a burning description of the raising of the flag," said Walkley, "while the brilliant Point buskies for food. And makes damn sure he gets it," he added fiercely.

Little Nell thereupon wandered over the face of the earth, threading out the story of the landing of the regiments. He only found about fifty men who had been the first American soldier to set foot on Cuba, and of these he took the most probable. The army was going forward in detail as soon as the pieces were landed. There was a house something like a crude country tavern; the soldiers in it were looking over their rifles and talking; there was a well of water, quite hot; more palm trees—an inscrutable background.

When he arrived again at Walkley's mansion he found the veranda crowded with correspondents in khaki, duck, dungaree and flannel. They wore riding-breeches, but that was mainly forethought. They could see now that Fate intended them to walk. Some were writing copy while Walkley discoursed from his hammock. Rhodes—doomed to be shot in action some days later —was trying to borrow a canteen from men who had canteens and from men who had none. Young Point, wan, utterly worn out, was asleep on the floor. Walkley pointed to him. "That is how he appears after his foraging journey, during which he ran all Cuba through a sieve. Oh, yes. A can of corn and half a bottle of lime juice."

"Say, does anybody know the name of the commander of the Twenty-sixth Infantry?"

"Who commands the first brigade of Kent's division?"

"What was the name of the chap that raised the flag?"

"What time is it?"

And a woful man was wandering here and there with a cold pipe, saying plaintively: "Who's got a match? Anybody here got a match?"

Little Nell's left boot hurt him at the heel, and so he removed it, taking great care and whistling through his teeth. The heated dust was upon them all, making everybody feel that bathing was unknown and shattering their tempers. Young Point developed a snore which brought grim sarcasm from all quarters. Always, below, hummed the traffic of the landing-place.

When night came Little Nell thought best not to go to bed until late, because he recognized the mackintosh as but a feeble comfort. The evening was a glory. A breeze came from the sea, fanning spurts of flame out of the ashes and charred remains of the sheds, while overhead lay a splendid summer-night sky aflash with great tranquil stars. In the street of the village were two or three fires, frequently and suddenly reddening with their glare the figures of low-voiced men who moved here and there. The lights of the transports blinked on the murmuring plain in front of the village, and far to the westward Little Nell could sometimes note a subtle indication of a playing searchlight which alone marked the presence of the invisible battle-ships half-mooned about the entrance of Santiago harbor, waiting— waiting—waiting.

When Little Nell returned to the veranda he stumbled along a man-strewn place until he came to the spot where he had left his mackintosh; but he found it gone. His curses mingled then with those of the men upon whose bodies he had trodden. Two English correspondents, lying awake to smoke a last pipe, reared and looked at him lazily. "What's wrong, old chap?" murmured one.

"Eh? Lost it, eh? Well, look here; come here and take a bit of my blanket. It's a jolly big one. Oh, no trouble at all, man. . . . There you are. Got enough? Comfy? . . . Good-night."

A sleepy voice arose in the darkness. "If this hammock breaks I shall hit at least ten of those Indians down there. Never mind. This is war!"

The men slept. Once the sound of three or four shots rang across the windy night, and one head uprose swiftly from the veranda, two eyes looked dazedly at nothing, and the head as swiftly sank. Again a sleepy voice was heard. "Usual thing; nervous sentries." The men slept. Before dawn a pulseless, penetrating chill came into the air, and the correspondents awakened shivering into a blue world. Some of the fires still smouldered. Walkley and Little Nell kicked vigorously into Point's framework. "Come on, Brilliance! Wake up, Talent! Don't be sogering. It's too cold to sleep, but it's not too cold to hustle." Point sat up dolefully. Upon his face was a childish expression. "Where we going to get breakfast?" he asked sulkily.

"There's no breakfast for you, you hound. Get up and hustle." Accordingly they hustled. With exceeding difficulty they learned that nothing emotional had happened during the night save the killing of two Cubans who were so secure in ignorance that they could not understand the challenge of two American sentries. Then Walkley ran a gamut of commanding officers, and Little Nell pumped privates for their impressions of Cuba. When his indignation at the absence of breakfast allowed him, Point made sketches. At the full break of day the *Adolphus*, an *Eclipse* dispatch-boat, sent a boat ashore with Tailor and Shackles in it, and Walkley departed tearlessly for Jamaica, soon after he had bestowed upon his friends much canned goods and blankets.

"Well, we've got our stuff off," said Little Nell. "Now Point and I must breakfast."

Shackles for some reason carried a great hunting-knife, and with it Little Nell opened a can of beans. "Fall to," he said amiably to Point.

There were some hard biscuits. Afterward they—the four of them—marched off on the route of the troops. They were well loaded with luggage, particularly young Point, who had somehow made a great gathering of unnecessary things. Hills covered with verdure soon enclosed them. They heard that the army had advanced some nine miles with no fighting. Evidences of the rapid advance were here and there; coats, gauntlets, blanket-rolls on the ground. Mule trains came herding back along the narrow trail to the sound of a little tinkling bell. Cubans were appropriating the tunics and blanket-rolls.

The four correspondents hurried onward. The surety of impending battle weighed upon them always, but there were a score of minor things more intimate. Little Nell's left heel had chafed until it must have been quite raw, and every moment he wished to take seat by the roadside and console himself from pain. Shackles and Point disliked each other extremely, and often they foolishly quarreled over something or over nothing. The blanket-rolls and packages for the hand oppressed everybody. It was like being burned out of a boarding-house and having to carry one's trunk eight miles to the nearest neighbor. Moreover, Point, since he had stupidly overloaded, with great wisdom placed various cameras and other trifles in the hands of his three less burdened and more sensible friends. This made them fume and gnash, but in complete silence, since he was hideously youthful and innocent and unaware. They all wished to rebel, but none of them saw their way clear because—they did not understand, but somehow it seemed a barbarous project—no one wanted to say anything—cursed him privately for a little ass, but—said nothing. For instance, Little Nell wished to remark: "Point, you are not a thoroughbred in a half of a way. You are an inconsiderate, thoughtless little swine." But in truth he said: "Point, when you started out you looked like a Christmas tree. If we keep on robbing you of your bundles there soon won't be anything left for the children." Point asked dubiously: "What do you mean?" Little Nell merely laughed with deceptive good nature.

They were always very thirsty. There was always a howl for the half bottle of lime juice. Five or six drops from it were simply heavenly in the warm water from the canteens. Point seemed to try to keep the lime juice in his possession in order that he might get more benefit of it. Before the war was ended the others found themselves declaring vehemently that they loathed Point, and yet when men asked them for reasons they grew quite inarticulate. The reasons seemed then so small, so childish, as the reasons of a lot of women. And yet at the time his offences loomed enormous.

The surety of impending battle still weighed upon them. Then it came that Shackles turned seriously ill. Suddenly he dropped his own and much of Point's traps upon the trail, wriggled out of his blanket-roll, flung it away, and took seat heavily at the roadside. They saw with surprise that his face was pale as death and yet streaming with sweat.

"Boys," he said in his ordinary voice, "I'm clean played out. I can't go another step. You fellows go on and leave me to come as soon as I am able."

"Oh, no, that wouldn't do at all," said Little Nell and Tailor together. Point moved over to a soft place and dropped amid whatever traps he was himself carrying.

"Don't know whether—it's—ancestral or merely from the—sun —but I've got a stroke," said Shackles, and gently slumped over to a prostrate position before either Little Nell or Tailor could reach him. Thereafter Shackles was parental; it was Little Nell and Tailor who were really suffering from a stroke—either ancestral or from the sun.

"Put my blanket-roll under my head, Nell, me son," he said gently. "There, now. That is very nice. It is delicious. Why, I'm all right, only—only tired." He closed his eyes and something like an easy slumber came over him. Once he opened his eyes. "Don't trouble about me," he remarked. But the two fussed about him, nervous, worried, discussing this plan and that plan.

It was Point who first made a business-like statement. Seated carelessly and indifferently upon his soft place, he finally blurted out: "Say. Look here. Some of us have got to go on. We can't all stay here. Some of us have got to go on."

It was quite true. The *Eclipse* could take no account of strokes. In the end Point and Tailor went on, leaving Little Nell to bring on Shackles as soon as possible. The latter two spent many hours in the grass by the roadside. They made numerous abrupt acquaintances with passing staff officers, privates, muleteers, many stopping to inquire the wherefore of the death-faced figure on the ground. Favors were done, often and often, by peer and peasant—small things—of no consequence and yet warming.

It was dark when Shackles and Little Nell had come slowly to where they could hear the murmur of the army's bivouac.

"Shack," gasped Little Nell to the man leaning forlornly upon him, "I guess we'd better bunk down here where we stand."

"All right, old boy. Anything you say," replied Shackles, in the bass and hollow voice which arrives with such condition.

They crawled into some bushes and distributed their belongings upon the ground. Little Nell spread out the blankets and generally played housemaid. Then they lay down, supperless, being too weary to eat. The men slept.

At dawn Little Nell awakened and looked wildly for Shackles, whose empty blanket was pressed flat like a wet newspaper on the ground. But at nearly the same moment Shackles appeared elate.

"Come on," he cried; "I've rustled an invitation for breakfast."

Little Nell came on with celerity. "Where? Who?" he said.

"Oh, some officers," replied Shackles airily. If he had been ill the previous day he showed it now only in some curious kind of deference he paid to Little Nell.

Shackles conducted his comrade, and soon they arrived at where a captain and his one subaltern arose courteously from where they were squatting near a fire of little sticks. They wore the wide white trouser-stripes of infantry officers, and upon the shoulders of their blue campaign shirts were the little marks of their rank, but otherwise there was little beyond their manners to render them different from the men who were busy with breakfast near them.

The captain was old, grizzled—a common type of captain in the tiny American army—overjoyed at the active service, confident of his business, and yet breathing out in some way a note of pathos. The war was come too late. Age was grappling him, and honors were only for his widow and his children—merely a better life insurance policy. He had spent his life policing Indians with much labor, cold and heat, but with no glory for him nor for his fellows. All he could do now was to die at the head of his men. If he had youthfully dreamed of a general's stars, they were now impossible to him, and he knew it. He was too old to leap so far; his sole honor was a new invitation to face death. And yet, with his ambitions lying half-strangled, he was going to take his men into any sort of holocaust because his traditions were of gentlemen and soldiers, and because . . . he loved it for itself . . . the thing itself . . . the whirl, the unknown. If he had been degraded at that moment to be a pot-wrestler, no power could have starved him from going through the campaign as a spectator. Why, the army! It was in each drop of his blood.

The lieutenant was very young. Perhaps he had been hurried out of West Point at the last moment, upon a shortage of officers appearing. To him all was opportunity. He was, in fact, in great luck. Instead of going off in 1898 to grill for an indefinite period on some God-forgotten heap of red-hot sand in New Mexico, he was here in Cuba—on real business—with his regiment. When the big engagement came he was sure to emerge from it either horizontally or at the head of a company, and what more could a boy ask? He was a very modest lad, and talked nothing of his frame of mind, but an expression of blissful contentment was ever upon his face. He really accounted himself the most fortunate boy of his time. And he felt almost certain that he would do well. . . . It was necessary to do well. . . . He would do well.

And yet in many ways these two were alike—the grizzled captain with his gently mournful countenance—"Too late"—and the elate young second lieutenant, his commisson hardly dry. Here again it was the influence of the army. After all they were both children of the army.

It is possible to spring into the future here and chronicle what happened later. The captain, after thirty-five years of waiting for his chance, took his Mauser bullet through the brain at the foot of San Juan Hill in the very beginning of the battle, and the boy arrived on the crest panting, sweating, but unscratched, and not sure whether he commanded one company or a whole battalion. Thus Fate dealt to the hosts of Shackles and Little Nell.

The breakfast was of canned tomatoes stewed with hard bread, more hard bread, and coffee. It was very good fare, almost royal. Shackles and Little Nell were absurdly grateful as they felt the hot bitter coffee tingle in them. But they departed joyfully before the sun was fairly up, and passed into Siboney. They never saw the captain again.

The beach at Siboney was furious with traffic, even as had been the beach at Daiquiri. Launches shouted, jack-tars prodded with their boathooks, and load of men followed load of men. Straight, parade-like, on the shore stood a trumpeter playing familiar calls to the troop-horses who swam toward him eagerly through the salt seas. Crowding closely into the cove were transports of all sizes and ages. To the left and to the right of the little landing-beach green hills shot upward like the wings in a theatre. They were scarred here and there with blockhouses and rifle-pits. Up one hill a regiment was crawling, seemingly inch by inch. Shackles and Little Nell walked among palms and scrubby bushes, near pools, over spaces of sand holding little monuments of biscuit boxes, ammunition boxes and supplies of all kinds. Some regiment was just collecting itself from the ships, and the men made great patches of blue on the brown sand.

Shackles asked a question of a man accidentally. "Where's that regiment going to?" He pointed to the force that was crawling up the hill. The man grinned and said: "They're goin' to look for a fight."

"Looking for a fight," said Shackles and Little Nell together. They stared into each other's eyes. Then they set off for the foot of the hill. The hill was long and toilsome. Below them spread wider and wider a vista of ships quiet on a grey sea; a busy, black disembarkation-place; tall, still, green hills; a village of well-separated cottages; palms; a bit of road; soldiers marching. They passed vacant Spanish trenches; little twelve-foot blockhouses. Soon they were on a fine upland near the sea. The path, under ordinary conditions, must have been a beautiful wooded way. It wound in the shade of thickets of fine trees, then through rank growths of bushes with revealed and fantastic roots, then through a grassy space which had all the beauty of a neglected orchard. But always from under their feet scuttled noisy land-crabs, demons to the nerves, which in some ways possessed a semblance of moon-like faces upon their blue or red bodies, and these faces were turned with expressions of deepest horror upon Shackles and Little Nell as they sped to overtake the pugnacious regiment. The route was paved with coats, hats, tent and blanket-rolls, ration-tins, haversacks—everything but ammunition belts, rifles and canteens.

They heard a dull noise of voices in front of them—men talking too loud for the etiquette of the forest—and presently they came upon two or three soldiers lying by the roadside, flame-faced, utterly spent from the hurried march in the heat. One man came limping back along the path. He looked to them anxiously for sympathy and comprehension. "Hurt m' knee. I swear I couldn't keep up with th' boys. I had to leave 'm. Wasn't that tough luck?" His collar rolled away from a red muscular neck, and his bare forearms were better than stanchions. Yet he was almost babyishly tearful in his attempt to make the two correspondents feel that he had not turned back because he was afraid. They gave him scant courtesy, tinctured with one drop of sympathetic yet cynical understanding. Soon they overtook the hospital squad—men addressing chaste language to some pack-mules—a talkative sergeant—two amiable cool-eyed young surgeons. Soon they were amid the rear troops of the dismounted volunteer cavalry regiment which was moving to attack. The men strode easily along, arguing one to another on ulterior matters. If they were going into battle they either did not know it or they concealed it well. They were more like men going into a bar at one o'clock in the morning. Their laughter rang through the Cuban woods. And in the meantime soft, mellow, sweet, sang the voice of the Cuban wood dove . . . the Spanish guerilla calling to his mate . . . forest music . . . on the flanks . . . deep back on both flanks . . . the adorable wood dove, singing only of love . . . some of the advancing Americans said it was beautiful . . . it *was* beautiful . . . the Spanish guerilla calling to his mate. . . . What could be more beautiful?

Shackles and Little Nell rushed precariously through waist-high bushes until they reached the centre of the single-filed regiment. The firing then broke out in front. All the woods set up a hot sputtering; the bullets sped along the path and across it from both sides. The thickets presented nothing but dense masses of light green foliage, out of which these swift steel things were born supernaturally.

It was a volunteer regiment going into its first action, against an enemy of unknown force, in a country where the vegetation was thicker than fur on a cat. There might have been a dreadful mess; but in military matters the only way to deal with a situation of this kind is to take it frankly by the throat and squeeze it to death. Shackles and Little Nell felt the thrill of the orders. "Come ahead, men! Keep right ahead, men! Come on!" The volunteer cavalry regiment, with all the willingness in the world, went ahead into the angle of a V-shaped Spanish formation.

It seemed that every leaf had turned into a soda-bottle and was popping its cork. Some of the explosions seemed to be against the men's very faces; others against the backs of their necks. "Now, men, keep goin' ahead. Keep on goin'." The forward troops were already engaged. They, at least, had something at which to shoot. . . . "Now, Captain, if you're ready." . . . "Stop that swearing there." . . . "Got a match?" . . . "Steady now, men."

A gate appeared in a barbed-wire fence. Within were billowy fields of long grass, dotted with palms and luxuriant mango trees. It was Elysian, a place for lovers, fair as Eden in its radiance of sun, under its blue sky. One might have expected to see white-robed figures walking slowly in the shadows. . . . A dead man, with a bloody face, lay twisted in a curious contortion at the waist. . . . Some one was shot in the leg—his pins knocked cleanly from under him. . . . "Keep goin', men." . . . The air roared, and the ground fled reelingly under their feet. . . . Light, shadow, trees, grass. . . . Bullets spat from every side. Once they were in a thicket, and the men, blanched and bewildered, turned one way and then another, not knowing which way to turn. "Keep goin', men." Soon they were in the sunlight again. They could see the long scant line which was being drained man by man—one might say drop by drop. The musketry rolled forth in great full measure from the magazine carbines. "Keep goin', men." . . . "Christ, I'm shot!" . . . "They're flankin' us, sir." . . . "We're bein' fired into by our own crowd, sir." . . . "Keep goin', men." A low ridge before them was a bottling establishment blowing up in detail. From the right—it seemed at that time to be the far right—they could hear steady, crashing volleys—the United States regulars in action.

Then suddenly—to use a phrase of the street—the whole bottom of the thing fell out. It was suddenly and mysteriously ended. The Spaniards had run away and some of the regulars were chasing them. It was a victory.

When the wounded men dropped in the tall grass they quite disappeared, as if they had sunk in water. Little Nell and Shackles were walking along through the fields, disputing.

"Well, damn it, man," cried Shackles, "we *must* get a list of the killed and wounded."

"That is not nearly so important," quoth Little Nell academically, "as to get the first account to New York of the first action of the army in Cuba."

They came upon Tailor lying with a bared torso and a small red hole through his left lung. He was calm, but evidently out of temper. "Good God, Tailor," they cried, dropping to their knees like two pagans, "are you hurt, old boy?"

"Hurt?" he said gently. "No, 'tis not so deep as a well nor so wide as a church door; but 'tis enough, d' you see? You understand, do you? Idiots."

Then he became very official. "Shackles, feel and see what's under my leg. It's a small stone or a burr or something. Don't be clumsy, now. Be careful. Be careful." Then he said angrily, "Oh, you didn't find it at all. Damn it!"

In reality there was nothing there, and so Shackles could not have removed it. "Sorry, old boy," he said meekly.

"Well, you may observe that I can't stay here more than a year," said Tailor with some oratory, "and the hospital people have their own work in hand. It behooves you, Nell, to fly to Siboney, arrest a dispatch-boat, get a cot and some other things, and some minions to carry me. If I get once down to the base I'm all right, but if I stay here I'm dead. Meantime Shackles can stay here and try to look as if he liked it."

There was no disobeying the man. Lying there with a little red hole in his left lung, he dominated them through his helplessness and through their fear that if they angered him he would move and—bleed.

"Well?" said Little Nell.

"Yes," said Shackles, nodding.

Little Nell departed. "That blanket you lent me," Tailor called after him, "is back there somewhere with Point."

Little Nell noted that many of the men who were wandering among the wounded seemed so spent with the toil and excitement of their first action that they could hardly drag one leg after the other. He found himself suddenly in the same condition. His face, his neck, even his mouth, felt dry as sun-baked bricks, and his legs were foreign to him. But he swung desperately into his five-mile task. On the way he passed many things —bleeding men carried by comrades—others making their way grimly with encrimsoned arms—then the little settlement of the hospital squad—men on the ground everywhere, many in the path—one young captain dying with great gasps, his body pale blue, and glistening, like the inside of a rabbit's skin. But the voice of the Cuban wood dove, soft, mellow, sweet, singing only of love, was no longer heard from the wealth of foliage.

Presently the hurrying correspondent met another regiment coming to assist—a line of a thousand men in single file through the jungle. "Well, how is it going, old man?" "How is it coming on?" "Are we doin' 'em?" Then after an interval came other regiments moving out. He had to take to the bush to let these long lines pass him, and he was delayed and had to flounder amid brambles. But at last, like a successful pilgrim, he arrived at the brow of the great hill overlooking Siboney. His practiced eye scanned the fine broad brow of the sea with its clustering ships, but he saw thereon no *Eclipse* dispatch-boats. He zigzagged heavily down the hill and arrived finally amid the dust and outcries of the base. He seemed to ask a thousand men if they had seen an *Eclipse* boat on the water or an *Eclipse* correspondent on the shore. They all answered "No."

He was like a poverty-stricken and unknown suppliant at a foreign court. Even his plea got only ill hearings. He had expected the news of the serious wounding of Tailor to appal the other correspondents, but they took it quite calmly. It was as if their sense of an impending great battle between two large armies had quite got them out of focus for these minor tragedies. Tailor was hurt—yes? They looked at Little Nell, dazed. How curious that Tailor should be almost the first; how *very* curious; yes. But as far as arousing them to any enthusiasm of active pity, it seemed impossible. He was lying up there in the grass, was he? Too bad, too bad, too bad!

Little Nell went alone and lay down in the sand with his back against a rock. Tailor was prostrate up there in the grass. Never mind. Nothing was to be done. The whole situation was too colossal. Then into his zone came Walkley the invincible.

"Walkley," yelled Little Nell. Walkley came quickly and Little Nell lay weakly against his rock and talked. In thirty seconds Walkley understood everything, had hurled a drink of whisky into Little Nell, had admonished him to lie quiet, and had gone to organize and manipulate. When he returned he was a trifle dubious and backward. Behind him was a singular squad of volunteers from the *Adolphus* carrying among them a wire-woven bed.

"Look here, Nell," said Walkley in bashful accents, "I've collected a battalion here which is willing to go bring Tailor, but—they say—you—can't you show them where he is?"

"Yes," said Little Nell, arising.

When the party arrived back at Siboney and deposited Tailor in the best place, Walkley had found a house and stocked it with canned soups. Therein Shackles and Little Nell revelled for a time and then rolled on the floor in their blankets. Little Nell tossed a great deal. "Oh, I'm so tired. Good God, I'm tired. I'm—tired."

In the morning a voice aroused them. It was a swollen, important circus voice, saying: "Where is Mr. Nell? I wish to see him immediately."

"Here I am, Rogers," cried Little Nell.

"Oh, Nell," said Rogers, "here's a dispatch to me which I thought you had better read."

Little Nell took the dispatch. It was: "Tell Nell can't understand his inaction. Tell him come home first steamer from Port Antonio, Jamaica.—*Eclipse*."

THE REVENGE OF THE *ADOLPHUS*

I

STAND by."

Shackles had come down from the bridge of the *Adolphus* and flung this command at three fellow-correspondents who in the galley were busy with pencils trying to write something exciting and interesting from four days quiet cruising. They looked up casually. "What for?" They did not intend to arouse for nothing. Ever since Shackles had heard the men of the navy directing each other to stand by for this thing and that thing, he had used the two words as his pet phrase and was continually telling his friends to stand by. Sometimes its portentous and emphatic reiteration became highly exasperating and men were apt to retort sharply. "Well, I *am* standing by, ain't I?" On this occasion they detected that he was serious. "Well, what for?" they repeated. In his answer Shackles was reproachful as well as impressive. "Stand by? Stand by for a Spanish gunboat. A Spanish gunboat in chase! Stand by for *two* Spanish gunboats—*both* of them in chase!"

The others looked at him for a brief space and were almost certain that they saw truth written upon his countenance. Whereupon they tumbled out of the galley and galloped up to the bridge. The cook with a mere inkling of tragedy was now out on deck bawling, "What's the matter? What's the matter? What's the matter?" Aft, the grimy head of a stoker was thrust suddenly up through the deck, so to speak. The eyes flashed in a quick look astern and then the head vanished. The correspondents were scrambling on the bridge. "Where's my opry glasses, damn it? Here—let me take a look. Are they Spaniards, Captain? Are you sure?"

The skipper of the *Adolphus* was at the wheel. The pilot-house was so arranged that he could not see astern without hanging forth from one of the side windows, but apparently he had made early investigation. He did not reply at once. At sea, he never replied at once to questions. At the very first Shackles had discovered the merits of this deliberate manner and had taken delight in it. He invariably detailed his talk with the captain to the other correspondents. "Look here. I've just been to see the skipper. I said: 'I would like to put into Cape Haytien.' Then he took a little think. Finally he said: 'All right.' Then I said: 'I suppose we'll need to take on more coal there?' He took another little think. Finally he said: 'Yes.' I said: 'Ever ran into that port before?' He took another little think. Finally he said: 'Yes.' I said: 'Have a cigar?' He took another little think. See? There's where I fooled 'im——"

While the correspondents spun the hurried questions at him, the captain of the *Adolphus* stood with his brown hands on the wheel and his cold glance aligned straight over the bow of his ship.

"Are they Spanish gunboats, Captain? Are they, Captain?"

After a profound pause, he said: "Yes." The four correspondents hastily and in perfect time presented their backs to him and fastened their gaze on the pursuing foe. They saw a dull grey curve of sea going to the feet of the high green and blue coastline of northeastern Cuba, and on this sea were two miniature ships with clouds of iron-colored smoke pouring from their funnels.

One of the correspondents strolled elaborately to the pilot-house. "Aw—Captain," he drawled, "do you think they can catch us?"

The captain's glance was still aligned over the bow of his ship. Ultimately he answered: "I don't know."

From the top of the little *Adolphus's* stack, thick dark smoke swept level for a few yards and then went rolling to leeward in great hot obscuring clouds. From time to time the grimy head was thrust through the deck, the eyes took the quick look astern and then the head vanished. The cook was trying to get somebody to listen to him. "Well, you know, damn it all, it won't be no fun to be ketched by them Spaniards. Be-Gawd, it *won't*. Look here, what do you think they'll do to us, hey? Say, I don't like this, you know. I'm damned if I do." The sea, cut by the hurried bow of the *Adolphus*, flung its waters astern in the formation of a wide angle and the lines of the angle ruffled and hissed as they fled, while the thumping screw tormented the water at the stern. The frame of the steamer underwent regular convulsions as in the strenuous sobbing of a child.

The mate was standing near the pilot-house. Without looking at him, the captain spoke his name. "Ed!"

"Yes, sir," cried the mate with alacrity.

The captain reflected for a moment. Then he said: "Are they gainin' on us?"

The mate took another anxious survey of the race. "No—o— yes, I think they are—a little."

After a pause the captain said: "Tell the chief to shake her up more."

The mate, glad of an occupation in these tense minutes, flew down to the engine-room door. "Skipper says shake 'er up more!" he bawled. The head of the chief engineer appeared, a grizzly head now wet with oil and sweat. "What?" he shouted angrily. It was as if he had been propelling the ship with his own arms. Now he was told that his best was not good enough. "What? Shake 'er up more? Why she can't carry another pound, I tell you! Not another ounce! We——" Suddenly he ran forward and climbed to the bridge. "Captain," he cried in the loud harsh voice of one who lived usually amid the thunder of machinery, "she can't do it, sir! Be-Gawd, she can't! She's turning over now faster than she ever did in her life and we'll all blow to hell——"

The low-toned, impassive voice of the captain suddenly checked the chief's clamor. "I'll blow her up," he said, "but I won't git ketched if I kin help it." Even then the listening correspondents found a second in which to marvel that the captain had actually explained his point of view to another human being.

The engineer stood blank. Then suddenly he cried: "All right, sir!" He threw a hurried look of despair at the correspondents, the deck of the *Adolphus*, the pursuing enemy, Cuba, the sky and the sea; he vanished in the direction of his post.

A correspondent was suddenly regifted with the power of prolonged speech. "Well, you see, the game is up, damn it. See? We can't get out of it. The skipper will blow up the whole bunch before he'll let his ship be taken, and the Spaniards are gaining.

Well, that's what comes from going to war in an eight-knot tub."
He bitterly accused himself, the others, and the dark, sightless,
indifferent world.

This certainty of coming evil affected each one differently.
One was made garrulous; one kept absent-mindedly snapping his
fingers and gazing at the sea; another stepped nervously to and
fro, looking everywhere as if for employment for his mind. As
for Shackles he was silent and smiling, but it was a new smile
that caused the lines about his mouth to betray quivering weakness. And each man looked at the others to discover their degree
of fear and did his best to conceal his own, holding his crackling
nerves with all his strength.

As the *Adolphus* rushed on, the sun suddenly emerged from
behind grey clouds and its rays dealt titanic blows so that in a
few minutes the sea was a glowing blue plain with the golden
shine dancing at the tips of the waves. The coast of Cuba glowed
with light. The pursuers displayed detail after detail in the new
atmosphere. The voice of the cook was heard in high vexation.
"Am I to git dinner as usual? How do I know? Nobody tells me
what to do! Am I to git dinner as usual?"

The mate answered ferociously. "Of course you are! What do
you s'pose? Ain't you the cook, you damn fool?"

The cook retorted in a mutinous scream. "Well, how would I
know? If this ship is goin' to blow up——"

II

The captain called from the pilot-house. "Mr. Shackles! Oh,
Mr. Shackles!" The correspondent moved hastily to a window.
"What is it, Captain?" The skipper of the *Adolphus* raised a
battered finger and pointed over the bows. "See 'er?" he asked,
laconic but quietly jubilant. Another steamer was smoking at
full speed over the sun-lit seas. A great billow of pure white was
on her bows. "Great Scott!" cried Shackles. "Another Spaniard?"

"No," said the captain, "that there is a United States cruiser!"

"What?" Shackles was dumfounded into muscular paralysis.
"No! Are you *sure*?"

The captain nodded. "Sure. Take the glass. See her ensign?
Two funnels, two masts with fighting tops. She ought to be the
Chancellorville."

Shackles choked. "Well, I'm blowed!"

"Ed!" said the captain.

"Yessir!"

"Tell the chief there is no hurry."

Shackles suddenly bethought him of his companions. He dashed to them and was full of quick scorn of their gloomy faces. "Hi, brace up there! Are you blind? Can't you see her?"

"See what?"

"Why, the *Chancellorville*, you blind mice!" roared Shackles. "See 'er? See 'er? See 'er?"

The others sprang, saw, and collapsed. Shackles was a madman for the purpose of distributing the news. "Cook!" he shrieked. "Don't you see 'er, cook? Good Gawd, man, don't you see 'er?" He ran to the lower deck and howled his information everywhere. Suddenly the whole ship smiled. Men clapped each other on the shoulder and joyously shouted. The captain thrust his head from the pilot-house to look back at the Spanish ships. Then he looked at the American cruiser. "Now, we'll see," he said grimly and vindictively to the mate. "Guess somebody else will do some runnin'." The mate chuckled.

The two gunboats were still headed hard for the *Adolphus* and she kept on her way. The American cruiser was coming swiftly. "It's the *Chancellorville*!" cried Shackles. "I know her! We'll see a fight at sea, my boys! A fight at sea!" The enthusiastic correspondents pranced in Indian revels.

The *Chancellorville*—2000 tons—18.6 knots—10 five-inch guns—came on tempestuously, sheering the water high with her sharp bow. From her funnels the smoke raced away in driven sheets. She loomed with extraordinary rapidity like a ship bulging and growing out of the sea. She swept by the *Adolphus* so close that one could have thrown a walnut on board. She was a glistening grey apparition with a blood-red water-line, with brown gun-muzzles and white-clothed motionless jack-tars; and in her rush she was silent, deadly silent. Probably there entered the mind of every man on board of the *Adolphus* a feeling of almost idolatry for this living thing, stern but, to their thought, incomparably beautiful. They would have cheered but that each man seemed to feel that a cheer would be too puny a tribute.

It was at first as if she did not see the *Adolphus*. She was going to pass without heeding this little vagabond of the high-seas. But suddenly a megaphone gaped over the rail of her bridge and a voice was heard measuredly, calmly intoning. "Halloa—there! Keep—well—to—the—north'ard—and—out of my—way—and I'll —go—in—and—see—what—those—people—want——" Then nothing was heard but the swirl of water. In a moment the *Adolphus* was looking at a high grey stern. On the quarter-deck sailors were poised about the breach of the after-pivot-gun.

The correspondents were revelling. "Captain," yelled Shackles, "we can't miss this! We must see it!" But the skipper had already flung over the wheel. "Sure," he answered almost at once. "We can't miss it."

The cook was arrogantly, grossly triumphant. His voice rang along the deck. "There, now! How will the Spinachers like that? Now, it's *our* turn! We've been doin' the runnin' away but now we'll do the chasin'!" Apparently feeling some twinge of nerves from the former strain, he suddenly demanded: "Say, who's got any whisky? I'm near dead for a drink."

When the *Adolphus* came about, she laid her course for a position to the northward of a coming battle, but the situation suddenly became complicated. When the Spanish ships discovered the identity of the ship that was steaming toward them, they did not hesitate over their plan of action. With one accord they turned and ran for port. Laughter arose from the *Adolphus*. The captain broke his orders, and, instead of keeping to the northward, he headed in the wake of the impetuous *Chancellorville*. The correspondents crowded on the bow.

The Spaniards when their broadsides became visible were seen to be ships of no importance, mere little gunboats for work in the shallows at the back of the reefs, and it was certainly discreet to refuse encounter with the five-inch guns of the *Chancellorville*. But the joyful *Adolphus* took no account of this discretion. The pursuit of the Spaniards had been so ferocious that the quick change to heels-over-head flight filled that corner of the mind which is devoted to the spirit of revenge. It was this that moved Shackles to yell taunts futilely at the far-away ships. "Well, how do you like it, eh? How do you like it?" The *Adolphus* was drinking compensation for her previous agony.

The mountains of the shore now shadowed high into the sky and the square white houses of a town could be seen near a vague cleft which seemed to mark the entrance to a port. The gunboats were now near to it.

Suddenly white smoke streamed from the bow of the *Chancellorville* and developed swiftly into a great bulb which drifted in fragments down the wind. Presently the deep-throated boom of the gun came to the ears on board the *Adolphus*. The shot kicked up a high jet of water into the air astern of the last gunboat. The black smoke from the funnels of the cruiser made her look like a collier on fire, and in her desperation she tried many more long shots, but presently the *Adolphus*, murmuring disappointment, saw the *Chancellorville* sheer from the chase.

In time they came up with her and she was an indignant ship. Gloom and wrath was on the forecastle and wrath and gloom was on the quarter-deck. A sad voice from the bridge said: "Just missed 'em." Shackles gained permission to board the cruiser, and in the cabin, he talked to Commander Surrey, tall, bald-headed and angry. "Shoals," said the captain of the *Chancellorville*. "I can't go any nearer and those gunboats could steam along a stone sidewalk if only it was wet." Then his bright eyes became brighter. "I tell you what! The *Chicken*, the *Holy Moses* and the *Mongolian* are on station off Nuevitas. If you will do me a favor—why, to-morrow I will give those people a game!"

III

The *Chancellorville* lay all night watching off the port ot the two gunboats and, soon after daylight, the lookout descried three smokes to the westward and they were later made out to be the *Chicken*, the *Holy Moses* and the *Adolphus*, the latter tagging hurriedly after the United States vessels.

The *Chicken* had been a harbor tug but she was now the U.S.S. *Chicken*, by your leave. She carried a six-pounder forward and a six-pounder aft and her main point was her conspicuous vulnerability. The *Holy Moses* had been the private yacht of a Philadelphia millionaire. She carried six six-pounders and her main point was the chaste beauty of the officers' quarters.

On the bridge of the *Chancellorville* Commander Surrey surveyed his squadron with considerable satisfaction. Presently he signalled to the lieutenant who commanded the *Holy Moses* and to the boatswain who commanded the *Chicken* to come aboard the cruiser. This was all very well for the captain of the yacht, but it was not so easy for the captain of the tugboat who had two heavy lifeboats swung fifteen feet above the water. He had been accustomed to talking with senior officers from his own pilot-house through the intercession of the blessed megaphone. However he got a lifeboat over-side and was pulled to the *Chancellor-ville* by three men—which cut his crew almost into halves.

In the cabin of the *Chancellorville* Surrey disclosed to his two captains his desires concerning the Spanish gunboats and they were glad of being ordered down from the Nuevitas station where life was very dull. He also announced that there was a shore battery containing, he believed, four field guns—three-point-twos. His draught—he spoke of it as *his* draught—would enable him to go in close enough to engage the battery at moderate range, but he pointed out that the main parts of the attempt to destroy the Spanish gunboats must be left to the *Holy Moses* and the *Chicken*. His business, he thought, could only be to keep the air so singing about the ears of the battery that the men at the guns would be unable to take an interest in the dash of the smaller American craft into the bay.

The officers spoke in their turns. The captain of the *Chicken* announced that he saw no difficulties. The squadron would follow the senior officer's ship in line ahead, the senior officer's ship would engage the batteries as soon as possible, she would turn to starboard when the depth of water forced her to do so and the *Holy Moses* and the *Chicken* would run past her into the bay and fight the Spanish ships wherever they were to be found. The captain of the *Holy Moses* after some moments of dignified thought said that he had no suggestions to make that would better this plan.

Surrey pressed an electric bell; a marine orderly appeared; he was sent with a message. The message brought the executive officer and the navigating officer of the *Chancellorville* to the cabin and the five men nosed over a chart.

In the end Surrey declared that he had made up his mind and the juniors remained in expectant silence for three minutes while he stared at the bulkhead. Then he said that the plan of the *Chicken's* captain seemed to him correct in the main. He would make one change. It was that he should first steam in and engage the battery and the other vessels should remain in their present positions until he signalled them to run into the bay. If the squadron steamed ahead in line, the battery could, if it chose, divide its fire between the S.O.P.'s ship and the vessels constituting the more important attack. He had no doubt, he said, that he could soon silence the battery by tumbling the earthworks on to the guns and driving away the men even if he did not succeed in hitting the pieces. Of course he had no doubt of being able to silence the battery in twenty minutes. Then he would signal for the *Holy Moses* and the *Chicken* to make their rush, and of course he would support them with his fire as much as conditions enabled him. He arose then indicating that the conference was at an end. The boatswain, who captained the *Chicken*, looked uncomfortable for a moment and then withdrew. He was not used to this cabin. In the few moments more the four men remained in the cabin, the talk changed its character completely. It was now unofficial, and the sharp badinage concealed furtive affections, academy friendships, the feelings of old-time shipmates, hiding everything under a veil of jokes. "Well, good luck to you, old boy! Don't get that valuable packet of yours sunk under you. Think how it would weaken the navy. Would you mind buying me three pairs of pyjamas in the town yonder? If your engines get disabled, tote her under your arm. You can do it. Good-bye, old man, don't forget to come out all right——"

When the captains of the *Holy Moses* and the *Chicken* came upon deck they strode it with a new step. They were proud men. The marine on duty above their boats looked at them curiously and with awe. He detected something which meant action, conflict. The boats' crews saw it also. As they pulled their steady stroke they studied fleetingly the face of the officer in the stern-sheets. In both cases they perceived a glad man and yet a man filled with a profound consideration of the future.

IV

"Beat to quarters!"

Bugles and drums stirred the decks of the *Chancellorville*. There was the noise of rushing feet, a clanging of scuttle-plates, a rattling of ammunition hoists, followed directly by the sinister, deep note of locking breech-plugs. As the cruiser turned her bow toward the shore, she happened to steam near the *Adolphus*. The usual calm voice hailed the despatch-boat. "Keep—that—gauze under-shirt of yours—well—out of the—line of fire."

"Ay, ay, sir!"

The cruiser then moved slowly toward the shore, watched by every eye in the smaller American vessels. She was deliberate and steady, and this was reasonable even to the impatience of the other craft because the wooded shore was likely to suddenly develop new factors. Slowly she swung to starboard, smoke belched over her and the roar of a gun came along the water.

The battery was indicated by a long thin streak of yellow earth. The first shot went high, ploughing the chaparral on the hillside. The *Chancellorville* wore an air for a moment of being deep in meditation. She flung another shell, which landed squarely on the earthwork, making a great dun cloud. Before the smoke had settled, there was a crimson flash from the battery. To the watchers at sea, it was smaller than a needle. The shot made a geyser of crystal water, four hundred yards from the *Chancellorville*.

The cruiser, having made up her mind, suddenly went at the battery hammer and tongs. She moved to and fro casually, but the thunder of her guns was swift and angry. Sometimes she was quite hidden in her own smoke, but with exceeding regularity the earth of the battery spurted into the air. The Spanish shells for the most part went high and wide of the cruiser, jetting the water far away.

Once a Spanish gunner took a festive side-show chance at the waiting group of the three nondescripts. It went like a flash over the *Adolphus*, singing a wistful metallic note. Whereupon the *Adolphus* broke hurriedly for the open sea, and men on the *Holy Moses* and the *Chicken* laughed hoarsely and cruelly. The correspondents had been standing excitedly on top of the pilot-house, but at the passing of the shell they promptly eliminated themselves by dropping with a thud to the deck below. The cook again was giving tongue. "Oh, say, this won't do! I'm damned if it will! We ain't no armored cruiser, you know. If one of them shells hits us—well, we finish right there. 'Tain't like as if it was our *busi-*

ness, foolin' 'round within the range of them guns. There's no sense in it. Them other fellows don't seem to mind it, but it's their *business*. If it's your *business*, you go ahead and do it, but if it ain't, you—look at that, would you?"

The *Chancellorville* had set up a spread of flags, and the *Holy Moses* and the *Chicken* were steaming in.

V

They on the *Chancellorville* sometimes could see into the bay, and they perceived the enemy's gunboats moving out as if to give battle. Surrey feared that this impulse would not endure or that it was some mere pretence for the edification of the townspeople and the garrison, so he hastily signalled the *Holy Moses* and the *Chicken* to go in. Thankful for small favors, they came on tumultuously. The battery had ceased firing. As the two auxiliaries passed under the stern of the cruiser, the megaphone hailed them. "You—will—see—the—en—em—y—soon—as—you —round—the—point. A—fine—chance. Good—luck."

As a matter of fact, the Spanish gunboats had not been informed of the presence of the *Holy Moses* and the *Chicken* off the bar, and they were just blustering down the bay over the protective shoals to make it appear that they scorned the *Chancellorville*. But suddenly from around the point there burst into view a steam yacht, closely followed by a harbor tug. The gunboats took one swift look at this horrible sight and fled screaming.

Lieutenant Reigate, commanding the *Holy Moses*, had under his feet a craft that was capable of some speed, although before a solemn tribunal one would have to admit that she conscientiously belied almost everything that the contractors had said of her originally. Boatswain Pent, commanding the *Chicken*, was in possession of an utterly different kind. The *Holy Moses* was an antelope; the *Chicken* was a man who could carry a piano on his back. In this race Pent had the mortification of seeing his vessel outstripped badly.

The entrance of the two American craft had had a curious effect upon the shores of the bay. Apparently everyone had slept in the assurance that the *Chancellorville* could not cross the bar, and that the *Chancellorville* was the only hostile ship. Consequently, the appearance of the *Holy Moses* and the *Chicken* created a curious and complex emotion. Reigate on the bridge of the *Holy Moses* laughed when he heard the bugles shrilling and saw through his glasses the wee figures of men running hither and thither on the shore. It was the panic of the china when the bull entered the shop. The whole bay was bright with sun. Every detail of the shore was plain. From a brown hut abeam of the *Holy Moses* some little men ran out waving their arms and turning their tiny faces to look at the enemy. Directly ahead, some four miles, appeared the scattered white houses of a town with a wharf and some schooners in front of it. The gunboats were making for the town. There was a stone fort on the hill overshadowing, but Reigate conjectured that there was no artillery in it.

There was a sense of something intimate and impudent in the minds of the Americans. It was like climbing over a wall and fighting a man in his own garden. It was not that they could be in any wise shaken in their resolve; it was simply that the overwhelmingly Spanish aspect of things made them feel like gruff intruders. Like many of the emotions of war time, this emotion had nothing at all to do with war.

Reigate's only commissioned subordinate called up from the bow gun. "May I open fire, sir? I think I can fetch that last one."

"Yes." Immediately the six-pounder crashed, and in the air was the spinning-wire noise of the flying shot. It struck so close to the last gunboat that it appeared that the spray went aboard. The swift-handed men at the gun spoke of it. "Gave 'm a bath that time, anyhow. First one they've ever had. Dry 'em off this time, Jim." The young ensign said: "Steady." And so the *Holy Moses* raced in, firing, until the whole town, fort, water-front and shipping was as plain as if it had been done on paper by a mechanical draftsman. The gunboats were trying to hide in the bosom of the town. One was frantically tying up to the wharf and the other was anchoring within a hundred yards of the shore. The Spanish infantry, of course, had dug trenches along the beach, and suddenly the air over the *Holy Moses* sung with bullets. The shore-line thrummed with musketry. Also some antique shells screamed.

VI

The *Chicken* was doing her best. Pent's posture at the wheel seemed to indicate that her best was about thirty-four knots. In his eagerness he was braced as if he alone was taking in a 10,000-ton battleship through Hell Gate.

But the *Chicken* was not too far in the rear and Pent could see clearly that he was to have no minor part to play. Some of the antique shells had struck the *Holy Moses* and he could see the escaped steam shooting up from her. She lay close inshore and was lashing out with four six-pounders as if this was the last opportunity she would have to fire them. She had made the Spanish gunboats very sick. A solitary gun on the one moored to the wharf was from time to time firing wildly; otherwise the gunboats were silent. But the beach in front of the town was a line of fire. The *Chicken* headed for the *Holy Moses* and, as soon as possible, the six-pounder in her bow began to crack at the gunboat moored to the wharf.

In the meantime the *Chancellorville* prowled off the bar, listening to the firing, anxious, acutely anxious, and feeling her impotency in every inch of her smart steel frame. And in the meantime the *Adolphus* squatted on the waves and brazenly waited for news. One could thoughtfully count the seconds and reckon that in this second and that second a man had died—if one chose. But no one did it. Undoubtedly the spirit was that the flag should come away with honor, honor complete, perfect, leaving no loose unfinished end over which the Spaniards could erect a monument of satisfaction, glorification. The distant guns boomed to the ears of the silent blue-jackets at their stations on the cruiser.

The *Chicken* steamed up to the *Holy Moses* and took into her nostrils the odor of steam, gunpowder and burnt things. Rifle bullets simply streamed over them both. In the merest flash of time, Pent took into his remembrance the body of a dead quartermaster on the bridge of his consort. The two megaphones uplifted together, but Pent's eager voice cried out first.

"Are you injured, sir?"

"No, not completely. My engines can get me out after—after

we have sunk those gunboats." The voice had been utterly conventional but it changed to sharpness. "Go in and sink that
gunboat at anchor."

As the *Chicken* rounded the *Holy Moses* and started inshore, a
man called to him from the depths of finished disgust. "They're
takin' to their boats, sir." Pent looked and saw the men of the
anchored gunboat lower their boats and pull like mad for shore.

The *Chicken*, assisted by the *Holy Moses*, began a methodical
killing of the anchored gunboat. The Spanish infantry on shore
fired frenziedly at the *Chicken*. Pent, giving the wheel to a
waiting sailor, stepped out to a point where he could see the men
at the guns. One bullet spanged past him and into the pilot-
house. He ducked his head into the window. "That hit you,
Murry?" he inquired with interest.

"No, sir," cheerfully responded the man at the wheel.

Pent became very busy superintending the fire of his absurd
battery. The anchored gunboat simply would not sink. It evinced
that unnatural stubbornness which is sometimes displayed by
inanimate objects. The gunboat at the wharf had sunk as if she
had been scuttled but this riddled thing at anchor would not even
take fire. Pent began to grow flurried—privately. He could not
stay there for ever. Why didn't the damned gunboat admit its
destruction. Why——

He was at the forward gun when one of his engine-room force
came to him and after saluting, said serenely: "The men at the
after-gun are all down, sir."

It was one of those curious lifts which an enlisted man,
without in any way knowing it, can give his officer. The impudent tranquillity of the man at once set Pent to rights and the
stoker departed admiring the extraordinary coolness of his captain.

The next few moments contained little but heat, an odor,
applied mechanics and an expectation of death. Pent developed
a fervid and amazed appreciation of the men, his men, men he
knew very well, but strange men. What explained them? He was
doing his best because he was captain of the *Chicken* and he
lived or died by the *Chicken*. But what could move these men to
watch his eye in bright anticipation of his orders and then obey
them with enthusiastic rapidity? What caused them to speak of

the action as some kind of joke—particularly when they knew he could overhear them? What manner of men? And he anointed them secretly with his fullest affection.

Perhaps Pent did not think all this during the battle. Perhaps he thought it so soon after the battle that his full mind became confused as to the time. At any rate, it stands as an expression of his feeling.

The enemy had gotten a field-gun down to the shore and with it they began to throw three-inch shells at the *Chicken*. In this war it was usual that the down-trodden Spaniards in their ignorance should use smokeless powder while the Americans, by the power of the consistent everlasting three-ply, wire-woven, double back-action imbecility of a hay-seed government, used powder which on sea and on land cried their position to heaven, and, accordingly, good men got killed without reason. At first Pent could not locate the field-gun at all, but as soon as he found it, he ran aft with one man and brought the after six-pounder again into action. He paid little heed to the old gun-crew. One was lying on his face apparently dead; another was prone with a wound in the chest, while the third sat with his back to the deck-house holding a smitten arm. This last one called out huskily, "Give 'm hell, sir."

The minutes of the battle were either days, years, or they were flashes of a second. Once Pent looking up was astonished to see three shell holes in the *Chicken's* funnel—made surreptitiously, so to speak. . . . "If we don't silence that field-gun she'll sink us, boys." . . . The eyes of the man sitting with his back against the deck-house were looking from out his ghastly face at the new gun-crew. He spoke with the supreme laziness of a wounded man. "Give 'm hell." . . . Pent felt a sudden twist of his shoulder. He was wounded—slightly. . . . The anchored gunboat was in flames.

VII

Pent took his little blood-stained tow-boat out to the *Holy Moses*. The yacht was already under way for the bay entrance. As they were passing out of range the Spaniards heroically redoubled their fire—which is their custom. Pent, moving busily about the decks, stopped suddenly at the door of the engine-room. His face was set and his eyes were steely. He spoke to one of the men. "During the action I saw you firing at the enemy with a rifle. I told you once to stop, and then I saw you at it again. Pegging away with a rifle is no part of your business. I want you to understand that you are in trouble." The humbled man did not raise his eyes from the deck. Presently the *Holy Moses* displayed an anxiety for the *Chicken's* health.

"One killed and four wounded, sir."

"Have you enough men left to work your ship?"

After deliberation, Pent answered: "No, sir."

"Shall I send you assistance?"

"No, sir. I can get to sea all right."

As they neared the point they were edified by the sudden appearance of a serio-comic ally. The *Chancellorville* at last had been unable to stand the strain, and had sent in her launch with an ensign, five seamen and a number of marksmen marines. She swept hot-foot around the point, bent on terrible slaughter; the one-pounder of her bow presented a formidable appearance. The *Holy Moses* and the *Chicken* laughed until they brought indignation to the brow of the young ensign. But he forgot it when with some of his men he boarded the *Chicken* to do what was possible for the wounded. The nearest surgeon was aboard the *Chancellorville*. There was absolute silence on board the cruiser as the *Holy Moses* steamed up to report. The blue-jackets listened with all their ears. The commander of the yacht spoke slowly into his megaphone: "We have—destroyed—the two—gunboats—sir." There was a burst of confused cheering on the forecastle of the *Chancellorville*, but an officer's cry quelled it.

"Very—good. Will—you—come aboard?"

Correspondents were already on the deck of the cruiser, and although for a time they learned only that the navy can preserve a classic silence, they in the end received the story which is here told. Before the last of the wounded were hoisted aboard the cruiser the *Adolphus* was on her way to Key West. When she arrived at that port of desolation Shackles fled to file the telegrams and the other correspondents fled to the hotel for clothes, good clothes, clean clothes; and food, good food, much food; and drink, much drink, any kind of drink.

Days afterward, when the officers of the noble squadron received the newspapers containing an account of their performance, they looked at each other somewhat dejectedly: "Heroic assault—grand daring of Boatswain Pent—superb accuracy of the *Holy Moses*' fire—gallant tars of the *Chicken*—their names should be remembered as long as America stands—terrible losses of the enemy——"

When the Secretary of the Navy ultimately read the report of Commander Surrey, S.O.P., he had to prick himself with a dagger in order to remember that anything at all out of the ordinary had occurred.

THE SERJEANT'S PRIVATE MAD-HOUSE

HE moonlight was almost steady blue flame and all this radiance was lavished out upon a still lifeless wilderness of stunted trees and cactus-plants. The shadows lay upon the ground, pools of black and sharply outlined, resembling substances, fabrics, and not shadows at all. From afar came the sound of the sea coughing among the hollows in the coral rocks.

The land was very empty; one could easily imagine that Cuba was a simple vast solitude; one could wonder at the moon taking all the trouble of this splendid illumination. There was no wind; nothing seemed to live.

But in a particular large group of shadows lay an outpost of some forty United States marines. If it had been possible to approach them from any direction without encountering one of their sentries, one could have gone stumbling among sleeping men and men who sat waiting, their blankets tented over their heads; one would have been in among them before one's mind could have decided whether they were men or devils. If a marine moved, he took the care and the time of one who walks across a death-chamber. The lieutenant in command reached for his watch and the nickel chain gave forth the faintest tinkling sound. He could see the glistening five or six pairs of eyes that slowly turned to regard him. His serjeant lay near him and he bent his face down to whisper. "Who's on post behind the big cactus-plant?"

"Dryden," rejoined the serjeant just over his breath.

After a pause the lieutenant murmured: "He's got too many nerves. I shouldn't have put him there." The serjeant asked if he should crawl down and look into affairs at Dryden's post. The young officer nodded assent and the serjeant, softly cocking his rifle, went away on his hands and knees. The lieutenant with his back to a dwarf tree, sat watching the serjeant's progress for the few moments that he could see him moving from one shadow to another. Afterward the officer waited to hear Dryden's quick but low-voiced challenge, but time passed and no sound came from the direction of the post behind the cactus-bush.

The serjeant, as he came nearer and nearer to this cactus-bush—a number of peculiarly dignified columns throwing shadows of inky darkness—had slowed his pace, for he did not wish to trifle with the feelings of the sentry, and he was expecting the stern hail and was ready with the immediate answer which turns away wrath. He was not made anxious by the fact that he could not yet see Dryden, for he knew that the man would be hidden in a way practiced by sentry marines since the time when two men had been killed by a disease of excessive confidence on picket. Indeed, as the serjeant went still nearer, he became more and more angry. Dryden was evidently a most proper sentry.

Finally he arrived at a point where he could see Dryden seated in the shadow, staring into the bushes ahead of him, his rifle ready on his knee. The serjeant in his rage longed for the peaceful precincts of the Washington Marine Barracks where there would have been no situation to prevent the most complete non-commissioned oratory. He felt indecent in his capacity of a man able to creep up to the back of a G Company member on guard duty. Never mind; in the morning back at camp——

But, suddenly, he felt afraid. There was something wrong with Dryden. He remembered old tales of comrades creeping out to find a picket seated against a tree perhaps, upright enough but stone dead. The serjeant paused and gave the inscrutable back of the sentry a long stare. Dubious he again moved forward. At three paces he hissed like a little snake. Dryden did not show a sign of hearing. At last the serjeant was in a position from which he was able to reach out and touch Dryden on the arm. Whereupon was turned to him the face of a man livid with mad fright. The serjeant grabbed him by the wrist and with discreet fury shook him. "Here! Pull yourself together!"

Dryden paid no heed but turned his wild face from the newcomer to the ground in front. "Don't you see 'em, Serjeant? Don't you see 'em?"

"Where?" whispered the serjeant.

"Ahead, and a little on the right flank. A reg'lar skirmish line. Don't you see 'em?"

"Naw," whispered the serjeant. Dryden began to shake. He

began moving one hand from his head to his knee and from his knee to his head rapidly, in a way that is without explanation. "I don't dare fire," he wept. "If I do they'll see me, and oh, how they'll pepper me!"

The serjeant lying on his belly, understood one thing. Dryden had gone mad. Dryden was the March Hare. The old man gulped down his uproarious emotions as well as he was able and used the most simple device. "Go," he said, "and tell the lieutenant while I cover your post for you."

"No! They'd see me! They'd see me! And then they'd pepper me! Oh, how they'd pepper me!"

The serjeant was face to face with the biggest situation of his life. In the first place he knew that at night a large or a small force of Spanish guerillas was never more than easy rifle-range from any marine outpost, both sides maintaining a secrecy as absolute as possible in regard to their real position and strength. Everything was on a watch-spring foundation. A loud word might be paid for by a night attack which would involve five hundred men who needed their earned sleep, not to speak of some of them who would need their lives. The slip of a foot and the rolling of a pint of gravel might go from consequence to consequence until various crews went to general quarters on their ships in the harbor, their batteries booming as the swift searchlight-flashes tore through the foliage. Men would get killed —notably the serjeant and Dryden—and outposts would be cut off and the whole night would be one pitiless turmoil. And so Serjeant George H. Peasley began to run his private mad-house behind the cactus-bush.

"Dryden," said the serjeant, "you do as I told you and go tell the lieutenant."

"I don't dare move," shivered the man. "They'll see me if I move. They'll see me. They're almost up now. Let's hide——"

"Well, then you stay here a moment and I'll go and——"

Dryden turned upon him a look so tigerish that the old man felt his hair move. "Don't you stir," he hissed. "You want to give me away. You want them to see me. Don't you stir." The serjeant decided not to stir.

He became aware of the slow wheeling of eternity, its majestic incomprehensibility of movement. Seconds, minutes, were quaint little things, tangible as toys, and there were billions of them, all alike. "Dryden," he whispered at the end of a century in which, curiously, he had never joined the marine corps at all but had taken to another walk of life and prospered greatly in it. "Dryden, this is all foolishness." He thought of the expedient of smashing the man over the head with his rifle, but Dryden was so supernaturally alert that there surely would issue some small scuffle and there could be not even the fraction of a scuffle. The serjeant relapsed into the contemplation of another century. His patient had one fine virtue. He was in such terror of the phantom skirmish line that his voice never went above a whisper, whereas his delusion might have expressed itself in hyena yells and shots from his rifle. The serjeant, shuddering, had visions of how it might have been—the mad private leaping into the air and howling and shooting at his friends and making them the centre of the enemy's eager attention. This, to his mind, would have been conventional conduct for a maniac. The trembling victim of an idea was somewhat puzzling. The serjeant decided that from time to time he would reason with his patient. "Look here, Dryden, you don't see any real Spaniards. You've been drinking or—something. Now——"

But Dryden only glared him into silence. Dryden was inspired with such a profound contempt of him that it was become hatred. "Don't you stir!" And it was clear that if the serjeant did stir, the mad private would introduce calamity. "Now," said Peasley to himself, "if those guerillas *should* take a crack at us to-night, they'd find a lunatic asylum right in the front and it would be astonishing."

The silence of the night was broken by the quick low voice of a sentry to the left some distance. The breathless stillness brought an effect to the words as if they had been spoken in one's ear.

"*Halt—who's there—halt or I'll fire!*" Bang!

At the moment of sudden attack particularly at night, it is improbable that a man registers much detail of either thought or action. He may afterward say: "I was here." He may say: "I was there." "I did this." "I did that." But there remains a great incoherency because of the tumultuous thought which seethes through the head. "Is this defeat?" At night in a wilderness and against skilful foes half seen, one does not trouble to ask if it is

also Death. Defeat is Death, then, save for the miraculous. But
the exaggerating magnifying first thought subsides in the ordered mind of the soldier and he knows, soon, what he is doing
and how much of it. The serjeant's immediate impulse had been
to squeeze close to the ground and listen—listen—above all else,
listen. But the next moment he grabbed his private asylum by
the scruff of its neck, jerked it to its feet and started to retreat
upon the main outpost.

To the left, rifle-flashes were bursting from the shadows. To
the rear, the lieutenant was giving some hoarse order or admonition. Through the air swept some Spanish bullets, very high, as
if they had been fired at a man in a tree. The private asylum
came on so hastily that the serjeant found he could remove his
grip, and soon they were in the midst of the men of the outpost.
Here there was no occasion for enlightening the lieutenant. In
the first place such surprises require statement, question and
answer. It is impossible to get a grossly original and fantastic
idea through a man's head in less than one minute of rapid talk,
and the serjeant knew the lieutenant could not spare the minute.
He himself had no minutes to devote to anything but the business of the outpost. And the madman disappeared from his ken
and he forgot about him.

It was a long night and the little fight was as long as the night.
It was heart-breaking work. The forty marines lay in an irregular oval. From all sides the Mauser bullets sang low and hard.
Their occupation was to prevent a rush, and to this end they
potted carefully at the flash of a Mauser—save when they got
excited for a moment, in which case their magazines rattled like
a great Waterbury watch. Then they settled again to a systematic potting.

The enemy were not of the regular Spanish forces. They were
of a corps of guerillas, native-born Cubans, who preferred the
flag of Spain. They were all men who knew the craft of the
woods and were all recruited from the district. They fought more
like red Indians than any people but the red Indians themselves.
Each seemed to possess an individuality, a fighting individuality,
which is only found in the highest order of irregular soldier.
Personally they were as distinct as possible, but through equality
of knowledge and experience they arrived at concert of action.

So long as they operated in the wilderness, they were formidable troops. It mattered little whether it was daylight or dark; they were mainly invisible. They had schooled from the Cubans insurgent to Spain. As the Cubans fought the Spanish troops, so would these particular Spanish troops fight the Americans. It was wisdom.

The marines thoroughly understood the game. They must lie close and fight until daylight when the guerillas promptly would go away. They had withstood other nights of this kind, and now their principal emotion was probably a sort of frantic annoyance.

Back at the main camp, whenever the roaring volleys lulled, the men in the trenches could hear their comrades of the outpost and the guerillas pattering away interminably. The moonlight faded and left an equal darkness upon the wilderness. A man could barely see the comrade at his side. Sometimes guerillas crept so close that the flame from their rifles seemed to scorch the faces of the marines, and the reports sounded as if from two or three inches of their very noses. If a pause came, one could hear the guerillas gabbling to each other in a kind of drunken delirium. The lieutenant was praying that the ammunition would last. Everybody was praying for daybreak.

A black hour came finally, when the men were not fit to have their troubles increase. The enemy made a wild attack on one portion of the oval which was held by about fifteen men. The remainder of the force was busy enough, and the fifteen were naturally left to their devices. Amid the whirl of it, a loud voice suddenly broke out in song:

"While shepherds watched their flocks by night,
All seated on the ground,
An angel of the Lord came down
And glory shone around."

"Who the hell is that?" demanded the lieutenant from a throat full of smoke. There was almost a full stop of the firing. The Americans were somewhat puzzled. Practical ones muttered that the fool should have a bayonet-hilt shoved down his throat. Others felt a thrill at the strangeness of the thing. Perhaps it was a sign!

> "The minstrel boy to the war is gone,
> In the ranks of death you'll find him,
> His father's sword he has girded on
> And his wild harp slung behind him."

This croak was as lugubrious as a coffin. "Who is it? Who is it?" snapped the lieutenant. "Stop him, somebody."

"It's Dryden, sir," said old Serjeant Peasley, as he felt around in the darkness for his mad-house. "I can't find him—yet."

> "Please, oh, please, oh, do not let me fall;
> You're—gurgh-ugh——"

The serjeant had pounced upon him.

This singing had had an effect upon the Spaniards. At first they had fired frenziedly at the voice, but they soon ceased, perhaps from sheer amazement. Both sides took a spell of meditation.

The serjeant was having some difficulty with his charge. "Here, you, grab 'im. Take 'im by the throat. Be quiet, you devil."

One of the fifteen men who had been hard pressed called out, "We've only got about one clip a-piece, Lieutenant. If they come again——"

The lieutenant crawled to and fro among his men, taking clips of cartridges from those who had many. He came upon the serjeant and his mad-house. He felt Dryden's belt and found it simply stuffed with ammunition. He examined Dryden's rifle and found in it a full clip. The mad-house had not fired a shot. The lieutenant distributed these valuable prizes among the fifteen men. As the men gratefully took them, one said: "If they had come again hard enough, they would have had us, sir—maybe."

But the Spaniards did not come again. At the first indication of daybreak they fired their customary good-bye volley. The marines lay tight while the slow dawn crept over the land. Finally the lieutenant arose among them, and he was a bewildered man, but very angry. "Now where is that idiot, Serjeant?"

"Here he is, sir," said the old man cheerfully. He was seated on the ground beside the recumbent Dryden who, with an innocent smile on his face, was sound asleep.

"Wake him up," said the lieutenant briefly.

The serjeant shook the sleeper. "Here, Minstrel Boy, turn out. The lieutenant wants you."

Dryden climbed to his feet and saluted the officer with a dazed and childish air. "Yes, sir."

The lieutenant was obviously having difficulty in governing his feelings, but he managed to say with calmness: "You seem to be fond of singing, Dryden? Serjeant, see if he has any whisky on him."

"Sir?" said the mad-house stupefied. "Singing—fond of singing?"

Here the serjeant interposed gently, and he and the lieutenant held palaver apart from the others. The marines, hitching more comfortably their almost empty belts, spoke with grins of the mad-house. "Well, the Minstrel Boy made 'em clear out. They couldn't stand it. But—I wouldn't want to be in his boots. He'll see fireworks when the old man interviews him on the uses of grand opera in modern warfare. How do you think he managed to smuggle a bottle along without us finding it out?"

When the weary outpost was relieved and marched back to camp, the men could not rest until they had told a tale of the voice in the wilderness. In the meantime the serjeant took Dryden aboard a ship, and to those who took charge of the man, he defined him as "the most useful —— —— crazy man in the service of the United States."

VIRTUE IN WAR

I

GATES had left the regular army in 1890, those parts of him which had not been frozen having been well fried. He took with him nothing but an oaken constitution and a knowledge of the plains and the best wishes of his fellow-officers. The Standard Oil Company differs from the United States Government in that it understands the value of the loyal and intelligent services of good men and is almost certain to reward them at the expense of incapable men. This curious practice emanates from no beneficent emotion of the Standard Oil Company, on whose feelings you could not make a scar with a hammer and chisel. It is simply that the Standard Oil Company knows more than the United States Government and makes use of virtue whenever virtue is to its advantage. In 1890 Gates really felt in his bones that, if he lived a rigorously correct life and several score of his class-mates and intimate friends died off, he would get command of a troop of horse by the time he was unfitted by age to be an active cavalry leader. He left the service of the United States and entered the service of the Standard Oil Company. In the course of time he knew that, if he lived a rigorously correct life, his position and income would develop strictly in parallel with the worth of his wisdom and experience and he would not have to walk on the corpses of his friends.

But he was not happier. Part of his heart was in a barracks, and it was not enough to discourse of the old regiment over the port and cigars to ears which were polite enough to betray a languid ignorance. Finally came the year 1898, and Gates dropped the Standard Oil Company as if it were hot. He hit the steel trail to Washington and there fought the first serious action of the war. Like most Americans, he had a native State, and one morning he found himself major in a volunteer infantry regiment whose voice had a peculiar sharp twang to it which he could remember from childhood. The colonel welcomed the West Pointer with loud cries of joy; the lieutenant-colonel looked at him with the pebbly eye of distrust; and the senior major, having had up to this time the best battalion in the regiment, strongly disapproved of him. There were only two majors, so the lieutenant-colonel commanded the first battalion, which gave him an occupation. Lieutenant-colonels under the new rules do not always have occupations. Gates got the third battalion—four companies commanded by intelligent officers who could gauge the opinions of their men at two thousand yards and govern themselves accordingly. The battalion was immensely interested in the new major. It thought it ought to develop views about him. It thought it was its blankety-blank business to find out immediately if it liked him personally. In the company streets the talk was nothing else. Among the non-commissioned officers there were eleven old soldiers of the regular army, and they knew—and cared—that Gates had held commission in the "Sixteenth Cavalry"—as *Harper's Weekly* says. Over this fact they rejoiced and were glad, and they stood by to jump lively when he took command. He would know his work and he would know *their* work, and then in battle there would be killed only what men were absolutely necessary and the sick list would be comparatively free of fools.

The commander of the second battalion had been called by an Atlanta paper, "Major Rickets C. Carmony, the commander of the second battalion of the 307th——, is when at home one of the biggest wholesale hardware dealers in his State. Last evening he had ice cream, at his own expense, served out at the regular mess of the battalion, and after dinner the men gathered about his tent where three hearty cheers for the popular major were given." Carmony had bought twelve copies of this newspaper and mailed them home to his friends.

In Gates's battalion there were more kicks than ice cream, and there was no ice cream at all. Indignation ran high at the rapid manner in which he proceeded to make soldiers of them. Some of his officers hinted finally that the men wouldn't stand it. They were saying that they had enlisted to fight for their country—yes, but they weren't going to be bullied day in and day out by a perfect stranger. They were patriots, they were, and just as good

men as ever stepped—just as good as Gates or anybody like
him. But, gradually, despite itself, the battalion progressed. The
men were not altogether conscious of it. They evolved rather
blindly. Presently there were fights with Carmony's crowd as to
which was the better battalion at drills, and at last there was no
argument. It was generally admitted that Gates commanded the
crack battalion. The men, believing that the beginning and the
end of all soldiering was in these drills of precision, were somewhat reconciled to their major when they began to understand
more of what he was trying to do for them, but they were still
fiery untamed patriots of lofty pride and they resented his manner toward them. It was abrupt and sharp.

The time came when everybody knew that the Fifth Army
Corps was the corps designated for the first active service in
Cuba. The officers and men of the 307th observed with despair
that their regiment was not in the Fifth Army Corps. The colonel
was a strategist. He understood everything in a flash. Without a
moment's hesitation he obtained leave and mounted the night
express for Washington. There he drove Senators and Congress-
men in span, tandem and four-in-hand. With the telegraph he
stirred so deeply the governor, the people and the newspapers of
his State that whenever on a quiet night the President put his
head out of the White House he could hear the distant vast
commonwealth humming with indignation. And as it is well
known that the Chief Executive listens to the voice of the people,
the 307th was transferred to the Fifth Army Corps. It was sent
at once to Tampa, where it was brigaded with two dusty regiments of regulars, who looked at it calmly and said nothing. The
brigade commander happened to be no less a person than Gates's
old colonel in the "Sixteenth Cavalry"—as *Harper's Weekly* says
—and Gates was cheered. The old man's rather solemn look
brightened when he saw Gates in the 307th. There was a great
deal of battering and pounding and banging for the 307th at
Tampa, but the men stood it more in wonder than in anger. The
two regular regiments carried them along when they could, and
when they couldn't waited impatiently for them to come up.
Undoubtedly the regulars wished the volunteers were in garrison
at Sitka, but they said practically nothing. They minded their
own regiments. The colonel was an invaluable man in a tele-

graph office. When came the scramble for transports the colonel retired to a telegraph office and talked so ably to Washington that the authorities pushed a number of corps aside and made way for the 307th, as if on it depended everything. The regiment got one of the best transports, and after a series of delays and some starts, and an equal number of returns, they finally sailed for Cuba.

II

Now Gates had a singular adventure on the second morning after his arrival at Atlanta to take his post as a major in the 307th.

He was in his tent, writing, when suddenly the flap was flung away and a tall young private stepped inside.

"Well, Maje," said the newcomer genially, "how goes it?"

The major's head flashed up, but he spoke without heat.

"Come to attention and salute."

"Huh!" said the private.

"Come to attention and salute."

The private looked at him in resentful amazement, and then inquired:

"Ye ain't mad, are ye? Ain't nothin' to get huffy about, is there?"

"I—— Come to attention and salute."

"Well," drawled the private, as he stared, "seein' as ye are so darn perticular, I don't care if I do—if it'll make yer meals set on yer stomick any better."

Drawing a long breath and grinning ironically, he lazily pulled his heels together and saluted with a flourish.

"There," he said, with a return to his earlier genial manner. "How's that suit ye, Maje?"

There was a silence which to an impartial observer would have seemed pregnant with dynamite and bloody death. Then the major cleared his throat and coldly said:

"And now, what is your business?"

"Who—me?" asked the private. "Oh, I just sorter dropped in." With a deeper meaning he added: "Sorter dropped in in a friendly way, thinkin' ye was mebbe a different kind of a feller from what ye be."

The inference was clearly marked.

It was now Gates's turn to stare, and stare he unfeignedly did.

"Go back to your quarters," he said at length.

The volunteer became very angry.

"Oh, ye needn't be so up-in-th'-air, need ye? Don't know's I'm dead anxious to inflict my company on yer since I've had a good look at ye. There may be men in this here battalion what's had just as much edjewcation as you have, and I'm damned if they ain't got better *manners*. Good mornin'," he said, with dignity; and, passing out of the tent, he flung the flap back in place with an air of slamming it as if it had been a door. He made his way back to his company street, striding high. He was furious. He met a large crowd of his comrades.

"What's the matter, Lige?" asked one, who noted his temper.

"Oh, nothin'," answered Lige, with terrible feeling. "Nothin'. I jest been lookin' over the new major—that's all."

"What's he like?" asked another.

"Like?" cried Lige. "He's like nothin'. He ain't out'n the same kittle as us. No. Gawd made him all by himself—sep'rate. He's a speshul produc', he is, an' he won't have no truck with jest common—*men*, like you be."

He made a venomous gesture which included them all.

"Did he set on ye?" asked a soldier.

"Set on me? No," replied Lige, with contempt. "I set on *him*. I sized 'm up in a minute. 'Oh, I don't know,' I says, as I was comin' out; 'guess you ain't the only man in the world,' I says."

For a time Lige Wigram was quite a hero. He endlessly repeated the tale of his adventure, and men admired him for so soon taking the conceit out of the new officer. Lige was proud to think of himself as a plain and simple patriot who had refused to endure any high-soaring nonsense.

But he came to believe that he had not disturbed the singular composure of the major, and this concreted his hatred. He hated Gates, not as a soldier sometimes hates an officer, a hatred half of fear. Lige hated as man to man. And he was enraged to see that so far from gaining any hatred in return, he seemed incapable of making Gates have any thought of him save as a unit in a body of three hundred men. Lige might just as well have gone and grimaced at the obelisk in Central Park.

When the battalion became the best in the regiment he had no part in the pride of the companies. He was sorry when men began to speak well of Gates. He was really a very consistent hater.

III

The transport occupied by the 307th was commanded by some sort of a Scandinavian, who was afraid of the shadows of his own topmasts. He would have run his steamer away from a floating Gainsborough hat, and, in fact, he ran her away from less on some occasions. The officers, wishing to arrive with the other transports, sometimes remonstrated, and to them he talked of his owners. Every officer in the convoying warships loathed him, for in case any hostile vessel should appear they did not see how they were going to protect this rabbit, who would probably manage during a fight to be in about a hundred places on the broad, broad sea, and all of them offensive to the navy's plan. When he was not talking of his owners he was remarking to the officers of the regiment that a steamer really was not like a valise, and that he was unable to take his ship under his arm and climb trees with it. He further said that "them naval fellows" were not near so smart as they thought they were.

From an indigo sea arose the lonely shore of Cuba. Ultimately, the fleet was near Santiago, and most of the transports were bidden to wait a minute while the leaders found out their minds. The skipper to whom the 307th were prisoners waited for thirty hours half way between Jamaica and Cuba. He explained that the Spanish fleet might emerge from Santiago Harbor at any time, and he did not propose to be caught. His owners—— Whereupon the colonel arose as one having nine hundred men at his back, and he passed up to the bridge and he spake with the captain. He explained indirectly that each individual of his nine hundred men had decided to be the first American soldier to land for this campaign, and that in order to accomplish the marvel it was necessary for the transport to be nearer than forty-five miles from the Cuban coast. If the skipper would only land the regiment the colonel would consent to his then taking his interesting old ship and going to h—— with it. And the skipper spake with the colonel. He pointed out that as far as he officially was concerned, the United States Government did not exist. He was responsible solely to his owners. The colonel pondered these sayings. He perceived that the skipper meant that he was running his ship as he deemed best, in consideration of the capital invested by his owners, and that he was not at all concerned with the feelings of a certain American military expedition to Cuba. He was a free son of the sea—he was a sovereign citizen of the republic of the waves. He was like Lige.

However, the skipper ultimately incurred the danger of taking his ship under the terrible guns of the *New York, Iowa, Oregon, Massachusetts, Indiana, Brooklyn, Texas* and a score of cruisers and gunboats. It was a brave act for the captain of a United States transport, and he was visibly nervous until he could again get to sea, where he offered praises that the accursed 307th was no longer sitting on his head. For almost a week he rambled at his cheerful will over the adjacent high seas, having in his hold a great quantity of military stores as successfully secreted as if they had been buried in a copper box in the corner-stone of a new public building in Boston. He had had his master's certificate for twenty-one years, and those people couldn't tell a marlin-spike from the starboard side of the ship.

The 307th was landed in Cuba, but to their disgust they found that about ten thousand regulars were ahead of them. They got immediate orders to move out from the base on the road to Santiago. Gates was interested to note that the only delay was caused by the fact that many men of the other battalions strayed off sight-seeing. In time the long regiment wound slowly among hills that shut them from sight of the sea.

For the men to admire, there were palm-trees, little brown huts, passive, uninterested Cuban soldiers much worn from carrying American rations inside and outside. The weather was not oppressively warm, and the journey was said to be only about seven miles. There were no rumors save that there had been one short fight and the army had advanced to within sight of Santiago. Having a peculiar faculty for the derision of the romantic, the 307th began to laugh. Actually there was not *anything* in the world which turned out to be as books describe it. Here they had landed from the transport expecting to be at once flung into line of battle and sent on some kind of furious charge, and now they were trudging along a quiet trail lined with somnolent trees and grass. The whole business so far struck them as being a highly tedious burlesque.

After a time they came to where the camps of regular regiments marked the sides of the road—little villages of tents no higher than a man's waist. The colonel found his brigade commander and the 307th was sent off into a field of long grass, where the men grew suddenly solemn with the importance of getting their supper.

In the early evening some regulars told one of Gates's companies that at daybreak this division would move to an attack upon something.

"How d'you know?" said the company, deeply awed.

"Heard it."

"Well, what are we to attack?"

"Dunno."

The 307th was not at all afraid, but each man began to imagine the morrow. The regulars seemed to have as much interest in the morrow as they did in the last Christmas. It was none of their affair, apparently.

"Look here," said Lige Wigram to a man in the 17th Regular Infantry, "whereabouts are we goin' ter-morrow an' who do we run up against—do ye know?"

The 17th soldier replied truculently: "If I ketch th' —— —— —— what stole my terbaccer, I'll whirl in an' break every —— —— bone in his body."

Gates's friends in the regular regiments asked him numerous questions as to the reliability of his organization. Would the 307th stand the racket? They were certainly not contemptuous; they simply did not seem to consider it important whether the 307th would or whether it would not.

"Well," said Gates, "they won't run the length of a tent-peg if they can gain any idea of what they're fighting; they won't bunch if they've about six acres of open ground to move in; they won't get rattled at all if they see you fellows taking it easy; and they'll fight like the devil as long as they thoroughly, completely, absolutely, satisfactorily, exhaustively understand what the business is. They're lawyers. All excepting my battalion."

IV

Lige awakened into a world obscured by blue fog. Somebody was gently shaking him. "Git up; we're going to move." The regiment was buckling up itself. From the trail came the loud creak of a light battery moving ahead. The tones of all men were low; the faces of the officers were composed, serious. The regiment found itself moving along behind the battery before it had time to ask itself more than a hundred questions. The trail wound through a dense tall jungle, dark, heavy with dew.

The battle broke with a snap—far ahead. Presently Lige heard from the air above him a faint low note as if somebody were blowing softly in the mouth of a bottle. It was a stray bullet which had wandered a mile to tell him that war was before him. He nearly broke his neck looking upward. "Did ye hear that?" But the men were fretting to get out of this gloomy jungle. They wanted to see something. The faint rup-rup-rrrrup-rup on in the front told them that the fight had begun; death was abroad, and so the mystery of this wilderness excited them. This wilderness was portentously still and dark.

They passed the battery aligned on a hill above the trail, and they had not gone far when the gruff guns began to roar and they could hear the rocket-like swish of the flying shells. Presently everybody must have called out for the assistance of the 307th. Aides and couriers came flying back to them.

"Is this the 307th? Hurry up your men, please, Colonel. You're needed more every minute."

Oh, they were, were they? Then the regulars were not going to do *all* the fighting? The old 307th was bitterly proud or proudly bitter. They left their blanket-rolls under the guard of God and pushed on, which is one of the reasons why the Cubans of that part of the country were, later, so well equipped. There began to appear fields, hot, golden-green in the sun. On some palm-dotted knolls before them they could see little lines of black dots—the American advance. A few men fell, struck down by other men who, perhaps half a mile away, were aiming at somebody else. The loss was wholly in Carmony's battalion, which immediately bunched and backed away, coming with a shock against Gates's advance company. This shock sent a tremor through all of Gates's battalion until men in the very last files cried out nervously, "Well, what in hell is up now?" There came an order to deploy and advance. An occasional hoarse yell from the regulars could be heard. The deploying made Gates's heart bleed for the colonel. The old man stood there directing the movement, straight, fearless, sombrely defiant of—everything. Carmony's four companies were like four herds. And all the time the bullets from no living man knows where kept pecking at them and pecking at them. Gates, the excellent Gates, the highly educated and strictly military Gates, grew rankly insubordinate. He knew that the regiment was suffering from nothing but the deadly range and oversweep of the modern rifle, of which many proud and confident nations know nothing save that they have killed savages with it, which is the least of all informations.

Gates rushed upon Carmony.

"—— —— it, man, if you can't get your people to deploy, for —— sake give me a chance! I'm stuck in the woods!"

Carmony gave nothing, but Gates took all he could get and his battalion deployed and advanced like men. The old colonel almost burst into tears, and he cast one quick glance of gratitude at Gates, which the younger officer wore on his heart like a secret decoration.

There was a wild scramble up hill, down dale, through thorny thickets. Death smote them with a kind of slow rhythm, leisurely taking a man now here, now there, but the cat-spit sound of the bullets was always. A large number of the men of Carmony's battalion came on with Gates. They were willing to do anything, anything. They had no real fault, unless it was that early conclusion that any brave high-minded youth was necessarily a good soldier immediately, from the beginning. In them had been born a swift feeling that the unpopular Gates knew everything, and they followed the trained soldier.

If they followed him, he certainly took them into it. As they swung heavily up one steep hill, like so many wind-blown horses, they came suddenly out into the real advance. Little blue groups of men were making frantic rushes forward and then flopping down on their bellies to fire volleys while other groups made rushes. Ahead they could see a heavy house-like fort which was inadequate to explain from whence came the myriad bullets. The remainder of the scene was landscape. Pale men, yellow men, blue men came out of this landscape quiet and sad-eyed with wounds. Often they were grimly facetious. There is nothing in the American regular so amazing as his conduct when he is wounded—his apologetic limp, his deprecatory arm-sling, his embarrassed and ashamed shot-hole through the lungs. The men of the 307th looked at calm creatures who had divers punctures and they were made better. These men told them that it was only necessary to keep a-going. They of the 307th lay on their bellies, red, sweating and panting, and heeded the voice of the elder brother.

Gates walked back of his line, very white of face, but hard and stern past anything his men knew of him. After they had violently adjured him to lie down and he had given weak backs a cold, stiff touch, the 307th charged by rushes. The hatless colonel made frenzied speech, but the man of the time was Gates. The men seemed to feel that this was his business. Some of the regular officers said afterward that the advance of the 307th was very respectable indeed. They were rather surprised, they said. At least five of the crack regiments of the regular army were in this division, and the 307th could win no more than a feeling of kindly appreciation.

Yes, it was very good, very good indeed, but did you notice what was being done at the same moment by the 12th, the 17th, the 7th, the 8th, the 25th, the——

Gates felt that his charge was being a success. He was carrying out a successful function. Two captains fell bang on the grass and a lieutenant slumped quietly down with a death wound. Many men sprawled suddenly. Gates was keeping his men almost even with the regulars, who were charging on his flanks. Suddenly he thought that he must have come close to the fort and that a Spaniard had tumbled a great stone block down upon his leg. Twelve hands reached out to help him, but he cried:

"No—d—— your souls—go on—go on!"

He closed his eyes for a moment, and it really was only for a moment. When he opened them he found himself alone with Lige Wigram, who lay on the ground near him.

"Maje," said Lige, "yer a good man. I've been a-follerin' ye all day an' I want to say yer a good man."

The major turned a coldly scornful eye upon the private. "Where are you wounded? Can you walk? Well, if you can, go to the rear and leave me alone. I'm bleeding to death, and you bother me."

Lige, despite the pain in his wounded shoulder, grew indignant.

"Well," he mumbled, "you and me have been on th' outs fer a long time, an' I only wanted to tell ye that what I seen of ye t'day has made me feel mighty diff'ent."

"Go to the rear—if you can walk," said the major.

"Now, Maje, look here. A little thing like that——"

"Go to the rear."

Lige gulped with sobs.

"Maje, I know I didn't understand ye at first, but ruther'n let a little thing like that come between us, I'd—I'd——"

"Go to the rear."

In this reiteration Lige discovered a resemblance to that first old offensive phrase, "Come to attention and salute." He pondered over the resemblance and he saw that nothing had changed. The man bleeding to death was the same man to whom he had once paid a friendly visit with unfriendly results. He thought now that he perceived a certain hopeless gulf, a gulf which is real or unreal, according to circumstances. Sometimes all men are equal; occasionally they are not. If Gates had ever criticized Lige's manipulation of a hay fork on the farm at home, Lige would have furiously disdained his hate or blame. He saw now that he must not openly approve the major's conduct in war. The major's pride was in his business, and his, Lige's, congratulations, were beyond all enduring.

The place where they were lying suddenly fell under a new heavy rain of bullets. They sputtered about the men, making the noise of large grasshoppers.

"Major!" cried Lige. "Major Gates! It won't do for ye to be left here, sir. Ye'll be killed."

"But you can't help it, lad. You take care of yourself."

"I'm damned if I do," said the private vehemently. "If I can't git *you* out, I'll stay and wait."

The officer gazed at his man with that same icy, contemptuous gaze.

"I'm—I'm a dead man anyhow. You go to the rear, do you hear?"

"No."

The dying major drew his revolver, cocked it and aimed it unsteadily at Lige's head.

"Will you obey orders?"

"No."

"One?"

"No."

"Two?"

"No."

Gates weakly dropped his revolver.

"Go to the devil, then. You're no soldier, but——" He tried to add something. "But——" He heaved a long moan. "But—you——you—oh, I'm so-o-o tired."

V

After the battle, three correspondents happened to meet on the trail. They were hot, dusty, weary, hungry and thirsty, and they repaired to the shade of a mango tree and sprawled luxuriously. Among them they mustered twoscore friends who on that day had gone to the far shore of the hereafter, but their senses were no longer resonant. Shackles was babbling plaintively about mint-juleps, and the others were bidding him to have done.

"By-the-way," said one at last, "it's too bad about poor old Gates of the 307th. He bled to death. His men were crazy. They were blubbering and cursing around there like wild people. It seems that when they got back there to look for him they found him just about gone, and another wounded man was trying to stop the flow with his hat! His hat, mind you. Poor old Gatesie!"

"Oh, no, Shackles!" said the third man of the party. "Oh, no; you're wrong. The best mint-juleps in the world are made right in New York, Philadelphia or Boston. That Kentucky idea is only a tradition."

A wounded man approached them. He had been shot through

the shoulder and his shirt had been diagonally cut away, leaving much bare skin. Over the bullet's point of entry there was a kind of a white spider, shaped from pieces of adhesive plaster. Over the point of departure there was a bloody bulb of cotton strapped to the flesh by other pieces of adhesive plaster. His eyes were dreamy, wistful, sad. "Say, gents, have any of ye got a bottle?" he asked.

A correspondent raised himself suddenly and looked with bright eyes at the soldier.

"Well, you have got a nerve!" he said, grinning. "Have we got a bottle, eh! Who in h—— do you think we are? If we had a bottle of good licker, do you suppose we could let the whole army drink out of it? You have too much faith in the generosity of men, my friend!"

The soldier stared, ox-like, and finally said, "Huh?"

"I say," continued the correspondent, somewhat more loudly, "that if we had had a bottle we would have probably finished it ourselves by this time."

"But," said the other, dazed, "I *meant* an empty bottle. I didn't mean no *full* bottle."

The correspondent was humorously irascible.

"An empty bottle! You must be crazy! Who ever heard of a man looking for an empty bottle? It isn't sense! I've seen a million men looking for full bottles, but you're the first man I ever saw who insisted on the bottle's being empty. What in the world do you want it for?"

"Well, ye see, mister," explained Lige, slowly, "our major he was killed this mornin' an' we're jes' goin' to bury him, an' I thought I'd jest take a look 'round an' see if I couldn't borry an empty bottle, an' then I'd take an' write his name an' reg'ment on a paper an' put it in th' bottle an' bury it with him, so's when they come fer to dig him up sometime an' take him home, there sure wouldn't be no mistake."

"Oh!"

MARINES SIGNALING UNDER FIRE
AT GUANTANAMO

THEY were four Guantanamo marines, officially known for the time as signalmen, and it was their duty to lie in the trenches of Camp McCalla, that faced the water, and, by day, signal the *Marblehead* with a flag and, by night, signal the *Marblehead* with lanterns. It was my good fortune—at that time I considered it my bad fortune, indeed—to be with them on two of the nights when a wild storm of fighting was pealing about the hill; and, of all the actions of the war, none were so hard on the nerves, none strained courage so near the panic point, as those swift nights in Camp McCalla. With a thousand rifles rattling; with the field-guns booming in your ears; with the diabolic Colt automatics clacking; with the roar of the *Marblehead* coming from the bay, and, last, with Mauser bullets sneering always in the air a few inches over one's head, and with this enduring from dusk to dawn, it is extremely doubtful if any one who was there will be able to forget it easily. The noise; the impenetrable darkness; the knowledge from the sound of the bullets that the enemy was on three sides of the camp; the infrequent bloody stumbling and death of some man with whom, perhaps, one had messed two hours previous; the weariness of the body, and the more terrible weariness of the mind, at the endlessness of the thing, made it wonderful that at least some of the men did not come out of it with their nerves hopelessly in shreds.

But, as this interesting ceremony proceeded in the darkness, it was necessary for the signal squad to coolly take and send messages. Captain McCalla always participated in the defense of the camp by raking the woods on two of its sides with the guns of the *Marblehead*. Moreover, he was the senior officer present, and he wanted to know what was happening. All night long the crews of the ships in the bay would stare sleeplessly into the blackness toward the roaring hill.

The signal squad had an old cracker-box placed on top of the trench. When not signaling, they hid the lanterns in this box; but as soon as an order to send a message was received, it became necessary for one of the men to stand up and expose the lights. And then—oh, my eye—how the guerillas hidden in the gulf of night would turn loose at those yellow gleams!

Signaling in this way is done by letting one lantern remain stationary—on top of the cracker-box, in this case—and moving the other over it to the left and right and so on in the regular gestures of the wig-wagging code. It is a very simple system of night communication, but one can see that it presents rare possibilities when used in front of an enemy who, a few hundred yards away, is overjoyed at sighting so definite a mark.

How, in the name of wonders, those four men at Camp McCalla were not riddled from head to foot and sent home more as repositories of Spanish ammunition than as marines is beyond all comprehension. To make a confession—when one of these men stood up to wave his lantern, I, lying in the trench, invariably rolled a little to the right or left, in order that, when he was shot, he would not fall on me. But the squad came off scathless, despite the best efforts of the most formidable corps in the Spanish army—the Escuadra de Guantanamo. That it was the most formidable corps in the Spanish army of occupation has been told me by many Spanish officers and also by General Menocal and other insurgent officers. General Menocal was Garcia's chief-of-staff when the latter was operating busily in Santiago province. The regiment was composed solely of *practicos*, or guides, who knew every shrub and tree on the ground over which they moved.

Whenever the adjutant, Lieutenant Draper, came plunging along through the darkness with an order—such as: "Ask the *Marblehead* to please shell the woods to the left"—my heart would come into my mouth, for I knew then that one of my pals was going to stand up behind the lanterns and have all Spain shoot at him.

The answer was always upon the instant: "Yes, sir." Then the bullets began to snap, snap, snap, at his head while all the woods began to crackle like burning straw. I could lie near and watch the face of the signalman, illumed as it was by the yellow shine of lantern light, and the absence of excitement, fright, or any emotion at all, on his countenance, was something to astonish all theories out of one's mind. The face was in every instance merely that of a man intent upon his business, the business of wig-wagging into the gulf of night where a light on the *Marble-head* was seen to move slowly.

These times on the hill resembled, in some days, those terrible scenes on the stage—scenes of intense gloom, blinding lightning, with a cloaked devil or assassin or other appropriate character muttering deeply amid the awful roll of the thunder-drums. It was theatric beyond words; one felt like a leaf in this booming chaos, this prolonged tragedy of the night. Amid it all one could see from time to time the yellow light on the face of a preoccupied signalman.

Possibly no man who was there ever before understood the true eloquence of the breaking of the day. We would lie staring into the east, fairly ravenous for the dawn. Utterly worn to rags, with our nerves standing on end like so many bristles, we lay and watched the east—the unspeakably obdurate and slow east. It was a wonder that the eyes of some of us did not turn to glass balls from the fixity of our gaze.

Then there would come into the sky a patch of faint blue light. It was like a piece of moonshine. Some would say it was the beginning of daybreak; others would declare it was nothing of the kind. Men would get very disgusted with each other in these low-toned arguments held in the trenches. For my part, this development in the eastern sky destroyed many of my ideas and theories concerning the dawning of the day; but then I had never before had occasion to give it such solemn attention.

This patch widened and whitened in about the speed of a man's accomplishment if he should be in the way of painting Madison Square Garden with a camel's hair brush. The guerillas always set out to whoop it up about this time, because they knew the occasion was approaching when it would be expedient for them to elope. I, at least, always grew furious with this wretched sunrise. I thought I could have walked around the world in the time required for the old thing to get up above the horizon.

One midnight, when an important message was to be sent to the *Marblehead*, Colonel Huntington came himself to the signal place with Adjutant Draper and Captain McCauley, the quartermaster. When the man stood up to signal, the colonel stood beside him. At sight of the lights, the Spaniards performed as usual. They drove enough bullets into that immediate vicinity to kill all the marines in the corps.

Lieutenant Draper was agitated for his chief. "Colonel, won't you step down, sir?"

"Why, I guess not," said the grey old veteran in his slow, sad, always-gentle way. "I'm in no more danger than the man."

"But, sir—" began the adjutant.

"Oh, it's all right, Draper."

So the colonel and the private stood side to side and took the heavy fire without either moving a muscle.

Day was always obliged to come at last, punctuated by a final exchange of scattering shots. And the light shone on the marines, the dumb guns, the flag. Grimy yellow face looked into grimy yellow face, and grinned with weary satisfaction. Coffee!

Usually it was impossible for many of the men to sleep at once. It always took me, for instance, some hours to get my nerves combed down. But then it was great joy to lie in the trench with the four signalmen, and understand thoroughly that that night was fully over at last, and that, although the future might have in store other bad nights, that one could never escape from the prison-house which we call the past.

At the wild little fight at Cusco there were some splendid exhibitions of wig-wagging under fire. Action began when an advanced detachment of marines under Lieutenant Lucas with the Cuban guides had reached the summit of a ridge overlooking a small valley where there was a house, a well, and a thicket of some kind of shrub with great broad, oily leaves. This thicket, which was perhaps an acre in extent, contained the guerillas. The valley was open to the sea. The distance from the top of the ridge to the thicket was barely two hundred yards.

The *Dolphin* had sailed up the coast in line with the marine advance, ready with her guns to assist in any action. Captain Elliott, who commanded the two hundred marines in this fight, suddenly called out for a signalman. He wanted a man to tell the *Dolphin* to open fire on the house and the thicket. It was a blazing, bitter hot day on top of the ridge with its shriveled chaparral and its straight, tall cactus plants. The sky was bare and blue, and hurt like brass. In two minutes the prostrate marines were red and sweating like so many hull-buried stokers in the tropics.

Captain Elliott called out:

"Where's a signalman? Who's a signalman here?"

A red-headed "mick"—I think his name was Clancy—at any rate, it will do to call him Clancy—twisted his head from where he lay on his stomach pumping his Lee, and, saluting, said that he was a signalman.

There was no regulation flag with the expedition, so Clancy was obliged to tie his blue polka-dot neckerchief on the end of his rifle. It did not make a very good flag. At first Clancy moved a ways down the safe side of the ridge and wig-wagged there very busily. But what with the flag being so poor for the purpose, and the background of ridge being so dark, those on the *Dolphin* did not see it. So Clancy had to return to the top of the ridge and outline himself and his flag against the sky.

The usual thing happened. As soon as the Spaniards caught sight of this silhouette, they let go like mad at it. To make things more comfortable for Clancy, the situation demanded that he face the sea and turn his back to the Spanish bullets. This was a hard game, mark you—to stand with the small of your back to volley firing. Clancy thought so. Everybody thought so. We all cleared out of his neighborhood. If he wanted sole possession of any particular spot on that hill, he could have it for all we would interfere with him.

It cannot be denied that Clancy was in a hurry. I watched him. He was so occupied with the bullets that snarled close to his ears that he was obliged to repeat the letters of his message softly to himself. It seemed an intolerable time before the *Dolphin* answered the little signal. Meanwhile, we gazed at him, marveling every second that he had not yet pitched headlong. He swore at times.

Finally the *Dolphin* replied to his frantic gesticulation, and he delivered his message. As his part of the transaction was quite finished—whoop!—he dropped like a brick into the firing line and began to shoot; began to get "hunky" with all those people who had been plugging at him. The blue polka-dot neckerchief still fluttered from the barrel of his rifle. I am quite certain that he let it remain there until the end of the fight.

The shells of the *Dolphin* began to plow up the thicket, kicking the bushes, stones, and soil into the air as if somebody was blasting there.

Meanwhile, this force of two hundred marines and fifty Cubans and the force of—probably—six companies of Spanish guerillas were making such an awful din that the distant Camp McCalla was all alive with excitement. Colonel Huntington sent out strong parties to critical points on the road to facilitate, if necessary, a safe retreat, and also sent forty men under Lieutenant Magill to come up on the left flank of the two companies in action under Captain Elliott. Lieutenant Magill and his men had crowned a hill which covered entirely the flank of the fighting companies, but when the *Dolphin* opened fire, it happened that Magill was in the line of the shots. It became necessary to stop the *Dolphin* at once. Captain Elliott was not near Clancy at this time, and he called hurriedly for another signalman.

Sergeant Quick arose, and announced that he was a signalman. He produced from somewhere a blue polka-dot neckerchief as large as a quilt. He tied it on a long, crooked stick. Then he went to the top of the ridge, and turning his back to the Spanish fire, began to signal to the *Dolphin*. Again we gave a man sole possession of a particular part of the ridge. We didn't want it. He could have it and welcome. If the young sergeant had had the smallpox, the cholera, and the yellow fever, we could not have slid out with more celerity.

As men have said often, it seemed as if there was in this war a God of Battles who held His mighty hand before the Americans. As I looked at Sergeant Quick wig-wagging there against the sky, I would not have given a tin tobacco-tag for his life. Escape for him seemed impossible. It seemed absurd to hope that he would not be hit; I only hoped that he would be hit just a little, little, in the arm, the shoulder, or the leg.

I watched his face, and it was as grave and serene as that of a man writing in his own library. He was the very embodiment of tranquillity in occupation. He stood there amid the animal-like babble of the Cubans, the crack of rifles, and the whistling snarl of the bullets, and wig-wagged whatever he had to wig-wag without heeding anything but his business. There was not a single trace of nervousness or haste.

To say the least, a fight at close range is absorbing as a spectacle. No man wants to take his eyes from it until that time comes when he makes up his mind to run away. To deliberately stand up and turn your back to a battle is in itself hard work. To deliberately stand up and turn your back to a battle and hear immediate evidences of the boundless enthusiasm with which a large company of the enemy shoot at you from an adjacent thicket is, to my mind at least, a very great feat. One need not dwell upon the detail of keeping the mind carefully upon a slow spelling of an important code message.

I saw Quick betray only one sign of emotion. As he swung his clumsy flag to and fro, an end of it once caught on a cactus pillar, and he looked sharply over his shoulder to see what had it. He gave the flag an impatient jerk. He looked annoyed.

THIS MAJESTIC LIE

I

IN THE twilight a great crowd was streaming up the Prado in Havana. The people had been down to the shore to laugh and twiddle their fingers at the American blockading fleet—mere colorless shapes on the edge of the sea. Gorgeous challenges had been issued to the far-away ships by little children and women while the men laughed. Havana was happy, for it was known that the illustrious sailor Don Patricio Montojo had with his fleet met the decaying ships of one Dewey and smitten them into stuffing for a baby's pillow. Of course the American sailors were drunk at the time, but the American sailors were always drunk. Newsboys galloped among the crowd crying *La Lucha* and *La Marina*. The papers said: "This is as we foretold. How could it be otherwise when the cowardly Yankees met our brave sailors?" But the tongues of the exuberant people ran more at large. One man said in a loud voice: "How unfortunate it is that we still have to buy meat in Havana when so much pork is floating in Manila Bay!" Amid the consequent laughter another man retorted: "Oh, never mind! That pork in Manila is rotten. It always was rotten." Still another man said: "But, little friend, it would make good manure for our fields if only we had it." And still another man said: "Ah, wait until our soldiers get with the wives of the Americans and there will be many little Yankees to serve hot on our tables. The men of the *Maine* simply made our appetites good. Never mind the pork in Manila. There will be plenty." Women laughed; children laughed because their mothers laughed; everybody laughed. And—a word with you—these people were cackling and chuckling and insulting their own dead, their own dead men of Spain, for if the poor green corpses floated then in Manila Bay they were not American corpses.

The newsboys came charging with an extra. The inhabitants

of Philadelphia had fled to the forests because of a Spanish bombardment and also Boston was besieged by the Apaches who had totally invested the town. The Apache artillery had proven singularly effective and an American garrison had been unable to face it. In Chicago millionaires were giving away their palaces for two or three loaves of bread. These despatches were from Madrid and every word was truth, but they added little to the enthusiasm because the crowd—God help mankind—was greatly occupied with visions of Yankee pork floating in Manila Bay. This will be thought to be embittered writing. Very well; the writer admits its untruthfulness in one particular. It is untruthful in that it fails to reproduce one-hundredth part of the grossness and indecency of popular expression in Havana up to the time when the people knew they were beaten.

There were no lights on the Prado or in other streets because of a military order. In the slow-moving crowd there was a young man and an old woman. Suddenly the young man laughed a strange metallic laugh and spoke in English, not cautiously. "That's damned hard to listen to."

The woman spoke quickly. "Hush, you little idiot. Do you want to be walkin' across that grass-plot in Cabanas with your arms tied behind you?" Then she murmured sadly: "Johnnie, I wonder if that's true—what they say about Manila?"

"I don't know," said Johnnie, "but I think they're lying."

As they crossed the Plaza they could see that the Café Tacon was crowded with Spanish officers in blue and white pyjama uniforms. Wine and brandy was being wildly consumed in honor of the victory at Manila. "Let's hear what they say," said Johnnie to his companion, and they moved across the street and in under the *portales*. The owner of the Café Tacon was standing on a table making a speech amid cheers. He was advocating the crucifixion of such Americans as fell into Spanish hands and—it was all very sweet and white and tender, but above all, it was chivalrous, because it is well known that the Spaniards are a chivalrous people. It has been remarked both by the English newspapers and by the bulls that are bred for the red death. And secretly the corpses in Manila Bay mocked this jubilee—the mocking, mocking corpses in Manila Bay.

To be blunt, Johnnie was an American spy. Once he had been

the manager of a sugar plantation in Pinar del Rio, and during the insurrection it had been his distinguished function to pay tribute of money, food and forage alike to Spanish columns and insurgent bands. He was performing this straddle with benefit to his crops and with mildew to his conscience when Spain and the United States agreed to skirmish, both in the name of honor. It then became a military necessity that he should change his base. Whatever of the province that was still alive was sorry to see him go for he had been a very dexterous man and food and wine had been in his house even when a man with a mango could gain the envy of an entire Spanish battalion. Without doubt he had been a mere trimmer, but it was because of his crop and he always wrote the word thus: C R O P. In those days a man of peace and commerce was in a position parallel to the watchmaker who essayed a task in the midst of a drunken brawl with oaths, bottles and bullets flying about his intent bowed head. So many of them—or all of them—were trimmers, and to any armed force they fervently said: "God assist you." And behold, the trimmers dwelt safely in a tumultuous land and without effort save that their little machines for trimming ran night and day. So many a plantation became covered with a maze of lies as if thick-webbing spiders had run from stalk to stalk in the cane. So sometimes a planter incurred an equal hatred from both sides and when in trouble there was no camp to which he could flee save, straight in air—the camp of the heavenly host.

If Johnnie had not had a crop he would have been plainly on the side of the insurgents, but his crop staked him down to the soil at a point where the Spaniards could always be sure of finding him—him or his crop—it is the same thing. But when war came between Spain and the United States he could no longer be the cleverest trimmer in Pinar del Rio. And he retreated upon Key West losing much of his baggage train, not because of panic but because of wisdom. In Key West he was no longer the manager of a big Cuban plantation; he was a little tan-faced refugee without much money. Mainly he listened; there was nought else to do. In the first place he was a young man of extremely slow speech and in the Key West Hotel tongues ran like pin-wheels. If he had projected his methodic way of thought and speech upon this hurricane he would have been as effective as the man who tries to smoke against the gale. This truth did not impress him. Really he was impressed with the fact that although he knew much of Cuba, he could not talk so rapidly and wisely of it as many war-correspondents who had not yet seen the island. Usually he brooded in silence over a bottle of beer and the loss of his crop. He received no sympathy, although there was a plentitude of tender souls. War's first step is to make expectation so high that all present things are fogged and darkened in a tense wonder of the future. None cared about the collapse of Johnnie's plantation when all were thinking of the probable collapse of cities and fleets.

In the meantime battle-ships, monitors, cruisers, gunboats and torpedo craft arrived, departed, arrived, departed. Rumors rang about the ears of warships hurriedly coaling. Rumors sang about the ears of warships leisurely coming to anchor. This happened and that happened and if the news arrived at Key West as a mouse, it was often enough cabled north as an ele- phant. The correspondents at Key West were perfectly capable of adjusting their perspective, but many of the editors in the United States were like deaf men at whom one has to roar. A few quiet words of information was not enough for them; one had to bawl into their ears a whirlwind tale of heroism, blood, death, victory or defeat—at any rate, a tragedy. The papers should have sent play-wrights to the first part of the war. Play-wrights are allowed to lower the curtain from time to time and say to the crowd: "Mark, ye, now! Three or four months are supposed to elapse." But the poor devils at Key West were obliged to keep the curtain up all the time. "This isn't a continuous performance." "Yes, it is; it's *got* to be a continuous performance. The welfare of the paper demands it. The people want news." Very well; continuous performance. It is strange how men of sense can go aslant at the bidding of other men of sense and combine to contribute to a general mess of exaggeration and bombast. But we did; and in the midst of the furor I remember the still figure of Johnnie, the planter, the ex-trimmer. He looked dazed.

This was in May.

We all liked him. From time to time some of us heard in his words the vibrant of a thoughtful experience. But it could not be well heard; it was only like the sound of a bell from under the floor. We were too busy with our own clatter. He was taciturn and competent while we solved the war in a babble of tongues. Soon we went about our peaceful paths saying ironically one to another: "War is hell." Meanwhile, managing editors fought us tooth and nail and we all were sent boxes of medals inscribed: "Incompetency." We became furious with ourselves. Why couldn't we send hair-raising despatches? Why couldn't we inflame the wires? All the ijjits did. If a first-class armored cruiser which had once been a tow-boat fired a six-pounder shot from her forward thirteen-inch gun turret the world heard of it, you bet. We were not idle men. We had come to report the war and we did it. Our good names and our salaries depended upon it and we were urged by our managing-editors to remember that the American people were a collection of super-nervous idiots who would immediately have convulsions if we did not throw them some news—any news. It was not true, at all. The American people were anxious for things decisive to happen; they were not anxious to be lulled to satisfaction with a drug. But we lulled them. We told them this and we told them that, and I warrant you our screaming sounded like the noise of a lot of sea-birds settling for the night among the black crags.

In the meantime, Johnnie stared and meditated. In his unhurried, unstartled manner he was singularly like another man who was flying the pennant as commander-in-chief of the North Atlantic Squadron. Johnnie was a refugee; the admiral was an admiral. And yet they were much akin, these two. Their brother was the Strategy Board—the only capable political institution of the war. At Key West the naval officers spoke of their business and were devoted to it and were bound to succeed in it, but when the flag-ship was in port the only two people who were independent and sane were the admiral and Johnnie. The rest of us were lulling the public with drugs.

There was much discussion of the new batteries at Havana. Johnnie was a typical American. In Europe a typical American is a man with a hard eye, chin-whiskers and a habit of speaking through his nose. Johnnie was a young man of great energy, ready to accomplish a colossal thing for the basic reason that he was ignorant of its magnitude. In fact he attacked all obstacles in life in a spirit of contempt, seeing them smaller than they were until he had actually surmounted them—when he was likely to be immensely pleased with himself. Somewhere in him there was a sentimental tenderness, but it was like a light seen afar at night; it came, went, appeared again in a new place, flickered, flared, went out, left you in a void and angry. And if his sentimental tenderness was a light, the darkness in which it puzzled you was his irony of soul. This irony was directed first at himself; then at you; then at the nation and the flag; then at God. It was a midnight in which you searched for the little elusive ashamed spark of tender sentiment. Sometimes you thought this was all pretext, the manner and the way of fear of the wit of others; sometimes you thought he was a hardened savage; usually you did not think but waited in the cheerful certainty that in time the little flare of light would appear in the gloom.

Johnnie decided that he would go and spy upon the fortifications of Havana. If any one wished to know of those batteries it was the admiral of the squadron, but the admiral of the squadron knew much. I feel sure that he knew the size and position of every gun. To be sure, new guns might be mounted at any time, but they would not be big guns, and doubtless he lacked in his cabin less information than would be worth a man's life. Still, Johnnie decided to be a spy. He would go and look. We of the newspapers pinned him fast to the tail of our kite and he was taken to see the admiral. I judge that the admiral did not display much interest in the plan. But at any rate it seems that he touched Johnnie smartly enough with a brush to make him, officially, a spy. Then Johnnie bowed and left the cabin. There was no other machinery. If Johnnie was to end his life and leave a little book about it no one cared—least of all Johnnie and the admiral. When he came aboard the tug he displayed his usual stalwart and rather selfish zest for fried eggs. It was all some kind of an ordinary matter. It was done every day. It was the business of packing pork, sewing shoes, binding hay. It was commonplace. No one could adjust it, get it in proportion, until —afterward. On a dark night they heaved him into a small boat and rowed him to the beach.

And one day he appeared at the door of a little lodging-house in Havana kept by Martha Clancy, born in Ireland, bred in New York, fifteen years married to a Spanish captain, and now a widow, keeping Cuban lodgers who had no money with which to pay her. She opened the door only a little way and looked down over her spectacles at him.

"Good-mornin', Martha," he said.

She looked a moment in silence. Then she made an indescribable gesture of weariness. "Come in," she said. He stepped inside. "And in God's name couldn't you keep your neck out of this rope? And so you had to come here, did you—to Havana? Upon my soul, Johnnie, my son, you are the biggest fool on two legs."

He moved past her into the court-yard and took his old chair at the table—between the winding stairway and the door—near the orange tree. "Why am I?" he demanded stoutly. She made no reply until she had taken seat in her rocking-chair and puffed several times upon a cigarette. Then through the smoke she said meditatively: "Everybody knows ye are a damned little mambi." Sometimes she spoke with an Irish accent.

He laughed. "I'm no more of a mambi than *you* are, anyhow."

"I'm no mambi. But your name is poison to half the Spaniards in Havana. That you know. And if you were once safe in Cayo Hueso, 'tis nobody but a born fool who would come blunderin' into Havana again. Have ye had your dinner?"

"What have you got?" he asked before committing himself.

She arose and spoke without confidence as she moved toward the cupboard. "There's some codfish salad."

"*What?*" said he.

"Codfish salad."

"*Codfish what?*"

"Codfish salad. Ain't it good enough for ye? Maybe this is Delmonico's—no? Maybe ye never heard that the Yankees have us blockaded, hey? Maybe ye think food can be picked in the streets here now, hey? I'll tell ye one thing, my son, if you stay here long you'll see the want of it and so you had best not throw it over your shoulder."

The spy settled determinedly in his chair and delivered himself of his final decision. "That may all be true, but I'm *damned* if I eat codfish salad."

Old Martha was a picture of quaint despair. "You'll not?"

"No!"

"Then," she sighed piously, "may the Lord have mercy on ye,

Johnnie, for you'll never do here. 'Tis not the time for you. You're due after the blockade. Will you do me the favor of translating why you won't eat codfish salad, you skinny little insurrecto?"

"Codfish salad!" he said with a deep sneer. "Who ever heard of it!"

Outside, on the jumbled pavement of the street, an occasional two-wheel cart passed with deafening thunder, making one think of the overturning of houses. Down from the pale sky over the patio came a heavy odor of Havana itself, a smell of old straw. The wild cries of vendors could be heard at intervals.

"You'll not?"

"No."

"And why not?"

"Codfish salad? Not by a blame sight!"

"Well—all right then. You are more of a pig-headed young imbecile than even I thought from seeing you come into Havana here where half the town knows you and the poorest Spaniard would give a gold piece to see you go into Cabanas and forget to come out. Did I tell you my son Alfred is sick? Yes, poor little fellow, he lies up in the room you used to have. The fever. And did you see Woodham in Key West? Heaven save us, what quick time he made in getting out. I hear Figtree and Button are working in the cable office over there—no? And when is the war going to end? Are the Yankees going to try to take Havana? It will be a hard job, Johnnie! The Spaniards say it is impossible. Everybody is laughing at the Yankees. I hate to go into the street and hear them. Is General Lee going to lead the army? What's become of Springer? I see you've got a new pair of shoes."

In the evening there was a sudden loud knock at the outer door. Martha looked at Johnnie and Johnnie looked at Martha. He was still sitting in the patio, smoking. She took the lamp and set it on a table in the little parlor. This parlor connected the street-door with the patio, and so Johnnie would be protected from the sight of the people who knocked by the broad illuminated tract. Martha moved in pensive fashion upon the latch. "Who's there?" she asked casually.

"The police!" There it was, an old melodramatic incident from the stage, from the romances. One could scarce believe it. It had all the dignity of a classic resurrection. "The police!" One sneers at its probability; it is too venerable. But so it happened.

"Who?" said Martha.

"The police!"

"What do you want here?"

"Open the door and we'll tell you."

Martha drew back the ordinary huge bolts of a Havana house and opened the door a trifle. "Tell me what you want and begone quickly," she said, "for my little boy is ill of the fever——"

She could see four or five dim figures, and now one of these suddenly placed a foot well within the door so that she might not close it. "We have come for Johnnie. We must search your house."

"Johnnie? Johnnie? Who is Johnnie?" said Martha in her best manner.

The police inspector grinned with the light upon his face. "Don't you know Señor Johnnie from Pinar del Rio?" he asked.

"Before the war—yes. But now—where is he—he must be in Key West?"

"He is in your house."

"He? In my house? Do me the favor to think that I have some intelligence. Would I be likely to be harboring a Yankee in these times? You must think I have no more head than an Orden Publico. And I'll not have you search my house, for there is no one here save my son—who is maybe dying of the fever—and the doctor. The doctor is with him because now is the crisis, and any one little thing may kill or cure my boy, and you will do me the favor to consider what may happen if I allow five or six heavy-footed policemen to go tramping all over my house. You may think——"

"Stop it," said the chief police officer at last. He was laughing and weary and angry.

Martha checked her flow of Spanish. "There," she thought, "I've done my best. He ought to fall in with it." But as the police entered she began on them again. "You will search the house whether I like it or no. Very well; but if anything happens to my boy? It is a nice way of conduct, anyhow—coming into the house of a widow at night and talking much about this Yankee and——"

"For God's sake, señora, hold your tongue. We——"

"Oh, yes, the señora can for God's sake very well hold her tongue, but that wouldn't assist you men into the street where you belong. Take care; if my sick boy suffers from this prowling! No, you'll find nothing in that wardrobe. And do you think he would be under the table? Don't overturn all that linen. Look you, when you go upstairs tread lightly."

Leaving a man on guard at the street door and another in the patio, the chief policeman and the remainder of his men ascended to the gallery from which opened three sleeping-rooms. They were followed by Martha adjuring them to make no noise. The first room was empty; the second room was empty; as they approached the door of the third room Martha whispered supplications. "Now, in the name of God, don't disturb my boy." The inspector motioned his men to pause and then he pushed open the door. Only one weak candle was burning in the room and its yellow light fell upon the bed whereon was stretched the figure of a little curly-headed boy in a white nightie. He was asleep, but his face was pink with fever and his lips were murmuring some half-coherent childish nonsense. At the head of the bed stood the motionless figure of a man. His back was to the door, but upon hearing a noise he held up a solemn hand. There was an odor of medicine. Out on the balcony, Martha apparently was weeping.

The inspector hesitated for a moment; then he noiselessly entered the room and with his yellow cane prodded under the bed, in the cupboard and behind the window-curtains. Nothing came of it. He shrugged his shoulders and went out to the balcony. He was smiling sheepishly. Evidently he knew that he had been beaten. "Very good, señora," he said. "You are clever; some day I shall be clever, too." He shook his finger at her. He was threatening her but he affected to be playful. "Then—beware! Beware!"

Martha replied blandly. "My late husband, El Capitan Señor Don Patricio de Castellon y Valladolid, was a cavalier of Spain and if he was alive to-night he would now be cutting the ears from the heads of you and your miserable men who smell frightfully of cognac."

"Por Dios!" muttered the inspector as followed by his band he made his way down the spiral staircase. "It is a tongue! One vast tongue!" At the street-door they made ironical bows; they departed; they were angry men.

Johnnie came down when he heard Martha bolting the door

behind the police. She brought back the lamp to the table in the patio and stood beside it, thinking. Johnnie dropped into his old chair. The expression on the spy's face was curious; it pictured glee, anxiety, self-complacency; above all it pictured self-complacency. Martha said nothing; she was still by the lamp, musing.

The long silence was suddenly broken by a tremendous guffaw from Johnnie. "Did you ever see sich a lot of fools!" He leaned his head far back and roared victorious merriment.

Martha was almost dancing in her apprehension. "Hush! Be quiet, you little demon! Hush! Do me the favor to allow them to get to the corner before you bellow like a walrus. Be quiet."

The spy ceased his laughter and spoke in indignation. "Why?" he demanded. "Ain't I got a right to laugh?"

"Not with a noise like a cow fallin' into a cucumber-frame," she answered sharply. "Do me the favor——" Then she seemed overwhelmed with a sense of the general hopelessness of Johnnie's character. She began to wag her head. "Oh, but you are the boy for gettin' yourself into the tiger's cage without even so much as the thought of a pocket-knife in your thick head. You would be a genius of the first water if you only had a little sense. And now you're here, what are you going to do?"

He grinned at her. "I'm goin' to hold an inspection of the land and sea defences of the city of Havana."

Martha's spectacles dropped low on her nose and, looking over the rims of them in grave meditation, she said: "If you can't put up with codfish salad you had better make short work of your inspection of the land and sea defences of the city of Havana. You are likely to starve in the meantime. A man who is particular about his food has come to the wrong town if he is in Havana now."

"No, but——" asked Johnnie seriously. "Haven't you any bread?"

"*Bread!*"

"Well, coffee then? Coffee alone will do."

"*Coffee!*"

Johnnie arose deliberately and took his hat. Martha eyed him. "And where do you think you are goin'?" she asked cuttingly.

Still deliberate, Johnnie moved in the direction of the street-door. "I'm goin' where I can get something to eat."

Martha sank into a chair with a moan which was a finished opinion—almost a definition—of Johnnie's behavior in life. "And where will you go?" she asked faintly.

"Oh, I don't know," he rejoined. "Some café. Guess I'll go to the Café Aguacate. They feed you well there. I remember——"

"*You* remember? *They* remember! They know you as well as if you were the sign over the door."

"Oh, they won't give me away," said Johnnie with stalwart confidence.

"Gi-give you away? Give you a-away?" stammered Martha.

The spy made no answer but went to the door, unbarred it and passed into the street. Martha caught her breath and ran after him and came face to face with him as he turned to shut the door. "Johnnie, if ye come back, bring a loaf of bread. I'm dyin' for one good honest bite in a slice of bread."

She heard his peculiar derisive laugh as she bolted the door. She returned to her chair in the patio. "Well, there," she said with affection, admiration and contempt. "There he goes! The most hard-headed little ignoramus in twenty nations! What does he care? Nothin'! And why is it? Pure bred-in-the-bone ignorance. Just because he can't stand codfish salad he goes out to a café! A café where they know him as if they had made him! . . . Well . . . . I won't see him again, probably. . . . But if he comes back, I hope he brings some bread. I'm near dead for it."

II

Johnnie strolled carelessly through dark narrow streets. Near every corner were two Orden Publicos—a kind of soldier-police —quiet in the shadow of some doorway, their Remingtons ready, their eyes shining. Johnnie walked past as if he owned them, and their eyes followed him with a sort of a lazy mechanical suspicion which was militant in none of its moods.

Johnnie was suffering from a desire to be splendidly imprudent. He wanted to make the situation gasp and thrill and tremble. From time to time he tried to conceive the idea of his being caught, but to save his eyes he could not imagine it. Such an event was impossible to his peculiar breed of fatalism which could not have conceded death until he had mouldered seven years.

He arrived at the Café Aguacate and found it much changed. The thick wooden shutters were up to keep light from shining into the street. Inside there were only a few Spanish officers. Johnnie walked to the private rooms at the rear. He found an empty one and pressed the electric button. When he had passed through the main part of the café no one had noted him. The first to recognize him was the waiter who answered the bell. This worthy man turned to stone before the presence of Johnnie.

"Buenos noche, Francisco," said the spy, enjoying himself. "I have hunger. Bring me bread, butter, eggs and coffee." There was a silence; the waiter did not move; Johnnie smiled casually at him.

The man's throat moved; then like one suddenly re-endowed with life, he bolted from the room. After a long time he returned with the proprietor of the place. In the wicked eye of the latter there gleamed the light of a plan. He did not respond to Johnnie's genial greeting, but at once proceeded to develop his position. "Johnnie," he said, "bread is very dear in Havana. It is very dear."

"Is it?" said Johnnie looking keenly at the speaker. He understood at once that here was some sort of an attack upon him.

"Yes," answered the proprietor of the Café Aguacate slowly and softly. "It is very dear. I think to-night one small bit of bread will cost you one centene—in advance." A centene approximates five dollars in gold.

The spy's face did not change. He appeared to reflect. "And how much for the butter?" he asked at last.

The proprietor gestured. "There is no butter. Do you think we can have everything with those Yankee pigs sitting out there on their ships?"

"And how much for the coffee?" asked Johnnie musingly.

Again the two men surveyed each other during a period of silence. Then the proprietor said gently: "I think your coffee will cost you about two centenes."

"And the eggs?"

"Eggs are very dear. I think eggs would cost you about three centenes for each one."

The new looked at the old; the North Atlantic looked at the Mediterranean; the wooden nutmeg looked at the olive. Johnnie slowly took six centenes from his pocket and laid them on the table. "That's for bread, coffee and *one* egg. I don't think I could eat more than one egg to-night. I'm not so hungry as I was."

The proprietor held a perpendicular finger and tapped the table with it. "Oh, señor," he said politely, "I think you would like two eggs."

Johnnie saw the finger. He understood it. "Ye-e-es," he drawled. "I would like two eggs." He placed three more centenes on the table.

"And a little thing for the waiter? I am sure his services will be excellent, invaluable."

"Ye-e-es, for the waiter." Another centene was laid on the table.

The proprietor bowed and preceded the waiter out of the room. There was a mirror on the wall and, springing to his feet, the spy thrust his face close to the honest glass. "Well, I'm damned!" he ejaculated. "Is this me or is this the Honorable D. Hayseed Whiskers of Kansas? Who am I, anyhow? Fifty dollars in gold! . . . Say, these people are clever. They know their business, they do. Bread, coffee and two eggs and not even sure of getting it! Fifty dol—— Never mind; wait until the war is over. Fifty dollars gold!" He sat for a long time; nothing happened. "Eh," he said at last, "that's the game." As the front door of the café closed upon him he heard the proprietor and one of the waiters burst into derisive laughter.

Martha was waiting for him. "And here ye are, safe back," she said with delight as she let him enter. "And did ye bring the bread? Did ye bring the bread?"

But she saw that he was raging like a lunatic. His face was red and swollen with temper; his eyes shot forth gleams. Presently he stood before her in the patio where the light fell on him. "Don't speak to me," he choked out waving his arms. "Don't speak to me! *Damn* your bread! I went to the Café Aguacate! Oh, yes, I went there! Of course, I did! And do you know what they did to me? No! Oh, they didn't do anything to me at all! Not a thing! Fifty dollars! Ten gold pieces!"

"May the saints guard us," cried Martha. "And what was that for?"

"Because they wanted them more than I did," snarled Johnnie. "Don't you see the game. I go into the Café Aguacate. The owner of the place says to himself, 'Hello! Here's that Yankee what they call Johnnie. He's got no right here in Havana. Guess I'll peach on him to the police. They'll put him in Cabanas as a spy.' Then he does a little more thinking, and finally he says, 'No; I guess I won't peach on him just this minute. First, I'll take a small flyer myself.' So in he comes and looks me right in the eye and says, 'Excuse me but it will be a centene for the bread, two centenes for the coffee, and eggs are at three centenes each. Besides there will be a small matter of another gold-piece for the waiter.' I think this over. I think it over hard. . . . He's clever anyhow. . . . When this cruel war is over I'll be after him. . . . I'm a nice secret agent of the United States government, I am. I come here to be too clever for all the Spanish police, and the first thing I do is get buncoed by a rotten little thimble-rigger in a café. Oh, yes, I'm all right."

"May the saints guard us!" cried Martha again. "I'm old enough to be your mother, or maybe, your grandmother, and I've seen a lot; but it's many a year since I laid eyes on such a ign'rant and wrong-headed little red Indian as ye are! Why didn't ye take my advice and stay here in the house with decency and comfort. But he must be all for doing everything high and mighty. The Café Aguacate, if ye please. No plain food for His Highness. He turns up his nose at codfish sal——"

"Thunder and lightnin', are you going to ram that thing down my throat every two minutes, are you?" And in truth she could see that one more reference to that illustrious viand would break the back of Johnnie's gentle disposition as one breaks a twig on the knee. She shifted with Celtic ease. "Did ye bring the bread?" she asked.

He gazed at her for a moment and suddenly laughed. "I forgot to mention," he informed her impressively, "that they did not take the trouble to give me either the bread, the coffee or the eggs."

"The powers!" cried Martha.

"But it's all right. I stopped at a shop." From his pockets, he brought a small loaf, some kind of German sausage and a flask of Jamaica rum. "About all I could get. And they didn't want to sell them either. They expect presently they can exchange a box of sardines for a grand piano."

" 'We are not blockaded by the Yankee war-ships; we are blockaded by our grocers,' " said Martha, quoting the epidemic Havana saying. But she did not delay long from the little loaf. She cut a slice from it and sat eagerly munching. Johnnie seemed more interested in the Jamaica rum. He looked up from his second glass, however, because he heard a peculiar sound. The old woman was weeping. "Hey, what's this?" he demanded in distress, but with the manner of a man who thinks gruffness is the only thing that will make people feel better and cease. "What's this anyhow? What are you cryin' for?"

"It's the bread," sobbed Martha. "It's the—the br-e-a-d-d-d."

"Huh? What's the matter with it?"

"It's so good, so g-good." The rain of tears did not prevent her from continuing her unusual report. "Oh, it's so good! This is the first in weeks. I didn't know bread could be so l-like heaven."

"Here," said Johnnie seriously. "Take a little mouthful of this rum. It will do you good."

"No; I only want the bub-bub-bread."

"Well, take the bread, too. . . . There you are. Now you feel better. . . . By jiminy, when I think of that Café Aguacate man! Fifty dollars gold! And then not to get anything either. Say, after the war I'm going there and I'm just going to raze that place to the ground. You see! I'll make him think he can charge ME fifteen dollars for an egg. . . . And then not give me the egg!"

III

Johnnie's subsequent activity in Havana could truthfully be related in part to a certain temporary price of eggs. It is interesting to note how close that famous event got to his eye so that, according to the law of perspective, it was as big as the Capitol at Washington, where centres the spirit of his nation. Around him he felt a similar and ferocious expression of life which informed him too plainly that if he was caught he was doomed. Neither the garrison nor the citizens of Havana would tolerate any nonsense in regard to him if he was caught. He would have the steel screw against his neck in short order. And what was the main thing to bear him up against the desire to run away before his work was done? A certain temporary price of eggs! It not only hid the Capitol at Washington; it obscured the dangers in Havana.

Something was learned of the Santa Clara battery because one morning an old lady in black accompanied by a young man—evidently her son—visited a house which was to rent on the height, in rear of the battery. The portero was too lazy and sleepy to show them over the premises, but he granted them permission to investigate for themselves. They spent most of their time on the flat parapeted roof of the house. At length they came down and said that the place did not suit them. The portero went to sleep again.

Johnnie was never discouraged by the thought that his operations would be of small benefit to the admiral commanding the fleet in adjacent waters and to the general commanding the army which was not going to attack Havana from the land side. At that time it was all the world's opinion that the army from Tampa would presently appear on the Cuban beach at some convenient point to the east or west of Havana. It turned out, of course, that the condition of the defences of Havana was of not the slightest military importance to the United States since the city was never attacked either by land or sea. But Johnnie could not foresee this. He continued to take his fancy risk, continued his majestic lie, with satisfaction, sometimes with delight, and with pride. And in the psychologic distance was old Martha dancing with fear and shouting: "Oh, Johnnie, me son, what a born fool ye are!"

Sometimes she would address him thus: "And when ye learn all this, how are ye goin' to get out with it?" She was contemptuous.

He would reply, as serious as a Cossack in his fatalism. "Oh, I'll get out some way."

His manœuvres in the vicinity of Regla and Guanabacoa were of a brilliant character. He haunted the sunny long grass in the manner of a jack-rabbit. Sometimes he slept under a palm, dreaming of the American advance fighting its way along the military road to the foot of the Spanish defences. Even when awake he often dreamed it and thought of the all-day crash and hot roar of an assault. Without consulting Washington, he had decided that Havana should be attacked from the south-east. An advance from the west could be contested right up to the bar of the Hotel Inglaterra, but when the first ridge in the south-east would be taken the whole city with most of its defences would lie under the American siege guns. And the approach to this position was as reasonable as is any approach toward the muzzles of magazine rifles. Johnnie viewed the grassy fields always as a prospective battle-ground, and one can see him lying there, filling the landscape with visions of slow-crawling black infantry columns, galloping batteries of artillery, streaks of faint blue smoke marking the modern firing lines, clouds of dust, a vision of ten thousand tragedies. And his ears heard the noises——

But he was no idle shepherd boy with a head haunted by sombre and glorious fancies. On the contrary, he was much occupied with practical matters. Some months after the close of the war, he asked me: "Were you ever fired at from very near?" I explained some experiences which I had stupidly esteemed as having been rather near. "But did you ever have 'm fire a volley on you from close—very close—say thirty feet?"

Highly scandalized I answered, "No; in that case, I would not be the crowning feature of the Smithsonian Institute."

"Well," he said, "it's a funny effect. You feel as if every hair on your head had been snatched out by the roots." Questioned further he said: "I walked right up on a Spanish outpost at daybreak once, and about twenty men let go at me. Thought I was a Cuban army, I suppose."

"What did you do?"

"I run."

"Did they hit you, at all?"

"Naw."

It had been arranged that some light ship of the squadron should rendezvous with him at a certain lonely spot on the coast on a certain day and hour and pick him up. He was to wave something white. His shirt was not white, but he waved it whenever he could see the signal-tops of a war-ship. It was a very tattered banner. After a ten-mile scramble through almost pathless thickets, he had very little on him which respectable men would call a shirt, and the less one says about his trousers the better. This naked savage then walked all day up and down a small bit of beach waving a brown rag. At night he slept in the sand. At full daybreak he began to wave his rag; at noon he was waving his rag; at nightfall he donned his rag and strove to think of it as a shirt. Thus passed two days and nothing had happened. Then he retraced a twenty-five mile way to the house of old Martha. At first she took him to be one of Havana's terrible beggars and cried, "And do you come here for alms? Look out that I do not beg of you." The one unchanged thing was his laugh of pure mockery. When she heard it she dragged him through the door. He paid no heed to her ejaculations but went straight to where he had hidden some gold. As he was untying a bit of string from the neck of a small bag, he said, "How is little Alfred?" "Recovered, thank Heaven." He handed Martha a piece of gold. "Take this and buy what you can on the corner. I'm hungry." Martha departed with expedition. Upon her return she was beaming. She had foraged a thin chicken, a bunch of radishes and two bottles of wine. Johnnie had finished the radishes and one bottle of wine when the chicken was still a long way from the table. He called stoutly for more, and so Martha passed again into the street with another gold piece. She bought more radishes, more wine and some cheese. They had a grand feast, with Johnnie audibly wondering until a late hour why he had waved his rag in vain.

There was no end to his suspense, no end to his work. He knew everything. He was an animate guide-book. After he knew a thing once, he verified it in several different ways in order to make sure. He fitted himself for a useful career, like a young man in a college—with the difference that the shadow of the garrote fell ever upon his way, and that he was occasionally shot at, and that he could not get enough to eat, and that his existence was apparently forgotten, and that he contracted the fever. But——

One cannot think of the terms in which to describe a futility so vast, so colossal. He had builded a little boat, and the sea had receded and left him and his boat a thousand miles inland on the top of a mountain. The war-fate had left Havana out of its plan and thus isolated Johnnie and his several pounds of useful information. The war-fate left Havana to become the somewhat indignant victim of a peaceful occupation at the close of the conflict, and Johnnie's data was worth as much as a carpenter's lien on the North Pole. He had suffered and labored for about as complete a bit of absolute nothing as one could invent. If the company which owned the sugar plantation had not generously continued his salary during the war he would not have been able to pay his expenses on the amount allowed him by the government, which, by the way, was a more complete bit of absolute nothing than one could possibly invent.

IV

I met Johnnie in Havana in October, 1898. If I remember rightly the U.S.S. *Resolute* and the U.S.S. *Scorpion* were in the harbor, but beyond these two terrible engines of destruction there was not as yet any of the more stern signs of the American success. Many Americans were to be seen in the streets of Havana where they were not in any way molested. Among them was Johnnie in white duck and a straw hat, cool, complacent and with eyes rather more steady than ever. I addressed him upon the subject of his supreme failure, but I could not perturb his philosophy. In reply he simply asked me to dinner. "Come to the Café Aguacate at half-past seven to-night," he said. "I haven't been there in a long time. We shall see if they cook as well as ever." I turned up promptly and found Johnnie in a private room smoking a cigar in the presence of a waiter who was blue in the gills. "I've ordered the dinner." he said cheerfully. "Now I want to see if you won't be surprised how well they can do here in Havana." I was surprised. I was dumfounded. Rarely in the history of the world have two rational men sat down to such a dinner. It must have taxed the ability and endurance of the entire working force of the establishment to provide it. The variety of dishes was of course related to the markets of Havana, but the abundance and general profligacy was related only to Johnnie's imagination. Neither of us had an appetite. Our fancies fled in confusion before this puzzling luxury. I looked at Johnnie as if he were a native of Thibet. I had thought him to be a most simple man, and here I found him revelling in food like a fat old senator of Rome's decadence. And if the dinner itself put me to open-eyed amazement, the names of the wines finished everything. Apparently Johnnie had had but one standard, and that was the cost. If a wine had been very expensive, he had ordered it. I began to think him probably a maniac. At any rate, I was sure that we were both fools. Seeing my fixed stare, he spoke with affected languor: "I wish peacocks' brains and melted pearls were to be had here in Havana. We'd have 'em." Then he grinned. As a mere skirmisher I said: "In New York we think we dine well; but really this, you know—well—Havana——"

Johnnie waved his hand pompously. "Oh, I know."

Directly after coffee Johnnie excused himself for a moment and left the room. When he returned he said briskly, "Well, are you ready to go?" As soon as we were in a cab and safely out of hearing of the Café Aguacate Johnnie lay back and laughed long and joyously.

But I was very serious. "Look here, Johnnie," I said to him solemnly, "when you invite me to dine with you don't you ever do *that* again. And I'll tell you one thing—when you dine with me you will probably get the ordinary table d'hôte." I was an older man.

"Oh, that's all right," he cried. And then he too grew serious. "Well, as far as I am concerned—as far as I am concerned," he said, "the war is now over."

WAR MEMORIES

BUT to get the real thing!" cried Vernall, the war correspondent. "It seems impossible! It is because war is neither
magnificent nor squalid; it is simply life, and an expression of life can always evade us. We can never tell life, one to
another, although sometimes we think we can."

When I climbed aboard the despatch-boat at Key West the
mate told me irritably that, as soon as we crossed the bar, we
would find ourselves monkey-climbing over heavy seas. It wasn't
my fault, but he seemed to insinuate that it was all a result of
my incapacity. There were four correspondents in the party. The
leader of us came aboard with a huge bunch of bananas, which
he hung like a chandelier in the centre of the tiny cabin. We
made acquaintance over, around, and under this bunch of bananas, which really occupied the cabin as a soldier occupies a
sentry box. But the bunch did not become really aggressive until
we were well at sea. Then it began to spar. With the first roll of
the ship, it launched its bulk at McCurdy and knocked him
wildly through the door to the deck-rail, where he hung cursing
hysterically. Without a moment's pause, it made for me. I flung
myself head-first into my bunk and watched the demon sweep
Brownlow into a corner and wedge his knee behind a sea-chest.
Kary gave a shrill cry and fled. The bunch of bananas swung to
and fro, silent, determined, ferocious, looking for more men. It
had cleared a space for itself. My comrades looked in at the door,
calling upon me to grab the thing and hold it. I pointed out to
them the security and comfort of my position. They were angry.
Finally the mate came and lashed the thing so that it could not
prowl about the cabin and assault innocent war correspondents.
You see? War! A bunch of bananas rampant because the ship
rolled.

In that early period of the war we were forced to continue our dreams. And we were all dreamers, envisioning the sea with death grapples, ship and ship. Even the navy grew cynical. Officers on the bridge lifted their megaphones and told you in resigned voices that they were out of ice, onions, and eggs. At other times they would shoot quite casually at us with six-pounders. This industry usually progressed in the night, but it sometimes happened in the day. There was never any resentment on our side, although at moments there was some nervousness. They were impressively quick with their lanyards; our means of replying to signals were correspondingly slow. They gave you opportunity to say, "Heaven guard me!" Then they shot. But we recognized the propriety of it. Everything was correct save the war, which lagged and lagged and lagged. It did not play; it was not a gory giant; it was a bunch of bananas swung in the middle of the cabin.

Once we had the honor of being rammed at midnight by the U.S.S. *Machias*. In fact the exceeding industry of the naval commanders of the Cuban blockading fleet caused a certain liveliness to at times penetrate our mediocre existence. We were all greatly entertained over an immediate prospect of being either killed by rapid fire guns, cut in half by the ram or merely drowned, but even our great longing for diversion could not cause us to ever again go near the *Machias* on a dark night. We had sailed from Key West on a mission that had nothing to do with the coast of Cuba, and steaming due east and some thirty-five miles from the Cuban land, we did not think we were liable to an affair with any of the fierce American cruisers. Suddenly a familiar signal of red and white lights flashed like a brooch of jewels on the pall that covered the sea. It was far away and tiny, but we knew all about it. It was the electric question of an American war-ship and it demanded a swift answer in kind. The man behind the gun! What about the man in front of the gun? The war-ship signals vanished and the sea presented nothing but a smoky black stretch lit with the hissing white tops of the flying waves. A thin line of flame swept from a gun.

Thereafter followed one of those silences which had become so peculiarly instructive to the blockade-runner. Somewhere in the darkness we knew that a slate-colored cruiser, red below the waterline and with a gold scroll on her bows, was flying over the waves toward us, while upon the dark decks the men stood at general quarters in silence about the long thin guns, and it was the law of life and death that we should make true answer in about the twelfth part of a second. Now I shall with regret disclose a certain dreadful secret of the despatch-boat service. Our signals, far from being electric, were two lanterns which we kept in a tub and covered with a tarpaulin. The tub was placed just forward of the pilot-house, and when we were accosted at night it was everybody's duty to scramble wildly for the tub and grab out the lanterns and wave them. It amounted to a slowness of speech. I remember a story of an army sentry who upon hearing a noise in his front one dark night called his usual sharp query. "Halt—who's there? Halt or I'll fire!" And getting no immediate response he fired even as he had said, killing a man with a hair-lip who unfortunately could not arrange his vocal machinery to reply in season. We were something like a boat with a hair-lip. And sometimes it was very trying to the nerves. . . . The pause was long. Then a voice spoke from the sea through a megaphone. It was faint but clear. "What ship is that?" No one hesitated over his answer in cases of this kind. Everybody was desirous of imparting fullest information. There was another pause. Then out of the darkness flew an American cruiser, silent as death, handled as ferociously as if the devil commanded her. Again the little voice hailed from the bridge. "What ship is that?" Evidently the reply to the first hail had been misunderstood or not heard. This time the voice rang with menace, menace of immediate and certain destruction, and the last word was intoned savagely and strangely across the windy darkness as if the officer would explain that the cruiser was after either fools or the common enemy. The yells in return did not stop her. She was hurling herself forward to ram us amidships, and the people on the little *Three Friends* looked at a tall swooping bow, and it was keener than any knife that has ever been made. As the cruiser lunged every man imagined the gallant and famous but frail *Three Friends* cut into two parts as neatly as if she had been cheese. But there was a sheer and a hard sheer to starboard, and down upon our quarter swung a monstrous thing larger than any ship in the world—the U.S.S. *Machias*. She had a freeboard of about three hundred feet and the top of her funnel was out of sight in the clouds like an Alp. I shouldn't wonder that at the top of that funnel there was a region of perpetual snow. And at a range which swiftly narrowed to nothing every gun in her port-battery swung deliberately into aim. It was closer, more deliciously intimate than a duel across a handkerchief. We all had an opportunity of looking miles down the muzzles of this festive artillery before came the collision. Then the *Machias* reeled her steel shoulder against the wooden side of the *Three Friends* and up went a roar as if a vast shingle roof had fallen. The poor little tug dipped as if she meant to pass under the war-ship, staggered and finally righted, trembling from head to foot. The cries of the splintered timbers ceased. The men on the tug gazed at each other with white faces shining faintly in the darkness. The *Machias* backed away even as the *Three Friends* drew slowly ahead, and again we were alone with the piping of the wind and the slash of the gale-driven water. Later, from some hidden part of the sea, the bullish eye of a search-light looked at us and the widening white rays bathed us in the glare. There was another hail. "Hello there, *Three Friends!*" "Ay, ay, sir!" "Are you injured?" Our first mate had taken a lantern and was studying the side of the tug, and we held our breath for his answer. I was sure that he was going to say that we were sinking. Surely there could be no other ending to this terrific bloodthirsty assault. But the first mate said, "No, sir." Instantly the glare of the search-light was gone; the *Machias* was gone; the incident was closed.

I was dining once on board the flagship, the *New York*, armored cruiser. It was the junior officers' mess, and when the coffee came, a young ensign went to the piano and began to bang out a popular tune. It was a cheerful scene and it resembled only a cheerful scene. Suddenly we heard the whistle of the bos'n's mate, and directly above us, it seemed, a voice, hoarse as that of a sea-lion, bellowed a command: "Man the port battery." In a moment the table was vacant; the popular tune ceased in a jangle. On the quarter-deck assembled a group of officers—spectators. The quiet evening sea, lit with faint red lights, went peacefully to the feet of a verdant shore. One could hear the far-away measured tumbling of surf upon a reef. Only this sound pulsed in the air. The great grey cruiser was as still as the earth, the sea, and the sky. Then they let off a four-inch gun directly under my feet. I thought it turned me a back-somersault. That was the effect upon my mind. But it appears I did not move. The shell went carousing off to the Cuban shore, and from the vegetation there spirted a cloud of dust. Some of the officers on the quarter-deck laughed. Through their glasses they had seen a Spanish column of cavalry much agitated by the appearance of this shell among them. As far as I was concerned, there was nothing but the spirt of dust from the side of a long-suffering island. When I returned to my coffee I found that most of the young officers had also returned. Japanese boys were bringing liquors. The piano's clattering of the popular air was often interrupted by the boom of a four-inch gun. A bunch of bananas!

One day, our despatch-boat found the shores of Guantanamo Bay flowing past on either side. It was at nightfall, and on the eastward point a small village was burning, and it happened that a fiery light was thrown upon some palm-trees so that it made them into enormous crimson feathers. The water was the color of blue steel; the Cuban woods were sombre; high shivered the gory feathers. The last boatloads of the marine battalion were pulling for the beach. The marine officers gave me generous hospitality to the camp on the hill. That night there was an alarm, and, amid a stern calling of orders and a rushing of men, I wandered in search of some other man who had no occupation. It turned out to be the young assistant-surgeon, Gibbs. We foregathered in the centre of a square of six companies of marines. There was no firing. We thought it rather comic. The next night there was an alarm; there was some firing; we lay on our bellies; it was no longer comic. On the third night the alarm came early; I went in search of Gibbs, but I soon gave over an active search for the more congenial occupation of lying flat and feeling the hot hiss of the bullets trying to cut my hair. For the moment I was no longer a cynic. I was a child who, in a fit of ignorance, had jumped into the vat of war. I heard somebody dying near me. He was dying hard. Hard. It took him a long time to die. He breathed as all noble machinery breathes when it is making its gallant strife against breaking, breaking. But he was going to break. He was going to break. It seemed to me, this breathing, the noise of a heroic pump which strives to subdue a mud which comes upon it in tons. The darkness was impenetrable. The man was lying in some depression within seven feet of me. Every wave, vibration, of his anguish beat upon my senses. He was long past groaning. There was only the bitter strife for air which pulsed out into the night in a clear penetrating whistle, with intervals of terrible silence in which I held my own breath in the common unconscious aspiration to help. I thought this man would never die. I wanted him to die. Ultimately he died. At the moment, the adjutant came bustling along erect amid the spitting bullets. I knew him by his voice. "Where's the doctor? There's some wounded men over there. Where's the doctor?" A man answered briskly: "Just died this minute, sir." It was as if he had said: "Just gone around the corner this minute, sir." Despite the horror of this night's business, the man's mind was somehow influenced by the coincidence of the adjutant's calling aloud for the doctor within a few seconds of the doctor's death. It—what shall I say?—It interested him, this coincidence.

The day broke by inches, with an obvious and maddening reluctance. From some unfathomable source I procured an opinion that my friend was not dead at all—the wild and quivering darkness had caused me to misinterpret a few shouted words. At length, the land brightened in a violet atmosphere, the perfect dawning of a tropic day, and in this light I saw a clump of men near me. At first I thought they were all dead. Then I thought they were all asleep. The truth was that a group of wan-faced exhausted men had gone to sleep about Gibbs' body so closely and in such abandoned attitudes that one's eye could not pick the living from the dead until one saw that a certain head had beneath it a great dark pool.

In the afternoon a lot of the men went bathing, and in the midst of this festivity firing was resumed. It was funny to see the men come scampering out of the water, grab at their rifles, and go into action attired in nought but their cartridge belts. The attack of the Spaniards had interrupted in some degree the services over the graves of Gibbs and some others. I remember Paine came ashore with a bottle of whisky which I took from him violently. My faithful shooting boots began to hurt me, and I went to the beach and poulticed my feet in wet clay, sitting on the little rickety pier near where the corrugated iron cable-station showed how the shells slivered through it. Some marines, desirous of mementoes, were poking with sticks in the smoking ruins of the hamlet. Down in the shallow water crabs were meandering among the weeds, and little fishes moved slowly in shoals.

The next day we went shooting. It was exactly like quail shooting. I'll tell you. These guerillas who so cursed our lives had a well some five miles away, and it was the only water supply within about twelve miles of the marine camp. It was decided that it would be correct to go forth and destroy the well. Captain Elliott of C company was to take his men with Captain Spicer's company, D, out to the well, beat the enemy away and destroy everything. He was to start at the next daybreak. He asked me if I cared to go, and, of course, I accepted with glee; but all that night I was afraid. Bitterly afraid. The moon was very bright, shedding a magnificent radiance upon the trenches. I watched the men of C and D companies lying so tranquilly—some snoring, confound them—whereas I was certain that I could never sleep with the weight of a coming battle upon my mind, a battle in which the poor life of a war correspondent might easily be taken by a careless enemy. But if I was frightened I was also very cold. It was a chill night, and I wanted a heavy top-coat almost as much as I wanted a certificate of immunity from rifle bullets. These two feelings were of equal importance to my mind. They were twins. Elliott came and flung a tent-fly over Lieutenant Bannon and me as we lay on the ground back of the men. Then I was no longer cold, but I was still afraid, for tent-flys cannot mend a fear. In the morning I wished for some mild attack of disease, something that would incapacitate me for the business of going out gratuitously to be bombarded. But I was in an awkwardly healthy state, and so I must needs smile and look pleased with my prospects. We were to be guided by fifty Cubans, and I gave up all dreams of a postponement when I saw them shambling off in single file through the cactus. We followed presently. "Where you people goin' to?" "Don't know, Jim." "Well, good luck to you, boys." This was the world's lazy inquiry and conventional God-speed. Then the mysterious wilderness swallowed us.

The men were silent because they were ordered to be silent, but whatever faces I could observe were marked with a look of serious meditation. As they trudged slowly in single file they were reflecting upon—what? I don't know. But at length we came to ground more open. The sea appeared on our right, and we saw the gunboat *Dolphin* steaming along in a line parallel to ours. I was as glad to see her as if she had called out my name. The trail wound about the bases of some high bare spurs. If the Spaniards had occupied them I don't see how we could have gone further. But upon them were only the dove-voiced guerilla scouts calling back into the hills the news of our approach. The effect of sound is of course relative. I am sure I have never heard such a horrible sound as the beautiful cooing of the wood-dove when I was certain that it came from the yellow throat of a guerilla. Elliott sent Lieutenant Lucas with his platoon to ascend the hills and cover our advance by the trail. We halted and watched them climb, a long black streak of men in the vivid sunshine of the hillside. We did not know how tall were these hills until we saw Lucas and his men on top, and they were no larger than specks. We marched on until, at last, we heard—it seemed in the sky— the sputter of firing. This devil's dance was begun. The proper strategic movement to cover the crisis seemed to me to be to run away home and swear I had never started on this expedition. But Elliott yelled: "Now, men; straight up this hill." The men charged up against the cactus, and, because I cared for the opinion of others, I found myself tagging along close at Elliott's heels. I don't know how I got up that hill, but I think it was because I was afraid to be left behind. The immediate rear did not look safe. The crowd of strong young marines afforded the only spectacle of provisional security. So I tagged along at Elliott's heels. The hill was as steep as a Swiss roof. From it sprang out great pillars of cactus, and the human instinct was to assist one's self in the ascent by grasping cactus with one's hands. I remember the watch I had to keep upon this human instinct even when the sound of the bullets was attracting my nervous attention. However, the great thing to my sense at the time was the fact that every man of the marines was also climbing away like mad. It was one thing for Elliott, Spicer, Neville, Shaw, and Bannon; it was another thing for me; but—what in the devil was it to the men? Not the same thing, surely. It was perfectly easy for any marine to get overcome by the burning heat and, lying down, bequeath the work and the danger to his comrades. The fine thing about "the men" is that you can't explain them. I mean when you take them collectively. They do a thing, and afterward you find that they have done it because they have done it. However, when Elliott arrived at the top of the ridge, myself and many other men were with him. But there was no battle scene. Off on another ridge we could see Lucas' men and the Cubans peppering away into a valley. The bullets about our ears were really intended to lodge in them. We went over there.

I walked along the firing line and looked at the men. I kept somewhat on what I shall call the *lee* side of the ridge. Why? Because I was afraid of being shot. No other reason. Most of the men as they lay flat, shooting, looked contented, almost happy. They were pleased, these men, at the situation. I don't know. I cannot imagine. But they were pleased, at any rate. I wasn't pleased. I was picturing defeat. I was saying to myself: "Now if they, the enemy, should suddenly do so-and-so, or so-and-so, why —what would become of me?" During these first few moments I did not see the Spanish position because—I was afraid to look at it. Bullets were hissing and spitting over the crest of the ridge in such showers as to make observation to be a task for a brave man. No, now, look here, why the deuce should I have stuck my head up, eh? Why? Well, at any rate, I didn't until it seemed to be a far less thing than most of the men were doing as if they liked it. Then I saw—nothing. At least it was only the bottom of a small valley. In this valley there was a thicket—a big thicket— and this thicket seemed to be crowded with a mysterious class of persons who were evidently trying to kill us. Our enemies? Yes —perhaps—I suppose so. Leave that to the people in the streets at home. They know and cry against the public enemy, but when men go into actual battle not one in a thousand concerns himself with an animus against the men who face him. The great desire is to beat them, beat them whoever they are, as a matter, first, of personal safety; second, of personal glory. It is always safest to make the other chap quickly run away. And as he runs away, one feels, as one tries to hit him in the back and knock him sprawling, that he must be a very good and sensible fellow. But these people apparently did not mean to run away. They clung to their thicket, and amid the roar of the firing one could sometimes hear their wild yells of insult and defiance. They were actually the most obstinate, headstrong, mulish people that you could ever imagine. The *Dolphin* was throwing shells into their immediate vicinity, and the fire from the marines and Cubans was very rapid and heavy, but still those incomprehensible mortals remained in their thicket. The scene on the top of the ridge was very wild, but there was only one truly romantic figure. This was a Cuban officer who held in one hand a great glittering machete and in the other a cocked revolver. He posed like a statue of victory. Afterward he confessed to me that he alone had been responsible for the winning of the fight. But outside of this splendid person it was simply a picture of men at work, men terribly hard at work, red-faced, sweating, gasping toilers. A Cuban negro soldier was shot through the heart, and one man took the body on his back and another took it by its feet and trundled away toward the rear looking precisely like a wheelbarrow. A man in C company was shot through the ankle, and he sat behind the line nursing his wound. Apparently he was pleased with it. It seemed to suit him. I don't know why. But beside him sat a comrade with a face drawn, solemn and responsible, like that of a New England spinster at the bedside of a sick child.

The fight banged away with a roar like a forest fire. Suddenly a marine wriggled out of the firing line and came frantically to me. "Say, young feller, I'll give you five dollars for a drink of whisky." He tried to force into my hand a gold piece. "Go to the devil," said I, deeply scandalized. "Besides, I haven't got any whisky." "No, but look here," he beseeched me. "If I don't get a drink I'll die. And I'll give you five dollars for it. Honest, I will." I finally tried to escape from him by walking away, but he followed at my heels, importuning me with all the exasperating persistence of a professional beggar and trying to force this ghastly gold piece into my hand. I could not shake him off, and amid that clatter of furious fighting I found myself intensely embarrassed, and glancing fearfully this way and that way to make sure that people did not see me, the villain and his gold. In vain I assured him that if I had any whisky I should place it at his disposal. He could not be turned away. I thought of the European expedient in such a crisis—to jump in a cab. But unfortunately—— In the meantime I had given up my occupation of tagging at Captain Elliott's heels, because his business required that he should go into places of great danger. But from time to time I was under his attention. Once he turned to me and said: "Mr. Vernall, will you go and satisfy yourself who those people are?" Some men had appeared on a hill about six hundred yards from our left flank. "Yes, sir," cried I with, I assure you, the finest alacrity and cheerfulness, and my tone proved to me that I had inherited histrionic abilities. This tone was of course a black lie, but I went off briskly and was as jaunty as a real soldier, while all the time my heart was in my boots and I was cursing the day that saw me landed on the shores of the tragic isle. If the men on the distant hill had been guerillas, my future might have been seriously jeopardized, but I had not gone far toward them when I was able to recognize the uniforms of the Marine Corps. Whereupon I scampered back to the firing line and with the same alacrity and cheerfulness reported my information. I mention to you that I was afraid because there were about me that day many men who did not seem to be afraid at all, men with quiet, composed faces, who went about this business as if they proceeded from a sense of habit. They were not old soldiers; they were mainly recruits, but many of them betrayed all the emotion and merely the emotion that one sees in the face of a man earnestly at work.

I don't know how long the action lasted. I remember deciding in my own mind that the Spaniards stood forty minutes. This was a mere arbitrary decision based on nothing. But at any rate we finally arrived at the satisfactory moment when the enemy began to run away. I shall never forget how my courage increased. And then began the great bird shooting. From the far side of the thicket arose an easy slope covered with plum-colored bush. The Spaniards broke in coveys of from six to fifteen men —or birds—and swarmed up this slope. The marines on our ridge then had some fine open field shooting. No charge could be made because the shells from the *Dolphin* were helping the Spaniards to evacuate the thicket, so the marines had to be content with this extraordinary paraphrase of a kind of sport. It was strangely like the original. The shells from the *Dolphin* were the dogs; dogs who went in and stirred out the game. The marines were suddenly gentlemen in leggings, alive with the sharp instinct which marks the hunter. The Spaniards were the birds. Yes, they were the birds, but I doubt if they would sympathize with my metaphors.

We destroyed their camp, and when the tiled roof of a burning house fell with a crash, it was so like the crash of a strong volley of musketry that we all turned with a start, fearing that we would have to fight again on that same day. And this struck me at least as being an impossible thing. They gave us water from the *Dolphin* and we filled our canteens. None of the men were particularly jubilant. They did not altogether appreciate their victory. They were occupied in being glad that the fight was over. I discovered to my amazement that we were on the summit of a hill so high that our released eyes seemed to sweep over half the world. The vast stretch of sea, shimmering like fragile blue silk in the breeze, lost itself ultimately in an indefinite pink haze, while in the other direction, ridge after ridge, ridge and ridge, rolled brown and arid into the north. The battle had been fought high in air, where rain-clouds might have been. That is why everybody's face was the color of beetroot, and men lay on the ground and only swore feebly when the cactus spurs sank into them.

Finally we started for camp, leaving our wounded, our cactus pin-cushions, and our heat-prostrated men on board the *Dolphin*. I did not see that the men were elate or even grinning with satisfaction. They seemed only anxious to get to food and rest. And yet it was plain that Elliott and his men had performed a service that would prove invaluable to the security and comfort of the entire battalion. They had driven the guerrillas to take a road along which they would have to proceed for fifteen miles before they could get as much water as would wet the point of a pin. And by the destruction of a well at the scene of the fight Elliott made an arid zone almost twenty miles wide between the enemy and the base camp. In Cuba this is the best of protection. However, a cup of coffee! Time enough to think of a brilliant success after one had had a cup of coffee. The long line plodded wearily through the dusky jungle, which was never again to be alive with ambushes.

It was dark when we stumbled into camp, and I was sad with an ungovernable sadness because I was too tired to remember where I had left my kit. But some of my colleagues were waiting on the beach, and they put me on a despatch-boat to take my news to a Jamaica cable-station. The appearance of this despatch-boat struck me with wonder. It was reminiscent of something with which I had been familiar in early years. I looked with dull surprise at three men of the engine-room force who sat aft on some bags of coal smoking their pipes and talking as if there had never been any battles fought anywhere. The sudden clang of the gong made me start and listen eagerly, as if I would be asking, "What was that?" The chunking of the screw affected me also, but I seemed to relate it to a former and pleasing experience. One of the correspondents on board immediately began to tell me of the chief engineer, who, he said, was a comic old character. I was taken to see this marvel, which presented itself as a grey-bearded man with an oil can, who had the cynical, malicious, egotistic eye of proclaimed and admired ignorance. I looked dazedly at the venerable impostor. What had he to do with battles—the humming click of the locks, the odor of burnt cotton, the bullets, the firing? My friend told the scoundrel that I was just returned from the afternoon's action. He said, "That so?" and looked at me with a smile, faintly, faintly derisive. You see? I had just come out of my life's most fiery time, and that old devil looked at me with that smile. What colossal conceit! The four-times-damned, doddering old head-mechanic of a derelict junk-shop! The whole trouble lay in the fact that I had not shouted out with mingled awe and joy as he stood there in his wisdom and experience with all his ancient saws and home-made epigrams ready to fire.

My friend took me to the cabin. What a squalid hole! My heart sank. The reward after the labor should have been a great airy chamber, a gigantic four-poster, iced melons, grilled birds, wine, and the delighted attendance of my friends. When I had finished my cablegram I retired to a little shelf of a berth, which reeked of oil, while the blankets had soaked recently with sea-water. The vessel heeled to leeward in spasmodic attempts to hurl me out, and I resisted with the last of my strength. The infamous pettiness of it all! I thought the night would never end. "But, never mind," I said to myself at last, "to-morrow in Port Antonio I shall have a great bath and fine raiment, and I shall dine grandly, and there will be lager beer on ice. And there will be attendants to run when I touch a bell, and I shall catch every interested romantist in the town and spin him the story of the fight at Cusco." We reached Port Antonio, and I fled from the cable office to the hotel. I procured the bath, and, as I donned whatever fine raiment I had foraged, I called the boy and pompously told him of a dinner—a Real Dinner, with furbelows and complications and yet with a basis of sincerity. He looked at me calf-like for a moment and then he went away. After a long interval the manager himself appeared and asked me some questions, which led me to see that he thought I had attempted to undermine and disintegrate the intellect of the boy by the elocution of Arabic incantations. Well, never mind! In the end the manager of the hotel elicited from me that great cry, that cry which during the war rang piteously from thousands of throats, that last grand cry of anguish and despair: *"Well, then, in the name of God, can I have a cold bottle of beer?"*

Well, you see to what war brings men? War is death, and a plague of the lack of small things, and toil. Nor did I catch my sentimentalists and pour forth my tale to them, and thrill, appal, and fascinate them. However, they did feel an interest in me, for I heard a lady at the hotel ask, "Who *is* that chap in the very dirty jack-boots?" So you see that, whereas you can be very much frightened upon going into action, you can also be greatly annoyed after you have come out.

Later, I fell into the hands of one of my closest friends, and he mercilessly outlined a scheme for landing to the west of Santiago and getting through the Spanish lines to some place from which we could view the Spanish squadron lying in the harbor. There was rumor that the *Viscaya* had escaped, he said, and it would be very nice to make sure of the truth. So we steamed to a point opposite a Cuban camp which my friend knew, and flung two crop-tailed Jamaica polo-ponies into the sea. We followed in a small boat and were met on the beach by a small Cuban detachment, who immediately caught our ponies and saddled them for us. I suppose we felt rather godlike. We were almost the first Americans they had seen, and they looked at us with eyes of grateful affection. I don't suppose many men have the experience of being looked at with eyes of grateful affection. They guided us to a Cuban camp where, in a little palm-bark hut, a black-faced lieutenant-colonel was lolling in a hammock. I couldn't understand what was said, but, at any rate, he must have ordered his half-naked orderly to make coffee, for it was done. It was a dark syrup in smoky tin cups, but it was better than the cold bottle of beer which I did not drink in Jamaica.

The Cuban camp was an expeditious affair of saplings and palm-bark tied with creepers. It could be burned to the ground in fifteen minutes, and in ten reduplicated. The soldiers were in appearance an absolutely good-natured set of half-starved raga-muffins. Their breeches hung in shreds about their black legs, and their shirts were as nothing. They looked like a collection of real tropic savages at whom some philanthropist had flung a bundle of rags, and some of the rags had stuck here and there. But their condition was now a habit. I doubt if they knew they were half-naked. Anyhow, they didn't care. No more they should; the weather was warm. This lieutenant-colonel gave us an escort of five or six men, and we went up into the mountains, lying flat on our Jamaica ponies while they went like rats up and down extraordinary trails. In the evening we reached the camp of a major who commanded the outposts. It was high, high in the hills. The stars were as big as cocoanuts. We lay in borrowed hammocks and watched the firelight gleam blood-red on the trees. I remember an utterly naked negro squatting, crimson, by the fire and cleaning an iron pot. Some voices were singing an Afric wail of forsaken love and death. And at dawn we were to try to steal through the Spanish lines! I was very, very sorry.

In the cold dawn, the situation was the same but somehow courage seemed to be in the breaking day. I went off with the others quite cheerfully. We came to where the pickets stood behind bulwarks of stone in frameworks of saplings. They were peering across a narrow cloud-steeped gulch at a dull fire mark-ing a Spanish post. There was some palaver and then, with fifteen men, we descended the side of this mountain, going down into the chill blue-and-grey clouds. We had left our horses with the Cuban pickets. We proceeded stealthily, for we were already within range of the Spanish pickets. At the bottom of the cañon it was still night. A brook, a regular salmon-stream, brawled over the rocks. There were grassy banks and most delightful trees.

The whole valley was a sylvan fragrance. But—the guide waved his arm and scowled warningly and in a moment we were off, threading thickets, climbing hills, crawling through fields on our hands and knees, sometimes sweeping like seventeen phantoms across a Spanish road. I was in a dream, but I kept my eye on the guide and halted to listen when he halted to listen and ambled onward when he ambled onward. Sometimes he turned and pantomimed as ably and fiercely as a man being stung by a thousand hornets. Then we knew that the situation was extremely delicate. We were now, of course, well inside the Spanish lines, and we ascended a great hill which overlooked the harbor of Santiago. There, tranquilly at anchor, lay the *Oquendo*, the *Maria Theresa*, the *Christobal Colon*, the *Viscaya*, the *Pluton*, the *Furor*. The bay was white in the sun, and the great black-hulled armored cruisers were impressive in a dignity massive yet graceful. We did not know that they were all doomed ships, soon to go out to a swift death. My friend drew maps and things, while I devoted myself to complete rest, blinking lazily at the Spanish squadron. We did not know that we were the last Americans to view them alive, and unhurt, and at peace. Then we retraced our way, at the same noiseless canter. I did not understand my condition until I considered that we were well through the Spanish lines and practically out of danger. Then I discovered that I was a dead man. The nervous force having evaporated I was a mere corpse. My limbs were of dough and my spinal cord burned within me as if it were a red-hot wire. But just at this time we were discovered by a Spanish patrol, and I ascertained that I was not dead at all. We ultimately reached the foot of the mother-mountain on whose shoulders were the Cuban pickets, and here I was so sure of safety that I could not resist the temptation to die again. I think I passed into eleven distinct stupors during the ascent of that mountain while the escort stood leaning on their Remingtons. We had done twenty-five miles at a sort of a man-gallop, never once using a beaten track, but always going promiscuously through the jungle and over the rocks. And many of the miles stood straight on end, so that it was as hard to come down as it was to go up. But during my stupors, the escort *stood*, mind you, and chatted in low voices. For all the signs they showed, we might have been starting. And they had had nothing to eat but mangoes for over eight days. Previous to the eight days, they had been living on mangoes and the carcass of a small lean pony. They were, in fact, of the stuff of Fenimore Cooper's Indians, only they made no preposterous orations. At the major's camp my friend and I agreed that if our worthy escort would send down a representative with us to the coast, we would send back to them whatever we could spare from the stores of our despatch-boat. With one voice the escort answered that they themselves would go the additional four leagues, as in these starving times they did not care to trust a representative, thank you. "They can't do it; they'll peg out; there must be a limit," I said. "No," answered my friend. "They're all right; they'd run three times around the whole island for a mouthful of beef." So we saddled up and put off with our fifteen Cuban infantrymen wagging along tirelessly behind us.

Sometimes, at foot of a precipitous hill a man asked permission to cling to my horse's tail, and then the Jamaica pony would snake him to the summit so swiftly that only his toes seemed to touch the rocks. And for this assistance the man was grateful. When we crowned the last great ridge we saw our squadron to the eastward spread in its patient semicircle about the mouth of the harbor. But as we wound toward the beach we saw a more dramatic thing—our own despatch-boat leaving the rendezvous and putting off to sea. Evidently we were late. Behind me were fifteen stomachs—empty. It was a frightful situation. My friend and I charged for the beach and those fifteen fools began to *run*.

It was no use. The despatch-boat went gaily away, trailing black smoke behind her. We turned in distress, wondering what we could say to that abused escort. If they massacred us I felt that it would be merely a virtuous reply to fate and they should in no ways be blamed. There are some things which a man's feelings will not allow him to endure after a diet of mangoes and pony. However, we perceived to our amazement that they were not indignant at all. They simply smiled and made a gesture which expressed an habitual pessimism. It was a philosophy which denied the existence of everything but mangoes and pony. It was the Americans who refused to be comforted. I made a deep vow with myself that I would come as soon as possible and play a regular Santa Claus to that splendid escort. But we put to sea in a dug-out, with two black boys. The escort waved us a hearty good-bye from the shore and I never saw them again. I hope they are all in the police force in the new Santiago.

In time we were rescued from the dug-out by our despatch-boat, and we relieved our feelings by over-rewarding the two black boys. In fact they reaped a harvest because of our emotion over our failure to fill the gallant stomachs of the escort. They were two rascals. We steamed to the flagship and were given permission to board her. Admiral Sampson is to me the most interesting personality of the war. I would not know how to sketch him for you even if I could pretend to sufficient material. Anyhow, imagine, first of all, a marble block of impassivity out of which is carved the figure of an old man. Endow this with life, and you've just begun. Then you must discard all your pictures of bluff, red-faced old gentlemen who roar against the gale, and understand that the quiet old man is a sailor and an admiral. This will be difficult; if I told you he was anything else it would be easy. He resembles other types; it is his distinction not to resemble the preconceived type of his standing. When first I met him I was impressed that he was immensely bored by the war and with the command of the North Atlantic Squadron. I perceived a manner where I thought I perceived a mood, a point of view. Later, he seemed so indifferent to small things which bore upon large things that I bowed to his apathy as a thing unprecedented, marvellous. Still I mistook a manner for a mood. Still I could not understand that this was the way of the man. I am not to blame, for my communication was slight and depended upon sufferance—upon, in fact, the traditional courtesy of the navy. But finally I saw that it was all manner, that hidden in his indifferent, even apathetic, manner, there was the alert, sure, fine mind of the best sea-captain that America has produced since—since Farragut? I don't know. I think—since Hull.

Men follow heartily when they are well led. They balk at trifles when a blockhead cries "Go on." For my part, an impressive thing of the war is the absolute devotion to Admiral Sampson's person—no, to his judgment and wisdom—which was paid by his ship commanders—Evans of the *Iowa*, Taylor of the *Oregon*, Higginson of the *Massachusetts*, Phillips of the *Texas*, and all the other captains—barring one. Once, afterward, they called upon him to avenge himself upon a rival—they were there and they would have to say—but he said no-o-o, he guessed it—wouldn't do—any—g-o-oo-o-d—to the—service.

Men feared him, but he never made threats; men tumbled heels over head to obey him, but he never gave a sharp order; men loved him, but he had said no word, kindly or unkindly; men cheered for him and he said: "Who are they yelling for?" Men behaved badly to him and he said nothing. Men thought of glory and he considered the management of ships. All without a sound. A noiseless campaign on his part. No bunting, no arches, no fireworks; nothing but the perfect management of a big fleet. That is a record for you. No trumpets, no cheers of the populace. Just plain, pure, unsauced accomplishment. But ultimately he will reap his reward in—in what? In text-books on sea campaigns. No more. The people choose their own and they choose the kind they like. Who has a better right? Anyhow he is a great man. And when you are once started you can continue to be a great man without the help of bouquets and banquets. He don't need them—bless your heart!

The flagship's battle-hatches were down, and between decks it was insufferable, despite the electric fans. I made my way somewhat forwards, past the smart orderly, past the companion, on to the den of the junior mess. Even there they were playing cards in somebody's cabin. "Hello, old man. Been ashore? How'd it look? It's your deal, Chick." There was nothing but steamy wet heat and the decent suppression of the consequent ill-tempers. The junior officers' quarters were no more comfortable than the admiral's cabin. I had expected it to be so because of my remembrance of their gay spirits. But they were not gay. They were sweltering. Hello, old man, had I been ashore? I fled to the deck, where other officers not on duty were smoking quiet cigars. The hospitality of the officers of the flagship is another charming memory of the war.

I rolled into my berth on the despatch-boat that night feeling a perfect wonder of the day. Was the figure that leaned over the card game on the flagship, the figure with a whisky-and-soda in its hand and a cigar in its teeth—was it identical with the figure scrambling, afraid of its life, through Cuban jungle? Was it the figure of the situation of the fifteen pathetic hungry men? It was the same, and it went to sleep, hard sleep. I don't know where we voyaged. I think it was Jamaica. But, at any rate, upon the morning of our return to the Cuban coast, we found the sea alive with transports—United States transports from Tampa, containing the Fifth Army Corps under Major-General Shafter. The rigging and the decks of these ships were black with men, and everybody wanted to land first. I landed, ultimately, and immediately began to look for an acquaintance. The boats were banged by the waves against a little flimsy dock. I fell ashore somehow, but I did not at once find an acquaintance. I talked to a private in the 2nd Massachusetts Volunteers, who told me that he was going to write war correspondence for a Boston newspaper. This statement did not surprise me.

There was a straggly village, but I followed the troops, who at this time seemed to be moving out by companies. I found three other correspondents, and it was luncheon time. Somebody had two bottles of Bass, but it was so warm that it squirted out in foam. There was no firing, no noise of any kind. An old shed was full of soldiers, loafing pleasantly in the shade. It was a hot, dusty, sleepy afternoon; bees hummed. We saw Major-General Lawton standing with his staff under a tree. He was smiling as if he would say: "Well, this will be better than chasing Apaches." His division had the advance, and so he had a right to be happy. A tall man with a grey moustache, lithe but very strong, an ideal cavalryman. He appealed to one all the more because of the vague rumors that his superiors—some of them—were going to take mighty good care that he shouldn't get much to do. It was rather sickening to hear such talk, but later we knew that most of it must have been mere lies.

Down by the landing-place a band of correspondents were making a sort of permanent camp. They worked like Trojans, carrying wall-tents, cots, and boxes of provisions. They asked me to join them, but I looked shrewdly at the sweat on their faces and backed away. The next day the army left this permanent camp eight miles to the rear. The day became tedious. I was glad when evening came. I sat by a camp-fire and listened to a soldier of the 8th Infantry, who told me he was the first enlisted man to land. I lay pretending to appreciate him, but in fact I considered him a great shameless liar. Less than a month ago, I learned that every word he said was gospel truth. I was much surprised. We went for breakfast to the camp of the 20th Infantry, where Captain Greene and his subaltern, Exton, gave us tomatoes stewed with hard bread, and coffee. Later, I discovered Greene and Exton down at the beach good-naturedly dodging the waves, which seemed to be trying to prevent them from washing the breakfast dishes. I felt tremendously ashamed because my cup and my plate were there, you know, and—— Fate provides some men greased opportunities for making dizzy jackasses of themselves, and I fell a victim to my flurry on this occasion. I *was* a blockhead. I walked away, blushing. What? The battles? Yes, I saw something of all of them. I made up my mind that the next time I met Greene and Exton, I'd say: "Look here; why didn't you tell me you had to wash your own dishes that morning, so that I could have helped? I felt beastly when I saw you scrubbing there. And me walking around idly." But I never saw Captain Greene again. I think he is in the Philippines now, fighting the Tagals. The next time I saw Exton—what? Yes, La Guasimas. That was the "rough-rider fight." However, the next time I saw Exton I—what do you think? I forgot to speak about it. But if ever I meet Greene or Exton again—even if it should be twenty years—I am going to say, first thing: "Why——" What? Yes. Roosevelt's regiment and the First and Tenth Regular Cavalry. I'll say, first thing: "Say, why didn't you tell me you had to wash your own dishes, that morning, so that I could have helped?" My stupidity will be on my conscience until I die, if, before that, I do not meet either Greene or Exton. Oh yes, you are howling for blood, but I tell you it is more emphatic that I lost my toothbrush. Did I tell you that? Well, I lost it, you see, and I thought of it for ten hours at a stretch. Oh yes—he? He was shot through the heart. But, look here, I contend that the French cable company buncoed us throughout the war. What? Him? My toothbrush I never found, but he died of his wound in time. Most of the regular soldiers carried their tooth-brushes stuck in the bands of their hats. It made a quaint military decoration. I have had a line of a thousand men pass me in the jungle and not a hat lacking the simple emblem.

The first of July? All right. My Jamaica polo-pony was not present. He was still in the hills to the westward of Santiago, but the Cubans had promised to fetch him to me. But my kit was easy to carry. It had nothing superfluous in it but a pair of spurs which made me indignant every time I looked at them. Oh, but I must tell you about a man I met directly after the La Guasimas fight. Edward Marshall, a correspondent whom I had known with a degree of intimacy for seven years, was terribly hit in that fight and asked me if I wouldn't go to Siboney—the base—and convey the news to his colleagues of the *New York Journal* and round-up some assistance. I went to Siboney, and there was not a *Journal* man to be seen, although usually you judged from appearances that the *Journal* staff was about as large as the army. Presently I met two correspondents, strangers to me, but I questioned them, saying that Marshall was badly shot and wished for such succor as *Journal* men could bring from their despatch-boat. And one of these correspondents replied. He is the man I wanted to describe. I love him as a brother. He said: "Marshall? Marshall? Why, Marshall isn't in Cuba at all. He left for New York just before the expedition sailed from Tampa." I said: "Beg pardon, but I remarked that Marshall was shot in the fight this morning, and have you seen any *Journal* people?" After a pause, he said: "I am sure Marshall is not down here at all. He's in New York." I said: "Pardon me, but I remarked that Marshall was shot in the fight this morning, and have you seen any *Journal* people?" He said: "No; now look here, you must have gotten two chaps mixed somehow. Marshall isn't in Cuba at all. How could he be shot?" I said: "Pardon me, but I remarked that Marshall was shot in the fight this morning, and have you seen any *Journal* people?" He said: "But it can't really be Marshall, you know, for the simple reason that he's not down here." I clasped my hands to my temples, gave one piercing cry to heaven and fled from his presence. I couldn't go on with him. He excelled me at all points. I have faced death by bullet, fire, water, and disease, but to die thus—to wilfully batter myself against the ironclad opinion of this mummy—no, no, not that. In the meantime, it was admitted that a correspondent was shot, be his name Marshall, Bismarck, or Louis XIV. Now, supposing the name of this wounded correspondent had been Bishop Potter? Or Jane Austen? Or Bernhardt? Or Henri Georges Stephane Adolphe Opper de Blowitz? What effect—never mind.

We will proceed to July 1. On that morning I marched with my kit—having everything essential save a tooth-brush—the entire army put me to shame, since there must have been at least fifteen thousand tooth-brushes in the invading force—I marched with my kit on the road to Santiago. It was a fine morning and everybody—the doomed and the immunes—how could we tell one from the other—everybody was in the highest spirits. We were enveloped in forest, but we could hear, from ahead, everybody peppering away at everybody. It was like the roll of many drums. This was Lawton over at El Caney. I reflected with complacency that Lawton's division did not concern me in a professional way. That was the affair of another man. My business was with Kent's division and Wheeler's division. We came to El Paso —a hill at nice artillery range from the Spanish defences. Here Grimes's battery was shooting a duel with one of the enemy's batteries. Scovel had established a little camp in the rear of the guns and a servant had made coffee. I invited Whigham to have coffee, and the servant added some hard biscuit and tinned tongue. I noted that Whigham was staring fixedly over my shoulder, and that he waved away the tinned tongue with some bitterness. It was a horse, a dead horse. Then a mule, which had been shot through the nose, wandered up and looked at Whigham. We ran away.

On top of the hill one had a fine view of the Spanish lines. We stared across almost a mile of jungle to ash-colored trenches on the military crest of a ridge. A goodly distance back of this position were white buildings, all flying great red-cross flags. The jungle beneath us rattled with firing and the Spanish trenches crackled out regular volleys, but all this time there was nothing to indicate a tangible enemy. In truth, there was a man in a Panama hat strolling to and fro behind one of the Spanish trenches, gesticulating at times with a walking-stick. A man in a Panama hat, walking with a stick! That was the strangest sight of my life—that symbol, that quaint figure of Mars. The battle, the thunderous row, was his possession. He was the master. He mystified us all with his infernal Panama hat and his wretched walking-stick. From near his feet came volleys and from near his side came roaring shells, but he stood there alone, visible, the one tangible thing. He was a Colossus and he was half as high as a pin, this being. Always somebody would be saying: "Who *can* that fellow be?"

Later, the American guns shelled the trenches and a block-house near them, and Mars vanished. It could not have been death. One cannot kill Mars. But there was one other figure, which rose to symbolic dignity. The balloon of our signal corps had swung over the tops of the jungle's trees toward the Spanish trenches. Whereat the balloon and the man in the Panama hat and with a walking-stick—whereat these two waged tremendous battle.

Suddenly the conflict became a human thing. A little group of blue figures appeared on the green of the terrible hillside. It was some of our infantry. The *attaché* of a great empire was at my shoulder, and he turned to me and spoke with incredulity and scorn. "Why, they're trying to take the position," he cried, and I admitted meekly that I thought they were. "But they can't do it, you know," he protested vehemently. "It's impossible." And—good fellow that he was—he began to grieve and wail over a useless sacrifice of gallant men. "It's plucky, you know! By Gawd, it's plucky! But *they can't do it!*" He was profoundly moved; his voice was quite broken. "It will simply be a hell of a slaughter with no good coming out of it."

The trail was already crowded with stretcher-bearers and with wounded men who could walk. One had to stem a tide of mute agony. But I don't know that it was mute agony. I only know that it was mute. It was something in which the silence or, more likely, the reticence was an appalling and inexplicable fact. One's sense seemed to demand that these men should cry out. But you could really find wounded men who exhibited all the signs of a pleased and contented mood. When thinking of it now it seems strange beyond words. But at the time—I don't know—it did not attract one's wonder. A man with a hole in his arm or his shoulder, or even in the leg below the knee, was often whimsical, comic. "Well, this ain't exactly what I enlisted for, boys. If I'd been told about this in Tampa, I'd have resigned from th' army. Oh yes, you can get the same thing if you keep on going. But I think the Spaniards may run out of ammunition in the course of a week or ten days." Then suddenly one would be confronted by the awful majesty of a man shot in the face. Particularly I remember one. He had a great dragoon moustache, and the blood streamed down his face to meet this moustache even as a torrent goes to meet the jammed log, and then swarmed out to the tips and fell in big slow drops. He looked steadily into my eyes; I was ashamed to return his glance. You understand? It is very curious—all that.

The two lines of battle were royally whacking away at each other, and there was no rest or peace in all that region. The modern bullet is a far-flying bird. It rakes the air with its hot spitting song at distances which, as a usual thing, place the whole landscape in the danger zone. There was no direction from which they did not come. A chart of their courses over one's head would have resembled a spider's web. My friend Jimmie, the photographer, mounted to the firing-line with me, and we gallivanted as much as we dared. The "sense of the meeting" was curious. Most of the men seemed to have no idea of a grand historic performance, but they were grimly satisfied with themselves. "Well, begawd, we done it." Then they wanted to know about other parts of the line. "How are things looking, old man? Everything all right?" "Yes, everything is all right if you can hold this ridge." "Aw, hell," said the men, "we'll hold the ridge. Don't you worry about that, son."

It was Jimmie's first action, and, as we cautiously were making our way to the right of our lines, the crash of the Spanish fire became uproarious, and the air simply whistled. I heard a quavering voice near my shoulder, and, turning, I beheld Jimmie— Jimmie—with a face bloodless, white as paper. He looked at me with eyes opened extremely wide. "Say," he said, "this is pretty hot, ain't it?" I was delighted. I knew exactly what he meant. He wanted to have the situation defined. If I had told him that this was the occasion of some mere idle desultory firing and recommended that he wait until the real battle began, I think he would have gone in a bee-line for the rear. But I told him truth. "Yes, Jimmie," I replied earnestly, "you can take it from me that this is patent, double-extra what-for." And immediately he nodded. "All right." If this was a big action, then he was willing to pay in his fright as a rational price for the privilege of being present. But if this was only a penny affray he considered the price exorbitant, and he would go away. He accepted my assurance with simple faith, and deported himself with kindly dignity as one moving amid great things. His face was still pale as paper, but that counted for nothing. The main point was his perfect willingness to be frightened for reasons. I wonder where is Jimmie? I lent him the Jamaica polo-pony one day and it ran away with him and flung him off in the middle of a ford. He appeared to me afterward and made bitter speech concerning this horse, which I had assured him was a gentle and pious animal. Then I never saw Jimmie again.

Then came the night of the first of July. A group of correspondents limped back to El Paso. It had been a day so long that the morning seemed as remote as a morning in a previous year. But I have forgotten to tell you about Reuben McNab. Many years ago I went to school at a place called Claverack in New York State, where there was a semi-military institution. Contemporaneous with me as a student was Reuben McNab, a long, lank boy, freckled, sandy-haired—an extraordinary boy in no way, and yet, I wager, a boy clearly marked in every recollection. Perhaps there is a good deal in that name. Reuben McNab. You can't fling that name carelessly over your shoulder and lose it. It follows you like the haunting memory of a sin. At any rate, Reuben McNab was identified intimately in my thought with the sunny irresponsible days at Claverack, when all the earth was a green field and all the sky was a rainless blue. Then I looked down into a miserable huddle at Bloody Bend, a huddle of hurt men, dying men, dead men. And there I saw Reuben McNab, a corporal in the 71st New York Volunteers, and with a hole through his lung. Also several holes through his clothing. "Well, they got me," he said in greeting. Usually they said that. There were no long speeches. "Well, they got me." That was sufficient. The duty of the upright, unhurt man is then difficult. I doubt if many of us learned how to speak to our own wounded. In the first place one had to play that the wound was nothing; oh, a mere nothing; a casual interference with movement, perhaps, but nothing more; oh, really nothing more. In the second place, one had to show a comrade's appreciation of this sad plight. As a result I think most of us bungled and stammered in the presence of our wounded friends. That's curious, eh? "Well, they got me," said Reuben McNab. I had looked upon five hundred wounded men with stolidity, or with a conscious indifference which filled me with amazement. But the apparition of Reuben McNab, the schoolmate lying there in the mud with a hole through his lung, awed me into stutterings, set me trembling with a sense of terrible intimacy with this war which theretofore I could have believed was a dream—almost. Twenty shot men rolled their eyes and looked at me. Only one man paid no heed. He was dying; he had no time. The bullets hummed low over them all. Death, having already struck, still insisted upon raising a venomous crest. "If you're goin' by the hospital, step in and see me," said Reuben McNab. That was all.

At the correspondents' camp at El Paso there was hot coffee. It was very good. I have a vague sense of being very selfish over my blanket and rubber-coat; I have a vague sense of spasmodic firing during my sleep; it rained, and then I awoke to hear that steady drumming of an infantry fire—something which was never to cease, it seemed. They were at it again. The trail from El Paso to the positions along San Juan ridge had become an exciting thoroughfare. Shots from large-bore rifles dropped in from almost every side. At this time the safest place was the extreme front. I remember in particular the one outcry I heard. A private in the 71st, without his rifle, had gone to a stream for some water and was returning, being but a little in rear of me. Suddenly I heard this cry—"Oh, my God, come quick"—and I was conscious then to having heard the hateful zip of a close shot. He lay on the ground, wriggling. He was hit in the hip. Two men came quickly. Presently everybody seemed to be getting knocked down. They went over like men of wet felt, quietly, calmly, with no more complaint than so many automatons. It was only that lad—"Oh, my God, come quick." Otherwise men seemed to consider that their hurts were not worthy of particular attention. A number of people got killed very courteously, tacitly absolving the rest of us from any care in the matter. A man fell; he turned blue; his face took on an expression of deep sorrow; and then his immediate friends worried about him, if he had friends. This was July 1. I crave the permission to leap back again to that date.

On the morning of July 2, I sat on San Juan Hill and watched Lawton's division come up. I was absolutely sheltered, but still where I could look into the faces of men who were trotting up under fire. There wasn't a high heroic face among them. They were all men intent on business. That was all. It may seem to you that I am trying to make everything a squalor. That would be wrong. I feel that things were often sublime. But they were *differently* sublime. They were not of our shallow and preposterous fictions. They stood out in a simple, majestic commonplace. It was the behavior of men on the street. It was the behavior of men. In one way, each man was just pegging along at the heels of the man before him, who was pegging along at the heels of still another man who—— It was that in the flat and obvious way. In another way it was pageantry, the pageantry of the accomplishment of naked duty. One cannot speak of it—the spectacle of the common man serenely doing his work, his appointed work. It is the one thing in the universe which makes one fling expression to the winds and be satisfied to simply feel. Thus they moved at San Juan—the soldiers of the United States Regular Army. One pays them the tribute of the toast of silence.

Lying near one of the enemy's trenches was a red-headed Spanish corpse. I wonder how many hundreds were cognizant of this red-headed Spanish corpse? It arose to the dignity of a landmark. There were many corpses, but only one with a red head. This red head. He was always there. Each time I approached that part of the field I prayed that I might find that he had been buried. But he was always there—red headed. His strong simple countenance was a malignant sneer at the system which was for ever killing the credulous peasants in a sort of black night of politics, where the peasants merely followed whatever somebody had told them was lofty and good. But nevertheless, the red-headed Spaniard was dead. He was irrevocably dead. And to what purpose? The honor of Spain? Surely the honor of Spain could have existed without the violent death of this poor red-headed peasant? Ah well, he was buried when the heavy firing ceased and men had time for such small things as funerals. The trench was turned over on top of him. It was a fine honorable soldierly fate—to be buried in a trench, the trench of the fight and the death. Sleep well, red-headed peasant. You came to another hemisphere to fight because—because you were told to, I suppose. Well, there you are, buried in your trench on San Juan Hill. That is the end of it. Your life has been taken—that is a flat, frank fact. And foreigners buried you expeditiously while speaking a strange tongue. Sleep well, red-headed mystery.

On the day before the destruction of Cervera's fleet, I steamed past our own squadron, doggedly lying in its usual semicircle, every nose pointing at the mouth of the harbor. I went to Jamaica, and on the placid evening of the next day I was again steaming past our own squadron, doggedly lying in its usual semicircle, every nose pointing at the mouth of the harbor. A megaphone hail from the bridge of one of the yacht-gunboats came casually over the water. "Hello! hear the news?" "No; what was it?" "The Spanish fleet came out this morning." "Oh, of course it did." "Honest, I mean." "Yes, I know; well, where are they now?" "Sunk." Was there ever such a preposterous statement? I was humiliated that my friend, the lieutenant on the yacht-gunboat, should have measured me as one likely to swallow this bad joke.

But it was all true; every word. I glanced back at our squadron, lying in its usual semicircle, every nose pointing at the mouth of the harbor. It would have been absurd to think that anything had happened. The squadron hadn't changed a button. There it sat without even a smile on the face of the tiger. And it had eaten four armored cruisers and two torpedo-boat destroyers while my back was turned for a moment. Courteously, but clearly, we announced across the waters that until despatch-boats came to be manned from the ranks of the celebrated horse-marines, the lieutenant's statement would probably remain unappreciated. He made a gesture, abandoning us to our scepticism. It infuriates an honorable and serious man to be taken for a liar or a joker at a time when he is supremely honorable and serious. However, when we went ashore, we found Siboney ringing with the news. It was true, then; that mishandled collection of sick ships had come out and taken the deadly thrashing which was rightfully the due of—I don't know —somebody in Spain—or perhaps nobody anywhere. One likes to wallop incapacity, but one has mingled emotions over the incapacity which is not so much personal as it is the development of centuries. This kind of incapacity cannot be centralized. You cannot hit the head which contains it all. This is the idea, I imagine, which moved the officers and men of our fleet. Almost immediately they began to speak of the Spanish admiral as "poor old boy," with a lucid suggestion in their tones that his fate appealed to them as being undue hard, undue cruel. And yet the Spanish guns hit nothing. If a man shoots, he should hit something occasionally, and men say that from the time the Spanish ships broke clear of the harbor entrance until they were one by one overpowered, they were each a band of flame. Well, one can only mumble out that when a man shoots he should be required to hit something occasionally.

In truth, the greatest fact of the whole campaign on land and sea seems to be the fact that the Spaniards could only hit by chance, by a fluke. If he had been an able marksman, no man of our two unsupported divisions would have set foot on San Juan Hill on July 1. They should have been blown to smithereens. The Spaniards had no immediate lack of ammunition, for they fired enough to kill the population of four big cities. I admit neither Velasquez nor Cervantes into this discussion, although they have appeared by authority as reasons for something which I do not clearly understand. Well, anyhow they couldn't hit anything. Velasquez? Yes. Cervantes? Yes. But the Spanish troops seemed only to try to make a very rapid fire. Thus we lost many men. We lost them because of the simple fury of the fire; never because the fire was well-directed, intelligent. But the Americans were called upon to be whipped because of Cervantes and Velasquez. It was impossible.

Out on the slope of San Juan the dog-tents shone white. Some kind of negotiations were going forward, and men sat on their trousers and waited. It was all rather a blur of talks with officers, and a craving for good food and good water. Once Leighton and I decided to ride over to El Caney, into which town the civilian refugees from Santiago were pouring. The road from the belea- guered city to the outlying village was a spectacle to make one moan. There were delicate gentle families on foot, the silly French boots of the girls twisting and turning in a sort of abso- lute paper futility; there were sons and grandsons carrying the venerable patriarch in his own armchair; there were exhausted mothers with babes who wailed; there were young dandies with their toilets in decay; there were puzzled, guideless women who didn't know what had happened. The first sentence one heard was the murmurous "What a damn shame!" We saw a godless young trooper of the Second Cavalry sharply halt a waggon. "Hold on a minute. You must carry this woman. She's fainted twice already." The virtuous driver of the United States army waggon mildly answered: "But I'm full-up now." "You can make room for her," said the private of the Second Cavalry, a young, young man with a straight mouth. It was merely a plain bit of nothing—at—all but, thank God, thank God, he seemed to have not the slightest sense of excellence. He said: "If you've got any man in there who can walk at all, you put him out and let this woman get in." "But," answered the teamster, "I'm filled up with a lot of cripples and grandmothers." Thereupon they discussed the point fairly, and ultimately the woman was lifted into the waggon.

The vivid thing was that these people did not visibly suffer. Somehow they were numb. There was not a tear. There was rarely a countenance which was not wondrously casual. There was no sign of fatalistic theory. It was simply that what was happening to-day had happened yesterday, as near as one could judge. I could fancy that these people had been thrown out of their homes every day. It was utterly, utterly casual. And they accepted the ministrations of our men in the same fashion. Everything was a matter of course. I had a filled canteen. I was frightfully conscious of this fact because a filled canteen was a pearl of price; it was a great thing. It was an enormous accident which led one to offer praises that he was luckier than ten thousand better men.

As Leighton and I rode along we came to a tree under which a refugee family had halted. They were a man, his wife, two handsome daughters and a pimply son. It was plain that they were superior people, because the girls had dressed for the exodus and wore corsets which captivated their forms with a steel-ribbed vehemence only proper for wear on a sun-blistered road to a distant town. They asked us for water. Water was the gold of the moment. Leighton was almost maudlin in his generosity. I remember being angry with him. He lavished upon them his whole canteen and he received in return, not even a glance of—what? Acknowledgment? No, they didn't even *admit* anything. Leighton wasn't a human being; he was some sort of a mountain spring. They accepted him on a basis of pure natural phenomena. His canteen was purely an occurrence. In the meantime the pimple face approached me. He asked for water and held out a pint cup. My response was immediate. I tilted my canteen and poured into his cup almost a pint of my treasure. He glanced into the cup and apparently he beheld there some innocent sediment for which he alone or his people were responsible. In the American camps the men were accustomed to a sediment. Well, he glanced at my poor cupful and then negligently poured it out on the ground and held up his cup for more. I gave him more; I gave him his cup full again, but there was something within me which made me swear him out completely. But he didn't understand a word. Afterward I watched if they were capable of being moved to help on their less able fellows on this miserable journey. Not they! Nor yet anybody else. Nobody cared for anybody, save my young friend of the Second Cavalry, who rode seriously to and fro doing his best for people, who took him as a result of a strange upheaval.

The fight at El Caney had been furious. General Vara del Rey with somewhat less than 1000 men—the Spanish accounts say 520—had there made such a stand that only about 80 battered soldiers ever emerged from it. The attack cost Lawton about 400 men. The magazine rifle! But the town was now a vast parrot-cage of chattering refugees. If, on the road, they were silent, stolid and serene, in the town they found their tongues, and set up such a cackle as one may seldom hear. Notably the women; it is they who invariably confuse the definition of situations, and one could wonder in amaze if this crowd of irresponsible, gabbling hens had already forgotten that this town was the death-bed, so to speak, of scores of gallant men whose blood was not yet dry; whose hands, of the hue of pale amber, stuck from the soil of the hasty burial. On the way to El Caney I had conjured a picture of the women of Santiago, proud in their pain, their despair, dealing glances of defiance, contempt, hatred at the invader; fiery ferocious ladies, so true to their vanquished and to their dead that they spurned the very existence of the low-bred churls who lacked both Velasquez and Cervantes. And instead, there was this mere noise, which reminded one alternately of a tea-party in Ireland, a village *fête* in the South of France, and the vacuous morning screech of a swarm of sea-gulls. "Good! There is Donna Maria. This will lower her high head. This will teach her better manners to her neighbors. She wasn't too grand to send her rascal of a servant to borrow a trifle of coffee of me in the morning, and then when I met her on the calle—por Dios, she was too blind to see me. But we are all equal here. No? Little Juan has a sore toe. Yes, Donna Maria; many thanks, many thanks. Juan, do me the favor to be quiet while Donna Maria is asking about your toe. Oh, Donna Maria, we were always poor, always. But you. My heart bleeds when I see how hard this is for you. The old cat! She gives me a head-shake."

Pushing through the throng in the plaza we came in sight of the door of the church, and here was a strange scene. The church had been turned into a hospital for Spanish wounded who had fallen into American hands. The interior of the church was too cavelike in its gloom for the eyes of the operating surgeons, so they had had the altar-table carried to the doorway, where there was a bright light. Framed then in the black archway was the altar-table with the figure of a man upon it. He was naked save for a breech-clout, and so close, so clear was the ecclesiastic suggestion, that one's mind leaped to a fantasy that this thin pale figure had just been torn down from a cross. The flash of the impression was like light, and for this instant it illumined all the dark recesses of one's remotest idea of sacrilege, ghastly and wanton. I bring this to you merely as an effect —an effect of mental light and shade, if you like; something done in thought similar to that which the French Impressionists do in color; something meaningless and at the same time overwhelming, crushing, monstrous. "Poor devil; I wonder if he'll pull through?" said Leighton. An American surgeon and his assistants were intent over the prone figure. They wore white aprons. Something small and silvery flashed in the surgeon's hand. An assistant held the merciful sponge close to the man's nostrils, but he was writhing and moaning in some horrible dream of this artificial sleep. As the surgeon's instrument played,

I fancied that the man dreamed that he was being gored by a bull. In his pleading, delirious babble occurred constantly the name of the Virgin, the Holy Mother. "Good morning," said the surgeon. He changed his knife to his left hand and gave me a wet palm. The tips of his fingers were wrinkled, shrunken, like those of a boy who has been in swimming too long. Now, in front of the door, there were three American sentries, and it was their business to—to do what? To keep this Spanish crowd from swarming over the operating-table! It was perforce a public clinic. They would not be denied. The weaker women and the children jostled according to their might in the rear, while the stronger people, gaping in the front rank, cried out impatiently when the pushing disturbed their long stares. One burned with a sudden gift of public oratory. One wanted to say: "Oh, go away, go away, go away. Leave the man decently alone with his pain, you gogglers! This is not the national sport."

But within the church there was an audience of another kind. This was of the other wounded men awaiting their turn. They lay on their brown blankets in rows along the stone floor. Their eyes, too, were fastened upon the operating-table, but—that was different. Meek-eyed little yellow men lying on the floor awaiting their turns.

One afternoon I was seated with a correspondent friend, on the porch of one of the houses at Siboney. A vast man on horseback came riding along at a foot pace. When he perceived my friend, he pulled up sharply. "Whoa! Where's that mule I lent you?" My friend arose and saluted. "I've got him all right, General, thank you," said my friend. The vast man shook his finger. "Don't you lose him now." "No, sir, I won't; thank you, sir." The vast man rode away. "Who the devil is that?" said I. My friend laughed. "That's General Shafter," said he.

I gave five dollars for the Bos'n—small, black, spry imp of Jamaica sin. When I first saw him he was the property of a fireman on the *Criton*. The fireman had found him—a little wharf rat—in Port Antonio. It was not the purchase of a slave; it was that the fireman believed that he had spent about five dollars on a lot of comic supplies for the Bos'n, including a little suit of sailor clothes. The Bos'n was an adroit and fantastic black gamin. His eyes were like white lights, and his teeth were a row of little piano keys; otherwise he was black. He had both been a jockey and a cabin-boy, and he had the manners of a gentleman. After he entered my service I don't think there was ever an occasion upon which he was useful, save when he told me quaint stories of Guatemala, in which country he seemed to have lived some portion of his infantile existence. Usually he ran funny errands like little foot-races, each about fifteen yards in length. At Siboney he slept under my hammock like a poodle, and I always expected that, through the breaking of a rope, I would some night descend and obliterate him. His incompetence was spectacular. When I wanted him to do a thing, the agony of supervision was worse than the agony of personal performance. It would have been easier to have gotten my own spurs or boots or blanket than to have the bother of this little incapable's service. But the good aspect was the humorous view. He was like a boy, a mouse, a scoundrel, and a devoted servitor. He was immensely popular. His name of Bos'n became a Siboney stock-word. Everybody knew it. It was a name like President McKinley, Admiral Sampson, General Shafter. The Bos'n became a figure. One day he approached me with four one-dollar notes in United States currency. He besought me to preserve them for him, and I pompously tucked them away in my riding-breeches, with an air which meant that his funds were now as safe as if they were in a national bank. Still, I asked with some surprise, where he had reaped all this money. He frankly admitted at once that it had been given to him by the enthusiastic soldiery as a tribute to his charm of person and manner. This was not astonishing for Siboney, where money was meaningless. Money was not worth carrying—"packing." However, a soldier came to our house one morning, and asked, "Got any more tobacco to sell?" As befitted men in virtuous poverty, we replied with indignation. "What tobacco?" "Why, that tobacco what the little nigger is sellin' round."

I said, "Bos'n!" He said, "Yes, mawstah." Wounded men on bloody stretchers were being carried into the hospital next door. "Bos'n, you've been stealing my tobacco." His defence was as glorious as the defence of that forlorn hope in romantic history, which drew itself up and mutely died. He lied as desperately, as savagely, as hopelessly as ever man fought.

One day a delegation from the 33rd Michigan came to me and said: "Are you the proprietor of the Bos'n?" I said: "Yes." And they said: "Well, would you please be so kind as to be so good as to give him to us?" A big battle was expected for the next day. "Why," I answered, "if you want him you can have him. But he's a thief, and I won't let him go save on his personal announcement." The big battle occurred the next day, and the Bos'n did not disappear in it; but he disappeared in my interest in the battle, even as a waif might disappear in a fog. My interest in the battle made the Bos'n dissolve before my eyes. Poor little rascal! I gave him up with pain. He was such an innocent villain. He knew no more of thievery than the whole of it. Anyhow one was fond of him. He was a natural scoundrel. He was not an educated scoundrel. One cannot bear the educated scoundrel. He was ingenuous, simple, honest, abashed ruffianism.

I hope the 33rd Michigan did not arrive home naked. I hope the Bos'n did not succeed in getting everything. If the Bos'n builds a palace in Detroit, I shall know where he got the money. He got it from the 33rd Michigan. Poor little man. He was only eleven years old. He vanished. I had thought to preserve him as a relic, even as one preserves forgotten bayonets and fragments of shell. And now as to the pocket of my riding-breeches. It contained four dollars in United States currency. Bos'n! Hey, Bos'n, where are you? The morning was the morning of battle.

I was on San Juan Hill when Lieutenant Hobson and the men of the *Merrimac* were exchanged and brought into the American lines. Many of us knew that the exchange was about to be made, and gathered to see the famous party. Some of our Staff officers rode out with three Spanish officers—prisoners—these latter being blindfolded before they were taken through the American position. The army was majestically minding its business in the long line of trenches when its eye caught sight of this little procession. "What's that? What they goin' to do?" "They're goin' to exchange Hobson." Wherefore every man who was foot-free staked out a claim where he could get a good view of the liberated heroes, and two bands prepared to collaborate on "The Star Spangled Banner." There was a very long wait through the sunshiny afternoon. In our impatience we imagined them—the Americans and Spaniards—dickering away out there under the big tree like so many peddlers. Once the massed bands, misled by a rumor, stiffened themselves into that dramatic and breathless moment when each man is ready to blow. But the rumor was exploded in the nick of time. We made ill jokes, saying one to another that the negotiators had found diplomacy to be a failure, and were playing freeze-out poker for the whole batch of prisoners.

But suddenly the moment came. Along the cut roadway, toward the crowded soldiers, rode three men, and it could be seen that the central one wore the undress uniform of an officer of the United States navy. Most of the soldiers were sprawled out on the grass, bored and wearied in the sunshine. However, they aroused at the old circus-parade, torchlight-procession cry, "Here they come." Then the men of the regular army did a thing. They arose *en masse* and came to "Attention." Then the men of the regular army did another thing. They slowly lifted every weather-beaten hat and drooped it until it touched the knee. Then there was a magnificent silence, broken only by the measured hoof-beats of the little company's horses as they rode through the gap. It was solemn, funereal, this splendid silent welcome of a brave man by men who stood on a hill which they had earned out of blood and death—simply, honestly, with no sense of excellence, earned out of blood and death.

Then suddenly the whole scene went to rubbish. Before he reached the bottom of the hill, Hobson was bowing to right and left like another Boulanger, and, above the thunder of the massed bands, one could hear the venerable outbreak, "Mr. Hobson, I'd like to shake the hand of the man who——" But the real welcome was that welcome of silence. However, one could thrill again when the tail of the procession appeared—an army waggon containing the blue-jackets of the *Merrimac* adventure. I remember grinning heads stuck out from under the canvas cover of the waggon. And the army spoke to the navy. "Well, Jackie, how does it feel?" And the navy up and answered: "Great! Much obliged to you fellers for comin' here." "Say, Jackie, what did they arrest ye fer anyhow? Stealin' a dawg?" The navy still grinned. Here was no rubbish. Here was the mere exchange of language between men.

Some of us fell in behind this small but royal procession and followed it to General Shafter's headquarters, some miles on the road to Siboney. I have a vague impression that I watched the meeting between Shafter and Hobson, but the impression ends there. However, I remember hearing a talk between them as to Hobson's men, and then the blue-jackets were called up to hear the congratulatory remarks of the general in command of the Fifth Army Corps. It was a scene in the fine shade of thickly-leaved trees. The general sat in his chair, his belly sticking ridiculously out before him as if he had adopted some form of artificial inflation. He looked like a joss. If the seamen had suddenly begun to burn a few sticks, most of the spectators would have exhibited no surprise. But the words he spoke were proper, clear, quiet, soldierly, the words of one man to others. The Jackies were comic. At the bidding of their officer they aligned themselves before the general, grinned with embarrassment one to the other, made funny attempts to correct the alignment, and—looked sheepish. They looked sheepish. They looked like bad little boys flagrantly caught. They had no sense of excellence. Here was no rubbish.

Very soon after this the end of the campaign came for me. I caught a fever. I am not sure to this day what kind of a fever it was. It was defined variously. I know, at any rate, that I first developed a languorous indifference to everything in the world. Then I developed a tendency to ride a horse even as a man lies on a cot. Then I—I am not sure—I think I grovelled and groaned about Siboney for several days. My colleagues, Scovel and George Rhea, found me and gave me of their best, but I didn't know whether London Bridge was falling down or whether there was a war with Spain. It was all the same. What of it? Nothing of it. Everything had happened, perhaps. But I cared not a jot. Life, death, dishonor—all were nothing to me. All I cared for was pickles. *Pickles* at any price! *Pickles*!!

If I had been the father of a hundred suffering daughters, I should have waved them all aside and remarked that they could be damned for all I cared. It was not a mood. One can defeat a mood. It was a physical situation. Sometimes one cannot defeat a physical situation. I heard the talk of Siboney and sometimes I answered, but I was as indifferent as the starfish flung to die on the sands. The only fact in the universe was that my veins burned and boiled. Rhea finally staggered me down to the army-surgeon who had charge of the proceedings, and the army-surgeon looked me over with a keen healthy eye. Then he gave a permit that I should be sent home. The manipulation from the shore to the transport was something which was Rhea's affair. I am not sure whether we went in a boat or a balloon. I think it was a boat. Rhea pushed me on board and I swayed meekly and unsteadily toward the captain of the ship, a corpulent, well-conditioned, impickled person pacing noisly on the spar-deck. "Ahem, yes; well; all right. Have you got your own food? I hope, for Christ's sake, you don't expect us to feed you, do you?" Whereupon I went to the rail and weakly yelled at Rhea, but he was already afar. The captain was, meantime, remarking in bellows that, for Christ's sake, I couldn't expect him to feed me. I didn't expect to be fed. I didn't care to be fed. I wished for nothing on earth but some form of painless pause, oblivion. The insults of this old pie-stuffed scoundrel did not affect me then; they affect me now. I would like to tell him that, although I like collies, fox-terriers, and even screw-curled poodles, I do not like him. He was free to call me superfluous and throw me overboard, but he was not free to coarsely speak to a somewhat sick man. I—in fact I hate him—it is all wrong—I lose whatever ethics I possessed—but—I hate him, and I demand that you should imagine a milch cow endowed with a knowledge of navigation and in command of a ship—and perfectly capable of commanding a ship—oh well, never mind.

I was crawling along the deck when somebody pounced violently upon me and thundered, "Who in hell are you, sir?" I said I was a correspondent. He asked me did I know that I had yellow fever. I said No. He yelled, "Well, by Gawd, you isolate yourself, sir." I said, "Where?" At this question he almost frothed at the mouth. I thought he was going to strike me. "Where?" he roared; "how in hell do I know, sir? I know as much about this ship as you do, sir. But you isolate yourself, sir." My clouded brain tried to comprehend these orders. This man was a doctor in the regular army, and it was necessary to obey him, so I bestirred myself to learn what he meant by these gorilla outcries. "All right, doctor; I'll isolate myself, but I wish you'd tell me where to go." And then he passed into such volcanic humor that I clung to the rail and gasped. "Isolate yourself, sir! Isolate yourself! That's all I've got to say, sir. I don't give a God damn where you go, but when you get there, stay there, sir." So I wandered away and ended up on the deck aft, with my head against the flagstaff and my limp body stretched on a little rug. I was not at all sorry for myself. I didn't care a tent-peg. And yet, as I look back upon it now, the situation was fairly exciting—a voyage of four or five days before me—no food—no friends—above all else, no friends —isolated on deck, and rather ill.

When I returned to the United States I was able to move my feminine friends to tears by an account of this voyage; but, after all, it wasn't so bad. They kept me on my small reservation aft, but plenty of kindness loomed soon enough. At mess-time they slid me a tin plate of something, usually stewed tomatoes and bread. Men are always good men. And, at any rate, most of the people were in worse condition than I—poor bandaged chaps looking sadly down at the waves. In a way I knew the kind. First lieutenants at forty years of age, captains at fifty, majors at 102, lieutenant-colonels at 620, full colonels at 1000, and brigadiers at 9,768,295 plus. A man had to live two billion years to gain eminent rank in the regular army at that time. And, of course, they all had trembling wives at remote Western posts waiting to hear the worst, the best, or the middle.

In rough weather, the officers made a sort of a common pool of all the sound legs and arms, and by dint of hanging hard to each other they managed to move from their deck chairs to their cabins and from their cabins again to their deck chairs. Thus they lived until the ship reached Hampton Roads. We slowed down opposite the curiously mingled hotels and batteries at Old Point Comfort, and at our mast-head we flew the yellow-flag, the grim ensign of the plague. Then we witnessed something which informed us that with all this ship-load of wounds and fevers and starvations we had forgotten the fourth element of war. We were flying the yellow-flag, but a launch came and circled swiftly about us. There was a little woman in the launch, and she kept looking and looking and looking. Our ship was so high that she could see only those who hung at the rail, but she kept looking and looking and looking. It was plain enough—it was all plain enough—but my heart sank with the fear that she was not going to find him. But presently there was a commotion among some black dough-boys of the 24th Infantry, and two of them ran aft to Colonel Liscum, its gallant commander. Their faces were wreathed in darkey grins of delight. "Kunnel, ain't dat Mis' Liscum, Kunnel?" "What?" said the old man. He got up quickly and appeared at the rail, his arm in a sling. He cried, "Alice!" The little woman saw him, and instantly she covered up her face with her hands as if blinded with a flash of white fire. She made no outcry; it was all in this simply swift gesture, but we—we knew them. It told us. It told us the other part. And in a vision we all saw our own harbor-lights. That is to say those of us who had harbor-lights.

I was almost well, and had defeated the yellow-fever charge which had been brought against me, and so I was allowed ashore among the first. And now happened a strange thing. A hard campaign, full of wants and lacks and absences, brings a man speedily back to an appreciation of things long disregarded or forgotten. In camp, somewhere in the woods between Siboney and Santiago, I happened to think of ice-cream-soda. I had done very well without it for many years; in fact I think I loathe it; but I got to dreaming of ice-cream-soda, and I came near dying of longing for it. I couldn't get it out of my mind, try as I would to concentrate my thoughts upon the land crabs and mud with which I was surrounded. It certainly had been an institution of my childhood, but to have a ravenous longing for it in the year 1898 was about as illogical as to have a ravenous longing for kerosene. All I could do was to swear to myself that if I reached the United States again, I would immediately go to the nearest soda-water-fountain and made it look like Spanish Fours. In a loud, firm voice, I would say, "Orange, please." And here is the strange thing; as soon as I was ashore I went to the nearest soda-water-fountain, and in a loud, firm voice I said, "Orange, please." I remember one man who went mad that way over tinned peaches, and who wandered over the face of the earth saying plaintively, "Have you any peaches?"

Most of the wounded and sick had to be tabulated and marshalled in sections and thoroughly officialized, so that I was in time to take a position on the verandah of Chamberlain's Hotel and see my late shipmates taken to the hospital. The verandah was crowded with women in light, charming summer dresses, and with spruce officers from the Fortress. It was like a bank of flowers. It filled me with awe. All this luxury and refinement and gentle care and fragrance and color seemed absolutely new. Then across the narrow street on the verandah of the hotel there was a similar bank of flowers. Two companies of volunteers dug a lane through the great crowd in the street and kept the way, and then through this lane there passed a curious procession. I had never known that they looked like that. Such a gang of dirty, ragged, emaciated, half-starved, bandaged cripples I had never seen. Naturally there were many men who couldn't walk, and some of these were loaded upon a big flat car which was in tow of a trolley-car. Then there were many stretchers, slow-moving. When that crowd began to pass the hotel the banks of flowers made a noise which could make one tremble. Perhaps it was a moan, perhaps it was a sob—but no, it was something beyond either a moan or a sob. Anyhow, the sound of women weeping was in it.—The sound of women weeping.

And how did these men of famous deeds appear when received thus by the people? Did they smirk and look as if they were bursting with the desire to tell everything which had happened? No they hung their heads like so many jail-birds. Most of them seemed to be suffering from something which was like stage-fright during the ordeal of this chance but supremely eloquent reception. No sense of excellence—that was it. Evidently they were willing to leave the clacking to all those natural born major-generals who after the war talked enough to make a great fall in the price of that commodity all over the world.

The episode was closed. And you can depend upon it that I have told you nothing at all, nothing at all, nothing at all.

THE SECOND GENERATION

I

CASPAR CADOGAN resolved to go to the tropic wars and do something. The air was blue and gold with the pomp of soldiering, and in every ear rang the music of military glory. Caspar's father was a United States Senator from the great State of Skowmulligan, where the war fever ran very high. Chill is the blood of many of the sons of millionaires, but Caspar took the fever and posted to Washington. His father had never denied him anything, and this time all that Caspar wanted was a little captaincy in the army—just a simple little captaincy.

The old man had just been entertaining a delegation of respectable bunco-steerers from Skowmulligan who had come to him on a matter which is none of the public's business. Bottles of whisky and boxes of cigars were still on the table in the sumptuous private parlor. The Senator had said: "Well, gentlemen, I'll do what I can for you." By this sentence he meant whatever he meant.

Then he turned to his eager son. "Well, Caspar?" The youth poured out his modest desires. It was not altogether his fault. Life had taught him a generous faith in his own abilities. If any one had told him that he was simply an ordinary damned fool he would have opened his eyes wide at the person's lack of judgment. All his life people had admired him.

The Skowmulligan war-horse looked with quick disapproval into the eyes of his son. "Well, Caspar," he said slowly, "I am of the opinion that they've got all the golf experts and tennis champions and cotillion leaders and piano tuners and billiard markers they really need as officers. Now, if you were a soldier——"

"I know," said the young man with a gesture, "but I'm not exactly a fool, I hope, and I think if I get a chance I can do something. I'd like to try. I would, indeed."

The Senator drank a neat whisky and lit a cigar. He assumed an attitude of ponderous reflection. "Y-yes, but this country is full of young men who are not fools. Full of 'em."

Caspar fidgeted in the desire to answer that while he admitted the profusion of young men who were not fools, he felt that he himself possessed interesting and peculiar qualifications which would allow him to make his mark in any field of effort which he seriously challenged. But he did not make this graceful statement, for he sometimes detected something ironic in his father's temperament. The Skowmulligan war-horse had not thought of expressing an opinion of his own ability since the year 1865, when he was young, like Caspar.

"Well, well," said the Senator finally, "I'll see about it. I'll see about it." The young man was obliged to await the end of his father's characteristic method of thought. The war-horse never gave a quick answer, and if people tried to hurry him they seemed able to arouse in him only a feeling of irritation against making a decision at all. His mind moved like the wind, but practice had placed a Mexican bit in the mouth of his judgment. This old man of light quick thought had taught himself to move like an ox cart. Caspar said, "Yes, sir." He withdrew to his club, where, to the affectionate inquiries of some envious friends, he replied: "The old man is letting the idea soak."

The mind of the war-horse was decided far sooner than Caspar expected. In Washington a large number of well-bred handsome young men were receiving appointments as lieutenants, as captains, and occasionally as majors. They were a strong, healthy, clear-eyed educated collection. They were a prime lot. A German field-marshal would have beamed with joy if he could have had them—to send to school. Anywhere in the world they would have made a grand show as material, but, intrinsically, they were not lieutenants, captains and majors. They were fine men. Individual to individual, American manhood overmatches the best in Europe; but manhood is only an essential part of a lieutenant, a captain or a major. But at any rate, it had all the logic of going to sea in a bathing-machine.

The Senator found himself reasoning that Caspar was as good as any of them, and better than many. Presently he was bleating here and there that his boy should have a chance. "The boy's all right, I tell you, Henery. He's wild to go, and I don't see why they shouldn't give him a show. He's got plenty of nerve, and he's keen as a whip-lash. I'm going to get him an appointment, and if you can do anything to help it along I wish you would." Then he betook himself to the White House and the War Department and made a stir. People think that administrations are always slavishly, abominably anxious to please the machine. They are not; they wish the machine sunk in red fire, for by the power of ten thousand past words, looks, gestures, writings, the machine comes along and takes the administration by the nose and twists it, and the administration dare not even yell. The huge force which carries an election to success looks reproachfully at the administration and says, "Give me a penny!" That is a very small amount with which to reward a colossus.

The Skowmulligan war-horse got his penny and took it to his hotel where Caspar was moodily reading war rumors. "Well, my boy, here you are." Caspar was a captain and commissary on the staff of Brigadier-General Reilly, commander of the Second Brigade of the First Division of the Thirtieth Army Corps. "I had to work for it," said the Senator grimly. "They talked to me as if they thought you were some sort of empty-headed idiot. None of 'em seemed to know you personally. They just sort of took it for granted. Finally I got pretty hot in the collar." He paused a moment; his heavy grooved face set hard; his blue eyes shone. He clapped a hand down upon the handle of his chair. "Caspar, I've got you into this thing, and I believe you'll do all right, and I'm not saying this because I distrust either your sense or your grit. But I want you to understand you've *got to make a go of it.* I'm not going to talk any twaddle about your country and your country's flag. You understand all about that. But now you're a soldier, and there'll be this to do and that to do, and fightin' to do, and you've got to do *every damned one of 'em* right up to the handle. I don't know how much of a shindy this thing is goin' to be, but any shindy is enough to show how much there is in a man. You've got your appointment, and that's all I can do for you; but I'll thrash you with my own hands if, when the army gets back, the other fellows say my son is 'nothin' but a good-lookin' dude.' "

He ceased, breathing heavily. Caspar looked bravely and frankly at his father, and answered in a voice which was not very tremulous. "I'll do my best. This is my chance. I'll do my best with it."

The Senator had a marvelous ability of transition from one manner to another. Suddenly he seemed very kind. "Well, that's all right, then. I guess you'll get along all right with Reilly. I know him well, and he'll see you through. I helped him along once. And now about this commissary business. As I understand it, a commissary is a sort of caterer in a big way—that is, he looks out for a good many more things than a caterer has to bother his head about. Reilly's brigade has probably from two to three thousand men in it, and in regard to certain things you've got to look out for every man of 'em every day. I know perfectly well you couldn't successfully run a boarding-house in Ocean Grove. How you goin' to manage for all these soldiers, hey? Thought about it?"

"No," said Caspar, injured. "I didn't want to be a commissary. I wanted to be a captain in the line."

"They wouldn't hear of it. They said you would have to take a staff appointment where people could look after you."

"Well, let them look after me," cried Caspar resentfully; "but when there's any fighting to be done I guess I won't necessarily be the last man."

"That's it," responded the Senator. "That's the spirit." They both thought that the problem of war would eliminate to an equation of actual battle.

Ultimately Caspar departed into the South to an encampment in salty grass under pine trees. Here lay an army corps twenty thousand strong. Caspar passed into the dusty sunshine of it, and for many weeks he was lost to view.

II

"Of course I don't know a damned thing about it," said Caspar frankly and modestly to a circle of his fellow staff officers. He was referring to the duties of his office.

Their faces became expressionless; they looked at him with

eyes in which he could fathom nothing. After a pause one politely said: "Don't you?" It was the inevitable two words of convention.

"Why," cried Caspar, "I didn't know what a commissary officer was until I *was* one. My old guv'nor told me. He'd looked it up in a book somewhere, I suppose; but *I* didn't know."

"Didn't you?"

The young man's face glowed with sudden humor. "Do you know, the word was intimately associated in my mind with camels. Funny, eh? I think it came from reading that rhyme of Kipling's about the commissariat camel."

"Did it?"

"Yes. Funny, isn't it? Camels!"

The brigade was ultimately landed at Siboney as part of an army to attack Santiago. The scene at the landing sometimes resembled the inspiriting daily drama at the approach to the Brooklyn Bridge. There was a great bustle, during which the wise man kept his property gripped in his hands lest it might march off into the wilderness in the pocket of one of the striding regiments. Truthfully, Caspar should have had frantic occupation, but men saw him wandering fecklessly here and there crying: "Has any one seen my saddle-bags? Why, if I lose 'em I'm ruined. I've got everything packed away in 'em. Everything!"

They looked at him gloomily and without attention. "No," they said. It was to intimate that they would not give three whoops in Hades if he had lost his nose, his teeth and his self-respect. Reilly's brigade collected itself from the boats and went off, each regiment's soul burning with anger because some other regiment was in advance of it. Moving along through the scrub and under the palms, men talked mostly of things that did not pertain to the business in hand.

General Reilly finally planted his headquarters in some tall grass under a mango tree. "Where's Cadogan?" he said suddenly as he took off his hat and smoothed the wet grey hair from his brow. Nobody knew. "I saw him looking for his saddle-bags down at the landing," said an officer dubiously. "Bother him," said the general contemptuously. "Let him stay there."

Three venerable regimental commanders came, saluted stiffly and sat in the grass. There was a pow-wow, during which Reilly explained much that the division-commander had told him. The venerable colonels nodded; they understood. Everything was smooth and clear to their minds. But still, the colonel of the Forty-fourth Regular Infantry murmured about the commissariat. His men—— And then he launched forth in a sentiment concerning the privations of his men in which you were confronted with his feeling that his men—his men were the only creatures of importance in the universe, which feeling was entirely correct for him. Reilly grunted. He did what most commanders did. He set the competent line to doing the work of the incompetent part of the staff.

In time Caspar came trudging along the road merrily swinging his saddle-bags. "Well, General," he cried as he saluted, "I found 'em." "Did you?" said Reilly. Later an officer rushed to him tragically. "General, Cadogan is off there in the bushes eatin' potted ham and crackers all by himself." The officer was sent back into the bushes for Caspar, and the general sent Caspar with an order. Then Reilly and the three venerable colonels, grinning, partook of potted ham and crackers. "Tashe a' right," said Reilly with his mouth full. "Dorsey, see if 'e got some'n else."

"Mush be selfish young pig," said one of the colonels, with his mouth full. "Who's he, General?"

"Son—Sen'tor Cad'gan—ol' frien' mine—damn 'im."

Caspar wrote a letter:

"Dear Father: I am sitting under a tree using the flattest part of my canteen for a desk. Even as I write the division ahead of us is moving forward and we don't know what moment the storm of battle may break out. I don't know what the plans are. General Reilly knows, but he is so good as to give me very little of his confidence. In fact, I might be part of a forlorn hope from all to the contrary I've heard from him. I understood you to say in Washington that you at one time had been of some service to him, but if that is true I can assure you he has completely forgotten it. At times his manner to me is little short of being offensive, but of course I understand that it is only the way of a crusty old soldier who has been made boorish and bearish by a long life among the Indians. I dare say I shall manage it all right without a row.

"When you hear that we have captured Santiago, please send me by first steamer a box of provisions and clothing, particularly sardines, pickles, and light-weight underwear. The other men on the staff are nice quiet chaps, but they seem a bit crude. There has been no fighting yet save the skirmish by Young's brigade. Reilly was furious because we couldn't get in it. I met General Peel yesterday. He was very nice. He said he knew you well when he was in Congress. Young Jack May is on Peel's staff. I knew him well in college. We spent an hour talking over old times. Give my love to all at home."

The march was leisurely. Reilly and his staff strolled out to the head of the long sinuous column and entered the sultry gloom of the forest. Some less fortunate regiments had to wait among the trees at the side of the trail, and as Reilly's brigade passed them, officer called to officer, classmate to classmate, in which rang a note of everything from West Point to Alaska. They were going into an action in which they, the officers, would lose over a hundred in killed and wounded—officers alone—and these greetings, in which many nicknames occurred, where in many cases farewells such as one pictures being given with ostentation, solemnity, fervor. "There goes Gory Widgeon! Hello, Gory! Where you starting for? Hey, Gory!"

Caspar communed with himself and decided that he was not frightened. He was eager and alert; he thought that now his obligation to his country, or himself, was to be faced, and he was mad to prove to old Reilly and the others that after all he was a very capable soldier.

III

Old Reilly was stumping along the line of his brigade and mumbling like a man with a mouthful of grass. The fire from the enemy's position was incredible in its swift fury, and Reilly's brigade was getting its share of a very bad ordeal. The old man's face was of the color of a tomato, and in his rage he mouthed and sputtered strangely. As he pranced along his thin line, scornfully erect, voices arose from the grass beseeching him to take care of himself. At his heels scrambled a bugler with pallid skin and clinched teeth, a chalky, trembling youth, who kept his eye on old Reilly's back and followed it.

The old gentleman was quite mad. Apparently he thought the whole thing a dreadful mess, but now that his brigade was irrevocably in it he was full-tilting here and everywhere to establish some irreproachable, immaculate kind of behavior on the part of every man jack in his brigade. The intentions of the three venerable colonels were the same. They stood behind their lines, quiet, stern, courteous old fellows, admonishing their regiments to be very pretty in the face of such a hail of magazine-rifle and machine-gun fire as has never in this world been confronted save by beardless savages when the white man has found occasion to take his burden to some new place.

And the regiments were pretty. The men lay on their little stomachs and got peppered according to the law, and said nothing as the good blood pumped out into the grass; and even if a solitary rookie tried to get a decent reason to move to some haven of rational men, the cold voice of an officer made him look criminal with a shame that was a credit to his regimental education. Behind Reilly's command was a bullet-torn jungle through which it could not move as a brigade; ahead of it were Spanish trenches on hills. Reilly considered that he was in a fix, no doubt, but he said this only to himself. Suddenly he saw on the right a little point of blue-shirted men already half-way up the hill. It was some pathetic fragment of the Sixth United States Infantry. Chagrined, shocked, horrified, Reilly bellowed to his bugler, and the chalk-faced youth unlocked his teeth and sounded the charges by rushes. The men formed hastily and grimly, and rushed. Apparently there awaited them only the fate of respectable soldiers. But they went because—of the opinions of others, perhaps. They went because—no low-down, loud-mouthed, pie-faced lot of jail-birds such as the Twenty-Seventh Infantry could do anything that they could not do better. They went because Reilly ordered it. They went because they went.

And yet not a man of them to this day has made a public speech explaining precisely how he did the whole thing and detailing with what initiative and ability he comprehended and defeated a situation which he did not comprehend at all.

Reilly never saw the top of the hill. He was heroically striving to keep up with his men when a bullet ripped quietly through his left lung, and he fell back into the arms of the bugler, who received him as he would have received a Christmas present. The three venerable colonels inherited the brigade in swift succession. The senior commanded for about fifty seconds, at the end of which he was mortally shot. Before they could get the news to the next in rank he, too, was shot. The junior colonel ultimately arrived with a lean and puffing little brigade at the top of the hill. The men lay down and fired volleys at whatever was practicable.

In and out of the ditch-like trenches lay the Spanish dead, lemon-faced corpses dressed in shabby blue and white ticking. Some were huddled down comfortably like sleeping children; one had died in the attitude of a man flung back in a dentist's chair; one sat in the trench with its chin sunk despondently to its breast; few preserved a record of the agitation of battle. With the greater number it was as if death had touched them so gently, so lightly, that they had not known of it. Death had come to them rather in the form of an opiate than of a bloody blow.

But the arrived men in the blue shirts had no thought of the sallow corpses. They were eagerly exchanging a hail of shots with the Spanish second line, whose ash-colored entrenchments barred the way to a city white amid trees. In the pauses the men talked.

"We done the best. Old E Company got there. Why, one time the hull of B Company was *behind* us. Hell!"

"Jones, he was the first man up. I saw 'im."

"*Which* Jones?"

"Did you see ol' Two-bars runnin' like a land-crab? Made good time, too. He hit only in the high places. He's all right."

"The lootenant is all right, too. He was a good ten yards ahead of the best of us. I hated him at the post, but for this here active service there's none of 'em can touch him."

"This is mighty different from being at the post."

"Well, we done it, an' it wasn't b'cause *I* thought it could be done. When we started, I ses to m'self: 'Well, here goes a lot a' damned fools.' "

" 'Tain't over yet."

"Oh, they'll never git us back from here. If they start to chase us back from here we'll pile 'em up so high the last ones can't climb over. We've come this far, an' we'll stay here. I ain't done pantin'."

"Anything is better than packin' through that jungle an' gettin' blistered from front, rear, an' both flanks. I'd rather tackle another hill than go trailin' in them woods, so thick you can't tell whether you are one man or a division of cav'lry."

"Where's that young kitchen-soldier, Cadogan, or whatever his name is? Ain't seen him to-day."

"Well, *I* seen him. He was right in with it. He got shot, too, about half up the hill, in the leg. I seen it. He's all right. Don't worry about him. He's all right."

"I seen 'im, too. He done his stunt. As soon as I can git this piece of barbed-wire entanglement out a' me throat I'll give 'm a cheer."

"He ain't shot at all, b'cause there he stands, there. See 'im?"

Rearward, the grassy slope was populous with little groups of men searching for the wounded. Reilly's brigade began to dig with its bayonets and shovel with its meat-ration cans.

IV

Senator Cadogan paced to and fro in his private parlor and smoked small brown weak cigars. These little wisps seemed utterly inadequate to console such a ponderous satrap.

It was the evening of the 1st of July, 1898, and the Senator was immensely excited, as could be seen from the superlatively calm way in which he called out to his private secretary, who was in an adjoining room. The voice was serene, gentle, affectionate, low. "Baker, I wish you'd go over again to the War Department and see if they've heard anything about Caspar."

A very bright-eyed hatchet-faced young man appeared in a doorway, pen still in hand. He was hiding a nettle-like irritation behind all the finished audacity of a smirk, sharp, lying, trustworthy young politician. "I've just got back from there, sir," he suggested.

The Skowmulligan war-horse lifted his eyes and looked for a short second into the eyes of his private secretary. It was not a glare or an eagle glance; it was something beyond the practice of an actor; it was simply meaning. The clever private secretary grabbed his hat and was at once enthusiastically away. "All right, sir," he cried. "I'll find out."

The War Department was ablaze with light, and messengers

were running. With the assurance of a retainer of an old house, Baker made his way through much small-calibre vociferation. There was rumor of a big victory; there was rumor of a big defeat. In the corridors various watchdogs arose from their armchairs and asked him of his business in tones of uncertainty which in no wise compared with their previous habitual deference to the private secretary of the war-horse of Skowmulligan.

Ultimately Baker arrived in a room where some kind of a head clerk sat writing feverishly at a roll-top desk. Baker asked a question, and the head clerk mumbled profanely without lifting his head. Apparently he said: "How in the blankety-blank blazes do I know?"

The private secretary let his jaw fall. Surely some new spirit had come suddenly upon the heart of Washington—a spirit which Baker understood to be almost defiantly indifferent to the wishes of Senator Cadogan, a spirit which was not even courteously oily. What could it mean? Baker's fox-like mind sprang wildly to a conception of overturned factions, changed friends, new combinations. The assurance which had come from experience of a broad political situation suddenly left him, and he would not have been amazed if some one had told him that Senator Cadogan now controlled only six votes in the State of Skowmulligan. "Well," he stammered in his bewilderment, "well —there isn't any news of the old man's son, hey?" Again the head clerk replied blasphemously.

Eventually Baker retreated in disorder from the presence of this head clerk, having learned that the latter did not give a —— —— if Caspar Cadogan was sailing through Hades on an ice yacht.

Baker stormed other and more formidable officials. In fact, he struck as high as he dared. They one and all flung him short hard words, even as men pelt an annoying cur with pebbles. He emerged from the brilliant light, from the groups of men with anxious puzzled faces, and as he walked back to the hotel he did not know if his name was Baker or Cholmondeley.

However, as he walked up the stairs to the Senator's rooms he contrived to concentrate his intellect upon a manner of speaking.

The war-horse was still pacing his parlor and smoking. He paused at Baker's entrance. "Well?"

"Mr. Cadogan," said the private secretary coolly, "they told me at the Department that they did not give a gawd damn whether your son was alive or dead."

The Senator looked at Baker and smiled gently. "What's that, my boy?" he asked in a soft and considerate voice.

"They said——" gulped Baker with a certain tenacity. "They said that they didn't give a gawd damn whether your son was alive or dead."

There was a silence for the space of three seconds. Baker stood like an image; he had no machinery for balancing the issues of this kind of a situation, and he seemed to feel that if he stood as still as a stone frog he would escape the ravages of a terrible Senatorial wrath which was about to break forth in a hurricane speech which would snap off trees and sweep away barns.

"Well," drawled the Senator lazily, "who did you see, Baker?"

The private secretary resumed a certain usual manner of breathing. He told the names of the men whom he had seen.

"Ye-e-es," remarked the Senator. He took another little brown cigar and held it with a thumb and first finger, staring at it with the calm and steady scrutiny of a scientist investigating a new thing. "So they don't care whether Caspar is alive or dead, eh? Well . . . maybe they don't. . . . That's all right. . . . However . . . I think I'll just look in on 'em and state my views."

When the Senator had gone, the private secretary ran to the window and leaned afar out. Pennsylvania Avenue was gleaming silver blue in the light of many arc-lamps; the cable trains groaned along to the clangor of gongs; from the window the walks presented a hardly diversified aspect of shirt-waists and straw hats. Sometimes a newsboy screeched.

Baker watched the tall heavy figure of the Senator moving out to intercept a cable train. "Great Scott!" cried the private secretary to himself, "there'll be three distinct kinds of grand, plain practical fireworks. The old man is going for 'em. I wouldn't be in Lascum's boots. Ye gods, what a row there'll be."

In due time the Senator was closeted with some kind of deputy third-assistant battery-horse in the offices of the War Department. The official obviously had been told off to make a supreme effort to pacify Cadogan, and he certainly was acting according to his instructions. He was almost in tears; he spread out his hands in supplication, and his voice whined and wheedled. "Why, really, you know, Senator, we can only beg you to look at the circumstances. Two scant divisions at the top of that hill; over a thousand men killed and wounded; the line so thin that any strong attack would smash our army to flinders. The Spaniards have probably received re-enforcements under Pando; Shafter seems to be too ill to be actively in command of our troops; Lawton can't get up with his division before to-morrow. We are actually expecting . . . no, I won't say expecting . . . but we would not be surprised . . . nobody in the Department would be surprised if before daybreak we were compelled to give to the country the news of a disaster which would be the worst blow the national pride has ever suffered. Don't you see? Can't you see our position, Senator?"

The Senator, with a pale but composed face, contemplated the official with eyes that gleamed in a way not usual with the big self-controlled politician.

"I'll tell you frankly, sir," continued the other. "I'll tell you frankly, that at this moment we don't know whether we are a-foot or a-horseback. Everything is in the air. We don't know whether we have won a glorious victory or simply got ourselves in a devil of a fix."

The Senator coughed. "I suppose my boy is with the two divisions at the top of that hill? He's with Reilly."

"Yes; Reilly's brigade is up there."

"And when do you suppose the War Department can tell me if he is all right? I want to know."

"My dear Senator—frankly, I don't know. Again I beg you to think of our position. The army in a muddle; its general thinking that he must fall back, and yet not sure that he *can* fall back without losing the army. Why, we're worrying about the lives of sixteen thousand men and the self-respect of the nation, Senator."

"I see," observed the Senator, nodding his head slowly. "And naturally the welfare of one man's son doesn't—how do they say it?—doesn't cut any ice."

V

And in Cuba it rained. In a few days Reilly's brigade discovered that by their successful charge they had gained the inestimable privilege of sitting in a wet trench and slowly but surely starving to death. Men's tempers crumbled like dry bread. The soldiers who so cheerfully, quietly and decently had captured positions which the foreign experts had said were impregnable, now in turn underwent an attack which was furious as well as insidious. The heat of the sun alternated with rains which boomed and roared in their falling like mountain cataracts. It seemed as if men took the fever through sheer lack of other occupation. During the days of battle none had had time to get even a tropic headache, but no sooner was that brisk period over than men began to shiver and shudder by squads and platoons. Rations were scarce enough to make a little fat strip of bacon seem of the size of a corner lot, and coffee grains were pearls. There would have been godless quarreling over fragments if it were not that with these fevers came a great listlessness, so that men were almost content to die, if death required no exertion.

It was an occasion which distinctly separated the sheep from the goats. The goats were few enough, but their qualities glared out like crimson spots.

One morning Jameson and Ripley, two captains in the Forty-fourth Foot, lay under a flimsy shelter of sticks and palm branches. Their dreamy dull eyes contemplated the men in the trench which went to left and right. To them came Caspar Cadogan, moaning. "By gawd," he said, as he flung himself wearily on the ground, "I can't stand much more of this, you know. It's killing me." A bristly beard sprouted through the grime on his face; his eyelids were crimson; an indescribably dirty shirt fell away from his roughened neck; and at the same time various lines of evil and greed were deepened on his face, until he practically stood forth as a revelation, a confession. "I can't stand it. By gawd, I can't."

Stanford, a lieutenant under Jameson, came stumbling along toward them. He was a lad of the class of '98 at West Point. It could be seen that he was flaming with fever. He rolled a calm eye at them. "Have you any water, sir?" he said to his captain. Jameson got upon his feet and helped Stanford to lay his shaking length under the shelter. "No, boy," he answered gloomily. "Not a drop. You got any, Rip?"

"No," answered Ripley, looking with anxiety upon the young officer. "Not a drop."

"You, Cadogan?"

Here Caspar hesitated oddly for a second, and then in a tone of deep regret made answer: "No, Captain; not a mouthful."

Jameson moved off weakly. "You lay quietly, Stanford, and I'll see what I can russle."

Presently Caspar felt that Ripley was steadily regarding him. He returned the look with one of half-guilty questioning. "God forgive you, Cadogan," said Ripley, "but you are a damned beast. Your canteen is full of water."

Even then the apathy in their veins prevented the scene from becoming as sharp as the words sound. Caspar sputtered like a child, and at length merely said: "No, it isn't." Stanford lifted his head to shoot a keen proud glance at Caspar, and then turned away his face.

"You lie," said Ripley. "I can tell the sound of a full canteen as far as I can hear it."

"Well, if it is, I—I must have forgotten it."

"You lie; no man in this army just now forgets whether his canteen is full or empty. Hand it over."

Fever is the physical counterpart of shame, and when a man has had the one he accepts the other with an ease which would revolt his healthy self. However, Caspar made a desperate struggle to preserve the forms. He arose and taking the string from his shoulder, passed the canteen to Ripley. But after all there was a whine in his voice, and the assumption of dignity was really a farce. "I think I had better go, Captain. You can have the water if you want it, I'm sure. But—but I fail to see—I fail to see what reason you have for insulting me."

"Do you?" said Ripley stolidly. "That's all right."

Caspar stood for a terrible moment. He simply did not have the strength to turn his back on this—this affair. It seemed to him that he must stand forever and face it. But when he found the audacity to look again at Ripley he saw the latter was not at all concerned with the situation. Ripley, too, had the fever. The fever changes all laws of proportion. Caspar went away.

"Here, youngster; here's your drink."

Stanford made a weak gesture. "I wouldn't touch a drop from his damned canteen if it was the last water in the world," he murmured in his high boyish voice.

"Don't you be a young jackass," quoth Ripley tenderly.

The boy stole a glance at the canteen. He felt the propriety of arising and hurling it after Caspar, but—he, too, had the fever. "Don't you be a young jackass," said Ripley again.

VI

Senator Cadogan was happy. His son had returned from Cuba, and the 8.30 train that evening would bring him to the station nearest to the stone and red shingle villa which the senator and his family occupied on the shores of Long Island Sound. The Senator's steam yacht lay some hundred yards from the beach. She had just returned from a trip to Montauk Point, where the Senator had made a gallant attempt to gain his son from the transport on which he was coming from Cuba. He had fought a brave sea-fight with sundry petty little doctors and ship's officers, who had raked him with broadsides describing the laws of quarantine and had used inelegant speech to a United States Senator as he stood on the bridge of his own steam yacht. These men had grimly asked him to tell exactly how much better was Caspar than any other returning soldier.

But the Senator had not given them a long fight. In fact, the truth came to him quickly, and with almost a blush he had ordered the yacht back to her anchorage off the villa. As a matter of fact, the trip to Montauk Point had been undertaken largely from impulse. Long ago the Senator had decided that when his boy returned the greeting should have something Spartan in it. He would make a welcome such as most soldiers get. There should be no flowers and carriages when the other poor fellows got none. He should consider Caspar as a soldier. That was the way to treat a man. But, in the end, a sharp acid of anxiety had worked upon the iron old man, until he had ordered the yacht to take him out and make a fool of him. The result filled him with a chagrin which caused him to delegate to the mother and sisters the entire business of succoring Caspar at Montauk Point Camp. He had remained at home conducting the huge correspondence of an active national politician and waiting for this son whom he so loved and whom he so wished to be a man of a certain strong taciturn shrewd ideal. The recent yacht voyage he now looked upon as a kind of confession of his weakness, and he was resolved that no more signs should escape him.

But yet his boy had been down there against the enemy and among the fevers. There had been grave perils, and his boy must have faced them. And he could not prevent himself from dreaming through the poetry of fine actions, in which visions his son's face shone out manly and generous. During these periods the people about him, accustomed as they were to his silence and calm in time of stress, considered that affairs in Skowmulligan might be most critical. In no other way could they account for this exaggerated phlegm.

On the night of Caspar's return he did not go to dinner, but had a tray sent to his library, where he remained writing. At last he heard the spin of the dog-cart's wheels on the gravel of the drive, and a moment later there penetrated to him the sound of joyful feminine cries. He lit another cigar; he knew that it was now his part to bide with dignity the moment when his son should shake off that other welcome and come to him. He could still hear them; in their exuberance they seemed to be capering like school-children. He was impatient, but this impatience took the form of a polar stolidity.

Presently there were quick steps and a jubilant knock at his door. "Come in," he said. In came Caspar, thin, yellow and in soiled khaki. "They almost tore me to pieces," he cried, laughing. "They danced around like wild things." Then as they shook hands he dutifully said, "How are you, sir?"

"How are you, my boy?" answered the Senator casually but kindly.

"Better than I might expect, sir," cried Caspar cheerfully. "We had a pretty hard time, you know."

"You look as if they'd given you a hard run," observed the father in a tone of slight interest.

Caspar was eager to tell. "Yes, sir," he said rapidly. "We did, indeed. Why, it was awful. We—any of us—were lucky to get out of it alive. It wasn't so much the Spaniards, you know. The army took care of them all right. It was the fever and the—you know, we couldn't get anything to eat. And the mismanagement. Why, it was frightful."

"Yes, I've heard," said the Senator. A certain wistful look came into his eyes, but he did not allow it to become prominent. Indeed, he suppressed it. "And you, Caspar? I suppose you did your duty?"

Caspar answered with becoming modesty. "Well, I didn't do more than anybody else, I don't suppose, but—well, I got along all right, I guess."

"And this great charge up San Juan Hill?" asked the father slowly. "Were you in that?"

"Well—yes; I was in it," replied the son.

The Senator brightened a trifle. "You were, eh? In the front of it? or just sort of going along?"

"Well—I don't know. I couldn't tell exactly. Sometimes I was in front of a lot of them, and sometimes I was—just sort of going along."

This time the Senator emphatically brightened. "That's all right, then. And of course—of *course* you performed your commissary duties correctly?"

The question seemed to make Caspar uncommunicative and sulky. "I did when there was anything to do," he answered. "But the whole thing was on the most unbusiness-like basis you can imagine. And they wouldn't tell you anything. Nobody would take time to instruct you in your duties, and of course if you didn't know a thing then your superior officer would swoop down on you and ask you why in hell such and such a thing wasn't done in such and such a way. Of course I did the best I could."

The Senator's countenance had again become sombrely indifferent. "I see. But you weren't directly rebuked for incapacity, were you? No; of course you weren't. But—I mean—did any of your superior officers suggest that you were 'no good,' or anything of that sort? I mean—did you come off with a clean slate?"

Caspar took a small time to digest his father's meaning. "Oh, yes, sir," he cried at the end of his reflection. "The commissary was in such a hopeless mess anyhow that nobody thought of doing anything but curse Washington."

"Of course," rejoined the Senator harshly. "But supposing that you had been a competent and well-trained commissary officer? What then?"

Again the son took time for consideration, and in the end deliberately replied: "Well, if I had been a competent and well-trained commissary I would have sat there and eaten up my heart and cursed Washington."

"Well, then, that's all right. And now about this charge up San Juan? Did any of the generals speak to you afterward and say that you had done well? Didn't any of them see you?"

"Why, n-n-no, I don't suppose they did . . . any more than I did them. You see, this charge was a big thing and covered lots of ground, and I hardly saw anybody excepting a lot of the men."

"Well, but didn't any of the men see you? Weren't you ahead some of the time, leading them on and waving your sword?"

Caspar burst into laughter. "Why, no. I had all I could do to scramble along and try to keep up. And I didn't want to go up at all."

"Why?" demanded the Senator.

"Because—because the Spaniards were shooting so much. And you could see men falling—and the bullets rushed around you in —by the bushel. And then at last it seemed that if we once drove them away from the top of the hill there would be less danger. So we all went up."

The Senator chuckled over this description. "And you didn't flinch at all?"

"Well," rejoined Caspar humorously, "I won't say I wasn't frightened."

"No, of course not. But then you did not let anybody know it?"

"Of course not."

"You understand, naturally, that I am bothering you with all these questions because I desire to hear how my only son behaved in the crisis. I don't want to worry you with it. But if you went through the San Juan charge with credit I'll have you made a major."

"Well," said Caspar, "I wouldn't say I went through that charge with credit. I went through it all good enough, but the enlisted men around went through in the same way."

"But weren't you encouraging them and leading them on by your example?"

Caspar smirked. He began to see a point. "Well, sir," he said with a charming hesitation. "Aw—er—I—well, I dare say I was doing my share of it."

The perfect form of the reply delighted the father. He could not endure blatancy; his admiration was to be won only by a bashful hero. Now he beat his hand impulsively down upon the table. "That's what I wanted to know. That's it exactly. I'll have you made a major next week. You've found your proper field at last. You stick to the army, Caspar, and I'll back you up. That's the thing. In a few years it will be a great career. The United States is pretty sure to have an army of about a hundred and fifty thousand men. And starting in when you did and with me to back you up—why, we'll make you a general in seven or eight years. That's the ticket. You stay in the army." The Senator's face was flushed with enthusiasm, and he looked eagerly and confidently at his son.

But Caspar had pulled a long face. "The army?" he said. "Stay in the army?"

The Senator continued to outline quite rapturously his idea of the future. "The army, evidently, is just the place for you. You know as well as I do that you have not been a howling success, exactly, in anything else which you have tried. But now the army just suits you. It is the kind of career which especially suits you. Well, then, go in, and go at it hard. Go in to win. Go at it."

"But——" began Caspar.

The Senator interrupted swiftly. "Oh, don't worry about that part of it. I'll take care of all that. You won't get jailed in some Arizona adobe for the rest of your natural life. There won't be much more of that, anyhow; and besides, as I say, I'll look after all that end of it. The chance is splendid. A young, healthy and intelligent man, with the start you've already got, and with my backing, can do anything—anything! There will be a lot of active service—oh, yes, I'm sure of it—and everybody who——"

"But," said Caspar, wan, desperate, heroic, "father, I don't care to stay in the army."

The Senator lifted his eyes and his face darkened. "What?" he said. "What's that?" He looked at Caspar.

The son became tightened and wizened like an old miser trying to withhold gold. He replied with a sort of idiot obstinacy, "I don't care to stay in the army."

The Senator's jaw clinched down, and he was dangerous. But, after all, there was something mournful somewhere. "Why, what do you mean?" he asked gruffly.

"Why, I couldn't get along, you know. The—the——"

"The what?" demanded the father, suddenly uplifted with thunderous anger. "The what?"

Caspar's pain found a sort of outlet in mere irresponsible talk. "Well, you know—the other men, you know. I couldn't get along with them, you know. They're peculiar, somehow; odd; I didn't understand them, and they didn't understand me. We—we didn't hitch, somehow. They're a queer lot. They've got funny ideas. I don't know how to explain it exactly, but—somehow—I don't like 'em. That's all there is to it. They're good fellows enough, I know, but——"

"Oh, well, Caspar," interrupted the Senator. Then he seemed to weigh a great fact in his mind. "I guess——" He paused again in profound consideration. "I guess——" He lit a small brown cigar. "I guess you are no damn good."

SPITZBERGEN TALES

THE KICKING TWELFTH

THE Spitzbergen army was backed by traditions of centuries of victory. In its chronicles, occasional defeats were not printed in italics but were likely to appear as glorious stands against overwhelming odds. A favorite way to dispose of them was to frankly attribute them to the blunders of the civilian heads of government. This was very good for the army and probably no army had more self-confidence. When it was announced that an expeditionary force was to be sent to Rostina to chastise an impudent people, a hundred barrack-squares filled with excited men and a hundred serjeant-majors hurried silently through the groups and succeeded in looking as if they were the repositories of the secrets of empire. Officers on leave sped joyfully back to their harness and recruits were abused with unflagging devotion by every man from colonels to privates of experience.

The Twelfth Regiment of the Line—the Kicking Twelfth—was consumed with a dread that it was not to be included in the expedition and the regiment formed itself into an informal indignation meeting. Just as they had proved that a great outrage was about to be perpetrated, warning orders arrived to hold themselves in readiness for active service abroad—in Rostina, in fact. The barrack-yard was in a flash transformed into a blue and buff pandemonium and the official bugle itself hardly had the power to quell the glad disturbance.

Thus it was that early in the spring the Kicking Twelfth—sixteen hundred men in service equipment—found itself crawling along a road in Rostina. They did not form part of the main force but belonged to a column of four regiments of foot, two batteries of field-guns, a battery of mountain howitzers, a regiment of horse and a company of engineers. Nothing had happened. The long column had crawled without amusement of any kind through a broad green valley. Big white farm-houses dotted the slopes but there was no sign of man nor beast and no smoke came from the chimneys. The column was operating from its own base and its general was expected to form a junction with the main body at a given point.

A squadron of the cavalry was fanned out ahead, scouting, and day by day the trudging infantry watched the blue uniforms of the horsemen as they came and went. Sometimes there would sound the faint thuds of a few shots but the cavalry was unable to find anything to seriously engage.

The Twelfth had no record of foreign service and it could hardly be said that it had served as a unit in the great civil war when His Majesty the King had whipped the Pretender. At that time the regiment had suffered from two opinions. So that it was impossible for either side to depend upon it. Many men had deserted to the standard of the Pretender and a number of officers had drawn their swords for him. When the King, a thorough soldier, looked at the remnant he saw that they lacked the spirit to be of great help to him in the tremendous battles which he was waging for his throne. And so this emaciated Twelfth was sent off to a corner of the kingdom to guard a dock-yard where some of the officers so plainly expressed their disapproval of this policy that the regiment received its steadfast name, the Kicking Twelfth.

At the time of which I am writing the Twelfth had a few veteran officers and well-bitten serjeants but the body of the regiment was composed of men who had never heard a shot fired excepting on the rifle-range. But it was an experience for which they longed and when it came the moment for the corps' cry— "Kim up, the Kickers"—there was not likely to be a man who would not go tumbling after his leaders.

Young Timothy Lean was a second-lieutenant in the First Company of the third battalion and just at this time he was pattering along at the flank of the men, keeping a fatherly look-out for boots that hurt and packs that sagged. He was extremely bored. The mere far-away sound of desultory shooting was not war as he had been led to believe it.

It did not appear that behind that freckled face and under that red hair there was a mind which dreamed of blood. He was not extremely anxious to kill somebody but he was very fond of soldiering—it had been the career of his father and of his grandfather—and he understood that the profession of arms lost much of its point unless a man shot at people and had people shoot at him. Strolling in the sun through a practically deserted country might be a proper occupation for a divinity student on a vacation but the soul of Timothy Lean was in revolt at it. Sometimes at night he would go morosely to the camp of the cavalry and hear the infant subalterns laughingly exaggerate the comedy side of adventures which they had had when out with small patrols far ahead. Lean would sit and listen in glum silence to these tales and dislike the young officers—many of them old military-school friends—for having had experience in modern warfare. "Anyhow," he said savagely, "presently you'll be getting in a lot of trouble and then the Foot will have to come along and pull you out. We always do. That's history."

"Oh, we can take care of ourselves," said the cavalry, with good-natured understanding of his mood.

But the next day even Lean blessed the cavalry for excited troopers came whirling back from the front, bending over their speeding horses and shouting wildly and hoarsely for the infantry to clear the way. Men yelled at them from the roadside, as courier followed courier and from the distance ahead sounded in quick succession six booms from field-guns. The information possessed by the couriers was no longer precious. Everybody knew what a battery meant when it spoke. The bugles cried out and the long column jolted into a halt. Old Colonel Sponge went bouncing in his saddle back to see the general and the regiment sat down in the grass by the roadside and waited in silence. Presently the second squadron of the cavalry trotted off along the road in a cloud of dust and in due time old Colonel Sponge came bouncing back and palavered his three majors and his adjutant. Then there was a bit more talk by the majors and gradually through the correct channels spread information which in due time reached Timothy Lean. The enemy, 5,000 strong, occupied a pass at the head of the valley some four miles beyond. They had three batteries well posted. Their infantry was intrenched. The ground in their front was crossed and lined with many ditches and hedges but the enemy's batteries were so posted that it was doubtful if a ditch would ever prove convenient as shelter for the Spitzbergen infantry. There was a fair position for the Spitzbergen artillery 2,300 yards from the enemy. The cavalry had succeeded in driving the enemy's skirmishers back upon the main body but of course had only tried to worry them a little. The position was almost inaccessible on the enemy's right owing to high, steep hills which had been crowned by small parties of infantry. The enemy's left although guarded by a much larger force was approachable and might be flanked. This was what the cavalry had to say and it added briefly a report of two troopers killed and five wounded.

Whereupon, Major-General Richie, commanding a force of 7,500 men of His Majesty of Spitzbergen, set in motion with a few simple words the machinery which would launch his army at the enemy. The Twelfth understood the orders when they saw the smart young aide approaching old Colonel Sponge and they rose as one man, apparently afraid that they would be late. There was a clank of accoutrements. Men shrugged their shoulders tighter against their packs and thrusting their thumbs between their belts and their tunics they wriggled into a closer fit with regard to the heavy ammunition equipment. It is curious to note that almost every man took off his cap and looked contemplatively into it as if to read a maker's name. Then they replaced their caps with great care. There was little talking; and it was observable that not a single soldier handed a token or left a comrade with a message to be delivered in case he should be killed. They did not seem to think of being killed; they seemed absorbed in a desire to know what would happen and what it would look like when it was happening. Men glanced continually at their officers in a plain desire to be quick to understand the very first order that would be given and officers looked gravely at their men, measuring them, feeling their temper, worrying about them.

A bugle called; there were sharp cries; and the Kicking Twelfth was off to battle.

The regiment had the right of the line in the infantry brigade and as the men tramped noisily along the white road every eye was strained ahead, but after all there was nothing to be seen but a dozen farms—in short, a country-side. It resembled the scenery in Spitzbergen; every man in the Kicking Twelfth had often confronted a dozen such farms with a composure which amounted to indifference. But still down the road there came galloping troopers who delivered informations to Colonel Sponge and then galloped on. In time the Twelfth came to the top of a rise and below them on a plain was the heavy black streak of a Spitzbergen squadron and back of the squadron loomed the grey bare hills of the Rostina position. There was a little of skirmish firing. The Twelfth reached a knoll which the officers easily recognized as the place described by the cavalry as suitable for the Spitzbergen guns. The men swarmed up it in a peculiar formation. They resembled a crowd coming off a race-track but nevertheless there were no stray sheep. It is simply that the ground on which actual battles are fought is not like a chess-board. And after them came swinging a six-gun battery, the guns wagging from side to side as the long line turned out of the road and the drivers using their whips as the leading horses scrambled at the hill. The halted Twelfth lifted its voice and spake amiably but with point to the battery. "Go on, Guns! We'll take care of you. Don't be afraid. Give it to them." The teams—lead, swing and wheel—struggled and slipped over the steep and uneven ground and the gunners as they clung to their springless positions wore their usual and natural airs of unhappiness. They made no reply to the infantry. Once upon the top of the hill, however, these guns were unlimbered in a flash and directly the infantry could hear the loud voice of an officer drawling out the time for the fuses. A moment later the first three-point-two bellowed out and there could be heard the swish and the snarl of a fleeting shell. Colonel Sponge and a number of officers climbed to the battery's position but the men of the regiment sat in the shelter of the hill like so many blindfolded people and wondered what they would have been able to see if they had been officers. Sometimes the shells of the enemy came sweeping over the top of the hill and burst in great brown explosions in the fields to the rear. The men looked after them and laughed. To the rear could be seen also the mountain-battery coming at a comic trot with every man obviously in a deep rage with every mule. If a man can put in long service with a mule battery and come out of it with an amiable disposition, he should be presented with a medal weighing many ounces. After the mule battery came a long black winding thing which was three regiments of Spitzbergen infantry and back of them and to the right was an inky square which was the remaining Spitzbergen guns. General Richie and his staff clattered up to the hill. The blindfolded Twelfth sat still. The inky square suddenly became a long racing line. The howitzers joined their little bark to the thunder of the guns on the hill and the three regiments of infantry came on. The Twelfth sat still.

Of a sudden a bugle rang its warning and the officers shouted. Some used the old cry, "Attention! Kim up, the Kickers!" and the Twelfth knew that it had been told to go in. The majority of the men expected to see great things as soon as they rounded the shoulder of the hill but there was nothing to be seen save a complicated plain and the grey knolls occupied by the enemy. Many company commanders in low voices worked at their men and said things which do not appear in the written reports. They talked soothingly; they talked indignantly; and they talked always like fathers. And the men heard no sentence completely. They heard no specific direction, these wide-eyed men. They understood that there was being delivered some kind of exhortation to do as they had been taught and they also understood that a superior intelligence was anxious over their behavior and welfare.

There was a great deal of floundering through hedges, a climbing of walls, a jumping of ditches. Curiously original privates tried to find new and easier ways for themselves instead of following the men in front of them. Officers had short fits of fury over these people. The more originality they possessed the more likely they were to become separated from their companies. Colonel Sponge was making an exciting progress on a big charger. When the first faint song of the bullets came from above, the men wondered why he sat so high. The charger seemed as tall as the Eiffel Tower. But if he was high in air, he had a fine view and that is supposedly why people ascend the Eiffel Tower. Very often he had been a joke to them but when they saw this fat old gentleman so coolly treating the strange new missiles which hummed in the air, it struck them suddenly that they had wronged him seriously and that a man who could attain the command of a Spitzbergen regiment was entitled to general respect. And they gave him a sudden quick affection, an affection that would make them follow him heartily, trustfully, grandly—this fat old gentleman, seated on a too-big horse. In a flash his towselled grey head, his short thick legs, even his paunch, had become specially and humorously endeared to them. And this is the way of soldiers.

But still the Twelfth had not yet come to the place where tumbling bodies begin their test of the very heart of a regiment. They backed through more hedges, jumped more ditches, slid over more walls. The Rostina artillery had seemed to have been asleep but suddenly the guns aroused like dogs from their kennels and around the Twelfth there began a wild swift screeching. There arose cries to hurry, to come on, and, as the rifle bullets began to plunge into them, the men saw the high formidable hills of the enemy's right and perfectly understood that they were doomed to storm them. The cheering thing was the sudden beginning of a tremendous uproar on the enemy's left.

Every man ran, hard, tense, breathless. When they reached the foot of the hills they thought they had won the charge already but they were electrified to see officers above them waving their swords and yelling with anger, surprise and shame. With a long murmurous out-cry the Twelfth began to climb the hill. And as they went and fell, they could hear frenzied shouts. "Kim up, the Kickers." The pace was slow. It was like the rising of a tide. It was determined, almost relentless in its appearance, but it was slow. If a man fell there was a chance that he would land twenty yards below the point where he was hit. The Kickers crawled, their rifles in their left hands as they pulled and tugged themselves up with their right hands. Ever arose the shout, "Kim up, the Kickers." Timothy Lean, his face flaming, his eyes wild, yelled it back as if he was delivering the Gospel.

The Kickers came up. The enemy—they had been in small force, thinking the hills safe enough from attack—retreated quickly from this preposterous advance and not a bayonet in the Twelfth saw blood. Bayonets very seldom do.

The homing of this successful charge wore an unromantic aspect. About twenty windless men suddenly arrived and threw themselves upon the crest of the hill and breathed. And these twenty were joined by others and still others until almost 1,100 men of the Twelfth lay upon the hill-top while the regiment's track was marked by body after body, in groups and singly. The first officer—perchance the first man—one never can be certain —the first officer to gain the top of the hill was Timothy Lean, and such was the situation that he had the honor to receive his colonel with a bashful salute.

The regiment knew exactly what it had done. It did not have to wait to be told by the Spitzbergen newspapers. It had taken a formidable position with the loss of about 500 men and it knew it. It knew too that it was great glory for the Kicking Twelfth and as the men lay rolling on their bellies they expressed their joy in a wild cry. "Kim up, the Kickers." For a moment there was nothing but joy and then suddenly company commanders were besieged by men who wished to go down the path of the charge and look for their mates. The answers were without the quality of mercy. They were short, snapped, quick words. "No; you can't."

The attack on the enemy's left was sounding in great rolling crashes. The shells in their flight through the air made a noise as of red-hot iron plunged into water and stray bullets nipped near the ears of the Kickers.

The Kickers looked and saw. The battle was below them. The enemy was indicated by a long noisy line of gossamer smoke, although there could be seen a toy battery with tiny men employed at the guns. All over the field the shrapnel was bursting, making quick bulbs of white smoke. Far away two regiments of Spitzbergen infantry were charging and at the distance this charge looked like a casual stroll. It appeared that small black groups of men were walking meditatively toward the Rostina intrenchments.

There would have been orders given sooner to the Twelfth but unfortunately Colonel Sponge arrived on top of the hill without a breath of wind in his body. He could not have given an order to save the regiment from being wiped off the earth. Finally he was able to gasp out something and point at the enemy. Timothy Lean ran along the line yelling to the men to sight at 800 yards and like a slow and ponderous machine the regiment again went to work. The fire flanked a great part of the enemy's trenches.

It could be said that there were only two prominent points of view expressed by the men after their victorious arrival on the crest. One was defined in the exulting use of the corps' cry. The other was a grief-stricken murmur which is invariably heard after a hard fight. "My God, we're all cut to pieces!"

Colonel Sponge sat on the ground and impatiently waited for his wind to return. As soon as it did, he arose and cried out: "Form up and we'll charge again! We will win this battle as soon as we can hit them!" The shouts of the officers sounded wild like men yelling on ship-board in a gale. And the obedient Kickers arose for their task. It was running down hill this time. The mob of panting men poured over the stones.

But the enemy had not been at all blind to the great advantage gained by the Twelfth and they now turned upon them a desperate fire of small arms. Men fell in every imaginable way and their accoutrements rattled on the rocky ground. Some landed with a crash, floored by some tremendous blow; others drooped gently down like sacks of meal; with others it would positively appear that some spirit had suddenly seized them by the ankles and jerked their legs from under them. Many officers were down but Colonel Sponge, stuttering and blowing, was still upright. He was almost the last man in the charge but not to his shame, rather to his stumpy legs. At one time it seemed that the assault would be lost. The effect of the fire was somewhat as if a terrible cyclone was blowing in the men's faces. They wavered, lowering their heads and shouldering weakly as if it were impossible to make headway against the wind of battle. It was the moment of despair, the moment of the heroism which comes to the chosen of the war-god. The colonel's cry broke and screeched absolute hatred. Other officers simply howled and the men silent, debased, seemed to tighten their muscles for one last effort. Again they pushed against this mysterious power of the air and once more the regiment was charging. Timothy Lean, agile and strong, was well in advance and afterward he reflected that the men who had been nearest to him were an old grizzled serjeant who would have gone to hell for the honor of the regiment and a pie-faced lad who had been obliged to lie about his age in order to get into the army.

There was no shock of meeting. The Twelfth came down on a

corner of the trenches and as soon as the enemy had ascertained that the Twelfth was certain to arrive, they scuttled out, running close to the earth and spending no time in glances backward. In these days it is not discreet to wait for a charge to come home. You observe the charge, you attempt to stop it, and if you find that you can't, it is better to retire immediately to some other place. The Rostina soldiers were not heroes perhaps but they were men of sense. A maddened and badly frightened mob of Kickers came tumbling into the trench and shot at the backs of fleeing men. And at that very moment the action was won, and won by the Kickers. The enemy's flank was entirely crumpled and knowing this, he did not await further and more disastrous information. The Twelfth looked at themselves and knew that they had a record. They sat down and grinned patronizingly as they saw the batteries galloping to advanced positions to shell the retreat and they really laughed as the cavalry swept tumultuously forward. The Twelfth had no more concern with the battle. They had won it and the subsequent proceedings were only amusing.

There was a call from the flank and the men wearily adjusted themselves as General Richie and his staff came trotting up. The young general, cold-eyed, stern and grim as a Roman, looked with his straight glance at a hammered and thin and dirty line of figures which was His Majesty's Twelfth Regiment of the Line. When opposite old Colonel Sponge, a pudgy figure standing at attention, the general's face set in still more grim and stern lines. He took off his helmet. "Kim up, the Kickers," said he. He replaced his helmet and rode off. Down the cheeks of the little fat colonel rolled tears. He stood like a stone for a long moment and then wheeled in supreme wrath upon his surprised adjutant. "Delahaye, you damn fool, don't stand there staring like a monkey. Go tell young Lean I want to see him." The adjutant jumped as if he was on springs and went after Lean. That young officer presented himself directly, his face covered with disgraceful smudges, and he had also torn his breeches. He had never seen the colonel in such a rage. "Lean, you young whelp, you—you're a good boy." And even as the general had turned away from the colonel, the colonel turned away from the lieutenant.

THE UPTURNED FACE

W HAT will we do now?" said the adjutant, troubled
and excited.
"Bury him," said Timothy Lean.
The two officers looked down close to their toes where lay the
body of their comrade. The face was chalk-blue; gleaming eyes
stared at the sky. Over the two upright figures was a windy
sound of bullets, and on the top of the hill, Lean's prostrate
company of Spitzbergen infantry was firing measured volleys.
"Don't you think it would be better——" began the adjutant.
"We might leave him until to-morrow."
"No," said Lean, "I can't hold that post an hour longer. I've got
to fall back, and we've got to bury old Bill."
"Of course," said the adjutant at once. "Your men got in-
trenching tools?"
Lean shouted back to his little firing line, and two men came
slowly, one with a pick, one with a shovel. They stared in the
direction of the Rostina sharpshooters. Bullets cracked near
their ears. "Dig here," said Lean gruffly. The men, thus caused to
lower their glances to the turf, became hurried and frightened
merely because they could not look to see whence the bullets
came. The dull beat of the pick striking the earth sounded amid
the swift snap of close bullets. Presently the other private began
to shovel.
"I suppose," said the adjutant, slowly, "we'd better search his
clothes for . . . things."
Lean nodded; together in curious abstraction they looked at
the body. Then Lean stirred his shoulders, suddenly arousing
himself. "Yes," he said, "we'd better see . . . what he's got." He
dropped to his knees and approached his hands to the body of
the dead officer. But his hands wavered over the buttons of the
tunic. The first button was brick-red with drying blood, and he
did not seem to dare to touch it.

"Go on," said the adjutant hoarsely.

Lean stretched his wooden hand, and his fingers fumbled blood-stained buttons. . . . At last he arose with a ghastly face. He had gathered a watch, a whistle, a pipe, a tobacco pouch, a handkerchief, a little case of cards and papers. He looked at the adjutant. There was a silence. The adjutant was feeling that he had been a coward to make Lean do all the grizzly business.

"Well," said Lean, "that's all, I think. You have his sword and revolver."

"Yes," said the adjutant, his face working. And then he burst out in a sudden strange fury at the two privates. "Why don't you hurry up with that grave? What are you doing, anyhow? Hurry, do you hear? I never saw such stupid——"

Even as he cried out in this passion, the two men were laboring for their lives. Ever overhead, the bullets were spitting.

The grave was finished. It was not a masterpiece—poor little shallow thing. Lean and the adjutant again looked at each other in a curious silent communication.

Suddenly the adjutant croaked out a weird laugh. It was a terrible laugh which had its origin in that part of the mind which is first moved by the singing of the nerves. "Well," he said humorously to Lean, "I suppose we had best tumble him in."

"Yes," said Lean. The two privates stood waiting bent over on their implements. "I suppose," said Lean, "it would be better if we laid him in ourselves."

"Yes," said the adjutant. Then apparently remembering that he had made Lean search the body, he stooped with great fortitude and took hold of the dead officer's clothing. Lean joined him. Both were particular that their fingers should not feel the corpse. They tugged away; the corpse lifted, heaved, toppled, flopped into the grave, and the two officers, straightening, looked again at each other—they were always looking at each other. They sighed with relief.

The adjutant said: "I suppose we should . . . we should say something. Do you know the service, Tim?"

"They don't read the service until the grave is filled in," said Lean, pressing his lips to an academic expression.

"Don't they?" said the adjutant, shocked that he had made the mistake. "Oh, well," he cried suddenly, "let us . . . let us say something while . . . while he can hear us."

"All right," said Lean. "Do you know the service?"

"I can't remember a line of it," said the adjutant.

Lean was extremely dubious. "I can repeat two lines but——"

"Well, do it," said the adjutant. "Go as far as you can. That's better than nothing. And . . . the beasts have got our range exactly."

Lean looked at his two men. "Attention!" he barked. The privates came to attention with a click, looking much aggrieved. The adjutant lowered his helmet to his knee. Lean, bare-headed, stood over the grave. The Rostina sharpshooters fired briskly.

"*O, Father, our friend has sunk in the deep waters of death, but his spirit has leaped toward Thee as the bubble arises from the lips of the drowning. Perceive, we beseech, O, Father, the little flying bubble and——*"

Lean, although husky and ashamed, had suffered no hesitation up to this point, but he stopped with a hopeless feeling and looked at the corpse.

The adjutant moved uneasily. "*And from Thy superb heights——*" he began, and then he, too, came to an end.

"*And from Thy superb heights,*" said Lean.

The adjutant suddenly remembered a phrase in the back part of the Spitzbergen burial service, and he exploited it with the triumphant manner of a man who has recalled everything and can go on.

"*O, God, have mercy——*"

"*O, God, have mercy——*" said Lean.

" '*Mercy,*' " repeated the adjutant in a quick failure.

" '*Mercy,*' " said Lean. And then he was moved by some violence of feeling, for he turned suddenly upon his two men and tigerishly said: "Throw the dirt in."

The fire of the Rostina sharpshooters was accurate and continuous.

II

One of the aggrieved privates came forward with his shovel. He lifted his first shovel load of earth and for a moment of inexplicable hesitation it was held poised above this corpse which from its chalk-blue face looked keenly out from the grave. Then the soldier emptied his shovel on—on the feet.

Timothy Lean felt as if tons had been swiftly lifted from off his forehead. He had felt that perhaps the private might empty the shovel on—on the face. It had been emptied on the feet. There was a great point gained there—ha, ha!—the first shovelful had been emptied on the feet. How satisfactory!

The adjutant began to babble. "Well, of course . . . a man we've messed with all these years . . . impossible . . . you can't, you know, leave your intimate friends rotting on the field. . . . Go on, for God's sake, and shovel, *you*."

The man with the shovel suddenly ducked, grabbed his left arm with his right hand and looked at his officer for orders. Lean picked the shovel from the ground. "Go to the rear," he said to the wounded man. He also addressed the other private. "You get under cover, too. I'll . . . I'll finish this business."

The wounded man scrambled hastily for the top of the ridge without devoting any glances to the direction from whence the bullets came and the other man followed at an equal pace but he was different in that he looked back anxiously three times. This is merely the way—often—of the hit and the unhit.

Timothy Lean filled the shovel, hesitated, and then in a movement which was like a gesture of abhorrence, he flung the dirt into the grave and as it landed it made a sound—plop. Lean suddenly paused and mopped his brow—a tired laborer.

"Perhaps we have been wrong," said the adjutant. His glance wavered stupidly. "It might have been better if we hadn't buried him just at this time. Of course, if we advance to-morrow, the body would have been——"

"Damn you," said Lean. "Shut your mouth." He was not the senior officer.

He again filled the shovel and flung in the earth. Always the earth made that sound—plop. For a space Lean worked frantically like a man digging himself out of danger.

Soon there was nothing to be seen but the chalk-blue face. Lean filled the shovel. . . . "Good God," he cried to the adjutant. "Why didn't you turn him somehow when you put him in? This——" Then Lean began to stutter.

The adjutant understood. He was pale to the lips. "Go on, man," he cried, beseechingly, almost in a shout. . . . Lean swung back the shovel; it went forward in a pendulum curve. When the earth landed it made a sound—plop.

THE SHRAPNEL OF THEIR FRIENDS

FOM far over the knolls came the tiny sound of a cavalry bugle singing out the recall, and later, detached parties of His Majesty's Second Hussars came trotting back to where the Spitzbergen infantry sat complacently on the captured Rostina position. The horsemen were well pleased, and they told how they had ridden thrice through the helter-skelter of the fleeing enemy. They had ultimately been checked by the great truth that when a good enemy runs away in daylight he sooner or later finds a place where he fetches up with a jolt and turns to face the pursuit—notably if it is a cavalry pursuit. The Hussars had discreetly withdrawn, displaying no foolish pride of corps at that time.

There was a general admission that the Kicking Twelfth had taken the chief honors of the day, but the Artillery added that if the guns had not shelled so accurately the Twelfth's charge could not have been made so successfully, and the three other regiments of infantry of course did not conceal their feeling that their attack on the enemy's left had withdrawn many rifles that otherwise would have been pelting at the Twelfth. The Cavalry simply said that but for them the victory would not have been complete.

Corps prides met each other face to face at every step, but the Kickers smiled easily and indulgently. A few recruits bragged, but they bragged because they were recruits. The older men did not wish it to appear that they were surprised and rejoiced at the performance of the regiment. If they were congratulated they simply smirked, suggesting that the ability of the Twelfth had long been known to them and that the charge had been a little thing, you know, just turned off in the way of an afternoon's work. Major-General Richie encamped his troops on the position which they had taken from the enemy. Old Colonel Sponge of the Twelfth redistributed his officers, and the losses had been so great that Timothy Lean got command of a company. It was not too much of a company. Fifty-three smudged and sweating men faced their new commander. The company had gone into action with a strength of eighty-six. The heart of Timothy Lean beat high with pride. He intended to be some day a general, and if he ever became a general that moment of promotion was not equal in joy to the moment when he looked at his new possession of fifty-three vagabonds. He scanned the faces and recognized with satisfaction one old serjeant and two bright young corporals. "Now," said he to himself, "I have here a snug little body of men with which I can do something." In him burned the usual fierce fire to make them the best company in the regiment. He had adopted them; they were his men. "I will do what I can for you," he said. "Do you the same for me."

The Twelfth bivouacked on the ridge. Little fires were built and there appeared among the men innumerable blackened tin cups, which were so treasured that a faint suspicion in connection with the loss of one could bring on the grimmest of fights. Meantime certain of the privates silently re-adjusted their kits as their names were called out by the serjeants. These were the men condemned to picket duty after a hard day of marching and fighting. The dusk came slowly, and the color of the countless fires, spotting the ridge and the plain, grew in the falling darkness. Far-away pickets fired at something.

One by one the men's heads were lowered to the earth until the ridge was marked by two long shadowy rows of men. Here and there an officer sat musing in his dark cloak with a ray of a weakening fire gleaming on his sword hilt. From the plain there came at times the sound of battery horses moving restlessly at their tethers, and one could imagine he heard the throaty grumbling curse of the aroused drivers. The moon dived swiftly through flying light clouds. Far-away pickets fired at something.

In the morning the infantry and guns breakfasted to the music of a racket between the cavalry and the enemy which was taking place some miles up the valley. The ambitious Hussars had apparently stirred some kind of a hornet's nest, and they were having a good fight with no officious friends near enough to interfere. The remainder of the army looked toward the fight musingly over the tops of tin cups. In time the column crawled lazily forward to see. The Twelfth, as it crawled, saw a regiment deploy to the right, and saw a battery dash to take position. The cavalry jingled back, grinning with pride and expecting to be greatly admired. Presently the Twelfth was bidden to take seat by the roadside and await its turn. Instantly the wise men—and there were more than three—came out of the east and announced that they had divined the whole plan. The Kicking Twelfth was to be held in reserve until the critical moment of the fight, and then they were to be sent forward to win a victory. In corroboration they pointed to the fact that the general in command was sticking close to them in order, they said, to give the word quickly at the proper moment. And in truth, on a small hill to the right Major-General Richie sat his horse and used his glasses, while back of him his staff and the orderlies bestrode their champing, dancing mounts.

It is always good to look hard at a general, and the Kickers were transfixed with interest. The wise men again came out of the east and told what was inside the Richie head, but even the wise men wondered what was inside the Richie head.

Suddenly an exciting thing happened. To the left and ahead was a pounding Spitzbergen battery, and a toy suddenly appeared on the slope behind the guns. The toy was a man with a flag—the flag was white save for a square of red in the centre. And this toy began to wig-wag wag-wig, and it spoke to General Richie under the authority of the captain of the battery. It said: "The Eighty-eighth are being driven on my centre and right."

Now when the Kicking Twelfth had left Spitzbergen there was an average of six signal-men in each company. A proportion of these signalers had been destroyed in the first engagement, but enough remained so that the Kicking Twelfth read, as a unit, the news of the Eighty-eighth. The word ran quickly. "The eighty-eighth are being driven on my centre and right."

Richie rode to where Colonel Sponge sat aloft on his big horse, and a moment later a cry rang along the column. "Kim up, the Kickers." A large number of the men were already in the road, hitching and twisting at their belts and packs. The Kickers moved forward.

They deployed and passed in a straggling line through the

battery and to the left and right of it. The gunners called out to them cheerfully, telling them not to be afraid.

The scene before them was startling. They were facing a country cut up by many steep-sided ravines, and over the resultant hills were retreating little squads of the Eighty-eighth. The Twelfth laughed in its exultation. The men could now tell by the volume of fire that the Eighty-eighth were retreating for reasons which were not sufficiently expressed in the noise of the Rostina shooting. Held together by the bugle, the Kickers swarmed up the first hill and laid on the crest. Parties of the Eighty-eighth went through their lines, and the Twelfth told them coarsely its several opinions. The sights were clicked up to 600 yards, and with a crashing volley the regiment entered its second battle.

A thousand yards away on the right the cavalry and a regiment of infantry were creeping onward. Sponge decided not to be backward, and the bugle told the Twelfth to go ahead once more. The Twelfth charged, followed by a rabble of rallied men of the Eighty-eighth, who were crying aloud that it had been all a mistake.

A charge in these days is not a running match. Those splendid pictures of leveled bayonets dashing at headlong pace toward the closed ranks of the enemy are absurd as soon as they are mistaken for the actuality of the present. In these days charges are likely to cover at least the half of a mile, and to go at the pace exhibited in the pictures, a man would be obliged to have a little steam engine inside of him.

The charge of the Kicking Twelfth somewhat resembled the advance of a great crowd of beaters who for some reason passionately desired to start the game. Men stumbled; men fell; men swore. There were cries: "This way! Come this way! Don't go that way! You can't get up that way." Over the rocks the Twelfth scrambled, red in the face, sweating and angry. Soldiers fell because they were struck by bullets and because they had not an ounce of strength left in them. Colonel Sponge, with a face like a red cushion, was being dragged windless up the steeps by devoted and athletic men. Three of the older captains lay afar back, and swearing with their eyes because their tongues were temporarily out of service.

And yet—and yet the speed of the charge was slow. From the

position of the battery, it looked as if the Kickers were taking a walk over some extremely difficult country.

The regiment ascended a superior height and found trenches and dead men. They took seat with the dead, satisfied with this company until they could get their wind. For thirty minutes purple-faced stragglers rejoined from the rear. Colonel Sponge looked behind him and saw that Richie, with his staff, had approached by another route, and had evidently been near enough to see the full extent of the Kickers' exertions. Presently Richie began to pick a way for his horse toward the captured position. He disappeared in a gully between two hills.

Now it came to pass that a Spitzbergen battery on the far right took occasion to mistake the identity of the Kicking Twelfth and the captain of these guns, not having anything to occupy him in front, directed his six 3.2's upon the ridge where the tired Kickers lay side by side with the Rostina dead. A shrapnel shell came swinging over the Kickers, seething and fuming. It burst directly over the trenches and the shrapnel, of course, scattered forward, hurting nobody. But a man screamed out to his officer, "By God, sir. That is one of our own batteries." The whole line quivered with fright. Five more shells streaked overhead and one flung its hail into the middle of the third battalion's line and the Kicking Twelfth shuddered to the very centre of its heart—and arose like one man—and fled.

Colonel Sponge, fighting, frothing at the mouth, dealing blows with his fist right and left, found himself confronting a fury on horseback. Richie was as pale as death and his eye sent out sparks. "What does this conduct mean?" he flashed out from between his fastened teeth.

Sponge could only gurgle, "The battery—the battery—the battery——"

"The battery?" cried Richie in a voice which sounded like pistol shots. "Are you afraid of the guns you almost took yesterday? Go back there, you white-livered cowards! You swine! You dogs! Curs!—curs!—curs! Go back there!"

Most of the men halted and crouched under the lashing tongue of their maddened general. But one man found desperate speech and he yelled: "General, it is our own battery that is firing on us!"

Many say that the general's face tightened until it looked like a mask. The Kicking Twelfth retired to a comfortable place where they were only under the fire of the Rostina artillery. The men saw a staff officer riding over the obstructions in a manner calculated to break his neck directly.

The Kickers were aggrieved but the heart of the old colonel was cut in twain. He even babbled to his majors, talking like a man who is about to die of simple rage. "Did you hear what he said to me? Did you hear what he called us? *Did you hear what he called us?*"

The majors searched their minds for words to heal a deep wound.

The Twelfth received orders to go into camp upon the hill where they had been insulted. Old Sponge looked as if he were about to knock the aide out of the saddle but he saluted and took the regiment back to the temporary companionship of the Rostina dead.

Major-General Richie never apologized to Colonel Sponge. When you are a commanding officer you do not adopt the custom of apologizing for the wrongs done to your subordinates. You ride away. And they understand and are confident of the restitution to honor. Richie never opened his stern young lips to Sponge in reference to the scene near the hill of the Rostina dead but in time there was a General Order No. 20 which spoke definitely of the gallantry of His Majesty's Twelfth Regiment of the Line and its colonel. In the end Sponge was given a high decoration because he had been badly used by Richie on that day. Richie knew that it is hard for men to withstand the shrapnel of their friends.

A few days later the Kickers, marching in column on the road, came upon their friend the battery halted in a field. And they addressed the battery. And the captain of the battery blanched to the tips of his ears. But the men of the battery told the Kickers to go to the devil—frankly, freely, placidly, told the Kickers to go to the devil.

And this story proves that it is sometimes better to be a private.

"AND IF HE WILLS, WE MUST DIE"

A SERJEANT, a corporal and fourteen men of the Twelfth Regiment of the Line had been sent out to occupy a house on the main highway. They would be at least a half of a mile in advance of any other picket of their own people. Serjeant Morton was deeply angry at being sent on this duty. He said that he was over-worked. There were at least two serjeants, he claimed furiously, whose turn it should have been to go on this arduous mission. He was treated unfairly; he was abused by his superiors; why did any damned fool ever join the army; as for him he would get out of it as soon as possible; he was sick of it; the life of a dog. All this he said to the corporal who listened attentively, giving grunts of respectful assent. On the way to this post, two privates took occasion to drop casually to the rear and pilfer in the orchard of a deserted plantation. When the serjeant discovered this absence, he grew black with a rage which was an accumulation of all his irritations. "Run, you!" he howled. "Bring them here! I'll show them——" A private ran swiftly to the rear. The remainder of the squad began to shout nervously at the two delinquents whose figures they could see in the deep shade of the orchard hurriedly picking fruit from the ground and cramming it within their shirts, next to their skins. The beseeching cries of their comrades stirred the criminals more than did the barking of the serjeant. They ran to rejoin the squad, while holding their loaded bosoms and with their mouths open with aggrieved explanations.

Jones faced the serjeant with a horrible cancer marked in bumps on his left side. The disease of Patterson showed quite around the front of his waist in many protuberances. "A nice pair!" said the serjeant with sudden frigidity. "You're the kind of soldiers a man wants to choose for dangerous out-post duty, ain't you?"

The two privates stood at attention, still looking much aggrieved. "We only——" began Jones huskily.

"Oh, you 'only'!" cried the serjeant. "Yes, you 'only'! I know all about that. But if you think you are going to trifle with me——"

A moment later, the squad moved on toward its station. Behind the serjeant's back Jones and Patterson were slyly passing apples and pears to their friends while the serjeant expounded eloquently to the corporal. "You see what kind of men are in the army now! Why, when I joined the regiment it was a very different thing, I can tell you. *Then*, a serjeant had some authority and if a man disobeyed orders, he had a very small chance of escaping something extremely serious. But now! Good God! If I report these men, the captain will look over a lot of beastly orderly sheets and say"—here the serjeant wrathfully imitated the voice of his captain—" 'Haw, eh, well, Serjeant Morton, these men seem to have very good records; very good records indeed. I can't be too hard on them; no; not too hard.' " Continued the serjeant: "I tell you, Flagler, the army is no place for a decent man."

Flagler, the corporal, answered with a sincerity of appreciation which with him had become a science. "I think you are right, serjeant," he answered.

Behind them the privates mumbled discreetly. "Damn this serjeant of ours. He thinks we are made of wood. I don't see any reason for all this strictness when we are on active service. It isn't like being at home in barracks. This is very different. He hammers us now worse than he did in barracks. There is no great harm in a couple of men dropping out to raid an orchard of the enemy when all the world knows that we haven't had a decent meal in twenty days."

The reddened face of Serjeant Morton suddenly showed to the rear. "A little more marching and much less talking," he said.

When he came to the house he had been ordered to occupy, the serjeant sniffed with disdain. "These people must have lived like cattle," he said angrily. To be sure, the place was not alluring. The ground-floor had been used for the housing of cattle and it was dark and terrible. A flight of steps led to the lofty first floor which was denuded but respectable. The serjeant's visage lightened when he saw the strong walls of stone and cement. "Unless they turn guns on us, they will never get us out of here," he said cheerfully to the squad. The men, anxious to keep him in an amiable mood, all hurriedly grinned and seemed very appreciative and pleased. "I'll make this into a fortress," he announced. He sent Jones and Patterson, the two orchard-thieves, out on sentry-duty. He worked the others then until he could think of no more things to tell them to do. Afterward he went forth, with a major-general's serious scowl, and examined the ground in front of his position. In returning he came to a sentry, Jones, munching an apple. He sternly commanded him to throw it away.

The men spread their blankets on the floors of the bare rooms, and putting their packs under their heads and lighting their pipes, they lived in lazy peace. Bees hummed in the garden and a scent of flowers came through the open window. A great fan-shaped bit of sunshine smote the face of one man and he indolently cursed as he moved his primitive bed to a shadier place.

Another private explained to a comrade: "This is all nonsense anyhow. No sense in occupying this post. They——"

"But of course," said the corporal, "when she told me herself she cared more for me than she did for him, I wasn't going to stand any of his talk——" The corporal's listener was so sleepy that he could only grunt his sympathy.

There was a sudden little spatter of shooting. A cry from Jones rang out. With no little intermediate scrambling, the serjeant leaped straight to his feet. "Now," he cried, "let us see what you are made of! If," he added bitterly, "you are made of anything."

A man yelled: "Good God, can't you see you're all tangled up in my cartridge belt?"

Another man yelled: "Keep off my legs! Can't you walk on the floor?"

To the windows there was a blind rush of slumberous men, who brushed hair from their eyes even as they made ready their rifles. Jones and Patterson came stumbling up the steps, crying dreadful information. Already the enemy's bullets were spitting and singing over the house.

The serjeant suddenly was stiff and cold with a sense of the importance of the thing. "Wait until you see one," he drawled loudly and calmly, "then shoot."

For some moments the enemy's bullets swung swifter than lightning over the house without anybody being able to discover a target. In this interval a man was shot in the throat. He gurgled and then lay down on the floor. The blood slowly waved down the brown skin of his neck while he looked meekly at his comrades.

There was a howl. "There they are! There they come!" The rifles crackled. A light smoke drifted idly through the rooms. There was a strong odor as from burnt paper and the powder of fire-crackers. The men were silent. Through the windows and about the house the bullets of an entirely invisible enemy moaned, hummed, spat, burst and sang.

The men began to curse. "Why can't we see them?" they muttered through their teeth. The serjeant was still frigid. He answered soothingly as if he were directly reprehensible for this behavior of the enemy. "Wait a moment. You will soon be able to see them. There! Give it to them!" A little skirt of black figures had appeared in a field. It was really like shooting at an upright needle from the full length of a ball-room. But the men's spirits improved as soon as the enemy—this mysterious enemy—became a tangible thing, and far off. They had believed the foe to be shooting at them from the adjacent garden.

"Now," said the serjeant ambitiously, "we can beat them off easily if you men are good enough."

A man called out in a tone of quick great interest. "See that fellow on horse-back, Bill? Isn't he on horse-back? I thought he was on horse-back."

There was a fusilade against another side of the house. The serjeant dashed into the room which commanded that situation. He found a dead soldier on the floor. He rushed out howling: "When was Knowles killed? When was Knowles killed? Damn it, when was Knowles killed?" It was absolutely essential to find out the exact moment this man died. A blackened private turned upon his serjeant and demanded: "How in hell do I know?" Serjeant Morton had a sense of anger so brief that in the next second he cried: "Patterson!" He had even forgotten his vital interest in the time of Knowles' death.

"Yes?" said Patterson, his face set with some deep-rooted quality of determination. Still, he was a mere farm-boy.

"Go in to Knowles' window and shoot at those people," said the serjeant hoarsely. Afterward he coughed. Some of the fumes of the fight had made way to his lungs.

Patterson looked at the door into this other room. He looked at it as if he suspected it was to be his death-chamber. Then he entered and stood across the body of Knowles and fired vigorously into a group of charming plum-trees.

"They can't take this house," declared the serjeant in a contemptuous and argumentative tone. He was apparently replying to somebody. The man who had been shot in the throat looked up at him. Eight men were firing from the windows. The serjeant detected in a corner three wounded men talking together feebly. "Don't you think there is anything to do?" he bawled. "Go and get Knowles' cartridges and give them to somebody that can use them! Take Simpson's too." The man who had been shot in the throat looked at him. Of the three wounded men who had been talking, one said: "My leg is all doubled up under me, serjeant." He spoke apologetically.

Meantime the serjeant was re-loading his rifle. His foot slipped in the blood of the man who had been shot in the throat and the military boot made a greasy red streak on the floor.

"Why, we can hold this place," shouted the serjeant jubilantly. "Who says we can't?"

Corporal Flagler suddenly spun away from his window and fell in a heap.

"Serjeant," murmured a man as he dropped to a seat on the floor out of danger, "I can't stand this. I swear I can't. I think we should run away."

Morton, with the kindly eyes of a good shepherd, looked at the man. "You are afraid Johnston, you are afraid," he said softly. The man struggled to his feet, cast upon the serjeant a gaze full of admiration, reproach and despair, and returned to his post. A moment later he pitched forward and thereafter his body hung out of the window, his arms straight and the fists clenched. Incidentally this corpse was pierced afterward by chance three times by bullets of the enemy.

The serjeant laid his rifle against the stone-work of the window-frame and shot with care until his magazine was empty. Behind him, a man simply grazed on the elbow was wildly sobbing like a girl. "Damn it, shut up," said Morton without turning his head. Before him was a vista of a garden, fields, clumps of trees, woods, populated at the time with little stealthy fleeting figures.

He grew furious. "Why didn't he send me orders?" he cried aloud. The emphasis on the word "he" was impressive. A mile back on the road, a galloper of the Hussars lay dead beside his dead horse.

The man who had been grazed on the elbow still set up his bleat. Morton's fury veered to this soldier. "Can't you shut up? Can't you shut up? Can't you shut up? Fight! That's the thing to do. Fight!"

A bullet struck Morton and he fell upon the man who had been shot in the throat. There was a sickening moment. Then the serjeant rolled off to a position upon the bloody floor. He turned himself with a last effort until he could look at the wounded who were able to look at him.

"Kim up, the Kickers," he said thickly. His arms weakened and he dropped on his face.

After an interval, a young subaltern of the enemy's infantry, followed by his eager men, burst into this reeking interior. But just over the threshold he halted before the scene of blood and death. He turned with a shrug to his serjeant. "God! I should have estimated them as at least one hundred strong."

Appendixes

TEXTUAL NOTES

3.9 grey] In order to preserve uniformity in the spelling of this common word throughout *The Little Regiment* stories, some of which read 'grey' from an authoritative source but others 'gray' in the only substantive editions, a special exception is made to the editorial principles governing copy-text and authority as applied in the present edition and Crane's invariable spelling 'grey' is uniformly adopted. That Ch here reads 'grey' in the English spelling is, of course, purely fortuitous so far as authority is concerned, although there can be no question of the manuscript spelling.

3.22 voice] The A1 change from the McC singular to the plural 'voices of the guns' is certainly unauthoritative and does not seem to be a necessary correction. The plural 'their' of the 'challenges and warnings' appears to refer back to 'guns', not to 'voice'. In short, it is the guns that Crane is taking as issuing challenges and warnings, not their voices. Moreover, 'voice' conforms to the singular 'word' at 3.24. The conventional plural at 7.21 does not seem to apply here.

6.32 bellowed] The A1 variant 'bellowing'—though without presumed authority—seems to be a rationalization of an ambiguous McC construction. If 'One by one the batteries on the northern shore aroused,' is an absolute construction, then the comma after 'aroused' is correct and the syntax sufficiently clear. However, if the sentence is instead made up of two independent clauses, then the comma would be a typescript (or manuscript) error for a semicolon (Crane was usually though not invariably careful about writing so-called 'comma-fault sentences'). Absolute constructions are rare in Crane; hence the odds favor the hypothesis that the sentence consists of two independent clauses without a conjunction but with the present comma punctuation.

15.21 crackling] The 'cracking' of all three texts would seem to represent an overlooked typist's error, like the 'match' at 11.7 and 'saw' at 21.11 that were caught in proof. At 13.37 Crane writes of the 'crackle of musketry'. In "Three Miraculous Soldiers" occurs 'the sharp crack of a distant shot' (44.2) but the firing 'was now expressed in spiteful crackles' (46.21).

15.25 young] This is the reading of Ch, whereas McC 'younger' is conjectured to be a compositorial error probably under the influence of the comparative 'older' that follows. It would seem that 'young officers' is to be taken as an absolute as indicated by the absence of a preceding article; that is, 'young officers' set themselves apart by their tenor voices, whereas 'the older officers' are then lumped together with 'hoarse and deep voices' in contrast but, of course, with any number of assumed gradations. All officers younger than 'older' officers would not necessarily have tenor voices.

THREE MIRACULOUS SOLDIERS

23.14 into] This is one of the group of neutral variants for which the A1 line of descent is taken as more trustworthy than the typist and compositor behind the McClure master proof. However, in this particular example some partial support for A1 'into' instead of N,EIM 'to the kitchen' can be summoned from 25.28–29 in which the girl 'marched down into' even though at 25.33 the mother 'came down to the kitchen'.

23.29 wood] Crane seems to have used 'wood' and 'woods' almost interchangeably so that the authority of the harder reading of A1 (found also in all texts at 22.21) is presumably better than the conventional plural of the McClure proof. For examples of 'wood' and 'woods' see "An Indiana Campaign" 62.5, 62.12, 62.33, 63.11 (wood), 64.6, 64.18, 65.9; "A Grey Sleeve" 69.9 (wood), 69.13, 69.20, 69.23; "An Episode of War" 89.18 (wood), 89.23 (wood), 90.34–35 (wood).

24.4 blue,] The variety of treatment given the end of this sentence suggests that the manuscript could not have been specific and hence different typists, and compositors, styled as they interpreted the meaning. Both N[4] and N[7] may show confusion by the draconian method of omitting 'them—' at 24.3 to read 'disclosed a dozen', but with the dash after 'blue'. N[1] punctuates as does EIM with a dash after 'them' and a comma after 'blue'; but N[2-3,5-8] print a comma after 'them' but a dash after 'blue'. A1 is unique and almost certainly wrong in making 'a dozen brown-faced troopers in blue' into a parenthetical phrase by enclosing it with dashes. The other texts use a single dash with the effect of a colon. The only question, then, is which is the intended revelation—the fact that the troopers in blue were *galloping*, as in N[2-3,5-8], or that the horsemen were *troopers in blue* who were, incidentally, galloping. When one surveys the way in which Crane has prepared this scene by keeping the setting in doubt, and thus the identity of the soldiers, it would seem that the fact of their galloping is not revelatory since nothing is made of this later. Instead, as indicated by the preliminary use of 'them' with the dash, and then the explanation of 'them' immediately following, the revelation is that these are troopers *in blue*. Thus the N[1] and EIM construction appears to be the right one, and it is possible to attribute the second A1 dash to a misconstruction of the same dash, wherever it was in the manuscript, which had got misplaced in the McClure proof, evidently, to follow 'blue'.

24.32 moment, "they've] Although 'they've' quite clearly continues the sentence begun with ' "But, ma," ', the fact that N[2-3,6-8] agree in 'moment. "They've' seems to indicate what the master proof read; hence N[1,4-5] and EIM have corrected their copy. Whether A1 in reading 'moment, "they've' was reproducing the reading of its copy or, as is a tendency in A1, was reducing such a construction to lower case after an exclamation is moot. Although the construction is certainly exclamatory, as shown by $N^{2-3,6-8}$, no text prints an exclamation point, and A1 would certainly have done so if it had been present in copy. Thus although the period and capital are probably closer to Crane's manuscript than the comma and lower case, the interpretation of the sentence is also affected by the comma after 'But', which seems to remove any exclamatory intent and is present in all texts. On the whole, A1 seems to print a reasonable compromise and has been followed in the present edition.

25.24 the step] This is one of the cases when an apparently indifferent variant between A1 and N can be resolved, and in favor of A1. Here $N,EIM 'a step' lacks the reference to preceding 'As she neared the last step' provided by A1 'the step'.

26.33 grey] In this story EIM, with its English spelling 'grey', fortuitously prints what was Crane's invariable spelling, americanized to 'gray' in all other documents. Above, at 26.23, and thereafter silently in a few other places where A1 is the only authority, the spelling is altered to 'grey' in order to conform. EIM, of course, can carry no authority. One would not bother with this refinement were it not for the spelling 'grey' in the title and in most of the texts of the American newspapers for "A Grey Sleeve"; hence an attempt is made in the present edition to make the spelling uniform throughout *The Little Regiment*.

27.13 No'm'm] This eccentric use of the apostrophe throughout the story in $N is not likely to have been the invention of the McClure typist or compositor but should have derived directly from the manuscript, which was attempting to reproduce the sound of Southern speech slurring this phrase into a single word. The A1 and EIM 'No, m'm' is apparently an independent styling without authority.

27.16 thah] The conventional 'thar', unique with A1, appears to be a sophistication. The attempt to distinguish the Southern soft drawl from the 'r' of ordinary country speech is exhibited in 'Keh-plunk' at 27.15, sophisticated to 'Ker-' only in N^1.

27.33 a clean] The case is doubtful but there is something to be said for $N,EIM 'a clean cloth' as the manuscript reading, with the 'a' dropped in the A1 editing because of the literal difficulties. Such anomalies are common enough in Crane's style.

28.31 Just . . . We'd] The concurrence of EIM with A1 in reading 'snack-like—just a snack—we'd——' is odd but appears to be editorial or compositorial in both. For a similar example in which some evidence exists for A1's use of dashes and lower case to escape just such short incomplete sentences, see the Textual Note to 43.26.

29.20 feed box] On the first appearance here of this frequently occurring compound only N^4 and EIM hyphenate, and these continue the hyphenated form throughout. Some of the other N representatives slide in and out of 'feed box', 'feed-box', or even 'feedbox', but several come to rest eventually with the hyphen, like N^7, which though unhyphenated at 29.20 begins hyphenation at 29.37 and 30.4. Perhaps arbitrarily, for the purposes of the present edition the A1 unhyphenated form has been accepted as standard. The irregular or regular hyphens in other documents are taken to be compositorial (EIM, for example, regularly hyphenates more compounds than any other text), and without further notice (except for two slips in A1 where emendation is required) the copy-text is followed without comment. However, the hyphen in A1 at 45.4 is retained in the adjectival construction.

29.38 knothole] At first sight the majority view of $N^{1,3-4,7}$, EIM here would suggest that the hyphenated compound form should be adopted as standard; but, very oddly, at the next appearance of the word the different authorities settle down to something of a formula, although not a completely invariable one, whereby only N^2, N^{7-8}, and EIM regularly hyphenate but $N^{1,4,6}$ adopt the A1 'knothole' form and $N^{3,5}$ print 'knot hole'. For convenience, therefore, the A1 copy-text 'knothole' is adopted throughout without further comment save where A1 varies.

30.34 ask] This is the reading of the first typescript, as attested by $N joined by EIM. The A1 variant 'go ask' may have been contaminated by 'go' from lines 38,39. It is not necessarily overrefined to point out that the officer would be unlikely to say 'go' until he had ascertained, in the next sentence, where the mother was. After learning that she is within the house, he then changes to 'go and ask' in lines 38,39.

31.6–7 there was] The $N,EIM reading 'there was' clashes with 'there was' at 31.8–9. The latter cannot be spared, but it is possible to believe that the A1 editor saw that the first could be omitted and the text smoothed. The phrase 'there was' is a particular favorite with Crane but seems to be the particular victim of editorial pruning, perhaps aided here by 'there to reply' at 31.8.

31.15 wailed] No doubt can exist that 'wailed' was the reading of the McClure proof, and a strong presumption may exist that it was present in the manuscript as well. The variant 'wail', then, poses a choice between a Crane revision or an editorial smoothing out. The preterite is so clumsily placed—the sequence being that the mother wailed and began to thrash about—as to bear the mark of Crane's own inscription, not likely to be authorially revised.

35.36 made her mind up] A1 'decided' might have been taken as one of the casual word substitutions from N (although a not very explicable one), but signs of textual disturbance support another interpretation. On the evidence of $N^{2,4,6}$ the McClure proof (and in this case, one assumes the manuscript) must have read in error 'made her mind'. Although the inevitable 'up' must have occurred to him, as it did to the compositors of $N^{1,3,5,8}$ and EIM, it would seem that the A1 editor took the occasion to mend the reading by substituting 'decide'.

35.37 camp-fires] Only EIM reproduces what from the manuscript fragment of "The Little Regiment" we know to be Crane's hyphenation of this compound, although in the nature of the transmission EIM, when unique, must be unauthoritative. On the other hand, the two lines of the text disagree, N¹⁻⁶ printing 'campfires' and A1 'camp fires'. The opportunity may be taken, therefore, to introduce an authoritative form even from an unauthoritative source. Whether the consistent lack of hyphenation in A1 has anything to do with its copy is problematical, although it should be noticed that the compositor of "The Little Regiment" follows his copy in reading 'camp-fire'. But of course he may have been a different workman from the compositor(s) who set "Three Miraculous Soldiers" in this area.

35.38 circles] A1 'circle' would mean, literally, that the campfires were arranged in a circle within the orchard, but there is no evidence that this was Crane's intention. For the use of 'circle' to describe the light from a single campfire, instead, see "The Little Regiment" 18.26–27: 'At last a soldier from a distant fire came into this circle of light.'

37.2 Sssh.] That A1 'S-s-s-h' is compositorial may be indicated by the same difference in "An Indiana Campaign" between N 'Sssh' and A1 'S-s-s-h'. The fact that in "An Indiana Campaign" the N reading does not invariably carry the exclamation point (as is the tendency in A1) may suggest that in the present case the period in N¹,³,⁵,⁷⁻⁸ is more authoritative than the exclamation in N²,⁴, EIM, and A1 where compositorial styling is almost inevitable.

39.3 ever] For the authority of A1 'ever' versus $N,EIM 'even' see "An Indiana Campaign" 58.8–10, 'the little boy stood before the major, struggling with a tale that was ever upon the tip of his tongue.'

39.37 glinted] One may be reluctant to emend the rare A1 'glintered' by the common 'glinted' of the other authorities. Although 'glinted' constantly appears in Crane, unfortunately at the moment of writing the present editor has not come upon another example of 'glintered'. It will no doubt be promptly observed by an early reader, in which case the correction can be made in a subsequent printing.

40.27–28 wildly . . . indifference] This is the first of the only two cuts in A1 from the McClure typescript (or of additions in the master proof) that are more than a word or two. In both cases (see the Textual Note to 41.21) no very strong reason exists for such an unusual omission as part of any systematic paring operation. On the other hand, in the present case a most literal-minded editor could object to a possible contradiction. That is, if the swishing continued until the head appeared, it would stop, presumably, at that moment if the 'until' is correct. Yet the next sentence indicates that the noise continued until they suppressed it by their gestures. Whether the Appleton editor (or Crane) was as finicky as this is open to question; on the other hand, the words do not read like an addition. Very likely the passage close by at 41.21 must be viewed as a unit with this at 40.27–28, and there a better case can be made against the hypothesis of addition. Yet if they are omissions, the agent and his reasons remain obscure. Two cases of eyeskip may be asking too much. Of course, it is possible that the two passages are not a unit (even though they occur suspiciously close together), in which case different explanations could be evolved. Although the whole matter is most obscure, the present editor is led to take the position that the two should be an integral part of the text and that in one way or another A1 is in error in omitting them.

41.21 A man . . . box?"] This omission gives a choice of the lady or the tiger. A discontinuity of a sort certainly exists in the identification of the 'He' who 'smiled' and the man who saw Captain Sawyer. If the passage is an omission (and only eyeskip can satisfactorily explain it), then the gap is accounted for. On the other hand, if the difficulty of reference were inadvertent (even though unnatural), Crane could have fixed it in reading over the typescript sent to McClure—if he indeed did have the typescript made up himself—and added the necessary reference. The problem seems slightly narrower than that at 40.27–28, but the answer is no clearer except that the material omitted in A1 should be a part of the text since it does not appear to be an excision and does not sound like an editorial addition.

43.26 anyhow. Even] The agreement of $N^{1-2,6-8}$ leaves no doubt that the McClure proof (and probably the typescript) read, 'That's some satisfaction anyhow. Even if you did bag me. You'll get a good walloping.' The variants seem to indicate that the other compositors objected to this series, including the incomplete sentence, and adjusted the modification according to their own lights. N^{4-5} read, with A1, 'anyhow, even . . . You'll . . . walloping.' This is manifestly wrong. Whether the A1 version is a revision or—like N^{4-5}—a compositorial (or editorial) sophistication is moot, but the odds seem to favor a sophistication, for the McClure typescript and proof reading is not a natural error. Moreover, A1 has something of a history of preferring joined syntax, with or without dashes, in similar cases.

45.39 at the orchard] On the analogy of unique N^2 'in', the A1 reading 'in' looks very much like a sophistication. So far as the account goes the fight was, strictly, not inside the orchard but *at* it, that is, contiguous with it, as in the McClure proof.

46.13 clinched] So far as the evidence of the manuscripts goes, Crane never wrote anything but 'clinched'. The $N,EIM 'clenched' very likely goes back to the first typist or compositor.

46.23 grimy,] The absence of a necessary comma after 'grimy' in A1 (although a comma appears after 'panting') suggests the possibility that the manuscript read 'grimly' as did the McClure proof and thus that 'grimy' is an unauthoritative albeit necessary correction both in EIM and in A1.

A MYSTERY OF HEROISM

48.27 grey] In order to provide uniformity in the spelling of this word throughout *The Little Regiment* so that all texts will agree with the authoritative spelling of the title "A Grey Sleeve," the invariable Crane spelling has been adopted in this story against the authority of all the documents reading 'gray'.

50.36 great] The unauthoritative change of 'great concern' in all other texts to 'little concern' in E1 (and E2) is an obvious sophistication, although a tempting one. However, Crane's use of 'great' here seems to be a bit of rather clumsy ironic understatement, and there is no reason to suppose that it is not what he wanted.

52.1 Collins's] Agreement of $N^{2,5}$ and NS in the error 'Collin's' suggests that this was a mistake in the master proof that was corrected according to the taste of the other compositors. The proper form may be suggested by the *McClure's* proof 'Sickleses colt' altered in the magazine text to 'Sickles's' (83.29,84.1–2) but corrupted in the derived *Chicago Tribune* printing to 'Sickles''. On the other hand, the late *O'Ruddy* manuscript always reads 's apostrophe'.

54.14 boiling] The agreement of N^{1-5} and NS in the error 'broiling' demonstrates the reading of the master proof. Thus the A1 correction 'boiling' need have no special authority, especially since N^6 made the same necessary alteration.

56.22 young] The agreement of N^3 and N^5 in the omissi.n of this word is odd, but it is simpler to conjecture independent error (especially since this is a long adjectival series) than to speculate that the basic proof could have been sent out in two stages of correctness.

AN INDIANA CAMPAIGN

57.26 extremely excited] The PM reading 'supremely' is certainly Crane's, but—though not impossible—'extremely' is not a natural compositorial change. It would seem that this is one of the handful of readings that Crane altered on review of the text, perhaps in typescript before setting but perhaps in proof.

57.29 who] This typically careless Crane grammar was definitely in the proof behind N, and it is unlikely that it was a compositorial slip. Moreover, on the evidence of N^3, which alters 'who' to 'that', it is probable that PM 'which' is also a compositorial sophistication. One cannot imagine Crane altering a manuscript or typescript reading 'which' to 'who' in the reviewed version of the text represented by the proof.

58.11 Major——"] The typescript behind N clearly must have read 'major' throughout, although N^{5-6} and EIM invariably style 'Major', as does PM. Whether all military titles are capitalized or not was a point of styling that divided compositors of this period, as is amply demonstrated in *Wounds in the Rain*. Although no evidence exists to suggest that Crane ever wrote military titles with anything but a minuscule (except for his uncertain practice with 'Colonel–colonel' in the late manuscript of *The O'Ruddy*), yet as a part of the necessary editorial preparation of a reading text it has seemed permissible to the present editor to adopt the common practice—although not one that is very common in the contemporary styling of Crane's texts—of using a capital when the title is in the vocative but lower case in all other instances.

59.5,6 Well?] The PM comma is almost certainly what stood in the manuscript, and is the invariable PM form in this usage. Peter, like the other characters, frequently prefaces a speech with 'Well', and at 62.27 the dash after 'Well' is only a sign of the same custom. But at 62.1, as at 59.5,6, a different use appears, marked as a question by the verb 'demanded'. Under these circumstances it seems proper to follow the $N question mark at 59.5,6 and to emend as necessary elsewhere (as at 64.8) when $N agrees with PM in the use of the comma although a query is indicated.

66.13 fence and mopping] The divergence of the copies presents a serious problem here. PM alone reads 'and still mopping', but $N^{2,6}$ omit the 'still' although retaining the participle. On the other hand, $N^{1,3-5}$, EIM, and A1 read 'and mopped', N^5, EIM, and A1 with a comma after 'fence' that turns 'still on the fence' into a parenthetical phrase. Oddly, E1, which was set from A1 copy, reads 'mopping'; and since sophistication is difficult to account for here the probable answer is that it reproduces the reading of the A1 proof that was subsequently altered by an Appleton reader to 'mopped'. This conjectural alteration joins with the evidence of $N^{2,6}$ to suggest that the Bacheller master proof read 'still on the fence and mopping his brow' and that the proof omission of 'still' before 'mopping', present in PM, offered such awkward syntax as to lead to general emendation to 'mopped'. That is, given the PM reading it is more probable to conjecture that 'mopped' is a sophistication of proof 'mopping' than that $N^{2,6}$ (and A1 early state?) 'mopping' is a sophistication of proof 'mopped', especially in view of the general lack of a period after 'fence'. This being accepted, the only question is the omission of 'still' in the Bacheller proof and its authority. Here one may only guess. The present editor feels that the odds favor the excision of the repetitious second 'still' as one of the various authorial revisions in the copy for N over the view that it was a compositorial corruption.

A Grey Sleeve

68.27 imperturbable] It is odd that N^3 joins N^1 in the misspelling 'imperturable'; but when the same error is found in N^2 at 76.33, it would seem that one of Crane's misspellings slipped into the master proof but was automatically corrected by most compositors.

72.16 house?] Although this is a natural question, the appearance of a comma in N^{3-5} and PM suggests that the master proof may have had a comma and that the question mark in N^1 and others is a compositorial correction.

72.20 Are] The evidence of the texts makes it certain that 'Is' stood in the Bacheller proof, and very likely in Crane's manuscript by a careless holdover from the first sentence. On the evidence of the unauthoritative DFM, which also altered 'Is' to 'Are', the A1 change is no doubt editorial. It is, nonetheless, necessary. In view of 'some of them' above at 72.19, the 'any' of 72.20 can only be in the plural, and 'one' following it cannot be understood since no parallel exists with the form of the original question at 72.16.

72.24 besides] Despite the numerical superiority of the texts reading 'besides', the example of A1 which alters to 'besides' its PM copy 'beside' suggests that the less correct reading 'beside' stood in the master proof (and probably in Crane's manuscript), only to be corrected by most compositors. The correction is a useful one and is adopted here on those grounds, not on authority.

75.7 clinched] Since FLW is the only authoritative document to preserve the invariable Crane form 'clinched' for 'clenched', the odds certainly require the Bacheller proof to have read 'clenched' and thus the FLW variant to be compositorial. However, Crane always wrote 'clinched', and though the source cannot be defended it may be worth while to preserve what must have been the manuscript reading behind the proof that is being reconstructed in the present edition.

79.11 need] The odd combination of texts that read 'need' ($N^{1-4,6}$,FLW) and 'heed' (N^5,PM,DFM,EIM,A1) might suggest the possibility of a broken 'h' in the proof that could have been misread by some compositors as 'n'. On the other hand, the example of the unauthoritative DFM reading 'heed' set from FLW 'need' indicates, instead, that Crane's quiet irony was not understood and that the compositors of N^5, PM, EIM, and DFM thought that they were correcting a simple misprint.

80.22 Never!] Agreement of N^{1-5} in the harder reading with the exclamation instead of the easier with the question mark suggests that the question in N^6, PM, FLW, EIM is a sophistication, perhaps referring back to 80.12. A1, of course, merely follows PM without independent authority.

80.32 this] This variant is an interesting example of sophistication. The concurrence of the majority of the texts establishes 'this' as the correct reading, as does the EIM variant 'the', as against the 'his' of $N^{1,6}$, DFM, and A1. But the two newspaper readings 'his' (and the unauthoritative DFM variant from FLW as well as the A1 change to 'his' of PM 'this') demonstrate the pull of referring a pronoun back to the captain and 'his return journey'. For a similar confusion, see the N^2,DFM error 'his' for 'this' at 70.39 and the N^1 error at 72.27.

An Episode of War

89.15 had winced] The perfect tense of all authorities clashes with the preterites that follow in the same sentence and must be wrong. A slight possibility may be considered that 'has' should be omitted and 'winced' made into a preterite in the series. However, it is also possible that the wincing was before the men saw the blood and cried out, in which case the past perfect is needed, slightly awkward as it is.

89.18–19 little puffs of white smoke] G must have repeated some unresolved change in the manuscript involving the position of 'white' or, perhaps more likely, the addition of 'of white smoke'. No reason exists to believe that E1 is authoritative here, but its assignment of the first 'white' as the error seems sound if the mistake arose by reason of addition. The adjective elsewhere in Crane is associated with *smoke*, not with *puffs*, as in 67.9 and 69.21.

THE LONE CHARGE OF WILLIAM B. PERKINS

114.30 had emanated] Crane's use of the past perfect often attracted the attention of editors, who were likely to reduce it to the preterite. The *Gazette* past perfect appears to be correct. That is, Perkins had just arrived and would have had no opportunity to observe the flocks of bullets, which obviously were not passing over in the short interval after his landing. The camp is quite peaceful in his experience until the firing of the jammed rifle causes the guerillas to reveal themselves.

115.38 sputter] WG 'splutter' versus McC 'sputter' may be correct, but the only occasion where 'splutter' is used to describe the sound of firing is in "The Price of the Harness" (100.33–34), 'the whole forest spluttered and fluttered with battle', where there is at least some chance that 'splutter' has been affected by 'flutter'. Otherwise, Crane's invariable word is 'sputter' as at 91.25, 150.35, 191.33, and 229.19. It is of some interest that 'splutter' seems to be an English preference, as suggested by the unauthoritative change of 'sputter' at page 87.14 of the 1852 American first edition of *A Wonder Book* to 'splutter' in the 1852 Bohn edition.

117.7 suppliant] The WG reading here, versus McC 'supplicant' may be supported by its use, also as a noun, in " 'God Rest Ye, Merry Gentlemen' " at 153.29. As an adjective, 'supplicant' is used in *Tales of Adventure*, p. 85.7.

THE CLAN OF NO-NAME

120.14 grass∧] N¹ is in the minority here in failing to punctuate, whereas both BW and A1 have commas; but the commas seem to be a case of independent styling. In setting off such phrases N¹ is lighter than BW,A1 four times and heavier twice. It must be observed that BW is very heavy indeed in punctuating these phrases, and in Parts I–V the first A1 compositor never lightens such a punctuation but eight times adds commas against N¹ and BW. Thus it is easy within this area of the text and for this particular syntactical construction for BW and A1 to have styled alike without regard for the practice of the typescript; thus the odds favor N¹'s lack of punctuation here as a reflection of copy.

120.30 quickly∧] In this case control examples suggest that BW,A1 are following copy by not punctuating with the N¹ comma. The particular construction here with dependent clauses and phrases is the most notable of N¹'s tendency to make the punctuation heavier, occurring four times in Parts I–V and eight times in all.

120.33 teeth$_\wedge$] This is a good example of what seems to be independent heavier styling by BW,A1 against minority but correct N^1. The first A1 compositor characteristically in this first section (3 times; 8 times total) sets off an inverted phrase and puts a comma after 'In the gloom of it'. Apparently this comma then affected what one assumes was a general heightening of the typescript punctuation because the parenthetical phrase 'with . . . teeth' was not set off by a comma before 'with' but instead was closed by a comma after 'teeth' (actually, a not uncharacteristic Crane habit). On the contrary, although it has some slight tendency to punctuate inverted phrases, BW has no comma here but, characteristically, sets off the parenthesis by commas before 'with' and after 'teeth'. N^1 has no commas anywhere. Thus BW is fully conscious of the parenthesis, A1 only partly so, and N^1 not at all. Either A1 or N^1 could reflect the typescript, but the light punctuation of N^1 is so unusual as to be worth preserving.

121.2 agony. He] A marked difference develops in the three documents in the treatment of short declarative sentences as independent units or as part of a longer sentence separated by semicolons. BW is especially prone to joining such short sentences since it does so eight times versus N^1,A1 agreement as against three times that it replaces a semicolon construction with a period and capital. Also, BW and A1 agree in the semicolon construction eight times against the N^1 period. (Uniquely, at 132.30 A1 substitutes a semicolon for an N^1 period where BW has a dash; the dash is probably BW's own styling of the same structure.) The preference for short sentences with periods may be independent styling in N^1 of course, but this usage is nearer Crane's than BW,A1. Of itself, A1 only once (126.20) uses a semicolon against N^1,BW period. But it is probable—if, as presumed, N^1 is closer in this matter to the typescript—that some of the seven BW,A1 agreements represent separate styling and not agreement in following copy. The majority is suspect here, then, and the copy-text N^1 forms have been followed.

121.5 data$_\wedge$ apparently$_\wedge$] Both BW and A1 set off 'apparently' in commas as against N^1. Crane's manuscripts are not entirely consistent, although he has a general tendency to ignore the marking off of parenthetical words and phrases. In this respect unauthoritative independent styling by BW and A1 is likely here. In Parts I–V A1 independently sets off six such phrases (in contrast to only one in Parts VI–IX), and BW sets off two, although it has a total of six to form its third heaviest punctuation habit. The odds in this respect favor N^1's minority view in Parts I–V.

121.8 incessant,] Although Crane himself ordinarily did not put a comma between two clauses of a compound sentence joined by a conjunction, the odds may favor the comma punctuation here and elsewhere when A1 agrees with BW as reproducing the typescript (which no doubt differed from the manuscript in various details). It is true that the punctuation of this sentence structure is BW's second strongest characteristic (seven times in all as against nine times for compound predicates). But, in contrast, A1 never independently inserts such punctuation, and in Parts I–V even removes it once. Thus when we find agreement, the possibility is there that A1 has added the comma by its own styling (particularly if in Parts I–V its treatment of compound predicates is a straw in the wind). Nonetheless, the probability seems stronger that the copy had a comma, and that this is a case where N^1 is styling the copy by lightening the punctuation. N^1 removes six such commas in which BW and A1 agree, three of these in Parts I–V.

122.5 half a league] This is an idiom so subject to compositorial or editorial styling as to make determination of the typescript phrase far from certain. In the present case N^1 and BW join in reading 'half a league' against A1 'a half league'. However, at 122.18 BW joins A1 in 'A half-mile' whereas N^1 has 'Half a mile'. The one constant factor is that N^1 reads 'half a' at 122.5 and 122.18. Either N^1 is styling a typescript that read 'a half' or else is following copy, as may perhaps be indicated by the BW agreement with N^1 at 122.5 against A1, which is as regular in 'a half' as N^1 is in the reverse. Other texts in this volume fail to decide the question. The earlier-composed "Three Miraculous Soldiers" also varies. There all the newspapers and the *English Illustrated Magazine* read 'a half mile' (all have common copy in a master proof), whereas A1, set from a typescript, reads 'half a mile' (22.17). In " 'God Rest Ye, Merry Gentlemen' " the *Saturday Evening Post* prints 'half a bottle' at 143.3, but *Cornhill* and A1 (which is derived from *Cornhill*) has 'a half-bottle'; yet at 145.33–34 all texts agree in 'a howl for the half bottle of lime juice'. In " 'God Rest Ye' " the case is particularly complicated by the unresolved question whether the 'half bottle' refers to the size of the bottle or—much more likely—to a bottle of normal size that was half full. With some timidity, in the present case the editor opts for 'half a', in some part mindful of 'at which the police had been swearing for the half of an hour' in *Maggie* as well as 'the half of a block' (*Bowery Tales*, pp. 23.15, 49.17–18).

122.5–6 General] A1 is the only text to use the lower-case 'general' here and elsewhere in the story, whereas N^1 and BW agree in 'General'; moreover, this usage coincides with A1 'colonel' but N^1,BW 'Colonel' at 132.13 *et seq.* Ordinarily one is accustomed to a diversity of styling in texts that involve military titles, with some compositors capitalizing all titles and others printing them in lower case. In the present story some reason exists to suspect that the typescript capitalized 'General' and 'Colonel' as the two commanding officers, although invariably leaving 'lieutenant' uncapitalized. If so, one must suppose that N^1's unique capitalization of 'captain' at 133.12,15 represents independent styling, especially because N^1 retains 'lieutenant' always in lower case. The matter of these titles is so variable that in this edition they are ordinarily capitalized only in the vocative, without regard for the copy-text custom. But "The Clan of No-Name" is unusual among these stories in distinguishing only the opposing commanding officers by capitals while not capitalizing the titles of their subordinates. Hence in deference to what clearly seems to have been the typescript differentiation of these two titles as if they were names throughout, the capitals have been retained.

127.15–16 away from the enemy . . . hundred yards] At 123.9–10 thirty men are assigned the task of engaging the blockhouse, and at 124.10–12 'the fight was opened by eight men who, snuggling in the grass within three hundred yards of the blockhouse, suddenly blazed away at the bed-ticking figure in the cupola'. A few sentences later Crane remarks, 'The eight men, as well as all other insurgents within fair range, had chosen good positions for lying close' (124.19–20). At 124.34 we learn that the insurgents were scattered on two sides of the blockhouse; but though we know from the results of their volley that the eight men within three hundred yards were all on one side of the blockhouse, no suggestion holds that the remaining twenty-two were on the other. Indeed, one could argue to the contrary since those 'within fair range' are not specifically located except that they are not in the advance group. Thus the normal assumption is that on the side of the blockhouse that is in question the firing party was composed of eight men who lay close within three hundred yards and an unspecified number who, though within fair range, were spaced farther back, in support, with Bas. If taken with complete literal-mindedness, the lieutenant's observation that others within three hundred yards' range were in greater danger than he was would apply only to the advance party of eight men, whereas of course the whole group was safer no matter how spaced. Another minor anomaly is that the lieutenant's progress is rapidly reported as 'five hundred—four hundred and fifty—four hundred yards away', but then the three following sentences (while presumably he is still running) ought to cover a further time that would bring him still nearer, whereas the first insurgent to reveal himself is Bas, who cannot have been among the eight forward men but was perhaps lying at a range of four hundred yards but no less than three hundred and fifty. Though it is conjectured that Crane did not read proof for BW, perhaps the editor recognized the difficulties presented by the details of the original and made the BW cut that clarified the situation. But the case is not basically confused if one supposes that the lieutenant saw only the smoke of the firing party at three hundred yards and was running toward them when intercepted farther back by Bas, whose group had not been firing. At any rate, it is a rather extraordinary fact that N[3]—although no connection exists between this text and BW—makes the same cut as does BW. This editorial attention must serve to throw considerable doubt on the authority of the same BW alteration, of course. On the whole, it seems better to retain the $N,A1 version, although rejecting as probably unauthoritative the A1 variant 'the others' for $N 'others'.

130.2 the wisdoms of bushwhacking.] The omission of this phrase ($N: the wisdom of bushwhacking) in BW might be an alteration by Crane, who, coming upon the phrase in proof, thought it somewhat repetitious but, no attractive alternative occurring to him, decided to cut it. Yet if the BW omission above at 127.15–16 is not authoritative, the present has less claim for consideration, and both must be put against the BW omission of a sentence at 120.25 that cannot be defended in any sense.

130.9 his mother] The true meaning is found in $N, which read 'His mother'; but Crane was often careless about capitalizing pronominal references to God and Christ and the present text would seem to reflect what he actually wrote in his manuscript.

134.6 heaven] Following 'or down to hell', unique with BW, may be editorial, but in some part (unless the editor were merely completing a commonplace) it relies on information not given the reader until 134.10–11 that Smith believed in her treachery. Just possibly this is independent censorship by N^1 and A1; but since BW has a full record of interfering with the text of this story, the possibility is not strong enough to warrant acceptance of the BW reading.

134.28 brooks] The BW substitution of 'coffee-mills' for 'brooks' (without altering 'babbled') is so unusual for an editor as to arouse some concern whether Crane in fact read proof and inserted the change. But no parallels elsewhere have been observed for the comparison. In dispatch #27, "Chased by a Big Spanish 'Man-o'-War'" (see *Reports of War*, WORKS, Vol. IX), Crane wrote, 'Blow her [the ship] into a semblance of the output of a compound, eleven-story, triple-tooth coffee-grinder.' The reference here is not to noise but to pulverization, however. As noted, also, 'coffee-mills' is a British phrase. A quite different kind of mill is found in "The Stove" (*Tales of Whilomville*, WORKS, VII, 199.12–14): "Then suddenly it [the tea-party] would be off like the wind, eight, fifteen or twenty-five tongues clattering with a noise like a cotton-mill combined with the noise of a few penny-whistles."

"GOD REST YE, MERRY GENTLEMEN"

142.37 canteens] The substitution of C 'one' looks suspiciously like the editorial smoothing out of a typical Crane repetition. See "The Clan of No-Name," 133.15–16, 'The captain shot from the corner of his eye a cynical glance at the guerilla, a glance which commented . . .' but N^1 'at the guerilla which commented . . .' but especially " 'God Rest Ye' " 145.13 in which C omits the repetitive 'over' and 145.39 in which the C change of SP 'for reasons' to 'the reason' seems dictated by 'the reasons' in 146.1. For the opposite in C, however, see 146.25 in which C prints the repetitive 'his eyes' which reads 'them' in SP.

143.24 street] If 140.10–11 is to be taken literally, the village had only one street and C,A1 are wrong in their plural 'streets' for the SP singular.

153.38 lying] SP 'dying' and C 'lying' are so close as to lead to the suspicion that one is a misreading. But the chance exists that 'dying' was the original form and got changed in the C proof because Tailor, although he had lain in the long grass (153.38) had not died there, and a misconstruction of the end of the story might be possible if the SP version were to hold. He is intended to survive.

THE REVENGE OF THE *Adolphus*

155.24 deck] The A1 change of the galley from the lower deck moves the correspondents to a better vantage point of observation, one nearer the bridge, and also serves to reserve the lower deck for the appearance of the stoker.

155.27 Captain] The A1 styling of titles follows that adopted for this edition; that is, an officer addressed by his title, has his title capitalized but not otherwise. Both CW and S use lower case for all titles under any circumstance.

156.9 Finally . . . Yes.'] The omission of this sentence from A1 seems more like compositorial eyeskip than authorial revision. Although the same sentence is repeated after the next question, part of the point is just such repetition. Each question must have an answer until the joke at the end, which depends upon the offer being withdrawn before the answer is produced.

159.20 runnin'." The mate chuckled.] The A1 variant 'running," the mate chuckled' would appear to be a misunderstanding just such as the one that distorts the meaning in A1 at 158.35. The concurrence of CW and S demonstrates what stood in their typescript; and unless the assignment of the speech was a typescript error Crane should have known who was to make the remark and not changed his mind in preparing copy for A1. Moreover, it is not idiomatic for him to have people 'chuckle' remarks.

160.29 at the back] For the probable authority of this CW,S variant from A1 'back' see "The Serjeant's Private Mad-house" 175.27, 'right in the front'. However, it must be admitted that both could derive from an English typist if such a one prepared both typescripts.

163.27–28 came upon deck] This S change takes account of Colwell's suggestion that the boatswain would visit the warrant officers' mess. The CW,A1 reading would be appropriate only if he had stayed in the cabin.

165.5 set] For the probable authority of this CW,S reading versus A1 'sent', see " 'God Rest Ye, Merry Gentlemen' " 142.10–11, 'Suddenly the man-crowded landing set up its cheer'.

166.28 'm] That ' 'em' was the reading of the typescript is pretty clear from the agreement of CW and S, not only here but also at 169.22,30 where A1 reads ' 'm'. It would be easy to take it that ' 'm' is merely a compositorial variant were it not that it is probable (although not absolutely certain) that a different compositor set 166.28 from the compositor of 169.22,30. Moreover, in " 'God Rest Ye, Merry Gentlemen' " 150.10 a change is made in *Cornhill*, and repeated in A1, of the *Post* ' 'em' to ' 'm' as part of a sentence also changing 'the' to 'th' '. Since Crane was often careful about his dialect forms, a real possibility exists that the A1 reading ' 'm' derives from the manuscript.

THE SERJEANT'S PRIVATE MAD-HOUSE

172.3,24 cactus-plants] Although EIM is alone in hyphenating this compound (and also *cactus-bush*), it may be that the hyphen that slips into *cactus-bush* in A1 at 174.28 represents a following of copy that otherwise had been restyled. The hyphenated form may have stood in the manuscript, therefore.

172.21 glistening] Whether A1 'glistening' is a sophistication of SP,E1 'glisten in', or 'glisten in' a misreading by the first typist of manuscript 'glistening', is impossible to demonstrate. The general authority of A1 here may lead to the acceptance of its reading, with the added reminder that although glistening eyes have figured prominently in the stories of this volume, 'glisten' has not been used as a noun.

172.22 serjeant] As remarked in the Textual Introduction, this is Crane's usual spelling and is found so in the autograph list of stories made up for *Wounds in the Rain*.

176.1 miraculous] SP,EIM 'miraculous ones' is so clumsy and obscure in reference as to call indifferently for authorial revision or compositorial sophistication. (The 'ones' seems to refer to soldiers miraculously spared and therefore 'miraculous soldiers'; but no referent 'soldiers' appears.)

177.24 increase] That A1 'increased' is an error for SP,EIM 'increase' may be suggested by the more obvious error of A1 'required' for SP,EIM 'require' at 176.16. The double error is certainly unusual.

THIS MAJESTIC LIE

201.7 Montojo] The reading of all texts is 'Patricio de Montojo' but Crane's memory is at fault here.

204.7 plentitude] The *O.E.D.* cites a few examples of this erroneous form, suggesting that it arose by confusion with 'plenty' and that some cases may represent misprints. On the evidence that 'plentitude' is the reading of N^{2-3} and, independently, of A1 as against N^{1a-b} 'plenitude', it would seem probable that 'plentitude' stood in Crane's own copy (or at least in the typescript and its carbon) whence it was transferred to the N galley proof in the uncorrected state sent out to the newspapers. However, one must conjecture that this single change was made in the galleys before they were sent to Congress for deposit, and then subsequently the galleys were more systematically read before printing in the *Herald* as N^{1b}. See note 88 in the Textual Introduction.

204.14 rang] Despite the general authority of A1, its reading 'sang' for N 'rang' seems affected more by an assumed need for conformity with 'sang' also in 204.14 than with the sense. For a rumor to *ring* is singularly appropriate for the noisy operation of coaling, whereas *sang* works out well enough for the leisurely anchoring, perhaps the musical sound of the lowered anchor chain. At any rate, it is easier to account for the presence of 'sang' in A1 than of 'rang' in N.

205.8 the ijjits] The A1 substitution of 'this we' seems to be a sophistication based on a misunderstanding of Crane's meaning. The correspondents ask themselves why they could not inflame the wires in the way that all 'the ijjits' did. An example of 'ijjit' reporting is then given in the next sentence about the armored cruiser, replete with ridiculous contradictions. The next sentence, however—'We were not idle men'—does not continue the thought, as the A1 editor supposed. Instead, although the good correspondents did not send ignorant dispatches like the one quoted, they were, nevertheless, busy men and they reported the war competently despite the urgings of the managing editors. The A1 reading would have the correspondents becoming like 'the ijjits' at the urging of their editors; Crane's sense is the exact opposite.

214.17 Fifty] The A1 variant 'Five' for N 'Fifty' could refer to Johnny's outrage at the size of the tip, but this—being 10 per cent—was no more outrageous than the other nonexistent items. His account in 215.8–9 lists the tip among the other charges but with no especial emphasis. On the whole the N reading with its triple repetition seems best to serve the context.

218.19–20 No . . . Institute.] The general meaning of the correspondent's answer to Johnnie seems to be fairly clear. That is, jocularly he anticipates his preservation after death in the Smithsonian Institution because of his fame. But if he were the victim of a volley at thirty feet, there would not be enough of him left to preserve.

WAR MEMORIES

229.34 great] According to the conjectured textual transmission, the A1 variant 'attractive' for AS 'great' cannot be authoritative here. One cannot tell, therefore, whether 'attractive' has been substituted by contamination from 'attracting' in the preceding sentence, or whether the compositor (or editor) was overcome with the possibilities of the wordplay on 'attract' as *to draw to* as well as *to be pleasing*. The attempt at wordplay ends in some confusion, if this is what is intended, since two things are attracting the correspondent—the sound of the bullets and the example of the marines—although he ends by stating that only the latter was 'the attractive thing to my sense at the time'. 'Great' is not much of a word, but it is neutral enough to pass muster even though it seems to have provoked dissatisfaction in the reprint A1. It is worth noting that another change between the two texts occurs in this passage, the alteration of ungrammatical AS 'the sound of the bullets were attracting my attention' to A1 'was attracting'. Almost certainly the same agent was responsible for both changes; and it would seem that the false grammar of the typescript reading 'were' (Crane's grammar sometimes being uncertain) was reproduced faithfully by the AS compositor but automatically corrected by the compositor or editor of A1, who also objected to the word 'great' in the same passage.

THE SECOND GENERATION

265.28 clear-eyed] Crane's invariable phrase is 'clear eye' or 'clear-eyed', used dozens of times, as in "Three Miraculous Soldiers" (45.36), "Twelve O'Clock" (TALES OF ADVENTURE, p. 172.21), or Chapter 1 of *The O'Ruddy*. Nowhere else except here (where it is supported by all three authorities) does 'clean-eyed' appear; the nearest parallel, which is not good enough, is the description of the old cab driver in "The Pace of Youth" (TALES OF ADVENTURE, p. 11.21–22) as 'dusty-eyed and tranquil'. The error may well have occurred in making the typescript, since the confusion of final 'r' and 'n' is not difficult.

268.21 fecklessly] That C 'fetlessly' is not a misprint but the copy reading is demonstrated by war dispatch No. 52, "Memoirs of a Private" (see

REPORTS OF WAR, Vol. IX), which reads, 'behold—you find the chair occupied by a doddering fetless old man', which was properly emended by
Fryckstedt at the first to *feckless.* (Fetless is unknown to *O.E.D.,* and
doubtless represents Crane's mishearing.) In "The Second Generation" it
follows that SP 'footlessly' is only a good guess, and AI 'bootlessly' a bad
one, for C and copy 'fetlessly'. On the evidence of the context in No. 52,
the indicated emendation is 'fecklessly'.

270.33 clinched] Although all authorities read 'clenched', the emendation
to Crane's invariable form in the manuscripts is justified by the appearance
of 'clinched' at 283.37.

THE KICKING TWELFTH

288.30 Kim up, the Kickers] The punctuation of this phrase is not at all
certain, in large part because the exact meaning is unknown. If 'Kickers'
is the direct object of the verb 'kim up', then no comma should separate
the two. On the other hand 'kim up' could be an imperative addressed to
the outside world, with some form of elision present, the general meaning
being, *watch out, here come the Kickers.* Or the imperative could be addressed to the Kickers themselves, or else 'Kickers' could be in the vocative. In these cases a comma would be required. Only a guess is possible,
but the present editor opts for a suggestion privately made by Professor
J. C. Levenson that 'kim up' may be intended to represent the dialect form
of the phrase 'come up'. This seems to be the best explanation yet offered
for the meaning of 'kim up' but it does not necessarily solve the problem
of the punctuation. If the general meaning were, *Bring on the regulars,*
then no comma would be appropriate, of course. On the other hand, some
order like *Come up* (or *Come on*) *to the line of battle* could be addressed
to the Kickers, in which case a comma would be required. The evidence of
the texts is conflicting. In the earliest story, "The Kicking Twelfth," the
first time the phrase is found in the Richie manuscript, at 288.30, a comma
appears. Then occurs one use without a comma at 292.11, but the next
with a comma at 293.25. Thereafter, in three more appearances (293.31,
294.13, and 296.27) no comma is present. Oddly, in *Ainslee's* no comma
appears in the phrase throughout, whereas in the *Pall Mall Magazine* the
cry always has a comma. It would be idle speculation to reconstruct the
circumstances by which the typescript could be taken as reproducing
the initial comma in MS at 288.30 but not thereafter, and PMM continued this styling, although the AM compositor preferred the general
practice of the typescript. We know nothing of the characteristics in this
respect of the lost typescript made from the Richie MS, and that conjecture
is dangerous may perhaps be suggested by the fact that the same distinction is found in "The Shrapnel of Their Friends" whereby at 303.35
Ainslee's prints no comma but a comma occurs in the *Black and White* text.
Under these circumstances it is impossible to determine which compositor
in "The Kicking Twelfth" or in "The Shrapnel" chose to interpret the
phrase in his own way, and no reconstruction of the lost typescripts is
possible. On the other hand, although a comma appears in the typescript
of " 'And If He Wills, We Must Die,' " at 312.18, both magazine texts—
Leslie's and the *Illustrated London News*—have no comma, and it may

well be that the lost typescript behind these two texts was wanting the punctuation, although the Barrett typescript, also deriving independently from the manuscript, possesses it. Under these conditions it is difficult to know what the manuscript read, although an assumption may hold that there was a comma in it. Some evidence favoring a comma, therefore, may be found in the various texts, although uncertainty must prevail. Finally, when one considers that the dictated Richie manuscript punctuated with a comma on its first appearance, and even though only once thereafter was a comma present, on that second occasion there is some suggestion that the comma was added after initial inscription, the comma may seem to be the authentic reading, especially when found in the typescript of " 'And If He Wills.' " For the sense, the reading in "The Kicking Twelfth" at 292.11–12 may be suggestive. That is, for the only time the corps' cry is here associated with a call to Attention: 'Some used the old cry, "Attention! Kim up, the Kickers!" ' and thereafter Crane proceeds 'and the Twelfth knew that it had been told to go in.' This context may perhaps indicate that the cry is, in fact, addressed to the Kickers themselves as a call to action and that the comma is required. If so, the textual evidence for the occasional presence of the comma corroborates the sense, and the times when the comma is wanting may be put down, as in the Richie MS, to carelessness, or in *Ainslee's* to a compositorial misinterpretation.

290.18 clank] This typescript reading for MS 'clink' is not certainly authoritative, but various parallels favor it. Although in "Three Miraculous Soldiers" (24.16) the troopers rode by with a 'tinkle of steel and tin', in "A Grey Sleeve" (68.8) occurs 'the jingle and clank of steel'. In addition, in "The Little Regiment" the detail 'clanked out of the kitchen' (12.39); in "Three Miraculous Soldiers" one reads 'They could faintly hear the thudding of many hoofs, the clank of arms' (28.38); in "A Mystery of Heroism" 'the clank of steel against steel' (49.27); and in "A Grey Sleeve" (78.21) 'his men clanked docilely after him.'

290.25 it was observable that not] MS read originally, 'it was not observable that a single soldier', but then 'not' was interlined with a caret after 'that'. Because inadvertently the original 'not' after 'was' was left undeleted, the typescript copied it and omitted the interlined revision, thus concealing the finally intended reading in favor of the rejected one.

THE SHRAPNEL OF THEIR FRIENDS

305.27 eye] The authority of MS singular against what must have been the typescript plural may be upheld by reference to "The Clan of No-Name" 123.30 in which the same natural sophistication appears. There the young lieutenant 'laughed at all their jests although his eye roved continually over the sunny grass-lands'. This is the reading of *Black and White* and of the Doubleday & McClure *Open Boat* collection. The newspaper version reads 'eyes'.

"AND IF HE WILLS, WE MUST DIE"

309.39 calmly, "then shoot] That this is the reading of FL and ILN instead of TMs 'calmly. "Then shoot' would ordinarily signify no more than that the lost typescript read so, and it is perhaps a natural modification of what could have seemed to be unnecessary abruptness. But when E1 agrees with FL,ILN, the question is raised whether E1 has independently sophisticated the reading (as is possible if one were to grant that the TMs form is so unusual as to trigger two such reactions). It is also possible to conjecture that in TMs[b] Cora by reference to the manuscript made this change, although failing to alter TMs[a], the Barrett typescript. Unusual as this operation would be, there may be thought sufficient chance of its probability to adopt the reading as modified.

EDITORIAL EMENDATIONS IN THE COPY-TEXT

[NOTE: Every editorial change from the copy-texts—whether manuscript, typescript, newspaper, magazine, or book versions, as chosen—is recorded for the substantives, and every change in the accidentals as well save for such silent typographical alterations as are remarked in "The Text of the Virginia Edition," prefixed to Volume I of this collected edition, with slight modification as indicated in the headnotes to the present apparatus. Only the direct source of the emendation, with its antecedents, is noticed; the Historical Collation may be consulted for the complete history, within the texts collated, of any substantive readings that qualify for inclusion in that listing. However, when as in syndicated newspaper versions a number of texts have equal claim to authority, all are noted in the Emendations listing. An alteration assigned to the Virginia edition (V) is made for the first time in the present edition if *by the first time* is understood *the first time in respect to the texts chosen for collation.* Asterisked readings are discussed in the Textual Notes. The note *et seq.* signifies that all following occurrences are identical, and thus the same emendation has been made without further notice. The wavy dash ($\sim$) represents the same word that appears before the bracket and is used exclusively in recording punctuation or other accidentals variants. An inferior caret ($_\wedge$) indicates the absence of a punctuation mark. The dollar sign ($\$$) is taken over from a convention of bibliographical description to signify *all* editions so identified. That is, if N represents newspaper versions in general, and N^{1-6} the six collated newspapers, then $\$N$ would be a shorthand symbol for all of these six texts and would be used even if one text owing to a more extensive cut than simple omission (always recorded in the Historical Collation) did not contain the reading in question. Occasionally a text subsumed under the $\$$ notation may be excluded from agreement by the use of the minus sign. Thus such a notation as $\$N(-N^4)$ would mean that all of the N texts agree with the noted reading to the left of the bracket except for N^4 which, by its absence from the $\$N$ list of agreements, must therefore agree with the reading to the right of the bracket unless otherwise specified. A lengthier way of expressing the same situation would be $N^{1-3,5-6}$. A plus sign may be used as a shorthand indication of the concurrence of all collated editions following the cited edition. For instance, if E1 and E2, listed after A1, agree in a reading with A1, the note may read A1+ instead of A1,E1–2. Rarely, in dealing with accidentals, when only general concurrence of the following editions is in question and exactness of detail would serve no useful purpose, the $\pm$ symbol may be used. Thus if an emendation line read 'said:] $\$N\pm$; $\sim$, PM' one should understand that the majority of the N texts have a colon instead of the PM comma, but some might have a period or some even a comma. The exact readings of these variant N texts would not, however, affect the conclusion that the basic proof from which the N texts radiate had the colon. If it seemed important to indicate that certain of these variant texts had such and such punctuation, then the listing would do so as most convenient.]

THE LITTLE REGIMENT

THE LITTLE REGIMENT

[The copy-text is McC: *McClure's Magazine*. The other text collated is Ch: *Chapman's Magazine*. A1, E1, and E2 are completely derived and without authority.]

*3.9 et seq. grey] Ch; gray McC
3.17 sudden₍] Ch; ~ , McC
*3.22 voice] stet McC
3.27 rain₍] Ch; ~ , McC
3.30 pockets₍] Ch; ~ , McC
4.10 afterward] A1; afterwards McC,Ch
4.28 vindictive] Ch; vindicative McC
5.6 town₍] Ch; ~ , McC
5.8 that₍] Ch; ~ , McC
6.3 derned] Ch; durned McC
6.17 hushed₍] Ch; ~ , McC
6.29 river₍] Ch; ~ , McC
*6.32 bellowed] stet McC
8.1 sliddering] Ch (slidering); sliding McC
8.7 halted₍] Ch; ~ , McC
9.4 side-walks] Ch; side-|walks McC
9.14 clouds] Ch; crowds McC
10.12 there₍] Ch; ~ , McC
11.16 vague₍] Ch; ~ , McC

11.21 hills₍] Ch; ~ , McC
12.36–37 head₍ . . . hair₍] Ch; ~ , . . . ~ , McC
13.4 again₍] Ch; ~ , McC
13.8 head₍] Ch; ~ , McC
14.15 damning] Ch; cursing McC
15.16 necks₍] Ch; ~ , McC
*15.21 crackling] V; cracking McC Ch
*15.25 young] Ch; younger McC
16.25 bridges₍] Ch; ~ , McC
17.7 wind-demons] Ch; ~ ₍ ~ McC
17.32 toppled₍] Ch; ~ , McC
18.9 side-walks] MS,Ch; sidewalks McC
18.28 closer₍] Ch; ~ , McC
19.30 to] Ch; omit McC
20.32–33 hands₍ . . . explaining₍] Ch; ~ , . . . ~ , McC
21.7 Damn] Ch; Curse McC

THREE MIRACULOUS SOLDIERS

[The copy-text is A1: *The Little Regiment*, Appleton, 1896. Other texts collated are N¹: *Saint Paul Pioneer Press*; N²: *Inter Ocean*; N³: *Kansas City Star*; N⁴: *San Francisco Examiner*; N⁵: *Omaha Daily Bee*; N⁶: *Boston Globe*; N⁷: *Philadelphia Inquirer*; N⁸: *Pittsburgh Leader*; EIM: *English Illustrated Magazine*.]

22.16 woods₍] $N(−N²); ~, N², EIM,A1
22.17 a half mile] $N,EIM; half a mile A1
22.21 sound₍] $N,EIM; ~ , A1
22.24 southeast₍] $N(−N²),EIM; ~ , N²,A1

22.26–27 excitement₍] $N (−N¹⁻²); ~ , N¹⁻²,EIM,A1
22.29 soft₍] N¹,⁵,⁸,EIM; ~ , N²⁻⁴, A1
23.4 neighborhood] V; neighbourhood A1,EIM
*23.14 into] stet A1

23.19 hand$_\Lambda$] \$N($-$N^2),EIM; $\sim$,
N^2,A1
23.21 up stairs] \$N($-$N^5);
upstairs N^5,EIM,A1
23.22 breath$_\Lambda$]   \$N($-$N^2),EIM;
$\sim$, N^2, A1
23.23 reproach$_\Lambda$] \$N($-$N^2); $\sim$,
N^2,EIM,A1
23.24 window$_\Lambda$] \$N($-$N^3), EIM;
$\sim$, N^3,A1
23.27 world.] \$N,EIM; $\sim$! A1
*23.29 wood] stet A1
23.31 woods.] \$N,EIM; $\sim$! A1
23.32 bended]   N$^{3-5,7-8}$; bent
N$^{1-2}$,EIM,A1
23.32–33 from   whence]   \$N
($-$N^1),EIM; from which N^1;
whence A1
23.37 bended]   N$^{3-5,8}$;   bent
N$^{1-2}$,EIM,A1
*24.4 blue,] N^1,EIM; $\sim$ — N$^{2-8}$,A1
24.5 look,] \$N($-$N^1); $\sim$! N^1,
EIM,A1
24.13 upward$_\Lambda$] N$^{1-3,6,8}$; $\sim$, N$^{4-5}$,
EIM,A1
24.15 At (no ¶)] \$N,EIM; ¶ A1
24.16 column$_\Lambda$]   \$N($-$N^1),EIM;
$\sim$, N^1,A1
*24.32 moment, "they've] stet A1
24.33 back,] \$N,EIM; $\sim$! A1
24.33 mother$_\Lambda$] \$N($-$N^5),EIM;
$\sim$, N^5,A1
24.35 Oh] V; O A1
24.37 locked.] \$N,EIM; $\sim$! A1
25.1 Mother——] \$N,EIM; $\sim$, A1
25.2 whispered:] \$N; $\sim$, EIM,
A1
25.3 Motionless (no ¶)] \$N,EIM;
¶ A1
25.4 quavered:]   \$N($-$N^6),EIM;
$\sim$, N^6,A1
25.12 there,] \$N,EIM; $\sim$! A1
*25.24 the step] stet A1
25.28 there.] \$N($-$N^2),EIM; $\sim$,
N^2; $\sim$! A1
25.31 here.] \$N,EIM; $\sim$! A1
25.34 had.] \$N; $\sim$! EIM,A1
26.9 do.] \$N,EIM; $\sim$ — A1
26.10 said:] \$N; $\sim$, EIM,A1
26.23 grey] V; gray A1

26.27 open$_\Lambda$] \$N($-$N^2); $\sim$, N^2,
EIM,A1
*26.33 et seq. grey] EIM; gray
\$N,A1
26.37 announced:] \$N,EIM; $\sim$,
A1
27.4 Oh,] \$N; $\sim$! EIM,A1
27.4 said. "You] \$N($-$N^{2,4}),
EIM; $\sim$; "you N^{2,4}; $\sim$, "you
A1
27.4 me.] \$N,EIM; $\sim$! A1
*27.13 et seq. No'm'm] \$N; No,
M'm EIM; No, m'm A1
27.15 arm.]   \$N($-$N^2),EIM; $\sim$,
N^2, A1
27.15 Keh-plunk] V; Keh-pluck
N$^{3-5,7-8}$, EIM; Ker-plunk N^1;
keh-pluck N^2; Kehplunk A1;
omit N^6
*27.16 thah] \$N,EIM; thar A1
27.21 indeedee.] \$N; $\sim$! EIM,A1
27.31 crown,] \$N,EIM; $\sim$; A1
*27.33 a clean] \$N,EIM; clean A1
*28.31 -like. Just a snack. We'd]
\$N; -like—just a snack—we'd
EIM,A1
28.34 Listen,] \$N,EIM; $\sim$! A1
28.35 was bended] N$^{3-5,8}$; was
bending N^{1,7}; bended N^2; was
bent EIM,A1
28.39 arms$_\Lambda$] \$N($-$N^2); $\sim$, N^2,
EIM,A1
29.1 Yanks.] \$N($-$N^{4,6}); $\sim$! N^4,
EIM,A1; Yankees ! N^6
29.8 hide,] N$^{1,3,5,7-8}$; $\sim$! N^{2,4,6},
EIM,A1
29.8 girl$_\Lambda$]   \$N($-$N^{4,6,8}),EIM;
$\sim$, N^{4,6,8},A1
29.10–11 hain't. . . . boys.] \$N
($-$N^6); $\sim$! . . . $\sim$! N^6,EIM,
A1
29.13 girl$_\Lambda$] \$N; $\sim$, EIM,A1
29.13 door$_\Lambda$] \$N($-$N^{5,8}); $\sim$, N^{5,8},
EIM,A1
29.15 hide.] \$N,EIM; $\sim$! A1
29.17 munching$_\Lambda$]   \$N($-$N^5),
EIM; $\sim$, N^5,A1
*29.20 feed box] stet A1
29.21 Here! Here!] \$N($-$N^4),
EIM; Here! here! N^4,A1

29.29 closer] $N,EIM; close A1

29.33 coats$_\wedge$] $N; ~ , EIM,A1

29.37 tip-toed] $N($-$N^{3,6}),EIM; tiptoed N^{3,6},A1

*29.38 knothole] *stet* A1

29.39 plainly:] $N; ~ , EIM,A1

*30.34 ask] $N,EIM; go ask A1

30.34 her$_\wedge$] $N($-$N^{2,7}),EIM; ~ , N^{2,7},A1

30.37 you.] $N,EIM; ~ ! A1

30.38 go and ask] $N,EIM; go ask A1

31.2,7 Ma,] $N($-$N^4); ~ ! N^4, EIM,A1

31.5 new$_\wedge$] $N($-$N^4); ~ , N^4, EIM,A1

*31.6 there] $N,EIM; *omit* A1

31.9 quilts$_\wedge$] $N($-$N^2); ~ , N^2, EIM,A1

31.10 Mary,] $N,EIM; ~ ! A1

31.13 box.] $N,EIM; ~ ! A1

31.13 The elder (*no* ¶)] $N,EIM; ¶ A1

31.15 thresh] N$^{1,4-5,7-8}$,EIM; thrash N$^{2-3,6}$,A1

*31.15 wailed] $N($-$N^5),EIM; wail N^5,A1

31.16 exclaimed. "And] $N; ~ , "and EIM,A1

31.16 barn,] $N($-$N^2); ~ $_\wedge$ N^2; ~ — EIM,A1

31.17 box.] $N; ~ ! EIM,A1

31.20 Ma,] $N; ~ ! EIM,A1

31.23 The old (*no* ¶)] $N($-$N^4), EIM; ¶ N^4,A1

31.26 recognized] $N; recognised EIM,A1

31.28 chevrons] $N,EIM; chevron A1

31.30 As (*no* ¶)] $N,EIM; ¶ A1

31.38 grey-beard] $N,EIM; graybeard A1

32.12 mar'] V; ~ $_\wedge$ A1

32.14 An'] E1; ~ $_\wedge$ A1

32.24–25 horses$_\wedge$ . . . accoutred$_\wedge$] $N($-$N^{2,4,8}),EIM; ~ , . . . ~ , N^{2,4},A1; ~ $_\wedge$ . . . ~ , N^8

33.23 engaged$_\wedge$ . . . doubt$_\wedge$] $N($-N^{3-4}$); ~ , . . . ~ , N$^{3-4}$, EIM,A1

34.5 grey-beard] $N($-$N^{3,8}),EIM; greybeard N^{3,8},A1 (graybeard)

34.15 not$_\wedge$ then$_\wedge$] $N($-$N^2),EIM; ~ , ~ , N^2,A1

34.21 fields$_\wedge$] $N($-$N^2); ~ , N^2, EIM,A1

34.24 color] $N; colour EIM,A1

35.10 labored] V; laboured A1

35.15 labor] V; labour A1

35.19 splendor] V; splendour A1

*35.36 made her mind up] V; made up her mind N^{1,3,5,8},EIM; made her mind N^{2,4,6}; decided A1

*35.37 *et seq.* camp-fires] EIM; campfires $N($-$N^8); ~ $_\wedge$ ~ N^8,A1

*35.38 circles] $N,EIM; circle A1

36.2 last$_\wedge$] $N($-$N^4),EIM; ~ , N^4,A1

36.3 it$_\wedge$] $N($-$N^2); ~ , N^2,EIM, A1

36.10 moment$_\wedge$] $N,EIM; ~ , A1

36.13 endless$_\wedge$] $N($-N^{3-4}$),EIM; ~ , N$^{3-4}$,A1

36.24 stick$_\wedge$] $N($-$N^8),EIM; ~ , N^8,A1

36.26 Finally$_\wedge$] $N; ~ , EIM,A1

36.37 —— ——] $N($-$N^3); dam N^3; —— EIM,A1

36.38 mar'.] $N,EIM (mare); ~ ! A1

*37.2 Sssh.] $N($-$N^{2,4}); ~ ! N^{2,4}, EIM; S-s-s-h! A1

37.2 Pete,] $N($-$N^{2,4}),EIM; ~ . N^2; ~ ; N^4,A1

37.9 stilettoes] N$^{3-4,7}$,EIM; stillettoes N$^{1-2,5-6}$; stilettos N^8,A1

37.12 thoughtfulness$_\wedge$] $N,EIM; ~ , A1

37.13 generalities$_\wedge$] $N($-$N^2); ~ , N^2,EIM,A1

37.20 gesture$_\wedge$] $N,EIM; ~ , A1

37.23 added$_\wedge$] N$^{3-4,6-8}$; ~ , N$^{1-2,5}$, EIM,A1

38.4 her$_\wedge$] $N($-$N^2); ~ , N^2, EIM,A1

38.4 and,] $N,EIM; ~ $_\wedge$ A1

38.9 calm$_\wedge$] $N($-$N^{2,6}),EIM; ~ , N^{2,6},A1

38.11 dangling$_\wedge$] \$N($-$N$^{2-3,6}$), EIM; ~ , N$^{2-3,6}$,A1

38.11 heels,] \$N,EIM; ~ $_\wedge$ A1

38.11 no wise] \$N($-$N^1),EIM; nowise N^1,A1

38.12 feed box] N$^{2-3,6}$; ~ - ~ N$^{4,7-8}$,EIM,A1; ~ - | ~ N^{1,5}

38.14 apart$_\wedge$] \$N($-$N^2); ~ , N^2, EIM,A1

38.19 blackness$_\wedge$] \$N($-$N^{2,4}), EIM; ~ , N^{2,4},A1

38.24 whiteness$_\wedge$] \$N($-$N^2); ~ , N^2,EIM,A1

38.33–34 from whence] \$N ($-$N^3),EIM; whence N^3; from which A1

38.35 vision,] \$N,EIM; ~ — A1

38.35 room$_\wedge$] \$N($-$N^{2,5}),EIM; ~ , N^{2,5},A1

*39.3 ever] *stet* A1

39.10 color] \$N; colour EIM,A1

39.11 form$_\wedge$] \$N; ~ , EIM,A1

39.16 *et seq.* marvelous] \$N; marvellous EIM,A1

39.25 said:] \$N($-$N^6); ~ , N^6, A1; ~ $_\wedge$ EIM

*39.37 glinted] \$N,EIM; glintered A1

39.37 wavered;] \$N($-$N^6),EIM; ~ , N^6,A1

40.1 breathed:] \$N($-$N^4); ~ $_\wedge$ EIM; ~ , N^4,A1

40.13 signaled] \$N($-$N^{1,4,8}); signalled N^{1,4,8},EIM,A1

40.16 In (*no* ¶)] \$N($-$N^6),EIM; ¶ N^6,A1

40.18 nodded$_\wedge$] \$N($-$N^6); ~ , N^6,EIM,A1

40.20 state$_\wedge$] \$N($-$N^2); ~ , N^2, EIM,A1

40.21 face$_\wedge$] \$N,EIM; ~ , A1

40.22 arms$_\wedge$] \$N($-$N^{2,6}); ~ , N^{2,6},EIM; ~ ; A1

40.22 mournfully$_\wedge$] \$N($-$N^6), EIM; ~ , N^6,A1

40.24 signaling] \$N; signalling EIM,A1

40.25 slow$_\wedge$] \$N($-$N$^{2-3}$),EIM; ~ , N$^{2-3}$,A1

*40.27–28 wildly . . . indifference] \$N,EIM; *omit* A1

40.35 said:] \$N($-$N^{1,4,8}); ~ , N^{1,4,8},EIM,A1

41.1 face$_\wedge$] \$N($-$N^{2,6}); ~ , N$^{2-6}$, EIM,A1

41.2 When (*no* ¶)] \$N($-$N^6), EIM; ¶ N^6,A1

41.2 together$_\wedge$] \$N,EIM; ~ , A1

41.5 tip-toed] \$N($-$N^{3,6}),EIM; tiptoed N^{3,6},A1

41.8 awhile] \$N($-$N^2); a while N^2,EIM,A1

41.17 undertone.] N$^{3,5,7-8}$,EIM; ~ : N$^{1-2,4,6}$,A1

*41.21 A man . . . box?"] \$N,EIM; *omit* A1

41.22 us$_\wedge$] \$N,EIM; ~ , A1

41.32 men$_\wedge$ . . . peril$_\wedge$] \$N; ~ , . . .~ , EIM,A1

42.1 another$_\wedge$] \$N($-$N^{2,6}),EIM; ~ , N^{2,6},A1

42.10 whispered:] \$N($-$N^1), EIM; ~ , N^1,A1

42.15 said:] \$N,EIM; ~ , A1

42.20 turning$_\wedge$] \$N($-$N^6); ~ , N^6,EIM,A1

42.23 girl$_\wedge$ . . . darkness$_\wedge$] \$N,EIM; ~ , . . .~ , A1

42.35 Instead$_\wedge$] \$N; ~ , EIM,A1

43.3 reinforced] \$N($-$N^{2,7}),EIM; re-enforced N^{2,7},A1

43.10 rat$_\wedge$] \$N($-$N$^{4-5}$),EIM; ~ , N$^{4-5}$,A1

43.11 rate$_\wedge$] \$N($-$N^4),EIM; ~ , N^4,A1

43.15 disheveled] \$N($-$N^{1,6,8}); dishevelled N^{1,6,8},EIM,A1

43.20 waxen$_\wedge$] \$N($-$N^{1,4}); ~ , N^{1,4},EIM,A1

43.23 Finally$_\wedge$] \$N($-$N^4),EIM; ~ , N^4,A1

43.23 box$_\wedge$ and$_\wedge$] \$N($-$N^{3,4}); ~ , ~ , N^4,EIM,A1; ~ $_\wedge$ ~ , N^3

43.26 satisfaction$_\wedge$] \$N($-$N^4); ~ , N^4,EIM,A1

*43.26 anyhow. Even . . . me. You'll] N$^{1-2,6-8}$; ~ . Even . . . me, you'll N^3,EIM; ~ , even . . . me. You'll N$^{4-5}$,A1

43.27 moment$_\wedge$] N$^{1-3,5,7-8}$,EIM; ~ , N^4,A1

43.29　damned] $N^{1-4,8}$,EIM;
　darned N^7; d—d N^5,A1
43.31　Nixey.] $N; ~ ? EIM; ~ !
　A1
43.33　And . . . And] $N; and
　. . . and EIM,A1
43.35　astonishment.] $N^{1,5,7-8}$; ~ ,
　$N^{4,6}$,A1; ~ : N^{2-3},EIM
43.36　did.] $N; ~ ! EIM,A1
43.39　was.] $N; ~ ! EIM,A1
44.6　distant$_\Lambda$] $N,EIM; ~ , A1
44.9　was] $N,EIM; were A1
44.12　shouted:] $N($−N^{1-2}),EIM;
　~ , N^{1-2},A1
44.16　intent$_\Lambda$] $N,EIM; ~ , A1
44.17　sternness:]　$N($−$N^{4,6}$),
　EIM; ~ , $N^{4,6}$,A1
44.18　are.] $N,EIM; ~ ! A1
44.21　Now! Now,] $N($−N^1);
　Now, now, N^1; Now—now$_\Lambda$
　EIM; Now—now, A1
44.25　that.] $N,EIM; ~ ! A1
44.25　move.] $N($−N^6),EIM; ~ !
　N^6,A1
44.28　mouth.] $N,EIM; ~ ! A1
44.30　row$_\Lambda$—] $N; ~ !— EIM,A1
44.35　mad$_\Lambda$]　$N^{1-3,7-8}$,EIM; ~ ,
　$N^{4,6}$,A1; ~ - N^5
44.39　clamor]　$N;　clamour
　EIM,A1
45.8　knothole] $N^{1,3,6}$; ~ $_\Lambda$ ~ $N^{2,5}$,
　A1; ~ - ~ N^4,EIM; ~ - | ~
　N^{7-8}
45.11　There$_\Lambda$ . . . her$_\Lambda$] $N,EIM;
　~ , . . . ~ , A1
45.15　forever.] $N,EIM; ~ ! A1
45.19　tall$_\Lambda$]　$N($−N^6),EIM; ~ ,
　N^6,A1
45.21–22　mission$_\Lambda$]　$N($−$N^{4,6}$);
　~ , $N^{4,6}$,EIM,A1

45.24　elbow,]　$N($−N^{7-8}),EIM;
　~ $_\Lambda$ N^{7-8}; ~ ; A1
45.25　there$_\Lambda$]　$N($−N^{2-3}); ~ ,
　N^{2-3},EIM,A1
45.27　arms$_\Lambda$ . . . all$_\Lambda$] $N
　(−$N^{1,3}$); ~ , . . . ~ , $N^{1,3}$,EIM,
　A1
45.28　tone.]　$N^{1-2,4,7-8}$,EIM; ~ :
　$N^{3,5-6}$,A1
45.32　back.] $N($−N^4); ~ ! N^4,
　EIM,A1
45.36　hard$_\Lambda$]　$N^{1,4,6-8}$,EIM; ~ ,
　$N^{2-3,5}$,A1
45.38　him.] $N,EIM; ~ ! A1
45.39　him.]　$N($−N^4),EIM; ~ !
　N^4,A1
*45.39　at] $N($−N^2),EIM; in N^2,
　A1
46.4　passage$_\Lambda$] $N($−N^1); ~ , N^1,
　EIM,A1
46.8　prisoner$_\Lambda$]　$N($−N^4),EIM;
　~ , N^4,A1
46.10　towered$_\Lambda$] $N($−$N^{1-2,7-8}$),
　EIM; ~ , $N^{1-2,7-8}$,A1
46.12　knothole] N^5; ~ $_\Lambda$ ~ N^3,A1;
　~ - ~ $N^{1-2,4,7-8}$,EIM
*46.13　clinched] *stet* A1
46.16　door$_\Lambda$] $N; ~ , EIM,A1
*46.23　grimy,] EIM; grimy$_\Lambda$ A1;
　grimly$_\Lambda$ $N
46.26　chorus:]　$N($−N^4),EIM;
　~ , N^4,A1
46.36　course.] $N,EIM; ~ ! A1
46.37　Oh,] $N; ~ ! EIM,A1
46.38　arise$_\Lambda$] $N; ~ , EIM,A1
47.7　rebel$_\Lambda$]　$N($−$N^{3,6}$); ~ ,
　$N^{3,6}$,EIM,A1
47.12　things,] $N,EIM; ~ ; A1
47.12　God.] $N,EIM; ~ ! A1

A Mystery of Heroism

[The copy-text is N^1: *Philadelphia Press*, August 1,2, 1895. Other texts collated are N^2: *Minneapolis Tribune*; N^3: *Omaha Daily Bee*; N^4: *Kansas City Star*; N^5: *San Francisco Chronicle*; N^6: Chicago *Times-Herald*; NS: *Novels and Stories* [1896]; A1: *The Little Regiment*, Appleton, 1896. The E1 and E2 texts are derived.]

48.14　Collins$_\Lambda$ . . . Company$_\Lambda$]
　N^{3-5}; ~ , . . . ~ , $N^{1-2,6}$,NS,A1

48.25　Sometimes$_\Lambda$] $N^{3-4,6}$,A1; ~ ,
　$N^{1-2,5}$,NS

*48.27 *et seq.* grey] V; gray $N, NS,A1

49.1 upward] N[3,6],A1; upwards $N(−N[3,6]),NS

49.3 woods] $N(−N[1])+; wood N[1]

49.10 questions] $N(−N[1])+; question N[1]

49.36 Collins_∧ . . . Company_∧] N[3-4]; ∼ , . . . ∼ , $N(−N[3-4]), NS,A1

50.14 winter] $N(−N[1])+; Winter N[1]

*50.36 great] *stet* $N,NS,A1

51.3 carelessly] $N(−N[1])+; carlessly N[1]

51.8 that] $N(−N[1])+; of N[1]

51.12 battery,] $N(−N[1])+; ∼ _∧ N[1]

51.23 Yeh'll] V; You'll $N+

51.33 colonel . . . captain] $N(−N[1,5]),NS,A1; Colonel . . . Captain N[1,5]

51.37 moment_∧] N[4-6]; ∼ , N[1-3], NS,A1

*52.1 Collins's] N[4],A1; Collins' N[1,3,6]; Collin's N[2,5],NS

52.14 sir.] N[3-4,6],NS; ∼ , N[1-2], A1; ∼ ; N[5]

52.39 business.] N[5-6],A1; ∼ ! N[1-4],NS

53.15 seemed] $N(−N[1])+; seemd N[1]

53.32 fifteen dollars] NS,A1; $15 $N

53.36 diabolical,] $N(−N[1]),NS; ∼ _∧ N[1]; ∼ ; A1

54.7 color-sergeant] N[2,5-6]; ∼ _∧ ∼ N[1,3-4],A1

*54.14 boiling] N[6],A1; broiling $N(−N[6]),NS

54.18 house_∧] N[3-6]; ∼ , N[1-2], NS,A1

54.26 well_∧] $N(−N[1]); ∼ , N[1], NS,A1

55.11 over,] $N(−N[1])+; ∼ _∧ N[1]

55.25 hoof prints] N[2,4,6]; ∼ - ∼ N[1,3,5]; hoofprints A1

56.21 waved] $N(−N[1])+; waived N[1]

*56.22 young] *stet* N[1-2,4,6],NS,A1

AN INDIANA CAMPAIGN

[The copy-text is PM: *Pocket Magazine*. Other texts collated are N[1]: *Kansas City Star*; N[2]: *Buffalo Commercial*; N[3]: *Nebraska State Journal*; N[4]: *Minneapolis Tribune*; N[5]: *San Francisco Chronicle*; N[6]: *St. Louis Post-Dispatch*; EIM: *English Illustrated Magazine*; A1: *The Little Regiment*, Appleton, 1896. The E1 and E2 texts are derived.]

57.0 I] A1; CHAPTER I N[6]; *omit* PM,N[1-5],EIM

57.7 an] $N, A1; *omit* PM,EIM

57.11 Northern] N[1],A1; northern PM,$N(−N[1]),EIM

57.13 day_∧] $N+; ∼ , PM

57.23 road_∧] $N+; ∼ , PM

*57.26 extremely] $N+; supremely PM

*57.29 who] $N(−N[3,6]), EIM, A1; which PM; that N[3,6]

58.3 little] $N+; *omit* PM

*58.11 Major——"] *stet* PM

58.13 What's]$N+; what's PM

58.13 th'] N[1,4-6],EIM,A1; the PM,N[2]; the' N[3]

58.30 hold] $N+; grip PM

58.35 down] $N+; *omit* PM

58.35 pegs] $N+; peg PM

58.35-36 smooth-bore] N[3,5],EIM; ∼ - | ∼ N[2,4,6],A1; smoothbore PM; ∼ _∧ ∼ N[1]

58.36 cap_∧]$N+; ∼ , PM

58.37 was] $N+; *omit* PM

58.37 removed it] $N+; removed PM

59.3 tavern_∧] $N+; ∼ , PM

*59.5,6 Well?] $N+; ∼ , PM

59.8 'Got'?] V; ' ∼ ?' $N(−N[1,5]), EIM,A1; _∧ ∼ _∧ ? PM, N[1,5]

59.9 sentence_∧] $N(−N[1]),A1; ∼ , PM,N[1],EIM

59.29 Smith's] $N+; Smiths's PM

59.29 is$_\wedge$] $N+; ~ , PM

59.34 Then,] $N+; ~ $_\wedge$ PM

60.10 moment$_\wedge$] $N+; ~ , PM

60.17 Finally$_\wedge$] $N(−N²); ~ , PM,N²,EIM,A1

60.17 a'] N²,EIM,A1; 'a PM,$N (−N²)

60.18 Petersen] $N(−N⁶)+; Peterson PM,N⁶

60.21 Jeroozel] N$^{1,5-6}$; Jerozel PM,N$^{2-4}$,EIM+

60.22 mus'] $N+; must PM

60.30 goin'] $N+; going PM

60.37 Petersen] V; Peterson PM+

61.3–4 could contain] $N+; contained PM

61.8 yellow] $N+; the yellow PM

61.8 tops] $N+; top PM

61.22.1 II] A1; PART II $N(−N⁶), EIM; CHAPTER II N⁶; omit (with space) PM

61.24 dignity] $N+; the dignity PM

61.30 last$_\wedge$] $N+; ~ , PM

61.32 a'] $N(−N⁶)+; a$_\wedge$ PM; a-N⁶

61.32 do?"] $N+; ~ ." PM

62.1 Well?] $N+; ~ , PM

62.7 Well?] EIM; ~ , PM,$N,A1

62.15 clambered] $N(−N³)+; climbed PM; clamored N³

62.19 nor nuthin'] $N+; or nothin' PM

62.20 'ud] $N+; $_\wedge$ud PM

62.21 an'] $N+; and PM

62.25 of] $N+; omit PM

62.25 'im] $N+; him PM

62.28 hain't] $N+; ain't PM

62.31 along,] $N,A1; ~ $_\wedge$ PM, EIM

62.31 th'] $N+; the PM

63.2–3 appeared. As . . . them$_\wedge$ it] A1; ~ $_\wedge$ as . . . them. It PM,$N,EIM

63.4 whispered:] $N+; ~ ,— PM

63.5 a'] A1; a$_\wedge$ PM(−N²)+; a-N²

63.5 here,$_\wedge$ . . . supposin'——"]

$N+; ~ , — . . . ~ ." PM

63.6 what?] $N+; ~ , PM

63.7 Supposin'——] $N+; ~ , PM

63.7 Peter] $N+; old Peter PM

63.9 Thunder!] $N+; ~ , PM

63.10 got] $N+; came PM

63.15 there's] $N+; there is PM

63.16 said] $N+; replied PM

63.18 hain't] V; ain't PM+

63.18 within$_\wedge$] $N+; ~' PM

63.22 turned] $N+; slowly turned PM

63.22 yeh] $N+; you PM

63.23 said] $N+; asked PM

63.25 "I (no ¶)] $N(−N⁶)+; ¶ PM,N⁶

63.26,32 heered] $N+; heerd PM

63.29 Sssh] $N(−N$^{5-6}$); Ssssh PM,N⁵; S-s-sh N⁶,A1

63.32,36 anythin'.] $N+; ~ ! PM

64.2 'im] $N+; him PM

64.5 this] $N(−N³)+; the PM; his N³

64.5 reproach$_\wedge$] $N(−N¹),EIM; ~ , PM,N¹,A1

64.8 Well?] N⁶; ~ , PM(−N⁶)+

64.9 upon] $N+; on PM

64.23 swift silent] $N+; silent swift PM

64.25 major] white space below $N(−N³); no space PM,N³, EIM,A1

64.29 Petersen] V; Peterson PM(−N³)+; Patterson N³

64.31 stopped$_\wedge$] $N(−N^{2,6}),A1; ~ , PM,N^{2,6},EIM

64.32 others:] $N,EIM; ~ , PM, A1

64.32 Why,] $N+; ~ $_\wedge$ PM

65.3 Here$_\wedge$] $N(−N⁶)+; ~ , PM, N⁶

65.15 gun$_\wedge$] $N+; ~ , PM

65.17 share] $N+; have a share PM

65.19 the gun] $N+; it PM

65.22 t'] $N+; to PM

65.22 'em] N^{1,5},A1; it PM; 'im N$^{2-4,6}$,EIM

65.29 and,] $N(−N⁴)+; ~ $_\wedge$ PM, N⁴

65.34 silken] $N+; *omit* PM
65.35 last$_A$] $N+; ~ , PM
65.36 toward] N$^{1,5-6}$,A1; towards PM,N$^{2-4}$,EIM
65.36 of a] $N(−N^1)+; of PM,N^1
66.5 on'y] N^3,EIM,A1; o'ny PM,N$^{4-5}$; o'ly N^2; only N^1

66.8 sudden$_A$] $N(−N^6)+; ~ , PM,N^6
66.10 Petersen] N$^{2-3,5}$,EIM,A1; Peterson PM,N^{1,4,6}
*66.13 mopping] N^{2,6}; still mopping PM; mopped $N(−N^{2,6})+
66.15 sure."] $N+; ~ . $_A$ PM

A GREY SLEEVE

[The copy-text is N^1: *Kansas City Star*. Other texts collated are N^2: *Minneapolis Tribune*; N^3: *Philadelphia Press*; N^4: *Omaha Weekly Bee*; N^5: *San Francisco Chronicle*; N^6: Chicago *Times-Herald*; PM: *Pocket Magazine*; FLW: *Frank Leslie's Weekly*; EIM: *English Illustrated Magazine*. A1, E1, and E2 are all derived texts, as is DFM.]

67.0 I] PM,FLW; PART I $N; *omit* EIM
67.5 him,] $N(−N^1),PM; ~ $_A$ N^1,FLW,EIM
67.12 far-away] N^5,FLW,EIM; faraway N$^{1-4}$,PM; ~ - | ~ N^6
67.15 but,] N$^{3-6}$+; ~ $_A$ N$^{1-2}$
67.21 column$_A$] $N(−N^1)+; ~ , N^1
68.8 tense$_A$] $N(−N^{1,5}), PM,EIM; ~ , N^{1,5},FLW
68.10 headlong] $N(−N^{1,3})+; ~ - ~ N^1; ~ - | ~ N^3
68.12 teeth,] $N(−N^1)+; ~ $_A$ N^1
68.13 at] $N(−N^1),PM,FLW; of N^1,EIM
68.16 paces] FLW; faces $N,PM,EIM
*68.27 imperturbable] $N(−N^{1,3})+; imperturable N^{1,3}
68.39 toward] $N(−N$^{1-2}$),FLW; towards N$^{1-2}$,PM,EIM
69.9 the wood] N$^{4-5}$; wood N$^{1-3,6}$+
69.21 grey] PM, EIM; gray $N,FLW
69.21 smoke] $N(−N^1)+; smok N^1
69.23 seen] $N(−N^1)+; sen N^1
69.39 there's] $N(−N^{1,6})+; There's N^{1,6}
70.1 house!] $N(−N^1)+; ~ . N^1
70.5 brown-faced] $N(−N$^{1-2}$)+; ~ $_A$ ~ N$^{1-2}$

70.13 blue-clothed] $N(−N$^{1-2}$)+; ~ $_A$ ~ N$^{1-2}$ (N^2: $_A$ coated)
70.31 something,'] N$^{2-3,6}$+; ~ $_A$ ' N$^{1,4-5}$
70.39 this] $N(−N^1); his N^1
71.5 to a] $N(−N^1)+; to his N^1
71.8 sleeve!] $N(−N^{1,6})+; ~ . N^{1,6}
71.10 t'——"] FLW; t' "—— $N,PM; it——" EIM
71.12 troopers] $N(−N^1)+; troops N^1
71.18.1 II] PM,FLW; PART II $N,EIM
71.23 marble-topped] $N(−N^1)+; ~ $_A$ ~ N^1
71.24 fireplace] $N(−N^1); ~ $_A$ ~ N^1; ~ - ~ PM,FLW; ~ - | ~ EIM
71.27 transfixed] $N(−N^1); tranfixed N^1
72.10 battle-howling] N$^{2-3,5}$+; ~ $_A$ ~ N^{1,4,6}; ~ -howlings EIM
*72.16 house?] *stet* N$^{1-2,6}$,FLW, EIM
72.18 maybe] $N(−N^{1,3})+; may be N^{1,3}
*72.20 Are] A1; Is $N,PM,FLW, EIM
*72.24 besides] *stet* $N(−N^{3,5}), FLW
72.27 this] $N(−N^1)+; his N^1
73.25 men$_A$] N^{2,4,6},FLW,EIM; ~ , N^{1,3,5},PM

75.5 somehow] N⁴⁻⁶+; ~ ∧ ~ N¹⁻³

75.6 her——"] $N(−N¹·³)+; ~"
—— N¹·³

*75.7 clinched] FLW; clenched $N,PM,EIM

75.9.1 III] PM,FLW; PART III $N,EIM

76.2 desolation.] $N(−N¹),FLW; ~ : N¹,EIM; ~ , PM

76.7 men] $N(−N¹)+; man N¹

76.11 trifle∧] N²·⁴·⁶,PM,FLW; ~ , N¹·³·⁵,EIM

76.11 and,] $N(−N¹),PM,FLW; ~ ∧ N¹,EIM

76.12 attitudes] $N(−N¹); attitude N¹

76.37 crackled] $N(−N¹)+; crackeld N¹

77.10 grey] PM,EIM; gray $N, FLW

77.18 an] $N(−N¹)+; omit N¹

78.24 blue-coated] N³·⁵⁻⁶+; ~ ∧ ~ N¹⁻²; bluecoated N⁴

78.30 ¶ "Did] $N(−N¹)+; no ¶ N¹

*79.11 need] stet $N(−N⁵),FLW

79.35 beds] $N(−N¹)+; heads N¹

79.36; 80.17 Good-bye!] $N(−N¹·⁵)±; ~ . N¹·⁵

80.13 'tain't] N⁶+; 'taint $N(−N⁶)

80.14 but——∧] $N(−N¹)+; ~ ——. N¹

80.17 said:] N⁶,PM+; ~ . N¹·³; ~ , N²·⁴⁻⁵

*80.22 Never!] stet $N(−N⁶)

80.25 mind] $N(−N¹)+; mind it N¹

80.31 panic-stricken] $N(−N¹⁻²)+; ~ ∧ ~ N¹⁻²

*80.32 this] $N(−N¹·⁶),PM,FLW; his N¹·⁶; the EIM

80.33 a] $N(−N¹); the N¹

80.35 please,] $N(−N¹·⁶),PM, EIM; ~ ∧ N¹·⁶,FLW

81.1 long-impending] N³⁻⁴·⁶+; ~ ∧ ~ N¹⁻²·⁵

81.2 a silence] $N(−N¹)+; silence N¹

THE VETERAN

[Copy-text is McC(p), the proofsheets of *McClure's Magazine*. The other texts—McC, SJB, N¹, A1, and E1—are derived.]

83.29; 84.1,2 Sickles's] McC; Sickleses McC(p); Sickles' N¹

84.19; 85.1 grey] SJB; gray McC(p),McC

84.34–35 trampling, and] McC; brampling, and McC(p)

AN EPISODE OF WAR

[Copy-text is G: *The Gentlewoman*. The other texts collated are derived: TMs: University of Virginia typescript; E1: *Last Words*, Digby, Long, 1902.]

*89.15 had] V; has G+

*89.18 little puffs] E1; little white puffs G,TMs

89.23 too∧] E1; ~ , G,TMs

90.14 Well∧] V; ~ , G+

92.29 answered:] TMs; ~ ; G

93.2 school-house] TMs; schoolhouse G

WOUNDS IN THE RAIN

THE PRICE OF THE HARNESS

[Copytext is Co: *Cosmopolitan Magazine*. The other text collated is B: *Blackwood's Edinburgh Magazine*. A1 is derived and without authority.]

97.0 THE . . . HARNESS] B; THE WOOF OF THIN RED

THREADS Co

97.6 guinea-grass∧] B; ~ , Co

97.10–11 to time$_\wedge$] B; ~ ~ , Co
97.11 sleek-sided$_\wedge$] B; ~ , Co
97.12 other way] B; other Co
97.18 Men (*no* ¶)] B; ¶ Co
97.22 hill$_\wedge$] B; ~ , Co
97.27 blue$_\wedge$] B; ~ , Co
98.7 eat,] B; ~ ? Co
98.11 *et seq.* grey] B; gray Co
98.23 of foliage] B; of the foliage Co
98.27 again$_\wedge$] B; ~ , Co
98.27 "Wonder (*no* ¶)] B; ¶ Co
98.30 "Them (*no* ¶)] B; ¶ Co
98.31 it,] B; ~ ! Co
98.31 th'] B; the Co
98.36 reappeared$_\wedge$] B; ~ , Co
98.37 said$_\wedge$] B; ~ , Co
99.3 arose$_\wedge$] B; ~ , Co
99.10 dawn$_\wedge$] B; ~ , Co
99.27 Now,] B; ~ $_\wedge$ Co
99.27 cried. "Hold] B; ~ : "hold Co
100.12 swords$_\wedge$] B; ~ , Co
100.30 fat$_\wedge$] B; ~ , Co
100.30 muscles$_\wedge$] B; ~ , Co
100.37 left$_\wedge$] B; ~ , Co
101.1 ahead$_\wedge$] B; ~ , Co
101.17 front$_\wedge$] B; ~ , Co
101.31 busy$_\wedge$ and] B; ~ , ~ Co
102.3 And (*no* ¶)] B; ¶ Co
102.14 On (*no* ¶)] B; ¶ Co
102.34 Horses$_\wedge$] B; ~ , Co
102.37 discussion$_\wedge$] B; ~ , Co
103.1 battalion$_\wedge$] B; ~ , Co
103.1 battalions$_\wedge$] B; ~ , Co
103.3 fact$_\wedge$] B; ~ , Co
103.5 great$_\wedge$] B; ~ , Co
103.9 shots$_\wedge$] B; ~ , Co
103.16 exhibited$_\wedge$ . . . length$_\wedge$] B; ~ , . . . ~ , Co
103.17 blue$_\wedge$] B; ~ , Co
103.19 Non-commissioned (*no* ¶)] B; ¶ Co
103.32 chimneys$_\wedge$] B; ~ , Co
103.33 swift$_\wedge$] B; ~ , Co
103.33 front$_\wedge$] B; ~ , Co
104.1 "Come (*no* ¶)] B; ¶ Co
104.7 To (*no* ¶)] B; ¶ Co
104.12 knolls$_\wedge$] B; ~ , Co
104.23 Jesus] B; Hell Co
104.32 shot$_\wedge$] B; ~ , Co

104.36 soothing$_\wedge$] B; ~ , Co
105.4 musketry$_\wedge$] B; ~ , Co
105.7 He (*no* ¶)] B; ¶ Co
105.21 lieutenant-colonel] B; Lieutenant-Colonel Co
105.23 captains] B; Captains Co
106.2 him$_\wedge$] B; ~ , Co
106.2 *et seq.* lieutenant] B; Lieutenant Co
106.15 arms$_\wedge$] B; ~ , Co
106.36 Following (*no* ¶)] B; ¶ Co
107.1 men$_\wedge$] B; ~ , Co
107.13 arose] B; rose Co
107.13 field$_\wedge$] B; ~ , Co
107.22–23 wounds$_\wedge$ . . . quaint-ly$_\wedge$] B; ~ , . . . ~ , Co
107.28–29 Here$_\wedge$ . . . bank$_\wedge$] B; ~ , . . . ~ , Co
107.33 incessant$_\wedge$] B; ~ , Co
107.36 Here,   what's] B; ~ ! What's Co
108.2 member$_\wedge$] B; ~ , Co
108.13 their rifles] B; *omit* Co
108.16 wound] B; wounds Co
108.21 Here,] B; ~ ! Co
108.26 said. "Here] B; ~ ; "here Co
109.5 pleaded$_\wedge$ . . . length$_\wedge$] B; ~ , . . . ~ , Co
109.32 prut] B; " ~ " Co
109.35 great$_\wedge$] B; ~ , Co
110.1 shoulders$_\wedge$ . . . hands$_\wedge$] B; ~ , . . . ~ , Co
110.2 blades$_\wedge$] B; ~ , Co
110.18 'em, . . . 'em.] B; ~ ! . . . ~ ! Co
110.18–19 He . . . mistress.] B; *omit* Co
110.19 aiming] B; aiming his rifle Co
110.35 charge$_\wedge$] B; ~ , Co
111.8 moment$_\wedge$] B; ~ , Co
111.19 "It (*no* ¶)] B; ¶ Co
111.32 *is*] B; is Co
112.1 temper. "See] B; ~ , "see Co
112.1 Grierson (*no* ¶)] B; ¶ Co
112.11.1 VI] B; *omit* Co
112.21 They (*no* ¶)] B; ¶ Co

112.34; 113.16 Martin_∧] B; ~ , 113.7 fever_∧] B; ~ , Co
Co 113.18 triangle] B; tangle Co

THE LONE CHARGE OF WILLIAM B. PERKINS

[Copy-text is WG: *Westminster Gazette*. The other text collated is McC: *McClure's Magazine*. The A1 text is derived.]

114.12 *et seq.* harbor] McC; harbour WG
114.19,25; 115.9 Perkins (*no ¶*)] McC; ¶ WG
114.25 nights of] McC; nights' WG
*114.30 had emanated] *stet* WG
115.6–7 and_∧ . . . way_∧] McC; ~ , . . . ~ , WG
115.14–15 where_∧ . . . exuberance_∧] McC; ~ , . . . ~ , WG
115.16 blasting] McC; blazing WG
115.18 Perkins_∧] McC; ~ , WG
115.27 But] McC; Now WG
115.28 and] McC; *omit* WG
115.29 six hundred] McC; 600 WG
*115.38 sputter] McC; splutter WG
115.39; 116.12 *fluttery-fluttery*] McC (*in roman*); *flutery-flutery* WG
116.6 one hundred and fifty] V; 150 WG,McC
116.12–13 *flllluttery*] McC (*in roman*); *flllllutery* WG
116.14 men_∧] McC; ~ , WG
116.16 The (*no ¶*)] McC; ¶ WG
116.16 five hundred] McC; 500 WG
116.16 In (*no ¶*)] McC; ¶ WG
116.27 As (*no ¶*)] McC; ¶ WG

116.39–117.1 that_∧ . . . imbecility_∧] McC; ~ , . . . ~ , WG
*117.7 suppliant] *stet* WG
117.7 chaparral] McC; chapparal WG
117.14 peace_∧] McC; ~ , WG
117.17 Boom-] McC; *Boom-* WG
117.17 -Pum] McC (-pum); *-Pum* WG
117.18 -crk_∧] McC (*in roman*); ~ , WG
117.26 was,] McC; ~ — WG
117.27 temple_∧ shining_∧] McC; ~ , ~ , WG
117.30 Then_∧] McC; ~ , WG
117.34 passed. The] McC; ~ ; the WG
117.34 *prut . . .*] McC (*in roman*); ~ *** WG
117.38 not able] McC; unable WG
118.1 again_∧] McC; ~ , WG
118.3 shouted,] McC; ~ ; WG
118.4 him_∧] McC; ~ , WG
118.10 did!] McC; ~ ? WG
118.10 boiler? Out] McC; ~ _∧ out WG
118.12 rusty] McC; old rusty WG
118.14–15 The patrol . . . blind.] McC; The party then laid down in the brush and laughed until every face was blazing red. WG

THE CLAN OF NO-NAME

[Copy-text is N[1]: *New York Herald*. Other texts collated are BW: *Black and White*; A1: *Wounds in the Rain*, Stokes, 1900. N[2-3] are derived texts.]

119.0 No-Name] A1; ~ _∧ ~ N[1], BW
119.1 riddle.] BW,A1; ~ ; N[1]

119.3 die,] BW; ~ . N[1]; ~ ; A1
119.9; 119.20 "Margharita (*no ¶*)] BW,A1; ¶ N[1]

119.9   Her (*no* ¶)] BW,A1; ¶ N¹

119.15   fish-pond] BW,A1; ~ ∧ ~ N¹

119.16   red-fins]   BW,A1; ~ ∧ ~ N¹

119.22   carelessly:] V; ~ :— N¹; ~ , BW,A1

119.22   "Oh (*no* ¶)] BW,A1; ¶ N¹

119.24   high-minded] BW,A1; ~ ∧ ~ N¹

120.11   bed-ticking] BW,A1; ~ ∧ ~ N¹

*120.14   grass∧] *stet* N¹

120.24   long∧] BW,A1; ~ , N¹

120.24   keen-angled] BW,A1; ~ ∧ ~ N¹

120.25   safety-pins] BW,A1; ~ ∧ ~ N¹

120.28   deadly-swift] BW,A1; ~ ∧ ~ N¹

*120.30   quickly∧] BW,A1; ~ , N¹

*120.33   teeth∧] *stet* N¹

120.34;121.4   loop-holes] BW, A1; loopholes N¹

*121.2   agony. He] *stet* N¹

121.2   repeated:] BW,A1; ~ :— N¹

121.3   ill-conditioned] BW,A1; ~ ∧ ~ N¹

*121.5   data∧ apparently∧] *stet* N¹

121.7   The (*no* ¶)] BW,A1; ¶ N¹

*121.8   incessant,] BW,A1; ~ ∧ N¹

121.10   men,] BW,A1; ~ ∧ N¹

121.10   out:] BW,A1; ~ :— N¹

121.12   linen∧] BW,A1; ~ , N¹

121.13   color∧] BW; ~ , N¹,A1

121.14   fact∧] BW,A1; ~ , N¹

121.17   sun-up] BW,A1; ~ ∧ ~ N¹

121.17   half-marked] BW,A1; ~ ∧ ~ N¹

121.19   half-shod] BW,A1; ~ ∧ ~ N¹

121.33   soldiers∧ . . . corporal∧] BW,A1; ~ , . . . ~ , N¹

121.34; 122.19; 123.10   block-house] BW,A1; ~ ~ N¹

121.36   Mariel] BW,A1; Manriel N¹

122.4   going] BW,A1; going on N¹

*122.5   half a league] *stet* BW,N¹

*122.5–6   General] *stet* N¹,BW

122.14   dissolution,] BW,A1; ~ ∧ N¹

122.16–17   a wood] BW,A1; the wood N¹

122.17   long-grassed∧] BW,A1; ~ ∧ ~ , N¹

122.18   A half-mile] BW,A1; Half a mile N¹

122.23   men∧] BW,A1; ~ , N¹

122.26   veteran-like] BW,A1; veteranlike N¹

123.2   task] BW,A1; one N¹

123.4   bayed] BW,A1; kept at bay N¹

123.16   for ever] BW,A1; forever N¹

123.26   very] BW,A1; *omit* N¹

123.27   cartouche] BW,A1; car-touch N¹

123.29   happy;] BW,A1; ~ , N¹

123.30   eye] BW,A1; eyes N¹

123.30   grass-lands] A1; ~ ∧ ~ N¹; grasslands BW

123.34   general;] BW,A1; ~ , N¹

124.3   out] BW,A1; *omit* N¹

124.9   enemy-crowded] BW,A1; ~ ∧ ~ N¹

124.10   men∧] BW,A1; ~ , N¹

124.10   snuggling] BW,A1; smuggling N¹

124.12   bed-ticking] BW, A1 (~ - | ~); bedticking N¹

124.13   door∧] BW,A1; ~ , N¹

124.19   all] BW,A1; the N¹

125.2   free-band]   BW,A1; ~ ∧ ~ N¹

125.6   ill-used] BW,A1; ~ ∧ ~ N¹

125.8   Yes?] BW,A1; ~ . N¹

125.8   right."] BW,A1; ~ . ∧ N¹

125.9   "Eat] BW,A1; ∧ ~ N¹

125.9   incredibly foul] BW,A1; *omit* N¹

125.15   was] BW,A1; were N¹

126.13   longingly:] BW,A1; ~ , N¹

126.17   for ever] BW,A1; forever N¹

126.19 know——"] BW,A1; ~ "
—— N¹
126.25 rifle-drumming] BW,A1;
~ ∧ ~ N¹
126.30 dun] BW,A1; dum N¹
126.31 foot-hills] BW,A1;
foothills N¹
126.32 et seq. aide] BW,A1; aid
N¹
126.34 march,] BW,A1; ~ ∧ N¹
127.6 severed] BW,A1; several
N¹
*127.15–16 away from the enemy
. . . hundred yards] stet N¹,A1
127.23 him:] BW,A1; ~ :— N¹
127.26 Bas. "You] BW,A1; ~ ;
"you N¹
127.28 life.] BW,A1; ~ ! N¹
127.29 no,] BW,A1; ~ ! N¹
127.31 never was] BW,A1; was
never N¹
127.34 ambition—] BW,A1; ~ ,
N¹
127.36–128.21 "Well . . . minute.] BW,A1; omit N¹
127.37 Bas∧] BW; ~ ,A1
127.37 killed∧] BW; ~ , A1
128.6 fight∧] BW; ~ , A1
128.10 expected. There] BW; ~ ;
there A1
128.13 him. There] BW; ~ ;
there A1
128.23 passed,] BW,A1; ~ ∧ N¹
128.23 wild-fowl] BW,A1; ~ ∧ ~
N¹
128.24 along a] BW,A1; a lone
N¹
128.24 sea-beach] BW,A1; ~ ∧ ~
N¹
128.28 it,] BW,A1; ~ ∧ N¹
128.33 disconsolately]   BW,A1;
omit N¹
128.34 foot-hills] BW,A1; ~ ∧ ~
N¹
128.36 rear-guard] BW,A1; ~ ∧
~ N¹
129.3 war-ship] A1; ~ ∧ ~ N¹;
warship BW
129.6 ladder-climbing] BW,A1;
~ ∧ ~ N¹

129.7 hurry,] BW,A1; ~ ∧ N¹
129.8 shoulders∧] BW,A1; ~ , N¹
129.9 courage:] BW,A1; ~ , N¹
129.9 mess!] BW,A1; ~ ? N¹
129.18 possible] BW,A1; impossible N¹
129.21 firing-line] BW,A1; ~ ∧ ~
N¹
129.22 emotional] BW,A1; emotioned N¹
129.35 despairingly; he] BW,A1;
~ . He N¹
129.38 reality∧] BW,A1; ~ , N¹
*130.2 wisdoms] A1; wisdom $N
*130.9 his] BW,A1; His N¹
130.9 mother,] BW,A1; ~ ∧ N¹
130.18 death; there] BW,A1; ~ .
There N¹
130.24 death-bed] BW,A1;
deathbed N¹
130.27 saucer-like] BW,A1; sau-
cerlike N¹
130.39 panic-stricken] BW,A1; ~
∧ ~ N¹
131.6,14 northern] BW,A1;
Northern N¹
131.6 ice-fields]   BW,A1; ~ ∧ ~
N¹
131.6,14 hot∧] BW,A1; ~ , N¹
131.6 jungles,] BW,A1; ~ ; N¹
131.7,15 unfamiliar] BW,A1;
familiar A1
131.14 ice-fields] BW; ~ ∧ ~ N¹;
icefields A1
131.18 stooped] BW,A1; stopped
N¹
131.21 simple∧] A1; ~ , N¹,BW
131.32 breast,] BW,A1; ~ ∧ N¹
131.35 slope,] BW,A1; ~ ∧ N¹
132.6 saucer,] BW,A1; ~ ∧ N¹
132.9 blood-greed] BW,A1; ~ ∧ ~
N¹
132.15 retreated∧] A1; ~ , N¹,
BW
132.26 expedition,] BW,A1; ~ ∧
N¹
132.26–27 brigadier-general]
BW,A1; ~ ∧ ~ N¹
132.28 man∧] BW,A1; ~ , N¹

132.34 muttering:] BW,A1; ~ ,
N¹
132.36 back$_\wedge$] BW,A1; ~ , N¹
132.37 fire-engine] BW,A1; ~ $_\wedge$
~ N¹
133.2 tongue-hanging] BW,A1;
~ $_\wedge$ ~ N¹
133.3 after-battle] BW,A1; ~ $_\wedge$ ~
N¹
133.5 and libidinous] BW,A1;
omit N¹
133.5–6 filled . . . life] BW,A1;
omit N¹
133.12,15 captain] BW,A1; Captain N¹
133.13 señor.] BW,A1; ~ ! N¹
133.16 guerilla,] A1; ~ $_\wedge$ N¹; ~
— BW
133.16 a glance] BW,A1; omit
N¹
133.17 M-m-m] BW,A1; M—m—
N¹
133.18 slow$_\wedge$] A1; ~ , N¹,BW
133.18–19 faint smile, . . .
love,] BW,A1; ~ ~ — . . .~
— N¹
133.20 presently,] BW,A1; ~ $_\wedge$
N¹
133.20–21 written: . . . this:]
BW,A1; ~ :— . . .~ :— N¹
133.23 half-minute] BW,A1; ~ $_\wedge$
~ N¹
133.24 slow$_\wedge$] A1; ~ , N¹,BW
133.24 Pobrecito] N³,E1; Pobrecetto N¹⁻²,BW,A1
133.28 earth, . . . heights,] BW,
A1; ~ $_\wedge$ . . .~ $_\wedge$ N¹
133.29 down-turned] BW,A1; ~ $_\wedge$
~ N¹
133.32 fish-pond] BW,A1;
fishpond N¹
134.1 air,] BW,A1; air$_\wedge$ and with
N¹
*134.6 heaven] stet N¹, A1

134.7 dream-rivals] BW,A1; ~ $_\wedge$
~ N¹
134.7 and] BW,A1; and that N¹
134.15 was] BW,A1; were N¹
134.23 say:] BW,A1; ~ , N¹
134.26 talk,] BW,A1; ~ $_\wedge$ N¹
134.27 incorrect$_\wedge$] BW,A1; ~ ,
N¹
*134.28 brooks] stet $N,A1
134.32 well-bred] BW,A1; ~ $_\wedge$ ~
N¹
134.33 ask:] BW,A1; ~ , N¹
134.35 head:] BW,A1; ~ :— N¹
134.36 Prat] BW,A1; Pratt N¹
135.1 that] BW,A1; omit N¹
135.5 star-like] BW,A1; starlike
N¹
135.5–6 rumpled . . . squalid]
BW,A1; reduced . . . abject
N¹
135.8 She (no ¶)] BW,A1; ¶ N¹
135.9 -o'-] BW,A1; -'o- N¹
135.18 when—presto—] BW,A1;
~ , ~ ! N¹
135.22 murmured$_\wedge$] BW,A1; ~ ,
135.24 lie of] BW,A1; omit N¹
135.28 of the] BW,A1; of N¹
135.31–32 glance, . . . glance,]
BW,A1; ~ — . . .~ — N¹
135.35–36 dressing-table] BW,
A1; ~ $_\wedge$ ~ N¹
135.38 written:] BW,A1; ~ :—
N¹
135.39 this:] BW,A1; ~ . N¹
136.1 only] BW,A1; omit N¹
136.1 who$_\wedge$] BW,A1; ~ , N¹
136.2 northern] BW,A1; Northern N¹
136.2 ice-fields] BW,A1; ~ $_\wedge$ ~
N¹
136.3 lies and] BW,A1; lines of
N¹

"GOD REST YE, MERRY GENTLEMEN"

[Copy-text is SP: *Saturday Evening Post*. The other text collated is C: *Cornhill Magazine*. A1 is a derived text but has authority between 299.23 and 301.25. E1, printed from A1 plates, has a few plate changes that are recorded when accepted.]

137.2 *et seq.* *New York Eclipse*] C; New York Eclipse SP

137.2 *Eclipse*, and at sea$_\wedge$] C; Eclipse. At sea, SP

137.3 -boats$_\wedge$] C; ~ , SP

137.3 pyjamas] C; pajamas SP

137.10 "Take (*no* ¶)] C; ¶ SP

137.10 If (*no* ¶)] C; ¶ SP

137.16 *et seq.* *Jefferson G. John-son*] C; Jefferson G. Johnson SP

137.29 Little (*no* ¶)] C; ¶ SP

138.3 condoled$_\wedge$] C; ~ , SP

138.6 They (*no* ¶)] C (But they); ¶ SP

138.7 cockleshell] C; cockleshells SP

138.8 flags,] C; ~ ; SP

138.10 The (*no* ¶)] C; ¶ SP

138.12 "Can't (*no* ¶)] C; ¶ SP

138.14 Tampa. Expected] C; ~ ; expected SP

138.15 immediately. Place] C; ~ ; place SP

138.17 high$_\wedge$] C; ~ , SP

138.18 fleets] C; fleet SP

138.22 At (*no* ¶)] C; ¶ SP

138.23 hour$_\wedge$] C; ~ , SP

138.25 *et seq.* grey] C; gray SP

138.26 lay] C; swung SP

138.27 thin$_\wedge$] C; ~ , SP

138.28 $_\wedge$boom . . . boom-boom$_\wedge$] C; " ~ . . . ~ — ~ " SP

138.34 ¶ The] C; *no* ¶ SP

138.36 cruiser$_\wedge$] C; ~ , SP

138.37 tars$_\wedge$] C; ~ , SP

138.38 cold$_\wedge$ blue$_\wedge$] C; ~ , ~ , SP

139.2 The (*no* ¶)] C; ¶ SP

139.8 chafed] C; chaffed SP

139.10 Then (*no* ¶)] C; ¶ SP

139.16 reality$_\wedge$] C; ~ , SP

139.19 high$_\wedge$ green$_\wedge$] C; ~ , ~ , SP

139.23 *et seq.* army] C; Army SP

139.23–24 landing— . . . part —] C; ~ ; . . . ~ ; SP

139.25 The (*no* ¶)] C; ¶ SP

139.29 boats$_\wedge$] C; ~ , SP

140.3 At (*no* ¶)] C; ¶ SP

140.9 ashes$_\wedge$] C; ~ , SP

140.9 Little (*no* ¶)] C; ¶ SP

140.13 Spanish] C; recent Spanish SP

140.21 It . . . warm.] C; *omit* SP

140.21 It was really (*no* ¶)] C; ¶ SP

140.30–31 who$_\wedge$ . . . nations$_\wedge$] C; ~ , . . . ~ , SP

140.36 Walkley$_\wedge$] C; ~ , SP

140.38 "Oh (*no* ¶)] C; ¶ SP

140.38 Nell, how] C; Nell," he cried, "how SP

141.6 seat on the steps] C; a seat SP

141.9 food$_\wedge$] C; ~ , SP

141.25 Rogers$_\wedge$] C; ~ , SP

141.34 A (*no* ¶)] C; ¶ SP

141.36 *and*] C; and SP

142.13 a great] C; the great SP

142.21 damn sure] C; sure that SP

142.21 fiercely] C; *omit* SP

142.23–24 only found] C; found only SP

142.36 days] C; two days SP

*142.37 canteens] *stet* SP

143.11–12 Anybody . . . match?] C; *omit* SP

143.16 unknown$_\wedge$] C; ~ , SP

*143.24 street] *stet* SP

143.27 The (*no* ¶)] C; ¶ SP

143.31 entrance of] C; entrance to SP

144.4 arose] C; rose SP

144.11 Before (*no* ¶)] C; ¶ SP

144.16 Point (*no* ¶)] C; ¶ SP

144.20 Accordingly (*no* ¶)] C; ¶ SP

144.24 Then (*no* ¶)] C; ¶ SP

144.27 *et seq.* *Adolphus*] C; Adolphus SP

144.36 ¶ There] C; *no* ¶ SP

144.36 Afterward (*no* ¶)] C; ¶ SP

144.36–37 they—the four of them—marched . . . troops.] C; the four of them marched off. SP

144.39 Hills (*no* ¶)] C; ¶ SP

145.1 enclosed] C; inclosed SP

145.11 seat] C; a seat SP

145.13–14 nothing. The] C; ~ : the SP

145.17 Moreover (*no* ¶)] C; ¶ SP

145.22–23 —they . . . project —] C; (~ . . . ~) SP

145.24–25 —cursed . . . nothing] C; *omit* SP

145.25 For (*no* ¶)] C; ¶ SP

145.26 a half] C; half SP

145.30 Point (*no* ¶)] C; ¶ SP

145.31 Little (*no* ¶)] C; ¶ SP

145.37 of] C; from SP

146.1 inarticulate. The] C; ~ : the SP

146.2 as] C; like SP

146.2 yet∧ . . . time∧] C; ~ , . . . ~ , SP

146.7 seat] C; a seat SP

146.22 me] C; my SP

146.24 He (*no* ¶)] C; ¶ SP

146.25 his eyes] C; them SP

146.28 business-like] C (~ - | ~),A1; businesslike SP

146.31 Some . . . on.] C; *omit* SP

146.33 end∧] C; ~ , SP

146.33 Point and Tailor] C; Tailor and Point SP

147.18 said] C; asked SP

147.23 *et seq.* captain] C; Captain SP

147.23 arose] C; rose SP

147.25 wide∧] C; ~ , SP

147.30–31 grizzled— . . . army —] A1; ~ , . . . ~ , SP

147.38 If (*no* ¶)] A1; ¶ SP

147.38 *et seq.* general's] A1; General's SP

148.6 the whirl,] A1; *omit* SP

148.6–9 If . . . blood.] A1; *omit* SP

148.10 *et seq.* lieutenant] A1; Lieutenant SP

148.10 very] A1; *omit* SP

148.18 He (*no* ¶)] A1; ¶ SP

148.23 yet∧ . . . ways∧] A1; ~ , . . . ~ , SP

148.24 gently∧] A1; gentle, SP

148.25 second] A1; Second SP

148.26 all∧] A1; ~ , SP

148.31 of the battle] A1; *omit* SP

148.32 crest∧] A1; ~ , SP

148.35–149.1 The . . . Siboney.] C; *omit* SP

149.1–2 They . . . again.] A1; *omit* SP, C

149.4 Daiquiri] E1; Daqueri SP,C,A1

149.6 parade-like] C; paradelike SP

149.7 -horses∧] C; ~ , SP

149.8 Crowding (*no* ¶)] C; ¶ SP

149.13–14 scrubby bushes, near pools,] C; *omit* SP

149.18 man∧] C; ~ , SP

149.24–28 The . . . blockhouses.] C; *omit* SP

149.28 blockhouses] A1; ~ - ~ C

149.29 Soon (*no* ¶)] C; ¶ SP

149.38 pugnacious] C; *omit* SP

150.1–3 The route . . . canteens.] C; *omit* SP

150.1–2 blanket-rolls] V; ~ ∧ ~ C,A1

150.4–7 —men . . . heat.] C; *omit* SP

150.10 th' . . . 'm] C; the . . . 'em SP

150.11 away] C; *omit* SP

150.11 red] C; great red SP

150.13 babyishly] C; babishly SP

150.15 They (*no* ¶)] C; ¶ SP

150.18–19 sergeant . . . sur-geons] C; Sergeant . . . Sur-geons SP
150.18 amiable_∧] C; ~ , SP
150.21 to] C; with SP
150.23–24 They . . . morning.] C; *omit* SP
150.39–151.8 It was . . . forma-tion.] C; *omit* SP
151.9 soda-bottle] C; soda-water bottle SP
151.26 trees] C; trees, vines SP
151.27 Once (*no* ¶)] C; ¶ SP
151.30 long_∧] C; ~ , SP
151.33 "Christ, I'm shot!"] C; *omit* SP
151.33 shot!" . . .] V; ~ !" _∧ C,A1
151.35 A (*no* ¶)] C; ¶ SP
151.38 *et seq.* regulars] C; Regu-lars SP
152.4–5 When . . . water.] C; *omit* SP
152.5 Little (*no* ¶)] C; ¶ SP
152.6 disputing] C; *omit* SP
152.7 damn] C; hang SP
152.12 lying] C; *omit* SP
152.13,33 left] C; right SP
152.16 Hurt?] C; ~ , SP
152.16 well_∧] C; ~ , SP
152.21–22 Then . . . it!"] C; *omit* SP
152.21 said_∧] V; ~ , C,A1
152.25 here more] C; here for more SP
152.29 get once] C; once get SP

152.34 that_∧ . . . him_∧] C; ~ , . . . ~ , SP
152.39 somewhere] C; *omit* SP
153.5 mouth,] C; ~ _∧ SP
153.7 task. On] C; task. ¶ Pres-ently the hurrying correspon-dent met another regiment coming to assist—a line of a thousand men in single file through the jungle. "Well, how is it going, old man?" "How is it coming on?" "Are we doin' 'em?" On SP
153.7 On (*no* ¶)] C; ¶ SP (Pres-ently)
153.11–12 his body . . . skin] C; *omit* SP
153.14 from . . . foliage] C; *omit* SP
153.15–18 ¶ Presently . . . 'em?"] C; *omit* SP (*see* 153.7 *above*)
153.18 Then (*no* ¶)] C; ¶ SP
153.23 fine broad] C; *omit* SP
153.35 —yes? . . . dazed] C; *omit* SP
*153.38 lying] C; dying SP
154.4 Walkley_∧] C; ~ , SP
154.5 ²Walkley] C; Walkly SP
154.16 arising] C; rising SP
154.16.1 *line space*] V; *omit* SP; . . . . . . C,A1+
154.21–22 tired. . . . tired. . . . —tired.] C; ~ ! . . . ~ ! . . . _∧ ~ ! SP
154.23 aroused] C; roused SP
154.24 Mr.] C; *omit* SP
154.29 "Tell (*no* ¶)] C; ¶ SP

THE REVENGE OF THE *Adolphus*

[Copy-text is A1: *Wounds in the Rain*, Stokes, 1900. Other texts collated are CW: *Collier's Weekly* and S: *Strand Magazine*. A few plate changes in E1 are recorded when accepted.]

155.6 for?"] CW,S; ~ ? _∧ A1
*155.24 deck] *stet* A1
155.26 opry] CW; *omit* S,A1
*155.27 Captain] *stet* A1
156.2 first_∧] CW,S; ~ , A1

156.6 said:] V; ~ , CW,S; ~ _∧ A1
*156.9 Finally . . . Yes.'] CW,S; *omit* A1
156.9 he said:] V; ~ ~ , CW,S

156.11 said:] E1; ~ , CW,S; ~ ∧ A1
156.22 northeastern] CW; ~ - ~ S,A1
156.23 *et seq.* -colored] CW; -coloured S,A1
156.30 *Adolphus's*] CW,S; *Adolphus'* A1
156.31 leeward] CW,S,E1; leaward A1
156.36 *won't*] CW; won't S,A1
157.20 Shake] V; shake A1; Hook CW,S
157.27 clamor] CW; clamour S,A1
158.20 do!] CW,S; ~ ? A1
158.35 Sure. Take] CW,S; Sure, take A1
*159.20 runnin'." The] CW,S; running," the A1
159.35 board of] CW,S; board A1
160.2 Halloa] CW,S; Hello A1
160.6 -deck∧] CW,S; ~ , A1
*160.29 at the] CW,S; *omit* A1
160.33 heels-over-head] CW,S; heels-overhead A1
161.16,34 Commander] S; Lieutenant-Commander CW,A1
161.22 favor] CW; favour S,A1
161.28 *et seq.* harbor] CW; harbour S,A1
161.28 U.S.S.] CW,S; *U.S.S.* A1
161.33 officers'] CW,S; officer's A1
161.34 *Chancellorville*∧] CW,S; ~ , A1
162.2 cruiser] V; flagship CW,S, A1
162.3 tugboat] CW; ~ - ~ S,A1
162.5–6 pilot-house] CW,S; ~ ∧ ~ A1
162.9 *Chancellorville*∧] S; ~ , CW,A1
162.11 of] CW,S; for A1
162.24 senior officer's ship] S; flagship CW; senior officer A1
162.24 senior officer's ship] S; flagship CW; *S.O.* A1
162.33–34 executive officer and the] S; *omit* CW,A1

162.35 five] S; four CW,A1
163.5 S.O.P.'s ship and the vessels] S; flagship and the vessels CW; cruiser and the gunboats A1
163.8 *et seq.* earthworks] CW,S; ~ - ~ A1
163.14–16 The boatswain . . . cabin.] S; *omit* CW,A1
163.17 the four] S; that all four CW,A1
163.19 academy] CW,S; Academy A1
163.20 shipmates] CW,S; ~ - ~ A1
163.23 pyjamas] S; pajamas CW,A1
*163.27–28 came upon deck∧] S; emerged from the cabin, CW,A1
163.28 it] S; the deck CW,A1
163.30–31 conflict.] CW,S,E1; ~ , A1
163.32 stroke∧] CW,S; ~ , A1
163.32–33 stern-sheets] CW,S; ~ ∧ ~ A1
163.35–164.2 "Beat . . . breechplugs.] S; A bird-like whistle stirred the decks of the *Chancellorville*. It was followed by the hoarse bellowings [A1: bellowing] of the boatswain's mate. CW,A1
164.4 despatch-boat] CW,S; ~ ∧ ~ A1
164.11 starboard,] CW,S; ~ ; A1
164.23 battery∧] CW,S; ~ , A1
164.24 swift] S; gruff CW,A1
164.26–27 shells∧ . . . part∧] CW,S; ~ , . . . ~ , A1
164.35 shell∧] CW,S; ~ , A1
164.38 armored] CW; armoured S,A1
165.4 you?] CW,S; ~ ! A1
*165.5 set] CW,S; sent A1
165.7 They∧ . . . *Chancellorville*∧] CW,S; ~ , . . . ~ , A1
165.10 townspeople] CW,S; town's people A1

165.12 favors] CW; favours S,A1

165.13 tumultuously] S; like charging horsemen CW; like charging bantams A1

165.21 suddenly$_\Lambda$ . . . point$_\Lambda$] CW,S; ~ , . . . ~ , A1

165.27 tribunal$_\Lambda$] CW,S; ~ , A1

165.29 her$_\Lambda$] CW,S; ~ , A1

166.2 Chicken$_\Lambda$] CW,S; ~ , A1

166.3 complex] S; complete CW,A1

166.3–4 Reigate$_\Lambda$ . . . Moses$_\Lambda$] CW,S; ~ , . . . ~ , A1

166.9 Moses$_\Lambda$] CW,S; ~ , A1

166.12 wharf$_\Lambda$] CW,S; ~ , A1

166.21 war time] CW,S; ~ - ~ A1

*166.28 'm] stet A1

166.29 time,] CW,S; ~ $_\Lambda$ A1

166.31 -front$_\Lambda$] CW; ~ , S,A1

166.32 was . . . it] CW,S; were . . . they A1

167.4 10,000-ton] CW,S; ~ $_\Lambda$ ~ A1

167.17,20 meantime$_\Lambda$] CW,S; ~ , A1

167.22 that$_\Lambda$ . . . that second$_\Lambda$] CW,S; ~ , . . . ~ ~ , A1

167.23 Undoubtedly$_\Lambda$] CW,S; ~ , A1

167.24 honor] CW; honour S,A1

167.30 et seq. odor] CW; odour S,A1

167.31 streamed] CW,S,E1; steamed A1

168.10 Chicken] CW,S; Chicken A1

168.24 engine-room] S; ~ $_\Lambda$ ~ A1

168.25 and$_\Lambda$] CW,S; ~ , A1

169.1 joke] CW,S; a joke A1

169.15 first$_\Lambda$] CW,S; ~ , A1

169.18 gun-crew] CW,S; ~ $_\Lambda$ ~ A1

169.26 -gun$_\Lambda$] CW,S; ~ , A1

170.3 men] S; engineers CW,A1

170.27 gunboats] CW; ~ - ~ S, A1

170.31 Correspondents] CW; Two correspondents S,A1

170.31–34 and although . . . told] CW; omit S,A1

THE SERJEANT'S PRIVATE MAD-HOUSE

[The copy-text is A1: *Wounds in the Rain*, Stokes, 1900. Other texts collated are SP: *Saturday Evening Post*; and EIM: *English Illustrated Magazine*. Plate changes in E1 are recorded when accepted.]

*172.3,24 cactus-plants] EIM (plant at 24); ~ $_\Lambda$ ~ SP,A1

172.6 rocks] SP,EIM; rock A1

*172.21 glistening] stet A1

*172.22 et seq. serjeant] V; sergeant SP,EIM,A1

173.1 Afterward$_\Lambda$] SP,EIM; ~ , A1

173.3 et seq. cactus-bush] EIM; ~ $_\Lambda$ ~ SP,A1 (except 174.27 ~ - ~ A1)

173.11 practiced] SP; practised EIM,A1

173.28 paces$_\Lambda$] SP,EIM; ~ , A1

173.29 last$_\Lambda$] SP,EIM; ~ , A1

173.35 "Don't] SP,EIM; $_\Lambda$ ~ A1

173.35 Serjeant] SP (Sergeant); sergeant EIM,A1

174.11 Oh] SP,EIM; O A1

174.13 a small] SP,EIM; small A1

174.14 rifle-range] SP,EIM; ~ $_\Lambda$ ~ A1

174.18 night$_\Lambda$attack] SP,EIM; ~ - ~ A1

174.23 harbor] SP; harbour EIM, A1

174.24 searchlight] SP,EIM; ~ - ~ A1

174.24 -flashes] EIM; $_\Lambda$ flashes A1

174.27 *et seq.* mad-house] EIM; madhouse SP,A1
174.29 told] SP,EIM; tell A1
175.9 His (*no ¶*)] SP,EIM; ¶ A1
175.39 half∧seen] SP,EIM; ~ - ~ A1
*176.1 miraculous] *stet* A1
176.16 require] SP,EIM; required A1
176.21 ken] SP,EIM; pen A1
176.24 was] SP,EIM; was a A1
176.25 sides∧] SP,EIM; ~ , A1
176.37 soldier] SP,EIM; soldiers A1
176.39 experience∧] SP,EIM; ~ , A1
177.13 outpost∧] SP,EIM; ~ , A1
*177.24 increase] SP,EIM; increased A1

177.25 oval∧] SP,EIM; ~ , A1
177.29 While] SP,EIM,E1; When A1
177.29 watched] SP,EIM,E1; guard A1
178.1 is] V; has SP+
178.9 oh . . . oh] SP,EIM; O . . . O A1
178.18 men∧ . . . pressed∧] SP, EIM; ~ , . . . ~ , A1
178.18 hard pressed] SP,EIM; ~ - | ~ A1
178.28 sir—] SP,EIM; ~ , — A1
178.30 daybreak∧] SP,EIM; ~ , A1
179.6 calmness:] SP,EIM; ~ , A1

VIRTUE IN WAR

[The copy-text is FL: *Frank Leslie's Popular Monthly*. The other text collated is ILN: *Illustrated London News*. A1 is a derived text, as is N[1].]

180.0 VIRTUE IN WAR] A1; WEST POINTER AND VOLUNTEER; OR, VIRTUE IN WAR FL,ILN
180.7 of good] ILN; ofgood FL
183.8 Now∧] ILN; ~ , FL
183.13 newcomer∧] ILN; ~ , FL
183.13 genially,] ILN; ~ ∧ FL
184.25 'm] ILN; 'im FL
185.24 skipper∧ . . . prisoners∧] ILN; ~ , . . . ~ , FL
187.22 Wigram∧] ILN; ~ , FL
187.23 ter-morrow] ILN; termorrow FL

187.25 replied∧] ILN; ~ , FL
187.36 easy;] ILN; ~ , FL
188.24 Colonel] ILN; colonel FL
188.28 blanket-rolls] ILN; ~ ∧ ~ FL
189.14 know] ILN; konw FL
191.30–31 congratulations,] A1; ~ ∧ FL,ILN
191.38 private∧] ILN; ~ , FL
192.26 one∧] ILN; ~ , FL
193.29 an] A1; an' FL,ILN

MARINES SIGNALING UNDER FIRE AT GUANTANAMO

[Copy-text is McC: *McClure's Magazine*. The other text collated is the derived A1: *Wounds in the Rain*, Stokes, 1900.]

194.4 *et seq.* Marblehead] A1; "Marblehead" McC
195.5 *et seq.* guerillas] A1; guerrillas McC
197.8 grey] A1; gray McC

197.28 advanced] A1; advance McC
197.34 *et seq.* Dolphin] A1; "Dolphin" McC

THIS MAJESTIC LIE

[Copy-text is A1: *Wounds in the Rain*, Stokes, 1900. The other text collated is N^1: *New York Herald*, both in its preserved proof N^{1a} and its published form N^{1b}. When both agree, notation will be simply N^1. N^{2-3} are derived texts. Plate changes in E1 are recorded when accepted.]

201.0   I] N^1; omit A1
201.1   twilight$_\wedge$] N^1; $\sim$, A1
201.4   colorless] N^1; colourless A1
*201.7   Montojo] V; de Montojo N^1,A1
201.17   laughter$_\wedge$] N^1; $\sim$, A1
202.16   crowd$_\wedge$] N^1; $\sim$, A1
202.25   Plaza$_\wedge$] N^1; $\sim$, A1
202.26   pyjama] N^{1a}; pajama N^{1b},A1
202.28   *et seq.* honor] N^1; honour A1
202.37   jubilee—] N^1; $\sim$; A1
203.25   air—] N^1; $\sim$, A1
203.26   crop$_\wedge$] N^1; $\sim$, A1
203.33   West$_\wedge$] N^1; $\sim$, A1
203.39   hurricane$_\wedge$] N^1; $\sim$, A1
204.2   Really$_\wedge$] N^1; $\sim$, A1
*204.7   plentitude] *stet* A1
204.12   meantime$_\wedge$] N^1; $\sim$, A1
204.13,14   Rumors] N^1; Rumours A1
*204.14   rang] N^1; sang A1
204.23   victory$_\wedge$] N^1; $\sim$ — A1
204.27   elapse."] E1; $\sim$. $_\wedge$ $N,A1
204.30   well;] V; $\sim$, N^1; $\sim$: A1
*205.8   the ijjits] $N; this we A1
205.8   armored] N^1; armoured A1
205.10   turret$_\wedge$] N^1; $\sim$, A1
206.10   elusive$_\wedge$] N^1; $\sim$, A1
206.10   Sometimes$_\wedge$] N^1; $\sim$, A1
206.29   it$_\wedge$] N^1; $\sim$, A1
206.29   all$_\wedge$] N^1; $\sim$, A1
206.30   tug$_\wedge$] N^1; $\sim$, A1
206.35   afterward] N^1; afterwards A1
206.35   night$_\wedge$] N^1; $\sim$, A1
207.35   of] N^1] omit A1
208.2   *et seq.* favor] N^1; favour A1
208.4,14   codfish] N^1; $\sim$ - $\sim$ A1

208.9   *et seq.* odor] N^1; odour A1
208.19   you$_\wedge$] N^1; $\sim$, A1
208.25   Johnnie!] V; $\sim$? N^1,A1
208.32   *et seq.* parlor] N^1; parlour A1
208.37   police!] N^1; $\sim$. A1
209.20   harboring] N^1; harbouring A1
209.31   There,] N^1; $\sim$! A1
210.1   care;] V; $\sim$! N^1; $\sim$: A1
210.4   upstairs$_\wedge$] N^1; $\sim$, A1
210.8   adjuring] N^1; abjuring A1
210.10   room$_\wedge$] N^1; $\sim$, A1
210.15   nightie] N^1; nightey A1
210.19   up] N^1; omit A1
210.26   señora] V; Señora N^1,A1
210.27   too."] E1,N^1; $\sim$. $_\wedge$ A1
210.30   blandly.] N^1; $\sim$, A1
210.31   Valladolid,] E1,N^1; $\sim$ $_\wedge$ A1
212.2   behavior] N^1; behaviour A1
212.10   a-away] N^1; a-way A1
213.3   Inside$_\wedge$] N^1; $\sim$, A1
213.7   recognize] N^1; recognise A1
213.14   time$_\wedge$] N^1; $\sim$, A1
213.25   gold.$_\wedge$] N^1; $\sim$." A1
213.33   gently:] V; $\sim$:— N^1; $\sim$, A1
214.1   coffee$_\wedge$] N^1; $\sim$, A1
214.16   Honorable] N^1; Honourable A1
*214.17   Fifty] N^1; Five A1
214.20   dol——] N^1; $\sim$ — . . . A1
214.23   him$_\wedge$] N^1; $\sim$, A1
215.7   two centenes] V; a centene N^1,A1
215.11   over$_\wedge$] N^1; $\sim$, A1
215.14   rotten$_\wedge$] N^1; $\sim$; A1
215.19   little$_\wedge$] N^1; $\sim$, A1
215.22–23   His Highness] N^1; his highness A1
215.23   codfish] N^1; $\sim$ - $\sim$ A1

216.11   br-e-a-d-d-d] N¹;
         br-e-a-ddd A1
216.20   jiminy] N¹; Jove A1
216.22   warᴧ . . . thereᴧ] N¹; ~ ,
         . . . ~ , A1
216.24   egg!] N¹; ~ . A1
216.28   at] N¹; of A1
216.29   himᴧ] N¹; ~ , A1
216.31   caughtᴧ] N¹; ~ , A1
217.3   batteryᴧ] N¹; ~ , A1
217.14   watersᴧ] N¹; ~ , A1
217.36   the Spanish] N¹; Spanish
         A1
217.37   awakeᴧ] N¹; ~ , A1
218.3   takenᴧ] N¹; ~ , A1
218.11   noises——] N¹; ~ . A1
218.18   sayᴧ] N¹; ~ , A1
218.19   scandalized] N¹; scandal-
         ised A1
*218.19–20 No . . . Institute.]
         stet $N,A1+
218.21   if] N¹; omit A1
218.23   said:] V; ~ :— N¹; ~ ,
         A1
218.38   savageᴧ thenᴧ] N¹; ~ ,
         ~ , A1

218.39   nightᴧ] N¹; ~ , A1
219.3   daysᴧ] N¹; ~ , A1
219.6   outᴧ] N¹; ~ , A1
219.8   itᴧ] N¹; ~ , A1
219.14   returnᴧ] N¹; ~ , A1
219.28   garrote] N¹; garote A1
219.39   was] N¹ᵃ; were N¹ᵇ, A1
220.1   North Pole] N¹; north pole
         A1
220.1   labored] N¹; laboured A1
220.4   warᴧ] N¹; ~ , A1
220.10   harbor] N¹; harbour A1
220.11   was] N¹ᵃ; were N¹ᵇ,A1
220.18   half-past seven] N¹; 7:30
         A1
220.22   dinner.] N¹; ~ , A1
220.33   fatᴧ] N¹; ~ , A1
220.36   Johnnie] N¹; Johnny A1
221.6   said:] V; ~ :— N¹; ~ , A1
221.6   Yorkᴧ] N¹; ~ , A1
221.9   coffeeᴧ] N¹; ~ , A1
221.12   Aguacateᴧ] N¹; ~ , A1
221.15   youᴧ] N¹; ~ , A1

WAR MEMORIES

[Copy-text is AS: *Anglo-Saxon Review*. The other text collated is A1: *Wounds in the Rain*, Stokes, 1900, which is substantive only in part.]

222.1 *et seq.* thing!"] A1; ~ !'
         (AS *uses single quotes throughout*)
222.6 *et seq.* despatch-boat] A1
         ~ ᴧ ~ AS (*irregularly*)
223.12 *et seq.* recognized] V;
         recognised AS,A1
223.16–225.25 Once . . . closed.]
         A1; *omit* AS
223.16 *et seq.* honor] V; honour
         A1
223.38 *et seq.* -colored] V; -col-
         oured A1
225.26   flagship] V; ~ - ~ AS,A1
225.26–27 *et seq.* armored] V;
         armoured AS,A1
228.39   marked] A1; market AS
229.8   further] A1; farther AS
229.17   they] A1; these AS
229.22   men;] A1; ~ : AS

229.33   was] A1; were AS
*229.34   great] *stet* AS
230.3   afterward] A1; afterwards
         AS
231.10   Afterward] V; Afterwards
         AS,A1
231.26   scandalized] V; scandal-
         ised AS,A1
232.13   jeopardized] V; jeopard-
         ised AS,A1
232.30   covered] A1; coveted AS
233.2   sympathize] V; sympathise
         AS,A1
234.18 *et seq.* odor] V; odour
         AS,A1
234.30   labor] V; labour AS,A1
235.29 *et seq.* harbor] V; har-
         bour AS,A1
235.30 *et seq.* rumor] V; ru-
         mour AS,A1

237.15 black-hulled] V; blacked-hull AS,A1

238.22 toward] V; towards AS,A1

239.33 balk] A1; baulk AS

240.36 flagship,] A1(∼ - ∼,); ∼ ∧ AS

240.37 teeth—] A1; ∼ ; AS

242.8 and—— Fate] A1; and—Fate AS

242.22 "Why——"] A1; '∼' — AS

242.38 July?] A1; ∼ . AS

243.14 succor] V; succour AS,A1

244.13 et seq. El Paso] V; El Poso AS,A1

245.21 it!"] A1; ∼ .' AS

249.1 Hill] V; hill AS,A1

249.10 et seq. behavior] V; behaviour AS,A1

249.23 cognizant] V; cognisant AS,A1

249.31 politics] A1; politic AS

251.2 centralized] V; centralised AS,A1

251.32 was] A1; is AS

254.7 neighbors] V; neighbours AS,A1

254.12 favor] V; favour AS,A1

255.23–257.24 One . . . battle.] omit AS

256.22 riding-breeches] V; ∼ ∧ ∼ A1

257.1 et seq. 33rd] V; 33d A1

260.18–22 I would . . . man.] A1; omit AS

260.23–26 him, and I . . . ²ship —oh] A1; him. Oh AS

260.27 ¶ I] A1; no ¶ AS

260.39 et seq. humor] V; humour AS,A1

261.24–263.28 In . . . world.] A1; Ultimately we arrived. We landed at Old Point Comfort—saintly name! AS

261.34 yellow-flag] V; ∼ ∧ ∼ A1

261.37 hung] V; rung A1

262.29 soda-water-fountain] V; ∼ - ∼ ∧ ∼ A1

262.37 officialized] V; officialised A1

THE SECOND GENERATION

[Copy-text is A1: *Wounds in the Rain*, Stokes, 1900. Other texts collated are SP: *Saturday Evening Post*, and C: *Cornhill Magazine*.]

264.9 et seq. captaincy] C; Captaincy SP,A1

264.10 just] C; omit SP,A1

264.12 Bottles (no ¶)] C; ¶ SP,A1

264.14 et seq. parlor] SP; parlour C,A1

264.14 said:] SP; ∼ , C,A1

264.20 damned] C; omit SP; d—d A1

264.27 they] C; that they SP,A1

265.1 drank a neat whisky and] C; omit SP,A1

265.2 Y-yes] C; Y—yes SP,A1

265.13 finally,] SP,C; ∼ . A1

265.17 in him] C; omit SP,A1

265.23 replied:] SP; ∼ , C,A1

265.26 et seq. lieutenants] C; Lieutenants SP,A1

265.27 captains] Captains SP,A1

265.27 et seq. majors] C; Majors SP,A1

*265.28 clear-eyed] V; clean-eyed SP,C,A1

265.29 field-marshal] C; Field-Marshal SP,A1

265.31 intrinsically,] SP,C; ∼ ∧ A1

265.33–34 men. Individual . . . but] C; men, though SP,A1

265.35 it] C; this arrangement SP,A1

266.1 Henery] C; Henry SP,A1

266.4 Then (no ¶)] C; ¶ SP,A1

266.6 administrations] C; Administrations SP,A1

266.7 et seq. machine] C; Machine SP,A1

266.13 penny!] C; bun. SP,A1
266.14 amount] C; thing SP,A1
266.14 colossus] C; Colossus SP,A1
266.15 penny] C; bun SP,A1
266.16 *et seq.* rumors] SP; rumours C,A1
266.17 *et seq.* commissary] C; Commissary SP,A1
266.19 "I (*no ¶*)] C; ¶ SP,A1
266.24 heavy∧] C; ~ , SP,A1
266.25 "Caspar (*no ¶*)] C; ¶ SP,A1
266.31 fightin'] C; fighting SP,A1
266.32 *damned*] C; d—d SP,A1
266.33 goin'] C; going SP,A1
266.36 *et seq.* army] C; Army SP,A1
266.37–38 nothin' . . . lookin'] C; nothing . . . looking SP,A1
267.5 marvelous] SP; marvellous C,A1
267.16 How you goin'] C; How are you going SP,A1
267.32 damned] V; blamed SP,A1; damn C
268.2 said:] SP,C; ~ , A1
268.5 guv'nor] C; Guv'nor SP,A1
268.8 humor] SP; humour C,A1
*268.21 fecklessly] V; footlessly SP; fetlessly C; bootlessly A1
268.22 crying:] SP,C; ~ , A1
268.22 'em] SP,C; them A1
268.25–26 three whoops in Hades] C; a rip SP,A1
268.37 *et seq.* general] V: General SP,C,A1
269.1 division-commander] C; Division Commander SP,A1
269.2 *et seq.* colonels] C; Colonels SP, A1
269.5 men—— And] C; men— and SP,A1
269.14 "Did (*no ¶*)] C; ¶ SP,A1
269.15 tragically.] C; ~ : SP,A1
269.20 Reilly∧] C; ~ , SP,A1
269.23 damn] C; dash SP,A1
270.9 long∧] C; ~ , SP,A1
270.12 in which] C; and in these greetings SP,A1

270.13 everything∧] C; ~ , SP, A1
270.18 fervor] SP; fervour C,A1
270.29 color] SP; colour C,A1
*270.33 clinched] V; clenched SP,C,A1
271.2 behavior] SP; behaviour C,A1
271.11–12 law , . . . nothing∧] SP,C; ~∧ . . . ~ , A1
271.12 grass;] SP,C; ~ , A1
271.18 fix,] SP,C; ~ ∧ A1
271.23 chalk-] C; chalked- SP,A1
271.24 The (*no ¶*)] C; ¶ SP,A1
271.27 low-down,] C; *omit* SP, A1
271.27 loud-mouthed,] C; ~ ∧ SP, A1
271.27–28 pie-faced] C; *omit* SP, A1
272.11 (*twice*) its] SP,C; his A1
272.22 Hell!] C; *omit* SP,A1
272.24 *Which*] C; Which SP,A1
272.27 lootenant] C; Lootenant SP,A1
272.32; 273.10 a'] C; of SP; o' A1
272.33 damned] C; blanked SP; d—d A1
273.5 is?] SP,C; ~ . A1
273.17 small∧] C; ~ , SP,A1
273.23 "Baker (*no ¶*)] C; ¶ SP, A1
273.25 -eyed∧] C; ~ , SP,A1
274.1 house,] SP,C; ~ ∧ A1
274.8 of a] SP,C; of A1
274.16 even] SP,C; *omit* A1
274.27 —— ——] SP; —— C, A1
274.28,34 was] C; were SP,A1
274.30 short∧] C; ~ , SP,A1
274.33 anxious∧] C; ~ , SP,A1
275.1,6 gawd damn] V; cuss SP,A1; gawd dam C
275.5 Baker∧] C; ~ , SP,A1
275.18 Ye-e-es] C; Ye—e—es SP,A1
275.27 clangor] SP; clangour C,A1
275.27 window∧] C; ~ , SP,A1

275.30 tall_Λ] C; ~ , SP,A1
275.40 "Why (*no* ¶)] C; ¶ SP,A1
276.9   Department] SP; department C,A1
276.11 *et seq.* national] SP,C; National A1
276.15 big_Λ] C; ~ , SP,A1
276.21 devil] C; deuce SP,A1
276.26 right?] SP,C; ~ . A1
276.27 Senator—] C; ~ , SP,A1
276.28 in] C; is in SP,A1
276.28 its] C; it's a SP,A1
276.35 it?—] SP,C; ~ _Λ— A1
277.22 dreamy_Λ] C; ~ , SP,A1
277.24,31 gawd] C; Jove SP,A1
278.3   answer:] C; ~ , SP,A1
278.5   russle] C; rustle SP,A1
278.7   "God (*no* ¶)] C; ¶ SP,A1
278.11 sound] C; sounded SP,A1
278.13 keen_Λ] C; ~ , SP,A1
278.21 had] SP,C; *omit* A1
278.36 here's] SP,C; here is A1
278.38 damned] C; blamed SP, A1
278.39 high_Λ] C; ~ , SP,A1
279.6   8.30] SP,C; 8:30 A1

279.10 Point,] SP,C; ~ _Λ A1
279.13 officers,] SP,C; ~ _Λ A1
279.14 broadsides_Λ]   SP,C; ~ , A1
279.28 But, . . . end,] SP,C; ~ _Λ . . . ~ _Λ A1
279.32 succoring] SP; succouring C,A1
279.36 strong_Λ taciturn_Λ] C; ~ , ~ , SP,A1
280.6   actions,] SP,C; ~ _Λ A1
280.18 him.] SP,C; ~ , A1
280.23 In (*no* ¶)] C; ¶ SP,A1
280.23 yellow_Λ] SP; ~ , C,A1
281.16 *course*] C; course SP,A1
281.23 then] C; *omit* SP,A1
281.24 hell] C; the deuce SP,A1
281.36 officer?] SP,C; ~ . A1
281.39 replied:] SP,C; ~ _Λ A1
282.6   n-n-no] V; n—n—no SP, A1; no-o-o C
282.10 time,] SP,C; ~ _Λ A1
282.16 falling—] C; ~ , SP,A1
283.10 face] C; cheek SP,A1
283.32 his face] C; *omit* SP,A1
284.14 small_Λ] C; ~ , SP,A1

SPITZBERGEN TALES

THE KICKING TWELFTH

[Copy-text is MS: New York Public Library manuscript, inscribed by Edith Richie. Other texts collated are AM: *Ainslee's Magazine,* and PMM: *Pall Mall Magazine.* TMs (University of Virginia typescript) and E1 are derived. Alterations within the MS are listed following the Historical Collation.]

287.0   THE KICKING TWELFTH] AM,PMM; *omit* MS
287.12 sped] AM,PMM; hurried MS
287.25 spring] AM,PMM; Spring MS
288.6   scouting,] AM,PMM; ~ _Λ MS
288.8   there] AM,PMM; *omit* MS
288.24 name, the] AM,PMM; name of the MS
*288.30 Kim up,] *stet* MS,PMM

288.34 along] AM,PMM; *omit* MS
288.38 ¶ It] AM,PMM; *no* ¶ MS
289.7-8 at night] PMM; in the camp at night MS,AM
289.10-11 far ahead] AM,PMM; farahead MS
289.39 enemy's] AM; enemie's MS; enemies' PMM
290.3   2,300] AM; 2300 MS,PMM
290.6   inaccessible] AM,PMM; inaccessable MS

290.12 Richie,] PMM,AM; ~ ∧ MS

290.13 His] AM,PMM; his MS

*290.18 clank] AM,PMM; clink MS

*290.25 observable] V; not observable MS, AM,PMM

290.38 ahead,] AM; ~ ∧ MS; ~ ; PMM

290.39 short,] AM,PMM; ~ ∧ MS

291.5 In] PMM; But in MS,AM

291.10 recognized] AM; recognised MS,PMM

291.17 horses] PMM; guns MS,AM

291.20 lead,] AM,PMM; ~ ∧ MS

291.31 blindfolded] PMM; ~ - ~ MS,AM

292.11 cry,] AM,PMM; ~ . MS

292.11 up,] PMM; ~ ∧ MS,AM

292.23–24 welfare] AM,PMM; well-fare MS

292.34,36 Eiffel] AM,PMM; Eifel MS

292.37 coolly] AM,PMM; cooly MS

293.14 on,] AM; ~ ∧ MS; ~ ; PMM

293.26 appearance,] AM,PMM; ~ ∧ MS

293.31; 294.13 up,] PMM; ~ ∧ MS,AM

294.5–6 Lean, and∧] AM,PMM; ~ ∧ ~ , MS

294.15 besieged] AM,PMM; beseiged MS

294.17 snapped,] PMM; ~ ∧ MS, AM

294.24–25 smoke, although] AM, PMM; ~ . Although MS

294.26 bursting,] AM,PMM; ~ ∧ MS

295.7 out:] V; ~ . MS; ~ , AM, PMM

295.24 fire] AM,PMM; terrible fire MS

295.30–31 debased,] AM,PMM; ~ ∧ MS

295.34 strong,] AM,PMM; ~ ∧ MS

296.10 won,] AM,PMM; ~ ∧ MS

296.14 patronizingly] AM; patronisingly MS,PMM

296.16 cavalry] AM,PMM; calvalry MS

296.20–21 adjusted themselves] PMM; came to attention MS,AM

296.27 up,] PMM; ~ ∧ MS,AM

The Upturned Face

[Copy-text is AM: *Ainslee's Magazine*. The other text collated is CP: *Crystal Palace Magazine*. TMs and E1 are derived texts.]

297.18 Lean∧] CP; ~ , AM

297.25 things."] CP; ~ . ∧ AM

298.1 adjutant∧] CP; ~ , AM

298.12–13 Hurry . . . stupid ——"] CP; omit AM

298.18 curious∧] CP; ~ , AM

298.21 said∧] CP; ~ , AM

298.32 again] CP; omit AM

298.32 —they . . . other] CP; omit AM

298.37 pressing . . . expression.] CP; omit AM

298.39 cried∧] CP; ~ , AM

298.40 something while] CP; something AM

299.3 but] CP; out AM

299.25,26 O] CP; Oh AM

299.27 adjutant∧] CP; ~ , AM

299.34 earth∧] CP; ~ , AM

299.36 which∧ . . . face∧] CP; ~ , . . . ~ , AM

300.3–4 —ha . . . satisfactory!] CP; omit AM

300.5 ¶ The] CP; no ¶ AM

300.7 field. . . .] V; ~ . . . AM; ~ —— CP

300.10 hand] CP; omit AM

300.12 "You (no ¶)] CP; ¶ AM

300.16 came∧] CP; ~ , AM

300.16 pace∧] CP; ~ , AM

300.21 grave$_\wedge$] CP; ~ , AM
300.27 mouth.". . . officer.$_\wedge$] CP;
~ . $_\wedge$ . . . ~ ." AM
300.29 earth.] CP; earth. . . . .
AM
300.29–30 Always. . . plop.] CP;
omit AM
300.30 space$_\wedge$] CP; ~ , AM

300.30–31 frantically$_\wedge$] CP; ~ ,
AM
300.31 danger.] CP; ~. . . . AM
300.32 ¶ Soon] CP; no ¶ AM
300.33 God] CP; Good AM
300.33–34 adjutant. "Why] CP;
~ , $_\wedge$ why AM
300.35 Then . . . stutter.] CP;
omit AM

THE SHRAPNEL OF THEIR FRIENDS

[Copy-text is AM: *Ainslee's Magazine*. Other texts collated are MS: Columbia University fragment, and BW: *Black and White*. TMs (University of Virginia typescript) and E1 are derived texts. Alterations within the MS are listed following the Historical Collation.]

301.8 a good enemy] BW; an enemy AM
301.11–12 at that time] BW; omit AM
301.17 infantry$_\wedge$ . . . course$_\wedge$]
BW; ~ , . . . ~ , AM
301.31–302.1 Sponge$_\wedge$ . . .
Twelfth$_\wedge$] BW; ~ , . . . ~ , AM
302.3,9 Fifty-three] BW; Forty-seven AM
302.6 be$_\wedge$ . . . day$_\wedge$] BW; ~ ,
. . . ~ , AM
302.7 general$_\wedge$] BW; ~ , AM
302.10,21 serjeant] V; sergeant
AM,BW
302.16 built$_\wedge$] BW; ~ , AM
302.17–18 tin$_\wedge$ cups] BW; ~ - | ~
AM
302.25,33 Far-away] BW; ~ $_\wedge$ ~
AM
302.27 long$_\wedge$] BW; ~ , AM
303.13 And$_\wedge$] BW; ~ , AM
303.25 wig-wag$_\wedge$ wag-wig] BW;
wig-wag, wig-wag AM
303.28 Now$_\wedge$] BW; ~ , AM
303.32 eighty-] V; eigty- AM;
88th BW
303.34 aloft$_\wedge$] BW; ~ , AM
303.35 up,] BW; ~ $_\wedge$ AM
304.10 the crest] BW; its crest
AM
304.14 right$_\wedge$] BW; ~ , AM

304.21 toward] V; towards
AM,BW
304.24 and$_\wedge$] BW; ~ , AM
304.28 beaters$_\wedge$] BW; ~ , AM
304.35 steeps] BW; steps AM
305.5 minutes$_\wedge$] BW; ~ , AM
305.12 Now$_\wedge$] MS,BW; ~ , AM
305.13 Twelfth$_\wedge$] MS; ~ , AM,
BW
305.16 shell] MS; omit AM,BW
305.16–18 came . . . the shrapnel] MS,BW; omit AM
305.18 shrapnel] BW; Shrapnel
MS
305.18 and the] MS,BW; A AM
305.20 sir. That] MS; ~ , that
AM,BW
305.21 streaked] MS,BW;
streamed AM
305.21 overhead$_\wedge$] MS; ~ , AM,
BW
305.22 line$_\wedge$] MS; ~ , AM,BW
305.27 death$_\wedge$] MS; ~ , AM,BW
*305.27 eye] MS; eyes AM,BW
305.34 You . . . You] MS,BW;
you . . . you AM
305.35 Curs!—curs!—curs!] V;
Curs!—curs—curs, MS; curs!
curs! curs! AM; Curs! Curs!
Curs! BW
305.38 speech$_\wedge$] MS; ~ , AM,BW
306.6 aggrieved$_\wedge$] MS; ~ , AM,
BW

306.15 saddle_∧] MS; ~ , AM,BW
306.20 wrongs_∧] MS; wrong AM,BW
306.23 dead_∧] MS; ~ , AM,BW
306.24 a] MS,BW; *omit* AM
306.24 20_∧] MS; ~ , AM,BW

306.30 ¶ A] MS,BW; *no* ¶ AM
306.31 friend_∧ . . . battery_∧] MS,BW; ~ , . . . ~ , AM
306.34 frankly,] BW; ~ ,— MS; ~ — AM

"AND IF HE WILLS, WE MUST DIE"

[Copy-text is TMs: University of Virginia typescript. Other texts collated are FL: *Frank Leslie's Popular Monthly*, and ILN: *Illustrated London News*. E1 is a derived text. TMs is distinguished when necessary as TMs(u), the original typing, or TMs(c) representing Cora's hand alterations.]

307.5,6,14,26,29; 308.3 Serjeant] V; Sergent TMs(u); Sergeant TMs(c),FL,ILN
307.9 damned] TMs(c); damn TMs(u)
307.10 as possible] TMs(c); as it was possible TMs(u)
307.13 casually] FL,ILN; *omit* TMs
307.20 orchard_∧] FL,ILN; ~ , TMs
307.22 stirred] FL,ILN; stired TMs
307.22 criminals] FL,ILN; criminals TMs
307.23 serjeant] V; sergent TMs; sergeant FL; Sergeant ILN
307.30 dangerous] FL,ILN; a dangerous TMs
307.30 ain't] FL,ILN; aint TMs
308.3 'only'!] V; '~ !' TMs; _∧ ~ _∧ , FL; _∧ ~ ! _∧ ILN
308.3 ²only'!] FL,ILN; '~'. TMs
308.5 its] FL,ILN; it's TMs
308.6,7,10,15,18 serjeant's] V; sergeant's TMs+
308.6 back_∧] FL,ILN; ~ , TMs
308.9 now!] FL,ILN; ~ . TMs
308.12 God!] FL,ILN; ~ ? TMs
308.14–15 here . . . captain—] FL,ILN (FL *in parentheses, not dashes*); *omit* TMs
308.15 " 'Haw] FL,ILN; _∧ '~ TMs
308.17; 309.28,30 can't] FL,ILN; cant TMs

308.22 right,] FL,ILN; ~ _∧ TMs
308.24 don't] FL,ILN; dont TMs
308.26 *et seq.* isn't] FL,ILN; isnt TMs
308.26–27 This . . . barracks.] FL,ILN; *omit* TMs
308.32 much] FL,ILN; *omit* TMs
308.32 said.] FL,ILN; ~ _∧ TMs
308.34 disdain] FL,ILN; dissain TMs
309.2 men,] FL,ILN; ~ _∧ TMs
309.5 -thieves] FL,ILN; _∧thiefs TMs
309.6 others_∧ then_∧] FL,ILN; ~ , ~ , TMs
309.7 Afterward_∧] FL,ILN; ~ , TMs
309.8 scowl,] FL,ILN; ~ _∧ TMs
309.9 to] FL,ILN; upon TMs
309.11 rooms,] FL,ILN; ~ _∧ TMs
309.13 lazy] FL,ILN; easy TMs
309.19 ¶ "But] FL,ILN; *no* ¶ TMs
309.24 little] FL,ILN; *omit* TMs
309.27 anything.] FL,ILN; ~ ! TMs
309.37 serjeant] V; sergeant TMs+
*309.39 calmly, "then] FL,ILN; ~ . "Then TMs
310.1 swung_∧] FL; ~ , TMs,ILN (sung,)
310.2 lightning] FL,ILN; lightening TMs
310.3 interval_∧] FL,ILN; ~ , TMs

310.8 crackled] FL,ILN; crack-
eled TMs
310.9 odor] FL; oder TMs; odour
ILN
310.9 as] FL,ILN; as if TMs
310.11 invisible] FL,ILN; invis-
able TMs
310.13 they] FL,ILN; They TMs
310.17 them!] FL,ILN; ~ . TMs
310.30 howling:] FL,ILN; ~ .
TMs
310.32 essential] FL,ILN; esential TMs
310.38 deep-rooted] FL,ILN;
~ ∧ ~ TMs
311.2 Afterward∧] FL; ~ , TMs,
ILN
311.5 as if he] FL,ILN; as if he
as if he TMs
311.6–7 vigorously] FL,ILN; vig-
erously TMs
311.7 charming] FL,ILN; omit
TMs
311.8–9 contemptuous] FL,ILN;
contempteous TMs
311.14 that] FL,ILN; who TMs

311.15 Simpson's∧] ILN; ~ ,
TMs,FL
311.18 apologetically] FL, ILN;
opologetically TMs
311.23 can't] ILN; cant TMs
311.27 danger,] FL,ILN; ~ .
TMs
311.27 swear] FL,ILN; sware
TMs
311.29 Morton,] FL,ILN; ~ ∧
TMs
311.29 shepherd] FL,ILN; shep-
erd TMs
311.32 despair] FL,ILN; dispair
TMs
311.33 later∧] FL,ILN; ~ , TMs
311.34 clenched.] ILN; ~ ∧ TMs
311.35 corpse] FL,ILN; corpes
TMs
311.35 afterward] V; afterwards
TMs,ILN
312.3 trees,] FL,ILN; ~ ∧ | TMs
312.3 stealthy∧] V; ~ , FL,ILN;
omit TMs
312.15 bloody] FL,ILN; blod
TMs
312.23 God!] ILN; ~ . TMs

WORD-DIVISION

1. End-of-the-Line Hyphenation in the Virginia Edition

[NOTE: No hyphenation of a possible compound at the end of a line in the Virginia text is present in the copy-texts except for the following readings, which are hyphenated within the line in the copy-texts. Except for these readings, all end-of-the-line hyphenation in the Virginia text may be ignored except for hyphenated compounds in which both elements are capitalized.]

4.17	blood-|smeared	162.13	three-|point-
15.5	horse-|hair	163.32	stern-|sheets
58.35	smooth-|bore	170.1	engine-|room
67.4	green-|shadowed	173.4	cactus-|bush
89.19	statue-|like	209.26	heavy-|footed
102.38	wire-|string	211.38	street-|door
103.19	Non-|commissioned	223.5	six-|pounders
103.33	battle-|sound	225.3	port-|battery
107.26	music-|hall	227.38	cable-|station
110.33	dream-|scenes	231.16	wheel-|barrow
111.1	barbed-|wire	234.3; 239.4; 243.14; 250.28 des-
116.34	-sing-|ing-		patch-|boat
116.38	Sshsh-|swing-	234.27	home-|made
120.28	poppety-|pop	242.28,32	tooth-|brush
132.26	brigadier-|general	245.4	block-|house
135.35	dressing-|table	252.36	steel-|ribbed
140.36	-and-|green	253.27	parrot-|cage
141.28	transport-|lame	256.17	stock-|word
141.33	God-|forsaken	259.7	thickly-|leaved
142.7	landing-|place	260.1	army-|surgeon
145.3	blanket-|rolls	271.27	pie-|faced
149.34	land-|crabs	277.20	Forty-|fourth
150.17	pack-|mules	281.39	well-|trained
150.32	waist-|high	291.14	chess-|board
154.11	wire-|woven	303.32	eighty-|eighth
156.21	coast-|line	309.14	fan-|shaped
156.25; 162.5; 168.12 pilot-|house			

2. *End-of-the-Line Hyphenations in the Copy-Texts*

[NOTE: The following compounds, or possible compounds, are hyphenated at the end of the line in the copy-texts. The form in which they have been transcribed in the Virginia text, listed below, represents the practices of the respective copy-texts so far as can be determined, and in cases of doubt the form is that generally found in Crane manuscripts.]

3.26	ankle-deep		169.28	deck-house
8.26	driftwood		174.25	outposts
8.32	riflemen		176.32	native-born
9.4	side-walks		179.16	fireworks
10.15	horse-hair		181.2,7	lieutenant-colonels
13.4	daybreak		188.21	rocket-like
13.9	night-time		191.34	grasshoppers
15.22	panther-like		196.10	thunder-drums
15.38	sun-light		196.24	daybreak
16.11	sideways		196.36	sunrise
31.31	grey-bearded		202.16	slow-moving
35.31; 36.26,29; 38.9	knotholes		203.14	watchmaker
35.35	headlong		204.24	play-wrights
41.26	low-like		207.13	rocking-chair
56.2	brass-bound		208.15	pig-headed
59.4	sooty-faced		211.26	codfish
85.19	work-horses		213.39	nutmeg
97.6	guinea-grass		214.2	to-night
97.11	pack-train		216.1	war-ships
98.21	blood-red		218.24	daybreak
98.37	to-night		219.2	nightfall
100.28	fore-arms		223.39	waterline
101.14	bloodshed		225.17	search-light
102.29	raw-boned		233.18	rain-clouds
106.30	outcries		234.25	junk-shop
109.24	marksmen		236.8	palm-bark
111.17	chowder-faced		239.1	dug-out
124.26	blockhouse		240.11	fireworks
138.1	half-starved		247.19	sandy-haired
138.7	cockleshell		251.11	overpowered
140.10	blockhouse		258.31	blue-jackets
142.11	man-crowded		260.19	fox-terriers
149.10	landing-beach		262.13	yellow-fever
149.12	rifle-pits		262.21	ice-cream-
149.36	moon-like		262.29	-water-fountain
159.32	water-line		266.3	whip-lash
162.7	over-side		268.22	saddle-bags
162.17	gunboats		272.25	land-crab
166.31	water-front		276.5	re-enforcements
167.30	gunpowder		276.7	to-morrow
169.2	overhear		280.20	school-children
169.12	three-ply		291.36	mountain-battery
			295.4	grief-stricken

3. *Special Cases*

[NOTE: In the following list the compound, or possible compound, is hyphenated at the end of the line in the copy-texts and in the Virginia edition.]

67.4   green-|shadowed]   green-|shadowed (i.e. green-shadowed)

97.11   bell-|mare] bell-|mare (i.e. bell-mare)

99.11   shelter-|tents] shelter-|tents (i.e. shelter-tents)

161.16   bald-|headed] bald-|headed (i.e. bald-headed)

162.5   pilot-|house]   pilot-|house (i.e. pilot-house)

223.25   thirty-|five] thirty-|five (i.e. thirty-five)

256.17   stock-|word]   stock-|word (i.e. stock-word)

HISTORICAL COLLATION

[Note: Substantive variants from the Virginia text are listed here, together with their appearances in the collated texts. Collated texts not noted for any reading agree with the Virginia-edition reading to the left of the bracket. Variations in paragraphing, for substantive editions only, may be recorded in a separate list if especially covenient but no record is made when such variations have been accepted as emendations and the facts have been noted in the list of Editorial Emendations in the Copy-Text. Paragraphing variation in derived texts is not recorded even when a basically derived text may have substantive authority because of authoritative revision. Typographical errors not forming acceptable words have not been recorded in editions after the first. The headnote to each story in the list of Editorial Emendations provides the necessary information about which texts are substantive and which derived, as does the Textual Introduction. Systematic cuts in a text are also separately listed if especially convenient. In the notation a plus sign indicates concurrence of all collated editions following the one cited. For this and for other conventions of shorthand notation, see the general headnote to the list of Editorial Emendations.]

THE LITTLE REGIMENT

The Little Regiment

[McC: *McClure's Magazine*; Ch: *Chapman's Magazine*; CL: *Current Literature*; A1: *The Little Regiment*, Appleton, 1896; E1: *The Little Regiment*, Heinemann, 1897.]

3.1   column of men] men of the column A1+

3.7   undertoned] undertone CL

3.10   long] low CL

3.15–16   the artillery] artillery Ch,CL

3.19   other] and of other Ch,CL

3.19   sounds] various sounds Ch,CL

3.19–20   near and remote] *omit* Ch,CL

3.22   voice] voices A1+

3.30   clothes] cloths A1+

4.10   afterward] afterwards McC, Ch, CL

5.19–20   would jump . . . drag] jumped . . . dragged A1+

6.1   rushed] flushed Ch

6.3   derned] durned McC,A1+

6.5   Afterward] Afterwards Ch

6.32   bellowed] bellowing A1+

7.12   his regiment] the regiment Ch

7.25   waved butterfly's] butterfly's waved A1+

7.33   It (*no* ¶)] ¶ Ch

7.34–35   forgotten] forgotten it A1+

8.1   sliddering] slidering Ch; sliding McC,A1+

8.3   at] after Ch
9.2–3   defying the guns, the . . . volleys; holding] defied the guns and the volleys and held Ch
9.8   board] sign A1+
9.9   wide-hatted] white-hatted Ch
9.14   clouds] crowds McC, A1
9.21   oration] orations Ch
9.32   argument] arguments Ch
9.35   Presently (*no* ¶)] ¶ Ch
9.39   "Funny (*no* ¶)] ¶ Ch
10.10   hoop-skirt . . . it] pair of hoop-skirts . . . them Ch
10.11   applause] applaud Ch
10.32   merely have] have merely Ch
10.34   grab] get Ch
11.7   matched] match Ch,A1+
11.15   proud] *omit* A1
11.22   "Shucks (*no* ¶)] ¶ Ch
11.24   During (*no* ¶)] ¶ Ch
12.30   men] the men Ch
12.35   "Them's (*no* ¶)] ¶ Ch
12.36   An (*no* ¶)] ¶ Ch
13.4   aroused] arose Ch
14.15   damning] cursing McC,A1+
14.16   the enemy] an enemy Ch
15.21   crackling] cracking McC+
15.25   young] younger McC,A1+
16.16   At (*no* ¶)] ¶ Ch

16.28   considerations] considera-tion CL
17.1   a madness] madness CL
17.2   miles . . . fury] to this fury miles in width A1+
17.7   arose] rose CL
17.20   unformed] uniformed CL
17.25   a muscular] muscular A1+
17.30   against] *omit* Ch,CL
17.36   never had] had never Ch
18.2   to coolly] coolly to A1+
18.4   the Little Regiment] "the lit-tle regiment" Ch
18.12   arose] rose Ch
18.16   a] a | a A1
18.28   "Got (*no* ¶)] ¶ Ch
19.3   He (*no* ¶)] ¶ Ch
19.5   "No (*no* ¶)] ¶ Ch
19.11   swan] swear Ch
19.30   to] *omit* McC
19.34   suddenly] had suddenly Ch
19.35   became] become Ch
20.20   reflection] reflections Ch
20.28–29   "Well . . . Dan!"] "Well . . .things!"   "Dan!   Dan!" "Look who's coming!" "Oh, Dan!" Ch
20.34   skin] face Ch, A1+
21.7   Damn] Curse McC,A1+
21.11   sat] saw Ch,A1+
21.14   Finally (*no* ¶)] ¶ Ch

THREE MIRACULOUS SOLDIERS

[N¹: *Saint Paul Pioneer Press*; N²: Chicago *Inter Ocean*; N³: *Kansas City Star*; N⁴: San Francisco *Examiner*; N⁵: *Omaha Daily Bee*; N⁶: *Boston Globe*; N⁷: *Philadelphia Inquirer*; N⁸: *Pittsburgh Leader*; EIM: *English Illustrated Magazine*; A1: *The Little Regiment*, Appleton, 1896; E1: *The Little Regiment*, Heinemann, 1897. The variant paragraphing of N⁶ and the cuts in N⁶ and N⁷ are separately listed at the end of the collation.]

22.0 *et seq.*   I] CHAPTER I N⁸
22.2–14   It . . . bureau.] *omit* $N,EIM
22.15   ¶ From] *no* ¶ $N,EIM
22.15   of the blinds] *omit* $N,EIM
22.17   where] when $N,EIM
22.17   a half mile] half a mile A1+
22.18   summer] *omit* N⁵

22.20   Occasional] Occasionally $N,EIM
22.22   winds] wind N³
22.25   little] *omit* N⁵
23.3–23.7   A voice . . . coming."] *omit* $N,EIM
23.8   shrillness] surliness N¹
23.11   streak] stream $N,EIM
23.14   into] to $N,EIM
23.20   skins] -skins N²

23.22 contriving] continuing $N,EIM

23.29 wood] woods $N,EIM

23.31 They're] They are $N,EIM

23.32,37 bended] bent N^{1-2},EIM, A1+

23.32–33 from whence] from which N^1; whence A1+

23.33 'em] them $N,EIM

23.34 swiftly] *omit* N^1

23.38 to still] still to EIM

24.3 them—] *omit* $N^{4,7}$

24.6–10 as if . . . hallucinations] *omit* $N,EIM

24.13 upward] upwards N^4

24.15 At the heels] At the rear N^1; At the head $N^{2-6,8}$; In the rear EIM

24.17–21 The . . . horse.] *omit* $N,EIM

24.26 note] notes N^5

24.26 expressed] express $N^{1-3,5,7-8}$

24.28 fer] for $N,EIM

24.29 Santo's] Danto's $N^{4-5,8}$

24.35 Oh . . . you?] *omit* $N,EIM

24.37 tragic] a tragic N^5,EIM

24.37 door] *omit* N^1

24.38 bended] bent N^2,EIM

25.11 stood] stoop N^3

25.12 elder] older $N,EIM

25.22 crackled] cracked N^8

25.22 the girl] she N^1

25.24 the step] a step $N,EIM

25.25 the—the fire] the fire $N,EIM

25.27 sudden] a sudden N^2

25.29 In] On $N,EIM

25.35–26.5 "Oh, ma . . . left——] *omit* $N,EIM

26.6 suddenly] *omit* $N,EIM

26.8 Oh,] Of, $N^{1,3,5,8}$; Of$_\Lambda$ N^2; Of— EIM

26.10 ¶ The] *no* ¶ $N

26.11 the] her N^2

26.12–15 "But . . . Mary!"] *omit* $N,EIM

26.16 out] *omit* $N,EIM

26.18 here] there $N,EIM

26.23–25 On . . . north.] *omit* $N,EIM

26.27 peg] pig $N,EIM

26.36 calm] *omit* N^2

27.4 You—] *omit* N^2

27.5 but] but we N^4

27.6 another] the other N^5

27.7 yere] here N^4

27.7 raikoned] raikined $N (—N^{1,4,7})$,EIM; raikened $N^{4,7}$; raikind N^1

27.12 The (*no* ¶)] ¶ $N,EIM

27.13 cotch] catch $N,EIM

27.14 mile] miles $N^{3,7}$

27.15 Keh-plunk] Ker-plunk N^1; keh-pluck N^2; Keh-pluck $N^{3-5,7-8}$,EIM; *omit* N^6

27.16 thah] thar A1+

27.16 Curious.] *omit* N^6

27.21 men] man N^2

27.25 very] *omit* N^1

27.27 in] for EIM

27.27 In the] Of their $N,EIM

27.29 corps] service N^4

27.29 emblem] emblems N^2

27.30 number] number still upon it $N,EIM

27.30 one] another N^2

27.30 great] great brown $N,EIM

27.32 man] *omit* N^1

27.33 a clean cloth] clean cloth A1; clean cloths E1

27.35 Leavitts] Heavitts $N,EIM

27.37–28.13 "Did . . . cavalry ——"] *omit* $N,EIM

28.21 and his] and N^1

28.21 forelock] forehead N^2

28.25 go] to go N^2

28.26 like] likely N^1

28.31 us] up $N(—N^6)$,EIM

28.34 had reached] could reach N^1; reached $N^{2,4}$

28.35 was bended] was bending $N^{1,7}$; bended N^2; was bent EIM,A1+

28.35 forward, her] ~ . Her $N(—N^{2-3})$; ~ —her EIM

28.38 thudding] thundering $N^{1,6}$

29.1 Yanks] Yankees N^6

29.5 intersected] intercepted $N,EIM

29.7 down] along $N,EIM

29.7   "Oh (*no* ¶)] ¶ $N,EIM
29.10   They're] They are $N,EIM
29.14   Where'll we hide?] *omit*
        N[2,4]
29.17   levyings] levying EIM
29.20   She (*no* ¶)] ¶ $N
29.22   the rear part of] *omit* N[2];
        the rear of N[1,6]
29.24   good] great N[4]
29.24–25   a tangle] tangle N[5]
29.25   last] least N[5]
29.25–26   at last were] were at last
        N[6]
29.29   closer] close A1+
29.32   shone] showed $N,EIM
29.34   under] round N[3]
29.34   black] *omit* N[2]
29.37   feed] food N[1]
29.37   "They've (*no* ¶)] ¶ N[5]
30.3   done] have done $N,EIM
30.10   coats] uniforms N[2]
30.11   the instant] that instant N[3];
        once N[7-8]
30.11–17   The . . . box."] omit
        $N,EIM
30.18   ¶ The] *no* ¶ $N(−N[7]),EIM
30.18   toward] towards N[1]
30.20   "You (*no* ¶)] ¶ N[2]
30.23   you'd] you'll N[4]
30.26   that] *omit* N[1]
30.29   on] at N[7]
30.31   [1]if] *omit* N[3]; in N[4]
30.32   officer] soldier N[1]
30.34   ask] go ask A1
30.38   Well, . . . then,] Will_∧ . . .
        then? $N,EIM
30.38   go and] go A1+
31.2   called] said N[3]
31.3   still] *omit* $N,EIM
31.5   new] now N[1]
31.6   there] *omit* A1+
31.10   a] *omit* N[2,5]
31.12   ma] me N[5]
31.12   a thousand] 1,000 $N(−N[3])
31.14   upon . . . daughter] *omit*
        N[4]
31.15   thresh] thrash N[2-3,6],A1
31.15   wailed] wail N[5],A1+
31.17   do, ma? What] do? Ma!

what   N[1,4-5,8]; ∼ ? ∼ !   What
        N[2]; ∼ ? ∼ , what N[3]
31.20   appealed] pleaded N[4]
31.22   peeked] peeped EIM
31.23   The (*no* ¶)] ¶ N[4]
31.23   the others] others N[2]
31.23   staring] starting N[1]
31.24   a proper] the proper $N,
        EIM
31.27   that] which $N(−N[5]),EIM
31.28   dim] *omit* N[2]
31.28   chevrons] chevron A1+
31.30   near to] near N[1]
31.31   first] *omit* N[5]
31.31   fine] *omit* $N,EIM
31.34   a] *omit* N[1]
31.36   coolly] very coolly N[2]
31.36   and with] with $N,EIM
31.36   interested] uninterested N[3]
31.37   so] to be so N[2]
31.37   he] that he N[2]
31.40   toward] towards EIM
32.3–20   The busy . . . dream-
        fully.] *omit* $N,EIM
32.22   leaned] leaning N[5]; leant
        EIM
32.27–36   Upon . . . girl.] *omit*
        $N,EIM
33.3   thought] thought that N[5]
33.4   that] *omit* N[2]
33.7   the three] three N[1,3,5-8],EIM
33.11–17   In all . . . question.]
        omit $N,EIM
33.18–19   the attempt] an attempt
        $N,EIM
33.20   of dreaming] and dreaming
        N[4-6,8]
33.22   with] *omit* N[2]
33.28–35   Heroines . . . circuit.]
        omit $N,EIM
33.35   One (*no* ¶)] ¶ $N,EIM
33.37   They . . . service.] *omit*
        $N,EIM
34.4   him] to him N[2]; upon him
        N[8]
34.13   that] *omit* $N,EIM
34.16   enabled] enables EIM
34.20   broad] the broad $N,EIM
34.25–35.20   The girl . . . steel.]
        omit $N,EIM

35.25   troopers] troops N[8]
35.26   sentries] the sentries $N, EIM
35.30–35   A picture . . . straw.] omit $N,EIM
35.36   Once] One N[1]
35.36   made her mind up] made her mind N[2,4,6]; made up her mind N[1,3,5,8],EIM; decided A1+
35.38   circles] circle A1+
35.38   mystic] omit N[1]
36.1   had] omit N[3]
36.5   ¶ For] no ¶ N[3]
36.7   reds] red N[2]
36.11   shrill] omit $N,EIM
36.14   plight] flight $N(−N[3]),EIM
36.17   This sound] This song $N (−N[1]),EIM; The song N[1]
36.20   blanch] blench EIM
36.20   Duty] duty $N,EIM
36.23   the light] her light N[2]
36.27   structure] barn N[7]
36.29   barely] scarcely N[5]
36.37   in your] in the N[1]
36.37   hull—— ——] hull dam N[3]; ~ —— EIM,A1
36.37   rod] rods $N,EIM
36.38   mar'] mare $N,EIM
37.3   apparently been] been apparently N[2]
37.7   "Everything (no ¶)] ¶ N[8]
37.7   all] is N[2]
37.9   This] The N[3]
37.15,22   What's] What is N[4]
37.21   scooped] scooped up N[4]
37.28   of] to N[4,7]
37.33   joy] rejoice EIM
38.6   stretched] stretching N[2,4]
38.15   three] omit N[3]
38.28   sort of a] sort of N[4]
38.29   here] there N[8]
38.31   was] was now $N,EIM
38.33–34   from whence] whence N[3]; from which A1+
38.39–39.1   blackness] darkness $N,EIM
39.2   see now] now see $N,EIM
39.3   She (no ¶)] ¶ $N,EIM
39.3   ever] even $N,EIM
39.11   suggestion] suggestions N[8]

39.16   come] have come EIM
39.18   this] the N[2]
39.24   sod] soil N[1]
39.28   stooped] stopped N[4]
39.35   beam] barn N[8]
39.36   miraculous] three miraculous $N,EIM
39.37   glinted] glintered A1+
39.37   finally] finely N[6]
39.38   became] become N[4]
40.1   right."] ~ ?" $N(−N[3]),EIM
40.6   forced] pushed N[8]
40.10   mechanically] technically N[8]
40.11   and his] and the $N,EIM
40.14   that their] their $N,EIM
40.16   this] the $N,EIM
40.22   their] his N[2]
40.27–28   wildly . . . indifference] omit A1+
40.31   this] the N[2,5-6]; their N[1,3-4,7-8],EIM
40.35   "Where's (no ¶)] ¶ N[2]
41.5   peered] peeped N[3]
41.11   others] other N[8]
41.17   Cap'n] Cap'in N[1-4,6,8]
41.21   A man . . . box?"] omit A1+
41.24   'round . . . 'round] ∧ ~ . . . ∧ ~ N[4,6],EIM
41.25   cotched] kotched N[1]
41.29   'im] 'em $N,EIM
41.30   that] omit N[5]
41.35   to reach] to be reaching N[6]
41.37   raikon] raiken N[4,7]
42.1   another] the other N[6]
42.2–9   Another . . . him.] omit $N,EIM
42.9   She] The girl $N,EIM
42.16   they∧hang] ~ — ~ EIM
42.17   No'm'm] No'm N[7]
42.17   Oh, no'm'm.] omit $N,EIM
42.18   a contemplation] the contemplation EIM
42.19   nor] or EIM
42.22   toward] towards N[4]
42.25–28   She . . . barn.] omit $N,EIM
42.29   ¶ When] no ¶ $N,EIM
42.32   again] in the dark N[1]
42.35   apparently] appeared N[5]

42.36 on] at N⁸
43.9–10 as small . . . been] *omit*
　　N²
43.13 to greatly] greatly to EIM
43.23 slipped] slid $N,EIM
43.23 raising] raised N¹
43.26 anyhow. Even] anyhow,
　　even N⁴⁻⁵,AI+
43.26 me. You'll] ∼ , you'll N³,
　　EIM
43.29 damned] darned N⁷; d—d
　　AI+
43.31 hey] hay N¹⁻²,⁴,⁶⁻⁸,EIM
43.31 hey? Nixey.] ∼ , ∼ ? EIM
43.32 lick us] lick some of us N²
43.38–39 Fine . . . was] *omit* N²
44.4 the hoarse] a hoarse N³
44.5 singing] telling N⁶
44.9 was] were AI+
44.9 the mellow] the hollow $N
　　(−N²),EIM; *omit* N²
44.11 and unhurried] *omit* N⁷
44.19 Expressions] Expression
　　N¹⁻³,⁷⁻⁸
44.20 "A (*no* ¶)] ¶ EIM
44.23 the barrel] his barrel N⁸
44.24 "Well (*no* ¶)] ¶ EIM
44.27 "I (*no* ¶)] ¶ EIM
44.28 "And . . . mouth."] *omit* N⁵
44.29 flung] swung N⁵
44.30 "Pete (*no* ¶)] ¶ EIM
44.30 Pete] Pere N¹
44.30 row] caw N¹; raw N⁵,⁸
44.33 plunged] dove $N; dived
　　EIM
45.2 blow] blown EIM
45.5 into] in N¹
45.6 no] not N⁵
45.9 orchard,] ∼ ∧ N³
45.14 a] an EIM
45.15 you'll] you will N¹
45.17 tired] tried N⁸
45.22 reappear] appear N⁴,EIM
45.36 clear] big clear N¹
45.38 "Oh (*no* ¶)] ¶ $N,EIM
45.39 at] in N²,AI+
45.39–46.1 the loud music] loud;
　　the music N¹
46.1 rioting] rolling $N,EIM
46.9 the sentry] sentry N¹⁻³,⁷⁻⁸,
　　EIM

46.10 arose] across N¹,³⁻⁴,⁶,⁸,EIM
46.13 clinched] clenched $N,
　　EIM,EI
46.14 her] all her N¹,⁵,EIM
46.21 crackles] cackles EIM
46.21 last] last few N¹
46.23 grimy] grimly $N
46.23 panting] painted N⁵
46.27 knelt] knelt weeping $N,
　　EIM
46.28 "He's (*no* ¶)] ¶ EIM
46.32 "Why (*no* ¶)] ¶ EIM
46.34 some] *omit* $N,EIM
46.35 feverishly] *omit* $N,EIM
46.36 better] all right $N,EIM
46.37 down] out N⁸
47.2 eyes] lips N⁵
47.4 lane] line N¹
47.7 rebel] a rebel $N,EIM
47.10 reflection] reflecting N¹

In the following places N⁶ *indents
to form new paragraphs where no
paragraphing is present in the other
texts:* 23.33 "Hush 24.27
"And 25.15 Her 26.29,32
She 27.31;29.15,25,30 The
30.19 But 30.27 "You 31.
23,34 She 31.26 Presently
31.31 The 36.10 Uncon-
sciously 36.23 Once 36.26
Finally 37.21 "You 38.9
When 38.14 From 38.20
Frequently 38.24 And 38.
31; 39.15 She 40.5 Wrig-
gling 40.9 When 40.16,31
In 40.19; 41.14 He 41.33
They 42.36 The 43.8,14
At 43.24 "Oh 44.5 A
44.14 An 45.3 When 45.
20 She 46.7 In

In the following places N⁶ *makes
unique cuts:* 22.17–24 It . . .
blue. 22.28–30 The pines . . .
house. 23.17–24 She . . . 'em!"
23.31–33 "Hush . . . emerged.
23.35–39 And . . . are!" 24.5–
6 "Oh . . . fascination 24.15–
24.24 At . . . sank. 24.37–25.3
Already . . . eyes. 25.5–12

The . . . woman. 25.18–20 But . . . fire. 25.23–26 But . . . hysterically. 25.29–32 In . . . it. 25.33–34 "Oh . . . has. 26.8–10 "Oh . . . Santo." 26.17 The . . . Mary!" 26.19–20 She . . . daring. 26.36–37 As . . . holler." 27.12 The . . . trembled. 27.19–23 "Was . . . m'm. 27.25–26 Their . . . tattered. 27.26–28 It . . . diversity. 27.33–36 "These . . . We——" 28.14 Mary . . . intention. 28.17–29 "No . . . something?" 28.35–37 Her . . . silence. 29.4–7 The . . . blue. 29.12–15 They . . . hide." 29. 16 It seemed true. 29.22–25 They . . . tangle. 29.29–30 No . . . situation. 29.34–36 The . . . there. 29.38–30.4 A . . . box. 30.26 He . . . assuringly. 30.29–30 The . . . it. 31.2–4 "Ma . . . floor. 31.5–6 The . . . nerves. 31.7–20 "Ma . . . Ma!" 31.30–31 As . . . again. 31.32–34 The . . . reply. 31. 36–37 He . . . prisoner 31. 39–32.2 A . . . box. 32.24–26 Four . . . post. 33.6–9 She . . . box. 33.21–27 There . . . ears. 34.1–12 The . . . unreasonable. 34.14–17 She . . . distressed. 34.20–24 The . . . grove. 35.23–29 Horses . . . instant. 35.39–36.4 She . . . darkness. 36.8–10 The . . . step. 36.12–17 High . . . trees. 36.17–23 This . . . door. 36. 29–37.4 She . . . manner. 37. 26–28 With . . . feed. 37.31–34 It . . . pass. 38.2–6 She . . . silence. 38.12–14 The . . . mused. 38.19–20 The . . . phosphorescently. 38.22–24 When . . . unreal. 38.33–36 As . . . sleeping. 39.3–7 She . . . approaches. 39.17–22 She . . . jury. 39.38–39 The . . . her. 40.13–16 The . . . meanings. 40.30–31 With . . . noise. 41.6–9 The . . . we——" 41. 12–14 The . . . spot. 41.19 "Cap'n . . . men. 41.28–33 And . . . it. 41.35–36 They . . . calamity. 42.12 He's been . . . time. 42.15–17 She . . . m'm. 42.30–31 She . . . nothing. 42.32–33 The . . . dangers. 42.35–36 The . . . reflecting. 43.1–4 She . . . men. 43.12–14 At . . . lights. 43. 17–18 The . . . silver. 43.20–22 The . . . eyes. 43.27–29 He . . . smart." 44.11–14 A . . . command. 44.26–28 The . . . mouth." 44.39–45.2 She . . . away. 45.8–12 Even . . . tragedy. 45.39–46.2 The . . . tragedy. 46.12–14 As . . . might. 46.30 They . . . forward. 46.35–36 "Are . . . awhile.

In the following places N⁷ *makes unique cuts*: 22.17–30 It lay . . . house. 23.29–31 The . . . flashes. 23.34–38 for . . . road. 24.2–3 It . . . shifted. 24.12–16 In . . . tin. 24.35–25.34 She . . . has." 26.6 coming . . . window 26.16–23 The . . . tour. 28.19–23 Santo . . . nose. 29.4–7 The . . . blue. 29.31–36 A . . . there. 31.1–11 the kitchen . . . thought ——" 31.16–20 "Ma . . . Ma!" 32.21–26 Over . . . post. 33. 17–27 Plainly . . . ears. 33. 35–34.12 One . . . unreasonable. 34.14–24 She . . . grove. 35. 36–36.2 Once . . . wavering. 36.5–21 For . . . noon. 37.36–38.6 The . . . silence. 38.16–26 The . . . mystery. 39.15–22 She . . . jury. 41.32–36 These . . . calamity.

In the following place N⁶,⁷ *join in the same cut*: 37.9–14 The . . . everything.

A MYSTERY OF HEROISM

[N¹: *Philadelphia Press*; N²: *Minneapolis Tribune*; N³: *Omaha Daily Bee*; N⁴: *Kansas City Star*; N⁵: *San Francisco Chronicle*; N⁶: Chicago *Times-Herald*; NS: *Novels and Stories* [1896]; A1: *The Little Regiment*, Appleton, 1896; E1: *The Little Regiment*, Heinemann, 1897. The unique cuts in NS are listed following the collation.]

48.0   A Detail . . . Battle] A Detail of a Battle N⁴; *omit* A1+
48.0   *omit*] I N⁴
48.7   blue] *omit* N⁵
48.11   groups] croups N²
48.13   infantry] infantrymen N³
48.14   A Company] Company A N⁶
48.14   wisht] wish N²; whisht NS
48.17   half of] half N³⁻⁴,A1+
48.19   leap] heap N²
48.25   a] the N⁶
48.27   ¹a] the N³
48.30   long] old N³
49.1   upward] upwards N¹⁻²,⁴⁻⁵,NS
49.2   had stood the barn] the barn had stood N³
49.3   woods] wood N¹
49.3   the sound] a sound N⁵
49.5   At (*no* ¶)] ¶ NS
49.5   appearances] appearance N⁶
49.7   often,] ~ ∧ N³,⁶,NS
49.8   it] *omit* N⁴
49.10   questions] question N¹
49.30   at all] *omit* NS
49.36   wisht] wish N⁶; whisht NS
49.38   how you] how are you N⁴
49.38   goin'] going N⁴
49.38   git] get N⁴,NS
50.9   any] *omit* NS
50.12   fragments] ragments N⁴
50.14   Indeed] *omit* NS
50.14   the infantry (*no* ¶)] ¶ N⁶
50.19   ¹was] were A1+
50.31   mystic] mysterious N³
50.32   "Well] "Yell N⁴
50.34   minnet] minute N²
50.34   shut] shet N⁶
50.36   great] little E1
51.3   held] *omit* N³
51.6   batt'ry] battery N²
51.8   that] of N¹
51.11   meadow] meadows N²

51.18   as stiff] stiff N³
51.20   A Company] Company A N⁶
51.21   faces] face N⁴
51.21   yeh] ye N⁴
51.22   t'] to N²
51.22   yeh] ye N²
51.23   Yeh'll] You'll N¹+
51.30   want] wan't E1
51.30   git] get A1+
51.33   the captain] captain N³
51.34   "You (*no* ¶)] ¶ N⁶,NS
52.1   Collins's] Collins' N¹,³,⁶; Collin's N²,⁵,NS
52.2   a voice] voice N⁴
52.6   toward] towards NS
52.6   his] *omit* N³
52.7   wether] whether N⁵
52.7   'tis] it is N⁵
52.13   other] *omit* N³
52.13   an'] and N⁵
52.21   *omit*] Second Part N¹⁻³,⁵; II N⁴,⁶
52.38   if] it N²
53.1,2   goin'] going NS
53.20   this] his N⁶
53.21   ¶ Too, he] He (*no* ¶) A1+
53.25   phenomena,] phenomenal ∧ N⁶
53.32–33   back the next] back next N²,NS
53.34   for] from N⁵
53.35   the] a N²
53.36   had come] came N²
54.8   ice] the ice N⁵
54.12   this] the N⁴
54.14   boiling] broiling N¹⁻⁵,NS
54.14   shore. In] shore in N²
54.20   by] on N²
54.22   of] of the N⁵
54.24   howls] and howls N⁶
54.31   face] white face N²

54.38 water] the water N⁴
54.38 as] are N⁴
55.6 withdrawing] drawing N²
55.11 turning] turned NS
55.15 screamed] scrambled N⁴
55.18 with] in NS
55.26 fallen] taken N⁵
55.36 this] his A1+
56.1 and] on N²
56.2 its] his N²
56.6 bended] bent A1+
56.7 was] were A1+
56.14 on] upon N⁵
56.15 from] of N²
56.21 waved] waived N¹
56.22 young] *omit* N³,⁵
56.28 from] among A1+

In the following places NS *makes unique cuts*: 48.7–13 When . . . infantry. 48.20–22 On . . . lances. 48.23–24 In . . . conflagration. 48.26–27 Its . . . breeze. 48.29–30 The . . .

post. 49.3–5 From . . . fighting. 49.14–27 The . . . steel. 49.33–35 He . . . meadow. 50.1–7 Its . . . maiden. 50. 11–14 A . . . Indeed 50.17– 18 Fewer . . . guns. 50.28–31 From . . . sky. 50.38–51.1 He . . . man. 51.7–9 The . . . him. 51.17–18 A . . . stake. 51.29–30 in those . . . knees. 52.2–3 "Look . . . lad— 52. 32–34 It . . . brow. 53.8–9 It . . . victor. 53.13–14 As . . . surprised. 53.16–17 He . . . great. 53.19–20 He . . . incident. 53.26–29 He . . . hero. 53.30 He . . . hero. 54.7–8 The . . . ice. 54.14–17 In . . . tinkling. 54.24–25 The . . . head. 55.3–7 There . . . furnace. 55.24–25 He . . . feet. 55.38–39 His . . . heels. 56.14–15 He . . . child.

AN INDIANA CAMPAIGN

[PM: *Pocket Magazine*; N¹: *Kansas City Star*; N²: *Buffalo Commercial*; N³: *Nebraska State Journal*; N⁴: *Minneapolis Tribune*; N⁵: *San Francisco Chronicle*; N⁶: *St. Louis Post-Dispatch*; EIM: *English Illustrated Magazine*; A1: *The Little Regiment*, Appleton, 1896; E1: *The Little Regiment*, Heinemann, 1897. Variant paragraphing in N⁶ is recorded after the collation.]

57.4–5 Everybody . . . affairs.] *omit* N⁴
57.6 the Migglesville] Migglesville $N+
57.7 an] *omit* PM,EIM
57.18 far] *omit* N⁶
57.22 fields] field $N+
57.26 extremely] supremely PM
57.28 terrific] terrible N¹
57.29 who] which PM; that N³,⁶
58.1 plainly] *omit* N⁶
58.2 them] him N³
58.3 rouse] arouse $N+
58.3 little] *omit* PM
58.5 chicken] chickens N²⁻³
58.10 his] the N³
58.12 aroused] roused $N+

58.13 th'] the PM,N²; the' N³
58.13 matter] matteh N³
58.14 th'] the N²
58.16 Lots] Lot's N¹⁻⁵
58.16 is] *omit* N⁴
58.16 th'] the N²
58.16 a] the N⁵
58.17 importance] impatience N³
58.17 'uz] us N⁶
58.18 an'—] ~ ∧ N⁶
58.18 now—] ~ ∧ N⁵
58.18 th'] the N⁶
58.19 th'] the $N+
58.23 pounced] bounced N⁶
58.25 yeh] you N⁵
58.25–26 How long ago? Where is he now?] *omit* N³

58.26 you] you $N+
58.28 He—] He's_∧ N⁶
58.30 hold] grip PM
58.31 Then he said:] omit N⁶
58.32 th'] the N²,⁶; the' N³
58.32 an'] and E1
58.33 yeh] you E1
58.35 down] omit PM
58.35 pegs] peg PM
58.37 was] omit PM
58.37 removed it] removed PM
59.1 of the condition] omit N²
59.4 Witheby] Whiteby N²
59.7 what] what's $N+
59.8 th'] the EIM
59.8 At (no ¶)] ¶ $N+
59.9 the boys] boys $N+
59.13 had] omit $N+
59.16 terrible] the terrible N⁶
59.17 major] mayor N⁴
59.28 All] All that $N(−N⁴)+
59.28 is] is that $N+
59.36 this] his N²
59.36 movement] moment $N+
60.4 stared] started N³
60.4 figure] figures EIM
60.4 pursuer] partner N³
60.5 Jeroze] Jeroozel N¹
60.9 at] off EIM; omit A1+
60.12 ways] way EIM,E1
60.17 up] omit N⁶
60.18 Petersen] Peterson PM,N⁶, E1
60.21 Jeroozel] Jerozel PM,N²⁻⁴, EIM+
60.22 mus'] must PM
60.23 everybody] everybody's orders N⁵
60.23 He (no ¶)] ¶ N⁵
60.27 upon] on N¹
60.28 Jeroze] Jeroozel N⁵⁻⁶
60.30 goin'] going PM
60.31 There] Then EIM
60.36 dangers] danger N⁶
60.37 Petersen] Peterson PM+
60.39 happen to] omit N⁶
61.3 It] I N²
61.3-4 could contain] contained PM
61.4-5 The . . . men.] omit N⁵

61.5 as] omit $N+
61.6 threats] now threats N⁶
61.8 yellow] the yellow PM
61.8 tops] top PM
61.11 the little] little N⁵
61.11 came to a halt] halted N⁵
61.14 "Well (no ¶)] ¶ $N+
61.19 fear] fears A1+
61.22.1 N¹⁻⁴ print the following (text from N¹): SYNOPSIS. While Major Boldin, a veteran of the Mexican war, is taking a nap on the bench in front of the tavern at Migglesville, a little boy comes running to tell the major that his ma's chickens have been stolen and that he has seen a "rebel" in the woods. The major is almost the only able-bodied man left in the village, the rest having volunteered for service in the Union army. By the time he has secured a rifle and is ready to hunt down the rebel, a large crowd of women and boys has gathered at the tavern. The major starts down the road with Peter Witheby. The women hesitate and finally follow.
61.24 the importance] importance $N(−N⁶),EIM
61.24 dignity] the dignity PM
61.25 forward swiftly] swiftly forward N¹
61.28 and] omit N⁵
62.11 legs] his legs N⁶
62.13 What] Well N⁶
62.14 anythin'] anything N⁶
62.15 ¶ The] no ¶ N²
62.15 clambered] climbed PM; clamored N³
62.19 hain't] han't N¹
62.19 nor nuthin'] or nothin' PM
62.21 an'] and PM
62.23 began Peter] Peter began N¹
62.25 of] omit PM
62.25 'im] him PM

62.28 hain't] ain't PM
62.31 th'] the PM
62.35 th'] the $N+
62.35 fer] for $N+
62.37 hain't] ain't A1+
63.1 then] men N³
63.1 wary] weary N³
63.2–3 appeared. As . . . them₍ᴧ₎
  it] appeared₍ᴧ₎ as . . . them. It
  PM,$N,EIM
63.5 here,] ~ ,— PM
63.5 supposin'——"] supposing'
  ——" N⁴
63.7 "Supposin'——] ~ , PM
63.7 Peter] old Peter PM
63.10 got] came PM
63.15 there's] there is PM
63.15,16 in] *omit* N⁶
63.16 said] replied PM
63.18 hain't] ain't PM+
63.18 a] *omit* N⁶
63.20 Lissen] Listen $N+
63.21 their] they N⁶
63.22 turned] slowly turned PM
63.22 yeh] you PM
63.23 said] asked PM
63.26,32 heered] heerd PM
63.29 shift] lift $N+
63.29 some] *omit* $N+
63.31 shucks] chucks N⁶
64.2 hain't] ain't A1+
64.2 'im] him PM
64.5 this] the PM; his N³
64.9 upon] on PM
64.21 should] could N³
64.22 this] the N³
64.23 swift silent] silent swift PM
64.24 go back and] *omit* N⁶
64.27 gliding] glittering $N+
64.29 Petersen] Peterson PM
  (−N³)+; Patterson N³
64.30 shoulder] shoulders N¹,⁴⁻⁶,
  EIM+
64.32 on'y] o'ny N¹⁻²,⁴⁻⁵
64.33–34 the swiftest] swiftest
  $N+

64.35 only] *omit* EIM+
65.3 an'] and $N+
65.3 George,] ~ ₍ᴧ₎ N⁴,⁶
65.10 can't yeh] can'e ye N⁶
65.17 share] have a share PM
65.17 one] ones N⁵
65.18 was . . . his] were . . .
  their N⁵
65.19 the gun] it PM
65.22 t'] to PM
65.22 'em] it PM; 'im N²⁻⁴,⁶,EIM
65.26 the other] other $N+
65.26 that] their N⁴
65.34 silken] *omit* PM
65.36 toward] towards PM,N²⁻⁴,
  EIM
65.36 of a] of PM,N¹
65.38 came] come N⁴
66.2 his rifle] the rifle N³
66.5 on'y] only N¹; o'ly N²; o'ny
  N⁴⁻⁵
66.10 Petersen] Peterson PM,
  N¹,⁴,⁶,EI
66.13 Yep] Yes EIM
66.13 mopping] still mopping PM;
  mopped $N(−N²,⁶),EIM,A1
66.18 one] *omit* A1+

In the following places N⁶ *in-*
dents to form new paragraphs
where no paragraphing is present
in the other texts: 58.13 "Come
58.25 "Where   58.28 "He
58.31 "By   59.5   "Well   59.
21 "What   59.23 Upon   59.
27 "Now   59.38 "Hol'   60.
17,29 "Well   60.21   "Come
61.13 "I'm   61.13 The   61.
21 "My   61.31; 62.2 "Well
62.13 "What   62.18   "If
63.5 "Say   63.15,25 "I   63.
20 "Lissen   63.22 "Did   63.
29 "Sssh   63.31,36   "Oh
63.34 "Shet   64.11   "You
64.32 "Why   65.3 "Here   66.
12 "Drunk

A GREY SLEEVE

[N¹: *Kansas City Star*; N²: *Minneapolis Tribune*; N³: *Philadelphia Press*; N⁴: *Omaha Weekly Bee*; N⁵: *San Francisco Chronicle*; N⁶: Chicago *Times-Herald*; PM: *Pocket Magazine*; FLW: *Frank Leslie's Weekly*; DFM: *Demorest's Family Magazine*; EIM: *English Illustrated Magazine*; A1: *The Little Regiment*, Appleton, 1896; E1: *The Little Regiment*, Heinemann, 1897.]

67.0   I] PART I $N; *omit* EIM
67.3   ¶ So] *no* ¶ N⁵
67.6   at us] us N⁶
67.10   an] *omit* N⁵
67.11   the eternal] he eternal FLW
67.17   him] *omit* N²
67.18   the] an N⁶
67.19   the brigade] a brigade EIM
67.22   the colors] colors EIM
67.23   shouts] shout DFM
67.25   troop] troops EIM
67.27   thundered] thudded EIM
67.30   the] *omit* EIM,DFM
68.4   if] *omit* N⁵
68.4   a giant] the giant N⁶
68.5   steady] sturdy A1,E1
68.6   his] their N⁴
68.8   tense] terse DFM
68.11   bended] bent EIM,A1,E1
68.13   in] to N³
68.13   at] of N¹,EIM
68.15   bended] bent EIM; compelled A1,E1
68.16   paces] faces $N,PM,EIM, A1,E1
68.16   a flight] the flight EIM
68.16   flight of] *omit* N³; fight of N⁴
68.16   harnessed] harassed N⁵
68.18   pace] place EIM
68.19   lithe] light EIM
68.19   was] was as EIM
68.21   calmly] calmly fixed DFM
68.22   from] *omit* EIM,A1,E1
68.22   picking] pecking EIM
68.24   in] with EIM
68.25   to] *omit* N⁵
68.26   why] way N⁵
68.27   imperturbable] imperturable N¹,³
68.29   a fence] the fence N⁵,EIM
68.34   soldierly] soldiery A1

68.36   ¶ Suddenly] *no* ¶ EIM
68.39   toward] towards N¹⁻²,PM, EIM
69.1   of the] *omit* EIM
69.9   the wood] wood N¹⁻³,⁶,PM, FLW,DFM,EIM; woods A1,E1
69.12   spanged] fired N⁵
69.17   as inscrutable] inscrutable EIM
69.19   more] *omit* EIM
69.20   gloom] *omit* EIM
69.20   burnt] burned A1,E1
69.24   in . . . volley] *omit* DFM
69.24   an] *omit* N⁵
69.29   minute] minutes N²
69.32   in] on EIM
69.38   field] fields EIM
70.1   Everyone] Every one N⁴⁻⁵, FLW+
70.6   each feature of them] with features DFM
70.11   girted] girded A1,E1
70.13   -clothed] ₐcoated N²
70.16   climb] climb over EIM
70.21   awe and doubt] doubt and awe N⁴
70.26   something——"] ~ ," EIM
70.26   the] a FLW,DFM
70.28,30–31   'something—something'] ₐ ~ — ~ ₐ EIM
70.29   "Send (*no* ¶)] ¶ N⁴
70.30   about] *omit* N³
70.30   your] *omit* EIM
70.32   damned] d—d N⁴,PM, FLW,DFM,A1,E1; —— N⁵; d—— N⁶
70.35   into] in N³
70.37   suddenly] *omit* EIM
70.39   this] his N¹, DFM
71.2   speculations] speculation EIM
71.5   to a] to his N¹

71.8 blinds. An] ~ — an E1
71.10 t'] it EIM
71.12 at the] in N³
71.12 troopers] troops N¹
71.18.1 II] SYNOPSIS. | The story begins in the midst of a lively skirmish during the Civil War. After it had finished the lieutenant of the artillery and the captain of the infantry, who had been companions in the fight, went forward with their men, and after going a short distance came suddenly upon a house which they found to be vacant. While about to make a nearer approach they were struck with awe by the sight of an arm moving the blinds, an arm with a grey sleeve. When they arrived in front of the house the troopers paused, while the captain went softly up the front steps. He stood before the large front door and studied it. Suddenly swore angrily and kicked the door with a loud crash and it flew open. | PART II. N³; PART II (no synopsis) N¹⁻², ⁴⁻⁶,EIM
71.19 lights] light N⁶
71.20 door] front door EIM
71.23 Further] Farther N⁵⁻⁶,EIM, A1,E1
71.28 wide] wide-open EIM
71.32 reddish, bronze] ~ - ~ EIM
71.33 hair] hair and N⁶
72.3 He . . . wary.] omit EIM
72.6 was] was really EIM
72.7 dusty] very dusty DFM
72.10 -howling] -howlings EIM
72.15 still with her hands] with her hands still N²
72.20 Are] Is $N,PM,FLW,EIM
72.20 there] omit DFM
72.24 here] there here N⁴
72.24 besides] beside N³,⁵,PM, EIM
72.25 his] the N⁴

72.26 there] omit EIM
72.27 answered] discovered N⁴
72.27 this] his N¹
72.28 then] omit EIM
72.35 had always] continually A1,E1
72.36 hands] hand EIM
72.37 as] like EIM
73.7 me;] ~ — EIM
73.10 behind me] omit EIM
73.13 "Well (no ¶)] ¶ EIM
73.15 that] omit N⁵
73.18–20 As . . . prisoner.] omit EIM
73.34 supreme] most supreme FLW,DFM
73.35 faced] she faced EIM
73.36 with] with a EIM
73.39 swiftly] omit N⁶
74.9 toward] towards PM,EIM
74.11 the] this EIM
74.13 Nothing!] ~ ? EIM,FLW
74.22 this] the N⁶,EIM
74.24 didn't] did not N²
74.25 And—and∧] ~ — ~ — DFM
74.25 know] knew EIM
74.26 they'd] they's N⁵
74.26 and—so] ~ ∧ ~ — EIM
74.27 pistol—] ~ , EIM
74.27 you kicked] kicked EIM
74.32 Ah] Oh, ah EIM
74.36 arm] arms DFM
74.38 I am] I'm EIM
75.2 being thus] thus being EIM
75.4 feller] fellow EIM
75.7 between] behind DFM
75.7 clinched] clenched $N,PM, EIM
75.9.1 III] PART III $N,EIM
75.17 of her] of DFM
75.19 shoulder] shoulders N⁶,EIM
75.21 here] omit N²
75.22 moaned. Because] ~ —because A1,E1
75.28 the fawn] a fawn EIM
75.33 ¶ Suddenly] no ¶ EIM
75.33 low] omit EIM
75.35 ¶ All] no ¶ EIM
75.35 toward] at EIM
75.36 there] omit EIM

75.36   in a] in N⁴
76.2   little] *omit* N²
76.7   toward] towards EIM
76.7   men] man N¹
76.11   had] *omit* EIM
76.12   attitudes] attitude N¹
76:12   were] *omit* EIM
76.21   Harry—] ~ ; EIM
76.25   upon] on EIM
76.27   glare] glance EIM
76.28   first] *omit* EIM
76.29   rang] rung EIM
76.31   sheathed] had sheathed N⁶
76.33   imperturbable] imperturable N²
76.33–34 You are mistaken.] You are mistaken. You are mistaken. EIM
77.12   nor] or DFM,EIM
77.14   hung] clung PM
77.14   railing] rail PM,A1,E1
77.18   toward] towards EIM
77.18   threw] drew EIM
77.18   an] *omit* N¹
77.24   it] him A1,E1
78.2   girl's efforts] young girl's effort EIM
78.8   there] here N²
78.9   others] more EIM
78.10   damned] d—d N⁴,PM,FLW, DFM,A1,E1; —— N⁵; d—— N⁶
78.13   place] whole place EIM
78.14   half] half of EIM
78.17   Oh,] Oh, come, EIM
78.20; 79.24 toward] towards EIM
78.21   docilely] meekly N⁵
78.22   the] a EIM,DFM
78.22   harsh] harsh harsh N²
78.26   hi!] allʌ N³; Oh! PM,A1,E1
78.26   look] looked N³
78.26   the] that N⁵
78.28   bang] a bang A1,E1
78.29   dulled] dull EIM
78.29   outside of] outside EIM
78.30   horses] horse N²

78.34   to] fo A1
79.3   at] with N⁴
79.6   me—and I'm—] ~ , and—and I'm EIM
79.11   need] heed N⁵,PM,DFM, EIM,A1,E1
79.13   anything] something EIM
79.15   frighten you] frighten N²,A1,E1
79.17   dusty] dusky EIM
79.26   there] *omit* EIM
79.27   bugle's] bugler's EIM
79.28   swung] sprang EIM
79.34   at the head] ahead EIM
79.35   horse] horse skilfully EIM
79.35   beds] heads N¹
79.37   trampled slowly] slowly tramped N²; tramped slowly FLW,DFM
79.38   Good-bye.] *omit* N²
80.2   seems] seemed EIM
80.4   around] round EIM
80.11   no] *omit* N⁶
80.11   we] you DFM,E1
80.14   it] *omit* EIM
80.19   blush] flush EIM
80.19   the curves of] *omit* DFM
80.22   Never!] ~ ? N⁶,PM,EIM
80.23   bended] bent N⁶,FLW+
80.23   a] the EIM
80.25   mind] mind it N¹
80.27   strong for she] strong. She EIM
80.32   this] his N¹,⁶,DFM,A1,E1; the EIM
80.33   a] the N¹
80.34   beseeched] besought DFM
80.37   drooped] dropped N³⁻⁴,EIM
80.39   stared] started EIM
80.39   at] to EIM
81.2   and] after DFM
81.2   a] *omit* N¹
81.4   perhaps—] *omit* EIM
81.4   while—] ~ ʌ EIM
81.5   tree—] ~ ʌ EIM

THE VETERAN

[McC(p): proofsheets of *McClure's Magazine*; McC: *McClure's Magazine*; SJB: *Saint James's Budget*; N[1]: *Chicago Tribune*; A1: *The Little Regiment*, Appleton, 1896; E1: *The Little Regiment*, Heinemann, 1897.]

82.3 Further] Farther McC,A1+	84.28–29 in front] from in front
82.7 grocery] grocery store SJB,N[1]	N[1]
82.11 at] *omit* N[1]	84.34–35 trampling and] bram-
83.14 afterward] afterwards	pling and McC(p)
SJB,N[1]	84.37 and sped] and sped and
83.17 pretty] pretty well A1+	sped N[1]
83.19 well] *omit* N[1]	85.11 opened] open N[1]
84.4 to] into McC,A1+	85.25 the cows] cows N[1]
84.26 toward] towards SJB	86.30 toward] towards SJB,N[1]

AN EPISODE OF WAR

[G: *The Gentlewoman*; TMs: University of Virginia typescript, distinguished when necessary as TMs(u) as originally typed and TMs(c) as altered in hand by Cora; E1: *Last Words*, Digby, Long, 1902.]

89.7 crevices] crevice| TMs	90.22 weight] weigh| TMs
89.15 had] has G+	90.28 them] him TMs,E1
89.18 little puffs] little white puffs	91.8 bloomed] boomed E1
G,TMs	91.35 with] in TMs(u)
89.21 had] ha| TMs; *omit* E1	92.20 that] *omit* TMs(u)
89.24 moment] instant TMs,E1	92.27–28 impatiently. What . . .
89.27–28 at once] *omit* TMs,E1	anyhow?] ~ , "what . . .~ ?"
90.2 miraculously] *omit* TMs,E1	E1
90.13 even] een E1	93.1–2 wrathfully. His] ~ ∧ | His
90.14 Well∧] ~ , G+	TMs; ~ , his E1

WOUNDS IN THE RAIN

THE PRICE OF THE HARNESS

[Co: *Cosmopolitan Magazine*; B: *Blackwood's Edinburgh Magazine*; A1: *Wounds in the Rain*, Stokes, 1900.]

97.0 THE PRICE OF THE HAR-	98.31 th'] the Co
NESS] THE WOOF OF THIN	99.22 grim] a grim B,A1
RED THREADS Co	100.15 battalion] battalions B,A1
97.6 Trees (*no* ¶)] ¶ B,A1	100.23 There (*no* ¶)] ¶ B,A1
97.12 came] come A1	101.14 bloodshed, death] blood-
97.12 other way] other Co	shed and death B,A1
97.24 ghastly] ghostly B,A1	101.25 up] *omit* B,A1
97.30 Figures (*no* ¶)] ¶ B,A1	102.21 deep] as deep B,A1
98.15 each] either B,A1	102.28 'way] way B,A1
98.17 low-cut] low-cart B,A1	102.34 an'] and B,A1
98.23 of foliage] of the foliage Co	102.35 know] knew B

103.7   than] when B,A1
103.9   as they] as these B,A1
103.17   by] with B,A1
103.21   column] columns B,A1
104.15   dirt₍] ~ , B,A1
104.23   Jesus] Hell Co
104.29   down] downward B,A1
105.3   pale] pale blue B,A1
105.16   the army was] was the army B,A1
105.18   that army was] was the army B,A1
105.29   tales] a tale B,A1
106.4   heeding the man just] just heeding the man B,A1
106.16   was] were B,A1
106.26   which] that B,A1
107.13   arose] rose Co
107.16   exchanged] they exchanged B,A1
107.22–23   wounds₍ . . . quaint-ly₍] ~ , . . . ~ , Co

108.13   their rifles] omit Co
108.16   wound] wounds Co
109.4   but was] but that he was B,A1
109.21   had] omit B,A1
110.18–19   He . . . mistress.] omit Co
110.19   aiming] aiming his rifle Co
111.18   boy] old boy B,A1
111.19   much, . . . think,] ~ . . . . ~ ₍ B,A1
111.28.31   lyin'] lying B,A1
111.32   is] is Co
112.11.1   VI] omit Co
112.13   afterward] afterwards B, A1
113.18   triangle] tangle Co
113.21   An'] And A1
113.26   ". . . Long . . . wave. . . ."] omit B,A1

THE LONE CHARGE OF WILLIAM B. PERKINS

[WG: *Westminster Gazette*; McC: *McClure's Magazine*; A1: *Wounds in the Rain*, Stokes, 1900.]

114.25   nights of] nights' WG
114.29   a thousand] 1,000 McC,A1
114.30   had] omit McC,A1
115.16   blasting] blazing WG
115.27   But] Now WG
115.28   and] omit WG
115.38   sputter] splutter WG
116.6   one hundred and fifty] 150 WG,McC,A1
117.7   suppliant] supplicant McC, A1
117.13   Then (*no* ¶)] ¶ McC,A1
117.16   *-wing-*] *-win-* McC,A1

117.27   temple₍ shining₍] ~ , ~ , WG
117.38   not able] unable WG
118.3   "It's (*no* ¶)] ¶ McC,A1
118.9   Like hell] Yes, McC,A1
118.12   patrol] party WG
118.12   rusty] old rusty WG
118.14–15   The patrol . . . blind.] The party then laid down in the brush and laughed until every face was blazing red. WG

THE CLAN OF NO-NAME

[N¹: *New York Herald*; N²: Chicago *Times-Herald*; N³: San Francisco *Examiner*; BW: *Black and White*; A1: *Wounds in the Rain*, Stokes, 1900; E1: *Wounds in the Rain*, Methuen, 1900.]

119.10   commercially] easily N²
119.28   stuck] struck N²,BW+
120.25–26   The sentry . . . lan-

guorously.] omit BW
120.33   breaths] breath N³

121.11   ²Por] Per A1,E1
121.14–21   It . . . lake.] *omit* N³
121.14   of a] of A1,E1
121.20   a] *omit* N²
121.36   Mariel] Manriel $N
122.4   going] going on $N
122.5   half a league] a half league A1
122.8–14   A moment . . . dreamed.] *omit* N³
122.16–17   a wood] the wood $N
122.18   A half-mile] Half a mile $N
122.22–34   Their . . . existence.] *omit* N³
122.31   to safely scoot] to scoot safely BW
123.2   task—] one— $N
123.4   bayed] kept at bay $N
123.26   very] *omit* $N
123.28   in a] in the BW
123.30   eye] eyes $N
123.31   his] in his N³
123.34   rapidly] *omit* N³
123.35   filed] filled N²
124.3   out] *omit* $N
124.10   snuggling] smuggling $N
124.15   surprise] surprised BW
124.19–125.3   The eight . . . lane.] *omit* N³
124.19   all] the N¹⁻²
124.23   men] the men N²
124.25   to long] long to BW
124.36   ragging] raging A1,E1
124.36   its] the N²
124.36   dirling] drilling N²
125.9–10   incredibly foul] *omit* $N
125.15   was] were $N
125.21   clatter] chatter BW
125.24   succeeded itself] itself succeeded BW
125.35   to . . . blockhouse] to circle the blockhouse widely BW
126.13   an] *omit* BW
126.17   for ever] forever $N
126.30   dun] dum N¹
126.32   in the west ceased] ceased in the west BW
127.5   tearing] leaving a bit of BW
127.6   severed] several $N

127.13   closer] close A1,E1
127.14   thought] though N²
127.15–16   away from . . . three hundred yards] *omit* N³,BW
127.15   others] the others A1,E1
127.31   never was] was never $N
127.36–128.20   "Well . . . minute.] *omit* $N
128.23   along a] a lone N¹; along N³
128.31   shoulders] shoulder N³
128.32   disconsolately] *omit* $N
129.10   for] *omit* N³
129.18   possible] impossible N¹
129.20   being] *omit* BW
129.22   emotional] emotioned $N
129.26   mowed] moved BW
129.34   were] was N²
130.2–3   in the wisdoms of bushwhacking] *omit* BW
130.2   wisdoms] wisdom $N
130.8   on] upon BW
130.9   his] His $N
130.25   insurgent] insurgents A1, E1
130.28   hot] the BW
130.37   himself] *omit* BW
130.39   in] *omit* BW
131.7,15   unfamiliar] familiar $N
131.16   the benediction] benediction BW
131.18   stooped] stopped $N
131.22   on] of N³
131.30   in] on BW
132.9   illimitable] illuminable BW
132.10   singular] single BW
132.21   purple] *omit* N²
132.28   who] and he BW
133.5   and libidinous] *omit* $N
133.5–6   filled . . . life] *omit* $N
133.16   a glance] *omit* $N
133.17   M-m-m] M-m $N
133.19   homes] home N²
133.24   Pobrecito] Pobrecetto N¹⁻², BW,A1
133.30   garden] gardens A1,E1
134.1   air,] air_∧ and with $N
134.6   heaven] heaven or down to hell BW

134.7　and] and that $N
134.8　And] And then BW
134.9　to then escape] to escape BW
134.9　any one] anyone BW
134.15　was] were $N
134.28　brooks] coffee-mills BW
134.33　please play?] play, please? BW
134.36　Prat] Pratt $N
135.1　that] *omit* $N

135.5–6　rumpled . . . squalid] reduced . . . abject $N
135.10　but at] at A1
135.14　room] rook BW
135.24　lie of] *omit* $N
135.25　"What (*no* ¶)] ¶ BW
135.25　do] did N²
135.28　of the] of $N
135.39　you."] you, Margharita." BW
136.1　only] *omit* $N
136.3　lies and] lines of $N

"GOD REST YE, MERRY GENTLEMEN"

[SP: *Saturday Evening Post*; C: *Cornhill Magazine*; A1: *Wounds in the Rain*, Stokes, 1900; E1: *Wounds in the Rain*, Methuen, 1900.]

137.0　"God . . . Gentlemn"] ∧ ~ . . . ~ ∧ A1+
137.2　*Eclipse,* and at] Eclipse. At SP
137.4　what] whatever C,A1+
137.10　cabled] cable C,A1+
137.18　canned] tinned C,A1+
138.6　They] But they C,A1+
138.7　cockleshell] cockleshells SP
138.18　fleets] fleet SP
138.26　lay] swung SP
139.3　the] a C,A1+
139.8　chafed] chaffed SP
140.8　Rogers] Rogers' C; Roger's A1+
140.10　to] *omit* C,A1+
140.13　Spanish] recent Spanish SP
140.21　It . . . warm.] *omit* SP
140.28　¶ And] *no* ¶ C,A1+
140.29　It (*no* ¶)] ¶ C,A1+
140.31　changing] change C,A1+
140.34　joys] joy C,A1+
140.38　Nell, how] Nell," he cried, "how SP
141.6　seat on the steps] a seat SP
141.14　A-hunger] ~ ∧ ~ C,A1+
141.33　here] *omit* C,A1+
141.34　little] *omit* C,A1+
141.35–36　Point, . . . genius;] ~ ! . . . ~ , C,A1+
142.3　Don't] Don' A1+

142.11　man-crowded] men-crowded C,A1+
142.13　a great] the great SP
142.21　damn] *omit* SP
142.21　sure] sure that SP
142.21　fiercely] *omit* SP
142.23–24　only found] found only SP
142.24　soldier] soldiers C
142.34　Fate] fate C,A1+
142.36　days] two days SP
142.37　canteens] one C,A1+
143.3　half a bottle] a half-bottle C,A1+
143.11–12　Anybody . . . match?] *omit* SP
143.24　street] streets C,A1+
143.31　of] to SP
143.34　had] *omit* C,A1+
143.37　reared] half rose C
144.4　arose] rose SP
144.15　sogering] sodgering C,A1+
144.17　Where] Where are C,A1+
144.18　sulkily] sulking C,A1+
144.27　an] and A1
144.30　canned] tinned C,A1+
144.34　can] tin C,A1+
144.34　"Fall (*no* ¶)] ¶ C,A1+
144.36　Afterward] Afterwards C,A1+
144.36–37　they— . . . troops.] the four of them marched off. SP

145.6   tunics] coats C,A1+
145.8   were] was C,A1+
145.11 seat] a seat SP
145.13 over   nothing]   nothing
        C,A1+
145.23 understand, but] ~ . But
        A1+
145.24–25 —cursed . . . nothing]
        omit SP
145.37 of] from SP
145.39 for reasons]   the reason
        C,A1+
146.2   as] like SP
146.7   seat] a seat SP
146.14 Point (no ¶)] ¶ C,A1+
146.16 whether—it's—] ~ ∧   ~ ∧
        C,A1+
146.19 Thereafter   (no   ¶)]   ¶
        C,A1+
146.22 (twice) me] my SP
146.25 his eyes] them SP
146.26 But (no ¶)] ¶ C,A1+
146.28 ¶ It] no ¶ C,A1+
146.30 Say (no ¶)] ¶ C,A1+
146.31 Some . . . on.] omit SP
146.33 Point and Tailor] Tailor
        and Point SP
147.18 "Where (no ¶)] ¶ C,A1+
147.18 said] asked SP
147.23 arose] rose SP
147.30–148.34 The captain . . .
        Nell.] omit C
147.30 ¶ The] no ¶ A1+
147.37 nor for] nor A1+
147.37 could do now] now could
        do A1+
148.6   the whirl,] omit SP
148.6–9 If . . . blood.] omit SP
148.10 very] omit SP
148.24 gently] gentle SP
148.31 of the battle] omit SP
148.35–149.2 The . . . again.]
        omit SP
149.1–2 They . . . again.] omit C
149.4   Daiquiri] Daqueri SP,C,A1
149.7   toward] towards C,A1+
149.13–14 scrubby . . . pools,]
        omit SP
149.20 goin'] going C,A1+

149.24–28 The . . . blockhouses.]
        omit SP
149.35 ways] way C,A1+
149.38 pugnacious] omit SP
150.1–3 The . . . canteens.] omit
        SP
150.4–7 —men . . . heat] omit SP
150.10 th' . . . 'm] the . . . 'em
        SP
150.11 away] omit SP
150.11 red] great red SP
150.13 babyishly] babishly SP
150.21 to] with SP
150.23–24 They . . . morning.]
        omit SP
150.39–151.8 It . . . formation.]
        omit SP
151.8   a] omit A1+
151.9   soda-bottle] soda-water bot-
        tle SP
151.23 Some one] Someone A1+
151.24 "Keep (no ¶)] ¶ C,A1+
151.26 trees] trees, vines SP
151.33 "Christ, I'm shot!"] omit
        SP
152.4–5 When . . . water.] omit
        SP
152.6   disputing] omit SP
152.7   damn] hang SP
152.12 lying] omit SP
152.13,33 left] right SP
152.21–22 Then . . . it!"] omit SP
152.25 here] here for SP
152.29 get once] once get SP
152.38 "That (no ¶)] ¶ C,A1+
152.39 somewhere] omit SP
153.7   On] Presently the hurrying
        correspondent   met   another
        regiment coming to assist—a
        line of a thousand men in
        single file through the jungle.
        "Well, how is it going, old
        man?" "How is it coming on?"
        "Are we doin' 'em?" On SP
153.11–12 his . . . skin] omit SP
153.14 from . . . foliage] omit SP
153.15–18 Presently . . . 'em?"
        omit SP
153.23 fine broad] omit SP

153.35	—yes? . . . dazed] *omit* SP	154.17	back] *omit* C,A1+
153.38	lying] dying SP	154.23	aroused] roused SP
154.16	arising] rising SP	154.24	Mr.] *omit* SP
		154.31	*Eclipse.*] *omit* C,A1+

THE REVENGE OF THE *Adolphus*

[CW: *Collier's Weekly*; S: *Strand Magazine*; A1: *Wounds in the Rain,* Stokes, 1900; E1: *Wounds in the Rain,* Methuen, 1900.]

155.5 days] days' CW,S
155.12 *am*] am CW
155.16–17 *two . . . both*] two . . . both CW
155.22 deck] the lower deck CW,S
155.26 opry] *omit* S,A1+
155.26 damn it] *omit* CW, curse it S
156.9 Finally . . . Yes.'] *omit* A1+
156.12 'im——"] ~ ." CW,S
156.25 strolled] strode CW
156.33 deck] lower deck CW,S
156.35 damn it all] my sons CW; hang it all S
156.36 Be-Gawd] By George CW; By Jove S
156.36 *won't*] won't S,A1+
156.38 damned] jiggered CW; blessed S
157.12,15,20 shake] hook CW,S
157.16 The (*no* ¶)] ¶ CW
157.24 Be-Gawd] By Gawd CW; By Heaven S
157.25 hell] blazes S
157.28 git] get CW,S
157.28 kin] can CW,S
157.34 the sky] to the sky CW
157.37 damn it] tight CW; curse it S
158.14 titanic] Titanic CW
158.22 damn fool] condemned ijit CW; blessed fool S
158.26,27 The (*no* ¶)] ¶ CW
158.27 "What (*no* ¶)] ¶ CW
158.31 "Great (*no* ¶)] ¶ CW
158.34 *sure*] sure CW
158.35 Sure. Take] Sure, take A1+

159.11 sprang] sprang up CW
159.13 Good Gawd] Great Scott CW; Good Heaven S
159.20 runnin'." The] running," the A1+
159.35 board of] board A1+
160.9 But (*no* ¶)] ¶ CW
160.13 along the deck] on the lower deck CW,S
160.14 *our*] our CW
160.21 toward] towards S
160.29 at the back] back A1+
161.13,14 was] were S
161.16,34 Commander] Lieutenant-Commander CW,A1
161.17 "Shoals (*no* ¶)] ¶ CW
161.33 officers'] officer's A1+
162.2 cruiser] flagship CW,S,A1+
162.11 of] for A1+
162.13–14 three-point-twos] three-decimal-twos CW
162.14 *his*] his CW
162.22,29,39 captain] commander CW
162.24 senior officer's ship] flagship CW; senior officer A1
162.24 line_∧ ahead,] ~ , ~ ∧ CW
162.24 ²senior officer's ship] flagship CW; S.O. A1+
162.33–34 executive officer and the] *omit* CW,A1+
162.35 five] four CW,A1+
163.5 S.O.P.'s ship and the vessels] flagship and the vessels CW; cruiser and the gunboats A1+
163.14–16 The boatswain . . . cabin.] *omit* CW,A1+

163.17 the four] that all four CW,AI+
163.26 right——"] ~ ." CW,S
163.27 captains] commanders CW
163.27–28 came upon deck] emerged from the cabin CW,AI+
163.28 it] the deck CW,AI+
163.35–164.2 "Beat . . . breech-plugs.] A bird-like whistle stirred the decks of the *Chancellorville*. It was followed by the hoarse bellowings [AI: bellowing] of the boastwain's mate. CW,AI+
164.24 swift] gruff CW,AI+
164.30 nondescripts] ships CW,S
164.37 I'm damned if it will!] Oh, this ain't no good! CW; I'm cursed if it will! S
164.39; 165.3 *business*] business CW
165.1 'round] round CW
165.5 set] sent AI+
165.10 townspeople] town's people AI+
165.11–12 signaled . . . go in] directed that signals be made ordering in the *Holy Moses* and the *Chicken* CW,S
165.13 tumultuously] like charging horsemen CW; like charging bantams AI+

165.34 had had] had S
166.3 complex] complete CW,AI+
166.25 Immediately (*no* ¶)] ¶ CW
166.28 'm] 'em CW,S
166.30 The (*no* ¶)] ¶ CW
166.31 fort] *omit* CW
166.32 was . . . it] were . . . they AI+
166.37 sung] sang CW,S
167.3 was] were CW,S
167.30 burnt] burned CW
167.31 streamed] steamed AI
167.35 ¶ "Are] *no* ¶ CW
168.22 damned] pig-headed CW; blessed S
168.24 engine-room force] engineers CW
168.30 stoker] engineer CW; man S
168.32 an] and CW
169.1 joke] a joke AI+
169.22,30 'm hell] 'em hell CW; it 'em hot S
170.3 men] engineers CW,AI+
170.16 had sent] sent CW
170.28 There (*no* ¶)] ¶ CW
170.31 Correspondents] Two correspondents S,AI+
170.31–34 and although . . . told] *omit* S,AI+
171.9 Commander] Lieutenant-Commander CW
171.9 S.O.P.] *omit* CW

THE SERJEANT'S PRIVATE MAD-HOUSE

[SP: *Saturday Evening Post*; EIM: *English Illustrated Magazine*; AI: *Wounds in the Rain*, Stokes, 1900; EI: *Wounds in the Rain*, Methuen, 1900.]

172.6 rocks] rock AI+
172.8 a simple] simply a EIM
172.11 particular] particularly EIM
172.18 the time] time EIM
172.20 faintest] slightest SP,EIM
172.21 glistening] glisten in SP,EIM
172.22 slowly] *omit* SP,EIM
172.24 plant] bush SP

172.28 affairs] the affairs EIM
172.31 dwarf] dwarfed EIM
173.1 Afterward] Afterwards EIM
173.7 sentry, and he] sentry. He SP
173.7–8 the stern] his stern SP,EIM
173.10 yet] as yet SP,EIM
173.15 Dryden] him SP; the man EIM

173.25   tree‸ perhaps,] ～ , ～ ‸ SP
173.40   Dryden (*no* ¶)] ¶ SP
174.10   ²They'd see me!] *omit* SP,EIM
174.10   then] *omit* SP,EIM
174.13   a small] small A1+
174.19   earned] *omit* SP,EIM
174.24   searchlight flashes tore] searchlight flashed SP
174.25   outposts] the outposts SP
174.29   told] tell A1+
174.39   minutes] moments SP,EIM
175.2   "Dryden (*no* ¶)] ¶ SP
175.5   He (*no* ¶)] ¶ SP
175.8   could be not even] could not even be EIM
175.12   hyena] coyote SP,EIM
175.23   was] had SP
175.27   right in the front] in front SP
175.32   "Halt . . . *fire!*"] "Halt . . . fire!" SP
175.35   afterward] afterwards EIM
175.38   "Is (*no* ¶)] ¶ SP
176.1   Death . . . Death] death . . . death SP,EIM
176.1   miraculous] miraculous ones SP,EIM
176.10   admonition] caution SP,EIM
176.16   require] required A1+
176.18   talk] talking EIM
176.19   knew] knew that SP,EIM
176.20   minutes] minute SP,EIM
176.21   ken] pen A1+
176.24   was] was a A1+

176.25   hard] swift SP,EIM
176.26   Their occupation] The occupation of the Americans SP,EIM
176.31–32   forces. They were of] forces, but of SP
176.37   soldier] soldiers A1+
177.3,4   Cubans . . . Cubans] Cuban . . . Cuban EIM
177.3   insurgent] insurgents EIM
177.8   promptly would] would promptly SP
177.10   probably] *omit* SP
177.13   the outpost] outpost EIM
177.18   from] within SP
177.20   drunken] *omit* SP
177.21–22   praying that . . . praying for] praying for EIM
177.24   increase] increased A1+
177.29–32   "While . . . around."] "The minstrel boy . . . him." SP
177.29   While] When A1
177.29   watched] guard A1
177.31   An] The SP
177.33   hell] deuce SP
177.35   somewhat] *omit* SP,EIM
178.1–4   "The minstrel . . . him."] "While . . . around." SP
178.1   is] has SP+
178.12   This] The SP
178.17   devil] idiot SP
178.18   hard] hardly EIM
178.27   the men] they SP,EIM
179.22   took] assumed SP,EIM
179.23   useful —— ——] *omit* SP; ～ —— EIM

VIRTUE IN WAR

[FL: *Frank Leslie's Popular Monthly*; N¹: Cincinnati *Enquirer* (June 10, 1900), p. 9; ILN: *Illustrated London News*; A1: *Wounds in the Rain*, Stokes, 1900.]

180.0   VIRTUE IN WAR] WEST POINTER AND VOLUNTEER; Or, VIRTUE IN WAR FL,ILN; CRANE'S LAST WAR STORY. | Based on His Cuban Campaign With | the Sixth Infan- try. | Keen Observation the Basis | of Clever Fiction From | Pen of the Dead | Writer. | Mr. Stephen Crane, the news of whose death at the early age of 30 has just been cabled from

Baden, was one of the most promising of America's younger writers. The story which follows is in his best style, and it will be of particular interest since one of the regular regiments in the brigade which the writer describes was the Sixth Infantry, which was stationed for a number of years at Ft. Thomas. The story appeared in the Frank Leslie's Magazine of November, 1899, under the title of "West Pointer and Regular, or Virtue in War." N[1]

181.3 eye] eyes N[1]
181.6 first battalion] 1st Battalion ILN
181.8 third battalion] 3rd Battalion ILN
181.17 held commission] held a commission ILN
181.20 *their*] their N[1]
181.24,26 second battalion] 2nd Battalion ILN
181.30 hearty] heartly N[1]
182.34 but] and N[1]
183.24 darn] darned ILN
184.4 very] *omit* N[1]
184.6 good] *omit* N[1]
184.8 edjewcation] adjewcation N[1]

184.8 damned] darned ILN
184.9 *manners*] manners N[1]
184.21 *men*] men N[1]
184.24 *him*] him N[1]
184.25 'm] 'im FL,N[1],A[1]
185.9–10 the other] other N[1]
185.16 he was] *omit* N[1]
185.20 so smart] as smart N[1]
186.15 get] go N[1]
186.27 men] *omit* N[1]
186.38 *anything*] anything N[1]
187.25 ketch] catch ILN
188.27 *all*] all N[1]
188.35 wholly] wholly coming N[1]
189.3 hell] h—— ILN
190.5 regular] regulars A[1]
190.19 afterward] afterwards ILN
190.36 d——] d—n N[1]
191.11 diff'ent] different A[1]
191.30 Lige's] (Lige) N[1]
191.38 damned] d—d N[1]; darned ILN
191.39 *you*] you N[1]
192.17.1 V] *omit* N[1]
193.12 licker] liquor ILN
193.15 The . . . Huh?"] *omit* N[1]
193.19 *meant*] meant N[1]
193.20 *full*] full N[1]
193.28 jes'] just ILN
193.29 an] an' FL,ILN
193.32 up] *omit* ILN

MARINES SIGNALING UNDER FIRE AT GUANTANAMO

[McC: *McClure's Magazine*; A[1]: *Wounds in the Rain*, Stokes, 1900.]

195.9 it] *omit* A[1]
195.36 "Yes (*no* ¶)] ¶ A[1]
197.1 Adjutant] Adjudant A[1]

197.9 I'm] I am A[1]
197.27 advanced] advance McC

THIS MAJESTIC LIE

[N[1]: *New York Herald*; N[2]: *Chicago Tribune*; N[3]: *St. Louis Globe-Democrat*; A[1]: *Wounds in the Rain*, Stokes, 1900; E[1]: *Wounds in the Rain*, Methuen, 1900. N[1a] is the proof; N[1b] is the published *Herald* text.]

201.0 I] *omit* N[3],A[1]; CHAPTER I N[2]

201.7 Montojo] de Montojo $N, A[1]+

201.12 and] *omit* N²
201.12 *La Marina*] "La Marine" N³
201.13 Yankees] Yankee $N
201.17 Amid (*no ¶*)] ¶ $N
201.21–25 And . . . plenty."] *omit* $N
202.3 proven] proved N¹,³
202.4 an] the $N
202.12 one-hundredth] one one-hundredth N¹ᵇ
202.16 was] were N²
202.19 damned] d—d N²
202.21 plot] plat N²
202.27 was] were $N,E₁
202.30 *portales*] portales $N
202.33 very] *omit* N²
203.3 of] *omit* N²
203.5 with mildew] mildew $N
203.9 very] *omit* N²
204.5 island] islands N¹,³
204.6 crop] crops $N
204.7 plentitude] plenitude N¹, E₁
204.14 rang] sang A₁+
204.26 now!ₐ] ~ !" $N
204.27 elapse."] ~ .ₐ $N,A₁
204.29 *got*] got $N
204.38–39 be well] well be $N
205.5 all were] were all $N
205.7 send] send our N²
205.8 the ijjits] this we A₁+
205.9 her] its N²
206.14 the gloom] he gloom N²
206.28 leave] live $N
206.35 afterward] afterwards A₁+
207.13 seat] a seat $N
207.15 damned] d—d N²
207.17 *you*] you $N
207.21 ye] you N³
207.25 *What?*] What? $N
207.27 *Codfish what?*] Codfish what? $N
207.29 ye] he N¹,³
207.30 blockaded] blocked here N³
207.30 picked] picked up N²
207.35 of] *omit* A₁+
207.35 all be] be all N³

207.35 *damned*] damned N¹,³; d—d N²
207.37 "You'll (*no ¶*)] ¶ $N
208.2 Will] Wull N¹⁻²
208.9 a heavy] the heavy $N
208.14 blame] blamed N¹ᵇ
208.16 thought] though N³
208.18 gold] good $N
208.19 little] *omit* N³
209.8 dim] *omit* $N
210.3 all] *omit* N³
210.8 adjuring] abjuring A₁
210.19 up] *omit* A₁+
210.21 for] *omit* N³
210.31 y] of $N
211.7 sich] such $N
211.18 gettin'] getting $N
211.33–35 *Bread! . . . Coffee!*] Bread! . . . Coffee? $N
212.6 *You . . . They*] You . . . They $N
212.10 a-away] a-way A₁+
212.14 ye] you $N
212.15 one] a $N
212.24.1 II] CHAPTER II N²
212.29 of a] of $N
213.1 Aguacate] Aquacate N¹ᵃ,²
213.3 street] streets $N
213.22;214.32 Aguacate] Aquacate N¹ᵃ,²⁻³
214.1 *one*] one $N
214.6 Ye-e-es] Y-e-es $N
214.11 Ye-e-es] Y-e-es N³
214.16 damned] d—d N²
214.17 Fifty] Five A₁+
214.32 *Damn*] Damn N¹,³; D—n N²
214.39 Aguacate] Aquacate N³
215.7 two centenes] a centene $N, A₁+
215.8 at] *omit* N³
215.14 get] to get $N
215.24 lightnin'] lightning $N
216.1–2 " 'We . . . grocers,' "] "ₐ ~ . . . ~ , ₐ" $N
216.8 gruffness] gruffiness $N
216.11 the—] *omit* $N
216.13 g-good] good $N
216.20 jiminy] Jove A₁+
216.23 ᴍᴇ] me $N

216.24.1   III] CHAPTER III   N²
216.28   law] laws $N
216.28   at] of   A1+
217.6   rear] the rear $N
217.36   the Spanish] Spanish   A1+
218.1   could] would $N
218.8   slow-crawling] ~ ∧ ~   N¹,³;
  ~ , ~   N²
218.15,36   very] omit   N²
218.17   'm] 'em $N
218.20   Institute] Institution $N
218.21   if] omit   A1+
218.30   had] has   N²
218.30   light ship] ~ - ~   N³
218.34   see] seen   N²
218.38   This (no ¶)] ¶ $N

219.19   bought] brought $N
219.39   was] were   N¹ᵇ,²
220.7.1   IV] CHAPTER IV   N²
220.9   U.S.S. . . . . Scorpion] United
  States steamships Resolute and
  Scorpion $N
220.11   was] were   N¹ᵇ,A1+
220.14   a] omit   N²
220.16   could] would $N
220.24   I was surprised (no ¶)] ¶
  $N
220.29   was] were   N²
221.1   very] omit   N²
221.4   peacocks'] peacock's $N
221.15   don't you] don't $N
221.16   that] that $N

WAR MEMORIES

[AS: Anglo-Saxon Review; A1: Wounds in the Rain, Stokes, 1900; E1:
Wounds in the Rain, Methuen, 1900.]

222.17   bulk] honest pounds   A1+
223.1   sea] seas   A1+
223.16–225.25   Once . . . closed.]
  omit AS
227.21   violet] violent   A1+
227.29   the men] men   A1+
228.4   shoals] schools   A1+
228.39   marked] market   AS
229.8   further] farther   AS
229.17   they] these   AS
229.33   was] were   AS
229.34   great] attractive   A1+
230.3   afterward] afterwards   AS
230.17   they] omit   A1+
231.10   Afterward]   Afterwards
  AS+
231.14   through] though   A1+
232.30   covered] coveted   AS
233.16   and ridge] after ridge   A1+
233.18   in air] in the air   A1+
233.18   where] where the   A1+
233.33   protection]   protections
  A1+
234.35   leeward] leaward   A1
234.38; 235.4   Port] Fort   A1
235.7   Real Dinner] real dinner
  A1+
236.1   guided] guide   A1+
236.11   shreds] threads   A1+

237.15   black-hulled] blacked-hull
  AS+
237.26   a] omit   A1+
238.14   beef] beer   A1+
238.16   ¶ Sometimes] no ¶   A1+
238.16   at foot] at the foot   A1+
238.21   semicircle]   semicircular
  A1+
238.22   toward] towards   AS+
238.39   But∧] ~ —   A1+
239.3   in] on   A1+
239.34   "Go on"] ∧ go on∧   A1+
240.6   had] omit   A1+
240.10   campaign∧] ~ —   A1+
241.23   a right] the right   A1+
241.24   lithe] light   A1+
241.37   he] that he   A1+
242.10   was] was   A1+
243.7   wouldn't] would not   A1+
243.32   bullet] bullets   A1+
244.1   1] 1st   A1+
244.13; 247.13; 248.14,20   El
  Paso] El Poso   AS+
244.26   a ridge] the ridge   A1+
245.5   vanished]   had   vanished
  A1+
245.7   rose] arose   A1+
245.29   sense] senses   A1+
246.35   truth] the truth   A1+

247.4   pale] as pale A1+
247.14   a previous] the previous A1+
249.12–13   who was . . . who——] who was pegging along at the heels of still another man, who was pegging along at the heels of still another man who—— A1+
249.30   for ever] forever A1+
249.31   politics] politic AS
251.30   slope] slopes A1+
251.32   was] is AS
252.3   toilets] toilettes A1+
252.19   was] was the fact A1+
253.3   *admit*] admit A1+

253.7   pimple face] pimple-faced A1+
253.23   Vara] Vera A1+
255.23–257.24   One . . . battle.] *omit* AS
258.5   negotiators] negotiations A1+
258.36   fer] for A1+
260.18–22   I would . . . man.] *omit* AS
260.23–26   him, and I . . . ship— oh] him. Oh AS
261.24–263.28   In . . . world.] Ultimately we arrived. We landed at Old Point Comfort—saintly name. AS
261.37   hung] rung A1+

THE SECOND GENERATION

[SP: *Saturday Evening Post*; C: *Cornhill Magazine*; A1: *Wounds in the Rain*, Stokes, 1900.]

264.0   I] *omit* SP
264.1   *et seq.* Caspar] Casper C
264.10   just] *omit* SP,A1
264.20   damned] *omit* SP; d—d A1
264.26   cotillion] cotillon SP
264.27   they] that they SP,A1
265.1   drank a neat whisky and] *omit* SP,A1
265.4   while] though SP
265.9   for] because C
265.17   in him] *omit* SP,A1
265.28   clear-eyed]   clean-eyed SP+
265.30   had] seen C
265.33–34   men. Individual . . . but] men, though SP,A1
265.35   it] this arrangement SP,A1
266.1   Henery] Henry SP,A1
266.11   dare] does C
266.13,15   penny] bun SP,A1
266.14   amount] thing SP,A1
266.18   Brigadier—] Brigade— C
266.31   fightin'] fighting SP,A1
266.32   *damned*] d—d SP,A1
266.33   goin'] going SP,A1
266.37–38   'nothin' . . . dude.'] ˄ *nothin' . . . dude.*˄ C

266.37–38   nothin' . . . -lookin'] nothing . . . looking SP,A1
267.3–4   I'll do my best with it"] *omit* SP; 'I'll . . . it.' C
267.6   kind] kindly C
267.16   How you goin'] How are you going SP,A1
267.22   them] 'em SP
267.31.1   II] Second Chapter SP
267.32   damned] blamed SP,A1; damn C
268.6   somewhere] *omit* SP
268.6   I] I C
268.21   fecklessly] footlessly SP; fetlessly C; bootlessly A1
268.22   'em] them A1
268.25–26   three whoops in Hades] a rip SP,A1
268.35   "I (*no* ¶)] ¶ C
268.36   "Bother (*no* ¶)] ¶ C
269.10   doing] do C
269.15   eatin'] eating SP
269.23   damn] dash SP,A1
269.25   ¶ "*Dear*] *no* ¶ C
269.26   for] as C
269.38   ¶ "When] *no* ¶ C
270.1   underwear] underclothing C

270.12 in which] and in these greetings SP,A1
270.13; 277.33 West Point] Westpoint C
270.19 Hey, Gory!] eh, Gory? C
270.24.1 III] Third Chapter SP
270.33 clinched] clenched SP,C, A1
271.7 confronted] fronted C
271.8 by] by the C
271.22 shocked] omit SP
271.23 chalk-] chalked- SP,A1
271.23 unlocked his teeth] omit SP
271.26 others] the others C
271.27 low-down] omit SP,A1
271.27–28 pie-faced] omit SP,A1
272.11 its] his A1
272.15 rather] more C
272.22 B] P C
272.22 Hell!] omit SP,A1
272.24 Which] Which SP,A1
272.26 He's all right.] omit SP
272.31; 273.12 b'cause] because SP
272.32; 273.10 a'] of SP; o' A1
272.33 damned] blanked SP; d—d A1
273.6 I] I C
273.9,12 'im] him SP
273.10 'm] him SP; 'im C
273.15.1 IV] Fourth Chapter SP
274.8 of a] of A1
274.9 writing feverishly] feverishly writing C
274.9 roll-top] roller-topped C
274.16 even] omit A1
274.19–20 experience of] omit C
274.21 would] could C
274.23 in his bewilderment] omit SP
274.27 —— ——] —— C,A1
274.28,34 was] were SP,A1
274.29 stormed] assailed C

274.36 contrived] continued C
275.1,6 gawd damn] cuss SP,A1; gawd dam C
275.31 Scott] Scot C
276.21 devil] deuce SP,A1
276.28 in] is in SP,A1
276.28 its] it's a SP,A1
276.35.1 V] Fifth Chapter SP
277.8 other] another C
277.20,32,36; 278.4 Jameson] Jamson C
277.24,31 gawd] Jove SP,A1
277.33 toward] towards C
278.5 russle] rustle SP,A1
278.8 damned] omit SP; damn C
278.11 sound] sounded SP,A1
278.11 sputtered] strutted C
278.14 his face] omit SP
278.21 had] omit A1
278.23 and] omit C
278.26 had] would SP
278.32 forever] for ever C
278.36 here's] here is A1
278.38 damned] blamed SP,A1
279.4.1 VI] Sixth Chapter SP
279.7 shingle] shingled C
279.13 ship's] ship C
279.15 had] they had C
279.26 should] would C
279.27 should] would SP
280.14 -cart's] -cart SP
280.24 "They (no ¶)] ¶ C
281.16 course] course SP,A1
281.23 then] omit SP,A1
281.24 hell] the deuce SP,A1
282.4 afterward] afterwards C
282.6 n-n-no] no-o-o C
282.20 this] his C
282.33 through] through it C
283.10 face] cheek SP,A1
283.19 especially] specially C
283.24 adobe] abode C
283.32 his face] omit SP,A1
284.15 damn] —— SP; omit C

SPITZBERGEN TALES

THE KICKING TWELFTH

[MS: New York Public Library, inscribed by Edith Richie; AM: *Ainslee's Magazine*; PMM: *Pall Mall Magazine*; TMs: University of Virginia typescript; E1: *Last Words*, Digby, Long, 1902. A record of all changes made in MS during and after inscription follows this Historical Collation.]

287.0 THE KICKING TWELFTH] omit MS
287.1 et seq. Spitzbergen] Spitzenberg AM
287.1 traditions] tradition TMs, E1
287.5 to frankly attribute them] to attribute them frankly AM; frankly to attribute them PMM+
287.7 When (no ¶)] ¶ AM
287.12 repositories] repositaries PMM,TMs
287.12 sped] hurried MS
287.21 in fact] omit PMM+
287.22 transformed] transferred PMM+
287.24 the power] power TMs, E1
287.27 a] ; TMs
288.2 nor] or AM+
288.3 came] omit TMs,E1
288.8 there] omit MS
288.10 to seriously engage] to engage seriously AM; to engage PMM+
288.11 foreign] foregin TMs
288.13,16 Pretender] pretender TMs
288.14 opinions. So] ~ , so PMM+
288.24 name, the] name of the MS
288.29 it came the moment] the moment came PMM+
288.34 along] omit MS
288.35 packs] packes TMs
288.39 He] He He TMs
289.7–8 at night] in the camp at night MS,AM
289.10 adventures] the adventures E1

289.10 when] omit E1
289.13 warfare] warfar TMs
289.13–14 "Anyhow (no ¶)] ¶ PMM+
289.14 in] into AM+
289.28 see] steer AM
289.33 a bit] omit PMM+
289.35 The (no ¶)] ¶ PMM+
289.39 enemy's] enemie's MS; enemies' PMM,TMs
290.7 high] omit TMs,E1
290.18 clank] clink MS
290.25 observable] not observable MS+
290.25 that not] that AM+
290.28–29 what it would look like] how it would look PMM+
290.36 the line] line TMs,E1
290.37 as] omit TMs,E1
291.3 there] omit TMs,E1
291.4 informations] information AM+
291.5 In] But in MS,AM
291.6 a plain] the plain TMs,E1
291.7 back of] behind PMM+
291.8 hills] hill AM+
291.13 were] was TMs,E1
291.13 is] was PMM+
291.17 horses] guns MS,AM
291.18 spake] spoke PMM+
291.23 airs] air AM
291.26 voice] voices TMs
291.27 the fuses] fuses TMs,E1
291.27 three-point-two] 3·2 PMM+
292.3 back] at the back PMM; at the backs TMs,E1
292.5 to] omit TMs,E1
292.12 in] on E1
292.19 sentence] sentences TMs, E1
292.23–24 welfare] well-fare MS

292.25–26 a climbing . . . a jumping] climbing . . . and jumping E1
292.27 tried] try AM
292.32 faint] *omit* TMs,E1
292.34 in air] in the air AM+
292.35 is supposedly] supposedly is TMs,E1
292.39 and that a] and a AM+
293.11 have been] be PMM+
293.32 was] were PMM+
294.2 hill-top while the] hilltop. The AM
294.11 great] a great AM,PMM
294.17 "No (*no* ¶)] ¶ AM
294.24 was] were PMM+
294.32 been orders] orders been TMs,E1
295.1 were] was TMs
295.5 hard] *omit* TMs,E1
295.13 at all] *omit* TMs,E1
295.17 blow] blows TMs,E1

295.17 drooped] dropped AM+
295.18 with] whith TMs
295.19 the ankles] their ankles TMs,E1
295.24 fire] terrible fire MS
295.25 was] were PMM+
295.34 afterward] afterwards PMM+
296.11 crumpled] crippled E1
296.15 advanced] advance AM+
296.15 positions] position TMs,E1
296.17 The (*no* ¶)] ¶ AM+
296.20–21 adjusted themselves] came to attention MS,AM
296.21 Richie] Ritchie PMM
296.21–22 and his staff . . . cold-eyed,] *omit* E1
296.25 pudgy] podgy PMM+
296.30 then] *omit* TMs,E1
296.31 damn] d—— PMM,TMs; d—d E1
296.33 was] were PMM+

ALTERATIONS IN THE MANUSCRIPT

[NOTE: All alterations listed were performed by Edith Richie and in the same ink as the inscription.]

287.3 italics] *following period deleted*
287.23 pandemonium] *followed by deleted period*
287.26; 290.21 equipment] 'eq' *over* 'ac'
287.28 column] *preceded by deleted* 'flying'
287.29 mountain] *altered from* 'mounted'
289.12 school] *followed by deleted hyphen*
289.16 do.] *followed by deleted* 'Cavalry'
289.17 cavalry] 'c' *over* 'C'
289.18 mood.] *following* 'But' *deleted*
289.31 and] 'a' *over a period*
290.1–2 convenient] *followed by deleted* 'for the'
290.3 2300] *final* 'o' *deleted*
290.4 enemy's] *altered from* 'enemie's'

290.5 had] 'h' *over* 't'
290.7 hills] *followed by deleted period*
290.13 Majesty] 'M' *over* 'm'
290.13 motion] *followed by deleted* 'that'
290.25 not] *interlined with a caret*
290.38 strained] *followed by deleted* 'in their'
290.39 farms] *followed by deleted period*
291.2 often] *added below line with a direction stroke*
291.2 a composure] 'a' *over* 'co'
291.4 troopers] *interlined with a direction above deleted* 'figures'
291.7 squadron] *followed by deleted period*
291.19 Guns] 'G' *over* 'g'
291.27 three-] 't' *over* '3'
291.29 officers] *following comma deleted*
292.15 knolls] 'k' *over* 'n'

292.16   men] *followed by deleted period*

292.21   understood] *preceded by deleted* 'heard a palaver'

292.26   Curiously] 's' *over* 'l'

292.27   for] *interlined above deleted* 'from'

292.28   men] *altered from* 'man'

292.39   a] *interlined with a caret*

293.8   Twelfth] *interlined above deleted* 'regiment'

293.17   sudden] *preceded by deleted* 'beg'

293.18   left.] *followed by deleted* 'Eve'

294.1   1,100] *preceded by deleted* '11,00'

294.2   the regiment's] 'the' *altered from* 'their'

294.4   officer] *followed by deleted* 'dashed'

294.13   a] *over* 't'

294.13   Kickers] 'K' *over* 'k'

294.16   look] *altered from* 'looked'

294.25–26   employed] 'o' *over* 'y'

295.18   meal;] *semicolon preceded by deleted period*

295.21   upright] *preceded by deleted* 'galopping along.'

295.22   shame,] *comma over period*

295.29   absolute] 'b' *over doubtful* 'n'

295.31–32   Again they] 'Again' *interlined with a caret;* 't' *over* 'T'

295.32   pushed] *followed by deleted* 'again'

296.7   Rostina] *preceded by deleted* 'soldie'

296.13   themselves] *interlined above deleted* 'itself'

296.16   as] 's' *over* 't'

296.19   amusing.] *followed by deleted* 'There was'

296.20   call] 'a' *over* 'l'

296.21   trotting] *altered from doubtful* 'trooping'

296.31–32   monkey.] *followed by deleted quotes*

296.32   Go tell] *written* 'Gotell' *but then separated by a stroke*

THE UPTURNED FACE

[AM: *Ainslee's Magazine;* CP: *Crystal Palace Magazine;* TMs: University of Virginia typescript; E1: *Last Words,* Digby, Long, 1902.]

297.15   firing] *omit* TMs,E1

297.16   stared] started TMs,E1

297.21   beat] heat TMs

297.27   shoulders, suddenly∧] ~ ∧ ~ , CP+

297.29   approached his hands to] his hands approached CP+

297.32   to touch] touch TMs,E1

298.2   fumbled] fumbled the CP+

298.3   arose] rose CP+

298.3   a ghastly] ghastly TMs,E1

298.12–13   Hurry . . . stupid—"] *omit* AM

298.14   this] his TMs,E1

298.16   poor] a poor CP+

298.23   on] *omit* CP+

298.32   again] *omit* AM

298.32   —they . . . other] *omit* AM

298.37   pressing . . . expression] *omit* AM

298.40   something while] something AM,E1

299.3   but] out AM

299.11–14 *et seq.* ital.] CP+ *print in roman*

299.16   point,] poin, TMs

299.27   in a] in TMs,E1

299.32.1   II] * * * * * * CP+

300.3–4   —ha . . . satisfactory!] *omit* AM

300.5   ¶ The] *no* ¶ AM

300.8   you] you CP+; ——you TMs *(pencil alteration)*

300.10	hand] *omit* AM	300.29	in] *omit* TMs,E1
300.13	. . . I'll] *omit* CP+	300.29–30	Always . . . plop.]
300.14	hastily] hard still CP+		*omit* AM
300.17	This (*no* ¶)] ¶ CP	300.33	God] Good AM
300.18	and the] and E1	300.35	Then . . . stutter.] *omit*
300.21	paused] stopped E1		AM

THE SHRAPNEL OF THEIR FRIENDS

[MS: Columbia University fragment; AM: *Ainslee's Magazine*; BW: *Black and White*; TMs: University of Virginia typescript; E1: *Last Words*, Digby, Long, 1902. TMs is distinguished when necessary as TMs(u) as originally typed or TMs(c) as altered in Cora's hand. TMs(u) readings are provided only when followed by E1. Alterations within the MS are listed after this collation.]

301.1 far] *omit* TMs,E1
301.3 Second] 2nd BW+
301.4 infantry] Infantry BW,TMs
301.7 that] and TMs(u),E1
301.8 a good] an AM
301.9 to] *omit* TMs(u),E1
301.11–12 at that time] *omit* AM
301.14 Artillery] artillery BW+
301.17 feeling] feelings E1 (TMs *has final 's' deleted by typed slant*)
301.19 otherwise] *omit* BW+
301.19 Cavalry] cavalry BW+
301.22 Corps] Corps' E1
301.25 rejoiced] rejoicing TMs(c),E1; rejoic | TMs(u)
301.28 long been] been long E1
301.30 Major- (*no* ¶)] ¶ BW+
301.31 taken] *omit* TMs,E1
302.3 too] *omit* BW+
302.3,9 Fifty-three] Forty-seven AM
302.32 aroused] *omit* TMs,E1
302.32 dived] died BW+
303.2 The (*no* ¶)] ¶ BW+
303.4 jingled] jingle TMs(u),E1
303.13 the proper] | proper TMs
303.14 sat] sat on BW+
303.25 wig-wag ∧ wag-wig] wig-wag, wig-wag AM
303.27 *et seq.* Eighty-Eighth] 88th BW+
303.30 signalers] signallers BW
303.35 rang] ran E1

304.2 cheerfully] carefully TMs, E1
304.10 laid] lay TMs(c)
304.10 the] its AM
304.21 toward] towards AM+
304.22 absurd] absured TMs
304.22 they] the TMs
304.35 steeps] steps AM
304.39 and∧] ~ — E1
305.10 toward] towards E1
305.16 shell] *omit* AM+
305.16–18 came . . . the shrapnel] *omit* AM
305.18 and the] A AM
305.21 streaked] streamed AM
305.22 third] 3rd MS,BW+
305.27 eye] eyes AM+
305.28 from] *omit* TMs,E1
305.31 battery——"] ~ !" BW+
305.38 he] *omit* TMs,E1
306.6 old] *omit* TMs,E1
306.7 majors] major TMs,E1
306.20 wrongs] wrong AM+
306.23 near] nearer MS
306.24 a] *omit* AM
306.25 Majesty's] Majesties MS
306.25 Twelfth] 12th MS,BW+
306.26 decoration] Order MS
306.27 because] partly because MS

ALTERATIONS IN THE MANUSCRIPT

305.16 shrapnel] 'h' *written over another letter that may be 'c'*

305.21 flung] *preceded by deleted* 'fo' *and then deleted* 'burst'
305.22 and the] 'the' *interlined with a caret*
305.23 centre] *interlined above deleted* 'middle'
305.26 fist] *final* 's' *deleted*
305.28 sparks] *final* 's' *written over* 'es'
305.32 Richie] *following period deleted by continuation* 'in'
305.38 our] *possibly added later in right margin*

306.8 hear] *final* 'ar' *written over* 're'
306.15 the saddle] 'the' *written over* 'his'
306.19 you are] *interlined above deleted* 'one is'
306.19 you do] *written over* 'one does'
306.20 your] *written over* 'ones'
306.26 decoration] *in MS the word is* 'Order' *followed by deleted* 'mainly' *and its substitute* 'partly' *in the right margin*
306.28 men] 'e' *written over* 'a'

"AND IF HE WILLS, WE MUST DIE"

[TMs: University of Virginia typescript, distinguished when necessary as TMs(u), the original typing, and TMs(c), Cora's hand alterations; FL: *Frank Leslie's Popular Monthly*; ILN: *Illustrated London News*; E1: *Last Words*, Digby, Long, 1902.]

307.0 "And . . . die"] THE END OF THE BATTLE. | . . . "*And if He wills, we must die.*" FL
307.7 whose] who's TMs(u)
307.8 mission] duty TMs(u)
307.9 damned] damn TMs(u); d—d FL; darned ILN
307.10 as possible] as it was possible TMs(u)
307.13 casually] *omit* TMs,E1
307.16 "Run (*no* ¶)] ¶ FL,ILN
307.17 them——] ~ ! ILN
307.30 dangerous] a dangerous TMs,E1
308.5 toward] towards ILN,E1
308.10 *Then*] Then E1
308.14–15 here . . . captain—] *omit* TMs,E1
308.17–18 hard.'" Continued . . . serjeant:] ~ ,'" continued . . . ~ ; FL; ~ ,'" continued . . . ~ . ILN
308.23 Damn] D—n FL; Darn ILN
308.26–27 This . . . barracks.] *omit* TMs,E1
308.31 face] force TMs(u)
308.32 much] *omit* TMs,E1

309.7 Afterward] Afterwards E1
309.9 to] upon TMs,E1
309.13 lazy] easy TMs,E1
309.19 herself] herself that E1
309.24 little] *omit* TMs,E1
309.35 spitting] spilling FL,ILN
310.1 swung] sung ILN
310.9 as] as if TMs,E1
310.18 a field] the field FL
310.31 Damn] D—n FL; Curse ILN
310.32 essential] esential TMs
310.34 hell] h—ll FL
310.37; 311.1,14 Knowles'] Knowles's ILN
311.2 Afterward] Afterwards FL, ILN,E1
311.5 as if he] as if he as if he TMs
311.7 charming] *omit* TMs,E1
311.14 that] who TMs,E1
311.15 Simpson's] Simpsons TMs(u)
311.15 had] has ILN
311.17 said] said apologetically FL
311.18 serjeant] *omit* FL

311.18   He . . .   apologetically.]
omit FL
311.18   apologetically]   opologetically TMs
311.23   Who . . . can't?"] omit FL
311.24   away] omit FL
311.33   hung] hung limply FL
311.34–36   his arms . . . enemy]
omit FL
311.34   the fists] his fists ILN
311.35   afterward]   afterwards
ILN,TMs,E1
312.1   Damn it] omit FL,ILN

312.2   a garden] omit FL
312.3   at the time] omit FL
312.3   stealthy] omit TMs,E1
312.5   he] he FL
312.15   bloody] blod TMs; blood
E1
312.19   dropped] fell TMs(u)
312.22–23   halted before. . . . He
turned] halted, and remarked
FL
312.23   God!] omit FL
312.24   as] omit E1

ADDENDUM

From "Things Stephen Says"

In the Special Collections of the Columbia University Libraries is a small notebook in Cora Crane's hand with the heading, 'Things Stephen Says'. Among the items are several that bear on material used for stories in *Wounds in the Rain*. The initial item in the notebook contains the seed for "Virtue in War." The altered form of the rank for the man wanting the bottle may perhaps support the present editor's speculation that in an earlier form of the story called "The Making of the 307th," the personal conflict with Lige may not have been the central thread:

> Story of Leiutenant of Cavelry [*what may indeed be* 'Cabelry' *is interlined with a caret above deleted* 'private'] asking for, and insisting upon having a bottle—finally saying he wanted to write the name of his dead pal, on a piece of paper and put it in the bottle—to bury it with the body of his freind.

The next items, associated with " 'God Rest Ye, Merry Gentlemen' " and with "War Memories," follow immediately after a short rule:

> Capt. Green & Leiuten—Exton of 20 infantry—gave Stephen and Marshall luncheon—Then as they were going away they saw these officers wash their—his dishes—having to walk some way to do it—made Stephen feel ashamed.

> When I ran back from the end of the rough-rider fight, to get help for Marshall, I met on a narrow wood path the whole 71st N.Y. Regiment and every one seemed to know me, principaly because I had been on their transport the night before. I had already passed three troops of the 9th Cavelry (collored.) and they had had absolutely no questions to ask but every body in the 71st Reg. set up a yell for information as I floundered through the bushes past their incredibley long line. (single file.) Afterward I passed in much the same way the 6th & the 16th Regular infantry reg's. And they preserved an absolute silence almost an indifference as to what had transpired when they had heard the heavy firing. It seemed as if they were solly occupied with their own business, and had no nerotic interest in matters which gave them no casualty report.

The next leaf but one has a note that may be the germ for "The Serjeant's Private Mad-house":

> Make an Open Boat story of Cusico(?) Start where marine went crazy and jumped over cliff killing himself, when the outpost was cut off— —Trumperts called "Music" Next day the "music" went to the edge of cliff & leens over, Capt Short called & said whats that damn red headed music gloating over then he called to him sharply——

The last page starts with Marshall of " 'God Rest Ye' ":

> Marshal lied about statement having money belt on when shot with $100— all he had was gun—Artist "Point" got that. I gave him my blanket in the morning & he told me where he left that.